ACCLAIM FOR

THE NOVELLAS OF

MARTHA GELLHORN

Martha Gellhorn has lived in France, Cuba, Mexico,
Italy, and Kenya, while travelling widely as a journal-
ist. Since the early fifties she has lived in London
and Wales.

ALSO BY MARTHA GELLHORN

SHORT STORIES
The Heart of Another
The Honeyed Peace

NOVELS
A Stricken Field
Liana
Point of No Return
   (The Wine of Astonishment)
His Own Man
The Lowest Trees Have Tops

NONFICTION
The Face of War
Travels with Myself and Another
The View From the Ground

THE NOVELLAS OF Martha Gellhorn

THE NOVELLAS OF *Martha Gellhorn*

VINTAGE BOOKS

A DIVISION OF RANDOM HOUSE, INC. NEW YORK

Library of Congress Cataloging-in-Publication Data
Gellhorn, Martha, 1908–
[Novellas. Selections]
The Novellas of Martha Gellhorn.—1st Vintage Books ed.
p.   cm.
ISBN 0-679-74369-3 (pbk.)
I. Title.
[PS3513.E46A6   1994]
813'.52—dc20   93-42194
CIP

Book design by Iris Weinstein

$\mathcal{C}$ONTENTS

Mrs Maddison

M RS M A D D I S O N
M A K E S   B O T H   E N D S   M E E T

Mrs Maddison stood before the mirror and tried tipping her hat first over the right eye and then over the left. The mirror was cracked and Mrs Maddison's reflected face looked a bit mixed up. But the hat was clear. It was of white straw, the pot shape that is cheapest and commonest; it had cost thirty cents and Mrs Maddison herself trimmed it, with a noisily pink starchy rose, in the centre front, like a miner's lamp. This flower was only pinned on (safety-pin inside, rubbing a little against Mrs Maddison's forehead) and therefore nodded as she walked, bowed before she did, and occasionally blew from side to side, petulantly. It was her best hat. With it she wore a dress of dark blue voile, with white squares printed on it, and a piece of tough machine lace making the collar. She also had white wash gloves, only one of which she wore because the other had been darned beyond endurance. Everything was very clean, very stiff; her shoes had been whitened and she had borrowed paint from one of the fishermen to rim the soles and worn heels. She got her hat on finally, deciding that straight across her forehead it looked most dignified. Peering and rising on one foot, she put her rouge on somehow; two carnation-red circles over the soft wrinkly skin. She almost never made this effort; she almost never looked so trim and certain, so easy with herself and the world; a woman who had clothes and a place to put them on nicely. She was going up-town to beg.

'One thing,' Mrs Maddison said to the hat, 'I'm certainly not gonna give anyone the satisfaction of thinking I need things. I'll get what's my right but I'll not have anyone thinking I'm charity.'

There was, in Mrs Maddison's mind, a certain doubt as to her right; for that reason she put on her best and only clothes, to reassure herself. There was also some snobbery in her dressing. She didn't want the relief people to put her in the same class with the negroes, who unconcernedly paraded their want.

She closed the front door but did not lock it, having lost the key some time ago and being, anyhow, vague about such matters, with reason.

The path went dustily beside the river, bordered on one side by tin cans, underbrush, moored houseboats, wrecks and the wide, flat, brown sweep of the Mississippi. On the land side, beneath the bluff, sat the shacks of her friends and neighbours. Next door there was Mrs MacIvor and her two boys, further down lived Lena who was a negro, but nobody cared. Then there was the Wilsons' tent: the Wilsons were not on Relief, Mr Wilson being an artist. He went about the countryside ornamenting beds, and in every negro shack, in every tenant farmer's slat house, one could see his art, gilt and black scrolls changing a worn four-poster into something half sinful, half circus. Old Maybelle lived in a box made of outworn pieces of corrugated tin roofing; these were temporary quarters. Her houseboat had sunk, and she was still repairing damages prior to moving back into her real home. Maybelle was a great friend of Mrs Maddison; some quality, casual bright and illegal about them both, held them together.

The path wound up the hillside to town, straight from the ferry landing. Beyond the landing her own children lived and a few fishermen and some people one whispered about; they claimed they were Spanish.

Mrs Maddison waved to everyone she saw. No one asked her where she was going; her clothes announced her intentions.

Maybelle was sitting on the river-bank looking at her houseboat with love and anxiety.

'Flora,' she said as Mrs Maddison passed, 'would Alec help me with the roofing? I'll have the money next week. Tar paper. But it's my weight; I'm afraid to get up on the roof, it's kinda frail, you know.'

Mrs Maddison looked at Maybelle, smiling. Maybelle was her own age, sixty-ish, and a great woman with strength in her arms. She had a weatherbeaten man's face, rough and browned, and wore her hair twisted tight on her head. She would have shaved it, but that would mean answering questions, and Maybelle disliked questions. She had given up feeling or acting like a woman long ago; but her prestige for having once been a river captain's mistress followed her still in her old age. She was not fat, but there was a lot of her, muscle and bone; and everything about her houseboat was frail. Mrs Maddison promised to speak to Alec, her son.

The path up the hill was steep. The spring sun, already swollen and hot and ready for summer, beat down on it. Mrs Maddison stopped every once in a while with her hand over her heart, taking her breath in gulps. When her heart was quiet she wiped her forehead with the unworn glove. She did this quickly, not wanting to be seen. She knew she ought to have a handkerchief—it isn't my fault, she said to herself, crossly; I know how a lady ought to act, but what can I do?

She could see the crowds around the Relief office when she was still several blocks away. She hurried a little from excitement. There was always the chance that some commodities had come in from the north; perhaps some canned beef, or canned milk; perhaps even butter. Or clothes, maybe . . . she was almost running now, taking small quick steps over the cobbles, but careful, despite her haste, not to get any horse dung on her newly whitened shoes. Clothes: she had in a requisition for a baby dress for her granddaughter. The last ones she'd seen had been sweet; with pale blue French knots on them and little puckered sleeves. Now did they mean the sleeves to be like that, she thought, or was it just those fool women in the sewing-room not knowing what's the difference between sewing and shovelling coal . . . it didn't matter. Those dresses had all been given away before she got in her application slip. She had to be content with three didies the last time. And did she have to lie. She enjoyed herself briefly thinking about that: about the fine scene she'd had with Mrs Cahill, her home visitor. Sticking up for her rights, that's what she'd done. Couldn't she tell a lie if she wanted to? Some country when a woman couldn't lie, doing no harm to anyone. She said to Mrs Cahill: Now you look here, Miss Lucy, I don't need any clothes for myself, I'm getting on fine, but I gotta right to clothes same's everybody else. So I'll just take clothes for my grandchild instead. Mrs Cahill said: Nonsense, you need everything yourself, you haven't a decent pair of shoes and when I put in a requisition it's going to be for you. You let that girl Tennessee scrounge around for her own child. I'll take no bossing from you, Miss Lucy, you're too young to have any sense, Mrs Maddison said, and who'd know better than me what I need? You just get me things for Tiny, like I said. Mrs Cahill objected that it was against the rules. Rules, Mrs Maddison sniffed, rules—well I never. Mrs Cahill gave up: the office was small; they had a certain leeway in allotting federal commodities and in making decisions. And she knew Mrs Maddison. A woman who wouldn't be ordered about and who only obeyed when necessary, and then you could feel her chuckling. Lord God, Mrs Maddison thought, I hope those niggers and those begging white folks don't get everything before I can push my way in.

The Relief office was an unused warehouse: it loitered over a city block, the panes out of the windows, pink paint peeling from the walls, great barn-like doors opening into damp shadows. Little grilles had been knocked into the walls and at these, separately, whites and negroes received their pay checks, for work done on the roads or in the sewing-room. The negroes leaned against the walls, smoking pipes or stubs of cigarettes, dressed in neat white clothes, shapeless, chatty, able apparently to lean against something in the sun and laugh and talk in half sentences for hours, or days if necessary. The white people were crisper in their demands and never had to wait quite as long. If there were any seats or benches empty, inside the warehouse, they marched in and sat down. They wore their faces according to their needs for the day or their characters. There were quiet women, marked with weariness and resignation: there were angry ones, sitting stiffly as if they didn't want anyone to think they even approved the chairs in this thieving place: there were plaintive and garrulous and shy men: and Mrs Maddison, elegant with her rose, shoved into the midst of all this and settled herself on a bench, something like a bird perching and something like a ship dropping anchor.

'Howdy, Miz Crowder,' she said, bowing to the woman next to her. 'What've they got today?'

'Some lady's nightgowns,' Mrs Crowder said. 'But I'm here to talk about my rent. I don't want no nightgown; they can keep their old clothes; they feel like burlap those things do. But my landlord sez they don't pay him and he wantsa put us out. And Harry, like a pretzel with rheumatism and these spring nights.'

Mrs Crowder sighed and Mrs Maddison nodded at her with bright sympathy. She turned to see who else was here, and what they were getting if they were lucky or talked loud enough.

There was that Wilkins man who ought to be shut up in jail for the way he treated Miz Wilkins. The woman was too patient; didn't step up and speak for herself. One child after another, and each year that woman looked more like something blowing down the street; an old bit of newspaper that'd been rained on. She frowned at Mr Wilkins, who didn't notice.

She saw a small girl, a share cropper's child, whom she knew by sight. Mamie was sitting beside her mother, her hands folded in patience on her lap. Every once in a while she blew off flies that circled too close about her head. Mrs Maddison did not approve of this. No place to bring children. Children shouldn't know about begging and waiting around: they should be brought up as if all this weren't going on. Or as nearly as possible. The child would get a sad old look long before she should. She'd hear things children needn't know for a while. There was Ruth Hodges crying over there in the corner: well, she had a right to cry if she couldn't help herself, but it was a bad thing to cry in front of other people, and hard times were something you managed by yourself: better to be angry about it if anything. The child worried her. She found herself getting slowly fretful, wanting to rise and sail out of this place, waving her pride around her head like a flag. She hated it. The days she came up to work she didn't mind: then she just sewed in the gloomy cavern of the warehouse and gossiped and argued when she was told to hurry and argued about not getting enough hours work. How'm I ever gonna give that Tiny orange juice, she thought, on $7.80 a month. None of their old business what she did with her money. Shouldn't spend it on Tiny, they kept saying. Lot they knew. If she didn't, who would be getting Tiny what she needed, the little smiling white radish.... Why couldn't people give Bill work then, and, if they couldn't, why fuss with her about her money. Little's I've got, she thought, and it's not as if I had everything I needed for myself: I gotta right to choose if I want things or Tiny gets orange juice. Her mind turned these thoughts over, knowing each one of them, there was nothing new to think about. It was just that each week, each day, it began all over. God in heaven, she said to herself, what a stingy world it is.

'Miss Lucy,' she called. Mrs Cahill smiled to her, said, just a minute Mrs Maddison, and hurried back behind the beaver board partitions into an inner office, airless and lighted all day by bulbs on cords, where the social workers wrote reports and hung their hats. I'm kinda sorry for that girl, Mrs Maddison thought. She's getting a lot more money than I'll ever get outa this place, but she didn't used to have to run around all over this State in a Ford like a mule. When she was little, Mrs Maddison thought ... long ago Lucy Harmsworth wore a blue hair-ribbon and played on the lawn in front of a white house with high slim pillars.... Mrs Maddison's son Alec was a child, too, and Mr Maddison, who had died and been missed and then forgotten, had work as time-keeper at the box factory, was it that or had they been farming? Anyhow, they had a house, and the two older boys were alive and looked as if they'd live forever, with faces like balloons and shouting their lungs out, and falling into everything and eating all day long.... Timmy, the first one, had been her favourite. She'd forgotten now really what her husband looked like, since he'd been dead twelve years. But she'd never forget what Timmy was like, dying in the charity hospital of typhoid. And Rupert close after him. We all had it better once, Mrs Maddison decided. We were real folks once; we had places to live, and we had families, and we knew what we'd be doing the next year and the next one. Now, now ... A familiar feeling of uncertainty overcame Mrs Maddison; a fear that everything would blow away even as she waited; things would change once again, there wouldn't even be this piddling work for her, this measly living. She jumped to her feet and walked to the back office and went in without knocking.

'I gotta talk to you right away, Miss Lucy,' she said, her voice sharp with the sudden terror she had felt.

'Yes, Mrs Maddison.'

'I gotta have more hours work. Nobody can live on that $7.80 a month I'm getting and I'm not complaining about the pay, mind you, though I must say fifteen cents 'n hour looks like nigger wages to me, and it's not much for niggers the way pork 'n meal's going up, but, anyhow, I gotta be working more.'

'I'll see what I can do.' Mrs Cahill was thirty; she wore a cheap and ugly gingham dress. Her hair came out in neglected strands from the bun on her neck, and wearily she shoved the loose ends into place.

Mrs Maddison was sorry for her again, and angry at herself: I didn't come here to be crying over Lucy Harmsworth, she thought; there's Tiny to be worrying about.

'No, you gotta say something sure. Now.'

'I can't, Mrs Maddison. You know I haven't got the money. It comes from the State headquarters, and first it comes from Washington. They give us what they can every month and we divide it up. If there's more money you'll get more work. I can't ...' Mrs Cahill said, thinking to herself, that proud old woman worrying her heart out about Tiny, who probably oughtn't to live, anyhow, or just won't. . . .

'I gotta know,' Mrs Maddison said, but her voice was dimming, and she felt tired and wanted to be sitting on her front porch watching the river but not thinking.

'Well.'

They waited in silence and a few flies buzzed crazily against the lamp bulbs, and outside the office they could hear the close droning voices of people telling their troubles, asking for help.

'Perhaps I could get you something from the Commodities,' Mrs Cahill said.

'I'm not asking you for favours, Lucy Harmsworth, I'm asking you for work. Like a self-respecting woman's gotta right to.'

'I know,' Mrs Cahill said. 'I don't mean to be giving favours. If there's anything there you've got a right to it.'

She led Mrs Maddison through a back hall to a small dark room with a counter across half of it. A young man with a pencil behind his ear, trying to look cheerfully like a grocer's clerk, presided.

'Johnny,' Mrs Cahill said, 'have you got anything?'

He rumpled some papers. And turned and looked at the shelves.

'The nightgowns are all gone. There's no clothes now, and most of the other visitors got their clients down for the food already. There's just a little canned salmon,' he said. 'About two cans left. We never got much. Would you want that?'

Mrs Cahill looked at Mrs Maddison and Mrs Maddison looked through the wall, obstinate and silent. She was thinking: if I get it we'll have something nice to-night for supper. I could ask over Tennessee and that no-count husband of hers and have a big plate of it with something on it; maybe I could earn a dime or something for some tomatoes. . . . Her face remained stony, asking for nothing.

'Yes,' Mrs Cahill said, and signed a slip and handed the two cans to Mrs Maddison.

Mrs Maddison held them in her arms, uncomfortably, with no expression on her face. She stood looking at Mrs Cahill and said nothing. 'I know,' Mrs Cahill said, 'I know you haven't got anything against me. Go on home and get Tennessee over to supper.'

Mrs Maddison smiled at her then and went out, but tactfully, by the back door, so as not to make anybody else feel badly, and also because she knew that if Ruth Hodges was still there crying she'd have to give her one of the cans and then Tennessee wouldn't be coming to-night. . . . A party, Mrs Maddison thought, gay at once, a party: and I'll act like I just bought the salmon with my own money, just went up-town to a store and bought it, and nobody has to give me anything.

Mrs Maddison asked one of the MacIvor boys to tell Tennessee that supper would be waiting for her and Bill, about six o'clock. She sent the message like that, a casual word, not letting them know ahead what a fine supper it would be. Maybelle loaned her a can of tomatoes, knowing she'd get them back, or a can of something else, when Mrs Maddison's Relief check came on Tuesday. The MacIvors and the Wilsons and Lena instantly heard that Mrs Maddison had extra food and was going to give her daughter Tennessee and Bill a surprise party. Mrs Maddison thought regretfully of her son Alec and Sabine, his wife: she wanted them too. But she'd have to postpone that until the next successful visit up-town; or, anyhow, until next week. She was nearly out of everything: salt, sugar, flour, coffee, and the tall can of milk was suspiciously light in her hands.

She put her hat carefully on a shelf and set about making her house ready for the evening. There was very little to do. She tended it always with passionate care: she had lived in it a year now, which was a long time for anyone to have the same house. When she came to it, sent by Mrs Cahill because the rent was practically non-existent, she had wept bitterly but alone, walking up and down the river-bank, holding her hands over her mouth to keep it secret. It had been a negro cabin: three rotting rooms, the floor splintered and in places gone. Paper, plastered over the walls against the rain, hung in greying streamers, with spiders and less possible bugs crawling and crackling in the loose pieces. There was no furniture beyond a rusting stove, whose chimney gaped where the rust had eaten away a ragged hole. There were no window panes, and water lay in pools wherever it could collect, souvenirs of the last rain and a hint of what to expect from the roof. When she went up the front steps she clung to the shaking handrail, frightened of going through the steps, and breaking her ankles. After she had walked along the river for an hour, wasting her anguish over this place where she would have to live, she came back and sat down on the edge of the porch. Growing on the river-bank in front of her was a thin exhausted weeping willow, and a little to the left, amazingly, a magnolia tree. It didn't look as if it would ever have the strength to bloom again, but the leaves were glossy if scant, and stood blackly against the afternoon sky. Beside her house a wire fence shut in the water works: the drone of the dynamo was friendly and soothing, like bees, like an old woman humming endlessly to herself. She sat there quietly for hours and then decided that since she was here she would make this house fit for a person to live in. She had at that time an old trunk corded up, holding what clothes she owned, a few plates and pots and pictures of her children as babies, very starched and solemn.

From Mrs Cahill and Mrs Cahill's friends she got old magazines; and she tore out the advertisements and pasted them all over the ripped and filthy newspaper of the walls. She did this with an eye to colour, not caring much what the advertisement was about, just so it looked bright and fresh. There was, above her bed, an intimate advertisement about articles of personal hygiene for women, and she hesitated a long time about a Listerine advertisement but finally didn't use it, though the paper was nice and shiny, because the woman's face looked so anxious. Campbell's soup was vaunted on her walls, chic red-coated people smoked cigarettes, a handsome man in a polo coat drove a Packard, a lovely mask-like face, swathed like a nun, proved how clever Helena

Rubinstein was with skin. . . . It had taken her several weeks, and finally she'd gone to the public library and been eager about wanting old magazines to read. 'I wouldn't tell them I used them on my walls,' she said to Maybelle. 'They'd think I was poor and begging for something. But just wanting to read; well, that's something even rich folks can do.'

Alec, who earned his living, or tried to, salvaging iron, got her a less used piece of stove pipe and cleaned up the stove. The Relief gave her a bed, and what with judicious scavenging, barter, economies and ingenuity, she'd fitted up her house. The Wilsons had been very helpful. Mrs Maddison sewed for Mrs Wilson and in return Mr Wilson ornamented her furniture. His favourite style was black and gold, but as that was fairly expensive paint he used up all his odds and ends of colour. Mrs Maddison's house had a wild brightness; two curtains on the same window being different material, each unstable chair boasting several shades of paint; but all she cared about was that it should look gay and be clean. For a year she had collected oddments, patched, painted, hammered, and now her house, she felt, was a place any woman might be proud to live in. There was the kitchen-dining-room-living-room, and two bedrooms. Some day, Mrs Maddison used to tell herself, when times are better, I'll fix up one of those bedrooms for a parlour. She knew this would never happen. Parlour furniture meant plush, and a big sideboard of some heavy varnished wood. But just saying it to herself made her happy, made her feel like a woman of property, and opened up alluring vistas of the future, when she'd be entertaining her friends in a fine room, with a big oil lamp covered by a shade, lighting them all up, and showing off the food on the sideboard. . . .

She cared for the magnolia tree and built a support for the weeping willow, which was about to bend over into the river, the bank having been drained away and silted back, with countless floods and countless dry summers. She thought of these two trees as 'my garden.' Finally the dynamo next door became hers also, a friend, and got a name.

She called it Jennie. Some nights it sang loudly, with sudden moaning jerks: 'Jennie's got rheumatism,' she'd tell herself and fall asleep thinking what a fine house she had, and such an unusual location: with the garden and the river view, bottles floating beside grapefruit rinds, and the ferry tooting its way across to Louisiana, and the fishermen's boats put-putting up the river, and the houseboats, like dingy garages, square, stuck in the mud, helplessly tied to the shore.

'Flora.'

'Hi there, Maybelle, come right on in.'

'I brought you something. Lena made it for me. But I can't use it yet. I wouldn't have no place to put it in that box of mine. When I get the houseboat fixed, o' course—but I thought you could put it on the table to-night seeing's you got a real supper.'

Maybelle came cautiously up the steps; she was haunted by the idea that things would break under her. She handed Mrs Maddison her loan-gift. It was a new tin can, cut half-way down into fine strips. These strips had been bent outwards and twisted to resemble flower stems and on the top of each stem sat gaily a little paper crepe flower.

'Oh,' Mrs Maddison said, and held it wonderingly in her hand. 'Oh, Maybelle, if that ain't the purtiest. . . .'

Maybelle smiled at her. 'The house looks grand,' she said. 'But you wait till you see my houseboat. Oh, man, is that old tub gonna be a floating palace.'

They grinned at each other. 'What'ja gonna wear?' Maybelle asked.

'Why, my blue dress, of course. What did you think I'd wear; my black satin trimmed with ermine?'

Maybelle clanked her massively on the back, laughing. 'No, ma'am,' she said, 'I thought you was gonna wear a black lace nightie like that girl in your stocking ad. Well, I gotta go home. I'm making me a rag rug for the kitchen. It's a helluva job; but nothing's too good for me. We'll have a housewarming, Flora, just us two old girls, you wait. I betcha I know where I'll get some stuff. It'll be one party, all right.'

'I wisht I could ask you to-night, Maybelle.'

'Don't you think about it. You feed up that Tennessee of yours; she's looking peaked.'

'And well she might, with Bill drunk all the time and acting like a crazy Eyetalian or something, shouting at her and Tiny and I don't know what besides.'

'Well,' Maybelle said, 'you can't blame him too much, Flora, he used to be a good kid. He just don't know what to do, sitting around all day.'

'There's plenty others had to do the same,' Mrs Maddison said and her voice was cold, 'or he could help Alec with the iron.'

'Sure. There's a lotta money in that. What's Alec making now, 'bout thirty cents a day, ain't he? All he needs is a helper so's he can split.'

'All right, Maybelle.'

'Sure. You gotta think about them things. It's tough on the kids, Flora; they ain't had the fun we did.'

'I know. But I get so mad sometimes thinking about Tennessee and Tiny, and you can't only think about what Bill used to be. She ain't living with the boy she married two years ago, she's living with this here Bill, getting drunk all the time and . . . oh, I dunno, I'm not gonna think about it. We'll have a real good supper and I just won't think about it.'

'That's right. Well, so long, Flora. Come by for me in the mornin' and we'll go up to the sewing-room together. Have a good time.'

She creaked carefully down the stairs and Mrs Maddison could hear the great amiable voice booming to Lena on her front porch and passing the time of day with Mrs Wilson.

I'm not gonna get mad at Bill, Mrs Maddison thought: I know he's a good boy and I'm not gonna think about the rest. He just can't help himself, I guess. I won't think about it. It's none of my business. She walked lightly about her house, preparing dinner, setting the table, trying various places to put the lovely flower centre-piece Maybelle had brought. At six, everything was ready and swiftly she inspected and admired her home a last time and then went to sit in a rocker on the porch, cooling off from the stove heat and the excitement. This way, too, she could see them coming. She rocked quietly, bowed to Mrs MacIvor on the next porch, and thought to herself about Tennessee, who was her baby. That girl, she said to herself, is just too pretty for her own good. If she hadn't been such a beauty to look at she wouldn't of got grabbed off so young and she'd not be married at all yet. Nineteen now, with that child and Bill.... Well, I was married when I was eighteen, Mrs Maddison thought, and it worked fine: but those were different times; that was when a man could work if only he wanted to and didn't have the rheumatism or his heart going feeble on him.... It was all different, she thought; people weren't so careless of each other then: there were lots of people like Maybelle, liking to see their neighbours happy. Well, she thought calmly, I'm getting old. It's only old women thinks such fine thoughts about the past.

She watched them coming up the path beside the river, with the dust shining around them, and the wind clicking in the sparse, dry trees. All her joy in the fine food waiting, and in the house she had garnished for their evening, faded and left her cold with wretchedness. Bill was drunk. She could see that. His head, young and nice but for the pallor and the fretful uncertain look about his mouth, lolled on his neck. He stumbled, with Tennessee holding and guiding him. Tennessee was talking to him as one would to a frightened horse or a feverish child: Mrs Maddison could hear little bits of it, in the quietness. 'No, Billy, of course she don't think you're a bum—there's no jobs, honey; we all know that—now, Billy, pick your feet up a bit, you'll be falling—no, I know you're not drunk, it's only the path's bum and you can't see in this light—hold on to me, darling....' Mrs Maddison took in her breath. She knew what the supper would be like: the lavish supper of salmon with tomatoes thick over it, potatoes steaming from the stove, and sweetened coffee and bread-pudding. Tennessee and she would sit in silence, choking down their food, not looking up from their plates, trying not to see what Bill was spilling on the oil cloth, on his clothes, how his hands wavered with the fork. They'd be nervous and tight, waiting for the evening quickly to finish. And from time to time, thickly, Bill would break out into argument, angry against her, and suddenly cruel with Tennessee. How can he be like that, Mrs Maddison thought: there are others with the courage to stay sober: and a young wife, she thought, watching Tennessee, half pulling Bill towards the house, a lovely young wife. . . .

'Howdy, ma,' Tennessee called; she couldn't wave, she was using her hands.

'Howdy, Tennessee. Howdy, Bill,' Mrs Maddison said, her voice gay. 'Hurry on up, everything's ready.'

She left the porch; she didn't want Tennessee to feel her watching that unsteady ascent, Bill with his hands on the handrail and his feet slipping. She moved about the room, lighting up the oil lamps on the kitchen table and in the bedroom. For a moment she stood and looked at her table, and Maybelle's flowers, and thought: I wish that man was dead. He's only bringing unhappiness to folks who got enough without that.

Tennessee came in first: 'Bill's not feeling good,' she said anxiously.

'Who said I wasn't feeling good?' Bill said. 'S'lie. M'feeling fine. M'feeling swell. Hi, there, Maw, how's the old girl?'

'I'm fine, Bill. Wanna give me your cap?' She took it from him and laid it on the bed. Tennessee wore no hat or coat; she stood watching Bill, leaning against the door. Her mother looked at her and thought: For nineteen that girl looks too tired, she's getting bad lines in her forehead.

Bill noticed Tennessee suddenly. 'Fine looking girl I got fer a wife, ain't she? Fine shape that girl's got.' Mrs Maddison turned her back on him. Tennessee moved out of the light and Bill sat down heavily at the table. Mrs Maddison dished out the food. 'Miss Lucy had them cans of salmon extra,' she said. 'That's nice,' Tennessee murmured. Bill ate in silence for a while. Suddenly he banged his glass against the table.

'Charity food, that's what I'm eating. Just old canned stuff they give to paupers and niggers. Can't git our own stuff; has to be give to us. I don't take any of that Relief; by God, I'd ruther starve.'

'It's a shame you don't take it,' Mrs Maddison said. So I'm a pauper or a nigger, she thought, her eyes smarting. 'It's about time you did, Bill Saunders. You been married to that girl two years and it wasn't only the first six months you was really keeping her like a man should. You been hanging around without jobs for a long time, long's some folks can remember. It's a fine thing to be proud but not when your own wife and baby gets skinny in the face with your old pride.'

Mrs Maddison's breath came like a clock ticking, fast and staccato, her hands were fluttering in her lap. I said it now, she thought: well, it's about time, too. Somebody's gotta. He just can't see there's anybody alive at all but him. And that girl and Tiny....

Bill's face was getting dark with blood. 'You nagging old busybody,' he said. 'You nosey old woman, meddling in other folks business. I'll do with my wife like I want to. Just because you're a beggar's no reason for the whole fambly to go around holding out their hats and whining for a little something to eat. I kin work and I'm not taking any of their old charity and if you don't like it.' His fist lay on the table, like carved wood. 'And, anyhow, I don't like coming here, and I don't like my wife coming here. Just to listen to you crabbing at me. So I guess we'll go. Come on, Tennessee.'

Mrs Maddison didn't move and she said nothing. She made no gesture towards Tennessee and she kept her eyes fixed on the salt cellar, waiting. Whining for a little something to eat, she thought, and felt very tired. That's what had happened to her party.

'No,' Tennessee said. 'I'm not coming, Bill. You can't talk that way to my mother, and you're drunk. How do you s'pose Tiny'd be alive now if it wasn't for ma getting her orange juice and things with her own Relief money? I don't like people who act like you. I'm not coming, Bill.'

Bill stared at her stupidly, his head a little on one side and back, as if she had slapped him. Suddenly he swung to his feet, cursing: 'Whose wife are you, anyhow?' He reached out his arm for her and she hit it away. He grabbed her by the shoulder cruelly and she twisted out of his reach: he thrust against the table to get her and she ran into the next room, and her eyes were black with fear. He didn't see where he was going and he kept talking, not words but just sounds of fury: and his hands were out before him like claws. Mrs Maddison sat in her chair unable to move; even her voice had gone. Her mind kept saying, scream out, get the MacIvors and Lena and Maybelle and everybody, help, help, but she sat staring into the next room, frozen silent. She heard Tennessee's voice lift: 'I'll throw the lamp at you, Bill. I'll throw the lamp sure's I'm standing here.' Everyone's breath sounded clearly in the house. Mrs Maddison waited. Bill came back out of the room, tearing at his cap.

'It's your doing,' he shouted at Mrs Maddison. 'It's all your doing. If you wasn't a withered ugly old woman I'd take and wring your neck.' He got down the steps somehow; they could hear him stumbling and cursing back towards the ferry landing.

Tennessee came into the room; her eyes were still wide and black but she moved listlessly. She sat down at the table and Mrs Maddison said in a tiny voice: 'Have some bread-pudding, honey.' They picked up their spoons and held them and neither touched the food. Then Tennessee began to cry. 'What's wrong with that boy?' she said. 'He used to be a good man and I love him, I love him. What'm I gonna do?' she said and wept, staring straight in front of her.

'If he gets a job he'll be all right,' Mrs Maddison said.

'He won't get a job; there aren't no jobs anywhere. It's Mr Murdoch gets him drinks up there at the saloon; he oughtn't to do that, just 'cause he's 'n old souse hisself. Why don't he leave my Bill alone?'

'I know, lovey, I know.' Mrs Maddison pulled her chair alongside Tennessee's and stroked her hair. 'Don't fret, lamb; don't you fret. You just sleep here to-night and he'll be sobered up to-morrow.'

'I can't do that. How 'bout Tiny?'

'Didn't you leave Tiny at Alec's?'

'Yes.'

'She'll be all right there. You get some rest here, honey. It'll be all right tomorrow.'

'No, it won't,' Tennessee said, 'and you know it. And not day after to-morrow neither, or next week, or anything. Not till he gets him some work like he ought to have and takes care of us.'

'What'll you do, then?'

'I dunno. Oh, ma, what can I do?'

'Guess you'll have to leave him, Tennessee, till he gets work, anyhow. Just gotta, I guess; Miss Lucy'll take care of you and Tiny; and you kin live here.'

Tennessee said nothing: but she had stopped crying.

'You don't like him, do you, ma?'

'Not when he treats you the way he does and goes and gets drunk and lets you starve on account he's too proud.'

'You don't like him anyhow.'

'Oh, Tennessee. . . . Remember when you got married. . . .'

'You don't. You never did. You're lying now.'

Mrs Maddison moved a little away from her, and her hands clasped tight together. There had been hate in Tennessee's voice: my own daughter, she thought, my own daughter.

'I'm gonna leave him cause there's nothing else I can do. But I'm not coming here to live knowing you hate him. I won't do that and listen to you talking against him.'

'Tennessee, I only want you to be happy honey, I only want you to get what you gotta eat, you and Tiny. . . .'

She was talking to an empty room: swiftly, without a word or a gesture, Tennessee had gone, and Mrs Maddison could hear her running down the path as if she hated the house she had been in, and the woman she'd left.

I fixed her up a veil outa muslin for her wedding and those pretty flowers I got at the dime store on her hair, Mrs Maddison said to herself: what shall I do with all the food that's left, nothing hardly eaten, and she looked around at the gay talkative walls, but it seemed bare and forlorn to her, and she wished it were to-morrow already, or next week, and then it might be better, or she'd have forgotten how it was, talking to her daughter's footsteps running away from her.

Maybelle sat on the ground before her box-house and smoked. It looked like a rolled leaf, the cigarette, and as it smelled pretty bad nobody had ever wanted to try one. She used to say mysteriously that she'd found the formula for making them sealed in a bottle floating on the river, and she didn't doubt but that the old Indian chiefs smoked cigarettes like hers. She enjoyed making up important stories, and then waiting very earnestly to see who'd believe them.

Mrs Maddison sat down on a keg beside her.

'I heard Bill going home last night,' Maybelle said presently. 'And Tennessee after him.' Mrs Maddison watched a grapefruit rind fighting in the current, being whirled round, filling, sinking.

'It's bad times, Flora.' Maybelle's great hand lay on Mrs Maddison's knee. 'It's not the kids, nor it's not you. It's just the times.'

Mrs Maddison stared across the river to Louisiana, remembering how, three years ago, she'd picked pecans over there, till her back felt like something made of rusty iron. And gone to sleep in a tent with the mosquitoes droning closer and closer, and the damp air from the marshlands settling foggily in her throat. Tennessee was working in the dime store in the afternoons and going to school; Mrs Maddison could send her a little money each week, staying there in Louisiana, for the movies and marcelles: so she wouldn't feel she was different from the girls who had homes and didn't think about money all the time. I didn't do enough, she thought; somewhere I should have been better for her.

'Don't think about it, Flora,' Maybelle said. 'It don't do no good. And they'll forget, and you, too. No sense gitting moody.'

Maybelle rose and shook the dirt from her. She went behind her hut and emerged with a discoloured wheelbarrow, which had a drunken lurch when it moved, its wheels being dissimilar. On this sat a Singer sewing machine of vast dimensions and antique make.

'Well, for heaven's sake,' Mrs Maddison said, 'whatever are you gonna do with that?'

'I'm gonna trundle it up the hill to the sewing-room,' Maybelle said. 'I can't use it, anyhow, till I get the boat fixed up and I'm sick of piddling around with those flimsy things they got up there. I'm scared I'll mash the damn things every time I put my foot on the pedals. And I sez, working's fine but you gotta think of the conditions.' With this ominous remark, but evidently pleased with the effect she was making on her friend, she started the wheelbarrow limping on its way.

They arrived at the sewing-room, breathless. A crowd collected at once. Everybody wanted to know what was the matter with Maybelle, had the poor woman taken leave of her wits, and besides, pushing a thing like that, big as a horse, up the river hill, in this sun, she must be crazy, she'd have a stroke . . . and, anyhow, why bring your own stuff to the Government? That didn't make sense; the Government was supposed to get its own machines.

'Great God,' Maybelle said. 'Would you all keep quiet? Can't a woman do what she wants with her own stuff? I never saw sotcha commotion as if something'd happened.'

She established her machine under a light bulb. Mrs Maddison sat down beside her. Soon, above the hum of the machines and the women gossiping, Maybelle began to speak to Mrs Maddison in her booming authoritative voice.

'It's better now,' she said.

'Good.'

'This old machine I got from Captain Mike; in them days they made good solid stuff.'

'Yes.'

'I wish that old man wasn't dead; I useta have a fine time getting drunk with him.'

Mrs Jenkins, on Mrs Maddison's left, sniffed; and young Mrs Harden, alongside Maybelle, giggled and almost stopped working, hoping she'd hear some more.

Maybelle took a deep breath, and for a minute Mrs Maddison wondered whether she was going to burst into song, a big noisy river song for men drinking.

Miss Sampson, who had charge of the sewing-room, appeared.

'Now, ladies, we've got to have all these dresses done by Friday,' she said. 'So get along, less talking, I think. . . .'

'Well,' Maybelle said, 'we kin work better if we talk. We're likely to fall asleep if we don't. Setting in this gloomy place doing the same old thing every time, makes you sleepy-like.'

'You ought to be glad you've got the work, Maybelle.'

'I am. Don't get yourself in a fret. I am. I'm happy like a bird. That's why I gotta talk; just bubbling up with good spirits.'

Mrs Harden tittered again and Miss Sampson left; it seemed useless to stay. The clients were dreadfully trying at times. She went into the commodities-room to check over work done: she always felt silly after she'd talked to Maybelle.

'The trouble,' Mrs Maddison said, 'is they act like they're doing you a favour, letting you work for fifteen cents an hour. Now I'm not kicking: I sez, times is bad, we gotta work for what we kin get. But work's work; it's no favour to nobody.'

'I'll have a race,' Maybelle shouted suddenly. 'I'll bet old Jemima against any of those fiddling machines you gals is working on. I'm starting on the right sleeve. I'll bet I kin get done faster than any of you.'

From all over the room the bet was taken up. 'You start us off, Flora,' Maybelle said. 'And no cheaters. Lissen, Miz Drew, you can't race, you already got one seam done. Nor you, neither, Susie Thatch. Come on, the rest of you bum seamstresses.' She bowed over her machine, like a quarterback ready to give signals, her feet poised over the great ornamental pedals.

'One, two, three: Go.'

Machines banged; women stopped working in other parts of the room and stood above the contestants, screaming over the hum of the machines. 'Damn!' Maybelle's voice shouted out. 'I broke my thread.' Furiously she fixed it; women were laughing and swearing, and those racing leaned nearer and nearer the cloth. Negroes collected outside the wide open doors and watched and laughed. Suddenly Maybelle's voice went up like a rocket. 'I'm done! I won!' All the women jammed around her to see the sleeve, to look at the wondrous and titanic Jemima which was a sturdier implement than any of the Government's contraptions. Miss Sampson walked into this bedlam. She spread order like a nurse, driving the children away from a pillow-fight and back into bed. Everyone was quiet, a little guilty and thoroughly subdued, except Maybelle and Mrs Maddison. Mrs Maddison leaned over her machine and laughed up and down the scale, wiping her tears away. 'If you could of seen yourself, Maybelle.'

'That's enough,' Miss Sampson said. 'This isn't kindergarten.'

'But you wanted them dresses done quick,' Maybelle said, trying to look wide-eyed and abused.

Mrs Maddison went on laughing. 'It's worth losing the job,' she said, 'just to of seen you. I never saw a woman look like that. You big old mountain, shaking like a jello over that fool machine of yours. . . .'

Mrs Cahill watched the two of them, thinking what a pair: they'd find some way to amuse themselves if the world was blowing away. They'd probably bet on which trees would blow off first.

'Tennessee came to see me this morning.' Mrs Maddison stopped laughing at once. 'She said she was leaving Bill and she made out her application for Relief.'

Mrs Maddison nodded. 'I'm sorry about it,' Mrs Cahill said. 'But I don't think there was anything else she could do. We'll get her on Relief as fast as we can.'

'Where's she gonna live?' Mrs Maddison asked, ashamed she had to find this out from Mrs Cahill, and trying to seem casual about it, as if she didn't know because she hadn't had time to see her daughter yet.

'She's moving in with Alec and Sabine.'

'That's a small place.'

'We can get a bed for her; I think she'll be all right there. They're happy to have her.'

'Yes.' And so would she be happy to have her; and she had a bed, and a fine bright room waiting. Alec's house was falling to pieces and the damp came through the walls in wide brown patches, and Sabine was no good as a housekeeper, she was too young to care or to know how pretty a house could be. 'Yes; well, that's fine,' Mrs Maddison said, wearing her pride all around her.

Mrs Cahill paused and then said: 'Would you like to help mother this afternoon? She's starting her spring house-cleaning and she'd like somebody who wouldn't wash them into holes to clean up the curtains. She'll give you a half-dollar, I guess . . . if you've got the time.'

'That'll be fine, Miss Lucy. I'll go right over from here.'

Maybelle had been listening, and when Mrs Cahill moved away she said: 'Anyhow, Flora, she's leaving Bill and that's better for her and you wanted that.'

'Yes.'

'And you kin see her just as much as you want at Alec's.'

'Yes.'

'It's better living alone when you're old, Flora. Young people's so messy, and Tiny and all.'

Mrs Maddison looked at her, saying nothing.

'All right, Flora, I know it's lonely and you want her but don't break your heart over it, she'll get over this in a week, you just wait.'

Mrs Maddison smiled and thought even a week was a long time. . . .

With the fifty cents she bought a quart of milk and some cream of wheat and oranges, and stopped by Alec's on her way home. She called at the door but no one came and no one spoke. She left the package on the step and went home. Her arms ached from scrubbing the curtains, and she refused to think about Tennessee. She ate quickly, almost nothing, and then, in the evening cool, she sat on her front porch and rocked and brushed her hair slowly in long soothing strokes.

After a while Mrs MacIvor came out and nodded, and then presently the small gay stars appeared over Louisiana. Mrs Maddison went indoors and got her harmonica and came out on the porch and began playing the few tunes she knew, sad lazy music that had been floating over the river as long as she could remember. Mrs MacIvor moved on to Mrs Maddison's steps and Lena wandered over with Maybelle. Mrs Wilson came and was given a seat because she had rheumatism. They burned some rags against the mosquitoes and no one talked, and softly, insistently, the music curled over them in a thin streamlike smoke. The dynamo hummed in the power house, but gently, making no interruption of the quiet, and more stars came out. The weeping willow swished above the water, and the old women sat on Mrs Maddison's porch, resting after the effort of having lived another day.

T W O

•

MRS MADDISON
RETURNS TO THE LAND

In the Relief office they had read the bulletins coming from Washington via State headquarters, and they had received a good many visitors called field supervisors and field representatives. Under pressure and feeling theirs-not-to-reason-why, they had shipped unemployed families back to the land. It was a program, which made it vast and important, possible of endless interpretation and confusion, and above all it had to be done quickly. Some of the Relief workers, who had lived long in these parts and knew conditions and what you had to have to farm, and what kind of land they were putting people on, and what the houses meant in ill-health, shook their heads grimly but in wise silence. Rural rehabilitation: in itself a magnificent idea. A chance for men to be again self-supporting; their own masters; captains of their destinies, souls, pocket-books. 'It's a fine idea,' Mrs Cahill said, 'only nobody seems to have thought much about those negro shanties we're putting our folks in.' Mrs Lewis, who worked out towards the sawmill district, said it certainly was a fine idea, but she thought there'd be some trouble about medical aid: she also shook her head. 'The malaria,' Mrs Lewis said. Miss Ogilvie, who had a sharper tongue than the others, and used to lie awake at night furtively being ashamed of herself for having such a nice bed, said: 'It sez, in the bulletins, $105.80 a year is the average cost to the govment for rural rehab. families; for everything personal. Lissen to me,' she said, with the sun shining on her eyeglasses. 'That just isn't human. And to think those northerners made all that fuss about slaves. I don't think they got their heads screwed on right up there.'

Mrs Cahill brooded over the present and future of Mrs Maddison and her children. She realized that Mrs Maddison was starving herself, doing some very fine and tricky work with her Relief money in order to coddle Tiny. She liked Mrs Maddison and thought Tennessee was stupid, sexually awake only, selfish, and that Tiny had so few chances of being a decent or healthy citizen that Mrs Maddison's sacrifice probably came under the heading of heroic if senseless gestures.

She wanted very much to get Mrs Maddison away from Tennessee's disaffection, and she also liked Alec, and thought he could do with something to eat for a change. But rural rehabilitation. . . . Something about the name upset Mrs Cahill, who was fairly simple and usually said what she meant. It was such a vast sound, such a stupendous and splendid idea, and when you got right down to it, it was a chance to live in an abandoned negro shanty or a badly made, too small, new house; without adequate water, heat or light, with inadequate provision for staple groceries or clothes or medical care: and work until your back broke to raise a crop for which there might or might not be buyers. Obviously it was easier to be in debt to the Government than to private landowners. The Government, being so much bigger, sometimes got a little entangled and forgot to collect on time or just lent you more money to pay back with. But the idea distressed her, still. She talked this problem over with the local administrator and finally she approached Alec, calling on him one day when he was sitting on the river-bank fishing quite hopelessly, but fooling himself into feeling busy.

'Alec,' Mrs Cahill said, 'have you ever thought about farming?'

'No'm.'

'Would you like to go on a farm?'

Alec thought. He thought about farms as he remembered them and they seemed not unpleasant. Anyhow, a lot better than this overcrowded hut he was living in. And vaguely he had an idea that his mother had baked pies. There would, of course, be a catch in it somewhere.

'I'm not gonna take no Relief,' he said rather sulkily.

'It isn't Relief, Alec, it's a loan the Government makes you and you've got some years to pay it back. They give you a certain amount of stuff, farm animals, and tools, and feed, and fertilizer, and seed, and groceries and such; and you make a crop and you pay some money back to the Government.'

'Like on shares,' Alec said.

'Well.' Mrs Cahill was a little embarrassed. She knew that most enlightened people did not feel the share-cropper system was all that might be hoped. However. 'Well. Sort of.'

'Who'll go, just me and Sabine or all of us?'

'Well, I thought if we could arrange it, you and your mother and your wife would go—the houses aren't very big and Tiny's so small, it might be better for her to stay here with Tennessee.'

'Where'll they live then? Tennessee can't live way off down here with that drunk husband of hers around.'

'No, I thought Tennessee could take Mrs Maddison's house while you're on the farm. That way it'd be all right.'

'I'll think about it.' Alec was careful not to show pleasure or surprise; he mistrusted the Government, and all employers, deeply. It always sounded better than what you got in the end. No sense acting happy; then they'd cut you down even more. But a series of new ideas started in his head: satisfactory images and plans. The first picture he evoked was one of a table groaning with food, home-made preserves and things from the garden and fried chicken from their own backyard and pitchers of milk and corn bread and good pale butter. He tightened his jeans around him and wandered back to find Sabine and tell her warily about the future.

Sabine was sick of their cabin and especially now that Tennessee and the baby were there, and it was so crowded she couldn't properly wash things out, or cook, or ever be quiet. Without saying anything to Alec or comparing notes she too had a vision of wonderful food. And maybe a good dress coming in to town after the first crop; and some new silk stockings and even a permanent. She said casually that it looked all right to her and better ask Mrs Maddison.

Mrs Maddison's reasons were very simple: Tennessee and the baby would have a nice house if she left and then she wouldn't have to go around acting to the neighbours as if she and Tennessee saw each other and behaved as daughter and mother should. When, in fact, Tennessee didn't speak and Mrs Maddison felt more and more lonely and unwanted every day. And she was getting headaches from the sewing-room; her ten cent store glasses didn't seem to be so good after all. And then again, food. And maybe a garden. She saw the house in her mind: a neat little white house with roses all over it and several large magnolia trees and things on shelves in jars, very good to eat, which she had made herself, and curtains at the windows. The Maddisons agreed. Mrs Cahill wangled. Many papers were made out and signed. Mrs Maddison had a grand time rushing up to the Relief office, panting and flushed and clamouring for her rights and being stern and saying, I know Mr Roosevelt wouldn't mean for us not to have oil lamps.

Finally after a month of negotiations they were put into an intimidated Ford truck with whatever baggage they thought necessary or pleasant, and driven to their new start in life. They returned to the land.

'Oh,' Mrs Maddison said. She stood with a rolled patchwork quilt under one arm, and in her other hand, a market basket full of oddments, notably an alarm clock, a potato masher, two bars of laundry soap and some rope for hanging up the wash.

Sabine stared too but she could find nothing to say; and behind her, alarmed but not realizing the extent of the disaster, stood Alec with his mouth open.

'Gimme a hand bud,' the truck-driver said. 'I'll help you get the big pieces in but I gotta hurry along; I got some other famblies moving out to-day.'

Alec helped lift down the rusted stove they had brought from his shack; bed-posts; a table; a chest. He went in the house finally, with a chair resting over his head, and stopped in the middle of the floor, looking about him. He didn't know what to do. His instinct and his first desire were to cry out to this man, who was going to leave, 'Don't go, don't leave us here.' And then quickly, he thought: if only we could go back with him. . . . They were so far away; they were so alone and so helpless. What would they do here; how could they live in this place? Suddenly he realized that farming was not a job like salvaging iron: you had to know what to do, and when. And also you had to know what to expect.

Sabine was crying softly behind him. 'They shoulda told us,' she kept saying. 'It ain't right.'

Mrs Maddison was still outside; she had not moved. She didn't notice that the handle of the market basket was eating into her hand and that her arm and shoulder were getting stiff, holding the quilt. These things took time: when you had made a picture, clear and neat in your mind, it took time to erase it. She saw plainly the house she had imagined: white, with roses growing untidily all over it. There should perhaps have been a grey cat asleep on the doorstep in the sun. The curtains would already be up.... Mrs Cahill had been very uncertain about moving white families into abandoned negro shanties: these houses weren't even desirable for negroes she had felt, and that—by local tradition—was saying a good deal. It's got a tired look, Mrs Maddison thought, tired and worn-out and dirty. The kind of place you thought you'd die in, on the days when you were blue. Mrs Maddison felt that it was too late to start again; what kind of God was it, who was after her? Driving her from one filthy rattle-trap shack to another, driving and driving. She had a right to be tired; she had a right not to try any more.

'Where's Ma?' Alec said.

'Outside.'

'C'mon in, Ma,' Alec shouted, and there was irritation and despair in his voice; 'c'mon in and see the fine house your Relief got us.'

She waited a moment longer. It would take a little more courage to go inside, though she could imagine how it was. And she thought: they're young and they're not used to things. I'm the one's got to say something cheerful.

She climbed up the rickety steps. There were two front rooms, both having doors on to the porch. Behind one of them there was a lean-to addition, for a kitchen. It was the simplest form of house. She looked at both rooms and bent a little getting through the low door into the kitchen.

'Well,' she said.

They waited. Somehow they felt this was her fault. She was older. She should have known the kind of place they were coming to. They looked at her without kindness.

'Well,' Mrs Maddison said, 'I reckon Sabine and me can fix it up so's it'll be all right. It'll be all right in a coupla years.'

Alec laughed: 'We'll be dead first. We'll freeze in this place in winter. Look,' he said. Angrily he ripped more of the torn paper from the walls; light showed through gaps in the wall. 'Rain,' he said, 'we'll be washed outa bed, that's what. And how're we gonna git warm in a place like this?' Sabine, catching his anger, kicked her heel hard against the floor and the planking splintered and went through.

'Don't do that,' Mrs Maddison said. 'You don't have to show me. But we gotta live here. We don't have no other place to live. So we better get busy about it.'

'Your Relief,' Alec said in fury. 'It's your Relief's doing.'

Mrs Maddison put down her bundles on the floor. She stood up before him, a thin, old woman with her hair tightly wobbed on top of her head, sharp-faced and tired, her cheeks fallen in where teeth were missing.

'Lissen to me, Alec Maddison. Don't you talk like that to me. And don't go on saying foolishness. I'd of been dead if it warn't for that Relief. And Miss Lucy's a good woman. And Mr Roosevelt's a fine man. He's got a good kind face and he's doing what he can for us. Only it takes time. They gotta make mistakes like everybody. But don't you go blaming everything on them. And you jest get busy and set up that bed there, and put the stove where it belongs, and get the pipe fixed up on it, and Sabine, you get busy with a broom and clean out this place and don't look like somebody's stole your last penny. If we gotta live here, we gotta live here. No sense talking.'

Resentfully they obeyed her. Mrs Maddison unpacked what china and pots and pans they had: put clothes and odd bits of linen into the chest. She sang thinly as she worked. She made a lot of noise, too, trying to keep a silence from settling on the house. It's up to me she thought, they're too young yet. They get discouraged. It's up to me. Suddenly she felt a great pride that their three lives and their happiness and success depended on her: that she was the one who would keep things going, and somehow make a triumph out of this gloomy and decrepit house. It had to be done; it was another job. One more thing to get through before she died. She'd manage it too. The worst thing, Mrs Maddison decided, would be ever to admit that you didn't have any hope left at all, and that living was too much for you.

Alec was a bad farmer, and Sabine an unwilling housewife. Mrs Maddison, with love, sought to make excuses for them. It was true that they had little to work with. The mule named Thomas was old, embittered and weary. It was no joke ploughing up the field, holding the plough down with blistered hands, behind that languid and uncertain animal. Thomas had a tendency to wander off, suddenly bored by the straight

line. It was also true that Alec had to haul water on a crude handmade
sled, from a well about fifteen minutes walking down the road. There
was no well on the place: they rationed water as if they were on a raft,
with the salt ocean swelling ominously about them. And she and Sabine
had to take their clothes to a pond over the hill, a greenish pond, where
mosquitoes sang their welcome, to wash them. And there were no
screens, and no mosquito-nets for the beds, so that sleeping was uneasy,
a drugged, resentful fight against the whining pests. And the house; oh
yes, Mrs Maddison told herself, it's bad. But still. She could not keep
herself from singing, a thin monotonous song, as she worked. In the
evenings she sat on the porch alone, beside her pot of evil-burning rags,
and looked over the land. With contentment, and a kind of proud
peacefulness that Alec and Sabine found maddening.

Alec was planting cotton: it was the only pay crop (if there were
buyers) and the Government demanded this. The farm was twenty acres
in all; and he intended to put in eight acres of cotton. By turns, and
depending on his anger or where he'd been ploughing, he said: the land's
clay ... it's nothing but sand, no cotton nor nothing else'll grow ...
rocks, rocks, God I oughta be ploughing with dynamite.... The vegetable garden became Mrs Maddison's affair: turnips and squash, peas,
beans, beets, carrots, lettuce, potatoes, corn and suddenly, from nowhere,
mysteriously, she produced flower seeds: larkspur and asters and a few
brown, frail-looking rose plants, carefully embedded by the porch pillars.
Mrs Maddison saw everything green and rich already. Later, she thought,
when we've made the crop, we'll buy chickens and a cow. The fullness
of life. There might be money for paint too, and new planks to nail over
the rotting floor boards, and windows later, and yards of bright print
for curtains. It would be a home. She'd live long enough to make it into
a home.

Sabine would get up in the morning, with a fretful look on her
mouth, and say 'T'aint no use doing anything with this house.' In silence
Alec hitched the plough behind Thomas and set out for the fields. Sabine
and Alec worked against their disgust, wearily, and came back at nights
to hate this place where they had to live. Mrs Maddison could find no
words to encourage them. Now, before the garden came up, they had
to live sparingly on corn bread and sorghum and turnip greens which
she bought at the cross roads store five miles away: and the coffee was
thin, trying to use as little of it as possible, only coloured water: and the
milk was oily and yellowish from the can.... But in June the garden
would be coming on, and there'd be flowers on the cotton. And all
summer afterwards they could eat their own things, the fresh green
things from their own land; and by September—only five months, only

five months—they'd be picking cotton. And then. Maybe Miss Lucy could get them a cow before then. She dreamed as she worked.

There wasn't much to do about the house. The grey, unpainted walls, darkened in places from smoke, always seemed dirty. But, being spring, the broken windows didn't matter so much. She thought about them a good deal and finally wrote a letter, with difficulty, to Mrs Cahill, saying that there were five windows in the house and all broken: now if she could get some cheese-cloth to tack over them, that would anyhow keep out the flies, and maybe when next Alec went to town he could pick up a few boards for shutters in case it rained. And so maybe it would be best if she just knocked out the windows altogether, since they were jagged-like and ugly; and could Mrs Cahill maybe get her some cheese-cloth. The cheese-cloth arrived, together with a box of tacks, and Mrs Maddison was as excited as if she'd suddenly been given velvet curtains to hang sumptuously over French windows.

She dug up the garden and planted the seeds. Alec and Sabine together planted the cotton seed in the brown narrow furrows of earth in the fields. Mrs Maddison was alone in the house all day. There wasn't much cooking to do, because, finally, it always seemed to be pan bread or corn bread and sorghum and whatever else she could find or invent or afford, to eke this out. She wanted the garden to be big and the Government had been generous with seeds. She wrote a few letters, almost drawing the words as if each one were a picture, asking for magazines—she would again paper the walls gaily and cleanly. Mrs Cahill, who could not forget the old woman in that evil, decaying shack, sent her several yards of cheap print in startling colours. Mrs Maddison made curtains and bed spreads, and hung a length of it over the low door to the kitchen, which at least shut off the sight of that place, if not the smell.

It grew hot. Alec was working without a hat in the fields and he would come back at noon ominously white with the heat. Sabine made a bonnet for herself from newspapers; she worked in bent, broken, high-heeled slippers, the heels catching in the earth, suddenly jerking her ankle sideways. Before they drank the last of the water that they'd hauled in a keg, it was warmish and had a grey flat taste. Mrs Maddison tended the garden with passion and delicacy, almost luring the seeds to take root and grow. She lay awake at nights thinking of the feathery short green things that would be coming out of the earth. She particularly thought of the flowers. Alec's and Sabine's room had the walls papered now with advertisements: there weren't enough magazines despite Mrs Cahill's efforts, to do both rooms. In the winter, Mrs Maddison thought, when there isn't so much work outside, Sabine and I can make rag rugs so it'll be warmer underfoot. In two years, in three years, this place would be a good place: safe and quiet, with things in jars for the winter and, every summer, plenty in the garden, and a little money coming from the cotton for extras. Safe and quiet: Tennessee and the baby could come too. They'd save money for timber and put up another room. She'd have her family around her. If only they could live it out until the first crop got sold. There were days when her head ached and the garden went black before her eyes: I'm getting old she thought. And then too she was so sick of the food they ate that it was hard to swallow; it rested uneasily on her stomach. She was thinner.

Alec and Sabine were hoeing now, cutting out the plants that grew too close together, weeding, keeping the grass off, breaking the light dry crust of earth that formed over the plants after rain. They never talked: all three of them lived in an agony of fatigue, hurrying, trying each day to keep ahead of the land which didn't want to be worked over and driven; caring for the seeds which seemed animate, each one of its own fragile and demanding life. At night after supper, Alec and Sabine went to bed. And Mrs Maddison, too weary for sleep, sat on the porch, leaning against one of the thin posts that held it up, trying to ease the aches in her body before she lay down. For a while she would sit quietly thinking of nothing; but only identifying the places in her body that meant pain: the shoulders, the centre of her back, her knees, her wrists. She waited for the aches to stop being sharp and separate, knowing that they'd merge into a general weariness that was not hard to bear. And then she could look out over the fields, and her garden beside the house. And look at the sky. Things seemed sure to her now: her life and her children's lives were no longer dependent on other people, on the strange fancies of employers, and the rules and regulations of the Government. Yes, they were in debt: but the Government was going to give them time to pay. It wasn't like being on shares or a tenant, when you never knew where you stood. As long as we grow things, Mrs Maddison thought. She liked the emptiness of the land before her. It's good land, Mrs Maddison said to herself, and we're making something to last. Something for the children. There's nothing wrong with being poor, Mrs Maddison decided proudly, if you've got your own place, and no one coming to holler about the rent and throw you out; and if you know there's food in your garden, and you don't need to go begging around at every store. It's the begging and not knowing where you're going to be next. 'And work,' she said suddenly aloud, 'Land's sake, no one's ever gonna call my chilrun no-count loafers.'

. . .

A man came and talked with Alec about the cotton; he said he was the farm supervisor for the rural rehabilitation families around here. A woman came and talked to Mrs Maddison about groceries and what they needed in the house: she was the home visitor out this way. The callers made Alec mutely angry. He didn't want anybody butting in his business. Even if they acted nice about it. He could get along. Next time they came Mrs Maddison could just tell them to get the hell out; he'd manage his own farm. Mrs Maddison, who had an entirely personal conception of Government, was encouraged by these visits. For her, simply, it meant that Mr Roosevelt and Mrs Cahill were not forgetting her. If they couldn't come themselves they'd send their people. She was glad of this: she knew Miss Lucy wasn't forgetting her because there was the cheese-cloth and the print. But those things were gifts and had nothing to do with the Government. The Government was supposed to be interested and come around every once in a while and ask how you were getting on and ask if they could help. Government was like that. She had been rather boastful with Miss Blythe, who was Mr Roosevelt's representative out that way. She'd shown off her not yet producing garden and her house, and extended her arm largely to exhibit their land, the acres which were theirs, which made them respectable, steady, rooted people with a future. Miss Blythe had been flattering about the house and said she'd try to get their grocery order raised. 'Of course,' Miss Blythe said, 'if you can manage with it being so small—well that's just that much less money to pay back later.' Mrs Maddison liked that too; she was borrowing money, she wasn't begging.

Mrs Maddison told Alec that Mr Roosevelt had some right nice people working for him out this way; but Alec was neither interested nor pleased.

Sabine and Alec were more than silent; they were sullen now. They hated everything about the farm, and they had no faith in it. Alec used to say bitterly he knew his cotton would be bad, or it'd rain too much later, or there'd be boll weevil; or no buyers. He didn't believe anything could come of this; he saw the future as a long half-starved drudgery, slaving for nothing. And the silent days and the silent nights. Sabine saw herself growing ugly, her hair straight and unkempt, her hands coarse; no clothes, no finery, no fun. No girls to gossip with and no dances or any of the things she wanted. At least, in town, they could get together with their friends and have a little drink and somebody could always play a fiddle and they could go uptown and look at the stores anyhow. But this: working yourself to death and nothing to show for it. Those hateful ugly selfish little cotton plants.

Mrs Maddison was going calling. She was in such a good humour that she had to share it. She walked over the dusty reddish roads, with her hat sitting up on top of her head, where it would shade her, but not press down and give her headache. Her gingham dress was darned till it seemed to be covered with white sores. None of this worried her; she was going graciously to pay a call on Mrs Lowry and pass the time of day, and talk brightly of the future.

Mrs Lowry was sitting on her porch fanning herself. She was about Mrs Maddison's age. Mrs Maddison said, 'Howdy, Mrs Lowry, fine weather we're having' and they sat down to talk. Mrs Lowry said it was a treat, she never saw anybody for a month of Sundays and she'd have come to see Mrs Maddison but they were that busy. 'Farming,' Mrs Lowry said; 'you just gotta keep at it every second till you die.' But she seemed proud of it on the whole. Mrs Maddison liked her. She thought it would be nice in the winter, when they had more time, and she and Mrs Lowry could swap recipes and patterns for crocheting. Later, when the vegetables had been canned and the cotton sold.

Mrs Lowry had been in her house a year. 'Lawd knows it's nothin' to look at,' she said. 'But you ought of seen it when we come. Dirty, I never seen such a place. Now we got our own vegetables put up, and such-like; we're gettin' on all right. It's worst the first year.'

Mrs Maddison agreed.

'The bad thing is the young folks,' Mrs Lowry said. 'There's no fun for them. And they don't have no patience, poor things.'

'Later,' Mrs Maddison said to Mrs Lowry, her eyes shining with the thought of it, 'when we're all fixed up and everybody's not working so hard, we'll get together and have a barn dance. I see you gotta barn here, and we could sweep it out and fix it up pretty, and everybody bring a little something themselves, and have a real party.'

She had said this breathlessly, hurrying before the vision failed her. In her mind, the barn was filled with young men and girls, dressed as she had been dressed when she was young and went to a party. They'd be doing square dances, and the fiddlers thumping with their feet on the floor to keep time. And apple-bobbing. And blind man's buff. All the neighbours there together, being gay and serene, and every man sure of his home, sure of to-morrow, and easy with to-day.

Mrs Lowry understood her excitement. 'If only the young folks'll wait,' she said. 'We'll have a good time yet before we die.'

Alec lay in his darkened room and Sabine talked to Mrs Maddison in savage whispers.

'We're going,' she said. 'Soon's he can move we're going. We're not gonna stay out here to get ourselves killed. Sunstroke,' she said, and her whisper was shrill. 'He'll be laying in the fields dead next. And me with the malaria. What kinda life is that? They can't make us stay. We hate this place n'we're going quick; n'we're never coming back. So.'

Mrs Maddison twisted her hands in her lap. There were roses now, climbing up the door posts, and even if the posts were unpainted and the house grey and streaked behind them, these were real roses. Next year there would be more and maybe paint, too. The garden was green and just looking at it made you feel rich and safe. She'd been serving her own vegetables now for weeks. Next year, if they had a cow, there'd be butter to put on the new tender carrots and the beets, and the fresh green peas. The cotton was coming out thinly in the fields, but it was only the beginning. She'd gone down and picked a boll, and held the soft white fluff in her hands gently. This was money; of course there'd be a buyer and fine prices. This was more lumber for another room, and shoes, and a buggy, maybe. The worst was over. Things were growing. Larkspur and roses and squash and potatoes and cotton. This was what life meant, if life was good. She'd even gotten her room papered in advertisements now. With money, they could buy boards, make furniture, a solid roof, a whole floor, and paint to make it clean and gay. They had only now to live a little carefully and everything would come to them. They were safe now and what lay ahead was more safety and even ease. In the winter, when they couldn't work after dark and there was nothing much to do anyhow, there were the neighbours. All the things she'd planned and dreamed.

'Sabine,' she said softly, 'he'll get over it in a day or so. N'you'll get over the malaria. Miss Blythe said she'd send some quinine. We done the work, Sabine. You can't go now. The worst is all over.'

'We're going. And don't you try to stop us, neither. You're old and you don't expect to get any fun outa life. But we're young. And we're not gonna stay around here and kill ourselves.'

'You won't have any fun back in that old shack of yours. You won't even have stuff to eat. What kinda life is that, then? Sabine, we worked so hard,' Mrs Maddison said. There were tears in her eyes, but she was not looking at the younger woman. She was looking out the door, at the roses. For the last month it had seemed to her that not only Mr Roosevelt and Mrs Cahill were remembering her, but God also. The things she wanted: a home, and roses, and food, and quiet when the work was over, and a place to live and be. Tennessee could come in the fall; when they had a little money, too. She was an old woman and she was a lucky one: she had everything she could want.

She cried out against this dreadful and wanton thing they meant to do: leave the land when things were growing; leave the cotton unpicked and the garden going to weeds and waste. And the house they'd made into something like a home; let it rot back again into a worn-out negro shanty. But she knew they wouldn't listen to her. Miss Blythe came and argued and so did the farm foreman: he even threatened Alec, saying 'You'll never get a loan again' and 'You're a low quitter, that's what you are.' Alec was ill, and hysterically obstinate; something had happened to him. He hated the land beyond any explanation. He would rather starve than stay there; it was a slavery to him and a bleak, empty, exhausting life, with none of the things that made for pleasure. Sabine chattered with chills and burned with fever, and cursed the home visitor and the farm foreman and Mrs Maddison, and said she'd crawl to town on her hands and knees if she had to, but she wasn't going to stay out here in this hole and kill herself, and get ugly, and go crazy with the work, and no fun ever, ever, ever.

The entire neighbourhood got drawn into this, and Mrs Lowry stood on the porch with Mrs Maddison, one day at sunset, looking out over the white beginnings of the cotton, and the greenness of the garden and said: 'It's a sin and a shame, Flora. They'll be sorry, too.'

Mrs Cahill drove out in her uncertain Ford and tried to talk to Alec, who wouldn't listen. Mrs Maddison could not stay on alone; the work was too much for her. She couldn't keep the cotton cultivated and do the garden too. 'You'd be having sunstroke next,' Mrs Cahill said and smiled.

'He did have a sunstroke,' Mrs Maddison said abruptly. 'It was a real bad sunstroke and he was sick's a baby.'

'I know.' Mrs Cahill put her hand on Mrs Maddison's shoulder. The old woman would defend those no-count children if they did murder.

'Would you like to take home some roses, Miss Lucy, or some larkspur? It's all gonna be wasted now.'

She stood beside her flowers weeping quietly and helplessly. 'All wasted,' she said. 'It all come to nothing.'

'Alec deserves a beating,' Mrs Cahill said furiously. 'He's selfish, and he's being stupid, too. Sabine's a fool and you couldn't expect anything else of her. But Alec. I'd like to get some big strong man to give him the beating of his life.'

'It's only that he's not hisself. He's still weakish from that there sunstroke. But it's gonna be too late when he sees what he done. We'll of lost the place then.'

Mrs Cahill put her arm around Mrs Maddison's shoulder. 'You've done your best, darling. Nobody'll ever blame you. You made a fine place here and somebody'll be lucky to get it, and they'll know what a good worker you are. We'll see you get taken care of all right in town. I'm sorry. I'm sorrier than I can tell you.'

'We were all fixed,' Mrs Maddison said. 'We could of lived like real people again. Well,' she said, 'how's things in the sewing-room, Miss Lucy?'

Finally Mrs Cahill drove Alec and Sabine back with her. She thought it would be easier for Mrs Maddison to have them out of the way. The driver would come with the truck to-morrow or the next day and move Mrs Maddison and their possessions back into town. The land couldn't be wasted; someone would have to work it and try to profit by it and pay back the debt. Mrs Cahill drove in angry silence. Once Sabine started to talk to her and she turned and said: 'You're a no-count girl, Sabine, and you've got a no-count husband, and I don't want any truck with you. You've broken that poor old woman's heart and you deserve anything that comes to you. I'll drive you to town but I won't act friendly with you.'

Mrs Maddison had something to do. Before it grew dark, before she slept. Now that her son had really done this thing; gone away, not caring for the land or the money he owed. She got out a block of ruled paper and a stubby pencil and began: Dear Mr Roosevelt:

It was a long letter. She explained Alec's sunstroke and Sabine's malaria, and how hard it had been for over four months, working with so little and the house cheerless and such poor food. She told about everything which excused Alec in his desertion; but loyally, she said too, that the garden was fine now, and the cotton coming up. She hoped he wouldn't be too disappointed in Alec, but Alec was young, and when you were young you were foolish, and did bad things without knowing. She hoped he would excuse Alec. She was grateful for the things Mr Roosevelt had done, and she would work to pay back the money they owed but she was afraid it would take a long time. Work was so hard to get and money so scarce. She enclosed a short spray of larkspur because she wanted him to know that it was a fine place she was leaving.

She sat alone on the front porch and watched the stars come out. It had all come to nothing. The safety and the ease that was ahead, and the good times, and having a place and being someone. Nothing. The land was fine and beautiful, she thought, and she could smell the roses in the dark.

M R S   M A D D I S O N
A N D   H E R   C H I L D R E N

Alec and Sabine were going to give a party to celebrate their return to
the land of the living. Tennessee had moved to their shack, as soon as
she heard her mother was leaving the farm. All three of them invited
their friends. It was going to be a fiddling party. Dancing was impossible
in Alec's home, both because of space and because of the weakness of
the flooring. But people could stamp time, and sing; and somehow,
without visible explanation, there would be whisky in jugs. Both Alec
and Sabine were thin and still frail from their illness, but they were in
fine spirits now. At last, something that was fun. After that hated farm,
those barren months which seemed years, and at the same time were
almost forgotten.

Mrs Maddison returned to her own house, the day of the party: but
she was not invited. It was a young people's party to begin with, and
beside that, her children did not feel tenderly towards her.

Bill had disappeared, and Tennessee, knowing this had to be, still
held rancour against her mother, as if in some mysterious way, Mrs
Maddison was the cause of Bill's drinking. Someone had told Tennessee
that Bill was looking for work in Biloxi. If only he found a job. He was
her man anyhow: her mother didn't have a right to judge him.

It was dark, and guests began to straggle along the narrow path to
their cabin. They could hear voices first and then people calling: the first
arrivals were the fiddlers.

The men stood around outside, a little shy, stamping their feet and laughing and talking with Alec. Then they came in: a young man and two old men, one with a stubble of whitish beard on his face. They had their fiddles under their arms. Some strings were always missing. And there was no certainty about the tuning. But they made a grand gay noise. Couples began to drift in: one young woman brought her child, a baby of about nine months, and put him on the bed, under the mosquito netting with Tiny. The children slept quietly through all the noise. There weren't enough chairs to go round; some of the guests sat on the floor and others leaned against the wall, or huddled together on the second bed. Water was dipped out of a bucket. The men passed the whisky jug around and swigged it straight; there were a few cups and these were given to the women and a little water was mixed with the whisky. There were fourteen people in the cabin by the time the last guest came: and it was hot.

Outside in the darkness, mosquitoes droned over the swampy land where the river had receded; and the thick rushing sound of the Mississippi slurred over all other noises. Two oil lamps lighted the cabin: there was only one room. Tennessee stood by the water bucket, and passed the whisky jug when it was required. Her face gleamed with sweat: it was sun-browned and now had an oiled shining look. She wore her hair to her shoulders, loose and thick, held herself well, and her body was firm and inviting beneath her gingham dress. She was barefooted as was Sabine: the other women had shoes over bare feet, because they had been walking through the woods to get here. One man suddenly ripped off his sweat-soaked shirt, and sat with the lamp-light picking out little threads of sweat on his naked chest. The fiddling went on.

Someone called out the name of a song and the young fiddler said humbly that he wasn't good enough. And they all said: 'Sure y'are Jakie, go ahead Jakie. Attaboy, you kin play that fiddle.' Another man took a few straws from a broom and settled himself beside Jakie: Jakie laid the fiddle on his knees. It was a quick tune; the straws were to keep the beat, and to syncopate it: they whined against the wood of the fiddle as Jakie plucked the strings. Feet thumped faster and faster. When it was over everybody had another swig from the jug and told Jakie how good he was. The music was making them dizzy, the music and the heat and the whisky. Now all the tunes were fast, fast and yet whining, the strange melancholy music of the river. They had a hypnotic quality, the insistence on one phrase, monotonous swift music. The women swayed a little as they tapped their heels against the floor. Tennessee lifted her arm slowly to push back her hair and the young fiddler watched her with covetous eyes. Everyone was getting drunk. A man sitting beside his wife on the bed, leaned across and kissed her at the opening of her dress, and they all noticed this almost as if it were a signal given.

The children slept without moving. The fiddlers were getting a little tired, so they played slower music and everyone sang the verses; the long saga-like songs, with the refrain always the same. Tennessee began to think about the young fiddler; he had black hair curling close to his head and a fine strong neck. She moved across the room to him, as if she were walking in her sleep. The young fiddler felt her coming: he stayed bowed over his fiddle, slowly plucking at the strings, as if he were calling to her that way. She sat down on the floor beside him and watched him. The jug went the rounds again.

Someone named another song; and the old fiddler took out a dirty red handkerchief and ran it all over his face and head, and asked for some whisky before he began.

Tennessee, softly, as if he and she were alone in the room, her eyes a little glazed from drink, moved alongside the young fiddler and leaned her back against his leg. He pressed his leg against her: he felt as if his whole side was suddenly against coals, burning, but not hurting. The fast music started again. Alec held Sabine on his lap, holding her back against him, a little stretched out, so that the cloth of her dress was tight over her stomach and legs. The men who had come without women were beginning to look enviously around them. The young fiddler dropped out, leaving the two others to carry the tune. He reached for the jug and took a long unhesitating drink. He wiped his face with his hand and shook the sweat from his eyes. Then slowly, he looked down at Tennessee. He leaned over her suddenly, putting his hands around her, on her breasts, and kissed her where her throat joined her shoulder. Tennessee didn't move: her body felt limp and easy. The young fiddler stayed so a moment, bent over her.

A voice from the door, a thick furious voice, said: 'Git your hands off my wife.'

The music stopped.

The young fiddler straightened up and Tennessee fell backwards from him, supporting herself on her elbow. Bill stood in the door. Bill was drunk obviously. His eyes couldn't seem to look straight at anything, but he had seen enough. His face was red and ugly; and he stood there in the door as if uncertain where to begin, as if he couldn't decide where to start his vengeance.

'You dirty whore,' he said to Tennessee; but nobody minded talk.

'I'm taking you home with me. I'm gonna give you such a beating you'll learn to go around whoring. I'm gonna beat your skin off of you. You seem to of forgot,' Bill said very carefully, 'I'm the one's your husband.' There was a silence. 'Any guy that thinks different can say so,' Bill said staring at the young fiddler.

Bill started across the floor towards Tennessee and no one stopped him; it was true, she was his wife, he had a right. He stood above Tennessee who watched him with black fascinated eyes, and suddenly he brought his fist smashing down on her bare shoulder, at the place where the young fiddler had kissed her.

'Alec,' Tennessee screamed, 'he'll kill me, he'll kill me.'

No one moved: they seemed all helpless with drink, confused, and unable to manage or direct their bodies.

Bill pulled her up from the floor by the arm, roughly, and started back towards the door. 'Alec, Alec, you won't let him, you won't let him, he'll kill me.' With the back of his hand, Bill struck her across the mouth to silence her. But Alec had finally understood. He shouted at Bill: 'Leave my sister here. Here's her home. Git on out; nobody told you to come here.'

Bill turned; it was the young fiddler he wanted to kill, but no one was going to tell him what he could or couldn't do with his wife.

He told Alec what he thought of him in short ugly words. Alec was drunk too, and anyhow no man could talk like that to him, and no man could beat up his sister, right in front of him too. He crossed the room to Bill and got him by the neck of his shirt and pulled him away from the door and from Tennessee. Quietly, people began to drift out of the cabin, into the darkness, with no words. This was a family fight. The old fiddler found his violin case under the bed and picked it up and got out; the young woman lifted her baby from the bed and holding the child as if he were a flour sack, dropped from the cabin to the ground, by the back door, and started home. No use getting mixed up in trouble. Someone took the young fiddler's arm and led him away; he was pretty far gone anyhow. He'd gotten mixed up about the fight; the only thing he could remember clearly was Tennessee's breasts.

Tennessee kneeled on the floor and watched; the men did not fight cleanly or well, they fought with their nails, kicked, butted with their heads, and cursed rhythmically, but not wasting much breath on it. Blood ran from Alec's mouth and Bill's shirt hung from him in shreds. They knocked over a lamp and Sabine screamed and hurled the water bucket on it; the men fought through broken glass, crunching it back and forth across the floor. Suddenly Bill reached for the whisky jug, grabbed it by the handle and swung it over his head. Tennessee rose like wind and pushed him from behind, at his knees so that his balance was lost and Alec flung himself against Bill with all his weight and Bill crashed backwards and sideways, dropping the jug, and fell with his head against the stove. He didn't move and nobody noticed him. Sabine went to Alec and tried to wipe off the blood and get him to lie down on the bed; and Tennessee, picking her way carefully over the broken glass, went to the bed where Tiny slept and crept in beside her. She wanted to close her eyes and sleep. There was nothing more to worry about now; for the time being she was safe. Alec looked at Bill, though the room was dim with only one light burning, and said: 'He'll come around in the mornin'.' He threw a few cupfuls of water down on Bill's head, without bending, or looking closely and went to bed with Sabine. The house was quiet in a few moments: they had all drunk a lot that night.

In the morning they found that Bill was dead.

Everyone knew of it before Mrs Maddison. It was decided that Maybelle should break the news to her. Maybelle didn't like the job and put it off until afternoon. By that time, many things had happened. Tennessee had called on Mrs Cahill for help: she had sent a telegram to Bill's parents in Jackson and gotten an answer. She was to take the body there for burial: and she was to take Tiny with her and stay. In a crazy despair—because, if he beat her or not, he was still her man, and now he was dead—she turned against Alec, screamed at him, accused him of murdering her husband, said she never wanted to see any of them again, she hated them, she hoped the law would get them. It was her Bill; he was the one she loved; and now they'd gone and killed him. Mrs Cahill's face twisted with disgust: she thought it would be a fine thing for everyone if Tennessee did leave for good. She thought of Mrs Maddison and arranged for the Relief truck to take Tennessee and Tiny and the coffin (covered with tarpaulin so as not to scare the negroes en route) to Jackson. The less accusing Tennessee did, the better. Alec was quiet, helpless and stunned. The worst was that he couldn't be sure he remembered things clearly. But he did know that he hadn't killed anybody. Not really killed. Killing was when you went at a man with your hands or a knife or a gun and tried to finish him. He'd been fighting. He knew that. The sheriff came and took him to jail and locked him up. 'For safe keeping,' he said soothingly to Sabine who was almost as crazy as Tennessee.

By afternoon, things were quiet again on the river-front. Alec's shack was empty because Sabine had moved to her family's house which was up-town behind the box factory. Tennessee and Tiny had gone. And Alec was sitting in jail, looking at his hands, saying to himself, 'I never killed him. I couldn't of.'

Maybelle explained it all to Mrs Maddison. She started in a rush and finished lamely, with pauses between her words. It was hard to say that Tennessee had turned against her brother, and gone away without saying good-bye to her mother. And that Alec was already in jail.

'He didn't kill him, Flora,' Maybelle said. 'Nobody thinks that, not even Sheriff. It was fighting; that's different. He fell and hit his head. That don't count the same. Even lawyers say that. It'll be all right, Flora.'

Mrs Maddison said nothing. She should at least cry, Maybelle thought, or get up or something. This silence frightened Maybelle. Her friend looked old; she looked like a thin, old woman who is too tired to think or feel.

'They got Alec in jail?' Mrs Maddison said finally.

'Yes, honey. But Sheriff knows it ain't like murder.'

'I gotta get a lawyer to talk for him,' Mrs Maddison said.

With what money, Maybelle thought, how's she gonna get money for lawyers and such. That costs; poor people don't have lawyers.

'Sure,' she said, without conviction.

Mrs Maddison sighed. 'Well,' she said, 'what's gotta be has gotta be.'

Maybelle wanted to cry. This was worse than she had imagined. This terrible weariness. She put her hand gently on Mrs Maddison's knee. 'If I kin do anything, Flora,' she said.

Mrs Maddison shook her head. Then she made a great effort and remembered Maybelle, and patted her hand, and smiled at her.

'The willow's grown since I was on the farm,' she said. 'I'm surprised it's so green. I kinda thought it would git all burned up, what with the heat. It's sure pretty. I'm lucky I got such a nice place to live in.'

Maybelle rose to go then.

'You're a fine woman, Flora,' she said.

Mrs Maddison smiled as if she hadn't heard: 'I'll be seeing you in the sewing-room. I'm gonna start work again to-morrow.'

Mrs Maddison dressed with care and climbed the hill in the sun. She stopped every few minutes, with her hand on her heart, breathing deeply, waiting for the heart-beats to slow. She couldn't understand yet, clearly, what had happened: and maybe I never will, she thought. I'm only a plain woman and maybe these things are too big for me to understand. Maybe I wasn't meant to. For, surely, there seemed no reason why this trouble should come to her family; they were not wicked people. She thought, with sorrow, of Tennessee. The girl was too young, she hadn't learned enough yet. It's your own fault, Flora Maddison, she said, you should never of let her marry Bill and we'd all be happy to-day. She hurried now: poor Alec, sitting there alone. She wouldn't let herself think of Tennessee turning against him.

Alec looked at her silently: he wasn't going to ask her the question; he didn't dare. What if she said . . .

'No, honey,' Mrs Maddison said, 'you didn't kill him. He just killed hisself. He fell back on the stove and killed hisself. I'm gonna get a big lawyer from Jackson to talk for you. Don't you worry, honey. We'll git everything fixed up fine.' She kissed him on the cheek and sat with him quietly for a time, holding his hands in hers.

'Sabine?' he said.

'Sabine's fine,' Mrs Maddison said, though she knew nothing about her. 'She knows he killed hisself too, honey. Sabine'll be right along now to visit with you. We all love you, son.' And she thought, with pain, of Tennessee, who was too young to know what she was doing.

September was viciously hot. There was no call for it, decently the summer should be over. Heat hung over the river-front, and only the river moved, swift, thick and brown between the caked mud banks. Mrs Maddison sat on her porch until late at night, almost until dawn, waiting for a little freshness to come into the air so that she could sleep. She played her harmonica very softly, cupping it in her hand. She didn't want to disturb Mrs MacIvor, who had the toothache. If only I could sleep, Mrs Maddison thought. I'm that tired. I'm old, she decided, but she had excuse enough for weariness. She found washing to do, fifty cents for a great bundle, bending over the tub in the heat; sometimes having to go and sit on the porch, without moving, waiting for the blackness to pass from her eyes. She made some children's dresses for a lady up-town, sewing at night by the oil lamp, until she couldn't see the stitches and stopped, knowing the lady wouldn't be pleased if the work came back, with great coarse stitches like basting, just because Mrs Maddison's eyes were old. She helped as an extra with the fall house-cleaning in the druggist's house and at the preacher's. People gave her work, if they could. They knew why the old woman was always on the streets, walking fast from one job to the next. Every nickel counted, every nickel was saved, there was Alec waiting.

The heat came at her like an angry hand, pushing up against her throat. It's cool in the jail, she thought; anyhow, there's that. Hurry, hurry. She had some curtains to make for Mrs Guthrie, who ran the hat shop. After the curtains were made, she could probably get some more cleaning, or washing. But how much money did she need? What if she could never get enough; lawyers cost a lot, more than doctors or anybody. Or so she'd heard. She'd never had use for one before.

Maybelle said: take the bus to Jackson and go and see him. Mrs

Cahill had mentioned a Mr Everett, who was a fine lawyer and would talk well for Alec, if they could get him. 'But I'll use up my money.'

'You gotta do it, anyhow. You can't write such things to folks. Besides, lawyers, you gotta talk a long time and tell them everything.'

She thought this over for a week, and finally decided to go.

Mr Everett received her in a dim room, which seemed cool and rich to Mrs Maddison. She was badly frightened. What if she could never get enough money? She blinked her eyes, getting used to the gloom, and slowly she told him the story. She told him many things he had no use for, but he let her talk. He watched her, desperate and still too proud to beg for help, and keeping, somehow, a control and restraint on her voice.

'You can pay me later, whatever you can manage,' he said. 'It doesn't look like a difficult case.'

At best, they'd get a verdict of justifiable homicide based on self-defence, and an acquittal; at worst manslaughter, and a lenient judge—Mrs Maddison would make an admirable witness—only a light sentence; ten years, maybe, or even less.

He encouraged her: 'It really isn't a bad case at all, Mrs Maddison. I'd be very surprised if he weren't acquitted. You just go back home and don't worry. I'll do everything that's necessary; and I'll get in touch with you, whenever I have to. Tell the boy to cheer up, too. I'll drive over and see him next week. There's not a thing to worry about.'

Mrs Maddison rose uncertainly and thanked him. She wanted to tell him that she loved him; that all her life she would never forget; that she would work until she dropped to get money to pay him. But she could never thank him for this feeling of being saved, of having someone kind and helping, now, when she was almost exhausted, almost unable to endure her trouble. She could find no words.

'God bless you,' she said, and Mr Everett looked at her, touched and a little amused. She was being a good deal more grateful than he deserved, he thought, but it was nice, anyhow. It made him feel fine. He shook her hand and led her to the door.

Mrs Maddison caught the bus that left at five. It rattled off dustily, and honked and barked through the twilight. She was safe again. Once more she had managed, somehow. She looked at her hands, and knew how old she was; but she had won, anyhow. Until to-morrow or until the next trouble. Her boy would be talked for: and some day Tennessee would learn the things she should know. Indomitably, Mrs Maddison made pictures for herself again: pictures of a reunited and contented family; of plenty, of a home, a garden, things on the shelves in jars.

Soothing and strengthening herself with the future, which never came, but was at least always there to dream about.

Dust hung in amber gauze shreds over the road. Trees so close together that they all seemed to grow from the same roots. Here and there stagnant water shone like oil and mosquitoes hummed in the dusk. Negroes got on and off the bus, laughing, their arms full of brown paper parcels, corn meal and flour and a can of sorghum squaring out the bundle. Everybody talked to everybody else; droning like weary flies. 'Here you are, auntie,' the driver said and handed down her parcels to a gaunt, root-gnarled negress. She stood, bent beside her parcels, in the dusty road and waved, and the bus lurched on. Towns made up of a gas station and two stores at a cross roads, and dust and wagons waiting, and negroes dressed in dusty overalls and straw hats, and white men squatting close to the pavement in the shade of the stores, smoking or chewing a long piece of grass. . . .

I'm safe, Mrs Maddison thought, I'm safe for a little while; anyhow, till to-morrow. She leaned her head on her hand and the bus creaked and swayed over the rutted roads, and she fell asleep as it grew dark.

JOE AND PETE

Wind blows flat and strong across the city and carries the rain with it. The sky is grey green: early November. Ferryville looks as if it had been made hastily by people who had their minds on something else: supply and demand, perhaps, how best to ship the stuff out.... A small radius around the city hall appears to prosper: those few squares where people eat, shop, go to the movies and otherwise spend money. Beyond the city hall, stretching to the river, are rows of small houses looking alike. The workers from the factories live in them. They are silent and the rain spatters and bounces on the cracked pavements.

The larger factories lie on a narrow low strip of land beside the river. The Minton soup factory is the biggest. In common with most big factories it hesitates in appearance between a hospital and a prison. It seems to have grown by some curious elementary process of nature: like the amoeba perhaps, dividing and multiplying. Parts are old, ramshackle, clinging to the new bricks and concrete. Runways span the street, the buildings weave and sprawl, dim, unshakable. Doors, like mouseholes, unreasonably pierce the walls anywhere; and faintly, distantly, one can hear the rattle and hum of machinery, see the windows vibrating.

Not today.

The picket lines were small, groups of men standing at all the thirty entrances, chaffing their hands, moving from foot to foot, mostly silent or saying something briefly to laugh.

'Some job,' a man said. 'Now, if only it was Florida. The next time I strike, I'm gonna do it in summer.'

'They'll be around soon with the coffee.'

'How much longer?'

'Two hours this shift.'

'One thing you gotta hand Joe, he sure has organized this thing. Jees when you think of it, thirty doors you gotta watch all the time, and men to feed and relief pickets and Christ knows how much stuff besides. And the stuff to the papers,' he said, his voice wandering with admiration.

'I wouldn't want Joe's job.'

'He sure knows how to do it.'

A negro with a red muffler tied over his cap, around his ears, came up. He had a water kettle full of coffee, a sack of clanking tin cups (everyone's tin cups), and a bag of sandwiches.

'Hi there.'

They hurried towards him, asking questions. 'How're the other guys, any trouble, anything doing, anybody go home, everything okay?'

'Sure,' the negro said smiling. 'Sure, sure. Everything's fine. You leave it to Joe. You leave it to me. I bring the coffee and Joe got the ideas. Hey, you, leave them sandwiches, one apiece like Joe said. Them sandwiches gotta feed 25 and 27 too.'

A man put one back. 'All right, Jakie.' They swatted him on the back and he walked off, lopsided, careful not to spill a drop of coffee. 'You keep it up till summer,' he said, 'and I'll bring you ice cold beer.'

'Yah!'

'Hey, Jakie, didn't you hear they were gonna have a meeting to-day, and we're all gonna get forty a week?'

'Listen to him,' Jakie said, laughing in his throat, 'listen to him. When we're daid man, then the Lord's gonna come up to us and say: "You boys get together and make a union and I'll give you what you ask for ef it's in reason." '

They laughed and moved about the door, stamping their feet, asking each other occasionally what time it was.

Presently the relief crew came up; Joe was with them. They could hear his voice, quiet, very sure, telling some joke about the manager, what the foreman had said when he passed the picket at 17.

The waiting men forgot the cold for a minute, gathering around Joe. 'What's the news, Joe, anything new, everybody all right, nobody went home yet . . . ?'

'I heard the Labor man from Washington would be here to-morrow,' Joe said. 'They'll have to talk then. It'll work out fine. They say those Department of Labor men are okay. They say they can get this stuff straight. How're you? Cold? We sure picked a fine time for our strike, didn't we? We could a had it just as well last spring.'

'Any old time,' one of them said, cheerfully, 'any old time practically since this here plant opened.'

'Well, Joe, we're betting on you,' one of the pickets said, 'you talk straight to them when they get here. You tell them how it is.'

'Yes,' Joe said. They all looked at him a moment, serenely. Their confidence, believing he alone could do what he knew none of them could do, not all of them together, frightened him. 'We gotta keep everybody's spirit up,' he said, 'that's the main thing. Do you hear anybody talking?' he asked.

'Hell no, we're behind this union.'

From nowhere, suddenly, still and swift as a bullet passing, came the word. Scabs. It was a whisper first, a rumor. They must have felt it, standing there, even before a man with red-rimmed eyes, shapeless in his coat, came up to them and hinted it; wondered what now, what shall we do Joe. They stood; Joe waiting, almost as if he expected to hear thunder, his eyes squinting, half shut, and his mouth tight.

Then it came, from the other side of the buildings, angry, deep but clear.

'Scabs! Scabs! Scabs!'

They had all started running, Joe ahead, and over his shoulder he kept saying: 'For God's sake, don't do nothing violent, it'll only hurt us, they'll only lock you up, we can't get away with it. For God's sake,' he said thinly, his breath failing, 'for God's sake, keep your shirts on.'

Around the door of 17, the men had crowded together shouting; there were only gestures now, fists black against the grey green sky, shoving, churning, cursing at a narrow line of men, walking in to the factory with their heads down, each one looking at the other's heels. A double row of police stood by, with their clubs ready, suddenly looking warier, thinner, more dangerous than they ever did on traffic duty. Behind the pickets, more police, the blue coats trim against the grey formless mass of strikers.

From every corner and at once, men came. They left the other doors hurrying to see, their faces strained and furious. Men like themselves, workers like themselves with as little as they, as much to want, coming here with police thick around them, to steal work, to break this strike. After three weeks of this cold, of waiting, of fear at night and the wives doubting, they should come to break the strike, people like themselves. There was a quality of wonder about their anger. This was something they had been prepared for, but could not believe. They could understand that the police were against them, the management, and the newspapers. But not others like themselves.

Joe was there, running between the police and his own men, taking an arm here and saying: 'For God's sake, don't, don't.' Pushing someone back, shouting: 'Don't give them a chance, this is what they want.' Pleading: 'Wait, the men from Washington will be here, we'll lose everything if. . . .'

A policeman pushed him, said: 'Get out of the way, youse, step back.' For one still moment, Joe's arm swung up, crisped, waited. Then he let it fall. 'No no,' he shouted. 'That's what they want. No, stop, will you,' he said to a man behind him, a man whose eyes had gone blind and bright with anger.

No one knew where it came from and it went wild. It must have been iron, a crowbar perhaps, from the clattering noise it made, breaking through a window pane and falling inside on the concrete factory floor. Then it was useless. Joe saw it; said to himself helplessly: 'They got us where they want us,' and around him he saw, felt, heard bodies thudding against each other, the sharp crack of clubs on bone, the bright swift smack of fists.

Sirens howled. Policemen were thick as dust over the street. On the curb at the end of the block were people, the public, half afraid, half curious, not knowing what to think, for whom to shout. Behind the crowds, the strikers' women pushed, trying to get through, crying for their men, fighting their way.

'Kill him, kill him.' Who was saying it? One of his men. 'No, for God's sake,' he said and suddenly, in gladness, with joy, he saw a policeman coming for him, the club high above his head. Joe let his fist go, hard for the blue-coated stomach, shouting not words, just sound, free and glad at last, not caring what happened now. 'Good,' he grunted, 'good,' and pushed through, striking crazily, half blows, sometimes hitting something that gave, felt soft, went down.

When they threw the first tear-gas bomb, it was all over. Blinded, dazed, bruised, they were packed in the wagons on top of each other, and the street cleared.

'I wonder if the scabs got in,' Joe asked, speaking to no one.

The silence was like sound itself, and final.

Pete was having a fine time. He didn't know what it was all about but now that didn't matter. He hit out with his arms, crazily, spinning like a weather-vane, and big and useless as a scarecrow. All the time he was saying: 'You sonuvabitch, you goddam bastard, you': but it was a song, it was glad and exulting. Then, from nowhere, a policeman's club clicked on his left temple, slanting and swift: and he fell. Many people walked over him unintentionally; there was very little space and it was full of men running and shouting and trying to hit each other. Presently, tear gas smoked over the crowd between the factory walls and the houses opposite, and there was panic and people stumbling helplessly, cursing. It ended rapidly, with the noise of police wagons, bells clanging, backfiring, shrieking gears. Pete came to in jail. His experience of a strike had been exactly three weeks of peaceful picketing and then this sudden hot exulting fine business of being able to hit back or hit all around him, for a little while at least.

He was in a cell with several other men. They were packed in carelessly because, any minute now, with perhaps a few words about being Reds or perhaps not, and maybe a bit of bruising (but that also was dictated by personal taste) they would be released. His head hurt badly, both on the temple and at the back, at the base of the skull, and his eyes seemed very small and painful to him. He was half-leaning against the wall of the cell, and he sat up and felt his temple softly and passed his hands over his eyes and shook himself a little and looked around. He had never been in jail before but then he had also never been in a strike. He wasn't unhappy about it; beyond the pain in his head he remembered those few minutes when he, Pete Hines, had seemed to be a powerful man, a free and dangerous man, hitting out for himself and everybody else. It was cheap at the price.

'How ya coming, brother.' He smiled vaguely at the man next to him and said: 'Okay.' Across the cell, a man was sucking his mouth carefully, two teeth were missing in front and he kept running his tongue over the empty bloody space and his face looked surprised. Some of the men were not marked beyond scraped knuckles or tears in their clothes: four others besides Pete had bruises on their heads, bruises that were drying now, into red, dirty-looking welts, and would soon be darkly coloured, blue and purple and later yellow and greenish. They all seemed to Pete to be feeling fine about it, the way he was.

'Jees,' he said, suddenly, to no one, 'that was swell. I'd do that again. That was good all right.'

A few of the men, listening, smiled back at him.

'Wonner where they got Joe,' someone said.

There was silence: saying that name made the strike again something that had a purpose, something that went from definite decisions to gestures, and was intended to have a final result.

Joe Barrow was the one who'd had the idea long ago, and talked about it at home, and then later, with other men at Dick's saloon and written away for information and advice, and finally organized the local union. He was the man who did the thinking. Pete considered him. He had nothing new in his mind, despite this surprising experience of feeling so fine and hitting out for himself. He still thought what he had the first time he listened to Joe talking to a meeting in the small hall of the Labor Temple. He thought what Joe said was true and he liked how he said it, and the way his face changed as he talked. He understood every word Joe said and, from what he could remember of listening to other people talking on platforms, people who wanted to get elected to something, he had either not clearly understood or not quite believed any other speaker before. It was enough for him that he liked the way Joe looked and that he believed what Joe was saying.

'You can put me down,' he'd said that night, leaving the hall; and he shook hands with Joe, and he had gone home feeling he was in with good guys and that things would be better now.

When the strike was called he went out with the others and reported where he was told to report, and did picket duty as instructed and helped at odd jobs—mostly errands or getting coffee and sandwiches around to the men at night on picket duty—anything they told him to do. He didn't talk much because he felt shy to ask questions, and he had no opinions about the strike, beyond believing in Joe.

A man with raw knuckles said: 'What the hell happened?'

A man whose head looked something like Pete's, and whose eyes were bloodshot, said: 'Some guy threw a brick, or a crowbar, or something.'

'Those goddam cops.'

'Yeah, but I bet they say it was Joe or one of the union.'

'We'll win anyhow.'

Pete thought about that. He knew they were striking because they had to work too fast, and one man had to do two men's jobs and didn't get paid enough for half a man. And then, too, he'd heard Joe explain this, they were striking for the right to organize and be a union. He liked the union very much. He felt safe with these men, and he'd had a fine time picketing. Kind of walking around and talking to your new friends, or listening, and he had a little money saved up, so it wasn't like some of the men that had to go on Relief. When you had to go on Relief it wasn't fine any more: you didn't feel the same.

'They got you good, didn't they, boy,' a man said to Pete.

He said 'Yeah' modestly. He was feeling fairly proud of his clouted head, and he was still wobbly and dazed, but glad to have been there when the trouble started.

'I hope Joe's all right,' someone said.

'Oh, sure.'

Presently a policeman came and unlocked the cell door and let them all out. Minton's Soup Factory wasn't too popular locally: the Mintons spent their money someplace else. The policeman was pretty nice about it all and the cold air of the street felt good to Pete. A man he had never seen before, who had a cut on his face, linked arms with Pete and said: 'Let's go to Dick's and get a beer.' Most of the crowd from the jail straggled off to Dick's to find out what the latest news was and what Joe was saying. Pete had a little money on him and everybody seemed to be buying everybody else beers, as if it were a holiday or late Saturday night, and soon he was pleasantly drunk and feeling light and happy. He was crazy about the union. He hadn't known what swell guys he worked with before, or how good it was to feel surrounded by friends and safe because there were so many of you. He kept thinking, Ferryville isn't such a bad burg after all; though he'd lived there all his life, and even in the same house for the last fifteen years. But he'd never found himself thinking about it, one way or the other, before.

'They say the Labor guy from Washington's gonna be here tomorrow.'

'I bet Joe'll fix up that arbitration committee okay.'

'They say Bignose is gonna talk for Minton on that committee.'

'Didja see the *Evening Gazette* yet? It says the strikers rioted. Hell, none of us slung that brick.'

'When we win this strike, I'm gonna get my little woman a new coat to celebrate. We'll get paid like we should then, I'm telling you.'

Pete drank his beer and smiled and said 'Sure' whenever he was called upon to make an answer, and felt fine about everything. They'd win the strike and then he wouldn't have to tear his arms out and break his back trying to dip twelve of those stinking 115 gallon cauldrons of soup into the machine, every hour: and Mabel would get a new coat too, or that electric washing machine she was always talking about, and he could go to union meetings at night and listen to the boys who knew how to talk. He went home unsteadily and late, singing. He thought he was having about the best time in his life.

He'd forgotten about Mabel. But she was waiting in the front room, wearing a lavender flannel wrapper and her face was hard with anger.

'So that's what your old union is for: to make you go out and fight with cops and get your dumb head cracked open and then make you go out and get drunk. It's a fine union, that is.'

He didn't want to argue with her; he was still feeling warm and pleased.

'Now Mabel,' he said dimly.

'Now Mabel, nothing. You act like we got money to burn. And how about the rent, Pete Hines, and how about the food for the time your damn old union keeps you from working and how about a lotta other things? I hate that union,' she said, 'everything was fine before that big loud-mouth, Joe Barrow, begun to shoot off his face.'

'Lissen,' he said, and his voice was not nearly as conciliatory.

'I will not lissen. Who do you think I am? You go out and get yourself drunk and me sitting here, never going to the movies, or anything I wanna do, and scrimping and saving and washing my hands to the bone with the laundry and everything and all because of that union.'

'The President,' he said with dignity, 'told us we should strike.'

'Yeah. I bet.'

'He did. You couldn't know because you never read the papers or go to meetings or anything. But he sure did. He said in that NRA we could all get together and make unions, and if we couldn't get the right wages and stuff, then we could strike. The President's on our side. He knows a lotta guys like Joe.'

'Yeah. I betcha. I bet Joe goes and stays down there in the White House with him, and he sez: "Joe, what would you do if you was me?" '

'You lissen, Mabel. . . .'

'You lissen yourself, Pete Hines. You're a damn fool and you're drunk and you better go to bed and sleep it off. And to-morrow you can stay home and help me some instead of running around with those fool union men and you'll be a lot more help here with the furnace than all that stuff about picketing. And if you ask me, Joe's a big-mouthed liar. And if you wanna know where this is gonna end, it's gonna end with us on Relief.'

He laughed at her. After all she was only a woman and what could she know about unions and strikes, and Labor people from Washington, and committees, and the NRA and things like that? How could she be expected to know that the union was fine and there were a lot of men in it, practically everyone, and they'd get what they wanted? She was only a woman and women didn't get around much. 'Relief,' he said, laughing. 'Say, I never heard such boloney. I'll be working when I'm sixty.'

Joe went in to them quietly, the last. Before him, he herded the other two men, his members of the arbitration committee. He wore a blue shirt with a lavish wine-red tie, satin, and a small dingy diamond tie-pin. He saw the bare important-looking room and the other men around the table, thinking about something else. If we get mad, he thought, if we get up and get sore, then it won't go. He was glad there were no Italians on his side: they got excited, they spoke bad, quick English, and had a way of shaking their fists. Samuels and Harding slinked in ahead of him and found seats. Their hands looked absurd, afterthoughts tacked to their sleeves. They looked at the other men, their heads a little down, frowning. The Government man sat at the head of the table. Joe was surprised to see how young he was, just about his own age, thirty-five perhaps, not soft-looking, not seeming to be a man who had simply sat all his life waiting for the money to roll in. He looked tired too, and Joe found himself glad of this; thinking, if he's tired, he'll understand better about us, he'll know about work.

Curley, the plant manager, was there, and Daniels, floor foreman, and the owner, Mr Minton. They seemed nervous, given to sudden smiles, as if to show that they were easy with this, knew they were right, as if the workers were being foolish, unreasonable, like spoiled but dangerous children.

The Government man was named Stevens. He greeted the strikers' committee and got to work, sorting papers before him, speaking abruptly with no words he could spare.

'Yes,' Joe would say. 'Yes, that's right. Yes, you got all that straight.'

Then it was Mr Minton's turn. He said: 'Mr Curley will speak for me, I don't keep up with the details of the management.' And then he made a little speech about the factory, its ideals, what it meant to the workers. They all listened impatiently, Stevens with his hand over his eyes. Joe thought: The worst of it is, the poor old cluck probably believes all that drip he's saying.

Presently the case was outlined, stood agreed between them, the points of the dispute singled out and named.

And then it began. Joe thought, in the week that followed, that he had spent the best part of his life in this room, angry and exhausted by turns, hopeless, harried, trying to keep Samuels and Harding quiet, sane, attempting in the intervals between meetings to still their anger, their desire to blow up the plant, everything, stay out on strike until they all starved, kidnap Minton, anything, anything. Would this haggling never end?

He knew himself, early, that they had lost; they would gain nothing from this except Minton's fear, Curley's bitterness, a growing palpable desire for revenge. Within himself he wondered how he would face the men, after those cold starved weeks, after all the hope and strain, and say: 'Boys, I got you this,' holding up between thumb and forefinger a crumb.

At last, because he saw nothing else for it, knowing they had no money left to fight, there would be no coffee, no sandwiches, no groceries to take home at night, knowing the men were tired and the women frightened, he gave in. He thought: I've failed them and what else can I do? This is only the beginning, this is nothing, but how can I tell them that or give them patience or anything to go on with?

They agreed on a raise of three cents an hour; and on certain operations it was decided to add another man, to lessen the strain of the stretch-out. No one would be fired for belonging to the union, for striking: and they could hold meetings, grow, continue.

The men went back to work, not glad but relieved. Joe watched them file in, in the morning with the sky grey, high and frozen, their faces still smeared with sleep.

He thought: Back to your nine dollars, twelve dollars, your fourteen dollars and the machines driving you, living through the day to provide for yourself a little house with a basement flooded and the rain coming through broken windows, and Sunday a day to recover from it, a day to be limp and asleep.

The men greeted him as they passed. 'Hello, Joe,' they said, friendly and confident, 'you sure told it to them all right. You sure got us a raise, boy; you know how to handle this stuff all right. . . .'

Finally Joe went in, to the dark, smooth machines where he worked, too ashamed to stand there and take thanks for nothing.

Pete sat in his front room reading the papers. He rocked back and forth and held the paper close to his eyes, frowning. Finally he began saying the words over with his lips. He had bought all the papers and he had read everything they printed about the strike and the arbitration committee, once. But he was not sure he understood. Newspapers said things so strangely, as if they were writing about dead people or people some place else. This was, of course, his strike, and Joe's, and all the other men's, the ones in jail and the ones on the picket line. But the small black print seemed very remote, the words were cold and indifferent, and he could not be sure he had really understood.

Mabel watched him from the kitchen door. 'You might keep your shoes on in the parlour,' she said. 'You won't be having shoes soon enough, and we're not bums yet, anyhow, Pete Hines.'

He felt under the greyish over-stuffed sofa for his shoes and put them on. 'Wouldja like me to wear my coat too, and my collar, and maybe I should even have a diamond stick-pin?'

'You can still try and look like somebody with a job,' she said bitterly and went back to the kitchen.

He sat with the paper on his lap and stared in front of him. He was looking at the Age of Innocence, framed and unbearably sweet against the mottled wallpaper, but he did not see it. He saw nothing of that room which had been brought together, object piled on object, for the last fifteen years: their married life. Their wedding picture and both their parents, the baby who had died, the calendar with an Indian girl and a vast American beauty rose on it; the table covered with a fringed cloth, and topped by a marble lamp, the straight chairs neat against the wall, the lace curtains with plush drapes over them: he knew it was all there. His front room, the place he felt prosperous and sure in. The kitchen behind it, with something Mabel called a dinette, where they ate; and the bedroom, with a kewpie-lamp on Mabel's dressing-table. He was better off than a lot of men who worked in Minton's, having all these things. All these solid and different things, proving how long and steadily he had worked, in one factory or another: and showing also that after the baby who died there had been no others. He was proud of his home: it gave him a feeling of being somebody, having a handsome place like this to come back to. He liked Mabel to get herself up, too, when they went to the movies or to a church social or a dance at Holliday Park in the summer; that showed also what a worker he was, that he could make money and provide a fine house for his wife and fine clothes. It wasn't possible that he had understood the papers. He began to read again.

'The arbitration committee, presided over by Mr Guy Stevens, special representative of the Department of Labor and formed of six members, three designated by Mr Minton of Minton's Soups Inc., and three chosen from the local Canner's Union, to-day reached a decision satisfactory to both parties, which terminates the Minton strike at the beginning of its fifth week. Mr Curley, plant manager at Minton's, and a member of the arbitration committee, expressed himself as "perfectly satisfied". Mr Barrow, speaking for the Canner's Union, stated that he "hoped it would all work out all right according to the decisions of the committee". Certain changes in work loads will be agreed upon later. An increase in wages of three cents an hour was decided on. The Canners' Union is recognized. . . .'

Three cents an hour, Pete said to himself. Pete fingered the paper and felt afraid. Of course, if the union was recognized, that meant Joe would go on talking with the bosses and trying to get something better.

He rocked back and forth and tried to understand all this. Of his $105 savings, only $35 was left. That money had been saved for sickness; or if there wasn't any sickness, it was supposed to add up slowly and some day buy him and Mabel a good funeral with coffins lined in quilted pink satin. He was glad to spend it all right for the strike: but what did it all mean? It didn't sound as if the strike had come to much. And still there were so many guys in it and they'd been so strong. He remembered the fine feeling of hitting out, and how important he had been for just a little while and how happy. He thought perhaps he'd better go over to Dick's and listen to what the boys were saying, because sitting here alone this way you got mixed up and didn't really understand things. It seemed suddenly lonely to him in his front room and he was uncertain of himself and the things he had so clearly believed. It would be better to go and see what the boys were doing. He felt hurried. The room was too little and too dark and he knew nothing, he understood nothing. He got his coat and hat and was putting on his collar and tie before the mirror in the front room when Mabel again came from the kitchen. She had flour on her arms and she looked hot.

'Where you going now?'

'Down to Dick's; I wanna see what the boys gotta say about this arbitration committee.'

'And get drunk, I guess; and talk all night and then what've you got?' He said nothing, yanking at his tie, hurried and nervous, needing a crowd of men about him, all taking assurance from each other's voices.

'You lost your strike,' Mabel said slowly. 'I always knew you would. Your fine friend, Joe, lost your strike and used up most of your money and now what're you gonna do?'

He pulled on his coat and, with his hat in his hand, went swiftly to the door. He turned and saw her standing there, arms crossed, hot from the stove, but not angry, only final and warning. He slammed the door behind him, to blot her out, because he was afraid she told the truth.

It seemed that the human body could no longer endure these relentless days, with the cold clawing through the bone, the boredom, the grey same hours. December, Joe thought, is a month for dying. The union meetings went on, but differently. There was fear in them somewhere, as the men came to the bleak little hall above the tyre shop. And they talked too loud, raising their voices against an unnamed threat.

One day Mr Curley called Joe; he went to the plant manager's office with his overalls on, his arms stained by grease.

Curley's smile was in his eyes, and beneath his skin; he was too wary to let it come out, spread, glow; and his voice was hearty like red apples, jovial and deep.

'I'm damn sorry, Joe, but we got to lay you off for a while; just nothing doing in your shop, slack season you know. We'll let you know when things pick up. We have to reduce the entire staff, about a third, I guess. Tough times ... the depression ... sorry....'

Joe took a pack of cigarettes from his pocket and lit one and flicked the match up towards the ceiling. It made a brittle noise, dropping on the floor. He stared at Curley and breathed the smoke out in long twin streamers.

'I certainly hope Mr Minton'll manage to make both ends meet,' he said, and smiled and went from the room.

Pete lay in bed acting as if he were asleep. He waited while Mabel paused, not sure whether she ought to wake him—mainly from spite—

or whether he would be less trouble in bed, out of the way. She got up and he heard her in the kitchen, making a lot of noise with the coffee-pot and the frying-pan. He screwed his eyes shut and lay rigid. He knew that to-day, sometime, he would have to go to Minton's and see Bignose Curley and get his job back. He didn't want to. His legs writhed under the sheets. He was nervous and dimly resentful. It seemed to him it was like having to apologise and make up, without really doing that, but at least implying it. He felt licked and embarrassed. He felt as if he had been caught at something. Suddenly, he had the dreadful idea that Bignose might laugh at him and the union and say: 'Well, you guys sure thought you knew a lot. . . .' By now he was sweating with humiliation. He'd postponed going back for a week: there were men you didn't mind seeing when you felt you had the worst of it, but not Bignose.

All right, he said to himself, get up, you cluck, and go and see Bignose. What the hell's the matter with you; scared you'll get your tail spanked or something?

Mabel gave him breakfast dourly.

Now he found that it was harder and harder to face this interview. He walked out of his way, towards the centre of Ferryville, past the shops. He had on his work clothes. He was walking with his head down and his shoulders hunched, not conscious of where he was, but stalling for time. He turned and saw himself reflected in a shop window and stopped dead and looked at himself. He went closer to the window. He hadn't thought about how he looked for years, not since he used to go for the girls. He saw a tall man, not old or young, thin and loosely and carelessly hinged together, who held himself stooped, with one shoulder higher than the other. He couldn't make anything of his face: it seemed to him like everybody else's face, like all those faces on the street. But what worried him now was the way this man, himself, walked. 'My God,' he said softly and aloud, 'I'm walking like I was unemployed.'

He turned and went very quickly towards Minton's, his chest out and breathing like a locomotive, with effort.

It was eleven-thirty and the factory shrieked outside the wood partition. He could hear steam escaping, the rolling thunder of the belts, the heavy metal clanking of the iron containers dragged over cement floors. He waited on a bench for a chance to see Mr Curley. He twisted his cap and scraped the floor with his toe and felt himself to be damp and hot all over.

A stenographer opened the glass door and said: 'Come on in.' Curley was busy with some papers and didn't look up. Pete stood there. He felt, suddenly, as if his arms were unnaturally long, like an ape's, hanging way down to the floor and loose. He couldn't make himself stand up straight, grin, and look the way he wanted Curley to think of him.

Curley looked up, very vague.

"Hullo, Mr Curley.'

There was a silence. 'I'm Pete Hines. I'm a soup dipper in number three.'

'Oh, yes.'

'Well. I just come to report back for work, to tell you like, you know, to get on the pay-roll again. Now the strike's over and everything.'

Curley wanted badly to say what he thought of strikers; disloyalty, Russian ideas, and the whole dirty pack of them. But he couldn't. On account of those Government snoops sticking their noses into business and making a mess of everything. Fool kids or college professors or something, they were always sending around from Washington. On the taxpayers' money too.

'I'm sorry, Hines, but we won't be able to take you back right now.'

Pete looked at him, stupidly.

'What,' he said, this was as bad as the newspapers and the arbitration committee and everything else. Nobody said anything simply, or anything you expected.

'Naturally, we had to get in other help during the strike to keep some of the plant open and, of course, those people get preference now and, of course, right after the strike, a lot of people came straight back and some new ones too, and we had to hire quickly to try to make up for all the lost time. I'll take your name, of course, and let you know as soon as anything comes up.'

'Oh. Sure.'

'Just leave your name with Miss Jones when you go out. It's probably only a temporary lay-off,' Mr Curley said and began to turn over the papers on his desk again.

Pete got out of the room, mumbled his name and address to Miss Jones, and somehow found himself again on the street, walking with a more pronounced stoop than before. But I'm outa work, he kept saying to himself, stupidly. I'm outa work. And it isn't the good season, either. I'm never outa work. I been working since I'm twelve. I don't see how it can be like that. I'm a good soup dipper; they never complained of my work. And I been there six years. Besides, the President said we should make unions, and if the bosses didn't act like they should, we could strike, and then the Labor men would come from Washington, and then we'd go back to our jobs and they'd fix everything up in Washington. By God, he thought suddenly, Curley can't fire me. The President won't have it. It's against the law.

. . .

They sat in Joe's office, which was a corner partitioned off from the main room of the union headquarters. A chipped soup plate was full of cigarette butts and chewed cigar ends. It wasn't very warm but the air was old and heavy. There were three folding chairs and a kitchen chair behind the desk, at which Joe sat. Joe passed his hand over his eyes, his face, trying to wipe off the weariness.

'I can't explain it to you, Pete,' he said. 'We'll get this stuff before the Labor Department whenever we can. I'll write the people in Washington. We got to keep the union going. That's all. It takes time. Everything's slow,' he said and hated the sound of his voice: flat and stale like the air he was breathing, toneless with discouragement.

They sat in silence. Everything's too slow, Joe thought. Sometimes, it seems like there must be millions of people not doing anything but waiting; all of them waiting for something to happen, or somebody to say something. And nothing does happen. Things just go on.

'It's cold too,' Pete said into the silence. 'People gotta have coal.'

'I know.'

'What'll they all do; all the guys got fired?'

'Relief.'

Pete shook his head mulishly. 'Not me. I'm as good as I was when I was twenty. I'm only thirty-nine now; men that ain't sick can get work.'

'There must be about twelve million guys in this country then, sick as hell.' he grinned at Pete. 'Lissen boy, go on out and try. You might be lucky.'

'What're you gonna do?'

'I got some life-insurance I can cash in. That'll keep me a coupla months. And I'm gonna hold the union together.'

Pete stood up. 'I'm gonna go out and get me a job.'

'Good luck.'

'Same to you.'

Joe opened the window and stood by it, looking over Ferryville. The city lay shapeless and murky before him, sloping to the river. It was late afternoon. He thought about the places people lived, and his own home: that would have to go now. He'd send his mother to his brother in Boston who still had work. And give up the flat and move into a furnished room. And save and do without and, somehow, manage for a while. All the men like Pete—whose names you couldn't remember because they looked alike—who didn't understand anything and were helpless, he was bound to them. He'd started the union, and he was responsible. It was going to be hard. Not the business of living in a dump and all that, but just having to sit here and wait for them to come in and ask questions he couldn't answer. He'd have to act cheerful, no matter how he felt. It wouldn't do them much good to know that they were licked now, and perhaps for a long time.

There are more of us, he thought. But we're like a long freight train without a locomotive. If he'd been to school more ... if all the others like Pete knew what was happening around them, and knew how to get together and obey and give orders, for a while. If they could even see what was happening. We get lied to, he thought, we're the easiest people there are to fool. He thought of how he and Samuels and Harding, at the arbitration committee meetings, had been impressed by the way Mr Minton and Curley and Daniels looked: their clothes. The way Minton especially sat and talked, as if he were used to having people listen to him and do what he said. The Government man was the same: education did that, and clothes, and having enough money, so cops could never tell you to get a move on.... Suddenly, he felt infinitely alone, and without a world, knowing that he was not really one with Pete and the others, separated from them by the few things he knew and the many more things he wanted. And as for the other world: he thought grimly, and not quite with laughter, of the kind of tie he wore and the kind of tie Mr Stevens wore; and the way his voice sounded, and his accent, and the way his hands looked, and how he walked.... I got to keep them going somehow. We've got to be building something up all the time and learning stuff, and how to fight back, and we've got to learn all the tricks they know. It's slow, he said to himself, and again he stumbled over the word. But what about me, he thought, what about my life? From somewhere in his mind came a phrase: all men have inalienable rights to life, liberty and the pursuit of happiness. He leaned his forehead against the cold window pane and tried, hopelessly, to laugh.

The trouble with Joe, Pete thought, is, he's discouraged. Then, too, Joe was in a tough spot: everybody'd be coming to him saying, 'What'll I do?' That was dumb: the thing to do was go out and get another job. No use crying over spilt milk. Any guy with a good work record and muscles and some sense could get a job: maybe have to look around a little. But that was nothing.

By now, Pete was enjoying himself. Life was simple again. He didn't have a job and he was going to get one. That was easy. Not like all the things he'd been trying to understand: the union and NRA and things. All he had to do was go around and tell his name, and what he could do, and then go back to Mabel and say 'Well, kid, I'm working for....'

Pause. For whom? He began to make lists, in his mind, frowning. It had been so long since he'd thought about all this, six years. He felt that probably, even when he was working for somebody else, he'd start out in the morning, dopey-like, and begin walking towards Mintons. Well. There was the Orpheus Victrola Company, The Susie Sweet Biscuit Company, The Florida Cigar factory, the Bridle Leather Works, the Parisian Shoe Company (he dismissed that; shoes had always seemed to him especially skilled work somehow, so he wouldn't even bother). And the Beverley Underwear Mills. That was about all in the way of factories. There was the Lampson Trucking firm though, and probably a lot of other jobs like that, driving a truck or hauling stuff or something. But he was a factory worker, always had been. Better stick to the factories. He went to the nearest: the Susie Sweet Biscuit Company. There wasn't anybody in the office. He waited a while and then wandered off to look for someone. He found a clerk and said he'd come about a job. The clerk laughed at him. 'Lissen, brother, we wouldn't know how to act around here if anybody got hired. All we do here is make "necessary retrenchments". You better go somewhere else.' Pete thought the clerk was being smart, but it didn't matter. There were a lot of other places.

He walked across town towards the Orpheus Victrola plant. It was cold and he hurried. Probably going to rain. No sense getting there soaked and looking like a bum. He was a little breathless when he arrived. At a desk, behind a counter in an empty room, sat a man with a green eye shade. Pete leaned on the counter and said: 'Hello.' The man nodded. 'Anything doing?' Pete said. The man looked up at him. 'Nope. You can leave your name there on a piece of paper, if you want. I'll let you know.' There was neither sincerity nor warmth in the man's voice, and Pete thought it would be a waste of paper. He pulled his coat collar up, when he got on the street. These refusals had happened so fast that he didn't have time to think about them, or be in any way distressed. He said to himself, guess people don't buy so many victrolas, now it's the depression, and set off again, zig-zagging across the town.

It was dark now, and he thought he'd go to the Parisian Shoe Company, anyhow, because it was nearest. It'd be too late to do anything more to-day. It was raining too.

He went into the office without knocking; it was a small room, lighted by one electric bulb hanging on a cord. Rain smeared against the windows. There was a woman in there, talking to a man, or pleading with him. Pete only saw her back: a broad, middle-aged woman, hatless, the dark hair knotted loose at the nape of her neck. She was leaning over a table behind which the man sat, holding herself up with one hand and beating on the table with the other, as if not knowing what she did.

She was crying and her voice came out in the choked, unclear way of someone who has been crying and talking for a long time. The man looked nervous and unhappy.

'I'm sorry, Maria,' he was saying. 'You know I'd take you on if I could. But we're not taking anybody. Later, for the Easter trade, maybe. I swear I'll get you back the first chance I get.'

'It's too late,' the woman said, 'I can't wait for Easter. I gotta have money now. It's Raphael, he's sick. The little one. I gotta have milk and oranges and the medicines the doctor says. He's so skinny,' she said, her voice suddenly rising, and the free hand fluttering against the table. 'You gotta give me work. He's sicker to-day than he was yesterday. Please, Mr Atkins, I always worked good here, I never done nothing wrong, I always worked steady. I'm fast too. You gotta....'

The man spread his hands in a gesture of helplessness; his face was lined and distressed. The woman was not talking, now, only making stifled sounds, with a handkerchief against her mouth.

It might be Mabel, only she's got brown hair, Pete thought, shocked and silent. So this was what it was coming to, women were crying to get work, women were crying like they might at home, but for only their husbands to see, in front of strangers.... And they couldn't get work anyhow. He turned, fumbling for the door-knob. He ran most of the way home, running and walking, with the rain falling now in long thin curtains over the empty streets. It might of been Mabel, he thought.

He got up early and he didn't wait for breakfast. He was at the Florida Cigar Company before it opened. He watched the workers straggling in, sombre in the cold smoky morning light. He thought they were lucky, just to be working.

The day's crop of applicants had collected before the employment office door. Pete held himself a little apart; he wanted it clear that he was used to working, and not at all used to hanging around factory doors. He filed in, in turn. But he didn't have a chance to say anything. A bored and sleepy voice told him: 'Nothing doing to-day, come back in about two weeks or leave your name and address.' A voice reciting doom and failure, as if it were announcing a weather report: but nothing nearly as important as a baseball score. None of the men who had come in the morning cold waited about the doors. Were they going some place else, Pete wondered. How long did a man keep it up? When did he just decide to stay in bed because what was the use anyhow?

That day, fearfully, he canvassed every factory in town. Between stops, he went into stores and asked if they needed any help—a grocery store, a café, and finally a garage. His feet ached, and he was beginning to worry about his shoes. How would he get them fixed, once they were worn out? He was hungry until about two o'clock, and then just weak, with a headache pulling and buzzing behind his eyes.

Presently, he noticed that he wasn't even walking any more. He was shuffling his feet over the pavement, sagging and exhausted. Nothing was clear to him now: he couldn't understand why he should be doing this, how it had all happened. Towards the end of the day, he went into offices mutely, and looked at some man behind a desk or table and that man, in equal silence, shook his head. They didn't even bother with words. There was nothing to say.

At dusk, he went past the Lampson Trucking Company and noticing the lighted office, entered. He said to a man he could hardly see, being dazed now with weariness and despair. 'Need a driver?'

The man looked at him and said carelessly. 'You're too old.' He stood swaying on his feet, but the man had nothing more to say. Very quietly, Pete left the office. He didn't know in what direction he was going, and he couldn't even feel his body. Old, he kept saying to himself, too old. But yesterday or years ago, he had walked firmly around the city, conscious of his muscles and all the good years ahead for a man who knew how to work. Old. Old. He must get home now, quickly. He must get inside among his own things, where he would be safe.

It was later than supper time, and Mabel opened the door, ready with anger. 'Late again,' she said. 'Your union, your fine union. It makes you lose your job, and you're never home like a decent man, and the supper spoiled, and you don't care what happens to me. You don't care about anything except your old union.'

He stood blinking in the light. They won't give me work, he thought. They say I'm too old. Suddenly he was terrified and lonely, and he wanted her to put her arms around him, the way she had when they were young, and kiss him and tell him he'd find a good job to-morrow or the next day. Tell him something. And hold him against her, and make him feel that it wasn't true about his being old, and no one needing him for work. He stretched out his arms, awkwardly. And Mabel, thinking he was perhaps drunk again and crazy—everything was wrong since the union—imagined he was going to strike her. She put her hand out to hold him off and shouted at him: 'Don't you touch me, Pete Hines, I'll call the cops. Don't you touch me, you bum, I won't take that from you. . . .'

Pretty soon, Joe thought, this place will stop being a worker's union, and turn into a club room for the unemployed. Practically no one, who was still working at Minton's, came to the union office. Even men who had daughters or wives, employed in the factory, stayed clear of the union, fearing to endanger other jobs besides their own. Afraid, Joe said to himself, everybody's afraid. Afraid and waiting. He felt no anger for this: and made no effort to force employed union members to meetings. I haven't got the right, he thought. There's rent and food and the children: you can't ask men to be brave every day in the week.

And besides, he added, I couldn't do it if I tried. They don't think enough of me any more. They're beginning to blame me, somehow. Perhaps that was to be expected: but still. Some days, when he sat alone in the office and only a few men came in, and then usually to talk to him as if everything were his personal fault, he had a hard time with his temper. Being what the newspapers called a union leader, Joe decided, was not a bunch of roses.

He heard the outer office door opening and some men coming in; they were stamping snow from their feet, the grey, slimy wet snow of a city. One of them called: 'You in there, Joe?'

'Yup. Come on in.'

There were three of them, and they took the folding chairs and tilted them against the wall for comfort, and asked for cigarettes.

'You got it soft here,' one man said.

'How d'you figure that?'

'You kin stay indoors all day.'

'Yeah, and not have to go around to the agencies and have the guys laugh in your face.'

'And you're not on Relief, neither.'

'And you ain't got a wife hollering at you, or kids you gotta feed when you can't even feed yourself decent.'

'Say,' Joe said. 'Cut it out. Any of you guys can have my job any time you want it. Right now. Just step up and take it.'

'What's the matter with it? Looks good to me.'

'Yeah? I guess you think I'm getting a big salary from the union, too.'

'Aw Joe, nobody said nothing about you making any money out of it.'

'Well, lay off of me. I'm not on Relief yet, but I will be, soon's my life-insurance money runs out. And I couldn't get a job around this town, not if they hired everybody in the place, starting to-morrow. And I'm so goddam sick of this room and sitting around here writing letters to Washington, I could puke. I said I'd do this job and I will. But I'm not gonna take any of that you-got-it-soft stuff.'

They're beginning to hate me, Joe thought with wonder. Not long ago, they thought I was the finest man in town and they all said: How's-the-boy-Joe and you-sure-know-how-to-manage-this-stuff. They'll probably accuse me of using the union funds for myself, next. And he thought: there's nobody to talk to. There isn't anybody who'd know what I was talking about if I said that I'm going crazy here. That I know nothing I do is any good, and I have to do it anyhow, so we won't look as licked as we are; and so things will go on. He lit another cigarette, he was smoking several packs a day, and he had to make an effort now, holding the match, to keep his hand from shaking. Funny, Joe thought, I guess a man can live with just about nothing, but he's got to have friends.

Some more men came in, they brought chairs from the outer room and one of them sat on the corner of the desk. The conversation became general.

'Didj'a know the bakeries dump the loaves of bread with torn wrappers out on the city dump-heap? A guy told me that, down-town yesterday. I went out there this morning, and I got two loaves, and kinda washed them off....' 'The Relief moved us, on account we can't pay our rent where we are. Jees, you oughta see them houses they put you in. The bedbugs crawl around on the ceiling and fall on the floor and make a little click. My wife has to put pans of water under the bed posts, and she's gonna have a baby in two months....'

'Did'ja hear about Sam Garvin's daughter? She got so sick sitting home and couldn't have any clothes or anything, so she went out on North Main Street on Saturday night and she got a coupla guys. And somebody told Sam, and he beat the hell out of her....' 'They're cutting wages over at the Parisian Shoe. They got a system about piece work, now, so they can gyp you outa lot of money; but you gotta sign the payroll like you got code wages....'

A man came in; he pushed the door so that it slammed back against the wall, and he came straight over to Joe. 'I gotta have a dollar, Joe. My kid's got a abscessed tooth and she's screaming off her head, it hurts so bad. And they don't have that Relief Dentist Clinic till Friday, and anyhow there ain't no time to sit around there and argue, and wait for a doctor's order or any of that. She's gotta get it pulled quick. She pukes up all her food and she can't sleep, and it's awful. The dentist won't do nothing till I pay him. Joe, lissen....'

'I'm sorry as hell, Bert. I haven't got it.'

There was a silence. The man who had come in stared around the room at the other people there, but not seeing them. He didn't know what to do, now. He turned slowly to leave, saying nothing. He would have to go home and watch his child. The other men looked at Joe, with disgust. He didn't have the money: he was living on $3.50 a week for himself, two meals a day, and spending $6 a week of his own money on the union, the rent and heat and light for the office, stamps.... It wouldn't last long anyhow. The union came first.

'Say, Bert,' a man said slowly, and he was looking at Joe as he talked. 'We can help you I guess. This whole gang'll go over there to Relief now, and just push in together and make them give you that dentist order. There's ten of us. You won't be coming, will you, Joe?'

'I'll go alone with Bert and talk to them,' Joe said. 'I think I can get that order.'

'Maybe it'll be better if we all go with Bert: things don't always come out like you think, Joe. Maybe we'll be better at it than you will. I guess Bert'll be better off with us.'

Joe half rose and sat down again in his chair.

He lit another cigarette and said: 'Suit yourselves. I gotta lot of work to do here, anyhow.'

Without good-byes, they filed out of the room. One of the men had his hand on Bert's arm. Bert himself seemed surprised by all this, not knowing exactly what had happened, or why, suddenly, the attitude of the men had grown cold and menacing. But what mattered was a medical order for his child. He let himself be led away.

Joe put his head down on his arms: his shoulders were flattened against the desk, and light coming from the window behind him picked out the frayed and shiny back of his suit. He thought: what is it makes men really love you for a while, and then turn away, with their faces closed and hating? Why am I doing this? Why not go away? I'm only a little man anyhow, why not give up this idea and go off somewhere and start over and take what comes my way and not think about it? What is it in me that keeps me here? And how about myself? I've got a right to something for myself, too, something like being happy.

A woman's voice said: 'Excuse me.'

He looked up, flushing with embarrassment. 'I was feeling sick,' he said uncertainly.

'Sure.'

'What can I do for you?'

'Nothing much. I'm a member of this union. I just was going by, and I came in to get warm. It's cold out.'

That's something we're good for here, anyhow, he thought. 'Where I live, they ran out of coal lately. It's a helluva life,' she said brightly.

She pulled a chair close to the radiator and sat hunched up against it. Any minute, Joe thought, she'll take off her shoes and stockings and hang them up to dry. She doesn't know I'm here. She looked a little blue around the mouth; her hands were clumsy with cold. She was not especially young, and not very fresh. Small and dark; with an imitation fur coat, that had never been rich or handsome and now showed the marks of time. Her make-up was on badly, and her face was curiously pallid with cold, around and behind the crooked geranium-red cheeks. He thought she was probably running out of everything, even rouge. Funny, how much sadder and poorer women could look. She took off a brilliant blue beret and began to smooth out and almost caress a long straight quill that stuck from it. The snow had dampened and softened the quill and it looked bad. Her face was wrinkled with concern, her mouth pursed up to make a little sound of dismay or despair, which didn't come out. She must be about thirty, he thought, or thirty-two, and every year had done something to her.

'You been in factory work long?' he asked.

'Nope, I was a stenographer till three years ago. But I couldn't get any more work in that, so I been peeling potatoes for a couple of years.' She smiled at him. 'Wonderful experience for a girl,' she said.

'They fired you at Minton's?'

'No, laid-off.'

'Because of the union?'

'Oh, no. They're just cutting down: one girl should do the work of two now—you know how it is. I don't think Curley ever got the idea I was a big Labor agitator. Just laying people off, you know. Happens all over the country.'

'What're you doing now?'

She looked at him with a bland stare. His questions were beginning to annoy her. After all, she had once paid her union dues, in fact three times, and she'd only come in to get warm.

'What's it to you?'

'I'm sorry,' he said. His voice was reassuring; he hadn't meant to snoop, he was only interested or concerned for her. That was his job anyhow, he was supposed to keep up on union members....

'Well, I'm on Relief. I live like Reilly,' she said. 'I get two dollars a week to live on and the Relief pays my landlady $1.75 for my room. I have just the swellest little life.'

He was beginning to like her. Thinking it over, he liked the arrogance of that stiff, upstanding feather in her hat. And she didn't seem to expect anything of him. She hadn't come to tell her troubles, or blame him for them.

'It's getting late,' he said. 'Do you want to go out and get something to eat?'

'Gee.'

'What?'

'Us girls don't usually get offered a dinner first.'

He was angry now. He hadn't planned anything about her; the offer of food had been his tribute to her hat and her spirit. Because he liked her. All right, if she wanted to act that way.

'What do the boys usually give you, sister?'

'Girls like me get a beer, if we're lucky,' she said. 'But then, that's nourishing, too.'

Pete pushed the door open and both of the women stared at him. Mabel had not expected him to come home so soon. Usually, he was out all day, looking for work. She had an idea, now, that he didn't often go to a factory or a store and apply for a job. She imagined that he was more likely just walking about the city, in that new way he had, dragging his feet. Every once in a while he would stand and stare at a shop window or read the signs in front of an employment agency. She had seen him once, when he didn't know she was there watching. Perhaps he even stopped people on the street and said: 'Could I clean your front steps? Could I wash your car....?' She didn't want to think of that. And when he came home, nights, there was no use asking him what luck he'd had. The way he held himself told enough, and the empty unfixed look in his eyes.

When she had used up the last coffee, when the lard pail was empty and there were no more potatoes or flour in the house, she had gone alone to Relief headquarters in the City Hall and made an application, marked urgent. Now the lady had come to visit, the social worker. Some part of Mabel had stopped thinking or feeling, and she was only glad that Miss Merton was being so polite about it. She had already accepted the idea that Miss Merton should be here, asking what questions the Relief thought necessary. And she was answering them, in a flat, unmoved voice. It would be all right. They'd get Relief. And Pete wouldn't be home until after Miss Merton had gone.

She looked at him feeling frightened; she couldn't remember when she had done anything important without asking him about it first. And she knew he did not want Relief: he had said he was able to work and no one was going to make charity out of him. Miss Merton inspected him uncertainly. He hadn't shaved for some days, his shoes were muddy and wet and he looked at once exhausted and desperate: as if anything would send him off into a raving anger against what he had become.

'This is Miss Merton, Pete.'

'Please ta meetcha.' He didn't gather who she was, or why she was there. He was tired. He wanted to lie down, rest, close his eyes, perhaps sleep a while and not think about anything.

He went past them into the bedroom and shut the door. Mabel

sighed. 'We'll just talk low so's he can't hear,' she explained. 'He takes all this awful hard.'

'Yes, I know. It is hard. Now would you mind telling me, Mrs Hines, have you any life insurance, you or your husband?'

'No.'

'Have you any relatives who could help you now?'

'No.'

'Would you mind giving me a list of your nearest living relatives and their addresses?'

Mabel pulled from her memory some ignored cousins and an aunt. People died or moved away. One was very alone. She felt tired, too. She knew this only had to happen once and she hoped that it would be quickly over.

'May I look?' Miss Merton said, jotting things down in a little black note-book. She went towards the kitchen. Had to make a more or less complete inventory of what these people owned: to see if any of it could be sold, if there were any resources they hadn't yet used up. Mabel misunderstood. She made a despairing gesture and she did it quietly. She opened the bread box and the ice box and the kitchen closet. 'Nothing in them,' she said.

'Oh, yes. Yes, of course. By the way, here's your Relief order for the week, Mrs Hines. For food. You can take it to your regular grocer, he'll accept it as if it were money.' This was always the most nervous part: Miss Merton looked at Mabel anxiously through her glasses. Some times the clients got very upset about these orders. They were dreadfully small.

But Mabel didn't look at the amount; she held the slip of paper in her hand and said: 'Do I take that to Mr Burg? This piece of paper?'

'Yes.'

'But then, he'll know I'm on Relief.'

'Well.'

'But I been buying there for over ten years regular. He knows me. He knows Pete, too; and the way we always lived and everything. I don't see how I can....' Her voice trailed into miserable silence. She saw herself sneaking into Mr Burg's store and waiting until everyone else had been served; she, who was an old and favoured customer. Mr Burg always came out cheerfully wiping his hands on his apron and said: 'Well, Mrs Hines, and what will it be to-day? Fine weather we're having.' He always waited on her himself. She wasn't like some that went to the store in any old clothes. She always wore a hat and fixed up before she went, as a decent woman should. A woman who was buying properly for her husband; and had a nice house and a bright clean kitchen to cook in. For years she'd been doing this. Always. And now.

She looked at the grocery order and saw that it was for $3 and raised her eyes to Miss Merton, blankly.

'For a week,' she said, 'three dollars?'

'Yes, I'm afraid so,' Miss Merton said quickly. 'That's the budget for families of two, now. Of course, your coal and rent and medicine and all that is extra. It's only for food.'

Mabel folded the green slip. There wasn't anything more to say. There was nothing even to think or understand or be sure of.

'What is the rent here?' Miss Merton asked.

'Twenty.'

'Oh, dear,'

'Why?'

'Well, I'm afraid that's more than Relief allows for rents. I'm afraid you'll have to find a cheaper place; unless your landlord would accept our usual rates or just give you credit until Mr Hines gets a job.'

'We'll have to move?'

'Well, I don't know. We'll have to work out something. That's more rent than we allow, you see.'

'But we can't,' Mabel said, and now she had forgotten Pete and her voice rose. 'We can't. It's our home. We been here since we're married. It's our place, it belongs to us. What would we do if we had to go somewhere else? Give it up,' she said, the tears sticky on her face. 'Give it up.'

'Who says we're gonna give it up?' Pete stood in the doorway of the bedroom in stocking feet, looking strangely thin and pale.

'What's that about our house?' he said.

'We were just discussing the rent,' Miss Merton said, and Mabel wiped at the tears with the back of her hand.

'Why?'

'Well, I'm from the Relief, you see.'

'Get out,' Pete said. It was just a statement.

Miss Merton looked perplexed and a little hurt.

'Get out,' Pete said. 'This is my house. I don't want nothing from the Relief.'

Miss Merton walked towards the front door. Mabel went with her. 'He'll get over it,' Mabel whispered. 'He'll hafta. I don't see what else. I'll come and see you at City Hall. But you better go.'

'Yes. Well, good-night, Mrs Hines.'

'Did you get her here?' Pete said.

'What else could I do? There's nothing to eat in this house, Pete Hines, and no more coal. We can't starve, can we? We can't lock up the house and die, can we?'

'Maybe not and maybe so,' Pete said darkly, 'but I won't have strangers coming in my house poking around. I can work,' Pete said. And then, suddenly, he shouted it, waving his arms crazily over his head. 'I can work! I can work!'

Mabel sat down in a rocker. She was too tired now to argue this thing. What did it matter, anyhow? There were only a certain number of reasons for living, and then you didn't have them any more. 'What's the difference?' she said slowly, and Pete stared at her, frightened by the dead quiet of her voice. 'We haven't got the baby, so it don't matter. We don't have to do all this. We don't have to.'

'What're you talking about, Mabel?' he was whispering to her, but he didn't know it.

'What've we got, anyhow, now? We'll be old soon.'

'But I been working all my life,' Pete protested. 'It oughtn't to be like this. I can still work. For a long time yet. I don't see,' he said.

'We had some good times, anyhow, Pete.'

'It's not all over yet, Mabel.' But he was begging her to comfort and reassure him, to promise him a future he couldn't see.

'We had fun that year we went to the beach for a week.'

'Mabel, it isn't over. Don't act like that. Oh, Mabel, Mabel.' Suddenly he was down on his knees by her chair, with his head on her lap, crying awkwardly and trying to stop himself. He wept in terror and she stroked his hair, saying to him dimly: 'There, there, Petie, it'll be all right.' He had his arms around her, and her hands were gentle. They stayed there as it grew dark, not talking, because neither of them could think of a comforting lie for the other to believe.

They had found out a lot about each other over a thirty-five cent plate dinner. And finally, when the waitresses grew restive and lights began to go off in the back of the restaurant, they left. It was cold, with the wind blowing sharp and foolishly from different directions. Every once in a while, as if by mistake, a gust of rain would curl over the streets. They walked for a while. Then Joe said: 'I've got a room; it's pretty bad but it's warm. If you want to come.'

Now she was taking off her hat and then placing her hands on the radiator and blotting herself against it, and saying: 'This is Roxy's compared to my place.'

He looked with distaste around the room; the patched, not too clean linoleum on the floor, yellowing lace curtains, and the bedstead, chipped. He had a liking for clean things, at least, and some place to put the books he'd gotten together during the last years.

'Where I lived before,' he said, and stopped. No. To-night, just tonight, now, he was going to forget. He was going to live to-night as if he wouldn't have to wake up and go back to that lonely and hostile office; as if he didn't hate this room; as if life were good. He was going to think of himself, to-night, and what he wanted: something like happiness.

'Are you warmer?'

'Yes.'

'You're a good kid, Anna.'

She looked at him, smiling. It was as if she said, you don't fool me, but I'll play any game you say. If we're going to tell lies to-night, okay by me. And she thought to herself, there's nothing to lose and probably there's nothing to gain. But that doesn't say we can't try to have a good time. . . .

'Do you like me?' Joe said.

'Sure.'

'Enough?'

'I couldn't tell you yet.' She was smiling again.

Joe didn't realize that he was standing in front of her, grinding his teeth the way he did when he was thinking, and frowning. I've got to put it up to her some way so she can get out of it if she doesn't want to. She's probably had guys getting tough on her: I don't want her that way. If it's going to be any good. . . .

'Listen,' he said. 'I don't want to do anything you don't want to. It's up to you, see? I don't want you to think I expect anything. I mean, I'm not that cheap a guy.'

'I know you're not.' She stretched out her hand towards him. 'You're a dope for being straight. You'll never get thanked for it. Not even from your union buddies.'

'I don't want to talk about that. Not now, anyhow.'

'Sure. Like I don't want to think about Relief. Or what the hell I'm gonna eat to-morrow. I know. To-night's out.'

Joe waited.

'Come here,' she said.

He took her in his arms and had the surprised feeling that his arms were empty. He kissed her on the mouth harder than he meant to, but she didn't draw back.

'Put out the light,' she said.

He went to the switch by the door and came back towards her in the darkness. But she wasn't there. She was sitting on the bed and dimly he saw her bending over as if she were taking off her shoes. She said nothing. He waited. He could hear himself breathing. But insistently, and he could not escape it, he thought, she had me turn out the light

so's I wouldn't see her underclothes, so I wouldn't see how poor and old
they are. She's thinking about that, too. He pulled his mind away from
this. He got his clothes off quickly, throwing them on a chair, and found
her again in bed.

For one moment, with his blood beating behind his eyes, he felt
lifted and reckless. Whatever reasons had moved him to bring her here
were forgotten: her poverty and his, and the senseless waiting of their
lives. He held her body with his hands, and drew her towards him. And
then, suddenly, he realised without wanting to that the bones of her
naked body were an outrage. This was a half-starved woman, no matter
how crisply and mockingly she might talk of her life. Hungry, he
thought: great God, the girl is probably always a little hungry. He was
not reckless and excited any more. He was back in something he knew,
something that pursued him. People not having enough. He caught his
breath and it was almost a sob. I can't think about it, he told himself,
not now, not now. Let's have this at least. Let's get drunk on this and
forget for a while; for the night, anyhow.

She had felt or guessed what he was thinking: it was for this she
had wanted the lights out, and the protection of darkness. I'm getting
old, she thought, and God, I must be ugly. In despair she reached for
him, and in despair he took her, brutally, trying to crush from both their
minds the knowledge that this was no glad and easy and fortunate
coupling. This was just two people in the dark.

They lay beside each other quietly; he had his arm under her head.

'Thank you, Anna.'

'You don't have to.'

'You're a swell kid. I mean it. I'll remember.'

'It's no use, is it?'

'No,' he said. 'No, I guess not. Not for people like us.'

After a time she moved and said: 'I got to be going. Don't get up.'
In the darkness she dressed. He could hear her feeling around the floor
for her shoes, and then a rustle as she pulled her dress on. He lay in
bed, looking at the ceiling. She came over to the bed and stood beside it.

'I'm going now,' she said.

He took her hand and held it against his mouth.

She waited a moment, looking down at him, and then she said,
shakily: 'Cheer up, dearie. All you gotta do is think how fine it's gonna
be a long time after we're dead.'

The door closed softly behind her and he could not hear her on the
stairs.

· · ·

The man who had called to him on the street was a miracle. He'd had
to call twice because Pete couldn't believe it had happened. But the man
actually wanted the gravel raked on his drive and the garage cleaned
out. Pete had looked so stupid when told this that the man almost sent
him away. It was just surprise. It was the first work Pete had been
offered in four months. The man said he'd give him a dollar and Pete
tried to keep from crying, or singing, or doing something he'd be
ashamed of.

'We're not gonna spend it on groceries, Mabel,' Pete said. 'Can't you
see it's my chance? I gotta start out in business. I gotta sell stuff. I'll
make a lotta dough and pay it back to Mr Aarons. If I can get him
something before the fifteenth we can stay here.'

'Business,' Mabel said. 'What kinda business?'

'I'm gonna sell shoe strings and chewing gum. I seen guys doing
that. A lotta people need shoe strings and everybody chews gum. You
can't lose. I can get the stuff wholesale.'

'Why don't you sell apples? Then we can use them if they don't all
get sold.'

'Naw, they're not selling apples any more. That was way back. This
is serious stuff. This is business.'

Mabel made him a tray from the top of a cardboard box she begged
from the cleaners. She found some old ribbon and hung the tray from
Pete's neck by a bit of dusty pink satin. She spread the shoe strings and
gum out neatly and Pete shaved. He was terribly excited. In his mind
he had it all worked out. This was the break he'd been waiting for. It
had to come. Probably business was better than factory work, anyhow.
He saw the rent paid, and the two of them safe again in their home.
But that was only the first step. After that he saw people crowding
around him, on Main Street, all buying. Then he'd enlarge his business
and sell Hershey bars and maybe cigarettes. He'd be off Relief by now.
God, he thought, off Relief. For a moment there was no need to go
further. But then active, and hopeful, his mind plotted the now luminous
future. He could probably get a store before he was through. People had
to buy things; had to. He knew about that. Groceries. Or meat. Something like that. Or shoes. He saw himself working again, from morning
until dark, regularly every day, and coming home to good hot dinners,
and Mabel wearing fine clothes at Holliday Park in the summer. He
walked towards Main Street holding his tray carefully against him,
considering his shoe laces and his chewing gum with love.

Then another thing, he thought, there's not so many of them on the
tray, so that looks like they've been bought and that'll encourage people.

He started on the corner but found people were too hurried here,

too interested in the traffic lights and ducking under the street cars.
Only the newsboys did business. He moved to the middle of the block,
and stood in the sun. It was pleasant just being there. Having something
to do. A working man; a business man you might really say.

A woman came by: she wore a fur coat and she was young. She
hesitated. She walked a little past him and then walked quickly back
and with embarrassment dropped a quarter on the tray and fled.

'Here's your gum, lady.' He held it out, running after her.

'I don't want it, thank you,' she said over her shoulder.

He came back to his place and thought this over. It wasn't right.
She must have made a mistake. He wasn't begging. Anybody could see
he wasn't begging: he had things to sell. He was somewhat angered, but
on the other hand two bits was two bits. He put it in his pocket, first
making sure that his pocket was whole.

Nothing happened. He hadn't known how hard it was to stand still
in the same place. He moved back and leaned against a wall. And then
decided that wasn't proper: it didn't look wide awake. Have to stand
out from the wall; maybe talk to people.

'Shoelaces?' he said to a man. 'Need some chewing gum?'

The man pushed him aside, roughly. He had used a stiff arm with
some energy behind it.

'Say, you,' Pete started to follow him. What the hell kind of guy did
he think he was, going around shoving folks on the street? But then he
thought, no. Might get in trouble with a cop. Maybe he ought just to
stand and not say anything to people.

In the course of five hours he sold twenty cents worth of gum. He
was desperately tired. He ached from his heels in straight shooting pains
up to his neck. It's only that I haven't built up a trade, he thought, takes
time to get regular customers.

He was hungry too, but he couldn't face the idea of going home to
Mabel with forty-five cents, for his day's work. Somehow, he felt Mabel
would be too upset about it, and they'd sit that night, as they had
uncounted nights before, silently, in the front room, not doing anything,
just waiting for it to get late enough to go to bed.

He had planned coming back to-night with $1.65, all sold out, and
ready to buy more gum and shoelaces for to-morrow.

He was thinking about this and putting words together in his mind,
for Mabel. To keep it from seeming bad to her, he'd talk about how you
had to build up your regular customers and everything and explain it
that way. . . .

Suddenly, he saw a man further down the block, standing, as he
was, against the wall, and sharply profiled in front of him was a tray,

like Pete's own. Goddam the bastard, Pete thought, here I been standing around all day getting this place for myself and building up my trade and now that guy comes along. There's not money in it for two, he said to himself, and he was already angrily walking up the block towards his rival. The ache in his back hurried him on, his hunger and his disappointment sharpened his anger. I'll smack him one, he decided, sneaking up on me like that and stealing my customers. Taking the bread outa my mouth. Couldn't the guy go somewhere else; he must just be mean, just be wanting to get in there and grab off the people who'd be buying from Pete otherwise.

'Hey you,' he called, but the man did not turn. That made Pete angrier. Trying to high-hat him was he, trying to act innocent-like. His fist shut, tight and hard. I'll paste him one, I don't care if the cops run me in or not, no guy's gonna get away with that. He saw his business destroyed, everything gone. He ran forward and grabbed the man by the shoulder and spun him around, his fist up, ready to smash him between the eyes, cops or no cops. And he found himself staring at a quiet, blank face, with sealed eyes, the eyelids close and shrivelled over the iris, and a small, hand-drawn sign on the man's chest said: 'I AM BLIND.'

He let go the man's shoulder and his fist fell. He stood there, trying to find some words to say to this man, to explain, but he couldn't. He, Pete Hines, was doing a blind man's job, he was stealing from the blind; he was a strong, healthy man with eyes, and the only thing he could get to do was blind man's work, and this man would be hungrier because of it. Blind man's work. What kind of world was it; what kind of country were they running anyhow? Something seemed to be screaming inside him, but there were no words, only a murderous fury and a feeling that this was the last time he was going to get caught and cheated and shamed. The last time. He was against them now, them and their world. He was against them as long as he lived, with the only thing he had—hate.

He tore the pink ribbon from his neck and dumped his shoe laces and gum on the blind man's tray. 'Here buddy. You take 'em. You sell. That's your work. I'm not blind, buddy,' he said protestingly, to convince the man, to make the man realize that it was a mistake for him to have these shoe laces and gum at all, they didn't belong to him, it wasn't his kind of work, my God, he wasn't blind.

Joe had known this would happen some day. But only in his mind. His heart rebelled against the idea, against the stupidity and injustice of it, and the waste. He looked at the men standing in front of him. Probably it was only his eyes, tired from writing there in the ill-lit office. The men seemed unusually tall, all the same height even, and black and they stood tall and strong like trees. There had been no shuffling or uncertainty, they'd come in together firmly, stood grouped around him with none of the coughing nervous sounds of unsure people, waited, given him time to understand what was happening before any words were said. And then Frankie Zaleski spoke for them. They didn't want him any more; he wasn't the man they wanted to represent them and talk for them and guide them. They didn't trust him. He'd muffed the job. He wasn't really trying. He didn't have the guts. They could run the union better without him. They had their own ideas. So he better just get out.

He hadn't the strength to stand up, and at least talk to them on their level and he felt himself at an unconquerable disadvantage, seated there before them. He felt weak and sick, and he kept thinking, there's only one on my side. But there were things he'd have to say. If he took it silently, it would seem that he agreed, that he admitted what they accused him of. It would seem that he was a man who had been caught mismanaging other men's affairs, and now that he was caught, he was scared, and would slink off. He would have to say something; but he couldn't speak in his own defence. That would be an apology, and there was no apology to make. He had done his best. And he was the only one who knew how little any man could do.

His voice disgusted him; it sounded quavery and thin.

'All right,' he said. 'You take it over and run it the way you want. You'll anyhow know what you're talking about, then. I been working at this steady for months, and there's no more a man could do. But if you don't see it like that.'

He felt his shoulders sagging. I've got a right to be sore, he thought, I've got a right to get up and curse them to hell. The fools. Who'd have done this work like I have, for nothing, putting his own money in it? None of them. But he wasn't angry. He was only tired.

'We elected Frankie to take on the job,' a man said.

He smiled at that. Frankie was a good guy, but he'd have a fine time trying to write a letter, or make a speech, or keep the dues straight, or argue with the bosses, or any of that stuff.

'Okay,' Joe said. 'If you come around tomorrow morning, I'll show you where all the stuff is, Frankie, and what you gotta do.'

'I guess I can figger it out all right by myself,' Frankie said.

Suddenly he was angry. That was extra, that was like kicking a man for the fun of it. That unneeded hint of suspicion and the blank crazy stupidity of it. He stood up now, leaning on his desk.

'Lissen, you poor half-witted cluck. You'll never figger it out. None of you. You haven't got enough brains all of you together. You'll sure make a fine business of this union. You'll make a joke of it; they'll sit around Washington and laugh like hell every time they get a letter. And Minton'll be so happy he'll probably buy you an office. You might as well close this place up and stop thinking about it. The union's bust. Now. And besides which, get the hell out. I pay the rent. I'll get my stuff out and you can come in to-morrow and run this union any way you want. I don't give a goddam. I'm through. You can make any kinda goddam fool of yourselves you want. But I'm not gonna sit here and lissen to a bunch of horses' behinds like you talking about stuff you don't know about. The door's right behind you. I'll take the whole bunch of you on if you don't get outa here in three seconds flat.'

They stared at him; it was a quick change.

'Say, who d'you think you're talking to?' Frankie said, and stepped out from the others.

'To you. You heard me. Get the hell outa here.'

'You can't get away with that, Joe Barrow. You been sitting here running this union cockeyed, and not getting a damn thing for us and playing in with the bosses, and a lotta things we don't think's so hot. And now you talk like you was God-a-mighty. What you need is to get your face smeared.'

'Yeah. Well try and do it.'

There was just that quiet breathless moment which heralds a fight, that single instant of uncertainty for both sides to decide and to start.

A man put his hand on Frankie's arm. 'Come on, Frankie. Leave him be. It'll only mess up the office. We'll come back to-morrow.'

The others muttered agreement. Frankie dusted his hands together as if he had already hit Joe and the fight was triumphantly finished. They left more awkwardly than they had come.

Joe sat down again, with his hands stretched out open on the desk in front of him, staring at the door. So this was how it ended. This was what you got for it. His anger, which had protected him, dropped. And he thought: what do I do next? There was nothing left, not the union, nor his friends, and the feeling of being wanted, not work. There was no place for him now. His life which had fitted in with other lives, was now something needless and limited. It was as if he didn't have a name any more. His mind babbled helplessly: what am I going to do, what am I going to do next...?

Someone kicked the door open and the glass in it rattled as it hit against the wall. He jerked up straight. Frankie coming back to get his fight.

'Lissen Joe,' Pete said.

So Pete was sticking with him, Joe thought, there was Pete anyhow. 'You tell Mabel,' Pete said. 'I'm not gonna go back there. You tell her. You tell her it was blind man's work. They can't do nothing more to me. I'm gonna get out. You go and tell her. To-night. So's she won't worry. But tell her I'm not coming back. I can't do nothing for her, and tell her good-bye. You'll do that Joe?'

'What're you talking about?'

'It's the way they're running this country,' Pete said and his voice fell. There was terror in his voice. 'They're trying to make us crazy. They're trying to make us do blind men's work. They tell you you're too old. They don't act like we was men. I'll show 'em,' Pete said, and Joe was frightened of the man's eyes, 'I'll show 'em if they can get away with that.'

'They all came in here a little while ago,' Joe said, 'and they told me to get out. They said I ran this union cockeyed, and they didn't want me around. They told me to get out.'

Pete focussed his attention on this, something else that had happened: they were against Joe too, then. 'They did that,' he said.

'Yeah.'

'The bastards,' Pete said wonderingly.

'Sure.'

'What're you gonna do?'

'Don't know.'

'You can come with me. We'll show 'em.'

'No,' Joe said, and was surprised himself that he had made this decision. That would after all be best: go away. Forget it. Stop trying to do anything.

'You'll tell Mabel?'

'If I go,' Joe said, talking for himself, 'they'll be sure to say I took some union money, and the whole union'll get a dirty name. Somebody'll make it out crooked. I still gotta stay,' Joe said to himself, and he was amazed to discover this, that there was a role left for him, something important which he had to do.

Pete was at the door. 'Good-bye, Joe. Make it all right with Mabel. Tell her it's blind man's work.'

The moon had come up: a raw wind drove streaky clouds over the sky. People were indoors now, eating. People with the rent paid, Pete thought. He was going away from this: this place had been his home, and now it was strange to him, and full of cruelty. But he understood nothing. He was walking bent against the wind, towards the river, and his mind churned with these things he knew he would never understand.

I worked all my life, he kept saying: I was only in jail once. I paid my taxes. At the street corners, the wind sprang out at him. Where did guys sleep that didn't have a home? And all the other men, the ones he'd seen mornings asking for work at the factories, the people standing in front of employment agencies. What about them too? Suddenly it frightened him more than he could bear, to think of the others who must be like himself. It made it worse. There was nothing you could be sure of.

He was walking with his head down and now he was conscious of an extra darkness, shutting out the moon. He looked up and saw the great unformed mass of the Minton factory, silent and empty. There was no one on the streets. It looked as if the factory had been abandoned for a long time, in this light: as if no men ever came in the doors, lumpish with sleep in the morning, and went home in the afternoon, glad to be leaving. He stopped and stood with his head back, studying the overgrown outline of this building, like carelessly-piled boxes against the sky. And then he had a thought. It grew so swiftly that it was no longer an idea but a plan, something he had been waiting for and always wanted to do. The last thing he could do.

He went back along a side street: they were repairing a tenement and he remembered a small pile of bricks lying before it.

He picked a brick, a whole one, holding it up for the moon to shine on, to make sure it was solid. He held it in his hand and amazingly it felt warm. He hurried to where he saw the factory, big and black over the surrounding houses.

'I'll show you,' Pete shouted: his voice was close to him and sharp and not very real. 'I'll show you if you can get away with it. You and all the others.'

He raised his arm to throw, and it stuck. The brick stayed in his hand, above his head. There was no one on the street, no cop's voice calling to stop him. Nothing. But he couldn't do it. This was the last thing for him, to show he was a man anyhow, and they couldn't cheat him and kick him around and make him crazy. But the factory was too big. He tightened his hold on the brick, but he couldn't throw it. He let it drop and it cracked on the pavement.

Then, close under the shadows of the factory, he ran towards the freight yards, where the trains crawled slowly all night, going someplace else.

Jim

ONE

•

JIM COMES HOME

Climbing up the dirt track to the house, he could hear them: his father
and his sister, Clara.

'I'll go out with anybody I please, anywhere I please, anytime I
please,' she said, her voice heavy and slow with anger. 'What do you
think you are, anyhow? What gives you a right to order me around?
What do you do for me? I don't care about that, but don't try to stop
me doing for myself.'

His father's voice rumbled: 'I'll teach you to talk to me like that.'

'If you touch me I'll get the police.'

Jim stood at the door, watching them. His father standing above
Clara with a milk-bottle in his raised hand; his mother in a corner
mending, not noticing the noise or the scene, which she knew by heart,
anyhow. Nothing had changed. Why should it; he had only been gone
six weeks.

'Happy days,' he said cheerfully, to his father's back and his sister's
suddenly turning, surprised face.

'Jim,' Clara said. 'We didn't know you'd be coming back so soon.'

'Hello, son.' Mrs Barr crossed the room and kissed him on the cheek.
'You're looking fine. Did they feed you good at the farm?'

'Yeah. It was fine. Hello, Dad.'

'Hello, Jim.'

'Well, that's lucky. You won't be getting much here. I don't understand that new Relief lady, she gives $8 a week to Mamie Hodges and her family and there's only three of them and she only gives us $6.50; it just ain't right. . . .' Jim patted her arm. It made it even worse to whine about it. Bad enough to have to take it, to be helpless, to be waiting in a line, interviewed, questioned, handed things with kindness. It made it even worse to whine. That way it looked as if you were accepting the gift all right, only you wanted more. He didn't accept, not in his mind. Nobody had to keep him, he was Jim Barr and young and could work and take care of his family. . . . Mrs Barr was talking again, about her heart and how she'd have to get a medical order from the Relief to go to a doctor. . . . 'Clara,' Jim said, despairingly, turning away.

'Oh, ma, when he just comes home,' Clara said. 'When he's just come in, can't you think of something cheerful to say?'

He put his arm around Clara and they walked into the next room. He shut the door. 'Got a new steady?' he said.

'Yeah, Alf Harmon, the boy who works at the grocery down-town. He gets good money, too; $10 a week. But it don't do him much good; he's got his mother and sister there to take care of and he don't get help from the Relief because he's working.' She was silent a moment. 'Anyhow, I'm glad of that. Even if we can't do much, me and him, I'm glad he's working. I'm glad he's not on Relief like us and always arguing, or hanging around with the other boys by the garage or somewheres.'

'Sure.'

'God, he's a swell guy, Jim.'

'What's the old man got against him?'

'Oh, he says Alf's got a name with the women; says he got that blonde girl over by Henderson—you know, her name's Lucy something—in trouble.'

'Did he?'

'I dunno. What if he did? He's not that way with me, anyhow.'

'Well?' Jim said.

'I made a little money while you were gone, taking care of Miz Newton's baby when her maid went out. And I gotta job for the winter doing the housework at Miz Carter's, before school and after, board and room.'

'Pay?'

'Two dollars a week, that'll be enough for spending money and books and clothes. I'm fixed all right.'

'Jees,' he said.

'What's wrong?'

'Two dollars.'

'Better than nothing.'

'I know; me, I can't make two cents.'

'Oh, now, Jim.' She put her hand on his arm. 'Sure you can. What'd you make on the harvest?'

'Thirty-one plunks; I got about twenty-seven left, for school and stuff. I only got three weeks pitching oats; been walking around the rest of the time. You know—asking...'

'It'll be fun going to school together. We can pass notes and play around.'

'You bet. I'm twenty-one. You're a girl and you're only seventeen. And we'll be in the same class. It'll be lotsa fun.'

'Jim, nobody thinks you're dumb. Everybody knows it's just 'cause of money. And you trying to work for the family. Don't let it get you down, about being older, I mean.'

'Oh, hell, no. It's fine. I should care. When I'm forty I'll graduate from college with big honours. And when I'm sixty I'll be out of medical school all ready to start life and have a swell practise. When I'm seventy I'll give you a high-class wedding with a white satin dress.'

'What's the use, Jim?'

'It's a joke.'

She looked at him. 'I almost never laugh,' she said.

Clara took him to school the first day. She was already staying at the Carters' and already, even before her school work started, she had purplish circles under her eyes and she moved limply.

'It isn't hard,' she said. 'It just never stops.'

He met her at the corner, smiled, and said: 'Don't leave me alone, Ma.'

In the hall, boys and girls came up to Clara to say hello, ask each other questions about classes, teachers, teams, parties, and laugh without knowing why.

'This is my brother....' 'Pleased ta meetcha.' One boy Jim knew—Dick Manfred's younger brother: too young to be included in their talk or plans when he went to Dick's house. Considered a pest, somebody to take care of unwillingly.

'Hello, son,' Jim said. Sam Manfred frowned: so did Clara.

'He's in your class,' Clara whispered. 'You can't treat him like a baby.'

'Oh.'

'Come and pick your desk,' Clara said.

They went to the study hall: a great square room smelling already of feet, damp sweaters, stale candy. The boys shoved, trying to sit near to or far from the present love. The girls giggled and coyly said I'm gonna sit here, and waited for a stampede and said it again louder: if nothing happened they chose their seats near someone else more favoured.

There were innumerable small worlds here: each living, centred around a mystically selected individual, glued to and following that lead. Each group pyramided up to the one led by a few senior girls whose fathers had money, owned stores, cars, securities. Each world secretly or openly despised the others: each one had defined positions in its own hierarchy; special names; a language. Everyone was eager; there seemed to be a purpose in their movements, guided, perhaps, by last year and the friendships of last year or things done together in the summer. Jim stood alone in all this: where he sat made no difference. He didn't want to whisper behind his desk lid, sigh down his lady's neck, throw spit balls at his enemies. He only wanted a place to keep his books: all the desks were alike.

'I'll sit near you,' Clara said. He smiled at her; how kind she was. Anxious and careful with him: wanting him to feel he belonged here, wanting to identify him with these kids whose faces even seemed to him soft and unformed. Could two years make all this difference? It had been two years since he'd come to this study hall and put his books in a desk and even then he was older, but it didn't seem to matter. There was Dick Manfred then, also nineteen, a senior. Dick had worked in Seattle, and been in a longshoremen's strike, and jerked sodas in San Francisco, and ridden the rails, and women had taken him in, too, and fed him, and been good to him, and he and Dick could talk about what things they understood. It seemed to him he knew something none of these babies knew: he knew it was hard to get work, he knew you couldn't get it at all most of the time, and when you did it was by the day, the week, using your muscles only as if you didn't have anything but arms, as if your head was just stuck up there for looks. He knew what it was to be saying to yourself, it's going to be like this all the time: people like me finally die hanging on to a shovel. Or a pitchfork. He knew also that his only chance was this high school, and after it college, and even that wasn't sure: but without it he could see nothing. He had to have an education: something that changed him enough to fool employers, so that the men behind desks wouldn't always write down after his name: common labor. What did these kids know? He chose a desk without thinking: on his left sat a fattish boy in a plaid lumberjack shirt, already busy aiming something at somebody's head: on the other side was a little girl who must have been a freshman—all classes studied together in a muted shuffling, sighing tumult—a nice, quiet, shy little girl with long yellow braids. He smiled at her and she smiled back, blushed and quickly put up her desk lid and rummaged around inside.

'But I'm over there,' Clara said, standing above him.

'That's all right, kid. You go on over and play with your friends. I'm fine here: I only came to this school to study. Don't you worry about me.'

'But, Jim, you won't be happy if you don't get in with a gang.'

'Happy,' he said. 'That's a good one.'

He had been in school a month: already his imitation leather coat, bought carefully with the harvest money, was scratched. Already he drew in against the cold, walking fast in the mornings. And still he could bring no order into his mind. Even sitting quietly like this in the hot stuffy hall was hard. He had to tell himself every day: it stops at three. Three isn't so far off. Nine to three is a short working day; better than factories or the docks or the farm. Better than sitting home. His shoulders twitched and he kept looking out the window; he had been painfully aware of the fall, quickly come and now almost gone. He thought he had counted each leaf falling from the tree outside; sometimes he thought he had heard them. And he was old, older than any of these kids, shabby and poor, getting thin again at home and feeling his body slump. He sat and waited for three o'clock and then unhurried, weary, disgusted with himself, he wandered home.

He kept saying to himself: It'll all come back. But his eyes strayed, and his mind handled half-remembered phrases thoughtlessly, like a woman shopping for something she doesn't want. Nothing focussed. He sat in the study hall with a worn blue book before him: American history. There were things here to be learned: the teacher had assigned twelve pages for the day's lesson. The civil war: where was it, anyhow; a part of the country he had never seen, some people from the east and others from the south, fighting about negroes. He didn't know much about negroes. On the whole he thought they were nice, cheerful and stupid. People paid them less and arrested them quicker. They had been freed: there was a war about it. Would there be a war, for instance, to free the unemployed, who were slaves too, in a way?

I must learn this, he thought, and imitated unconsciously the bland dead look of his classmates and moved his lips, saying again and again, Lee lost the final battle of the war at Appomattox on 9 April 1865. He had been doing this for perhaps ten minutes: he stopped and enquired of himself what he had been saying, something about Lee, a battle. . . .

He passed his hand over his eyes, ready for tears, or furious flight. What's the use, he said, I can't do it. I don't give a damn for that stuff. That civil war is all over, long ago. And then he thought: is knowing about Lee and his battles what gets you jobs? Because that's what I want: the hell with everything else, I want a job. A good regular job you can count on all year, that isn't going to kill you before you're forty and you can live like a decent man, not the way they do at home, not like some kind of animal that feels and talks about it. . . .

The bell rang. The boys and girls shoved each other getting out of the room: shoving was a special sport, preferably one shoved a girl, one's favourite girl. Jim had spoken of this once to Clara, seeing her gay and argumentative, being pushed along by a boy whose hands on her shoulders, then hips, were possessive, interested.

'Why not climb into bed?' Jim suggested to her. 'It's more fun.'

She was angry with him, saying that he had a dirty mind and they were all friends here, just kids, they didn't mean anything by it. He had said nothing but he was ashamed, thinking perhaps she was right and they were all too sappy to know what they were about. Anyhow, Clara had so little that made her eyes bright, or made her laugh. None of his business: and that day again he had felt himself to be old and grey, carrying winter around with him.

He walked behind everyone else, in no hurry, to class. He chose his seat simply because no one else was sitting in it. The teacher, Mr Watkins, shuffled papers on his desk and made ominous marks with a blue pencil. Play acting, Jim thought. The second bell rang. Like light fading, the class dimmed, slouched into as comfortable positions as were possible on the straight chairs, leaned their heads on their hands, crossed their knees, their eyes mute and dazed. Mr Watkins came into his own, but without gladness, from habit. As if speaking to stone, he asked questions and usually led the pupil until he got something resembling an answer. He had done this for years. He has a family, Jim thought, and they're not rich enough to keep up a good front. He has to do this. Jim, too, slumped in his chair, a feeling of horrible weariness over him. Mr Watkins' voice went on: the dead talking to the sleeping, Jim decided. Would anything excite them; would anything make them uncross their knees and jerk up in their chairs? Now, if Mr Watkins just said, suddenly, 'Anybody who plays football is a fairy. . . .' He grinned.

'Share your joke, Barr.' Mr Watkins' voice was cold. There were limits to everything. He was used to talking to those glaucous eyes which the young turned on him. He was used to the awful parrotry of their replies or the uneasy shuffling when memory failed them. He was used to saying to himself: I am a fourth-rate teacher in a sixth-rate high-school in a small western town. But he wasn't going to be laughed at. He was too old now; there was nothing he could do to change this.

Jim sat up, he wasn't aware that he had smiled, but he knew he couldn't tell that joke, even if it was one.

'I was thinking about something.'

'Remarkable,' Mr Watkins said, knowing, with disgust, that this was the easiest, the cheapest reply.

The class tittered.

Suddenly Jim was angry, angry because the room was hot and thick with much-breathed air; angry at the lumpishness of the class and Mr Watkins feebly protecting his dignity, and at himself.

'I think, once in a while, to keep from going nuts.'

'You find it so dull here?'

'Worse than that. Dead.'

'You are not forced to attend school, I believe—you have passed the age limit.' Mr Watkins knew he would feel sick, flushing and weak with shame for this, later. But now, it was Watkins or Barr. I can't be laughed at, he thought, if I am, I'm finished, and I've got to keep my job.

'I wanted to look like somebody who's been to school, so I'd get a decent job,' Jim said. 'But I don't learn and I can't take it.'

He rose, sweeping note-books and pencils off the chair arm.

'Don't be ridiculous, Jim,' Mr Watkins said. 'It's the end of the day, we're all tired.'

'Listen,' Jim said. 'I know about jobs. How you gotta get them and then you gotta keep them because of grocery bills. I know about that. I'm sorry for you, too.'

The door closed behind him noiselessly on automatic springs.

Mr Watkins was aware of a small chirping noise, smothered: Clara was crying.

For a while he enjoyed simply being able to yawn out loud; being able to dawdle around the house, looking for a comfortable or fairly quiet place to sit, reading the papers or books chosen with care and excitement at the public library. For a week, perhaps more, it was a satisfaction in itself to know that he didn't have to go to school. He stopped shaving and abandoned the mustard-coloured jacket for a torn, soft sweater. When sufficiently pressed he helped his mother, sweeping or wiping dishes or collecting wood outside. He tried not to see his father. He had reasons for this. He had loved his father and thought there was nobody like Walt Barr in Harriston. He used to watch his father at work, building neatly with his hands, neatly and carefully; making the furniture that they sold at C. D. Magnus' furniture store, or making handsome pieces to order for Dr Swivelton and Mrs Maxwell, who was the town's great lady, and for others who wanted good work done and could pay. His father worked very slowly: he liked the special orders best, because he could then buy finer quality wood, and he used to explain woods to Jim, talking to him about seasoning, and staining, and polishing, and the rich real colour you could get. Being a hand cabinetmaker he never made much money: there were machines, and who in Harriston knew or really cared about the pride and love Walt Barr lavished on each drawer and panel and chair-back and bed-post? Who knew about the feel of wood and the way its colours rippled in a good light? Still, he had made enough money to keep his family decently, and there had been pieces of furniture in their own home, a home long before this one, which Walt used to stand and look at, saying nothing. He had taught Jim the word 'skill' when the boy was little. His own father had made great chests high as a man, Walt Barr said, and he also knew how to carve, but he was a finer craftsman: that was in England. He himself read only about cabinet making: but he took Jim to the public library in Harriston when he was twelve years old and said: 'Don't come home till dark.' Six years ago C. D. Magnus decided to buy only factory furniture. Slowly the people who lived on Oakdale Road and Harriston Drive stopped ordering furniture since they already had furniture, and you had to make a choice, now that there was a depression. One day, without saying anything, Walt Barr had gone out and gotten a pick and shovel job on the roads. But he was not young and he hated the work, and finally he couldn't even find work that needed no skill whatever.

He had sold the furniture in his home and at last, in a rage that no words would fit, he had taken an axe to his dining-room table, chopped the fine polished walnut into kindling and carried it to the lake and thrown it away. For the last two years he had avoided his family, hating to see his own failure in them. Clara was too young to remember clearly the other house, the other life: but Jim knew. For years he had been too sorry for his father to speak; and now he was too absorbed in his own problems to care about the older man. Mr Barr was glad of this. He had a habit of disappearing all day. No one knew where he went and no one asked. He would eat breakfast in silence and leave the house quickly, walking towards the woods as if he had a meeting planned or even, wonderfully, a job to do.

The days were very quiet. Mrs Barr talked to herself at times, in a soft whining voice. Occasionally Jim heard her making conversation with unknown neighbours about new things she had in the house, her new curtains, the lovely new bed Walt had made. He managed to get away, when that started: we're all lying to ourselves, he thought; we can't any of us, except Clara perhaps, admit that our lives are really like this.

Clara came home some evenings, or late in the afternoon. She was always hurried; the Carters ate, changed their clothes, mussed their rooms, slept in their beds. All of this was Clara's concern. 'Dirty and lazy,' Clara would say in her brief passage. 'I gotta hurry back: there's always more work than I can do, anyhow, in the day.'

'How's school?' Jim would ask.

'Oh, fine.' But she didn't want to talk about it. Jim had been a wash-out at school. She thought it was better to be nice to him and not talk about it. He was a sweet kid, anyhow: perhaps it wasn't his fault. . . . With quick hatred she would stare at the clogged kitchen where they all lived, ate, read, quarrelled, and hurry back to the Carters.

Jim got up later and later in the mornings. He used as much of the day as he could sleeping: and for hours, silent, frowning in concentration, he read. As it grew colder he chose books about warm countries. About travel: men who were surprised by things happening in far off places which bore no resemblance to the civilization they knew. He didn't have a wide choice in the public library but he managed to lose himself almost steadily in books about Tahiti and Borneo, Java, Bali, India. He began to build stories from these books with himself as hero: himself discovering incredible plants which cured cancer: finding a flower dust that stopped tuberculosis—but none of this with agony, working too hard; feeling any of the heat he imagined around him as a blessing. It just happened: Jim Barr in white shorts, an open-necked shirt and a sun helmet, still young. . . .

One day he rose very late and told himself simply: this morning I have tropical fever and can't go out in the jungle. Unaware of his mother, the silence that was his father's and Clara's absence, he fumbled for soap at the sink, washing himself, thinking about what he would work over in his laboratory to-day. He had almost decided on a small vermilion berry, properties as well as name unknown, when he looked into the mirror above the sink. He saw there, as amazingly as if he were looking at a stranger's face, a yellowish mask, unevenly grown with beard. The face looked old and, in some disgusting way, slipped, smeared, like rotten fruit, he thought, or something that's been dug up. He stood before his own face in silence; not touching himself, not moving. Finally it became clear to him that this was Jim Barr: this was the way he looked for everyone to see and probably he himself was like this face. He tore his jacket from a peg and ran out into the morning, with a wilted dandruffy snow falling.

He went to the pool-room: it took what may have been hours, running through the thin snow. He went without noticing directions and without plan. He stopped from time to time, stood still and passed his hand over his face. He could feel the stubble of beard and the flesh felt loose. Anyone who saw him, bent a little with the cold, stroking his face, thought: that boy is drunk. He had no reason for going to the pool-room except that he saw it before him suddenly, lighted up against the grey morning, and it looked warm inside.

'Lo, Jim.' . . . 'Got two bits?' . . . 'Wanna drink?' . . .

He heard that. He wanted a drink badly. Presently, he found that he was something of an authority on billiards, standing over the green tables, urging and advising, groaning at a stupid or failed play, slapping people on the back. Later, he even thought what a fine thing it was to live in a town where you knew everyone and there were such swell guys around in the morning to talk to. Friends. That was what mattered, people you could talk to. People just like you. Finally, he remembered vaguely that something had shocked him that morning, something disgusting. His own face, by God. He wandered to a mirror and looked at himself until he could see what he was looking at. Then he thought it was a pretty good face, like everybody else's, like his friends' faces. That was just a nut idea—the kind of thing you thought when you were alone, and no swell guys to talk to. He fell asleep on one of the benches along the wall, but the proprietor didn't put him out, he liked Jim all right and it was still snowing.

Mr Barr spoke frequently now about the way his son was a bum, and what was the use in having a son if he only grew up to be a drunk and it was a funny thing that a boy couldn't get any decent work, but he could loaf around and get free drinks easy. Mr Barr lived bitterly with his idleness and Mrs Barr lived with her ailments and her sense of being cheated by the Relief. Jim, between bouts of drinking and queasy hangovers, paid no attention to either of them.

He had found it was hard to talk to the men at the pool-room unless he was tight. Perhaps he was shy, he thought, or too young. But there was Dick Manfred, who came home for Sundays and started getting drunk Saturday night and rolled back to Ferguson, where the mines were, Monday morning, shaken, but sober enough to work.

In the short period before they were both too happy or too sodden to talk, Dick told him about the mines.

'The first day I was scared outa my pants, I thought sure everything was gonna fall in; I was at the eighteen-hundred level just shoving slush around on the wagons. I went up the ladders to watch the guys drilling, and I was so scared and excited I almost passed out. I thought: By God, this is some work! None of your old desk jobs for me, I thought. And then I figured I'd take a correspondence course in mining and engineering, and get to be one of the guys in high boots who go around inspecting and then I'd be the manager.'

Jim listened: he knew about this: he had told himself these stories too. An interne whom nobody noticed: just standing around, holding things or maybe putting iodine on cuts. But one day he'd have to do a major operation because nobody else was there, and save a life, and everybody would swat him on the back, and he'd be resident surgeon. And then he'd discover cures. And then and then....

'Well, what about it?' he said.

'Oh,' Dick Manfred was looking around in his mind for the right words. He wasn't drunk yet and he felt too tired, too disgusted, it was hard telling Jim about this. He could talk to lots of the young guys in the mines and they'd know. 'Listen,' he said. 'I can't quit on account of my mother, and my father was a miner and she don't seem to know what it's like. She's so used to all that, she thinks it's the way people live. I gotta take care of her. But don't you do it. Don't you do it, boy. Jesus,' he said. 'Hey, Sam, where's that whisky?'

'But work,' Jim said, still sober. 'There's times I think anything would be swell. Anything; not just hanging around, waiting for the time to pass.'

'That's the bunk. The kinda world we live in, people like us only got a choice between how they wanta conk out. Me, I'd a damn sight rather go at it easy and slow. If I was free, boy, I'd grab rides on the freights and see the world.'

'You would, wouldja? I've done it. The freight bulls are pretty boys, I wanna tell you. And people take a look at you and say "Bums" and slam the door or call a cop. You can't sit anywhere or lie anywhere. Every time you look around you get run in for vagrancy. See the world is right, running like hell with some guy running after you. You know a lot.'

'Well, what can we do then?'

'I dunno. Get an education I guess; get so you can be an engineer or a doctor or something like that. Then you can work like a real guy and make money and people think something of you. As long as you're just common labor you can't do a thing.'

'And I guess you're gonna pay for the education with smiles and many thanks. That's a good one too.'

There was a silence. 'Sam, how about the whisky?' Jim said.

Finally, while he was still shaping his words clearly, Jim said: 'There's nothing for us. We're the guys who don't count.'

'Take some whisky,' Dick said, 'I got some money left. Go ahead and drink. It'll be Monday soon enough.'

The pool-room closed at one on Saturday nights. Dick Manfred, having finally realised that it was necessary to leave, arose, draped his coat around him with a large if imprecise gesture and rocketted through the door and across the street. Calling for him to wait, Jim followed. A truck, doing night hauling between Spokane and Lewiston, rumbled around the corner, swung out a little, righted itself and drove towards Jim. There were no street lights at this hour: Jim's dark wavering figure appeared like a sudden shadow, before the square high nose of the truck closed him out. The brakes howled and the truck, with the sudden stopping, lurched sharply sidewise and hit a lamp-post. The driver dropped from his seat to find what he had killed, shouting curses, terrified. They picked Jim up across the street against the curb, limp, his hair wet and dark with blood. Dick Manfred leaned against a store and watched all this: his mind said soberly, Jim's dead, but he could not move, only the wall behind him kept his legs from melting under the weight of his body. The truck driver got Sam to shut the pool-room at once and drive his car to the hospital. The truck driver held Jim on the back seat, swearing the boy had run under the truck, how could a guy see on a dark street and Sam said don't you worry he was drunk, but it's too bad, he was a good kid that one.

At the hospital a sleepy but pleased interne (something important to do at last) examined Jim on the operating table. The whole thing disgusted him beyond reason: aside from a dinky cut on the head, probably from the curb stone, there was nothing the matter with this guy. Perhaps shock. Damn good thing too; teach him not to run under trucks. He deserved at least a double fracture of the arm, or an amputated leg. But nothing. Stinking drunk and limp; got brushed by the far wheel and thrown; just folded up soft like a handkerchief. The interne took eight stitches in Jim's head, cursing everybody with soft regularity and told the truck driver and Sam to get the hell out so he could sleep.

In the morning, the interne explained the accident to Jim angrily. The next time, he said, we'll let you bleed to death; you don't deserve much more. You kids can't hold your liquor; there ought to be jail sentences for goddam mugs walking under trucks.

Jim watched the life of the hospital: the nurse carrying things to him on glass trays, such clean orderly things and the way she handled them, as if she could see germs and was politely avoiding contact with them. His fever chart. The interne who relented after a day and told him stories about operations. He thought: It's a funny way to get into this kind of place where I've always wanted to be, but it's worth being hit by ten trucks, at least.

He asked questions until the interne said listen I've got some books you can have but for God's sake fella there're other people in here. He lay on his bed with his head hanging down towards the floor, to get flushed and hot, praying for fever, a slight infection, anything that would keep him here longer. He opened every closet, when he was allowed to get up, and hung around the operating room door white with excitement. They let him watch an appendectomy, against all the rules, but because his eyes were there outside the door, enormous, desperately pleading. He had a fever that day from joy, feeling that he had at last come where he belonged. And in his mind he placed every detail of the operating room, to hold it sharply forever. The silence, the precision, the white-clothed people working: instruments passed without orders, without words, according to ritual: the quick deft hands of the surgeon, the feeling of absolute safety: this thing could not fail now or ever; these men were skilled, were above other men, any kind of men. He lay in his bed that afternoon and stared at his hands, smiling, released of doubt about the future. When the nurse came in at night he said: 'Are my hands all right, have I got hands to be a surgeon?' She took them in hers and stroked his hair: he's good-looking enough to get in the movies, she thought, what a mutt to want to be a doctor. 'Sure you have, fine hands,' she said. And took his temperature. He slept happily. He had seen again clearly where he wanted to go; and now he had only to get there.

They had turned him down pleasantly in Harriston: the bakery, the garage, the Horny-Hand Café, Schultz's grocery, the Mammoth Construction Company, the Beaver Saw Mills, the Apex Drug Store. In Ferguson they were less chatty about it and just said, sorry nothing doing. By the time he got to Newberry Forks, he looked like a tramp and was hungry. They didn't know him there, and strangers were just more labor unwanted, or else guys bumming a meal. The constable told him to get a move on. He knew that phrase; he knew a lot about vagrancy charges. In all it took him a week to prove to himself again that there wasn't any work for people like him, though no doubt internes were besieged with offers of fine positions in hospitals. When his mother asked him about his luck, he said: 'Oh, I had a fine walk. Nothing like exercise to keep a man healthy.' His stomach was so shrunken, he could scarcely eat. He told his mother not to worry, he was fine. Didn't she know that he was twenty-one, the finest years of a man's life: and he could probably always get a job in the army unless his arches had fallen somewhere on the state highway.

He was too tired the first night to notice that something was more wrong than usual.

He finally wondered what they were keeping so quiet about. Mr Barr appeared only at breakfast and dinner. Mrs Barr went about the house complaining softly. But there was something more. She would pick up a plate to dry it and stand with it in her hand staring at the floor, aimless and uncertain. He would see her sitting on the side of the bed in her room, holding a mop, her eyes blank, weeping without knowing it.

Clara came to dinner on her night off: only because food was free, at home. Jim knew that: but he watched his father, feeling everyone's silence, these people who usually shouted at each other in anger. Finally he asked: 'What's biting you? What's wrong, Dad? Anything worse than it always is? And Clara for Christ's sake stop sitting there looking like you had a mouth full of worms.'

She stared at him.

Mr Barr said nothing. 'What is it?' Jim said. 'For God's sake let me in on your fun.'

Mr Barr stopped eating. He put his knife and fork down, carefully crossed on his plate.

'All right,' he said, 'I'll tell you. That girl is no good. She's a whore.'

For a moment no one spoke. Then Clara stood up, very quietly, and said: 'Shut your dirty mouth.'

'You see she don't deny it,' Mr Barr said, with grim pleasure. 'Because she can't. I know all right. All the neighbours are talking; if you weren't always drunk or away somewheres you'd have heard it too. Maybe they make jokes about her at the pool-room.'

'I'll kill you,' Clara said. 'Keep your dirty mouth shut.'

Mrs Barr silently, without moving, wept; she watched them with stupid eyes, and the tears ran down her face.

'What are you talking about?' Jim said.

'What beats me is how they do it,' Mr Barr's voice had gone high and false. 'In the back of the grocery truck, maybe. It's too cold outa doors, and they can't go to a hotel. Unless they take one of them rooms with bedbugs down at the Lone Star for fifty cents. It must be swell, isn't it, Clara, rolling around with the bedbugs?'

The plate she threw sailed over his head and smashed against the wall. Jim turned to his father fiercely and said: 'Shut up.'

'Clara,' he said. 'Listen kid. What is all this? Go ahead and tell me.'

'He's talking about me and Alf Harmon. Sure it's true. What about it? What else can we do? Get married I guess. That's a hot one. What would we be getting married on? On the Relief I guess. Not me. Besides,' she turned towards her father, 'who're you to talk? What do you do for me? You pulling this my daughter stuff and fallen woman and such crap. What're you? You're nothing but a man who can't get a job. I'm free, get that. I don't owe nothing to nobody: I'll do what I want.'

She was standing above them, white-faced, with the black rings around her eyes looking painted on. Thin and sharp: seventeen, Jim thought, seventeen and bitter and tired.

'And it's the only thing I know that don't cost money,' Clara said, and suddenly crazily laughed.

He got up and put his arm around her. He took her to the only chair in the room that wasn't unsteady, and sat down and held her on his lap. She leaned against his shoulder and wept, saying: 'What else can we do, what else can we do? I love him; I gotta have something in my life. What fun do they think it is for me to live? I'm working all the time and I ain't got anything I want or need and he's the only person makes me forget what it's like all day.'

Jim stroked her hair, and said quietly: 'Sure, honey, it's all right.'

'Oh, it's all right, is it?' Mr Barr said. 'It's fine; it's a fine thing to do, is it? Who do you think will marry her now? Just a little cheap whore you can have for nothing. Why don't she act like other girls her age?'

Over Clara's head Jim said to his father: 'Keep quiet. How can she act like other girls: do you want her to be like Nancy Tredway that's got a Chrysler maybe, or Sally Allison that goes to Seattle for Christmas vacation and the winter sports? Can't you see the kid's tired to death and there isn't anything for her that's fun? Do you think she'd be doing this if she had a good home, and clothes, and could go to the movies sometimes, and have boys in to supper and things like that?'

'I love him,' Clara said.

'Sure you do. Sure you do. I'm sorry as hell for you, kid.'

'She's a whore, that's all,' Mr Barr said. 'And she can just get outa here and go back to her grocery truck.'

'Listen,' Jim said. 'You shut up or I'll knock you out. Just being my father isn't so much. She can stay here as long as she wants. She belongs here. And if she has fun with Alf, you leave her alone. She's got a right to something. She's got a right to whatever she can get.'

He held Clara tightly in his arms. 'Don't cry, kid. Don't cry. It's all right. We don't care. It's all right.'

Suddenly Mrs Barr got up and came towards Clara. 'It's time for bed, dear,' she said, her voice a soft whisper in the room. 'Come along, mother'll undress you and you can say your prayers. I'll fix you a nice picnic to-morrow and you can go swimming with Jimmy. Don't cry: that old tooth won't be hurting for long.'

All three of them, silent, stared at her. Clara shrank back against Jim. Mrs Barr's eyes saw nothing, settled nowhere, and her hand stretched out towards Clara. The room seemed to have grown cold.

The doctor kept saying it's nothing at all, nothing at all. Happens all the time, these days. Just a breakdown from worry, you know, nerve strain. Fix her up in a few weeks, just needs a rest. The family sat and listened to him with wooden faces. Even if he could fix it up in a few weeks it shouldn't have happened, ever. They were all ashamed, realizing they had left this complaining bewildered woman entirely alone with whatever thoughts haunted her. The social worker in charge of their family came and was gentle and took Mrs Barr away; Mrs Barr was very sweet about going. She said she'd be back in the afternoon and for the children to be careful not to get their feet wet. She said the spring weather is so dangerous; you never know when colds will turn into pneumonia. They stood and waved at her, and as she left they could hear her saying to Mrs Meredith, the social worker: doesn't Clara look lovely with that pink hair-ribbon, she's going to grow up to be a beautiful woman.

Clara came home: they needed her and she didn't question this. The house ran very quietly, probably better than when Mrs Barr's patient but ineffectual hands cared for it. Mr Barr, shocked into deeper silence, spoke not at all; didn't seem to know Clara was there, and even ignored Alf Harmon when he came some nights in the grocery truck to fetch Clara.

Clara, Jim thought, is lucky. At least she's needed: we need her here. I could die and nobody would notice it. Clara had school, too: she would finish, she was younger, younger, there was time for Clara. And he sat in the kitchen and looked at his hands and felt his thoughts slipping and skidding, in terror. But he was very quiet, speaking to no one of this.

He thought when Mr Peck hired him that it could only be from pity. Why else would he get a job? He was used now to being refused and it seemed to him that the reason had to be himself, this unemployment was a personal thing based on his own unfitness. To be ashamed of, as you'd be ashamed of a club foot or ranking last at school. He was apart from other men and felt himself marked and degraded. And he was terribly frightened. I'll be fired, he thought, I'll be fired right away. And this will be the last chance I ever have.

He drove the J. P. Peck's General Clothing Emporium truck as slowly as it would go, without rattling to a halt. His hands on the wheel were cold and trembled. He never rang door-bells more than once, for fear the customers would complain of impoliteness on the part of the driver-delivery boy. He said nothing when Saturday rush meant driving until ten at night through a sticky swirling snow. He stayed awake at night thinking about the roads, the tyres on the truck, should he say good morning when he handed the package to the lady at the door, or just give it to her without saying anything. It was more than a job now. It was something he had to prove to himself: the last thing in the world to hold, his feeling that he was a worker, he was capable of work and meant to work. He earned five dollars a week.

He had worked a month before he realized what his work was, how the days passed. He began to notice more than the back firing of the truck, the way the brakes screamed and the grinding of the gears. Or the fact that some ladies smiled and some just grabbed the parcels that he delivered. He began to think about his hours and the pay. But mostly he thought of being a doctor, of the hospital and the operating-room. He looked at his hands, raw and chapped, and wondered what sense there was in living. In the spring he would be twenty-two and the only job he could get was driving a truck for five dollars a week. He learned nothing. He could also have driven a truck when he was sixteen.

He gave Clara his five dollars and she took it without looking at him or saying anything. But he knew that she wanted to give it back and say to him, go away, get out, let's both get out somehow. If only there was some place to go where it would be any different, if only they could kid themselves about that....

He didn't know quite what it was: but probably it was Dick Manfred. One night, when Jim had finished his deliveries, Dick tied a sled on behind the truck and picked up a girl named Holly and hugged her as the sled skidded across the road. Then he told Jim to go out and hang on to the girl, who was a pleasure to hang on to, and drove the truck himself. The snow was icy and stinging on Jim's face and the sled rocketted in a straight line and then swung wide like a deranged pendulum and Holly screamed and held his arms very tight around her, so that above the noise and speed and the fine feeling of wind down his throat he knew she had good breasts. He went home that night singing Jingle Bells at the top of his lungs and his father looked at him darkly, thinking him drunk again. He decided that it was possible to have a swell time now and again if you stopped worrying about to-morrow and all the things you never would have. He told Clara defiantly: 'I'm going to have some fun.' She smiled at him and said: 'Good for you.' He also said to her: 'I got to keep a little of my own money, Clara. I got to.'

'Keep it all. You got a right to it. I can fix it up with Mrs Meredith. She's all right; she knows it's tough the way we gotta live. My God, if a man hasn't a right to five dollars he makes, it's a lousy world.'

'I'll only keep a little.'

'You keep it all unless we run outa groceries.'

Five dollars, he thought: five dollars to spend. Not for something he needed. What he needed couldn't be bought with five dollars. He needed ten years to study, or almost that, and he needed clothes, and a home, and food, and warmth, and safety for his family. If he thought about his needs five dollars was an insult, a piece of paper to burn in disgust. But if he was thinking only of his happiness . . . he sat near the stove that night and turned over ideas in his mind. He scarcely knew where to begin. Automatically he thought of clothes: he could get a sheep-skin at the miner's store in Ferguson for five dollars, at least a worn one. And he was cold all the time. He threw that out: no, it was five dollars as a luxury, for something to enjoy. He thought of books, but he hadn't read everything in the public library yet and it was a waste to buy something he could get free. After work at night he walked along the main street of Harriston looking in the store windows and thinking. He was waiting for Friday, and his five dollars, but he had to be ready. If he didn't know what he wanted he might spend the money in a silly trickle on pool and movies and drinks. It couldn't be that way, he would have to get something to keep, to look at every day and be sure that he had bought it himself because he'd earned it and wanted it.

He had to leave the truck one night at a garage to get the brakes tightened. There was a bedraggled second-hand store next to the garage. He never looked at it: the windows were clogged with old china and flat irons, broken porcelain lamps, ragged shawls. But to-night he saw something red and bright, and stopped. It was a small accordion, with some roses painted on as decoration, and the keyboard was very neat, and it sat jauntily on its side, a little pulled out, gay among the broken oddments of the window display. He stood before it shivering and wondered how long it took to learn to play it. And he saw himself at home at night playing grand music sounding like an organ, and being happy, and far away from the kitchen. He went in and asked the little grey man who ran the store, how much it cost.

'Six dollars.'

'It's not worth it,' he said and hoped his voice didn't tremble.

'It's not worth it? Are you crazy? You couldn't get this accordion in Spokane for twenty dollars. I wouldn't have such a fine instrument here, only a crazy miner came down and got drunk and sold it for whisky. And I'm letting it go cheap because folks around here don't know nothing about music and fine instruments like that. I'm giving it away for six.'

'It's not worth it, but I'll give you five for it, and you can take it or leave it and see if I care.'

There was a silence; casually he fingered a broken china shepherdess and studied a fork with one prong missing. He tried to look careless, and he thought, I'll break his nose if he doesn't take five. I've got to have it, I've got to have it. He could hear the music already: the Blue Danube and the Volga boat song. He knew he would be able to play the accordion at once, because he wanted to. He saw himself playing it under the trees by the lake, in spring, with a beautiful girl listening. It was reason enough to live until spring. The great surgeon Dr James Barr who is also a talented performer on the accordion. . . .

'All right,' the little man said. 'Cash.'

'I'll come for it to-morrow night at six.' He walked out. When he was out of sight he began running. He wouldn't tell anyone until he had it, but he wanted to run to keep from shouting to the whole town that he, Jim Barr, was a musician not a truck driver.

He put it on a shelf by itself, in the kitchen. Clara said it was beautiful, she had never seen anything so pretty and what could he play on it? He said that he didn't know yet and it might take a little while to figure it out, but he thought he would play wonderful things. Mr Barr didn't see it at first. Then he said: 'What's that thing?'

'It's my new accordion.'

'Where'd you get it?'

'I bought it at Raphaelson's junk shop; it was a bargain. Only five dollars. It's a fine expensive instrument.'

Clara watched her father. She could see the muscles in his face tightening.

'You mean to say you went and spent five dollars on that thing when you know we need clothes and coal and food? Are you crazy,' he shouted, 'or what kinda hog are you?'

Clara got up from the table. 'He's got a right,' she began.

'Keep quiet, Clara,' Jim said, and turning to his father: 'You listen to me. I've given my money to the family for months. I never bought anything I wanted just for fun, just because it was nice and I wanted it. I make that money. And, besides, who in hell are you to squawk? If anybody has a right to kick it's the Relief. They're keeping this family, them and me. You just board here, free.'

'This is still my house.'

'And how do you figure that? We pay rent on it, or we're supposed to. Where does the money come from, I wanta know? I guess you'll say you pay the rent on the quiet without telling us, out of all the money you earn when you're not sitting here in the kitchen doing nothing.'

'I'm your father anyhow, I'm older than you. You haven't got a right to throw away money.'

'I got a right to be happy if I can sometimes. If I don't think of myself I wanta know who will. You leave us alone, Clara and me. We'll do what we gotta do for ourselves, and we'll get some fun any old way we know. We don't say anything to you so you keep your mouth shut about us.'

'I'm older,' Walt Barr said, and stood up. He wandered around the room, pushing the chairs out of his way, his eyes dark and bewildered. 'I'm older. He's my son. I'm the one who ought to give orders.'

Clara put some more potatoes on her father's plate. She didn't look at Jim. Jim was thinking, he used to work with his hands and he loved the things he made. He used to play spelling games with me so I'd learn words and how to write them. He isn't like this. Everything has gone wrong for him, but he isn't really like this.

'Dad,' he said. 'I take it all back. Only I want that accordion and it's mine. I'm sorry I said what I did.'

'If I could get some work,' Walt Barr said, as if he were talking to himself. 'If I could get anything. We wouldn't need their money; they could spend it the way they wanted and go ahead and live for themselves and have their own things. I'm too old.'

'Dad,' Clara said. 'Your potatoes are getting cold. I got some butter to put on them from the Relief commodities to-day and they're real good. Come and eat your dinner.'

Jim said: 'You had a fiddle when I was a kid, I remember it. Maybe you could play the accordion right off.'

'My hands aren't any good now,' Mr Barr said.

TWO

•

JIM AND LOU

It made an interesting noise, but it was definitely a noise. He had waited until Sunday morning before he gave himself up to the luxury of being a musician. It was now Sunday afternoon and Clara was worn-out.

'I don't want to be mean, Jim, but it's not awful cold to-day, and you could borrow Dad's coat. Would you mind taking it outside to practise for a while? When you're playing pieces it'll be different.'

He put on whatever warm clothes he could find around the house, finishing off with a bright wool scarf of Clara's, known as her 'sports outfit'. He walked fast to store up heat for sitting still later. In a pine clearing in the woods, he found a log which would do as a chair. He thought it was a wonderful day, and this was really a nicer place to practise. He whistled busily and tried everything the accordion would do. It was exciting and full of surprises: sometimes it sounded like a piano and sometimes like an organ and sometimes it was just sound. He was very happy.

The girl had come up behind him, but he wouldn't have noticed her anyhow.

She said: 'It's music, isn't it?'

He looked up at her. She had a market basket over her arm and it was almost full of wood. She was hatless, and her hair rumpled darkly over her head. She was very small.

'Do you like music?' Jim asked.

'Sure. I been listening to you for a long time. I heard you about five miles away and I been running all over the woods to see what it was. I didn't think it was a man,' she said doubtfully. She looked a little disappointed.

'It's an accordion.'

'Oh,' she said. Then she sat down beside him on the log, and put her basket on the ground. 'I'll just sit here and listen till I have to take this wood home.'

'Where do you live?'

'About three miles up the Ferguson road. I gotta pick up wood. We don't have any coal. Till Thursday.' He looked at her. He thought she was lovely; she had a face for the woods, for the woods in spring. She was so much smaller and neater than most girls, with a tiny nose as if she were sniffing cookies baking; and brown eyes.

'What's your name?' he said.

'Lou.'

'Mine's Jim. Pleased to meetcha. I guess I'll go on practising.'

He bent over the accordion, pulling it out and in fast and slow, moving his fingers over the keys, waiting to see what would come forth. She was as quiet as the trees. He felt sure she was watching him, her eyes bright and intent like a squirrel. And he kept thinking isn't it fine that she can sit still and not jerk around the way everybody does. It grew colder, and the sun was brushed out behind the pines. Once or twice he felt her shiver.

At last he said: 'It's getting dark. I gotta be going.'

'I had a swell time,' Lou said. 'Thanks for the music.'

They stood up.

'How old're you?'

'Seventeen,' she said.

'Do you go to school?' he said.

She looked at him.

'You ask a lotta questions, don't you? I'll tell you all about me if you wanta know. I don't do anything. We're on Relief. We been on Relief a year and sometimes I think we were always on it. We moved here six months ago because Dad thought they'd get him on farming, there's Relief farms you know. He's nutty: he never had experience farming. He was a book-keeper, he did the work for a hotel in San Francisco and they laid him off cause he's old now. So we moved to Chipsaw, that's north of here, where he was born, but there wasn't anything there either. We live in a bum house, and there's no money for me to get clothes and go to school and I hate it all. I hate the people who fired him and I hate this town and everything about it. Now you know.'

'Lou,' he said, 'we'll have fun with the accordion and with Dick's sled. Honest we will. If you don't think about it too much you can have a swell time.'

'I went to high school in San Francisco and had clothes like everybody else. And here. I wash dishes and make beds and I wish I was dead most of the time.'

'I know about that,' he said.

'Well, if you want to come to see me, my last name's Weylin. I live out towards Ferguson, about three miles, there's a side road with a gas station where they cross. I live just up the hill.'

'Lou.' He slung his accordion on his back like a knapsack and took her basket of wood from her hands and set it on the ground.

'Lou, kiss me.'

'Yes,' she said. 'Oh, sure. It don't cost a thing. We're giving them away for samples.'

'Lou,' he said, 'I'm crazy about you.'

She leaned against him. 'That's fine,' she said. 'I'm cold. How about you?'

'Oh, sure.'

'Never mind, it'll soon be spring. And then it'll be summer and we can be hot for a change. But I guess we better start walking now, Jim.'

Brown like an acorn, and little and quick like a squirrel, he thought. He took her hand and pirouetted her, elegantly, as if they were dancing the minuet. Then pulling her after him, stumbling and laughing, they ran out of the woods. 'Hurry Lou, Hurry Lou, the icicles are after you.'

'Hey, stop. Gosh how I'd like to sit down and get warm.'

'If I could make a dollar saving a millionaire's life, we could go to a hotel.'

'I won't go to hotels.'

'I know you won't, honey. You're shy.'

'I am not shy: don't be a fool, Jim Barr.'

'Tough as hell.'

'Come on, you sap.'

'Stop dead in your tracks so I can kiss you.'

He took her in his arms: it's like holding a bird, he thought. Little and soft and cold; I must be very careful of her. I'm going to get a fine job soon, and have things to give her, and a place for her to live. . . .

'Let's pick us a house to-day,' he said.

They had done this before, but there were endless possibilities. Lou started it one day when they were very cold: the woods she said are fine, but me, I want a house with a furnace, so let's go and pick one and have it sent to us next week. They had walked around Harriston, up the rich streets, looking at the houses: it was dusk and the snow made everything distant and more graceful than it really was. Lou said: 'I think that one will be fine.' Jim stood considering it, and then he said: 'No, it would be awful when there's no snow on it; besides we have to have a house with a side door and a drive up to it, so I can have my office in the house and my patients won't be embarrassed, and of course so the children won't get in the way.' Lou thought about that: 'The children,' she said. 'I forgot.'

'A fine kind of mother you are.'

Now they walked up Harriston Drive, holding hands. Lou was not very well dressed for winter: she had a thin serge coat, obviously taken in for her, and shiny. They had never mentioned their clothes to each other. Jim thought about her coat steadily, he had a feeling of guilt and anger against its ugliness and thinness. He wanted to see her wearing warm soft clothes, brown he decided, like fur or fine wood. He told himself stories about the dresses and coats and shoes he'd give her, when he was driving the truck: and every once in a while, waiting in J. P. Peck's for the parcels he had to deliver, he would loaf over towards the ladies' department and watch the girls selling. He almost never saw anything he thought was beautiful enough for Lou.

Now they walked fast, and Jim said: 'We could hopscotch, it makes you plenty hot, I remember from when I was a child. . . .' Suddenly she saw a house, it was set back from the street with pine trees neat around it. It was low and wandered over the snowy lawn, as if it were comfortable sprawling that way. It was made of white slats and the curtains behind the windows were white and soft, and 'Look,' she said, 'the curtains look like beat-up egg whites. I bet it's a clean, pretty house inside.' Jim studied it carefully, there was a carriage drive with white gravel on it, between the pines: and a low step led up to the side door. 'We'd have to build on some rooms,' he said. 'But it's all right for a start.'

'Jimmy, it's a wonderful house. It'll do us for ten years, anyhow.'

'It's all right.'

'It's wonderful.'

She stood in the street, rubbing her hands together, and shifting from foot to foot. 'We can build a playhouse in back for the children so's they won't make any noise for your patients.'

'Dad could make up the plans for that.'

'All right. Only a little playhouse, though. We don't want to spoil them.'

'No, we got to be careful about that. I'll tell them "Your Dad got everything he has, himself, you got to learn to make your own way." '

'All right, Jimmy, but don't sound mean will you?'

'You're spoiling them already.'

'I know, I know....'

'I wonder whose house it is?'

'I think it's the MacIntyres. I never met Mrs MacIntyre at any of the parties I go to.'

'You mean that old MacIntyre who owns the Drug Store.'

'That's the gent.'

'Oh, Lou, that old man, that old man and an old woman, living there, and us standing in the street.'

'Now,' she said. 'Don't act silly. We're just standing here deciding if we'll buy the house. Just because our own house is too little....'

He put his arm around her. 'Lou, I love you better than anything in the world.'

The lights on the second floor went on. Lou looked at the sky.

'My God, it's late,' she said, 'I got to get home.'

'Not yet.'

'Yes, honey. I got to make dinner, and put the kid to bed and see that Mother and Dad don't fight, and listen to Mother crying if I wake up and hear her because Jack didn't write for a month and Frank's in jail for being a hobo in New Mexico. Oh, sure, I got to get home.'

'Lou, it won't be long now. We'll have our own place in the spring and you won't have to work like a nigger and everything. I'm gonna get a fine house for you and take care of you, sweetheart. It's only a little while longer now.'

She took his hand and held it. He couldn't see her face in the darkness. She was looking at him tenderly, smiling, the way a woman would look at a little boy wearing a cocked hat made of newspaper, playing Napoleon with a broom for a horse....

Clara got a letter. Nobody in their house ever got a letter. Jim waited before going to work to see what it was about; even Mr Barr, instead of disappearing right after breakfast, lingered with his hand on the door-knob. Clara sat on a chair by the stove and opened it. It took her a long time to read, but Jim could see that it was only a few lines. She didn't say anything; but her body stiffened, and the muscles in her cheeks moved as if she were keeping her teeth closed on any sound she might make.

Mr Barr looked at her and quietly opened the door and went away.

'Clara,' Jim said. He went to her and put his hand gently on her hair. 'Clara dear.'

She turned to him; he was afraid of her eyes.

'Look at it,' she handed him the letter.

It was written in purple ink on ruled paper: 'Clara, we don't get anywhere, and we can go on like this till we go crazy. I'll never get any money. It isn't that I don't love you. I'm going away. Some guy told me that in Florida. . . .'

'As if,' Clara said, 'the name of the State makes any difference if you're outa work.'

'The bum,' Jim said. 'The goddamn lousy bum. Walking out on you. He could of stayed and gone on anyhow, or at least taken you.'

'Sure,' Clara said. 'It's fun being hungry together. He's not a bum. He's right. Now,' she said, 'I can go on getting up every morning and going to bed every night.'

'Oh, Clara.'

'Listen, Jim, you marry Lou. Don't wait for anything, and don't think you'll get anything. Just marry her. Jobs,' she said, her voice rising. 'Jobs. And enough money and a decent place to live and clothes and food. Oh, Christ, if I knew how I'd laugh my head off.'

'You poor little kid.'

'Don't worry.' She got up. She took the letter and put it in the stove. Her eyes when she turned to him were like pebbles, smooth and hard. 'Don't worry. I don't give a damn now, and it'll maybe be a lot easier for me. There are lots of men for a girl like me, and maybe I can get myself a fake fur coat if I work hard enough.'

He put his hands on her shoulders. 'Come with me to-day, in the truck. I got to go now, kiddo, but come on with me. I'd just like to have you around.'

'No. But thanks. And don't you worry.'

He thought about Clara all day. But he kept saying 'Lou' to himself, whenever he could, stealing back to her for comfort. It wouldn't be that way with him and Lou: everything was wrong but not Lou. Lou would never leave, and he'd be able to put his hand out and touch her and be safe. Nothing would ever be entirely ugly or destroyed for him, because there was that little brown girl wrinkling her nose and smiling. . . . Clara, he thought, God what can we do for you: we have nothing to give you.

'This is the last delivery to-day, Jim,' Mr Smithers said. 'And here's your money for four days' work. I'm sorry, kid, but one of the sales-clerks can do what delivering we need: March is a slack month. We'll be getting you back around Easter when it picks up again.'

Jim held out his hand as if he weren't sure whose hand it was. His mind lay numb: not a job, not even this job, and how about him and Lou, didn't they know about him and Lou and what they were planning, and how hurried they were because they had no place to be together, and how they couldn't wait.... 'But,' he said.

'I know, Jim, it's tough. You're a fine kid and we don't get any complaints about you. We all like you fine. But March's a lousy month. The store's losing money you know. Around Easter. And'—Mr Smithers looked at the empty store: he felt uneasy about this. Was the boy going to cry. 'Here's a pair of gloves for you, Jim. Just keep your hands warm till Easter.' He patted Jim on the back. And thrust the gloves into that still outstretched hand. They were bargain gloves, on sale as odd lots for forty-nine cents a pair. Jim walked to Lou's house with them in his hand, out in front of him as if they were made of glass or dynamite.

'I hate those people,' Lou said, 'Smithers and Peck and the bums at Dad's hotel. I'm coming over to your house to-night soon's the dishes are done. But don't look like that. It wasn't such a good job. Anyhow, damn them,' she said quietly. 'Damn them. Damn them. Don't let them make you look that way. I'm coming over later. How's Clara?'

He told her about the letter, Alf heading for Florida believing in the sun probably or that a man could live on oranges.

'Go home and be good to her,' Lou said. 'She's got real trouble. Your job doesn't matter. We'll get something better, soon. Honey boy.' She took his head in her hands and kissed his eyes softly. 'I'll eat awfully fast and wash everything in a minute. I'll be there before you will.'

Clara was not home. Mr Barr had made some supper. 'I don't know where she is,' Walt Barr said, and Jim thought this is the last thing he can stand; his voice sounds as if he were never going to try again. 'I don't know what to do, Jim.'

'We can't do anything about her. We haven't got anything to give her.'

He told his father about being laid off while he ate. He said: 'Look at the swell gloves they gave me. We can pawn them and live for two years on what we get.'

'Yes,' Mr Barr said. He got up and went to the bedroom. 'I'll sleep in here,' he said, 'since Clara's gone.'

'She'll come back later. Don't you worry, Dad.'

Lou stood in the doorway and watched him go. 'Where's Clara?'

'We don't know.'

'I'll wait with you, Jimmy. And we got to get married soon, sweetheart. Your house and my house and sometimes I think I'll go crazy with it all.'

'We'll get married on what?'

'On Relief.'

'Are you nuts, Lou? What do you think I am? Do you think I'm going to start off that way? We're going to get married like real people, and we're going to have a decent home, and we're not going to be beggars all our lives. We're going to be a man and his wife and not two Relief clients.'

'All right, Jim.'

He put his arm around her. 'Come and sit on my lap. You're such a skinny little thing I guess we can both sit on this chair.'

She put her head against his cheek; her hair was soft, and smelled of wood smoke. 'I wish we could sleep together, Lou.'

Her arms were around his neck. 'All right, Jimmy. Any time. I don't care where or anything. We got to take whatever we can.'

'When it's spring,' he said.

'Sure. That spring. I forgot about it.'

He rocked gently. 'If Dad wasn't sleeping I'd play the accordion for you.'

She mussed his hair. He could now play the Blue Danube definitely, or almost the Blue Danube. She knew every note by heart, she even knew the notes he missed.

The dollar alarm clock ticked with a sound of clattering tinware and they dozed.

The door opened so hard that it slammed against the inside wall of the kitchen. Clara swayed in the doorway, dusting snow from her shoulders. She was drunk. She looked at them for a while and then recognized them. "Lo, kids. How's everything? How's every little thing?' She pulled the door and it slammed heavily behind her. She walked over to the table and leaned on it. She opened her coat and from the neck of her sweater she pulled out a crushed five-dollar bill.

'Easy money,' she said. 'And there's a lot more where that came from, or from two other guys. It's a fine thing to be a working girl.'

Lou buried her head against Jim's shoulder and neither of them spoke.

'If this damn slush ever melts I bet you a violet or something would come up.'

'Walk over here,' Lou said. 'My shoe's got a big hole.'

'I was thinking: I can maybe get a job at the Jenkins again in the summer; they know me now. If I go early maybe I can follow the harvest. Three months, if I was lucky. I can save the money and that'd be a little for us to get married on.'

'But, Jimmy, you said the spring.'

'I know, honey, but I won't have the money. If I start at Peck's around the middle of April and spring is May first about, isn't it?'

'There's the Relief,' she said stubbornly.

'Lou.'

'I won't wait all our lives. I won't do it. You said spring.'

'But, sweetheart, I won't have money to buy you a dress to get married in.'

'Do you think I'm worrying about dresses? Do you love me? Do you want to get married to me or don't you?'

'Lou,' he said, with horror. 'Lou, how could you say that even if you're sore? It isn't that way with us. We're always going to love each other.'

'Put your arms around me, Jimmy and marry me quick. The winter's been long enough.'

He picked her up and snuggled his face against her throat. 'Spring is here,' he sang off key, noisily. 'Spring is here.'

She laughed at him. 'You're tickling me.'

'All right, walk on your own feet, pee wee.'

She put her hand in his and smiled at him. 'Let's go and sit on our log.' They found a fallen tree which had served them all winter, when it wasn't too cold to sit down.

'How's Clara?' she said suddenly.

'She comes home sometimes. She has money.'

They sat and watched some clouds like white rabbits, jumping before the wind.

'Dad's funny, too. He's getting so quiet. He always was quiet, but it was different. Like he'd bite you if you talked to him. Now he's quiet, like a blind man, some way.'

'It's better your mother's away.'

'Yes,' Jim said. 'But it's pretty funny when you're glad your own mother is shut away somewhere. It's pretty funny thinking she's better off like that.'

'I hate where we live,' Lou said, beating with a small fist on the log. 'I'm sorry for our families, it isn't their fault. My father isn't a mean man and my mother didn't used to be crying all the time, and we had a good house and clothes, and went to school and parties and everything. Your family's all right, too. But it's awful now and even us, when we're together we got to be careful a lot of the time, not to argue about getting married and things. I hate it. I won't stay in it any more. We got to get married.'

'Lou, baby. Come here.' He held her head against his shoulder and rumpled the short brown hair. 'You can cry if you want to. I guess I know how you feel. But you're wrong about us. We don't have to be careful about arguing. I'll do anything you want.'

'Will you marry me the next day after we see the first crocus?'

'Yes.'

She sighed. 'Everything's all right then. I don't want to cry.'

'Well, then, come on and walk, my seat's getting wet from this log.'

'All right. But I got to get home soon. The kid's got a cold and mother's sure it'll be pneumonia, so she can't do anything except cry, thinking he's going to die. Oh, hell,' she said very slowly, very carefully. 'Oh, hell.'

'You tell me what you did to-day and then I'll tell you.'

It was a game Jim had invented since he no longer drove the truck, and his days were empty and marked only by the dishes he washed, or the wood he cut.

'Well,' Lou said, taking a deep breath, 'this morning I thought what a fine day it was, so I put on my riding clothes and I rode Black Beauty out to Narrow Lake and back, and galloped.'

'You did?'

'You bet I did.'

'I didn't know you could ride like that.'

'I'm good.'

'And then what?'

'Then I got dressed in a nifty sports outfit and got into my Chrysler....'

'Did I see that car?'

'No, it's my new one. It's a black sports roadster with red wheels. Then I drove out to the Country Club and I had a swell lunch.'

'What did you eat?'

'Creamed chicken and peas.'

'God,' he said reverently.

'I knew you'd be jealous about that.'

'Hell, no. I ate at my men's club down-town and I had lobster.'

'I bet you don't even know what it looks like.'

'I had steak then.'

'I bet it was horse meat.'

'Meanie.'

'No, but if you don't want to know about the rest of the day....'

'Go ahead.'

'Well, I talked to Mrs Drayton about the kids. We figured it was about time to send little Jimmy to school in San Francisco so he could begin studying for college.'

'Oh, Lou.'

'What?'

'That's not fair. He isn't ready for school yet; he's only about three.'

'All right.'

'And, anyhow, he's going to Andover.'

'What's Andover?'

'I don't know. It's a school somewheres, I read some boys books about it. It sounded like lotsa fun for the kids.'

'All right, but I'm going to pick little Lou's school.'

'Hey,' Jim said, 'isn't that smoke? Don't you smell it? It looks like smoke.'

'Can't be a forest fire, everything's too wet.'

'Come on.' He took her hand and pulled her after him, jumping fallen logs and scratching their legs against stiff bare bushes.

'It's over this way,' Jim said. 'Of all the crazy things, a forest fire when everything's soaking. . . .'

It was hard running and they walked: from habit and practice they made very little noise and they were too out of breath to talk.

They came into a clearing: a bonfire burned in the middle of it and sitting beside the fire, turned sidewise to them was a man. He was sitting on a three-legged hand-made stool. A little shack of the lean-to variety was behind him, roofed with twigs, lurching unsteadily towards the trees. He was making something, and around him on the ground were other things he had made. Chairs and tables, suitable for a big doll or a very small baby: a bed, a bookshelf. He was at work now weaving some split twigs together to make a rush seat for an arm-chair. He had few tools: a small cheap hammer, a little saw, a hatchet, a plane, and a matchbox beside him full of nails. He was working steadily with clumsy intent hands. It was Walt Barr.

They stood watching him: Jim could not even feel himself breathing.

Mr Barr finished what he was doing: he nailed the woven twigs over the framework of the chair, stood it beside him on the ground and stared at it. Then he frowned. He picked it up and carefully pulled out as many nails as he could and began all over again, trying to make the chair better.

'He's been coming here then,' Jim whispered. 'All the days he went away right after breakfast and came back after dark. Every day he's been coming here, making things to keep from going nuts.'

He felt Lou's hand gripping his, her fingers like cold wire.

'God,' Jim said. 'Oh, my God.'

Lou pulled him back silently and still pulling, led him quickly and noiselessly away.

'You can't look at things like that,' she said.

'He never said anything. He never told us and we treated him like dirt.'

'Jimmy,' she said, 'for God's sake let's get out before we get like that too.'

'He used to make fine furniture,' Jim said. 'He even knew how to carve some.'

He had been driving the truck again for a week. He was tired. Where the hell do all these people get money to buy clothes, he thought. Easter. An Easter bonnet. Myself, I would like some Easter b.v.d.'s and my girl could do with some shoes that had more on them than the shoe laces. Five dollars. You're just starting life, young man. If you save that five dollars in fifty years it will be ten dollars and you can go out and get stinking drunk on rubbing alcohol.

'How's things, boy?' It was Dick Manfred. These last months Jim had not seen him. Lou wouldn't want him to hang around the poolroom and besides ... two bits to waste. Two bits: five cans of soup by God; the things you had to have, not the things you wanted.

'Well, this truck now,' Jim said, 'named Man o' War. I'm still driving it. That's how things is, my man. And how're the mines?'

'Fun. Lotsa fun.' Dick's face was yellowish in the morning light. He looked thin but principally his eyes looked desperate and lonely. 'Wanta drink?' Dick said.

'Can't, Dick. Gotta deliver parcels to Mrs Whoosis with the fat behind who just bought a new corset for Easter.'

'It's better than working in the cellar.'

'Sure.'

'I'll see you in ten years,' Dick Manfred said. 'And we can say just the same things. So now I'm gonna get drunk.'

No, Jim thought. No, by God. Not me. Lou, my darling, in ten years we'll be wondering if it was really true, all this winter, all this long hell winter. Lou, darling, darling....

The days were longer and the sun spread after it was behind the mountains and the sky turned gold high up and green along the horizon.

Spring. And spring, like winter, meant five dollars a week, if he was lucky. There would certainly be a slack season after Easter—they can't buy clothes for ever, the bastards—and five dollars would be a fabulous memory. So living was that: spring and summer, the harvest and the winter and snow and waiting. Lou, darling, what can we do? We've got to hurry, there's so little time and I have nothing to hope for, but it's spring now....

He was very tired. 'It'll smell good in the woods,' Lou said. 'Let's take a little walk and then you go to bed.'

She held his hand. She thought: he must marry me now, soon. He said we would in the spring. And if he won't do that because he's afraid to think of us starting all over just like our parents, then we've got to be lovers. We must have something, we must have something.

She was watching her feet, her head lowered against the golden sky. Oppressed with the soft air and the rich warmth of the earth and the smell of rotting wood and new leaves. She almost crushed it with her foot and jumped as if it were a snake.

'What is it?' Jim grabbed her arm. 'What's the matter, Lou?'

Her face was very pale. She stooped and gently uprooted it.

'It's a crocus,' she said.

He passed his hand over his eyes, his forehead: too tired to think. What was there to do now? What could he offer her? Could he bear to look at his wife and know that she wasn't his at all, that something as remote as the Government and as immediate as a social worker was providing for her?

'Jimmy, if you don't want to get married, all right. But let's show it's spring, anyhow, and we did get through the winter. I'll be proud to be lovers with you.'

'I can't give you anything, Lou.'

'I want you, Jimmy. I don't want anything else at all. I don't care how I live or anything if I have you.'

'You're so beautiful, Lou. What if a rich man came along . . . ?'

She put her hand over his mouth quickly. 'Jimmy. You can't say things like that.'

'It is a crocus,' he said and took it from her, holding it carefully, the white flower bright against the stained palm of his hand. 'It's spring, Lou.'

He looked at her as if he wanted to remember her when she wouldn't be there. She thought swiftly, this is the best, this is the best, anyhow, no matter what happens later. The woods are ours and there would be nothing as fine as this anywhere even for the people with money. And we're young and this is love, no matter what things ever happen to us.

'I love you, Jim.'

He picked her up in his arms tenderly; he felt that he was walking under water, everything swayed around him, he had a feeling of being carried on the air, only touching the ground lightly as someone who dances, flies, floats in green clear water. He walked with her towards a place where the pines grew close together, and behind them the narrow clean trunks of the birches rose with little leaves like green smoke high against the high gold sky. There was moss on the ground, and a tiny unceasing noise as of things moving faintly, insects, buds opening, the air sliding among the leaves and curling under the moss. It was in his eyes and his throat, this small steady pulse of the woods, and his body was shaken and warm with it. He could not feel her weight in his arms, and he knelt to ease her on the moss. She looked up at him with clear welcoming eyes and the crocus fell from his hand and was crushed between them.

Every day he waited for Mr Smithers' voice to rise at him cordially saying: 'It's slack now, Jim, we don't need you any more.' I wonder what he'll give me this time: a pair of ear muffs or a purple tie? He watched Mr Smithers with fear and hatred and was surprised each day when Mr Smithers only said good night.

He lived now for the end of the day, after supper, meeting Lou in the woods, with the sky still golden and staying until the sky was blue like not too deep water and then, later, like black fur. They had different places where they met, sometimes under the pines, with the fallen needles a little damp, but slippery and smelling a cool male smell. Sometimes on the moss, the moss sagging softly under them and green and staining their clothes. They watched the birch leaves uncurl and grow until they were like close-woven gauze across the sky: they picked out different trees and each day waited for them to hasten ahead to summer. They spoke very little because there was nothing to say; there was only the moment, the hour, to live and to be glad of. And they were afraid to think for fear thinking would mean planning. They could make no plans. Five dollars was five dollars.

'Lou,' he said. 'Are you happy?'

'I think I'm dreaming.'

'If you ever left me or got tired or didn't love me, I wouldn't want to live.'

'Yes,' she said. 'Don't be a sap.'

One night he had just said: 'You know what? I think you're more beautiful than Marlene Dietrich.'

She said: 'Jim, I got to talk to you.'

'Do you want to be introduced, Miss Weylin?'

'No, it's serious.'

'All right.' He tightened his arm around her shoulder and watched his cigarette, like an anchored glow-worm before him.

'We have to get married, at least I think so,' she said.

He said nothing.

'You got to say something, Jim.'

'I don't know how to say it. I'm sorry as hell because it's my fault, and it isn't fair on you. And the other thing is, I don't want to do anything except marry you. That's all I got to say.'

She was crying now, as softly as the air moving in the leaves. Her body felt limp beside him. 'I was afraid you wouldn't want me. I was afraid you'd do it because you'd have to.'

'Oh, Lou, are you crazy, sweetheart, don't you know anything, don't you know anything at all?'

'And it isn't any different now from what it was.' She drew in her breath and said it: 'We'll still have to go on Relief, specially with a baby.'

'Little Jimmy,' he said, 'who's going to Andover.'

He felt her turning her head away from him, against the moss.

'I didn't mean it like that, Lou.'

'Yes, you did.'

'He'll be a fine baby.'

They lay there quietly and a star perched like a bird on the top of a tall pine.

Suddenly, Lou sat up. 'Listen Jim. Listen to me. This is the last time I'm going to say any of this to you and either you got to understand or we won't have that baby and we don't have to get married. I'll go on being lovers anyhow. But, if we're going to get married, you got to get this straight.' He was sitting up too, leaning against a tree trunk, seeing her profile in the darkness, the little chin hard and her voice quiet, an older voice than hers had ever been, and sure.

'We will have to go on Relief. That's not our fault. You work when you can and you work as hard as any man could. You'd do anything you got a chance to. It isn't your fault if we have to go on Relief. It's their fault. It's the fault of the rich people who run things, it's not the fault of people like us. We'll take what we can get from the Relief and not go around thanking them either. If we can work and want to work, we're not beggars, no matter what anybody says. If we get married, Jim, and have to get help because they messed up everything, we will. But we *can't* be ashamed Jim. We *can't* be ashamed. We may as well go ahead and die if we're ashamed.'

Her body was bent with sobs. The words came out in jerks, but her voice was clear, and rang in the woods, with anger and with passion. He sat watching her, he hadn't known she was able to talk this way, and he knew, suddenly, that she was right. A man without two bits in his pocket was a bum, a man without a job was unemployed, the same thing as saying unfit, a loafer, a drain on society. But that was what they thought, and they were the ones who had let this mess happen. She was right. He knew it, and she did. No matter what the other people, with jobs and money in the bank and taxes to pay, might think. He and Lou could stand together and take it. They were all right. He had his goddam hands and his goddam muscles and anybody could hire them. If nobody wanted them, that wasn't his fault. It might make his life hell and hers too, and it was nothing to bring a baby to, but anyhow it wasn't shameful. They could stand together. . . .

'Lou,' he said, 'we'll get married and we'll maybe manage to live on what I can get. And maybe we'll have to go on Relief sometimes. But anyhow we won't be licked.'

'Then it's all right,' she said.

'It's all right now.'

She slept on his shoulder thinking, until winter anyhow we won't need any money for rent, and I read a story once about shipwrecked people living on berries. . . .

They were going to be married tomorrow, Sunday. He had lain awake all night thinking of it. He kept saying to himself: 'We can't be ashamed. We aren't beggars if we can work and want to work.' And all the time he was thinking: we're young and we'll only get married once. We're young. She's so lovely that little girl with her brown face and her brown hair and her hard, smooth legs. And we'll only get married once. It ought to be grand and fine and happy and everything like the spring; I ought to be able to give her. . . . We can't be ashamed. . . . But we ought to be fine and good-looking and well dressed and everything if only once, if only now, when this is happening to us. Only to-morrow, only once will anyone say, 'And I pronounce you man and wife.' Man and wife. Jim Barr and the little brown-skinned girl; I won't be a truck driver waiting to be unemployed; my wife is not going to be married in a dingy dress she got handed out to her by the Red Cross or the Relief or somebody. My wife, my beautiful little wife. We are not ashamed. We are young and it's only going to happen once. . . .

He could hardly see the turns on the road all day; he sweated at the wheel and his hands trembled, and all day he refused to tell himself what he knew he was going to do. He had it planned in his mind, but he wouldn't give it a name. He kept saying to himself, 'Supposing a guy. . . .' But he knew he would do it. His stomach churned and writhed with the fear of it, and he knew he'd do it anyhow. His head began to ache thinking all around it, but never giving it a name, and he kept wondering isn't it almost time?

Mr Smithers gave him the last parcels, and Jim said, 'I'll turn out the lights. I'll just be a second, gotta go upstairs,' he said, pointing to where the toilet was.

'Okay,' Mr Smithers said. 'See you Monday.'

'Yes sir, good night.' The doors locked automatically. The clothes were stacked on tables under sheets, put in drawers, hung behind glass. He went upstairs and vomited into the toilet.

The shades were all pulled down in the show windows and he heard no steps on the concrete outside the door. Swiftly, but with his eyes stinging and his hands frozen and clumsy, he grabbed what he wanted. A little red dress of heavy, good crepe, cut plainly; a pair of slippers. He tore a white shirt from a box, hoping to God it was the right size, a tie, a pair of shoes from the show-case, thinking, if they're too small it's only once, it's only once. Then he went to the glass case where the good suits hung. He saw one of rich brown tweed and he could even read the price-tag on the sleeve. Thirty-five bucks, he whispered to himself and his courage almost failed. For a tormented instant he thought the glass door was locked: it stuck and squeaked as it opened, and he choked for breath. A hat for Lou, a hat for Lou, but by now there was blood before his eyes and his terror rode him. He seized the first thing he saw on a counter, a bargain counter, in his hands it felt like velvet, a little velvet beret, marked down because it was winter wear. . . .

He bundled them all together inside the suit, turned out the lights and holding himself so stiffy that he walked like a soldier on parade, to keep from running, to keep from screaming in blind panic and running down the street, he got into the truck. He drove it out near his house, left the clothes in a dry ditch, and took the truck back to the garage.

He did not sleep. The clothes were in the house; every noise was the police, and when, for an instant, he dozed he started awake sure that a flashlight had gone on in his face, sure he had heard a voice saying: 'Here he is.'

And all night he said to himself: 'Dearest Lou, we're only going to do this once; it's the only thing we're sure we'll have, it must be fine, it's going to be hard and ugly and poor afterwards, but this has to be fine. Lou, Lou. . . .' Oh, God, he thought, I hope she likes the dress.

He got up at sunrise and dressed and left the house. He walked in the woods and had to lie down, feeling weak and dizzy. He got to Lou's house, having skirted the town so that no one would see him. They were going to be married in a little church on the Ferguson Road, early, before the regular service. He wouldn't have to go through town again. Clara and Mrs Weylin were the only people who were coming, as witnesses. He waked Lou; the Weylins had no reason to lock their door.

'Jimmy,' she said. 'I'm going to be a bride.'

'I got a wedding dress for you.'

She sat up fully awake and looked at him. 'Jim,' she said, and asked no questions.

She took the red dress and held it up before her and said, 'I never saw anything so beautiful.'

'Mr Smithers loaned me the things for us to get married in,' he said. 'Oh.'

She gave him some black coffee but he was sick again, running outside. When he came back she was dressed, and Mrs Weylin was walking ahead of them, down the road towards the church.

He took Lou's hand and said: 'You love me, don't you? You'll always love me.'

'I love you better than anything in the world,' she said. 'For always.'

When they were almost at the church, she said: 'We're swell looking people, we're a swell looking couple getting married. I'm proud of us, and I'm so happy I could sing.'

That made it all right. She was glad to be lovely; the dress fitted her, the little beret sat gaily on her brown hair, and he stood beside her at the church door, thinking it was worth it, no matter what happens, it was worth it. For just this once. For just this once to have something good, to have enough, not to look and feel like people who never have anything they want.

The minister wanted to be sure to get finished before the congregation arrived, and he cut sections out of the marriage service, and there was no music. Clara looked at their clothes questioningly and said nothing, and fortunately the minister was not a worldly man, and he would never have noticed unless they had been inadequately covered. Jim held Lou's hand, and she smiled at him, and he thought there's no one in the world so beautiful, no rich girl in Seattle or Spokane is as beautiful as she is. He heard nothing except the minister's voice saying: 'I pronounce you man and wife.' Her lips were trembling as he bent to kiss her. Clara's face, gaunt in the morning and tired and hurt, smiled at him as if she had lived longer than any of them, understood everything, and Mrs Weylin said: 'I hope you'll be happy. Be good to her, Jimmy. God bless you.'

They shook hands with the minister, and walked out into the sunlight. Lou stood for a minute on the church steps, preening herself, with her hand on Jim's arm. 'Mrs James Barr,' she said. 'Oh, Jimmy! Oh, Jimmy!'

I should have stolen a ring, Jim thought. I should at least. Mrs

Weylin had lent hers, and now Lou gave it back but gaily, not as if she minded.

'Good luck to you kids,' Clara said. 'See you later. I guess I'll go home and get Dad his lunch.' Mrs Weylin kissed Lou.

I pronounce you man and wife, Jim thought; and for once we are as good as anybody, married in a church and looking fine, looking like people who have a home to go to and a job. . . .

'Well, good morning.'

He noticed then that old Mrs Sankey from Harriston was walking up the path to the church; she would get there early. Wanting a front row seat and a chance to look at everybody as they came in.

'What're you kids doing here? Didn't know you belonged to this congregation.'

'We don't,' Lou said, and her voice sang, and the sun flashed off her. 'We just got married. This is my husband. I'm his wife.'

'Well, congratulations. It's a fine day to be getting married.' She was closer now. She stopped and stared at them curiously. 'And my heavens if you aren't swell, you're sure dressed up for your wedding all right. Where'd you got those fine clothes; I haven't seen anything so pretty for a month of Sundays, not up here in a poor congregation, though you might see such things down to the Reverend Johnstone's church.'

'We . . .' Lou started and Jim tightened his hold on her arm until she bent a little towards him, silenced, startled, her face responding to the pain.

'Santa Claus,' Jim said. 'He takes care of good little children. We got to hurry. We're taking the day off for our honeymoon.' He waved to her and walked Lou swiftly down the path to the road.

'I stole them,' he said. 'The clothes. I had to. We couldn't get married as if it was any old day.'

She pressed his hand against her cheek, but they did not stop.

'I loved our wedding, Jimmy. I'm glad you did it. And it's all right. We'll go away quick to another state, Washington or something, and have the baby, and they'll forget all about us.'

'It's a fine thing to ask your wife to run away like you're a murderer.' He was whispering to her, but he didn't know it.

'If you were a murderer, I wouldn't care.'

'You can't come; they'll find us, I know they will, they always get you, I'm not going to let them get you in prison, Lou. Oh Lou, I love you, you know how it was.'

'I don't care at all,' she said. 'I'm glad you did it. And it's not running away. It's just our honeymoon.'

He stared at her: was it true, was it possible anyone could be so serene and not frightened by anything, not by the police or hiding or all the things they didn't even know about that lay ahead? Could anyone love him like this?

'It'll be swell having the accordion,' she said in a clear voice.

He stopped then and kissed her. There were things he couldn't say, he didn't know how to thank her. Suddenly he heard voices behind them, coming towards them. Whose voices, what were they saying, whose voices? His hand clamped on her arm, and he pulled her with him, down the road, away from the voices, faster faster, the dust streaking over their new stolen shoes. Don't run, he said to himself, oh for God's sake don't run, don't run! . . .

$\mathcal{R}$UBY

Ruby let the wind push her head back. Her coat, made from her father's old one, flapped out behind, and one of her stockings tore loose from its safety pin fastener and rumpled around her ankle. 'Hoo-wee,' Ruby shouted. The coaster bounced every time it went over a crack in the pavement and Ruby hung on tight and shrieked with fear and joy. 'Lookit, lookit!' she screamed seeing Myra standing on the corner down the street. 'Lookit me! Lookit how fast I'm going.' The coaster all but flew across a crack, and Ruby bent over the wooden handle and prayed that it wouldn't break. 'Hey Ruby, you be careful,' Johnny yelled from up the block, cupping his hands around his mouth to make the words carry. 'You be careful of my coaster.' Ruby didn't answer. Her hair lifted from her head in brown wisps and floated like water weed; her hands were cracked and chapped with cold, but she didn't notice. She gripped the wooden handle bar until her knuckles stood out white, and sang to herself not opening her lips. Lookit me, lookit me, I'm flying! . . . Finally it had to end. She bumped off the curb at the end of the street, and Johnny screamed with fury, saying: 'Damn you, Ruby, you'll go and break my coaster; what do you think it's made of anyhow, iron? I'll never never let you ride on my coaster again.'

She turned and pushed it up the street. 'I didn't mean to, Johnny; it just wouldn't stop, it was flying. But it's all right,' she said, and slowly, lovingly, ran her stiff hands over the coaster. Johnny had made it himself. Johnny was twelve: Ruby thought he was the smartest man alive.

'Come here,' Johnny said, 'gimme that coaster. You don't deserve getting a ride the way you do with it, bumping it. Looks like you're just trying to break it.'

'I wasn't, Johnny. I wouldn't break it. Please, Johnny,' Ruby said very sweetly, blinking up at him, 'please, Johnny, can I ride it again?'

'No, I gotta go somewheres on it. I got work to do to-day.' Johnny pushed off, going very fast, grating down the hill. Myra came up and sat on the front steps with Ruby.

'It's cold,' she said, rubbing her hands together. 'I wish I had gloves.'
'Me too.'
'You got any coal at your house?'
'Yes, some. The Relief lady come to us Tuesday. You wanna come in and get warm?'
'Yes. We ain't got none. We ain't had none for four days. My Pa sez he's gonna steal some off the railroad tracks to-night, but Ma sez no, he oughtn't, because Miz Hammerstein's husband got arrested for stealing coal off the tracks.'

'Oh,' Ruby said, not hearing or remembering, 'well my seat is cold, too, come on in. Listen, Myra, d'ju think we could make a coaster, d'ju think we could find that lumber place and all?'

'Where'd we get the wheels from?'

'Maybe they got old wheels in garbage cans; I saw ole Maria down by the river poking in garbage cans and she gets a lotta junk.'

'Well,' Myra said, settling the matter judicially.

They went into the house. All the houses in that block, and in the blocks around it, were brick, two and three stories high. Most of them seemed empty; dirty windows or none at all, and cold and barren with no one moving around them or in them. Being winter still, or the bleak beginning of spring, the street was quiet. No one could afford to go outside and get cold.

Six families lived in the house. Ruby lived with her mother in one room. There was a stove and a streaked sink in it for washing dishes and bodies and clothes. In the hall on the second floor the bathroom, grey and unlighted, boasted a choked-up tub and a toilet with a broken seat.

Ruby said hullo casually to a little boy who peeked out of a door on the first floor. 'Hullo, Tim,' Myra said. Tim was Johnny's littlest brother, he was three years old; there were four others and then Johnny: the Durkins lived in three rooms, the biggest apartment in the house.

Ruby knew her way up the steps: the gloom of the stair well was something she could remember always, from all the other houses, ever since she could walk. Steps were something you felt but didn't see. 'Hey,' Myra said, 'where's the bad step?'

'Up here, come on. I'll show you.' Ruby waited. 'There, better step up two, the other one's about gone too.'

They opened a door on the third floor. Mrs Mayer was washing clothes in the sink.

'Hullo, Miz Mayer,' Myra said. 'S'nice and warm here. We ain't got no coal at our house.'

'Oh,' Mrs Mayer said. 'Well, sit down by the stove and get your hands froze out. Ruby,' she said suddenly, 'what have you done to your stockings; you know you ain't got any others, and now you've gone and tore off most all the top. I've a mind to spank you.'

'I didn't mean to, only I was flying,' Ruby said, her face cloudy and dazed with the lovely memory, 'flying through the air with the wind yelling at me.'

'She means she was coasting on Johnny's coaster,' Myra said.

Myra pulled out a handful of something—it might have been a cushion, or a wad of blanket or just rags, and sat down on the floor by the stove. Her mother had said that the Mayers were even worse off than some; there was a kitchen table and two uncertain chairs in the room, and against the wall, heaped-up, a mass of greyish-brownish something; old clothes and rags and rests of blankets. Mrs Mayer and her daughter slept on this; pulling it under them for softness, and over them for warmth. Mrs Mayer was nice, Myra thought to herself, but her house was awful. Still it was warm; they were good and lucky to have got their coal this week.

'Our Relief lady didn't come this week,' Myra said chattily, realizing it was her duty as guest to keep the conversation going.

'Who is she now?'

'Mizz McAdams. She's purty and young, but she don't know nuthin' Ma sez.'

'Well, if she's good to you that all that counts,' Mrs Mayer said. 'Ours is purty good, Mizz Sanders. About coal anyhow, and she sez she's gonna get Ruby some shoes. But my, we do have to scrounge on food. She's only giving us $3.50 a week, and that child likes to eat.'

Ruby sat on one of the uncertain chairs and dangled her legs, thinking about the coaster. Of course, Johnny was twelve and she was only ten, and he was a boy and they could do more than girls, and they were smarter; but still she didn't see why she couldn't find wood and wheels and things, and then if she couldn't *make* the coaster Myra would help, and Myra was as old as Johnny so she ought to know how to do things.

Myra's hands were a normal colour now, and she felt warm enough to leave. 'Guess I'll go,' she said. 'Thanks, Miz Mayer.'

'I'm coming too,' Ruby said. 'G'bye Ma, I'll be back for supper.'

'Yes,' Mrs Mayer said, bending her back over the sink. The door slammed and she could hear Ruby saying: 'Look out, that's the bad step'; and she scrubbed the thin remains of Ruby's night-gown and her own and her one pair of underpants and Ruby's other dress and two towels. God, she thought, she sure will be here for supper and breakfast and lunch. If only people could get along without food, Mrs Mayer thought, it would be easier for all of us. And she thought with almost horror of bread soaked in soup again another night; thinking to herself it would be a lovely thing now to have a nice hamburger steak and some canned peaches. . . . She kicked the rags back against the wall and hung the family wardrobe on the line to dry. And then sat down on a chair and looked at her idle, ugly hands, without seeing them.

Myra went home, and Ruby, saying nothing about her plans, drifted down the street. When she was out of sight of her block she walked fast and surely towards the river. Presently she stopped and, looking behind to be sure she knew no one in this neighbourhood, she walked into an alley. When she began on the first garbage-pail it seemed to her a hard thing she had decided to do. She found a stick and prodded around, wrinkling her nose and trying to hold her breath. She couldn't find anything. She stood off and looked at the pail and her heart went out of her work. 'Stinking,' she said to herself. 'What awful smells there are.' She turned and started back but remembered suddenly, with passion, the wind flying down the hill and how her heart thudded with the speed and the dangerous exciting way the coaster leapt the cracks.

'No,' she said aloud. 'No, I'm gonna find wheels.'

The alley was long. Every other house had a garbage-pail, and a few houses had regular ash-pits, twice as tall as Ruby. Her stocking furled around her ankle, and the brown weedy hair fell over her eyes. Her hands were cold and slowly dirtier, stained and evil, with coffee grounds under the nails and grease from other people's waste food. She dug in with her hands now furiously, tearing out egg-shells and old cans, and once she cut her hand and stopped, not hurt but disgusted to see her blood running on to the clammy rests of food. For over an hour Ruby zigzagged down the alley from one garbage-pail to another, stirring the tops of the ash-pits, when she could reach them, wearily. She found a broken comb and in an ash-pit an old sewing-basket that had once been green raffia trimmed with red. She kept these. But there were no roller skates. Night came down, and she couldn't see what her hands were getting into, but only feel the slime of food over them. A cat scraped against her bare leg and she screamed softly. It was cold. Her hands and her legs and the foot which had only half a sole to keep it from the ground, tingled and ached with the cold. There weren't any roller skates; not even just old wheels, any kind of wheels at all.

She put the basket under her coat and got both her hands inside the sleeves to warm them, and limping a little, to try to keep the almost bare foot off the alley cobbles, she walked home.

Mrs Mayer was angry, because she had had to keep the soup on longer, waiting for Ruby. Some had boiled away, and that made less to eat when already there was so little. She shook Ruby and said what are you doing out so late, don't you know, and how about dinner, you're a naughty girl, and what have you got there?

Ruby gave her the basket and Mrs Mayer looked at it not knowing what to do with it: it wasn't pretty or useful, but the child had brought it. 'Where did you get it, Ruby?'

'I found it,' she said, her voice heavy and toneless with fatigue and disappointment.

'Thank you, Ruby, it was nice of you.'

'All right.'

Ruby sat opposite her mother at the kitchen table and soaked her bread in the soup and swallowed it without tasting it or thinking that she was hungry and it was good to eat. No wheels anywhere. Lucky there was only the oil lamp and her mother not a very noticing woman anyhow. She'd wiped her hands on a piece of paper, blowing down the street, and then on her coat. But still there were coffee grounds under the nails and they smelled. 'Can I wash after supper?' she said.

'Sure, but whatever for, in this cold weather?'

'Well,' Ruby said.

They slopped up the damp bread.

Ruby thought, with misery, of the afternoon; there was no use in anything. Even if she could go to every garbage-pail in the whole city she wouldn't find the wheels. Inside her eyelids, tears filmed and blurred the soup plate.

'Ma,' she said, 'what do you do when you got to have something?'

'Oh, got to have something.' Mrs Mayer laughed. 'You don't got to have something. You just don't get it, so I guess you don't got to have it.'

'But I mean got to have, got to have, can't not have,' Ruby insisted.

'Well, there's two kinda things I guess,' Mrs Mayer said, and her voice sounded remote and gentle. 'Some things you ask God for, Ruby, and some things you ask the Relief lady, and sometimes you get them.'

Presently Mrs Mayer said, 'All right, Ruby,' and Ruby said, 'Yes, g'night Ma,' and Mrs Mayer blew out the oil lamp.

Ruby lay under her share of the rags and whispered softly, so that only God could hear and not her mother: 'God, if you got time, please put a garbage-pail somewhere I can find it with an ole roller skate inside. I'll be awful good if you do.' She lay quietly a moment, wondering if that would be enough. She knew this wasn't the kind of thing you could ask the Relief lady for. She understood about Relief; it was the

Government. It gave you food and coal, and if you died, so her mother said, it would pay for the funeral. But it didn't care about her and Johnny and coasters and things you just got to have.

Ruby hurried past the gate, walking sideways, as if to protect herself from attack, looking over her shoulder. Two big girls with rouge put crookedly on their cheeks sat on the gate, swung their legs and jibed at two boys. This was their way of flirting, a kind of bet-you-can't technique. They were all from the eighth grade. Ruby didn't know them, but she could tell by their size. She was in the third grade herself. Looking at them, she suddenly wondered whether she would ever get through all the rooms that separated her from them, all the blackboards, all the teachers, all the mornings with her stomach empty and growling to itself. She walked across the brick yard. There was a slide, overrun by children; they crowded up it and slid down it at the same time; the younger children stood in line waiting, with the patience of the weak, while some big boys directed the performance, shouting orders and yanking smaller children off, in mid-air, if they disobeyed. Children slid down head first, ran down, went down on their knees with their hands pressed together as if in prayer. The littlest ones crawled around underneath the supports and the whole thing seemed about to crack, crushing everyone in an uproar of arms, legs, bricks and torn tin. The yard itself was square, fenced in by an iron rail, bricked, and behind it rose the square, dead, brick wall of the school. Aside from the slide there was nothing to play with or on. Some children, the rich or the clever, had old tennis balls, or chipped golf balls, and they batted these against the brick wall of the school, surging forward and backward like pennants in the wind, shouting. One very small child, named Alice, walked about with great dignity, and held a conversation with herself. If you stood near enough you could hear shreds of it, hints of the main plan: 'I beg your pardon, Miz Schultz, I certainly didn't mean to step on your baby . . . if you can't give me thirteen dozen of the bestest eggs you've got, Mr Hoffman, I don't s'pose I'll bother, my family is very, very big, and eats most all the time. . . .' Alice bowed to imaginary people, busy adults like herself, talked, and looked about her with blind eyes. Myra was playing post tag: she waved at Ruby, and returned to the game. Ruby scuffed her feet over the bricks and wandered around, trying to find someone she knew well enough to talk to. She sniffed the air a little, with pleasure; it was still cold, but the sun had come through and made lemon-coloured marks on the brick yard. It was March. The wind would stop in a little while, Ruby thought, and then it wouldn't matter not having gloves. The noise of the children on the slide beat around

her, and she walked aimlessly, dragging her feet, trying to remember
what spring was like. It got warm, and when it was warm it was nicer:
you could play hopscotch, if you had some chalk to mark the squares
with, in the street after supper while the sky was still light. You could
sit on the front steps after school and do nothing and feel the sun on your
back and watch the ants. There was also the sandpile she remembered,
thinking hard; it was on the river, somewhere by a factory. She had
found it when last it was warm weather, and it was as big as a mountain,
and she had rolled in it and built castles and filled her shoes and then
fallen asleep. When the waterwagon came through the streets, at the
end of the day, you could run out and get a shower, and Myra had told
her, but then it was too late, that in a park somewhere, there was a
wading pool for poor children, and anybody could go and splash around.
It would be warm soon, she thought, with great contentment, and maybe
Mother could get a pair of shoes for her from the Relief lady, so the
pavement wouldn't burn that one bare hole on her left foot and she
could drink lemonade. . . . She stopped: no, there wouldn't be any lemonade. You had to have a nickel. She hadn't had a nickel as long as she
could remember, not since Daddy had a job, long before he went away.
She decided not to think about the lemonade, but just to think about
the sandpile. It was scary because it was so high and lovely and soft and
warm. She smiled to herself and dimly watched her battered shoes
scraping over the bricks.

Suddenly, like thunder and like mosquitoes, she was surrounded by
children. Girls, because the boys never descended to mere girls' fights.
She was in a circle with children dancing all about her, jumping up and
down and shouting. What had she done, she thought, frightened and
bewildered: she hadn't been playing with anybody, she'd just been walking alone, thinking about her sandpile.

'Poor little Ruby, poor little Ruby,' the voices sang at her, sticky-
sweet and cruel. 'Won't anybody play with you, Ruby, won't anybody
play with you cuz you're too dirty, cuz you smell like old rags . . . where's
your Pa, Ruby, why don't he take care of you and get you some clothes . . .
why don't you lissen to teacher, Ruby, why're you always last in class,
why're you always asleep, Ruby, don't your mother get you enough to
eat . . . poor little Ruby, nobody loves little Ruby. . . .' The voices whined
and chanted and the circle grew: other little girls thought perhaps it was
a new game, and came to see the fun, and Ruby stood in the middle,
blinking her eyes and staring, unable to believe that this awful thing
had happened to her. What had she done, what had she done to any of
them?

Then Myra came, Myra was bigger than Ruby and she shoved her

way through the circle and stood beside Ruby, put her arm around
Ruby's shoulder and said: 'Shut up, youse, you're not so good yerselves.'
'Yah, Myra loves Ruby,' the voices said.
'She's my friend.'
'Funny kinda friends you got, your friends never wash.'
'Shut up,' Myra said. 'You oughta see where she lives, you wouldn't
be so proud then. She ain't got nothing, nor her mother neither. And
her Pa went away. Besides she's on Relief, and a lot of you is on Relief
too, so don't talk.'
'Not me,' a little girl with curly blonde hair and a hair ribbon stepped
out, her chin up, and very pleased. 'My Daddy works at the gas house,
he works steady; we ain't on no Relief, and we're not gonna be.'
'Well,' Myra said. 'Perhaps your Pa does work, Betty Perkins, but
Julia's Pa don't, and Sadie's don't, and Jane's don't, and Ruth's don't,
and most of your ole Pas don't. Mine don't. But anyhow Ruby hasn't
even got a Pa what don't work. He's gone, and she's only got one room
to live in, and nothing much in it. And I bet all your Mas gets more
Relief than her Ma does. I know my Ma does. We get $6.60 a week and
she only gets $3.50.'
'Well, why don't she get some clothes from her Relief lady, and why
don't her mother keep her clean? Ruth's mother only gets $4.20 a week
and there's more in her fambly and Ruth's clean.' Ruth shone with
delight at this tribute, and stood a little apart so that everyone could see
her.
Suddenly Ruby shouted: 'Stop.' Her voice came out of her in a
groan, harsh and deep, and they were all silent, astonished and a little
afraid. She shook off Myra's arm and stood alone, her feet planted stiff
on the bricks, her face white and the skin seeming stretched over it.
'Stop,' she said again. 'And you listen to me,' she said, 'all of you.
Don't you never talk like this to me again. I'll tear your eyes out. I'll
wait in the street for you, and kill you when you go by in the dark. You
listen,' she said, 'Myra don't know what she's talking about. I got a purty
house with lampshades and beds and a big white tub in it and 'lectricity,
and my Ma gets $10 from the Relief, and we have chicken every Sunday,
and I don't wear my good clothes here cause I don't want to spoil them,
but I put on a coat with fur every Sunday and go up to the west end to
see my Grandma, who has a big house, and my Ma beats me for getting
dirty, I'm just dirty because I wanna be, and my Pa didn't go away,' she
said. There was a pause, and even the children on the slide were quiet
and the big girls stopped swinging on the gate. 'He's dead.'
She turned and walked across the brickyard. Her feet moved very
well she was surprised to see. She held her head up high and stiff, and

stared in front of her, seeing across the street, in red and gold, the sign of the A & P grocery store. She walked out the gate and no one spoke and no one stopped her, and turning, still with purpose and dignity, she walked up the street and lost the school from sight. Then she sat down on the curb and put her face in her hands.

After the soup and bread had all been swallowed and Mrs Mayer had put out the oil lamp Ruby called to her in the darkness, across the rags.

'Ma.'

'Yes.'

'Where has Daddy gone?'

'I don't know.'

'When did he go?'

'It's more'n a year, now.' And Mrs Mayer turned over on the rags, easing her back, turning her face to the wall, because these things didn't bear thinking about.

'Why did he go?'

' 'Cause he said it made him crazy to sit around here all day and nothing to do. He went every day to get work, but he couldn't find nothing, and then he just got so disgusted....' For six months, Mrs Mayer thought. Looking and looking, and coming back at night with his eyes tired, and then, towards the end, he'd come home and his eyes were fierce and angry, and he wouldn't talk. Had Ruby forgotten, she wondered, how it was, towards the end; how he beat the child for no reason and how he'd shout at Ruby if she made any noise, and how jumpy and queer he was.

'He was a good Daddy, Ruby,' Mrs Mayer said, 'and when you was little he had steady work and we used to live in a nice place with three rooms and beds, but you wouldn't remember. They laid him off with a lot of others and then he couldn't find nothing. He useta work at the shoe factory. Can you remember how he looked?' Mrs Mayer asked. 'He was a big strong man,' she said softly, remembering his arms around her when they were young and he was being nice. 'When we went on Relief he went away and didn't come back for three days, and when the lady come to the house he sat and didn't say nothing, just said to me, "Gertie, you tell the lady what she wants to know." And when she left he went around the house like a crazy man and said he wouldn't let nobody come into his house and ask him questions. But she was a nice lady. I don't guess she likes to ask all them questions but she hasta. And then, when he couldn't find no work and we had to move all the time and fin'ly we got here, he just said he was going, he couldn't stand it, it would make him crazy. If he gets work he'll come back, I guess, or send us something. . . .' Her voice drifted off. Work, she thought, remembering how it had been when he earned $20 a week and they had three rooms. She kept them nice then, but now she didn't have the heart, not in this place. They'd owned their furniture, but it all got sold the last year, when they were moving to smaller places, and finally the living-room set they'd been buying for five years got sold too. After that, she didn't much care, now she didn't care about anything: you just went on living, and perhaps Bert would come back some day, if there was work for people.

Ruby rolled around on her pile of rags and shoved some under her shoulders to make it softer. She lay in the dark, thinking about her father working, and how once they had had three rooms, perhaps rooms as she'd said this afternoon, with lamp-shades and beds and a bath. 'I wonder what'sa matter,' Ruby said to herself, doubtfully. 'I wonder what'sa matter with everything.'

Ruby trod the pavement as though it were rose petals, delicately, carrying her pride within her and smiling. In her hand she held a purple tooth-brush, covered by a glass tube. She put it up before her so that the light shone through. She had won it at school for deportment.

Miss Vincent had said that she was going to give a prize to the child who had the best record for behaviour during the week. And she said also that this was Hygiene Week, so they made posters about eating apples and drinking milk, and Miss Vincent talked to them about washing and toothbrushing. Ruby had been deeply interested by all this. Especially by the pictures of the apples, which looked as good as or better than the ones at Schultz's grocery store or at the A & P. She knew, though, that you couldn't eat them because of the Relief money; you could mainly eat bread and soup and sometimes pork and potatoes and things like that, or turnip greens, which she hated. She was more hungry than usual the mornings of that week, listening to her stomach growling over the breakfast of bread and syrup, and looking at the pictures of apples and fat milk bottles. Miss Vincent made a little speech about how good Ruby had been all week and gave her the purple toothbrush and said 'Use it every night and every morning.' Some of the other girls called her teacher's pet when she went home, because they were cross they hadn't won, but she didn't care. She stroked the glass covering gently so as not to break it and felt proud and important.

'Lookit, Ma. Lookit what I got.' She showed her mother the tooth-brush and her mother asked, as she always did, with the suspicion of those who have nothing and don't get things easily: 'Who gave it to you? Where'd you get it?' Ruby explained about the prize and how they'd had lessons about brushing teeth.

'Well,' Mrs Mayer said, 'it's very purty and you can keep it on the shelf. I don't guess you can use it, because you haven't got any toothpaste.'

Ruby grabbed it and held it against her heart. No one was going to take the toothbrush and put it away; she was supposed to use it every night and morning, the way Miss Vincent said. 'I'll get toothpaste. You'll see,' she said. 'It's my toothbrush and I won it for a prize and I'm gonna use it, I'm gonna.' There was fury in her voice; this was the only thing she had of her own and she wanted it, she had a right to it, and she would keep it.

'All right,' Mrs Mayer said, soothingly, 'you get your toothpaste and use your brush and you can keep it anywheres you want.'

So Ruby smiled and held the glass case in her hand, patting it. It was the prettiest thing in their room, she thought, and at once began brooding on ways to get toothpaste.

'Well, you go on out and play, Ruby, I gotta work.'

Ruby had intended to go out and tell Johnny about her toothbrush, but she stopped and stared at her mother. What work? Doing the house was called doing the house, that wasn't work. Work was what you got paid for.

'Miz Burk, up on Elk Street, give me some washing to do for her,' Mrs Mayer explained. 'It's not much to do and she's gonna give me fifty cents. She's gotta baby coming soon so she can't do it herself. Fifty cents,' Mrs Mayer said again, with pleasure in her voice. 'We'll get some hamburger and some canned peaches and have a real supper to-morrow night, Ruby.'

'Oh,' Ruby said and sat down on one of the chairs to take time to imagine this.

'There'll be a dime left over. What shall we do with that?'

'Candy,' Ruby said instantly. 'Some heavenly hash like they have in the window at the Greek's.'

'Oh, no, we oughtn't to do that. We ought to get something nourishing. We could get a can of spaghetti for the next night.'

'Please, Ma. Please, Ma.'

'Now, don't be silly, Ruby, it isn't often I can pick up a piece of work and we gotta get all the extra food we can. I've walked around here till I thought my feet would fall off, looking for some washing to do or some cleaning, and you know it isn't often I get anything. You'll just have to wait for your candy till Daddy gets a job and comes back, I guess.'

Ruby wandered down the street, thinking how stupid grown people were. I'm gonna buy candy for myself as soon as I'm big and got a job, she said; I sure am. She wondered how long it would be before she was big enough to get a job. Johnny whizzed by on his coaster. She noticed that he had nailed a box on to the floor board and that it was full of something.

'Hey, Johnny, where you going?'

'Can't stop now, going to work. See you to-morrow,' he said and was gone. It seemed very queer to Ruby that suddenly everyone was working, generally nobody had anything to do. She thought perhaps it's spread all over the city and got quite excited; saying to herself, I bet everybody's got a job now and soon Daddy'll come back and have a job and get me some toothpaste. She walked to Myra's house to see if Mr Herman, Myra's father, had a job, but when she got near the house she could hear Mrs Herman shouting at him, saying: 'Get outa here and stay out for awhile, will ya? You're just in the way, and stop picking on the kids. They ain't done nothing; it's you. You aren't much help around the house, you aren't, just sitting there and eating. If you haven't got anything else to do, go on up to the Relief and see if you can't get them shoes they promised for Louise.' And Mr Herman came out of the house, with a black, angry face, and started up the street, his shoulders hunched together and his feet dragging. I guess everybody hasn't got jobs, Ruby thought hopelessly, and never will, and Daddy won't come back.

At supper Mrs Mayer had more news.

'The Relief lady come to-day. She's got something for you.'

Mrs Mayer waited for Ruby to be curious and eager, and Ruby looked at her, questioning, expecting always and indomitably, some lovely surprise.

'She's gonna get you a pair of shoes and a gingham dress.'

'Oh,' Ruby said. 'Oh, hoo-wee . . . they won't tease me then at school and I can be clean and purty,' she said, and her mother looked at her and thought: I had it better when I was a child, this is nothing for a child to grow up into.

'Yes, Ruby.'

'Is she gonna raise our grocery order this month?' Ruby asked.

'No, she can't do that; they got all their money already give out.'

'Well, you know Bessie Norton who goes to my school; she lives with her grandmother and there's only two of them, just like us, and she said they got $4.25.'

'Yes, I know,' Mrs Mayer said wearily. 'But it don't do any good arguing, and besides, I hate to. And I guess we ought to be thankful we're getting anything. Times like they is, we'd starve if it weren't for this Relief. I can't get nothing to do, Ruby, so we better just take it and be glad it ain't worse.

'And she said that there's canned beef,' Mrs Mayer went on, and Ruby wrinkled her nose remembering it. One month the Relief lady had given them ten cans of it and she thought finally she'd rather not eat than go on with it, but luckily none had come since. 'She said it made the Golden children sick. It wasn't the beef, she said that's all right, but just they had to eat it twice a day every day for about two weeks becuz Mrs Golden's new on Relief and she don't know how to get along. And so the children all taken to vomiting, so they took them to the clinic and now they're getting milk and apples and it's all right.'

For a moment an idea, like a skyrocket, gleamed swiftly across Ruby's mind. She thought milk and apples, like the ones we put on the posters, and the soup tasted weak to her and she remembered it from many nights before, tasting the same way. Now if only I could vomit, Ruby thought, we'd get milk and apples. But then she knew she couldn't do it; she wouldn't know how. But it would be wonderful to have things like that for supper.

'Well, that's all, Ruby, so go to bed.'

Ruby took her toothbrush and laid it on the floor near her head, so that she'd see it first thing when she woke up. Presently, Mrs Mayer put out the light.

'To-morrow night we'll have hamburger and canned peaches,' she said.

'Yes, and then I'll have my dress and shoes, and I already got my toothbrush,' Ruby said. She sighed gently to herself. 'It's not such a bad life after all,' she said.

Mrs Mayer laughed quietly at the child's voice and thought to herself that Ruby sounded like an old woman, comfortable in her fat.

Ruby saw Johnny getting on a street car and was filled with wonder. Where did he get the money? He waved to her and his face, flushed and pompous, gave her to understand he was going forth on grave business. She stared after the street car a moment and went on her way. She was going down to the river. Spring had almost come; a little grass pushed up tentatively on the bruised front lawns of her block; and the air, at noon, was gentle with sun. The thought of the sandpile now ranked first in her mind, with thoughts of candy and toothpaste, and she was going to the river to see if she could again find that golden slippery mountain, near a factory, where she had played in the spring sun, last year.

She said hello to some women who were drawing water from a

spigot on the railroad tracks. She knew them by sight; they lived in the hand-built huts along the river front. Ruby had tried in vain to persuade her mother to move down here: it was so lively and exciting, with boats going by and all the little shacks lurching amiably together; and getting water at the spigot a quarter-mile away and chatting to one's friends was fun. Besides, she knew that everyone here was on Relief, and no one would shout mean things at her. None of the children looked any better than she did.

She stopped at old Maria's. Behind a shack, in a tiny littered yard, Maria's hut leaned wearily towards the ground. She had made it herself out of packing-cases and brown paper principally, and some said it stood up stiff with its own dirt. Maria was very old and very dirty and very proud. She had never applied for Relief; she ravaged the garbage pails and ate stew made of dead cats; but one day some neighbors found her fainted of hunger and then they spoke to the Relief lady, thinking it was high time. Maria had refused to answer any questions and when the Relief order came in for groceries, she quietly tore it up and let it float out in small pieces onto the river. The neighbors argued with her but she said she wanted only to be left alone: that was the way she had lived and she could well afford to die that way. Ruby loved her because she would sit in the sun, not noticing time, and tell stories of gypsies and talk to her dogs as if they were human, discussing with them how they felt about life and what kind of funeral they preferred. She found Maria home, making a pillow out of a burlap sack she had salvaged. She was wearing a greenish-black broadcloth jacket with silken frogs and puffed sleeves, which dated from the last century. She greeted Ruby politely and invited her to sit beside her on the dirt, in the sun.

'How're you, Maria?'

'I am being robbed,' Maria said amiably. 'I don't mind that at all but I do mind having that woman always poking and snooping about and never, never leaving me alone for a minute.'

That woman was the owner of the shack in front of Maria's. Ruby always saw her standing in the yard combing her hair. She had black hair, straight and stiff like a paint brush, and Ruby didn't care for her face. It was too square and her eyes were like raisins and never laughed.

'What's Emma doing to you?' She lowered her voice because Emma, they said, could hear every word that was spoken all up and down the river front, and she was a bad woman to anger.

'Oh, she takes all my grocery orders; she makes me go to the store and get things, and then she takes it all,' Maria said.

Ruby looked at Maria in amazement; why wasn't she crying or hating Emma, why wasn't she doing something about it? That was the very worst thing that could happen to you, to have your food stolen; since food was the only thing you had.

'Do you hate her, Maria? I hate her, I hate her for you.'

'No, it doesn't matter about the food. I can get on very well without it. I go around and find things, and they give me the stale bread at the bakery ... but she's so afraid I'll tell the Relief lady or some of the neighbours that she stays around all the time watching me, and I never have a minute. I'm going to have to move,' Maria said. 'There's a very nice cabin up above the warehouse selling for $4.00, but God knows where I'll find the money. However,' she said, 'and how are you, Ruby?'

'Oh, I'm all right. I just came down to-day looking for the sandpile.'

'The barge, you mean? Well, it's right up the river, about fifteen minutes walking for me. Take care you don't roll off and down, though I've often thought it would be a nice way to die.'

'I don't wanna die.'

'No, of course you don't.'

'Specially now it's almost spring.'

'Yes, of course,' Maria said, 'now it's almost spring.'

Ruby got up and bid Maria good-bye, and said she'd call again. She wandered up the street, waving to women on their porches, stopped to talk to some boys who were fishing hopelessly but with interest from the river-bank, looked with admiration at a new toilet Mr Holz had put up right in front of his house, in the centre of his river view, scuffed her feet, practised walking on the rails and hopping from one tie to the next, and sang to herself, with pleasure. Presently she came to the barge. It looked even more golden than she had remembered. Far below it the river ran smooth, thick, and grey. Across the flat water lay Illinois, with the trees sticking out of the river, and she could even see little houses, like Maria's hut, half standing in water, ready to float if they hadn't been so soggy. Farther down the river thin chimneys like asparagus pointed up into a sky made grey with their own smoke. And a little way up men were busy pushing boxes and sacks around the warehouse, and a string of barges floated on the water, waiting to be filled.

The sand barge was tied up alone; the sand rose like a giant golden loaf, steep up the sides and round on the top. Ruby slid down the bank and jumped the distance between the barge and the land. Slowly she crawled up the sides of the pile feeling the sand running down the neck of her dress and scratchy and warm against her legs. Her shoes were filled, and the damp top sand stuck to her hands and arms. She hummed to herself, thinking that now spring had really come, and soon school would stop, and she could play here every day all summer long. Perhaps she would even bring Myra and Johnny with her. Ruby sat on the top of the barge and surveyed the world. Those little match boxes down the river were the homes of her friends; those funny small rabbits scurrying around were the warehouse men; she was on a par with the factory chimneys, for size and height, she thought, and up here one could talk rather bossily even to God. She sat straight and began making speeches to the small inferior lives below her. 'Miz Sanders, you fix it right away so my Daddy comes home and gets a big job, and we are moved to a fine house with 'lectricity. . . . Hello, Hello, is this the Green Street Drug Store? This is Ruby Mayer talking. Please send me a dozen tubes of toothpaste to my new house, the most expensive kind you have. . . . Well, Johnny, I'll give you $1 for your coaster, and I think you're making a lot on it. . . .'

'Pooh,' she said suddenly and largely, and waved her hand to encompass the whole city, the entire world she knew, 'Pooh, for you. Nothing. You're nothing at all. You and your ole Relief and everything. Me, I'm queen of the sand mountain.' Whereupon she rolled down her stockings so that her legs were bare to the sun, pulled her dress up as far as it would go and opened it at the throat, lay down on her back, and went to sleep, dreaming of nothing more definite than light and warmth.

'Hey kid,' a voice shouted, 'Hey, you kid, come down from there.' She sat up, blinking at the sun, and saw the man standing with his head back and his eyes shaded, shouting at her. It made her furious. Who was this man to wake her up, to wake her up on the sand which was her own, and come into her private world like that, noisily bossing people when he had no right to?

'Why?'

' 'Cause that sand belongs to the Government, and nobody's supposed to mess it up.'

'I don't care. I don't know the Government.'

'You come on down, anyhow, or I'll come up and get you and give you a good beating for it.'

'Don't you dare,' she screamed. 'Don't you dare. You leave me alone. If you come up here I'll jump in the river and drown myself. I will so. Don't you dare come up here. It's mine. It's the only place I have, and I'm gonna keep it.'

'Hey, now,' the man said, in a different voice. 'Don't you do that, kid, don't you jump in no river. All right, you stay up there then, but don't come here again.' He turned and walked towards the houses, and Ruby shouted at his back: 'I will so. I'll come whenever I want to. It's my sand. You tell your ole Government to stay away from me, or I'll drown myself.'

The man was out of sight, and slowly her heart stopped thumping with anger and the terrible fear that perhaps he would climb up anyhow, and she'd have to jump. She spread her legs apart, and scooped a mound of sand towards her, and began fashioning a house. This is my new house, she told herself, a very big one, with trees and a room for me, and a bed. . . .

The water shone and went black as the sun set and wind furled the sand into ridges. Ruby climbed down, having waited until goose flesh crawled out on her legs, to be sure she was too cold to stay longer.

Mrs Baker saw her coming down the path, called street, and waved to her and said, 'Come on in Ruby, and have supper with the girls. Minnie May earned some money working for a lady to-day, and we got canned tomatoes and pie.' Ruby couldn't believe what she had heard.

'Did you say I was to come and eat with you?'

'Sure.'

Ruby stood in the dusk and teetered on her feet, and turned this new and amazing idea over in her mind. People did not give and receive invitations, that she knew of. She had always eaten at home in the room that was sometimes dining room, sometimes kitchen, sometimes both and bedroom as well, depending on where they lived. This, she supposed, was what you would call a party.

'I'm not awful clean, I haven't got on a nice dress,' she said, doubtfully.

'Neither have we,' Minnie May shouted from behind her mother. 'What do you think we are anyhow? Come on in.'

Ruby sat at the Bakers' table, and noticed that their oil lamp had a nice red shade; and that there were two rocking chairs and three beds in the room, and oilcloth on the table, and quite a few cups and saucers and plates and things. The food tasted good to her, and it was surprising to have something besides soup and bread for supper. Minnie May was fourteen, and the heroine of the evening, because she had provided the money for this feast. 'I gotta job doing some cleaning for a lady,' she said, and Ruby looked at her with awe, because Minnie May was smart and big and could earn money. There was Ellen who was Ruby's age, but not very smart; she just sat at home all day and talked to herself. Everybody was nice to her, but she frightened Ruby a little, because her eyes looked blind, and she never seemed to hear anything that was said. Ruby ate and looked at the room with envy, whenever she thought the Bakers couldn't see her. And Mr Baker talked about how bad times were, saying to Mrs Baker, 'They tell me they're laying men off at the Chevrolet even now; and the shoe factory is gonna move outa town, and the box factory went bust; even them poor wops working at the spaghetti factory is getting fired.'

And he said to Mrs Baker, 'It's a terrible thing when the only person in this family can make a little money is that Minnie May, and her just a kid still.'

'Well,' Mrs Baker said, 'we gotta be thankful at least she can.'

After supper Minnie May said to Ruby: 'You wanna come with me to the Pentecost meeting up-town? It's kinda church, but not really.'

And Ruby, who never did anything but go to bed at night, thought it was surely Christmas, or a dream, so many things happening at once.

On the way, Ruby asked about jobs: 'Do you think I could maybe get something cleaning? We need money at our house awful bad.'

'You'd be purty enough if you washed your hair and face, and had a clean dress,' Minnie May said thoughtfully. 'You got a kinda cute little face.'

'Do you have to be purty to get jobs cleaning,' Ruby asked with despair, because she knew then she'd never find anything.

'I don't clean,' Minnie May said, with scorn, laughing to herself. 'That's what I tell Pa and Ma.'

'What do you do?' This was getting more exciting and mysterious as it went on, and Ruby looked up at Minnie May with admiration. That was a girl who knew how to get what she wanted. Smart like Johnny. But, perhaps, she thought, when I'm as big and as old as they are, I'll be smart too.

'Oh I dunno, I'll tell you sometime, maybe. And maybe you can work with me.'

The Pentecost church was just a meeting-room, with board benches and bare walls, and electric-light bulbs hanging from cords. They slipped in and found seats near some other children. A man was walking up and down the platform, like a caged polar bear, and also like a cricket, jumping and prowling, clapping his hands, saying 'Praise God,' as punctuation for his sentences, and the rest of the time rambling off into a shouted discourse, without sequence, to which no one listened. Ruby looked around and saw a lot of children she knew at school, and some of the river-front people. She wondered if they came often, because it wasn't very funny, this man just saying a lot of words.

Then people sang and Ruby was jealous seeing Betty Perkins and her sister, in clean dresses and hair-ribbons, singing on the platform. They sung songs that whined and twanged, and presently there was a collection, and the meeting ended.

Ruby was going home, but Minnie May said 'Now's when the fun begins. You see,' Minnie May explained, 'There's always somebody wants to get the Holy Ghost, and now is when they start.'

They moved up front and watched. Women at one end, men at the other; two feet from the floor was a board, for praying. The woman rocked, shouted, prayed; and a girl of about seventeen came forward: a process of hypnosis by noise, shouting the same things over and over, began. The girl aided by clenching her fists, holding her body rigid, and generally working herself into a frenzy. She wept and trembled, and the shouting went on.

'Why are they so mean to her,' Ruby whispered, 'what did she do?'

'Nothing, silly, she's getting the Holy Ghost. You wait, she'll pass out in a little while and begin talking funny.'

With their eyes wide and gleaming the old women bent over the girl, shouting at her: 'Sinner Repent; Open up your heart; Make ready for the Holy Ghost....' Their bodies swayed and curled like spaghetti boiling in a pot, and they shouted and leaned over the girl, their breasts hanging above her, their eyes evil and alight. Her face grew mottled, and her hair was damp on her forehead; the backbone made a neat line under her rayon dress as she bowed and tossed, in the agony of prayer. Ruby stood on the bench and watched with horror. It was too mean, why didn't they leave the girl alone, why did they have to go on shouting at her that way? She moved off, to escape the sight, if not the sound. A little boy of four was sitting on a chair, looking at his feet. 'Do you like it?' she asked him.

'No.'

'It's awful noisy, isn't it?'

'Oh thas all right. Noise here, noise at home. Thas all right.'

She sat by him in silence, and was frightened. There was a man too, at his end of the praying-board, and the men took turns, shouting over him, exhorting and pleading; but their gestures were hammer-strokes up and down, not the writhing and coiling and twisting of the women.

Presently there was a shout and a silence; the girl had fallen backwards on the floor, in a faint. The old women waited, hanging over her, and suddenly her body came alive, and lashed against the floor, and strange words, senseless and jumbled, came from her mouth. 'She's got it,' Minnie May whispered. 'She's got the Holy Ghost. It's kinda scary don't you think?'

'It's awful,' Ruby said. 'I wanna go home.'

Minnie May and she walked out into the darkness. Ruby was relieved when they got out of the sound of those voices, and she blinked to forget what she had seen.

'Why do you go there, Minnie May?'

'Where else kin I go? You can't just go to bed every night, all the time. Gotta go somewheres. That's the only place I know it don't cost nuthin. That's why all us kids go. In summer you kin go and sit with a boy on the river,' she said; 'but it's too cold yet. Jest gotta do something. Anything's good enough if you ain't got the money.'

'Tim's sick,' Johnny said.
'What's he got?'
'Difteria.'
'Oh.' Ruby knew that was a bad thing to have, worse than measles for instance; you could probably die of difteria.
'They ain't got the money to give him what he should have.'
Ruby said nothing; of course they didn't. Mr Durkin didn't have a job either. Johnny said once to her that his pa never would have a job again. His pa was a motor-man. 'They don't want street-cars anymore,' Johnny said, 'they want buses. He ain't any good with automobiles.'
They sat on the front steps and shivered inside their coats. It had stopped being spring; Ruby was still damp from walking to school in a fine wiry rain that streamed flat over the city all morning. Later the rain billowed in gauzy clouds. Now the wind came up, lean and sharp, and circled coldly around their feet and shoulders.
'This weather too,' Johnny said. 'It's cold in there.'
'We got some coal.'
'Yeah. Your ma already give it to us.'
'Shall I go in and play with him?'
'He can't play; he's too sick.'
Suddenly Johnny reached in his pocket and brought out a handful of nickles and pennies.
'Gawd,' Ruby said with reverence.
Johnny counted them carefully, it came to forty-three cents.
'Where'd you get it, Johnny?'
'From my business.'
'You gotta business?'
'Yeah. I'm a salesman.'
Ruby waited. Johnny was too wonderful, too smart. There was nobody like him, not even Minnie May.
'Remember, Ruby, when you saw me getting on the street car?'
Ruby nodded, her mouth open, seeing the words before she heard them.
'Well, I was going out to sell. I get these dogs and kewpies and things made out of plaster—ain't you ever seen them, you know, at fairs or Luna Park, or beside the road sometimes? They're kind of ornermints. You put them on the mantel or on the table in the parlour. They're kinda cheap stuff, break easy and I don't think they're purty. But some women buy them. Well, I get them from a guy over on Maple Street,

and I sell them for twenty-five cents and I keep five cents. First I took them on the coaster, but then I made enough profit to take the street car, and that way you can get out farther into better neighbourhoods.'

'What do you do when you get there; how do you start?'

'I just ring door-bells. You gotta be smart, Ruby. Y'see these things ain't really nice so you can't take them to swell houses where people wouldn't want to put them in the parlour. Then you can't take them to houses like ours, where everybody's on Relief and ain't got a quarter. So you just have to pick the neighborhood, where people got enough money, but not too much.'

'Yes,' she said, marvelling at all this.

'I ring the door-bell,' Johnny went on, 'and I take off my cap and I say would you please buy one of these purty ornermints please, lady. I'm taking care of my old sick mother.'

'But your Ma isn't old or sick.'

'I know, but they 'spect you to say something like that. Anyhow, she might just as well be; she ain't got nothing. Sometimes I say my little brother's dying. . . .'

They stared at each other in sudden fear. Johnny rose.

'I'm gonna buy him some milk and some apples,' he said. 'Wait for me.'

Ruby waited and thought about Johnny and how smart he was, and about Tim and difteria, and how it must be wonderful to work and make money and buy things when you wanted them.

Johnny ran into the house with his gifts and came out again, his face shining. 'I'll take care of them,' he said. 'They don't need to worry. I'll get Tim everything he needs. When my business is better I guess we'll move from this neighbourhood so he can be outdoors more and get some sun. . . .'

Ruby put her hand in his speechlessly, to show how much she admired him. Johnny swelled noticeably under this treatment.

'And I ain't like some,' he said darkly. 'I'm honest I mean. I get my money the right way, by working.'

'What. . . .'

'There's some I know, and you too Ruby, who gets it other ways.'

'How?'

'You know those Sweeney boys on the next block? Well, they gotta gang and they steal,' he said almost whispering.

Ruby shivered.

'Their Mas will find out,' she said.

'Mas! Christ, that don't count. It's the police.'

'Johnny,' Ruby said, after a silence. 'Lissen, I gotta have some money too. How'm I gonna get it? I'm too little to work, nobody will let me do nuthin'. And I gotta.'

'What do you want to buy?'

'Well, there's my toothbrush, and I can't use it.'

'Yeah, I forgot that.'

'And Johnny, I'd *love* some candy....'

'Well, Ruby.'

She held his hand tighter; he was going to tell her now, and perhaps to-morrow she'd have all the things she wanted, needed.

'Well, Ruby, I know how some girls get money, and it's work too really, but then it's like stealing too, because if the police catch you and anyhow....'

'What is it, Johnny?'

'It's men.'

'What about men?'

'Don't you know? Don't you know about what men do? Don't you know about those women over on Sarah Street what sit behind the windows, and wave at men and walk around the streets at night?'

There was a pause; not awkward or significant, just a silence while Ruby thought hard, wrinkling her forehead.

She remembered Sarah Street, though it was not a place she played, and she didn't think she knew any children up there. Those women: and men. She had heard something a long time ago, the older girls talking at school in the playground, but the older girls always talked about something that you never listened to much, about clothes and boys and things that didn't matter. Something the men did with those women, she remembered dimly it had something to do with being naked and you had to be in bed and it was wicked, but she couldn't think what exactly had been said.

'I heard about men once,' she said, 'but I don't zackly remember. I guess those are bad women up there anyhow aren't they, Johnny? Not like Mrs Herman and Mrs Baker and Ma.'

'Well.'

'What is it anyhow? What's those women and men and things got to do with me? You said it was girls got money.'

'No, you can't do it, Ruby. It isn't any good and you're too little. If you don't even *know*. And besides your Ma would beat you.'

'I don't care if Ma does beat me if I get the money first.'

'How about the police?'

'Oh,' Ruby said. 'Oh.' She hunched her shoulders against the wind and put her hands inside her sleeves. Then slowly she got up. 'No, I

can't do it if it's like stealing,' she said, and walked up the front steps.
She turned at the door. 'But I don't see why I can't have something too.
I never have nuthin',' she shouted. 'Nuthin', nuthin', nuthin'!' and ran
into the house with tears smearing dirtily down her face.

The sun got into their room somehow. It spattered feebly over the rags.
Ruby woke up smiling. She pushed off the rags and crawled to her
mother.

'Ma, wake up, wake up. It's my birthday. I'm eleven.'

'Is it, Ruby? Well, go back to sleep now, it's early. We can't do
nothing about a birthday anyhow.'

Ruby crept back to the rags and pulled them up around her and
turned her face to the wall. She didn't cry. She had no courage left to
cry. But why were there cakes in the bakery if not to eat them on one's
birthday, cakes with candles? And there must be some children who
woke up on their birthdays and got presents. . . . I'll get them for myself
someday, I'll get them for myself. Nobody will give me anything ever.

She didn't mention birthdays again; and all day long she kept telling
herself, it isn't my birthday, it's only Tuesday. . . .

Ruby stood in front of the shoe store window and admired her reflection.
The Relief lady had sent a new dress—it was pink, with white and
yellow daisies on it—and a pair of new brown oxfords. Mrs Mayer,
again and joyfully, had found some washing to do: Ruby wore new
underwear and a new pair of short pink socks to match the dress. She
twitched the dress where it stuck to her back with sweat, and turned
her head, ogling over her shoulder, to see how she looked from the side.
She put one foot out before her and stared at the smooth chocolate-
coloured shoes, with complete soles, and no scratches; and her socks,
like the pink cream filling of the bakery pastries, filled her with pride.

She moved into the shade of the shop doorway. Spring had been as
brief as a hand-waving. It had fluttered softly for a week or two and
gone. Now it was summer. People's heels stuck in the asphalt of the
streets and heat ricocheted from the pavements to the brick walls of the
houses. The air seemed to hiss like steam, at noon, and all day Ruby felt
little lacings of sweat weaving about beneath her clothes. At night the
room on the third floor, under the roof, was agony to endure. Finally,
she and her mother sat on the front steps, saying nothing, just waiting
for time to go by. Until at last they were too tired to notice and climbed
upstairs and lay naked on the rags. They woke with their heads thick
or aching and their mouths tasting like cotton. Ruby watched other
children in the evening, playing hopscotch, and wondered where they

got money for chalk, to mark the pavement into squares. During the day she walked about the city and licked her lips and felt her throat long and ragged with thirst, and sometimes she thought she would scream if she had to go on wanting ice cream cones and lemon pop and not getting them.

She had trained herself now bitterly not to stop at the bakery window, not to look at the candy store, or linger near the man with the little ice-cream wagon.

At the end of the afternoon when the glare no longer hurt her eyes she walked to the sand barge on the river, looked swiftly to see that no man was there to threaten her in the name of the government, and climbed up. But her thirst was always with her.

'Well,' she said to herself, waiting in the shade, having no particular place to go and nothing to do. 'Well, anyhow I'm not cold and that's something.'

And she thought, if my hair were pretty the way Minnie May's is, and if I could have big shining white teeth, from my brush, I would be very nice now with my new clothes. But, she thought, I don't want clothes and curly hair and things like Minnie May does nearly as much as I want roller skates and a jumping rope. It was funny about Minnie May anyhow; Ruby could remember how Minnie May actually had roller skates two summers ago, but now she just walked around and giggled with the other big girls and sort of teased at the boys. Ruby had seen her coming out of the ten cent store a few days ago and she showed Ruby what she'd bought: a lipstick. Ruby thought Minnie May must be getting silly or something; going and throwing money away on a lipstick as if she had a lot of it and there weren't things you really had to have. If you had as much money as all that you might as well get a bathing-suit so you could run out under the water wagon when it came through the streets. Perhaps Minnie May wasn't so smart, or perhaps it was just because she was older and people always got funny when they got older. Still Minnie May had a job. Perhaps, she thought, now that I have a new dress, I could get a job cleaning.

She cooled her forehead against the window meditating on this; after a few days she might make fifty cents. Fifty cents. She put her hand out in front of her trying to imagine how it would look with the silver half dollar in it. I could get, she started: then her mind balked. No, I won't get a cleaning job or anything. I don't get things, and I'd best just not think about it.

Hurriedly, escaping from herself and from that hated future without anything she wanted or needed, she walked towards the river.

Near the spigot she saw Minnie May and two other girls. Minnie May's hair was marcelled, very orderly and glued with wave lotion. She had on a fresh gingham dress, too, and a vast pink ice cream cone slid in and out of her mouth, slowly wasting away, but keeping a fine round shape as it went.

Ruby turned to go back. How did that girl manage, she wondered, where was all this money coming from? Minnie May had everything. Perhaps Mr Baker worked now and then and didn't tell the Relief lady so he could give dimes to Minnie May. Well, she didn't have a Daddy to cheat the Relief lady. That was like everything else.

'ROO-BEE.'

'What?'

'C'mere.'

She walked towards them; they stared at her, Minnie May with her head a little on the side.

'She's awful poor,' she said to the others. 'Let's let her.'

'But she's too little, she's only about nine.'

'No, she's eleven. And that don't matter. They don't care, I don't think.'

'Her dress is nice,' one of the girls remarked, a dark girl with a chocolate ice-cream cone and a ten-cent store ring, signs of wealth. 'But her face is kinda dirty. And her hair.' She paused, in doubt.

'I bet we can fix her up,' Minnie May said. 'And she's really awful poor.' Then turning to Ruby she asked: 'Could you do with some money, Ruby?'

'Oh.' She couldn't say anything more. Perhaps Minnie May did know of a cleaning job then, or anything, anything.

Minnie May saw the way Ruby was looking at her ice cream.

'Here,' she said generously. 'Take a lick at it; don't bite, just lick it.'

Ruby rolled her tongue over the smooth strawberry mound and looked at Minnie May with love.

'Lissen, Myrtle,' Minnie May said to the one with the ten-cent store ring. 'You're only thirteen and that's only two years different, and Sally's only thirteen and a half. Lissen, let's get some soap and wash her hair and see how she looks.'

They agreed and turned towards Minnie May's house, with Ruby hopping around them, in a fever of happiness, saying: 'Am I gonna get a job, too, Minnie May, am I gonna get some money too?'

Mrs Baker lent them soap and they returned to the spigot. Myrtle and Sally made a circle, holding their skirts as a screen, with some difficulty so that the ice cream wouldn't roll off the cones. Ruby got out of her clothes and laid them on a box beside the spigot and Minnie May, who had eaten her ice cream cone in great bites, crunching the cone between her teeth, began on her hair.

'Bend over.' Ruby put her head under the spigot and the cool water ran over her body. Minnie May scrubbed and rinsed and soaped the hair ('Gosh, don't you ever wash it') and rinsed again. Then she gave Ruby the soap and Ruby, scarcely having to bend at all, washed and took a shower under the spigot.

'Jump up and down and you'll get dry quicker,' Minnie May ordered.

Ruby obeyed. She put her clothes back on to a cool damp body and Minnie May ran her fingers through Ruby's hair, drying it and fluffing it. From out of her bloomers she produced a little pink celluloid comb and combed Ruby's hair. It waved gently, and fell in a soft ripple over her forehead.

'Let's look,' Minnie May said, standing with her feet apart, critical. Ruby felt shy with them staring at her.

'She's pretty,' Sally said and Ruby blushed for pleasure. The small face showed up clear with faint colour in the cheeks. The lines of it were delicate and soft except for a hollowing in the cheeks, a little tightness, a little hunger about the mouth. The weedy hair was light and fine, and grew well about the face. She raised her pointed chin and stared back at them, feeling suddenly, now that she was pretty, much older and more important.

'She'll do,' Myrtle said. 'And we can say she's twelve anyhow.'

'All right,' Minnie May said. 'You can come with us to-morrow, Ruby, but you gotta promise not to tell anybody, specially not your Ma.'

'Is it stealing?' Ruby asked, because she couldn't do that, and again at once she saw all her hopes, everything she wanted, destroyed, lost. Her mouth drooped.

Sally laughed. 'Hell,' she said. 'It is not. You earn your money all right.'

Then everything was perfect and Ruby smiled at them, shining, grateful. 'Can I bring Myra?' she asked. 'Myra needs a job too.'

'No.' They were quick and unanimous. 'And lissen, Ruby,' Minnie May said. 'If you tell *anybody*, even Myra, we'll twist your arm up in back—this way.'

She grabbed Ruby by the arm and wrenched it up behind her, and Ruby, astonished at this abrupt cruelty, didn't scream, but only said: 'Minnie May, Minnie May.'

'All right then, but you promise not to tell.'

'I promise,' she said, her eyes wide and tears in them from the pain that hadn't had time to bring tears all the way out.

'You can get your own cones,' Myrtle said, 'only you got to come down here and wash pretty often because if you aren't clean then maybe we won't get any work.'

Ruby promised that too.

'You meet us here at the spigot to-morrow about this time,' Minnie May said. 'About five. You can go by the drug store and look at the clock so you'll be sure to be here.'

The three older girls walked back towards the river. In the afternoon sun Minnie May's blonde hair glinted; she patted it elegantly and swung her hips a little as she walked. Ruby could hear them talking. 'We had to have at least one more,' Minnie May said. 'There's too many for us now. And she really is awful poor. That kid hasn't got anything. You see her ole man even went away so when he could p'raps pick up a job now and then, he ain't even here. Though, I must say,' she said, very important and old, the oldest of them all, 'I make a lot more money than my Pa ever does.'

She knew the cabin: it was old Lucy's. It sat between the railroad tracks and the river, isolated, half in the white territory and half in the black. It was bigger than negro cabins usually were: it was really a house, deserving the dignity of the name. It didn't leak, being firmly and entirely covered with tar-paper; it didn't even sag. Lucy had actually bought it: she was one of the early settlers here, having come in 1929 when things officially began to go bad for many people. Things had been bad for Lucy and her friends for many years, or perhaps forever, and she decided to buy herself a house in her old age before it was too late and there were no jobs left at all. She had worked as a cleaning woman at night, down-town in the office buildings and found her new home both healthy and convenient. During two years she paid for it out of her wages: then there were no more wages. She lived on Relief, easily. It was not much money, but it was sure. And there were always little ways of ekeing things out. Her house was an admirable investment; she kept it nicely and was praised by the Relief lady who was unaccustomed to seeing anyone in that neighbourhood tidy or possessive. She had rented a room to a man who became known as Mr Lucy, he stayed so long and obeyed her so well. But finally he left, and when she was looking for something else to provide the luxury money, she met a man prowling about the river front on obvious business and it gave her an idea. She thought it would be less trouble to rent her rooms just for a few hours at a time, and perhaps more profitable. She met Minnie May at the spigot and gradually, with no one ever saying anything first, this little affair had grown up. For several months now Lucy had been able to buy all the small things she needed; she was even putting away some money for repairs on the house, next spring. Like any good business woman she was thinking to herself, cautiously, of enlargements and improvements.

When they came near the house Lucy rose from a rocker on the front porch, smiled, said nothing and went away. She never stayed; if anything happened she didn't want to be there. The people who came didn't steal, anyhow; they weren't after that. She kept her money in a pouch hanging between her breasts and no one would notice it as a small bulge in the swelling, uninterrupted, calico-covered mound formed by her bosom resting on her stomach.

'Why,' Ruby said, 'it's Lucy's cabin; are we gonna clean it?' with some wonder. 'And ole Maria lives right near here; we can go by and see her on the way home.'

'Gawd, isn't she dumb,' Myrtle said resignedly. 'Now you lissen, Ruby, lissen to me. You're not gonna go and see Maria and no one is gonna know you was down here this afternoon. If your Ma asks where you was you just say you was down at the sand barge like you always are. And don't you go waving at Maria. You just come down here quiet so nobody notices anything and then you go home quiet and you tell your Ma you was playing on the sand barge.'

'Yes,' Ruby said, thinking it all over carefully and trying to remember: not to speak to Maria, not tell Ma, sand barge ... well, it certainly wasn't cleaning then: but what was it?

Minnie May explained her duties briskly.

'Ruby,' she said, 'to-day you can watch on the porch to see nobody comes. Somebody has gotta. You watch and if you see anybody you knock on the door loud enough so's we can hear. We each give you a dime from what we get: that makes thirty cents. The days you go inside you do the same, you give a dime to the kid who watches and you keep the rest. Two days a week we give everything we make to Lucy. That's the way we work it.'

'Yes,' Ruby said, in growing amazement. Thirty cents, she thought, almost fifty cents, for doing nothing but sitting on a porch. It didn't seem true and it certainly didn't seem right. Somebody would surely take it from her in the end, things didn't happen like that, not easily that way, not for nothing, almost free. It was like giving money away, and nobody would do that, ever.

'Come in and look now before they come,' Minnie May said.

The cabin had three rooms, the floors were covered with linoleum. There were three beds, one in each room, small iron affairs. They looked odd to Ruby; she felt something was missing on them. Oh, yes, they just had one sheet spread over the mattress and a pillow. No covering. Well, perhaps that was because of the heat, but still. . . . And then who slept in them she wondered: there was only old Lucy living here.

The living-room had a table and chairs, and a lamp with a shade, and two calendars with pictures. Odd bits of furniture, not matching, not new, but all clean, sat rather uselessly in the other rooms. Outside, in a lean-to, Lucy did her cooking. The only thing Ruby finally noticed or remembered were the beds like hospital cots, glaringly white and ready.

'Now,' Sally said, 'you get outside, they'll be here soon. I'll tell you when you have to begin watching for people we don't want.'

A man came up to the porch. Ruby made the note in her mind: 'a man'. She stopped thinking about him. He was a man like people's fathers, a grown-up man. He had no collar on. He said nothing to her and went inside. A door closed. She heard Minnie May's voice but no words; just the sound of her voice. Presently everything was quiet. Another man appeared, entered in silence, and before the door closed she could hear Myrtle saying: 'Oh, hello, you back again.' When the third man went in Sally came out on to the porch, and without greeting him said to Ruby: 'Now keep your eyes open, we don't want anybody else for a while.'

Dim things began to form in Ruby's mind. She sat on the porch and waited and tried to give shape and meaning to her thoughts. Things she knew or had known once, a long time ago, and not thought of particularly. Things about men. Something. Something Johnny had said too, about the women who lived on Sarah Street. The minutes went past smoothly and she sat on the steps, not daring to use old Lucy's rocker, wrinkled her forehead and tried to remember. Then the door opened, it didn't seem very long, and a man came out—perhaps the first one, Ruby thought, but they all looked alike, just grown-up men, the way grown-up men always looked. She stared shyly at her feet; he stopped, standing above her on the steps and said: 'Hello.' She looked at him but didn't speak. 'See you sometime,' he said, and walked down the railroad tracks toward the city. Minnie May came out. She was combing her glued, flatly-waved hair. Her dress was unbuttoned at the neck.

'I'll sit with you unless another comes.'

They waited. Ruby went on thinking, kicking up a little dust around her shoes, her forehead ridged and anxious. She wanted to ask Minnie May about the men but somehow she didn't dare. Minnie May, she felt, might be angry or laugh.

In an hour, or less, the other two men had gone and the girls sat together on the porch. They stayed there until after the sun had gone down and then Minnie May said: 'No one will come now, we better get back for supper.' She whistled rather loudly for Lucy, who was waiting to hear, and as they saw Lucy, square against the evening sky, humping slowly over the railroad tracks, they started walking home. Ruby followed a little behind the others.

'I got sixty cents this time,' Myrtle said.

'Lucky.' There was envy in Minnie May's tone. 'If we had a few more men I wouldn't let that Bill come. I don't like him. I don't like what he does; not like the others.'

Ruby listened, her mind churning with doubt, memory, wonder, and somewhere, vaguely, something like fear.

'To-morrow,' Sally said over her shoulder, 'you can go in.'

Ruby thought waiting was good enough; she would be contented with thirty cents. But she kept silent; this was their work, they planned it, she was only to do what she was told and then have money—money....

At the spigot they stopped.

'Hold out your hand,' Minnie May said.

She stood with her hand out and each one put a dime in it.

'Be back here at five to-morrow,' Myrtle called, but she was shouting at Ruby's back. Ruby had started running; she was afraid they might change their minds and not want to give her money for doing nothing. And she had never had thirty cents, or not since she could remember. She ran up the street, half laughing, half crying, holding the dimes until she could feel their shape pressed into her hand.

For half an hour, tormented, she walked in front of the stores. Where was she going to start, what should she buy first? Now that she had money after this long waiting, after all the wanting and planning, she couldn't decide. With the dimes firm in her hand, and in luxury and pain of spirit, she walked between the bakery and the candy store and the drug store, saying, how will I decide, how can I decide? Finally, she bought a nickel's worth of heavenly hash, since it was evening now and she was more hungry than hot or thirsty. And a small tube of toothpaste for a dime, and then—fighting herself at every step but thinking I oughta, I oughta—she went into the grocery store and bought a can of peaches.

She walked home the longest way, slowly eating her candy, sucking it before she chewed it, letting it slip in an agony of sweetness from her tongue down her throat. When it was all gone she turned the sack inside out and ate a few squarish crumbs of milk chocolate.

She held the toothpaste in its cardboard box, with light and reverent fingers. She saw herself taking the lovely purple brush out of the glass case and spreading a pink cream band on it and brushing her teeth until her mouth was full of pink suds, and rinsing and brushing and rinsing. . . . In the morning and at night, and she would have white shining big teeth. She had to feel the little box to be sure she had it, after all this time. The toothpaste ought to last all summer, she thought; I'll be careful of it and make it last.

She lied to her mother easily, surprised herself at how simple it was to make up a story.

'I was walking along Oak Street and a woman called me and said, will you take this package up to my daughter's on Olive Street, and I said yes, and she said, when you're done come back and I'll give you something. Her daughter gave me a dime (that's for the toothpaste) and I went back, anyhow, and she gave me fifteen cents, so I got the peaches for you, Ma.' It wasn't a very sound story but she told it with conviction and Mrs Mayer, delighted by the peaches, made no comment.

Poor Ma, Ruby thought, she has to work all day doing washing and only gets fifty cents, and all I have to do is sit on a porch awhile and I make almost as much. I guess I'll be making more soon, she thought, and the doubt came back and the brief flash of fear. But she looked at her mother, opening the can of peaches, and there was her toothpaste on the table, and she hoped it would be to-morrow quickly.

'I'll watch to-day,' Minnie May said, 'I'm tired.'

Sally led Ruby into the farthest room. She fidgeted a little, her hand on the door-knob ready to go. 'Ruby,' she said and paused. Ruby had not spoken since they came. This, she knew, was the work part. Sitting on the porch, and getting paid for it, was too good to last. She watched Sally. She wanted to ask questions and yet she didn't. I'll find out, she thought, what it is, may as well wait. I'll find out later, when the men come.

'Ruby,' Sally said again. 'Lissen. I want to tell you something. It'll hurt, Ruby. Sometimes it hurts bad but only the first time. And all you gotta do is think about the money and how you can get marcelles and lipstick, and go to the movies, and everything you want, afterwards. That's all you got to do. It don't last long. It only hurts the first time, really.'

What, Ruby said in her mind. What. What; what is this thing? What am I waiting for? She kept silent for a moment and then said: 'I don't want marcelles or lipstick or the movies; I want a jumping rope and roller skates mostly, besides cones, of course, and candy. I got my toothpaste already.'

Sally stopped, she was a little frightened of this. It wasn't right, somehow; Ruby was too young. Myrtle had told Minnie May but Minnie May said 'No.' Still, Ruby was young. Imagine wanting roller skates instead of marcelles or clothes.

'Well,' she said. 'Well. All right, get what you want. Now just wait.' She closed the door and Ruby sat lightly on the edge of the bed, careful not to rumple it. She waited, her ears strained for the first heavy step on the front porch; but not thinking, just listening and waiting. The palms of her hands sweated. That surprised her. And her eyes ached from staring at the door.

Quite suddenly, before Ruby realized she had heard them coming, the door-knob turned. Minnie May came in; behind her was a man.

'This is Ruby,' Minnie May said in a funny voice, thin and nervous. 'Well,' she said and scratched one foot against her leg and hung on to the door-knob, swaying a little, uncertain. 'Well, g'bye.'

The man closed the door firmly. He turned and looked at Ruby; he doesn't see me, she thought, that's funny. He's looking at me but he doesn't know it's me. He hasn't even looked at my face.

'My name's Ruby,' she said helpfully, and then because he still seemed indefinite, strange in this room and not seeing her at all, though he was looking hard enough, she added: 'What's yours?'

'Hank,' he said. She jumped a little at the sound of his voice. Of course he would have a voice like that; it was silly to expect he'd have a voice like Johnny's. His voice was like Daddy's or Myra's father: a grown-up man's voice. And he was old too, old as anybody's father.

The man walked towards her across the room, slowly, a little doubtfully.

She didn't move, but felt her skin drawing back, felt herself pressing backwards on the bed. But his face looked all right; it didn't look as if he were going to be ugly or mean. She waited, staring up at him.

'What're you doing here?' he said.

There was no answer; that was what he should tell her, that was what she was waiting to find out.

'I'm gonna get some money,' she said in a thin voice, and the man laughed, relaxed, at ease again. She didn't like his laugh.

'Oh,' he said, 'so that's it? Like the others? Well, that's all right then.'

He sat down on the bed beside her and said: 'Now what?' But his voice was no longer hesitating and half gentle, half angry, bemused. It was a joking voice, a rough, easy joking voice.

She turned a little and looked at him, and he noticed that there were fine blonde hairs on her arms, soft, small, child arms, if thin. He picked her up and put her on his lap. Her arms hung limp and he said: 'Put your arms around my neck.' She obeyed, and suddenly the man found himself embarrassed; it was like visiting his sister on Sunday and taking his little niece on his knees. He told himself that he was a fool, these kids started young, they were all tarts and wanted the money, and hell, it wasn't any of his business, if it wasn't him it would be some other man, so what's the difference. . . . But he told her to take her arms away, and told her gruffly. She yanked them away in terror. That sounded like Daddy's voice, remembered now in fear, long ago, when he had started to beat her for nothing, for no reason, just because she was there.

Hank decided he was wasting his time. For reasons he could neither name nor understand he was feeling cross and put upon.

'I'll call Minnie May or Myrtle,' he said.

'No, no, please.' If he called them she would get scolded; nobody had called her when she was waiting on the porch. That wasn't the way they worked it. The man just came in and then later he went away. If he called they wouldn't let her come any more. He was going to call because she was younger, that was it. People never let her do anything because she was too little. Her lips trembled trying not to cry; the man was going to call and she would be sent away and never get any money again. No skates, no chalk for hopscotch, no cones. ⟡

'I'm thirteen,' she said doggedly. 'I'm thirteen. I'm as old as they are. I just look little.'

'Oh.' Then suddenly, and Ruby unprepared, astonished, he began to pull off her dress. He tugged at it, pulling her around on his knees, hurried and ungentle. She was breathless and frightened and worried about her dress. 'Please be careful. Please be careful. You'll tear my dress. You'll spoil my dress. It's my new one, too.'

The man didn't hear her. Anyhow, he didn't stop. He seemed to be breathing strangely too. Or talking to himself or laughing or something. Ruby felt herself getting cold. She wanted to hit out at him and shout stop, but she couldn't do that. Minnie May was on the porch and Sally in the next room, and they'd hear and not let her come, and then all summer she'd have nothing, nothing.

The man held her up in his arms, the naked child's body, white and narrow, neat, soft legs, no hips, and no breasts at all, just two tiny points. Ruby stared back at him with wide eyes, all pupil, black and terrified, but she could not speak now if she wanted, or even scream. It seemed to her that this had been going on for ever. If she held her breath and was very quiet and waited, perhaps it would soon end and she could get back into the street, into the sun, on the sand barge, back to the things she knew about.

He tossed her lightly backwards on the bed and Ruby's hands, useless as flowers, waved up against him, and were crushed down. There was blackness in her mind, neither thought nor feeling, and she lay as dead until she began to scream. Her voice curved out, thin, wailing, fierce, and the man put his hand heavily on her mouth. The sound died and she began to sob without noise, her whole body shaking and bruised. She said nothing, did nothing, and the sobbing tore out of her quietly. The man rose, looked at her, at the bed, pulled his clothes about him in fury, threw a dollar bill on her naked body, and ran from the house shouting at Minnie May on the porch as he went: 'You bitch, you goddam little whore,' he shouted, 'what're you trying to do here, goddam you?' Minnie May, for a horrified moment, stared after him running down the railroad tracks, dragging at his clothes, cursing distantly.

She crept in to Ruby and watched her, lying on her back on the bed, with open eyes, the tears flowing down her face and her body retching sobs, in long silent gasps now.

'Ruby, what is it? What's the matter with you?'

From between the sobs, slowly, Ruby said: 'It hurts, it hurts.'

The house emptied and the other two girls stood watching with Minnie May, helpless, scared, not speaking.

They knew that you had to stop crying sometime; had to, that was the way it was. They could only wait. Finally Ruby lay on the bed, the tears drying on her face.

'I'll help you get dressed,' Sally said.

They didn't speak again. Ruby walked home a little behind them, limping, dazed, holding the dollar bill in one hand. She did not think and had no questions to ask. She walked carefully because she was afraid she would tear in two.

She hid the dollar bill in a hole under the front steps, looking first at the windows to make sure no one saw her, and she told her mother she had fallen from the sand barge, was sick, wanted nothing to eat, let her alone, let her sleep, let her sleep. . . .

They did not expect to see her again. They had hardly spoken of it to each other, feeling that the picture of Ruby lying on the bed was best darkened and forgotten. Minnie May said once, briefly: 'I only hope she don't tell.' For two days they had gone about their business, sobered and stubborn. They did not see her on the streets anywhere, nor going to the sand barge: they asked no questions about her.

On the third day, just as they had passed the spigot, walking to Lucy's cabin, they heard a shout. Turning they saw Ruby at the top of

the street, coming down the hill towards the railroad tracks. 'Lookit,'
Ruby shouted. 'Lookit me on my roller skates! Lookit how fast I go!'
They stood silently and waited. As the speed increased Ruby
crouched down, and her hair blew back from her damp forehead and
her dress sailed out behind her. She did not look up, intent on keeping
her balance, concentrated, smiling. And then, bumping off the curb, she
stopped on the cinders, and stood up.

'I'm here,' she said.

They did not answer.

'I've come back,' she said. 'I bought these skates with the dollar.
They're lovely. I go fast as anything.'

Still there was silence.

'I'll do it again,' Ruby said, her chin hard, staring at them. 'I'll do
it again. Sally said it only hurt the first time.'

Minnie May looked at Myrtle, but got no help from her. Sally also
waited, making no sign.

'I guess you can watch,' Minnie May said. 'You can just watch from
now on.'

'No. I'll do it again. I'll do it the way you do.'

'You'll lose us our customers,' Sally said, coming alive at last. 'We
can't have that. You'll lose us all our customers.'

'No, I won't. You said it only hurt once.'

They turned and started walking towards the cabin, without answering, not sure yet of what they intended. Ruby took off her skates and
followed them. Her face was obstinate: she lowered her head, glaring
at the cinders.

'All right,' Minnie May said, on the porch. 'All right, you can try
once more. If you cry you have to go. You can't come any more if you
cry. Go in to-day. We'll see.'

Ruby left her skates, crossed on top of each other, carefully, tenderly,
in a corner of the porch.

She went back to the room, looked at the bed for one moment, wild
and ready to escape. She shook herself and again her face set in obstinate
lines. I know what it is now, she thought, I know what it is they want.
That makes it easier.... And then she wasn't sure; no, perhaps not,
because ahead of time, before they came, she could think what was going
to happen, how it would be. And all she thought now was: I hope it's
quick, I hope it doesn't take very long.

The man who came in found a little girl with dark dilated eyes,
staring at him, standing up, her arms stiff at her sides, her nostrils
pressed out and the line of her jaw clear over gritted teeth. He stopped

and looked at her a moment, startled, not knowing what to do next. But Ruby was ready.

'I'll take off my dress,' she said, whispered, urgent, hurried, her voice coming out between closed teeth. 'I'll take it off myself.'

Myrtle was on the porch in Lucy's rocker when she came out. Ruby sat on the steps, bowed over her knees, holding her arms tight across her stomach, and swayed a little to and fro, whimpering.

'What's the matter?' Myrtle said.

Ruby didn't answer. Minnie May had said not to cry. She held the tears back and hunched her body over.

'Did it hurt?'

'Yes,' Ruby said. 'Yes.'

They sat silently waiting for the others.

'Bill came again,' Myrtle said. 'He likes Minnie May but she don't like him. When I get older I'm gonna get married and go on Relief. I don't like this work. I'm tired.'

Ruby opened her hand and looked at the silver coins. 'He only gave me fifty cents,' she said.

'*Only*,' Myrtle snorted. 'Say, who do you think you are? I never got a dollar. You only got it cause it was your first time anyhow. *Only*. Lissen, that's a lotta money for kids. A big girl I know does this work says she gets a quarter, mostly. You oughta be glad. And lissen, you gotta pay your dime today, same's we do. We let you off last time, but you gotta pay to-day.'

Ruby looked at the money.

'I need it,' she said darkly, 'I need it. But I wish I could get me a cleaning job instead.'

The newspapers said it was the hottest summer on record, and every day, braggingly, listed deaths by sunstroke, heat prostration. The people on the block suffered like animals, going leadenly through the days, their eyes aching and glazed from heat, thirsty, unable to sleep at night in the closed, airless rooms. The pavement burned through shoe soles, and the slight, unhealthy grass withered into a brown crust. Mrs Mayer endured this summer, as she had others before it. She said nothing, since it was useless to complain, and she looked forward to nothing, realizing that the winter would merely be a change to enduring cold. She was only glad dimly, that Ruby seemed so gay and contented, since she had found that rich old woman up-town, to give her presents.

Ruby invented this lie, finally, with Minnie May's aid. It became a tax on her imagination to think up a fresh story every night, explaining away the sudden flow of cones, the chalk for hopscotch, the jumping-rope, and the various foods she brought home in bright cans. She broached the subject to Minnie May, asking how Minnie May got around her wealth. Minnie May had invented a legendary woman on Maple Street, for whom she did cleaning. But Minnie May was older, and Ruby knew her mother would not believe she had work. Then, one day, an old woman, who seemed incredibly rich-looking to Ruby, because she had on a real hat and proper shoes, actually spoke to her on the street and gave her a dime. From this incident, they elaborated the tale of a rich old woman living up town, who had no children of her own and was lonely. Ruby said that she went up to see this lady every afternoon, and always came away with presents. It was hard for Mrs Mayer to believe at first: though it seemed natural to her that any woman would find Ruby sweet, and want to have her near. But what she couldn't imagine was anyone with money enough to give some away every day. Ruby talked about the old lady's house, describing the lamp-shades, the beds ('with covers on them of pink,' she said, and then, breathlessly, risking everything, 'pink satin'). And, gradually, this mythical philanthropist took shape, became real, part of their lives, until Ruby began repeating her conversation in detail, and believing the story herself.

Slowly, she came not to notice her afternoon's work. It was only an hour or so, and she found that, if she thought hard about something else all the time, it passed quickly. She became casual and easy, if not friendly, with the customers. She never knew their names and never recognized them, even if they came back several times. Minnie May once complained of this, saying: 'You treat them like they was ghosts, or not in the room or something. You gotta say "hello" and their names at least.' But Ruby could not remember; she went through a routine automatically, and, as none of the men objected, Minnie May let the matter drop.

Ruby, now rich, now glutted with everything she needed, hurtled around the block on roller skates, played hopscotch as the light faded over the brick houses and the air cooled, sucked cones, luxuriously, drank lemon pop, proudly and busily bought presents for her mother: canned peaches, oranges, sometimes even a bottle of pop and once, daringly, she had spent her entire forty cents getting her mother jewellery at the ten cent store. Myra believed the story about the old lady and Ruby bought her cones, magnanimously, enjoying the reverence in Myra's eyes as she shelled out nickels. It was a lovely summer.

Johnny was going to have a birthday. Ruby had not seen him much this summer. He was working hard and often out of the neighborhood, peddling his clay dogs and kewpies up and down the burning streets, until late at night. Things were not going very well. At this time of year people did not want ornaments for their parlors: they wanted coca-cola and bathing suits and electric fans. They sat on their porches in the dusk and rocked and fanned themselves with folded newspapers. Johnny was wondering whether he could contact some big business man who sold soft drinks. Then he could carry a box slung from his shoulders, with ice and bottles inside. That would have more sale, now. And the box wouldn't be much heavier than the basket with clay animals. He looked thin and weary. He didn't have to bother now with stories about his old sick mother; his own face was sales-talk enough.

Ruby went to the ten cent store and shopped carefully. She dragged her feet, elbowing people, touching things on the counter, thinking to herself about Johnny, and what he would like. Finally, she bought him a belt and a big bag of pink candy, and two handkerchiefs with J. in green machine embroidery, in the corner. She took the gifts home and made a package and greeted Johnny, early in the morning, before he started off on the day's work, jumping up and down and shouting, 'Happy birthday. Happy birthday.'

Johnny took the package. He held it a minute, without opening it, smiling at her. For two birthdays now, he had received no presents, and he had forgotten what it was like. Birthdays and Christmas: days like all the other days. His mother had kissed him that morning, which was rare enough, and said, 'You're a good boy, Johnny,' but that was all she could do. He held Ruby's hand and then leaned over and kissed her cheek quickly, a little embarrassed.

'Oh,' Ruby said and blushed, and ran back into the house. She stood inside the house, hiding behind the door, and watched him open the package slowly, and hold everything up to look at it. He whistled softly over the handkerchiefs. Then she hurried upstairs, to avoid him, as he came back to show the presents to his mother and leave them for the day.

He found her, that night, playing hopscotch with Myra.

'Lissen, come down aways with me. I wanta ask you something.'

'I'll be back, Myra,' she said, and walked with Johnny, feeling proud, possessive, delighted, his hand upon her arm.

They walked to the next block and sat on a stranger's steps.

'I been thinking,' Johnny said. 'It was nice of you to get me those presents. They're awful purty, and the candy's awful good.'

Ruby smiled in the darkness, and put her hand in his.

'But lissen, Ruby, where did you get the money?'

There was a pause. Ruby swallowed. Her voice came out rather shaky and high. 'From my old lady up-town, you know, Johnny.'

'No,' he said firmly. 'No, you can't have. There isn't anybody in the world like that, there isn't anybody gives you something every day, just to come and see them. I know. I seen a lot of people. Your ma believes it, but grown-ups don't know much. They don't get around. I know, though. Where did you get it, Ruby?'

'I told you.'

'All right.' He got up, sighed, and turned to go. 'I should think you could tell me. When you know we're gonna get married some day.'

'Johnny,' she said, 'come back. I'll tell you.'

She found it hard to begin. She stammered a little, and then, hopeless of finding any way to say it well, she blurted it out. 'I go every afternoon to Lucy's cabin down by the tracks, with some other girls. And men come and they do something to you, and then they give you fifty cents.'

Johnny did not speak. His shoulders bent over and he sat apart. He took his hand away from hers.

'Well,' he said.

'I had to have some money,' Ruby went on. 'You know. I had to. And there wasn't any cleaning I could do.'

'Yes,' he said. 'I know. Boys steal, and girls do that, if they hafta. I know. I wish you didn't, though.'

'Why?'

'Oh, well. Nothing. Only, I don't guess we can get married then.'

'Oh, Johnny.'

'Well, a man can't marry women like that. They just don't.'

'What kinda women?'

'Nothing,' Johnny said wearily.

'Johnny, I didn't know you'd care like that. I just didn't tell you cause Minnie May said not to tell, not anybody. But I don't see why you care, Johnny. It's just working. It's all I can do. I'm too little to get me a real job.'

'Sure. Oh sure. You better not tell anybody either. They catch you for that, just like stealing. The cops come and catch you. I know.'

'But how can they, Johnny? It isn't stealing. I don't steal nuthin.'

'I dunno how they can. They do. Specially if you're little. You better be careful, Ruby.'

She shivered. Minnie May had never said this. She didn't know the cops would care. It wasn't stealing. Her hands went cold. But if Minnie May hadn't told her, then perhaps Johnny was wrong.

'Johnny,' she said, and slipped her hand back in his, 'are you still sore? Aren't you gonna marry me when we get big? When I'm big I'm gonna get a cleaning job, and then you won't hafta be sore. Please, Johnny. Don't be mean. I can't do anything else.'

She took his hand and laid it against her cheek, and said again softly, 'Please, Johnny.'

'All right. I guess I will, anyhow. Only you gotta do cleaning when you're big. You gotta stop this. I can't marry you if the cops get you, and you're in jail, can I?'

She hung on to his hand, frightened. 'Don't say that. Don't say that. You wouldn't let them, would you, Johnny?'

'I can't do nuthin about cops, Ruby. Kids like us gotta do what the cops say.' Then he put his arm around her, and said, 'No, Ruby, don't cry. It's all right. Come on back and let's play lamp-post tag.'

The newspapers rarely mentioned deaths from heat now, and the sun sank earlier. There were shadows, like pieces from a jig-saw puzzle, over the railroad tracks as Ruby walked home. She had forgotten Johnny's warning. The days went on, each one the same, with delights enough. Nourished on ice-cream, washed under the spigot, smooth and content in spirit, she looked plump, fresh, and wore the meaningless general expression of happiness one expects in children. She bounced her new golf-ball up the hill, throwing it a little ahead of her, so that she had to run to catch up with it, and hummed to herself. The summer she thought would go on, the sun would slant over the barge as she lay dozing on the top, she would buy cones to lick slowly with her tongue curved and careful, she would play hopscotch in the evenings, and roar around the block on her roller skates. The summer would go on.

And one day, as she bent to put her roller skates in the corner of the porch, a hand came down on her shoulder. Not roughly, but quietly, finally. She straightened up, seeing dark blue pants, and above them brass buttons, and then a tanned policeman's face. She stared at him, her mouth open, with horror prickling up and down her back.

'Come along,' he said. Simply, nothing more, not ugly or mean, just definitely. She knew there was no use arguing.

'Can I take my skates?'

'No. You won't want them. Just leave them here.'

At that, something went wrong inside her; terror soared over her mind; helplessness; being caught; allowed nothing any more, nothing of her own. She wept with abandon, her head forward on her breast, and the policeman led her by the arm, because her eyes were blind with tears.

'She don't look like one,' he kept saying to himself, 'she don't look like one. She just looks like a nice little girl.'

. . .

They were all quiet. 'The new girls,' the tall, bony woman had said, and the door slammed shut, and a key turned. 'This is where you sleep,' she said, and herded them before her, saying nothing, but just her gestures showing that now you obeyed, now you did what you were told, and didn't talk back about it.

She pointed to their beds, and, as if hypnotized, each one went and sat down. 'You can stay there till supper,' she said, and left. Myrtle and Sally and Minnie May and Ruby. They sat with their hands folded in their laps, and stared ahead at the brownish concrete wall, with barred windows across it. There was nothing to do now. Except wait, wait, wait. Ruby whimpered softly, and the other three turned to look at her as if their heads were heavy, stiff, pulled on wires, and then looked away.

They went in to supper and met the other girls. Some were older, some must have been at least sixteen, Ruby thought. The dining room was bare like the dormitory, but had three long tables in it. On one of them, they ate. The oilcloth cover was stained, and, in places, had worn away to the brown lining threads. For supper they had soup and bread and stewed apricots. She noticed the girls eating; they screwed up their faces and shovelled the food in, gulping it.

She discovered, to her surprise, that the girls almost always whispered, instead of talking out, though nothing they said was bad or a secret. 'You never can tell,' a girl with heavy red hair explained, 'they punish you for breathing.'

'They treat the coloured girls worse than us,' one girl told her. 'They don't beat us, but they do them. The food,' she said, 'gets worse and worse, till you think you'll puke if you hafta eat it. And there's nothing to do.'

'How long you been here?' Ruby asked.

'Three weeks. I'm waiting to go to court.'

Three weeks, Ruby thought, three weeks. She tried to think what that would be in days, and it seemed to her unimaginable and terrible, to stay in this brown cold place, with bars before the windows, whispering, waiting, for three weeks. She looked out of the window at people in white clothes, walking carelessly on the streets, having all the streets they wanted to walk on. She reached her hand involuntarily through the bars, reaching it out to be free, grabbing at the air and the house warden came in and pulled her back and said: 'You can't look out the windows, nobody can, it's against the rules, go and stand on the line in the hall for an hour.'

This meant standing on one of the cracks of the tiled floor, not moving. It was the usual punishment, varying in length according to the crime. It was hard to do. She was tired when she went to bed.

'I ran away,' it was the little girl with freckles, talking. She was thirteen, but small. She had a nice tweed suit and Ruby thought her teeth were wonderful, small round gleaming. They sat at one end of the long table, with their backs to the barred window. No one ever said anything about that; automatically they chose their places that way, to shut out the free world, and the bars before it.

'I ran away,' she said again. 'I live three thousand miles from here. None of you ever been there. The sea comes up on the beach in a big grey roll and makes foam all over. It's Conneckticut,' she said.

'It sounds nice,' Ruby said timidly. 'Water's nice. I like the river. There's a sand barge,' she did not finish, not wanting to speak of this place which was hers, had been hers, before.

'Oh, it's beautiful,' the freckled girl said. 'It's not like this where I come from.'

'Why did you leave then?' Myrtle wanted to know.

'Couldn't eat enough, couldn't get any clothes, nothing. My father don't work. He just sits around.'

They all knew about that.

'He useta work. He had a swell job. He worked in a store. We had a house with a swing behind and flowers. I had lotsa clothes; I had a pink taffeta dress for parties. But not now. Nor for a long time. And they're so crabby. Gee.'

'It was fun coming,' the girl from Connecticut went on. 'Everybody was nice to us, me and my girl friend. We got rides all the way. We ast people for something to eat and they gave it to us. It was nice everywhere till we got here. Then they run us in. This is a hole, I mean.'

'Were you going to California?' the girl with the scar asked.

'Yeah. Imagine. They say you just get food off the ground, oranges and things. We didn't get there though. I sure hate this place. I never been in a jail before, and I don't wanna be again.'

'Me either,' Minnie May said, fervently.

'Did you hear those coloured girls yelling this morning?' the girl with the scar said.

'Yeah.'

'Gee, I'm sorry for that one they call Hazel. I listened to her, when I was standing in the line this morning. She was crying.'

'Why?' And Ruby thought why not, it's enough to make anyone cry all the time, all day long and all night. It's the only thing you feel like doing, here.

'Oh, they're gonna send her to the reform school for three years. Seems she's pregnant.' (Ruby rumpled her forehead, doubtfully, and Myrtle leaned over and explained, whispering, 'Gonna have a baby, that means.') 'She ain't married to her boy and she was crying and saying: "How'm I gonna find that boy when I get out, how'm I gonna make that boy marry me when I get out, where'll he be three years from now? They don't do nothing to him, they just grab me. They're bustin' up homes here, that's what they're doing." She cried like that for an hour. Seems as if she loved that man.'

They were silent.

The days went on. Ruby tried to count. It seemed to her that weeks moved by, grey and unmarked. It was only four days. She began to get pale like the others, and the faint sun-gilding wore off. She lay about most of the day, feeling ill, wanting to roller skate, play hopscotch, run, laugh, roll in the sand on the barge. Her body felt limp and heavy and her stomach turned over, at every meal, with the soggy grey food on her tongue.

Gradually, though no one said these things publicly, but by whispering at night, from bed to bed, she found out why the other girls were there, waiting, like herself. Running away, stealing, going with men. She was surprised to find that others had thought of the same way to earn money: surprised and comforted.

One morning after breakfast, Miss Mayfield, the house warden, told them that they should get ready, they'd be going down to the clinic later. 'You four,' she said, pointing to Minnie May, Myrtle, Sally and Ruby.

They shuffled down the basement, hanging back, each one wanting the other to be first. Miss Mayfield, grey and sharp behind them, harried them with a voice like a scythe. 'That's enough, that's enough,' she said, 'pick up your feet and get along.'

The door to the clinic stood open. Inside a long hall, lined with benches, showed up dimly under dirty electric lights. There was a waiting-room; on one side negro women sat holding their children about them, hushing them, keeping them quiet and patient, softly. On the other side were the white women, hard-faced, shoddy, scolding their children, forgetting, calling to them. Some girls, about sixteen years old, sat alone and chewed gum and giggled with each other. There were a few children on the benches in the hall, waiting by themselves. Nurses came and went and in one room they could hear a murmur of conversation, brief professional talk, from the doctor to his patients. It was all dark, brown, with dead air. Not dirty, but used, worn-out, a place for the poor.

Miss Mayfield left them sitting on the wooden benches in the hall, and went to talk to the secretary in her office. The girls swung their legs nervously, and stared around them. Beside Ruby, sat another child. She was about thirteen and held a baby of three or so, by the hand. 'Now, Ruthie,' she would say. 'Now, Ruthie, just sit quiet, dear, and we'll go soon.' Her voice was a perfect imitation of a mother's or a nurse, except piping. Her hair was lank and unbrushed, and she smiled at Ruby suddenly, warmly, with the lovely unexpected friendliness of children.

'It's awful, ain't it?' she said. 'We gotta walk up from the south side, takes us about an hour. They won't let you eat before you come for them shots, and we just wobble when we get here. We all come,' she said brightly, 'the two boys and Ruthie and me.'

'Shots?' Ruby said, startled.

'Sure, didn't you come before?'

Ruby shook her head.

'Oh, well, you go in there, and the doctor rolls up your sleeve or sometimes takes down your pants, depends, and they give you a shot. It's for bad blood,' she said helpfully. 'You gotta come or they 'rest you. Ruthie cries, so does Mickey.'

'Does it hurt?'

'Nah, not much. Not after a while. They say I got it from a man. I went with a man once. Did you?'

'Yes.'

'Well then, that's what it is, I guess. I guess you got it too. The man said he'd give me a bicycle, but he didn't give me nothing, he just went away.'

They heard a scream, short and high, instantly stopped.

Ruby jumped, turned towards the door and looked back at the girl next her, questioning.

She was shaking her head. 'It's Mickey,' she said. 'I don't know what'sa matter with that child. Sometimes he pukes too. It don't hurt him like that, he just screams 'cause he's scared.'

'Oh,' Ruby said in a tiny tight voice.

The nurse came out in the hall and said: 'Ruby Mayer, this way.'

She put her hand against the wall to steady herself; she was trembling. The nurse took her by the shoulder and guided her to the operating table. 'Just lie down there,' she said.

Hurriedly and not too gently the doctor examined her. She held her breath in tight and looked at the cracks on the ceiling. She had never been in a clinic or hospital before. It seemed to her that now they had her, the other people, the people like policemen and Miss Mayfield, they could do anything to her, send her anywhere, hurt her when they wanted, boss her and punish her, all the time without reason. And she couldn't cry, she couldn't say anything. She would just have to wait and hope the days would go by quickly.

'The same, they're all the same,' the doctor said. The nurse wrote something on a card. 'I'll just give her a blood test.'

Ruby remembered Mickey screaming. No, no, they wouldn't. They couldn't hurt her any more. It wasn't fair, she hadn't been as bad as all that. They didn't have a right, they didn't have a right. She wouldn't have people sticking needles or knives or things into her. She had never done anything bad enough for this, for the bars and the long days and the food and Miss Mayfield punishing them for nothing and the doctor hurting her and not caring, not seeing her, not knowing who she was. . . .

'No,' she said, her voice low and urgent. 'No, you won't. I'm not gonna be hurt anymore.'

'It won't hurt,' the doctor said, taking the syringe from a tray.

He turned with it in his hand. Ruby looked at the long fine needle, with horror; the man would drive it into her, all through her, and her blood would spill all over the floor, no, no, they didn't have the right . . . She opened her mouth and screamed. 'No, no, I won't let you, I won't!'

'God, what is the matter with these kids?' the doctor said wearily. 'They yell like we were going to murder them. Be quiet, you dumb child, this doesn't hurt, it only takes a minute.'

She struck out at him and he got angry. 'Hold her arms,' he told the nurse. Swiftly, his face irritated and cold, he stuck the needle into Ruby's arm. She shut her eyes and screamed in terror. The nurse pushed her to get up, and she went out in the hall, holding cotton against the little purple circle, making a muffled sound of crying, her eyelashes shining with tears.

'That's nonsense, Ruby,' Miss Mayfield said. 'You had no business making that racket. You'll just do without your play this afternoon, as punishment.'

Ruby wanted to laugh, stick out her tongue at Miss Mayfield and jeer. Play! That was their idea, their word. She knew what playing was, it was running, and sun on your face, and being free. Play! What kind of people were they, anyhow?

'Your mother's come to see you, Ruby.'

She was frightened to go into the house warden's office. Mrs Mayer would be there, stiff, angry, and she'd get spanked. She couldn't remember many spankings, but they had been good ones, when she got them. She put her hands behind her back and sidled in. But, when she saw her mother, bowed in the chair, ungloved hands red, empty and tired in her lap, her eyes glossy with tears, looking towards her, she ran forward and put her arms around Mrs Mayer's neck, climbed up on her lap and wept.

'Poor little Ruby,' Mrs Mayer said, patting the soft brown hair, rumpling it, bending to kiss it, her arms tight about the small shaking body. 'I'm sorry you hadta. I should of got you the things you needed, I should of, but I couldn't. If your Daddy had been here, working,' she said, and her voice ached, 'it wouldn't of been like this. We never had no trouble when your Daddy was working. My little girl,' she said. 'Little Ruby.'

Ruby clung to her, feeling safe. Her mother had come, and would take her home. She would climb up the steps at night and go to sleep on the rags and wake and find her mother and the things she was used to, around her. She would go back to school soon, and it was still sunny enough to play on the barge. She wouldn't go to Lucy's cabin because the policeman might come, but she didn't care any more about cones; she only wanted to go home, and know her mother was there, waiting for her, and she could climb up on her lap and be hugged.

She cried gently to herself, from joy, because the waiting was over, the long days and the bars and the cold, mean people and the things that hurt.

'Shall we go now, Ma? Everything's all right. I haven't even got bad blood,' she said, smiling, wiping the tears from her eyelashes with her hand. 'Shall we go home now, Ma?'

There was silence. Mrs Mayer held her tighter, pressed against her own thin body, and above Ruby's head, her eyes fixed on the door with hatred. 'I can't take you, Ruby.' Ruby's body went hard in her mother's arms. 'They won't let me take you home. They say I'm not fit to keep you. They say I should of known what you were doing, and if I didn't then I'm not a good mother.' Her voice stopped, as if there were no more breath inside; came to a stop from emptiness, as if there were nothing to say anymore, ever.

Ruby wept. She did not speak, but held her arms around her mother's neck, pressing her cheek against her mother's, sobbing. They were going to take her mother: they were going to keep her, alone, away, shut inside a house until she died because it was useless to live. Her mother couldn't do anything against them either. Her body was weak with crying: she heard the sound of her own voice, rising, crazy with fear: 'No, no . . . no. . . .'

'You'd better go, Mrs Mayer.' Miss Mayfield stood in the door, impersonal as wood, and waited.

'Good-bye,' Mrs Mayer said. 'Good-bye, Ruby. Good-bye, darling.'

She lifted Ruby's arms from her neck, gently, and stood up.

Miss Mayfield took Ruby's shoulder, holding the thin bones tight in her hand, and pushed the child through the door.

'Oh,' Mrs Mayer said, stepping forward to catch Ruby, to lead her, to make it easier for her. 'Oh, don't—not like that.'

Miss Mayfield stood in the doorway and looked at her, not angry, not menacing; indifferent, dry, blank.

I'm not her mother any more, Mrs Mayer thought, they've got her. I'm not a good mother . . . Miss Mayfield locked the door behind her.

Ruby, not even crying now, still and hopeless, leaned her head against the bars and watched her mother dragging down the street.

'She's going the wrong way,' Minnie May said. 'That's not the way to your house.'

FOR BETTER FOR WORSE

The Baltic aunt smiled mischievously and reported that she, the gardener and the cobbler had stolen a horse from the Germans and taken it to the hills to the Partigiani. Her sister, the old Princess, sat straight-backed, faded, handsome, wearing regal pearls, and dealt herself another hand at solitaire. 'You must be prudent, Liza,' she said as though recommending the use of an umbrella on a wet day. The old Prince, in a chair pulled close to the cheap radio, cupped his hand around his ear and listened to music. All broadcasting sounded German now, equally loud and pompous. *Carmen* bellowed through the cold drawing room. The French cousin, who had no personality except as a bridge fourth, stood almost inside the stone fireplace, where small logs sputtered, and said, 'The Americans are coming.' No one ever listened to Count d'Arenville and, besides, he had been saying this for months.

Kitty watched her husband, the young Prince—young no more, none of them were young; they had lived in this castle too long. Andrea drank his barley coffee as if it were poison and he wished to die from it. He ran his hand through his hair in a gesture which Kitty dreaded. The long, fine hand trembled. The family, to Kitty, seemed no worse tonight than any night. She must have missed the exact word or look that, this minute, enraged Andrea. For fourteen years she had watched her husband, listened for the family's careless, wounding words, soothed and placated them all, prevented scenes.

I wonder what they will look like, Kitty thought, and found she could make no picture of her compatriots, those Americans whom Cousin Raoul was continually prophesying. She tried to be interested in this war; yet it was only scenery or climate, another background to the permanent war between the old Prince and the young. If she could not win one battle for her husband, how was she expected to be useful in a sprawling outside war which she did not understand? At least she knew what the struggle between the father and the son was for: it was for the land. His father's death was Andrea's only hope of victory. The father declined to die; the Ferentinos, as a rule, lived forever.

'I'm going to bed,' Kitty said. 'I have a headache.' She did have headaches. She caught them from watching Andrea. No love, no headaches, Kitty thought; it was not a feasible bargain.

'Take a Veganin,' her mother-in-law said.

'There is no Veganin,' the aunt said. 'You know that, Caterina.'

'I did not remember,' the old Princess answered. There had been no Veganin for some time; she did not care to remember anything uncomfortable. She did not care to notice the lives around her, which were immensely uncomfortable. Her detachment irritated her Baltic sister and sometimes penetrated the weariness of her American daughter-in-law, who would then resent it. But her husband and her son found her perfect.

'Good night,' Kitty said, and was bowed to from various corners of the room.

If only one could walk at night, to think and to stop thinking; but the Germans in the village were severe with their curfew, especially now that they were frightened and probably losing the war. She could not afford to be shot by a sentry. What would become of Andrea?

Kitty picked up a candle in the hall and walked toward the rooms which Andrea and she had been given, as bride and groom, when they came here to live after their wedding trip. The rooms had been arranged by her father-in-law and were dark and ornate, as his taste was. They would not have had a smaller apartment, Kitty thought, if they had lived in Chicago, where she was born, and Andrea earned a clerk's salary at Marshall Field's. There were four high-ceilinged boxes in a row— Andrea's room, the sitting room, her bedroom and their bath. Below their windows the garden displayed pebble-bordered triangles, squares, circles of stiff ill-placed flowers, or in winter a muddy look of decay like an untended public park.

Andrea had taken steps about the bathroom; it was blue-tiled, gleaming, and for the castle unbelievably modern. Kitty had removed a few black oils and replaced them with the sort of thing Andrea liked— English hunting scenes, ducks flying. She had ordered a bookcase. Beyond that she had done nothing; the walls of each room were still covered with red brocade for Andrea, green for her, yellow for the sitting room. With her money they could have bought a castle twice as big as this one and furnished it throughout in any way that cost a great deal; but she had come directly from her parents' home to her parents'-in-law. She had never made a place to live and had no opinion. Andrea seemed to think it was all right, as long as Andrea was pleased. . . .

At any rate these rooms were convenient. The library, the drawing room, the dining room were all on this floor, and when Kitty first came she was relieved not to lose herself in the stone labyrinth of this building, with its long, cold corridors, its meaningless sudden halls, its six interior staircases, each steeper and gloomier than the last. Now she knew the castle and the village around it and the land so well that she did not see them or think of them. She knew nothing else. They would live in their four rooms, childless, a woman of thirty-three and a man of forty now, until it was their turn to move into the old Princess's tower, the old Prince's murky apartment in the west wing.

Long ago, rebelling, Kitty had carried Andrea off, as far away as she could imagine, to Australia and to Brazil. It was useless; they had had to return. She offered Andrea other land, free and wider than this, as beautiful, and he could not live; Kitty recognized that he could not live. He had to come home; for him, this was the only land on earth. And it was all lovely, from the high hills and the bushy forests, down along the dirt roads under the olive trees, through the fields and vine-yards to the pinewoods and the yellow curve of the beach. Andrea had taught her his land as carefully as he had taught her love, and with much the same passion. When Kitty did not hate Torrenova, as she would hate a victorious enemy, she admired and cherished it.

They had been here since the beginning of the war; the occasional trips to Rome, the occasional visits to friends in huge houses on other lands, were stopped. For almost a year Kitty had not been outside the boundaries of the Ferentino estate. The war made no difference to her life; or, rather, she ought to be grateful to the war. Andrea was, at times, in some ways, happier. She could thank the Germans for speaking their disgusting language; Andrea was the only one who understood it. Since he had to treat with the Germans, his father was forced to give him more power. Within the limitations of war, the Germans, and his father's constant objection to change, Andrea had had more freedom to manage this coveted land than ever before.

The German officers were quiet tonight on the second floor. The German soldiers in the village were quiet; they could be heard moving in the rain as a deeper slurring whisper. Perhaps Cousin Raoul was finally right and the Americans were coming. But surely the Germans would fight before they left, even if they were only service troops, gray, heavy men who handled horses and carts and confiscated lumber from the sawmill. They are bound to fight, Kitty thought. Anything German is a soldier obeying orders. And their people would be killed, these peasants who had been here almost as long as the Ferentinos. Why did the peasants never move away? The Ferentinos had held this land for eight hundred years, and to lose only a little, century after century, to hold and remain, was the one purpose of their existence. But why should the peasants be so fixed in their station, father to son, generation following generation, on the same plot of earth, the new houses built on the foundations of the old? What was this madness of Europe which made people regard as a great good simply staying in one place?

Tomorrow, Kitty thought, I must make sure the cellars are in order—blankets, mattresses, chairs, candles, water, food, medicines, the old Princess's card table, the old Prince's portable radio. And also she must make sure, by reminding the doctor and the priest and the agent and Signora Grandi at the store, that the peasants knew they were to come to the cellars immediately when they heard the guns. This, probably, was what the cellars had been built for, as much as for storing wine, and had been so used by Ferentinos and their people since longer ago than Kitty could imagine. The castle itself burned down with tedious regularity every hundred years or so and was reconstructed according to the dire original plans; but the cellars remained, from the first castle, ancient and vast. The people would be safe there.

Kitty was reading in bed when Andrea opened the door of the sitting room, went to the liquor cupboard and poured himself a long drink of whisky, which he disliked. Kitty saw that something new had happened. She thought she understood the cause of each of Andrea's emotions; she felt herself to be not a person but a barometer, registering fickle weather. She must get ready now for whatever this was; Andrea needed some different understanding, which she would have to find in herself, quickly.

'Kitty, we should speak English all the time. Talk to me in English.'

French was the common language of this house. 'Why? What shall I say?'

'The Americans. Cousin Raoul is right. I have almost forgotten how to speak it. I must learn. When they come, what will they say to me? They will say I am a coward.'

'Oh, darling, how *can* you? They are our friends.'

'The Americans were not allies of Hitler. They have never lived like strangers in their own country and tried only not to do a bad thing because there is no clear good thing left to do. All they will see is a man of forty, here, not fighting.'

'Fighting?' She could not consider this war as belonging to people; it was a disaster, like a tidal wave or a creeping ice floe. You did not struggle against it, or with it. You tried to keep life going where you were, while the war went tragically on and on, wherever it was. She imagined the whole world as a series of Torrenovas, little huddled communities isolated from each other, intent on making soap and finding leather and rationing food and firewood and staving off sickness. There were the Germans, and the other armies, groups of displaced men in uniform, no doubt also trying to keep alive in their way. Beyond all of them were the remote mad dictators who wanted this and gave orders. She had seen no fighting.

'Talk in English,' Andrea commanded.

'Yes, Andrea.'

'If I can speak English perhaps they will give me employment.'

'"Give me a job," I think. I don't believe you say "give me employment."'

'They could use me,' Andrea said.

My God, Kitty thought, his voice.

'They must use me. I know all the land around here. I can talk to the peasants. I could show them where to go. Kitty, would they let me go with them?'

'I don't know. I don't know about armies.'

'If it were the English I think it would be all right. They would see why I stayed here. But the Americans. How can they understand that we could do nothing except stay in our own place and look after our own people? They have come here; it is not their own place.'

'But, Andrea, the Germans weren't in their country. It isn't the same. Please, please don't make something terrible out of this. The Americans will come and we will be at peace and then the war will be over.'

'Oh, Kitty,' he said tenderly and with disappointment, 'you have lived here so long that you think like Cousin Raoul and the aunt and Mama and Papa. No, no,' Andrea said violently and banged his glass on a table. 'It is not so easy.'

'It hasn't been easy,' Kitty murmured.

Andrea looked at his wife with shame. No, it had not been easy. It was easy enough to deal with the lumpish, blundering Germans, to hide from them always enough to keep the village going, to warn and disperse the peasants whenever the Germans had one of their crazy moods for discipline or punishment. The work on the land was bad—nothing could be improved, nothing new could be tried; still, it was possible to convince the Germans that the work must go on. But how had he failed to notice Kitty's forehead, lined as if a sharp pen had drawn marks across it? She had always been small and smooth and with a velvet softness; now she was thin and dried out. He had watched this wearing away of Kitty, day by day, and seen nothing.

He managed the land while Kitty managed the lives of the people.

Everyone said how good and wise she was, the young Princess; she is all kindness. So she was the one they brought their terrors to—the sons who ran away to join the Partigiani in the hills; the husbands who never came back from the first part of the war, when the Government drove unwilling men to go and fight for the Germans; the sick with the medicines giving out; the daily, hourly problems of needles, thread, shoes, matches and where to get an extra blanket for a new baby.

'How is your headache, my little Kitty?' Andrea sat on the edge of the bed and put his arms around her. His arms had protected her from nothing, yet she leaned against him, warm with the old indomitable joy, feeling that, with those arms around her, she was safe.

'Must we speak any more English?'

'No, my dearest, you sleep now.'

'Will you stay here, Andrea?'

'Yes. Turn off the light. I will be back.'

He stopped himself from walking up and down his room; Kitty would hear and lie awake, worrying. His mind cleared of the anxiety that was like fever and he gave himself up to a fantasy: the Americans would come; they would shake hands; he would bring out the best champagne; they would celebrate; the Americans would give him an old uniform; and he would go away with them, in the company of men, the living, and they would like him because he could show them all the roads and explain to them how the land formed and where the Germans might be hiding. He would be free to go to their war because Torrenova would be beyond harm, in the care of friends, Americans.

They were in the cellars and no one complained except Andrea. He did not protest against the damp discomfort of their life; he raged that he should be here, instead of above ground where the fighting was. They did not know what was happening; and the guns or bombs, or whatever made the noise, were heard as muffled thuds, felt rather than heard. When the sounds came nearer, or the earth beneath them seemed to rise and settle, Andrea said, 'I must go to the Americans! If they come down the road the Germans can wipe them out, from the hill behind the sawmill. I must tell them.'

'Don't be a fool,' his aunt said. She was herself in a torment of impatience; she could not bear to miss this excitement. 'What would you do? Walk up to an American officer who is busy with a machine gun and say, 'Prince Ferentino, at your service'? They would shoot you; they have no time for Ferentinos. Sit down, Andrea. You are making a great fuss.'

He could not strike an old woman of sixty-five, even if she was as strong as rope, hard, harsh; he could not shout insults at her; he could, in fact, only sit down. Cruel, cruel, Kitty thought. Don't you see that you kill him every day? It would be easier to be shot by a soldier than killed a little every day by an aunt, a cousin, a father, a mother.

'I hope the Americans do not damage the chapel,' Andrea's father said.

'Chapel, castle, village, the Ferentino land,' Aunt Liza said, 'do you think the Americans care about those? They have damaged better things. They are fighting a war; they are not a Commission for the Preservation of Monuments. If you had been in Russia,' the aunt said with her unfailing contempt, 'you would not talk in this absurd way.'

It was her power over them; it was why she could shake her fine carved head in disgust and glare over her arrogant nose. She had seen real life, where it did not matter if you were a Ferentino, or the wife of a great Russian landowner, a lady of the court. Her husband had been killed in the Revolution; she herself had been jailed with prostitutes and criminals. She had proudly refused to answer when called 'Comrade Voudransky', saying always, 'I am Countess Voudransky. Address me by my name if you wish to speak to me.' And she had lived for twenty-four years as the guest of her sister and brother-in-law; had there been a revolution in this soft country, the Ferentinos would have come to her; it was natural and nothing to be thankful for. For all these years Liza Voudransky had withered with boredom in the calm of Torrenova and was revived when the Germans came and she could take up a life of patriotic crime—hiding the young men, leading them to the hills, stealing from the Germans—and she had learned with ravishment about sugar in gasoline tanks. Countess Voudransky was the most reckless resistant in the village. The Ferentinos, in her opinion, were provincial aristocrats who understood nothing of the world, not even enough to know that you could not wander around a battle and expect to be treated courteously, as in a Roman drawing room.

The peasants were quiet, frightened of the battle, thinking of the houses they had left behind to be destroyed or looted, since all armies were alike; thinking of their fields, trampled over by men or gouged by shells. They were also aware of being visitors; to live in the cellars of the castle was a troubling experience.

The hierarchy of the village was maintained in the cellars: one room for the family, one room for the family's house servants; one large storage closet for the priest; one room for the teacher and the agent and the doctor and their relatives; one room for the little bourgeoisie of the village—the postmaster, the shopkeeper, the seamstress, the man who ran the bicycle-repair shop, the cobbler, the smith and their wives and children; and the remaining room and passages of the cellar for the peasants, who arranged themselves as they liked, taking into account their own social standing and feuds.

Several times a day the old Prince would walk through this constricted, ill-lighted kingdom and everyone would stand as he came by. He had a strange way of speaking to his people, as if shy of them or as if nothing, after living with them all his life, suggested itself to his mind. 'Well?' he would say. 'So? Good. Yes. Well, glad to see you. Then, how are you? That's right, that's right.' Sometimes he asked a question, if he managed to connect one face with another: 'How is your daughter, Luchetti?' But generally he had moved away before he heard the answer. The old Princess, who walked with a cane because of her rheumatism, and always looked more wonderful than any of them—tall, pale and serene, beautiful without effort—made one tour of the cellar. She said nothing, only smiled. It baffled Kitty that the villagers adored the old Princess, whom they knew as a quietly smiling, infrequent apparition and nothing more, for the old Princess had never been able to move from the gentle dream where she lived into association with these people. She had not concentrated long enough to supervise even one school graduation or the decoration of the chapel for one Easter Mass.

Cousin Raoul wrote persistently in his journal. What did he have to say? Kitty wondered. Nothing happened to any of them; less happened to him. Perhaps he thought these were his last words; he was using a great deal of kerosene in his lamp. If the battle lasted many days, Kitty would have to ration Cousin Raoul's journal.

Andrea, sitting in a corner of the family's cellar, brushed his dogs, cleaned the rifle he had hidden from the Germans and, though still, gave the impression of a man furiously walking the floor. He would not visit the other rooms; he was ashamed to be in this cellar. If his people thought it only proper (did not think but accepted) that the young Prince should stay with them and his family, this proved that his people too were without quality. All my life, Andrea thought, I have done what is considered suitable for a Ferentino and never what is right for a man— never, never. Except Kitty. Kitty was his own choice; Kitty was the only proof that he had a will like other men and a mind that belonged to him and was not simply an inherited property. If it were not for Kitty, he thought, and was suddenly lighted and warmed by his love for her, I would be nothing, only a name.

Kitty, knitting and thinking practical, anxious thoughts—the water supply, the increasingly bad air, the increasing loathsomeness of the make-shift latrines at the end of the cellars—was surprised to feel her husband standing over her. She knew it was Andrea without looking up, and when she raised her head she was dazzled by his eyes. Andrea knelt beside her chair and softly, once, stroked her cheek. He had told her what he wanted to tell her, this way; she heard it clearly: I love you, I need you, you are my whole life. But in all the years of their marriage, Andrea had scarcely touched her hand in public; his manners were faultless and grave and equal; he had a mania for privacy.

Kitty forgot the family, the people in the cellars; Andrea came first always. Anything she did, besides being his wife, was accidental and an outgrowth from her wifehood. She smoothed the brown hair back from his forehead and said, 'My dearest, my only love.' The family could have heard, although she whispered, but their own manners operated as deafness. Andrea smiled at her, the way he sometimes did when they were out with their guns, kicking up pheasants in the lower woods; smiled with confidence and gaiety and went back to his corner. He seemed now to be sitting still, to be occupied and at ease. Kitty, hearing voices in one of the farther rooms, got up to investigate. She looked once at Andrea. No, he was all right; he did not need her, but there might be a quarrel to resolve out there, or someone sick to help.

It did not happen as Andrea had dreamed. In the beginning there were tired, dirty, red-eyed men who looked old (surely Americans were young; that was the one known quality of Americans). They were as badly dressed as the Germans had been, but seemed thinner. They stared at this cowering world in the cellars with an inactive hatred, which they felt probably for all people not in uniform, all people who had a fixed place to cower and the right to save their lives. There had been a pounding on the wooden nail-studded door and it was Kitty, listening near it, who recognized that the muffled voices outside were talking English. She opened the door. She had expected a huge crowd, blond and tall and laughing, and there were five rather short, swarthy men at the door.

'What goes on here?' one of them said.

'Have the Germans left?' Kitty asked.

The man did not seem surprised that she answered in English. 'Yeah,' he said. 'Tell the folks you're liberated now.' He laughed then. 'You can all come up and get some nice fresh air.'

'So long,' one of the others said.

Kitty was terrified for a moment; these men were stranger to her than any others. She had imagined she would feel, instantly, some link between them; and she felt nothing. Except humility. She knew they were more tired than she had ever been and that she would never understand what had made them so numb and so aloof.

They wanted wine and food but hardly had time to eat or drink, and then they were moving on, slowly, as if it did not matter any longer where they went. Andrea had scarcely spoken; there was nothing to say to these men or to their officers, also old-young, thin, dirty, with the same despising eyes. He could not offer to go with them; he felt his own cleanliness as a brand of shame.

The peasants went back to their scattered houses; the villagers went home; the family moved upstairs. The chapel had been hit and the old Prince stood for a long time, saying nothing, but looking at jewel-colored fragments from windows which were famous throughout Italy and his special love. The castle was chipped and there were broken roof tiles; several peasant homes had been smashed and those families wept and crouched before them, as if the battered houses were full of their dead. Andrea ordered them to be silent, telling them a house could and would be rebuilt; the Americans must not see this paltry grief and feel even greater contempt. There were shell holes in the fields, damaged barns, glass in the village streets; nothing. It had been a small, insignificant engagement. Torrenova became the rear at once.

Torrenova seemed destined to be a place where men looked after transport, a sort of parking lot and repair shop. The organization of any army was beyond Kitty's comprehension, but at least she knew that this would not help Andrea. These were not the Americans who would take him away as he so passionately hoped. And then it happened by accident. An officer and his jeep driver came into Torrenova after dark; something was wrong with the jeep. The officer belonged to a different branch of the army—everything was initials, as it had been with the Germans— OSS he said, Kitty thought; and he was sick of sleeping in a tent or on the floor in a crowded house his army had requisitioned. He wanted a bath and a bed, since he was delayed anyhow; and he came to the castle. He was made welcome, as if he had been at least the Allied Commander-in-Chief instead of a young captain who by now was disgusted with every aspect of war. He talked to them with pleasure when he found they could all speak English, although the old Princess was too shy or else too far away to talk, but only listened and nodded and told the butler to bring more wine. When Andrea learned that this captain needed Italian in his work and had, as he said, a GI interpreter who was too dumb to live and could only get a job in the OSS, Andrea timidly offered himself. The captain liked this family; it was a joy to see clean, calm women, to sit in a decent room, to be washed and about to sleep in a bed. And why not? he thought. Anyhow I'll take him up and ask Colonel Harris.

'Might be a good idea,' the young captain said. 'I guess people would talk to you better, you being Italian.'

Kitty held her breath and prayed. Among other things, she prayed that the old people would not have understood and would not now say something dreadful, reprimanding Andrea as a child for the folly of his plan. What would Torrenova do without him? Quite impossible; Ferentinos served no one but their King.

Andrea could not sleep, and Kitty stayed awake with him, saying over and over, 'I'm sure he'll take you, darling,' and then saying, 'I know Colonel Harris will want you as soon as he talks to you.' It did not occur to Kitty that she was sending her husband, the center and the meaning of her life, off to war, which was—whatever else one did not know about it—dangerous and often fatal. She was sending Andrea where he had to go, and she considered nothing else.

Andrea was up, dressed and waiting, at six o'clock. At six-thirty the young captain came downstairs from one of the rooms lately vacated by a German officer and said he'd go and see how the jeep was, and Andrea said there would be breakfast for him when he got back. Kitty came into the hall, wearing a shapeless flannel bathrobe, to find Andrea standing there with no expression on his face.

'What did he say?'

'Nothing,' Andrea said in a dead voice. 'Nothing about taking me.'

Then the captain returned and said they'd have to eat quick and get cracking. 'English talk,' he explained. 'Picked it up from the Limeys.'

'You all ready?' he inquired, with egg in his mouth.

'Yes,' Andrea said. 'One minute.' Andrea ran down the hall to Kitty's room and took her in his arms and kissed her with great excitement, saying. 'He's taking me, I'm going,' and got out his raincoat, its pockets stuffed with a razor and toothbrush and extra socks and handkerchiefs, and kissed her again, and said, 'Explain to Papa and Mama, Kitty. Goodbye, my beloved,' and was gone.

Kitty sat in her bed, very still and very cold, and realized that, after fourteen years, she and Andrea were separated; after fourteen years she would have the days and the nights, the waking and the going to sleep, alone.

It was late summer then and, although the seasons changed in their recognized way, time was solid and did not move. The family surprised Kitty. She had never had a clear opinion of them; she only saw them as they affected Andrea, so that for some days or weeks she approved of one or the other, in case that one had been considerate of Andrea. Now she began to know them as themselves, and her first impression was that they were mad. She had explained Andrea's departure, his desire to help in the war, and she had waited for outbursts of anger from Andrea's father, derision from his aunt, anxiety from his mother, and mumblings from Cousin Raoul, who never committed himself. Instead, all of them had taken this news and Andrea's absence calmly; they seemed rather pleased, as if Kitty had announced that Andrea was off on a hunting trip with nice people—acceptable, well-born people, to be accurate, whose connections the Ferentinos knew and approved. No one had said, or apparently thought, that it might be dangerous. Only Kitty thought this, night after night, with anguish, and ordered herself not to be selfish, not to hamper Andrea with her fear.

Andrea's status seemed to be unclear, a former enemy alien become co-belligerent yet still civilian, so he did not have something called a serial number or something called an APO, both of which were evidently coveted honors. Kitty wrote to Andrea, addressing the envelopes to Andrea's first benefactor, the young captain: then the captain was transferred to another unit, and for two months she did not know where to write. Every night, after the fatigue and loneliness of the day, Kitty had gone to their rooms and written pages and pages on thin gray paper; she could hear what she was writing as though she talked to her husband. Perhaps she had never talked so much before, since her function was to listen; it had been another way of serving him. To be mute now made her feel that she was not Andrea's wife; she was really separated and was no one but herself.

Occasional scrubby letters arrived for Kitty, which Andrea managed to send by Americans who would be passing near Torrenova on one of the many incomprehensible errands of war. The Ferentino family received the message-bearers with warmth and the blessings of comfort; they spread the news of this castle, full of friendly people who spoke English, where the food and drink were good, the baths frequent, the beds soft. The castle became a favorite resort of the initiated; the Ferentinos thought their American soldier-visitors charming. Kitty recognized, with pleasure, the wide variety of these men by their speech and manners. But if the old Princess found a young man in her drawing room, lying on his spine with his feet on a table, who rose slowly and said, 'It's sure good to be in a real home again, ma'am, with the water working and all,' she thought this was the style of American gentlemen, and she found it delightfully original. The old Prince, his hand cupped about his ear as he used to listen to the radio, heard with enchantment the stories the visitors told: 'So we gave this Kraut the works and he couldn't talk fast enough. . . . So this lieutenant was there with five guys and one lousy machine gun and you could hear that tank like a mountain of tin cans coming along. . . .' Most of them had seen Andrea. 'He's okay,' they'd say. 'He's doing a good job. It's better if you got an Italian to talk to Italians, they open up better. He's good with Krauts, too—he can talk their stuff.' There were also reserved young men who did not seem very different from Andrea's usual friends and so failed to impress the Ferentinos as deeply. These would rather ask questions about the castle and the paintings in the chapel and the customs of Torrenova than tell the stories which the family loved.

Kitty could make no picture of Andrea in this energetic, chaotic world. None of the visitors ever spoke of war as dangerous; none spoke of death and wounds, except in an unreal way, saying someone caught it or someone got mucked up, which meant nothing to the family. They spoke a great deal about the bliss of home life; Kitty knew Andrea would not regret a bliss which had only tormented him. Then, somehow, Andrea got a serial number and an APO and Kitty was as proud as if he had been decorated for valor by the President of the United States. She could write to him freely, telling him of the life of his land, which was still very hard but quite different from when the Germans were here; it was hard but it was friendly. The peasants grumbled, because they had expected order and plenty when the Americans came; they believed that when Torrenova was freed there would be peace all over the world. But grumbling was not fear; they were never afraid of the Americans. It was decided at once in Torrenova that the Americans were clever, noisy children, and whatever they did was forgiven on the grounds of their good intentions and their obvious national lack of judgment.

Kitty discovered, in her loneliness for Andrea, that she needed more and more to be alone. It was a surprise to find she had needs, and she understood that Andrea's constant silent demands on her had been a gift, using her life and preventing her from criticizing or judging it. Now, in the rain and mud of November and December, she began to take long walks in the wood which Andrea had made into his private kingdom when he was a child. In summer the wood was a magical place. In winter it was sodden with rotted leaves, brown water ran in the stream, and the trees looked starved. Kitty did not see this nor notice the weather; she was reviewing her life.

Everyone said she was gentle and kind and good; but in fact, Kitty thought, I am a coward. She decided nothing; she never insisted. At what point did this so-called talent for understanding become a disease? Would it not have been better for Andrea if she had refused to understand anything, made her own demands, broken the mould of life at Torrenova by rejecting it? I have always thought I wanted to love, Kitty told herself, but perhaps I wanted to be loved, and this soft agreement with everyone is the trick I have used to win love. She was very hard on herself, plodding through the mud, hard and impatient.

She went back over her life, with suspicion, doubting her motives and her actions. There had been her father, whom she loved, a short, stout, red-faced man full of jollity and a desire to give presents. His name was Green—not much of a name. Her mother, born Winthrop, had added an *e* to it, in futile snobbery. Her father was a self-made man, as he used to say with pride until her mother cured him of mentioning an all too obvious fact. Much of his jollity disappeared in her mother's successive cures. How he adored her mother, how he admired her, how rare and flawless he found her; but really, Kitty thought, he was the rare one. Kitty could not decide, now, why her mother had ever married Fred Green, later Frederick Greene, who began life working in a drugstore, married when he owned a chain of drugstores, and died as a millionaire manufacturer of pharmaceutical products. Elise Winthrop came of a good family, by the standards of the Middle West, standards which would have embarrassed the Ferentinos and stimulated the aunt to loud, mocking laughter. Mrs Greene was a tall, handsome woman, but perhaps when she was young she was too tall, not handsome yet, only overpowering; perhaps she did not have many suitors as a girl, and surely none as dazzled and malleable as Fred Green, a coming man.

The Winthrops were certainly not poor, but they had to consider money; the Greenes were beyond such considerations. Kitty was too modest to be corrupted by the arrogance her mother practiced. They had sent Kitty to finishing schools in Paris and Florence; she returned to make a stupendous debut in Chicago. She was lovely in a delicate, quiet way which was unusual in her world; she was a great success, but she did not want any of the young men who proposed to her. Her mother shipped her off to Rome, to rest from the rigors of balls and luncheons and tea dances and receptions and theater parties. Elise Greene's sister Gladys had married a pleasant, lazy Roman nobleman; at nineteen, Kitty found herself established in their sunburned palace on the Via Gregoriana. Aunt Gladys and Uncle Ludovico had firm orders from Mrs Greene to chaperon Kitty carefully and see that no common fortune hunter beguiled her.

Kitty met Andrea at a ball; their courtship was highly suitable, being carried on through notes delivered and called for by Kitty's maid, their meetings always supervised by someone, Aunt Gladys or other respectable middle-aged ladies, friends of Aunt Gladys'. There were also secret meetings, in the Forum or the English Cemetery, or eating ices in the teashop at the Spanish Steps. These rendezvous were splendidly exciting because such devious lies had to precede them. There was the proposal, standing by a hidden fountain in the Borghese Gardens, and then the long involved business of the two families meeting and agreeing, and lawyers and the marriage contract. Kitty did not suspect that the Ferentinos were horrified at the news that their only son, the heir, wished to marry an unknown American, and that Kitty's charm and the welcome fact that she was immensely rich turned what might have been a bitter family row into open-armed acceptance.

I loved him, Kitty thought, from the first minute I saw him; I have never done anything for him except love him. If she loved him gladly, as the entire reason and occupation of her life, Andrea loved her more fiercely, almost with desperation. They were regarded as a not quite believable couple; such faithfulness was unique in their world.

Andrea had gone home with Kitty, in 1935, when her father died. She had never discovered what Andrea thought of Chicago and her home and the people her family knew; besides, an occasion of grief was not a fair test. Kitty remembered only that she could not get warm. It seemed to her that the very walls of their house were frozen, and she wondered if her father had always been cold in it. Her mother had died only two years ago and there was no question of going home for the funeral; Kitty received the news through the Swiss Red Cross. She had no family of her own now. She had no place and no people and no life except Torrenova. It has taken a long time, Kitty thought, but now I am as trapped as Andrea.

It will never stop raining, Kitty decided. There has never been such a year. Before, in March, the peasants in the fields took off their shirts to feel the new spring sun on their shoulders, and all the land bloomed as if smoked over with green. This year cold rain dripped from a steel sky, and Kitty stood at the window considering the dismal world, and herself, grown shabby, stringy, so tired that she often forgot to love Andrea or to want anything. But there was old Signora Polletti, dying of cancer, a fantastic irony to die slowly nowadays when people had learned to die so fast; and the Polletti family expected the visits of the young Princess and appreciated them. If one had nothing to give except one's presence, it was still necessary to move about and speak and listen. Kitty took a brown felt hat and squashed it on her head, noticing that her dark hair was ragged and an unbecoming length, and wrapped herself in a dirty Burberry. The once excellent tweed suit bagged; her shoes were soled like workmen's boots; her stockings of ribbed lisle would not stay up. If Andrea ever comes home, Kitty thought wearily, he will be appalled by me. I don't have to look quite so ghastly; I could try. But for what, for whom? Why shouldn't women be hideous anyhow? They didn't make wars; it was their right to be hideous.

The front door was open and the butler fidgeted in the rain. He could not learn how to receive jeeps, especially a jeep like this one, sticky with mud and overflowing with large, muddy men and musette bags. Some villagers had appeared and also stood in the rain, looking pleased. More friends of Andrea's, Kitty thought, and arranged her tired face in a smile.

One of the large muddy men turned, shouted 'Kitty,' lifted her from the ground, kissed her, hugged her like a bear, kissed her again, and set her down with a bump. Kitty, breathless, stared at this stranger who was Andrea. Her voice was gone, she could only smile and wink back the ignoble tears.

'Get out of the rain, darling,' Andrea said, and plunged into the jeep, hurling down musette bags, telling the driver where to find the garage, urging the others to hurry. His voice was new. He had never sounded so sure, so gay, and so hearty. And he had grown. No, Kitty told herself, a man of forty does not grow. He had been a man who could turn pale with fatigue; but nothing would tire him now. She did not recognize this Andrea, with his wind-burned, open, untroubled face, his certain voice, his tremendous shoulders. He had become an American.

Now they were standing in the vaulted stone hall, laughing for no reason, and Andrea, with his arm around Kitty, said, 'My wife.' He seemed taller than the others because he could say those words; he had a wife and she was here.

Kitty was suddenly grasping strong rain-wet hands.

'Well, hi, Kitty! Andy's been telling us about you. Only twenty-four hours a day, that's all.'

'Sure glad to meet you, Kitty!'

'So this is Kitty! By God, you're lucky, Andy. My wife's in Miami. If I still got her.'

Andrea led his friends up the stone stairs to the east wing and showed them their rooms.

'Nice little place you got here, Andy!'

'You said it was a house. You didn't say it was a damn sight bigger than the Statler.'

'Man, what a bed! You ever see a bed that size?'

Andrea told a maid to build a fire in the copper boiler that heated the bath water, warned his friends that a bell like a fire alarm announced dinner, asked if they still had a bottle because the family did not provide cocktails, and said they should take it easy, whereupon they said he should take it easy too. The stone corridor echoed with their voices and their hilarity.

They were at last in their own rooms and Andrea held Kitty in his arms and kissed her, slowly and tenderly, and looked at her, remembering all of her and seeing her as new.

'My little Kitty, you're tired.'

'Andrea, Andrea,' she said, and wept, and he lifted her on his knees as if she were a child, and stroked her hair and waited for the weeping to stop.

'Darling,' Andrea said. 'Darling, it won't be long now. The war's almost over.'

But was there regret in his voice? Did he speak as a man who accepts an inevitable loss?

'And when it's over,' Andrea said, 'I'm going to take you out of here.' He studied their brocaded sitting room, and he seemed amused but contemptuous. He reminded Kitty of the first Americans who had come to liberate them.

'I hate this place,' Andrea said quietly. Kitty shivered. 'I'll never live here again. It's old, its dead, it's all wrong.'

Kitty found herself wanting to protest, but she was too bewildered. Yet Andrea must know that they had worked hard if not heroically; they had done their best; they had kept life going. Could he forget so easily the little wood, green and secret in the summer; the long pine-needled galoppade by the beach; the autumn smell in the hills; the peasants who honored them and relied on them? It was not fair to speak with this loathing distaste of their home.

'I should have listened to you long ago, Kitty,' Andrea went on. 'I was a fool. But I've learned. You can't know what it's meant to me to work, to be with men, friends, to be somebody on my own.'

'Yes,' Kitty whispered.

'We will have our life and we will be free. I hate to think what I've been all these years, Kitty. I hate to think what I've done to you, hanging on you, hanging on you.'

'Oh, no! No!'

Andrea rocked her gently and said, 'I'm going to look after you, for a change. It's about time.'

She had felt safe in Andrea's arms because he needed her, because she gave him strength. But now she was the one in need. Andrea was hard and quiet as stone; he would make his decisions without help. He had become what he was, alone. Kitty felt herself suddenly old, a burden on a young man who was planning the future with hope. She could not plan; she wanted only to rest. And what would Andrea do with her in that new life, except carry her along, as an obligation and a habit?

Andrea kissed her eyes. 'We'll have time to talk tonight, darling. I must see Papa and Mama.'

'How long will you have here, Andrea?'

'Until tomorrow morning.'

There was no use crying out against time and war. 'I'll have your bath ready,' Kitty said.

She did not move when Andrea left, but sat on a chair staring at her folded hands. She could not think beyond the terror of leaving Torrenova, where she belonged, with her husband whom she did not know. The war had cleaned his mind of the obsession for this land; the war had turned him against his home. The war had rooted her here so that she could imagine no other life, nor desire any other. It cannot be true, Kitty thought in fear. Seven months cannot have done this to us. It is a mistake; it is the shock of meeting; it is the shortness of time. She went to the mirror and studied her face and found it defeated, lined, gray; whereas Andrea had come back to her triumphant. No, no, Kitty told herself, and she searched for lipstick and rouge and tried to brush life into her limp hair. I must, I must, she thought, not knowing what she must do; only that she must seem or be or become something else, quickly, even before Andrea returned to the room. Then she remembered the bath water.

'This bathroom,' Andrea said, standing at the door, 'is the only livable place in the castle. They seem all right, Mama and Papa.'

'Did you tell them? About leaving?'

'Of course not, darling. There's plenty of time for that. No sense in worrying the poor old things.'

He spoke as if they were feeble-minded. He spoke as if, when the moment came, he would tell them some soothing lie and pat them on the head and leave them and forget them. He has forgotten them already, Kitty thought. She was choked with pity for the old Prince and the old Princess. They had committed sins of stupidity against their son, but they were old, they were all old in this house, and helpless. It was a virtue to carry on, with dignity and calm, as Andrea's parents had, in a nightmare world which they could not understand. They deserved something better; they could not be discarded with a careless heart.

'The bath's ready,' Kitty murmured.

Kitty had sent Andrea's uniform to be brushed and pressed, knowing he would not want to wear civilian clothes before his friends, knowing even that he loved his uniform. Andrea, in a dressing grown, with a whisky in his hand, explained his friends while he waited to dress.

'You'll like them, Kitty. Sam, he's the major, is my boss; he comes from Miami; he's got a garage there. He wanted me to go in with him after the war, but it's not my line. Ray, that's the one with the mustache, the lieutenant, works in a bank in Peoria. He's a fine boy. Hank, the captain, is my partner; we've been together from the beginning. He owns a piece of a ranch in Montana. We've talked a lot about it. That's where we're going, Kitty. Hank will find land for us and help us get started. I've seen pictures of it. It's wonderful country.'

'I remember hearing that Montana is very beautiful.'

'Beautiful and big and empty,' Andrea said in a dreaming voice. 'If we had more time, I'd get Hank to tell you about it. But I'd take Hank's word for anything. He'll find us a place near him. The only reason I want the war to end,' Andrea said with terrifying candor, 'is Montana.'

'I must get dressed,' Kitty said, hoping her voice was steady. This was a world that Andrea had never had and Kitty had never seen. This was the world that belonged to men, in which women were cherished visitors. The men knew what they wanted and went after it, supported by their friends; and the women followed. That was how it would be in Montana. She would be Andrea's pleasure, his rest; but he would make his own life, with other men. I am jealous, Kitty thought in horror; I am jealous that he belongs to himself. I want him to depend on me and be torn and lost without me. I am like the old Prince, she thought in a blaze of understanding. I want him to stay weak so that I shall have power. This was too ugly. It was more than ugly; it was wicked, and she would not allow it in herself. It would be better to leave Andrea than to destroy him again.

Kitty tried to stop thinking now, and turn herself into an attractive woman. In the closet, her evening clothes looked soggy; she no longer dressed for dinner. The house was too cold; there was no one to be pretty for. She selected an old Paris dress, remembered as flattering, and took out her diamonds, which seemed dusty from disuse. When Kitty joined Andrea in the yellow-walled sitting room, the admiration in his eyes gave her courage. Perhaps if she concentrated, studied, cared with her whole heart, she could be beautiful for Andrea; and he would be proud of her. It was another way to be a wife. It did not seem much, but it was something, and any way to serve him was good.

Andrea's friends were impressed and entertained by the trailing velvet gowns, the lengthy pearls, the waved, netted hairdos of the old Princess and the Countess Voudransky. Cousin Raoul, as usual, rattled inside his dinner jacket; but Andrea's father with his well-brushed white mane, his haughty straightness, his ancient dress shirt and jeweled buttons, looked princely enough, even by American standards. When the family lapsed into torrential French, the young men in khaki were delighted.

Kitty felt herself tight with nerves. The family must not shame Andrea before his friends. The aunt had observed, with some asperity, that Andrea ate better in the army than they ate at Torrenova, since none of them had put on twenty pounds; but this remark only made Andrea laugh. Cousin Raoul asked peevishly when the war would be over as he really must get back to France, he couldn't think what would have happened to his property in all these years. Andrea ignored this, and his friends were amused by Cousin Raoul's tone; he sounded like a man who had just missed a train.

Then the old Prince said, with the kindly condescension he always used to his son, 'And what is your work, Andrea?'

Kitty trembled. Now Andrea's friends would see how Andrea was treated here, and they would condemn him for tolerating such disrespect.

'I take orders, Papa,' Andrea said casually.

The old Prince was offended by this answer. The Americans were charming and of course allies, but a son of his should do more than take orders from his inferiors.

'Is that all?'

'He takes pretty tough orders,' Hank said. What did the old boy mean: 'Is that all?' What the hell did the old boy think this war was anyhow? 'Three times behind the Kraut lines, in civvies.'

'Civvies?' asked the aunt.

'Civilian clothes,' Hank said. 'Out of uniform.'

'Surely,' the old Prince said, 'in an army, one wears a uniform?'

'You mean,' the aunt interrupted, 'going where the Germans are, causing trouble, like the Partigiani?' This was really interesting. She preferred the old days, when the Germans were here; it had been much more diverting to cause trouble than to be obedient and grateful, as now, with the Americans.

'Something like that,' Hank said shortly.

'But what if he were caught?' Kitty cried. She had forgotten the family; she was thinking, in terror, of how the Germans would deal with spies.

'If you're caught on that kind of job,' Hank said, 'it's curtains.' He was furiously angry with them and with himself. What did they think Andy was, a desk type who sat on his can in a headquarters? But he had not meant to talk of the war, not now or ever. The war was what they knew and not what they talked about; he was acting like a loud-mouth headquarters type himself.

'Curtains?' asked the aunt.

'Cut it, Hank,' Andrea said.

Hank looked sulkily at his plate. Sam, the major, thinking that Andy would naturally not want his family to know the chances he took and so become worried and a general nuisance, said to the old Prince, 'All any of us do is take orders, sir. We have a fine time. You know they call us the Cloak-and-Dagger boys.'

The old Prince was definitely displeased. It would seem that Andrea was in some absurd branch of the army, doing some kind of secondary work in which not even uniforms were worn.

'I am afraid I do not understand,' he said, dismissing the subject. 'I daresay the lack of previous military training counts against Andrea.'

No, Kitty thought, I cannot pity them; they bring it on themselves. They deserve to be abandoned; they deserve to be forgotten. They are more than ignorant. They have no faith; and they make a practice of cruelty. Yes, we will go, she told herself, we will go as soon as we can and we will never come back.

'I am sure Andrea is a very good soldier,' the old Princess said, as if she were defending a scolded child, or comforting him for a bruise or a scratched knee.

Kitty dug her fingernails into her hand, afraid to look at Andrea. But when she raised her head, she saw Andrea's face clear and amused; only Hank was angry. Hank was keeping his mouth shut with difficulty. The other two winked at Andrea; obviously Andy's family was not very bright, but then they were old and didn't know anything so you couldn't blame them.

They honor Andrea, Kitty thought, they admire him; nothing the family says can change that. And Andrea himself was beyond the family, untouched by them, free. I'm glad, Kitty said to herself, and felt the blood hot in her face. She wanted to shout to the old Prince: You couldn't destroy him; he doesn't need any of us, he's whole, he's his own man. Andrea looked across the table at his wife, who was beautiful, and Sam and Ray and Hank knew it as well as he did. He was astonished to see Kitty's eyes bright with tears.

Before dawn, Kitty woke with a sense of new, almost painfully sweet, luxury. This was what it was to follow, to be given to, and finally to rest. I have nothing to fear, Kitty thought, I shall be beautiful for him and his pleasure. How could she have felt this was a poor part; why had she not seen at once that their baffled, grasping life at Torrenova, the emptiness of the war, had been only training for this joy? Kitty leaned over Andrea and kissed his throat, his shoulders, his mouth. Andrea smiled in the darkness.

'My darling,' Kitty said, 'I can hardly wait for Montana.'

Countess Voudransky brought the news from the doctor's house, where she had been making a democratic call and listening to the radio. The old Prince would have heard it too, but later, since he did not feel it suitable to turn on the radio until after dinner. Kitty and Cousin Raoul and the old Prince and Princess were having tea in the library when the aunt stumped in.

'The war's over,' she said.

'Bravo,' said Cousin Raoul, 'I must start packing at once. My dear Caterina, my dear Stefano, I trust you will forgive this hurried departure; my properties. . . .'

No one listened, as usual. The old Prince and Princess stared at Kitty, who had fallen like a scarf over the sofa and was now weeping in deep rough sobs.

'I must say,' Aunt Liza remarked, 'it scarcely seems a time for tears.'

They had noticed a change in Kitty; they could not fail to notice. The aunt believed that Kitty and Andrea had quarreled in March. The old Princess decided dimly that Kitty had a weak chest. Kitty had lost her looks, that was sure; she was nothing but dull eyes circled with black, and alarmingly visible bones.

'Dear Kitty,' said the old Princess, rising with the aid of her cane, 'Andrea will be home now, from one day to the next.' She patted Kitty's shoulder. 'Will you have tea, Liza?' she asked, turning her mind away from the spectacle of her uncontrolled daughter-in-law.

Since March, when Kitty learned what Andrea did in the Americans' army, she had feared by day and dreamed by night of his being captured and tortured. She imagined Andrea's beloved body maimed; she would wake from nightmares in which she heard Andrea's voice screaming. She could not share her horror with the family; she could not write it to Andrea. The relief from fear was as overwhelming as the fear itself.

But Andrea did not come home from one day to the next. He wrote that it seemed as hard to send the army back to the United States as it was to bring the army to Europe. Later he wrote that he did not see how the Americans had managed without him and his apparently unique talent for speaking, writing and reading Italian. Later still he wrote that Hank had gone, presumably to fight in Japan, but since he, Andrea, did not speak Japanese, he was stuck here, a stenographer, a file clerk, a man drowned in papers. He was bored and lonely. There had to be eight copies of everything, sometimes more, Kitty could not imagine.

Think of the summer wasted. Ray had gone, Sam had gone. Only he was left. Why didn't Kitty drive to Rome and have some fun? There was no need for both of them to perish of ennui. What a way to celebrate the end of the war.

Surprisingly, the aunt agreed with Andrea. 'For heaven's sake go, Kitty. It is unbearable to see you fidgeting around all day. Go and buy yourself some clothes and find a good coiffeur. You are a sight. I would never have let myself get into such a condition,' said the aunt, 'not even in prison.'

It was like emerging from a tunnel into white sunshine. Rome was beautiful, flowered, lavish, crowded and gay. You had to search the outlying poor streets to find bomb ruins. No one seemed changed. Lola Gradara said you had to give war one thing—it collected masses of attractive men, unhampered by their women; the English had been simply divine, and the Poles were bliss. Lola said she would take Kitty, who indeed looked a fright, to her dressmaker, who had managed wonderfully all during the war, really not giving in for a moment. She had the new models from Paris and her material was perfect quality. Vera Mignelli sent Kitty her lingerie woman who, Vera said, had exactly the same silk as before the war. There were even nylon stockings and American and prewar French cosmetics. The tradespeople had been too good, Franca Suvereto told Kitty, they'd carried on. Perhaps the buying was a little furtive, and certainly very costly, but there was no excuse for a woman being dowdy, Lucia Astalli explained, war or peace.

In ten days, Kitty had collected a trousseau. She was sleek and lacquered, like a mannequin, she thought, and refreshed by the change. When her friends, who seemed like mad, affected children, tired her, she would walk through the streets, adoring the ocher beauty of the city and preening herself because men turned to watch her. These clothes would be useless in Montana, but they would charm Andrea when he first came home. And he would need a few weeks' rest, before they set out. Kitty rehearsed what she knew of Montana, culled from the encyclopedia: Topography, Fauna, Flora, Lumbering, Livestock. She tried to imagine her new home but only saw it as a large, uneven, pink rectangle on the map, larger than all Italy. She would buy her Montana clothes in Butte; cowboy boots and a shirt and blue jeans such as the centaur girls wore in Western movies.

Kitty told no one of Montana. Montana was Andrea's discovery and he could announce this new life when the time came. Their friends would think them insane. After all, Andrea's father was seventy-four and Torrenova was agreeable, at least for the summer and week-ends, and who would want to go to some unheard-of wilderness in

America, when here was Rome, so lovely, so lighthearted, and even so comfortable?

In September, Andrea came home. The land was golden under a lazy sun, a slow, ripe heat breathed out of the earth, and the summer dust still whitened the trees and hedges. Andrea had hitched a ride on a truck, and dropped off on the main road at the entrance to the pine alley. Some peasants, repairing the roof of a farmhouse, saw him and shouted greetings and called to other men working in the fields. They carried Andrea's musette bag and duffel bag; they followed him up the long lane under the straight dark trees. It was a triumphal procession to welcome the warrior home. Inside the castle the servants ran about, making unusual noise; Kitty, hearing them, hurried to the front door. The moment she saw Andrea she knew he had changed again. The summer indoors, forgotten at a desk, working with strangers, had been too long. He was hollowed out.

The family took Andrea's return as calmly as they had taken his departure; and immediately the old Prince assigned to Andrea those daily minor duties which had been his only work on the estate. Andrea said that the agent was perfectly competent; they had managed all right without him; he did not feel like doing anything for a while. The old Princess prevented her husband from criticizing or nagging; she explained that Andrea was tired. He was tired, he needed rest; but also, Kitty thought, Andrea will never be interested in Torrenova again: we are only visitors here now.

Kitty took Andrea off to picnic on the beach, where the clear green river, that started in the hills, cut through the sand and made a small delta in the sea: it was their favorite place. They shot pheasant and snipe and woodcock: they rode their elderly horses on the hill trails. Kitty's chief concern was to insulate Andrea from his family; but she need not have troubled. Andrea seemed indifferent to everything and everyone, except his wife. He would not speak of the war and he did not mention his plans for the future. He asked Kitty about her life, while he had been away: he wanted to know what she had done and felt and said and worn. When had she been cold, when bored, when lonely; what had she read, whom had she written to, how had she slept, what pleasures had she found for herself? Kitty, at first, was touched by this meticulous interest; then feared it. She understood that Andrea was building her back into his heart, as if she were a neglected shrine which he must now ornament and tend. She did not want to become his religion again; she wanted him to be that man she had briefly seen, who would take her with him where he was going.

The tiredness went from Andrea's body but remained in his mind, as lassitude. He seemed to have no wishes of his own. 'Whatever you like, Kitty,' he said. Perhaps if they went to Rome, if they visited friends in other country houses, he would revive. But after a week in Rome, Andrea said that everything seemed very much the same, didn't it. And after three visits in the country, he said that since they had boar at Torrenova, it was really less trouble to hunt there, and didn't Kitty find the evenings rather dull, so much talk, so much pointless talk. Only Paolo Gradara's horses interested him. Andrea observed that the horses at Torrenova were a scandal and it might be a good idea to buy a few mares and a stallion from Paolo and breed them; it might be fun; it would be something new. Kitty was surprised that Andrea wanted to buy horses when they were leaving so soon, and surely they would not take horses to Montana, which was already full of them. Perhaps Andrea planned to learn horse-breeding in preparation for their life on a ranch.

Before Christmas, Kitty decided she must speak, yet she did not want to hurry Andrea. She brought out the old encyclopedia, the volume *Maryb to Mushe*, and opened it to Montana.

'I've been studying. Andrea,' she said.

'You have?' Andrea turned the pages idly, remarking that they certainly had a lot of trees; look at this; and the cattle; and the mining; they seemed to have about everything.

'It does sound wonderful, Andrea. I'm so glad we're going to live there.'

'Yes,' Andrea said vaguely.

'But when, darling? Oughtn't we to be making plans?'

'You know, Kitty, I think we'd better wait. You see, I'm Italian; after all they lost a lot of their men here, their sons, their husbands, brothers. We were the enemy. I don't think they'd feel very friendly to Italians just yet, considering how their people got killed here.'

'But you were in the American Army.'

'I know. But everything's different after the war.'

'Oh.'

'And then, Kitty, it's hard to go just now. Transportation. Boats. It's still awfully messed up.'

'Oh.'

Andrea bought more horses. He was enthusiastic about his stable and planned to increase it. In the spring, they would go to England for the sales. There was no reason for Paolo Gradara to have a better stable in Lombardy. The aunt encouraged Andrea; even the old Prince was pleased. Horses were not inimical and alien like tractors; the old Prince was glad to see Andrea occupied with something reasonable, forgetting his wrongheaded ideas about modernizing the land. Kitty told herself that a man had to recuperate from war as from a sickness; she must be patient. Besides it was right that Andrea should learn all he could about horses; the time was not wasted.

'Have you heard from Hank, Andrea?'

'No.'

'Have you written him?'

'Well, no, Kitty. I thought I'd wait. I don't want to be a nuisance.'

'But surely you should write?'

'He'll write to me, if he feels like it. It's so far away. It's so different there. He might have gone home and wondered why he got tied up with me, you know, a foreigner, an Italian. He might have changed his mind.'

'Oh, Andrea, how can you!' Kitty cried. 'Hank's your friend. You know that. People don't change.'

'No, people don't change, do they? Even if they want to. Even if they try. I am still Andrea Ferentino, no matter how much I wish I were Hank Duncan of Whitefish, Montana.'

Then seeing the look of blank shock on her face, Andrea knelt by her chair, with his arms around her waist.

'Kitty, Kitty.' He seemed to be begging for something.

'I dreamed them,' Andrea said. His face was in Kitty's lap and his voice was broken, like a man crying. 'I dreamed them. I dreamed myself. I dreamed it all. It will never happen.'

So Torrenova was stronger than war. If Andrea could have gone with Hank, in March, they would be there now, in that wide strange land, and Andrea would be saved, in the company of others who made their own lives. I don't know what a ranch house looks like, Kitty thought. Logs? Brick? Plaster? She knew the old Princess's tower very well, and it was the future. They would never be free of Torrenova. There might not have been a war, for nothing had changed.

The knowledge of this defeat stood between them, and they feared it. Andrea feared that Kitty would despise him, as he despised himself, and Kitty knew this and fought against it. For if Andrea believed that she could abandon him in her heart, then he was entirely alone. She did not abandon him, or despise him; she pitied him. Kitty's headaches returned. It was a relentless strain to keep Andrea from hating himself.

And slowly Andrea slipped back into his disgust with the ways of Torrenova. At night, in their sitting room, he would walk the floor and tell Kitty of the stupidity, the backwardness, the waste that was Torrenova. Sometimes he raged against his father and sometimes against the peasants. Why didn't the peasants themselves demand reform? Why didn't they strike? They weren't serfs, after all. Why did they accept life without electricity and running water? Why did they agree to work like animals when machines would do that work? They were as bad as the old Prince, as unimaginative, as imbecile.

Perhaps Kitty was tired of listening, or perhaps she thought the old Prince might recognize that the time had come to abdicate; surely a man of seventy-five would weary of power at last.

'Why don't you go to your father and tell him what you want to do, and insist that you be given the authority to do it?'

Andrea stopped walking, stared at Kitty in amazement, and then, slowly, as if he were taking a dare, said, 'I will. It's the only way.'

The aunt and the old Princess had gone to bed and the old Prince sat alone by the fire in the library, reading *Manon Lescaut* for the tenth time. Kitty had followed Andrea, with some obscure notion of keeping him company, or being near to help him. She stood in the hall, beside the closed door, rearranging flowers on a table. The interview was brief. The door opened and the old Prince, standing very straight, said, 'You must wait a little longer, Andrea.' The old Prince, in his anger, did not see Kitty, but marched down the corridor, past the coats of armor and the dark portraits of his ancestors, to his own rooms.

Andrea sprawled in a leather chair, with his feet on the fender. He did not look up.

'He may be right, for all I know.' Andrea said.

'Right in what?'

'He says that for eight centuries, Ferentinos and their people have lived on this land in peace, or as much peace as they could manage. Anyhow, the trouble did not come from here. He says no one has suffered without help, no one has gone hungry. Everyone knows his place. He says there has been change everywhere, and it doesn't seem to have brought happiness or virtue. He says my way will make Torrenova like the world: the old people will be bewildered, the young people will be dissatisfied and want to leave for the cities. He says if the land has supported us all for eight centuries in this wasteful way, it will probably last for another eight centuries; and that being richer is no use and electric light is no use. What matters is knowing who you are and accepting the order of your life.'

Kitty said nothing; she did not know what Andrea wanted her to say.

'Have a night cap?' Andrea asked.

Paolo Gradara telephoned to say that they had four plane tickets for London and their rooms at the Ritz, and that Lord Thane, after all, was going to put up his yearlings for sale; be sure to tell Andrea. Kitty decided to drive down to the galoppade, where Andrea was exercising a new horse. It was May and the late afternoon sky flashed with pale opal light. They might swim before coming home.

Kitty left her car and walked under the umbrella pines to the far end of the galoppade. She wanted to watch Andrea coming toward her, along the straight brown pine-needled stretch of track. It was marvelous to think that in fifteen years she had never seen his face without excitement, nor ever wanted to look at another.

Kitty heard Andrea, far up the ride; he was singing or shouting. Then she saw him, standing Western style in the light English saddle. He seemed to be singing a shanty based on the word 'giddap', and he was slapping the horse's flank, in a free, loose way, and the wind blew his hair and he was laughing. The horse thundered by with the noise of a stampeding herd.

Andrea dismounted at the end of the galoppade and walked the horse back to where Kitty waited.

'What are you doing, Andrea?'

'Cowboy stuff,' Andrea said. 'That's the way they ride in Montana; at least I think it is, from what Hank said. We may not have the wide open spaces here, but I'm teaching Herod to be a cow pony. All I need now is a ten-gallon hat.'

Kitty stumbled across the track to Andrea and threw her arms around him. 'We can still go! You think of it, you want to go! Please, Andrea! We'd be so happy. Why should we stay here?'

Andrea dropped the bridle and held his wife against him. She clung to him, crying. When she was quiet, Andrea loosened her arms and said, 'I waited too long, Kitty.'

Do I look the way he does? Kitty thought. It seemed to her that now they faced the truth; there was nothing ahead except the years of their life.

'Darling,' Andrea said. 'Darling, don't. . . .'

Kitty pulled out a handkerchief, to wipe her eyes and to hide them.

'I'll give Herod one more run,' Andrea said in a carefully brisk voice, 'and drive back with you.'

'Fine,' Kitty said, matching his tone.

I failed him, Kitty thought, there was something I should have given him and I didn't, I couldn't. Faith? Courage? Love had not been enough.

The old Princess's dreaming detachment no longer seemed cowardice or frailty; it appeared a most wise solution. Perhaps, once, the old Prince had wished to be free and himself, longed to make something new; like all men, needed for his life's sake to build. Perhaps he had been refused his chance, and accepted the refusal. In due course, Kitty thought, Andrea may see his father's point. It was at least arguable; you could hardly say that change benefited people much, looking around you at the changes. But there would be no son, no man after Andrea to wait and eat his life out in waiting, born trapped, belonging only here. There will be no son, she told herself; and understood with grief that her failure had turned into triumph.

It would be easier now. Andrea would not fight any more, he knew how his life must go, he would learn to be happy. It is really not so bad, she thought, and saw, clearly, the small salon in the tower where the old Princess sat doing needlework in the afternoons; it is not so bad, it is all we have known, and we need never speak of it again.

FOR RICHER
FOR POORER

'I must say I liked Rose better when she was waiting for old Lord Adderford to die.' Lady Harriet leaned closer to the looking glass and frowned at the exquisite curve of her mouth. She thought about Rose Answell and her new lipstick; both irritated her.

Rose Answell had been irritating, you might even say maddening, for at least twenty years. First there was a long stretch of life when no one knew Rose or had heard of her; then suddenly Rose appeared as the girl bride of Bertie Radway, whom everybody knew and deplored. Bertie was a young man who fell down, owing to incurable drunkenness, at debutante parties. No one would have dreamed of marrying him, although he was far from hideous and quite rich, and his papa, Lord Adderford, owned half of Gloucestershire and a perfectly acceptable stately home. Rose, a total stranger and married to a famous sot, had the insolence, even then, to snub other girls who had not yet got their man.

After Bertie broke his neck on the Cresta Run, Rose became one of the most maddening young widows you could hope to meet. People said how brave she was, infuriating in itself, and Rose adopted the attitude that she was now a Great Thinker or something of the sort. Normally sane men started to quote Rose's opinions; and one had to swallow that nonsense for fear of seeming jealous.

Then, just when it looked as though Rose might be a widow forever, which was some consolation, she married Alan Answell, whom everyone had always adored, and who was vaguely an MP, whereupon Rose immediately became an authority on politics. No matter what Rose did, she succeeded in being maddening. She could not come into Maude Calhoun's bedroom to powder her nose, while the gentlemen were swigging port after dinner, without making you see at once that your own lipstick was smudged.

Lady Harriet scooped away, with a fingernail, a pink hairbreadth's streak of her new lipstick. Disgusting color; someone had told her you could eat like a horse and it never smeared; what rot one believed; and the stuff could only be bought in Switzerland, costing a fortune, and, to top it all, smelled like cough medicine and was called Kizmi.

Lady Harriet began to realize that, as usual, Rose Answell had put her in a temper.

Standing before the long glass, Lady Harriet's dearest friend, Mrs Bobby Braithewaite, was taking short, fierce breaths and tugging at something invisible above her bosom and something invisible below her hips.

'It's not possible,' Betsy Braithewaite announced. 'The anguish. Have you ever seen these Dior stays, Harriet? I mean, one all by itself, standing up?'

Lady Harriet turned to study her friend.

'It makes your waist a dream,' she observed.

'Well, yes, but is it worth it? *What* an evening. Of course your Dick's always angelic but that would be like trying to lure one's brother. And Maude's regular Duke who is well known to be blind and deaf. And Tippy, for heaven's sake. And Bobby who hasn't noticed my figure since before the war.'

'And Alan Answell,' Lady Harriet suggested.

'Alan! Can you see Alan daring to look at anyone, with Rose about? I can't bear her. Neither gold-digging nor political. Simply cannot bear her. Never could.'

The bathroom door opened and Chloe Ashe Vernham, a creamy vision in cream-colored satin and pearls, yawned comfortably in the doorway. She carried her slippers in her hand.

'Who're you talking about?' she asked.

'Rose Answell,' said Lady Harriet.

'I cannot imagine why we talk so much about Rose Answell.' Mrs Ashe Vernham dropped her slippers in the middle of the floor and proceeded to the dressing table. 'Push over, Harriet. Your hair's perfect, dear girl. It always is. I must make some repairs, although it's hardly an evening to bring out one's fighting spirit. I do wish Maude would stop giving dinner parties; I've begged her to, for years. Tippy. That's what I've had—solid Tippy bumbling on and on. It's a miracle to me that one's letters ever get delivered, considering he's in charge.'

'You can scarcely say the telephone's a complete success, and he runs that too,' Mrs Braithewaite remarked from the chaise longue where she was stretched out, resting from her stays.

'Poor Alan,' Lady Harriet said. 'He used to be so brainless and beautiful and such fun before Rose got her claws on him.'

'Nonsense,' Mrs Ashe Vernham said, flapping a swansdown puff at her nose. 'He worships her. She's a wonderful wife to him. No one can deny that Rose writes all his speeches.'

'I am told,' said Lady Harriet, 'that Alan's speeches are lethal.'

'Doesn't matter a bit. The thing is to make a lot of them and sooner or later you end up in the Cabinet.'

'Why do you suppose Rose bothered to come?' Mrs Braithewaite asked. 'I can't see there's anyone useful.'

'She probably thought she'd find Geoffrey,' Mrs Ashe Vernham said. 'She might have known I can't drag Geoffrey to Maude's dinners.'

'Ah, yes, Geoffrey,' Mrs Braithewaite said with satisfaction.

Geoffrey Ashe Vernham was really important; he was Home Secretary and odds-on favorite to be next Prime Minister—unlike Tippy who was only Postmaster General.

'All set?' Mrs Ashe Vernham inquired. 'Come on then, rally round one's childhood chums; we can't leave poor Maude alone with Rose. Maude's got such a good heart she never knows when people are being horrid to her. Someone must pry Tippy off me. I count on you girls. I've done you a great many favors in my time. We can leave at half past eleven. Agreed?'

'You bet,' Mrs Braithewaite said, in American.

Beautiful, elegant, serene, trained to please, able and sportingly willing to please, the ladies went down to the drawing room.

Rose Answell knew exactly why she was there. She had been rather miffed to find herself, at dinner, between an insignificant Duke who collected hourglasses and Harriet's husband, Dick Chace, who was an ordinary rich banker. Still, it was probably for the best, because now she had a clear run on Tippy. She drew Tippy, without effort, and sat, graceful and devastatingly attentive, while Tippy maundered on.

She watched Tippy with a practiced, almost a scientific, eye. She had seen this happen so often: the male blooming, expanding, flowering, and not because one took any real trouble, simply because one listened. Years of successful experiment had taught her that she need, in fact, hardly listen at all. It was done with a gleaming, approving look, while thinking of whatever one chose to think about; with an encouraging or admiring smile—you could always sense, either by their expressions or the note of their voices, when the moment had come to enlarge the smile into a delighted laugh; with an occasional frown of sympathetic agreement. It was unbelievable that women actually went to bed with men to get what they wanted, when all you had to do to ensnare the gentlemen was listen or seem to listen. Heavens, Rose thought, while Tippy's voice droned senselessly around her, *how* I listened to darling

Alan. It was a completely safe and infallible method, and the first thing mothers should tell their daughters.

Rose sank into smiling, rapt deafness. She had already found out what she wanted to know. Tippy confirmed the rumor which Cynthia Delafield reported last week. Ogilvie-Beck was going to resign before Christmas. 'Poor old O.B.,' Tippy said, 'He's had a dreadful time with those niggers. Niggers quite out of hand, worrying O.B. to death, and he gets no thanks for it. The Socialists spoiled them, that's what it is. O.B. says he can't wait to get back to Needers and have time for shooting. Hates the job, always has; he only took it to oblige the PM. As soon as this last flap dies down, he's going to get out. By Christmas in any case. Of course, this is between us, Rose.'

Now Tippy, soothed and elated by Rose's intelligent interest, chatted about his cows. Rose rested her arm along the back of the sofa, leaned her head on her hand, a pretty pose and almost as comfortable as sleeping, and glowed at Tippy. He remarked, with pleasure, her fine black eyes, her wide mouth which smiled so adorably as he scored his points about fodder and breeding, her heart-shaped face. She was wearing black and that was how he had first known her, in black, a quiet young widow. Most women had lost the art of quietness.

Alan Answell was a lucky fellow, and all the ladies who criticized Rose were nicely confused when Rose married him. Splendid fellow, Alan, Jock's nephew; everyone liked him; handsome fellow too, but not a bean to his name. Which proved how wrong the ladies were, years ago, when they said Rose married Bertie Radway for his money, or rather for old Adderford's money to come. Rose was hardly more than a child at the time; she couldn't possibly have known that poor Bertie was a hopeless drunk, never seemed to sober up except in the winter so he could go hurtling down the Cresta Run. Terrible when he got killed on it; bobsledding was an asinine sport.

Rose knew Tippy only slightly, but she also knew that nothing pleased aging men more than to feel they were intimate friends of much younger women. Tippy was purring as foreseen; soon she would slip in the few bits she meant him to remember, and they could leave this tedious party.

Alan was having a fine old time with Harriet and Betsy. Harriet and Betsy were the end, Rose thought; she had known them since they were eighteen; Harriet willowy, dark, with promising eyes; Betsy an auburn-haired baby-face; both assured of being the year's most glamorous debutantes, both assured of doing nothing at all, happily, for the rest of their lives. She was then a married woman of nineteen, and occupied in joining their world. She did join it, but she had never belonged. Due,

Rose thought, to the fact that one cannot be entirely half-witted no matter how hard one tries.

The Radway period was a phase Rose preferred to forget; if she hadn't been so young and in such a hurry, she would never have troubled with Bertie. However, behold Betsy and Harriet now: Betsy tied to a bridge player who hadn't stirred out of White's for the last fifteen years except occasionally during the war, and Harriet saddled with that dreary banker. Whereas she had Alan. Rose smiled at Alan, a wifely smile, which concealed the titanic pride of an artist in his work. They would all be astonished to see how far Alan was going. Very far. To the top.

At a quarter past eleven Rose said, 'I can hardly bear to leave, dear Tippy. But we must go, alas.' He had been glued to her for an hour.

Tippy kissed her hand, at a loss for words to express his infinite delight in her company. Rose's understanding of hornless Red Polls was unique; he was determined to see her more. So stupid the way one never saw the people one really wanted to see.

'Dear Maude,' Rose said, 'what a lovely evening.' She kissed the air in the neighborhood of Lady Calhoun's cheek.

'So sweet of you to come,' Lady Calhoun said. 'I know how terribly busy you and Alan always are. We must do it again soon.'

'Yes, we must,' Rose said. She looked around the room and thought it unnecessary to make any special farewells; instead she sent out a sweeping circular smile and murmured good night. Alan Answell, having seen his wife rise, made very special farewells to Betsy Braithewaite and Harriet Chace.

'What a charming couple,' Lady Calhoun said, when Rose and Alan had gone.

'Couldn't agree more,' Tippy said. Lady Harriet and Mrs Braithewaite did not commit themselves.

The Braithewaites gave Mrs Ashe Vernham a lift. In the car, Betsy Braithewaite said, 'Well, anyhow, Rose saved you from Tippy.'

'Butter wouldn't have melted in the old boy's mouth,' Mr Braithewaite observed. 'I thought he was going to burst into song. Very nice of Rose, really.'

'Most extraordinary,' said Mrs Ashe Vernham.

Alan Answell drove an ancient, loved, lovingly cared-for Bentley. He treated it with the affection he would have shown a horse.

'Shall we take a quick whisk through the park?' he asked, having some notion of exercising his car.

'Oh, Alan.' This was the tone of reproof his wife used with the children.

'All right.'

'Well,' Rose sighed and snuggled down in the seat. 'Tippy was most informative. O.B. is sure to resign and high time too. Helston will probably move over from the Board of Trade, and that cipher Plimsoll will get Education. Thus leaving the Minister of State for Colonial Affairs a gaping hole in the Government. All very satisfactory.'

Alan said nothing. When they were alone, Rose, who was the public listener, talked a great deal. It was a rest. Rose insisted that he must express himself to people; it was the only way to put one's ideas over. Have confidence in yourself, or how can you hope to convince others? His natural form was to laugh easily and impartially, enjoying everyone's jokes. He also listened with respect, conscious that anyone else knew more than he did. He had overcome these failings as best he could, helped by Rose's criticism and advice.

It had to happen sooner or later, Alan thought, but he regretted his long-lost, nice, obscure job. He had been so comfortable as one of three Parliamentary Secretaries to the Minister of Agriculture. He loved the Pig Scheme and he never had to make a speech. It was torture when the Socialists got in, and he became a Back Bencher, and Rose goaded him to talk all the time. Rose would not allow him to slink back into the blessed silence of Agriculture, although he could have had the job when the Conservatives took power again. She pointed out that agriculture was necessary as everyone knew, but he must remain free for his mission, the Colonies. Farmers did not need help, or rather they were able to look after themselves, but Alan had his special duty to Britain and to those varied, helpless, brown, yellow and black people who depended on Britain. To that end Alan became a free-wheeling expert on Colonial affairs and made thoughtful pronouncements in the House and at dinner parties; to that end he was always being scheduled to address meetings. It was amazing how many people would get together, how often, in miserable hired halls, to listen to ghastly lectures on the problems of Empire.

'I will be glad to creep into bed,' Rose said. 'Tippy is surely the dullest man alive.'

The old boy had looked so pleased with himself when he said good night to Rose. Poor old boy, Alan thought, but then Tippy would never know.

He dismissed Tippy, and thought instead of Chloe, Harriet and Betsy: their beauty was a public service. And they were always so gay, so soft, so leisurely. He was grateful, as if something precious had been saved from the lava-flow of time.

'I thought Chloe was looking a treat,' Alan said.

'Oh, did you? I thought she seemed rather haggard. And she never varies, does she? I find that tiddly talk quite exasperating in the long run.'

Sensible and funny and generous. Alan thought, what more could anyone be? But there was something more, and better, and he did not know exactly what it was.

'She's a very good friend.'

'Oh, Alan, what a *pointless* thing to say.'

'Although my Right Honorable friend, the Member for West Hammering, has handled the deplorable riot in Pethantikynia with great tact and efficiency, it is surely the better part of wisdom to acknowledge the very real power of Kwak an Sung and, accepting all the implications, attempt to gain his confidence and co-operation by including him in the Provisional Government. Having known Kwak an Sung for years, I can testify to his loyalty and. . . .' He was saying it aloud, standing before the electric fire in his study. Once, leaving this room to get himself a needed whisky, he had found the children crouched outside the door, where they were listening to Daddy intone. They raised their heads and looked at him with wide, pitying eyes; clearly they thought he was insane, and were very sorry.

I do not give a damn, Alan Answell said to himself, whether Kwak an Sung lives or dies, let alone gets into any known government.

The desirable thing would be to drive to Queen's and play two hard sets of tennis before lunch. The editor of the *Record* and the famous American political commentator Ralph Gorman and Max Berthold who did that BBC panel and a few other assorted blights were coming today. It was one of Rose's publicity parties.

Alan teetered before the fire, wondering how he had reached this position of being a great authority on awful people like Kwak an Sung. He would not trust, farther than he could throw them, any of the brown, yellow, black politicians he had met thus far; although in justice the same could be said of white politicians, with the exception of a few Englishmen. How did I get here? Alan asked himself, worrying over the steps in the journey.

Lady Irene Answell had absent-mindedly launched her younger son into politics. The MP for Modesbury had not changed practically within the memory of living man, so it was no surprise when he died in 1939 just before the Easter Recess. The Chairman and three important members of the local Conservative Association came to consult Mr Answell about a successor: it was their habit to consult Mr Answell. Modesbury had no industry except Modesbury College, with its famed ancient buildings which housed six hundred privileged boys in a state of black hardship. Since Mr Answell was the Headmaster, he was naturally the right man to go to for advice. The Chairman and company arrived at teatime to find Lady Irene present, with garden shears, trowel, muddy shoes and a certain amount of mud under her fingernails. Mr Answell could think of no one for the job; he was not really interested; at the moment he was fretting over a very nasty problem, kleptomania in the Third Form. Lady Irene said dimly, 'Well, why not Alan? He's young and healthy and not apt to die in the middle of things.'

The representatives of the Conservative Association were at first amazed but later thought it an excellent idea. They were a proud, Bolshie lot and never took orders from the Central Office in London and turned a cold eye on ambitious outsiders who believed that a fat contribution to the yokels' Association would buy a safe seat. It had to be a Modesbury man, and indeed why not Alan Answell? Fresh blood, finest type of young Tory, splendid at games, backbone of England. Alan's boss was sorry to lose such a talented salesman of Bentleys. His friends were delighted; what fun for all, they would rally round and help him in the by-election. Alan was agreeable to any passing babies who could bring in the mothers' vote, and drank beer in the Stag-at-Bay with the male electorate and saw at once that no one wanted heavy thinking about world events, but simply a good grumbling gossip about conditions in Modesbury.

Alan made his three spaced bows, took the Oath, shook hands with the Speaker, and thus became a Member of Parliament in May 1939. In September he was in the army.

He had malaria in Burma and later got an MC which at least ten other men deserved as much, and he hated it all, and meantime Mark, his older brother, the clever one, the cream of the family, was killed in the RAF. That was when he began to think, during those hot, wet, lonely years, with Mark dead.

He knew he had a very ordinary mind, but he saw that he had a duty and must do his best. He wasn't sure how he could help, he was only sure that he hated war and the cruel suffering it brought to these small brown people, who were not fighting folk at all and were ploughed under by passing foreign armies, through no fault of their own. He could never put into words what he felt about the Burmese, not to himself nor to anyone else; but those feelings ruled his life. It had something to do with Mark's not being dead for nothing, and something to do with England being like Mr Answell, stern and just, but also kind and a protector. But there was more to it than that.

He realized that the Burmese were very backward, as backwardness went nowadays, and had an attitude of helpless innocence toward all machinery, and possessed most alarming notions of hygiene, and were no doubt given to many antique and superstitious forms of private behavior. Still they were beautiful as he had not before known beauty, and gentle and sane in their own enduring way. They were not weak people; they were only defenseless. They were stronger, in their defenselessness, than the various khaki-clad people who overran them, used them, bossed them, and left them to whatever fate other khaki-clad people would deal out. He honored the Burmese, the country people, the people in rotten huts in lost villages; and he knew they needed help because they hadn't learned all the dirty tricks of the modern world. He wanted to help them; he wanted really to save for them what they had, but he could not explain exactly what they did have. And he had no idea how to serve them, but decided that when the war was over he would go back into Parliament, this time with a purpose.

When he finally did return to London, after what seemed a lifetime's exile, he met Rose, or met her again; they belonged to the same small world in London and had known each other unseeingly for years. It would be right to say that he recognized Rose for the first time in the autumn of 1945. She had a splendid mind, quite superior to his, and she understood his serious intentions and sympathized and agreed. It was too wonderful to find this fascinating woman who would let him talk about what concerned him. She also knew exactly what he must do. He must become Secretary of State for the Colonies. In that governing position he would be able to show what Britain was capable of in wisdom and mercy. She made him feel that he could protect her as well as all the dark-skinned millions, and he longed to do just that. She was so lovely and so alone. Six weeks after their first dinner together, they were married in the church at Modesbury.

Alan looked glumly at his notes. 'Testify to his loyalty and high intelligence.' Kwak an Sung had been at Balliol; he used to play tennis with the shifty little clot. Damn good, very quick; and probably the only reason Kwak an Sung didn't cheat was because it was too hard to do with people watching.

There was a knock at the door, immediately followed by Rose.

'How is it going?' she said.

'It's one more speech.'

'Darling, it is *not*. It's frightfully important. Let me see.' She took the wad of scribbled notes and settled herself in his armchair to read.

He was no longer touched by Rose's interest in his speeches. He knew by now that it would not matter to Rose if he talked about elm blight or the disappearing titmarsh, as long as that would make him, quickly, Minister of State for Colonial Affairs. Rose had lowered her sights from Secretary to Minister, explaining that one had to mount the ladder of command halfway up, and besides the junior men really did the work.

'Give me a cigarette, please,' Rose said. 'Couldn't you put in something about Burma?'

'What about Burma?' Alan asked, handing her the cigarette box.

'Oh, you know, your war years there and all. Excellent effect.'

'No,' he said stonily.

'Really? Why not?'

'Just no.'

'Oh, well. Never mind. Now, darling, I think you ought to tone it down here, about O.B. You mustn't seem to be blaming him for the mess. After all he is about to resign, and it never does to look disloyal in the House. And of course everyone will realize that your suggestions for Kwak an Sung are your own, but it would be more tactful if you could make it appear that you were only quoting O.B.'s ideas. I'm sure it will be a great success.'

Since Rose was pleased, it might be a good plan to discuss something which did concern him, unlike Kwak an Sung.

'Rose, John is really a very little boy.'

'What?' Rose said. She looked at her watch. She was not at all sure that Mrs Zadzicza had timed the soufflé safely. 'Darling, is it important about John, now? I've so much to do.'

'We never seem to have a minute to talk about John.'

'All right, Alan, but be quick.'

'I said, he's a very little boy. He's only seven. It isn't fair to be so hard on him. He went to bed in tears last night.'

'He cries far too much. I do hate a cry-baby boy. And he must stop being so lazy, Alan. His writing is dreadful and I told him to make a perfect copy of that exercise, and he didn't finish, and besides it was unreadable. He can't learn too soon to get things right.'

'He's only seven, for God's sake, Rose. By the time he grows up, everyone will be using typewriters, anyhow.'

'Personally I think you spoil him and that's one of the reasons he's so soft. Alan, I really must speak to Mrs Zadzicza; the people will be here in ten minutes.'

The dining room was papered with squashy cabbage roses; tasseled and fringed red corduroy curtains hid the gloom of a gray, drizzling November sky; the guests sat on well-sprung tufted chairs; bead pictures and comically virtuous embroidered mottoes hung on the walls; a small

coal fire twinkled under a chimney piece ornamented with an absurd
clock and pyramids of glass-encased wax flowers. Rose's dining room
was a stylish joke; the company nestled down to their food, as if ranged
inside a Victorian sewing basket.

Chatting busily and importantly, the guests, all men, tucked away
billowy cheese soufflé, an imposing baked fish bedded on bay leaves,
French peas with tiny onions, tomatoes in a casserole, flaky jam tarts.
Rose did her own marketing; it was a special point of pride to feed so
many people so well for so little. This new hock which she had bought
last week at a wine sale at Haver's was a glorious bargain, as happy
smiles and flushed faces proved.

It was now time to give Berthold a brief chance to shine. Without
effort, Rose turned the attention of the table to a small, donnish fat man,
who performed gratefully. So much less trouble than women, Rose
thought. She often gave woman-free luncheon parties, and never took
chances on unknown wives.

Mr Gorman, the American, was very nice and useful; pity he looked
like a potato wearing spectacles. He'd said, 'I can see your husband has
a great political future, Mrs Answell. I'll be keeping my eye on him.'
He would certainly cable a bit about Alan, mentioning his speech today.
How odd that she hadn't realized until lately the value of having some
reputation in America too; it seemed to blow back across the Atlantic.

Daunton, the editor of the *Record*, was a boor; the next time she saw
Lord Hasleton she would suggest that Daunton didn't seem to her quite
the thing. Fancy saying, 'You run a wonderful press conference, Mrs
Answell.' We can do without Daunton, Rose thought.

There must be, now, just enough talk of Alan in the press and not
too much. Alan seemed tired, poor lamb; no one ever felt well in
November. Still, with a little prodding, he played up very nicely.

The men had returned to the world's work, leaving Rose alone in
the drawing room. This room was all pale gray-blue; elegance and space
had been her object. She loved her home, she thought it the most
attractive house in London and envied no one. Alan had jibbed at
borrowing from the bank to buy it, but she had insisted, how rightly.
Barton Street was exactly the place to be, division bell downstairs, everyone dropping in from the House; and there was always food and drink
and Rose, interested in their work. Alan would have settled, the sweet
dolt, for something inexpensive on a shabby Kensington square.

She must be sure to compliment Mrs Zadzicza on the fish; she
always cheered Mrs Zadzicza with praise. The Zadziczas were pearls:
White Poles, ruined gentlefolk, an ex-officer, an ex-lady, you would
never think they'd make the best servants in London. She was spared

all the usual whining and tea guzzling and sluttishness. Alan worried about the Zadziczas' wages, but she said he had it all wrong, as he did. The Zadziczas did not care for money, they cared about having a nice home and being appreciated. And Miss Jenkins, whom she had found through the Dean of the London School of Economics, was a treasure too. Miss J. trundled the children around after school every day, for the reasonable sum of one pound fifteen a week and bus fares. The children were by now perfectly able to have their baths and dress themselves, and to get to bed alone if she was busy. It was a great saving, and a great relief, to be through with Nannie.

Rose rested on the blue sofa by the fire, listened to the rain, and basked in her own weather. Alan was a young man still, and Minister of State for Colonial Affairs was only the beginning. Darling Alan, Rose thought, what would have become of him if I hadn't taken him in hand? When he returned from the war, looking too beautiful for words, brown and lean and rather tragic in an exciting way, he was chock-a-block with the most woolly notions for doing good. Heaven knew he came by woolly notions legitimately: Lady Irene and her potty garden, and old Mr Answell champing away about education being a training in honor or some such. However, Alan's parents were ideal caretakers for the children during holidays, and never came to London, so she was well satisfied with them too.

After Bertie died in Switzerland she swore she would never marry again. She had had five years with Bertie to realize her mistake: money was not everything. Bertie's world was all fortunes, titles, and futility; no one paid the slightest attention to it except dressmakers and hotel keepers. The rich, when you studied the matter carefully, existed to provide comforts for the powerful: think how gratified Press lords were if they could persuade Geoffrey Ashe Vernham and Chloe to go on their yachts; think how unnecessary it was for Geoffrey to own a yacht himself.

People probably expected her to wither away when she was left with old Lord Adderford's grudging pittance as her only capital, but she had no such intention. She stepped smartly out of Bertie's enclave of gilded drones into the premises of Messrs Marcus and Faversham, Publishers. Publishing, an amateur profession, always had room for another amateur.

Within two years, Marcus and Faversham turned over their public relations to young Lady Radway, who had the most extraordinary talent for getting results. From that to being boss of those traveling debates for soldiers was like putting one foot in front of the other. She loved that job, it was great fun, and she saw to it that the Big Names, the people who really ran the world, took time off to enlighten her soldiers. At thirty-two, with the war ended, she was a power in her own right; all kinds of people were flattered to be asked to her house in Eaton Mews.

She had been rather tired in 1945, as who wasn't, and had lately ended a long, irritating affair with Peter Lavery who would probably finish as Lord Chancellor, but meantime was too selfish and inconsiderate. Alan's being so in love simply swept her off her feet. Also, at the back of her mind, she preserved a nagging anger against Lord Adderford and his famous remarks on her inability to produce an heir. There were plenty of men to have as lovers if one wanted them, and unlimited men to use for everything else. But marriage was a public undertaking— house, career, children, position—and you absolutely had to succeed together as a couple. There were few enough men to build all that on; none, as far as she was concerned, except Alan.

I am a perfectly happy woman, Rose thought. Could any of her friends say the same? She had everything she wanted: a competent, handsome, adoring husband; two beautiful, healthy, well brought up children, except for that slight taint of Answell woolliness in John which she would eradicate; a heavenly house, ideal servants. And all, she thought, amused by the phrase, handmade. There was the constant thrill of planning, building, making it come true, and going on, from gain to gamble, gamble turning into gain.

Gamble, Rose thought, at once disliking the word. Gamblers sometimes lost. She could not and would not lose. She was not gambling, she was playing to win. No one really wanted anyone else to win; that was natural enough. But a mutual aid system applied to a whole world: people were automatically helped to win; you were born into the Old School Tie Protective Association. She had not been born into it, no one had helped her; she had done it alone. She was infinitely beyond the Harriets and Betsys and Chloes; she was proud of her own will and her nerve. Alan of course did not realize the problem, and she would never dream of talking to him about it. Alan was so sweet, and also so foolish, that he no doubt thought they got where they were because people were nice, and liked them.

What Alan also did not know, and what no one else would ever be allowed to know, was the strain of winning. Money in itself was nothing; but there had to be enough of it, and there was not. Not enough to do what she had to do; even the miserable extra wages of a Junior Minister were now essential. Alan had no notion of how she schemed and combined, paid some bills, left others unpaid, to keep the appearance of their life so easy. It could not go on much longer; she knew she was tiring. This victory, the most important because the first was always the hardest, had to come now. And though she was still young, she was not as young as she had been, looked better by candlelight, had to hold her head in a certain way to avoid slightly scrawny shadows under the chin, and sometimes woke feeling dingy and longing for a forbidden rest.

They were all right; they had done splendidly; but they must now get firmly into a safe position for the climb ahead. There was also a curious and deadly trick about timing; the difference between a coming man and a man who would never make the grade was an odd matter of months, at the critical moment. If everything were not in fact going so well, everything would be desperate.

Rose shook off these unwanted thoughts. If you let yourself brood on being over forty and living beyond your means, it began to show, mysteriously, in your manner, your voice: people smelled anxiety. Nothing was more dangerous. What people were meant to see and value were one's blessings, one's happiness, one's success. The true picture, in short. I cannot loll here, Rose told herself briskly, there is lots to do. It would be a good time to give another Colonial cocktail party. The children, anyhow, doted on them; they spied through the banisters. The tattooed medical student from Uganda was their favorite.

Rose settled herself at the Regency writing table that she had bought in Brighton for a song. She began to arrange the shape of the next three weeks. After this, life would become almost too easy. Once in the Government, there was no reason ever to leave it; it was musical chairs simply, you got ever better and better jobs, until you got the best.

Alan, leafing through his notes, saw how he could cut his speech in half. He felt the usual stage fright; dry mouth, queasy stomach, thumping heart. He knew he would not show this, but it was a filthy way to feel. The House was always pleasant to him; he was not the sort of speaker who called forth furious Oh! Oh! Oh's! nor did he ever win bellows of laughter. His colleagues suffered him in amiable patience, as he knew. In the middle of his shortened speech, Alan looked across the floor of the House and saw Bill Farr, the Member for Middle Paddle (Lab). Bill Farr had been at Oxford with him and was an old friend. Furthermore, Bill Farr had been at Balliol and knew Kwak an Sung much better than he did. As that odious name pealed from his lips for the dozenth time, he was sure he saw Bill Farr wink.

He deserved it. How could Bill Farr know that he meant something he could not say and that made no sense if you said it? He meant: The people are afraid of everything; they are afraid of hunger, as they've reason to be; and of us whom they can't understand, and why should they, we don't understand them; and of their own leaders who are largely swine but still their own; and afraid of the jungle, and the revolting sicknesses they die from, and war and guns and noise and all the changes. Well, what could you make of that? Nothing. And the years of speeches had hardly added up to any salvation for those distant dark people who so closely concerned him. The end justifies the means. Alan told himself, but what if the means were ineffective and you could not see the end clear?

Bill Farr no doubt thought that his old friend Alan was talking his way to the Front Bench. If his old friend Alan wanted to use that unreliable little twister, Kwak an Sung, as a means to get a job, it was all right with Bill Farr. He liked Alan, he would rather see him in the Colonial Office than lots of other men, he didn't really care. The Colonies were not his thing. Good luck to Alan. Give him a nice cheering wink, and hope he made it as he wanted.

As soon as courtesy allowed, Alan left the chamber, went to check his speech with the official reporter, and finally came to rest in the smoking room. No one found Alan a bore here; he was unassuming and ready to laugh. And he made everyone feel that he was interested in them and wished them well; he gave this endearing impression because it was true.

Rose, who had been telephoning in Alan's study, hurried to open the door for him. She never went to the House when Alan was speaking. She believed that wives who hovered over their husbands had a damaging effect. She threw her arms around Alan's neck, kissed him on the cheek and said, 'Darling, I've already heard. Tippy telephoned, wasn't it sweet of him? He said O.B. was very pleased and the House was most attentive. Everyone thought you were absolutely right.'

'Oh, Rose.'

'Darling, you must not be so modest. It's like an affectation. I asked Tippy to come round for a drink when he leaves the House.'

'You'll have to look after him. I'm going up to the children.'

'You can see the children any day. Really, Alan.'

'The point is I hardly see the children any day, and this is the only time I have. Don't fuss, Rose. You can cope with Tippy perfectly well.'

As a matter of fact she could, so she let him go. Alan climbed the stairs, feeling how long they were and how heavy his legs. Annual flu, he decided; the stairs hadn't grown steeper overnight.

The children were bathed, pink, glistening, and looked like Teddy bears in their little camel's-hair bathrobes and fur slippers. They sat at the low table in the nursery, eating their supper with dutiful good manners, and conversing. When their father came in, the joy on their faces shamed him.

'May I sit with you?'

They hurried to bring him Nannie's old chair, they were speechless with pleasure. Then Alice said, 'Would you like a cup of milk, Daddy?'

'Yes, I would, I'd love one, thank you.'

At least John could beat Alice to the cupboard to get an extra cup. Alice poured the milk, copying her mother's tea-table manner, except for bouncing a bit from excitement and making small gurgled sounds.

'What are you two talking about?'

'About summer,' Alice said. 'About what happens in summer. In Grandma's pond. John says Grandma's goldfishes talk to each other. They sing, he says, not exactly talk. Is it true, Daddy?'

John was distressed; this was a secret he had told Alice.

'I'm sure it's true,' Alan said. 'And John is very lucky to have heard them. Not everyone can.'

'Oh.' Alice looked rather dashed. She thought John often fibbed. Mummy said he did. But if Daddy said it was true, then it was.

'Daddy?'

'Yes, John?'

'Can you stay long enough to tuck us in?'

'Of course I can.'

'Oh, good,' John said, and Alan felt something like pain.

'And tell us a story?' Alice asked.

'Yes, darling.'

'Let's eat faster,' Alice said. 'For the story.'

They brushed their teeth in a cursory manner, they hung their bathrobes neatly over their chairs, they knelt by their beds and raced through their prayers, and Alan stood, very tall in the pretty white and yellow room, and looked at them and thought what hopeless fools he and Rose were. Years of London cocktail hours stretched behind them, buzzing billions of words, and so they let this delight escape them. Without his noticing it, these two had stopped being babies and become children; if he was not careful he would lose it all.

'Sit there, Daddy,' Alice said. 'That's where Nannie used to sit for stories.'

And no doubt they missed her badly, Alan thought. Boring old woman, Rose had said, but Nannie was their property, and steady and comfortable and a lap to sit on and company on their way to sleep. He was suddenly afraid he would find nothing in his head that his children could use. To his surprise, he managed to invent a circus of rabbits and squirrels and ferrets and birds, in Modesbury woods.

'That was a lovely story,' John said.

'Daddy,' Alice said.

'Yes, my dear?'

'You couldn't come and tell it to us again tomorrow, could you?' John was alarmed. Alice should not have asked that. It made Mummy angry when they begged for things.

'Yes indeed I will,' Alan said. He went to John's bed to kiss the boy good night, and John reached up and seized him around the neck and clung with all the strength of his arms and rubbed his cheek against Alan's and said, 'Daddy, Daddy.' Alan held the little body and stroked the child's hair and thought: They're lonely, that's what it is. We're worse than fools. They live up here by themselves and do exactly what they're told and never complain and are lonely.

'Good night, old man,' Alan said.

Wiggling her toes under the blankets, Alice waited her turn, youngest last.

'You're my favorite little daughter. You're a very good, very pretty little girl. Will you sleep quickly now?' he asked, and they promised they would and thanked him for his visit. He raised the window and turned out the light. John was afraid of the dark but Rose would not allow that. He left the light on in the hall and the door open.

From the third-floor landing he could hear Tippy's voice nattering away over cocktails. He went into his dressing room, took off his coat and shoes, loosened his tie and lay down on the bed.

Rose waked him, saying, 'Poor darling, you must be tired to sleep in your clothes. You remember Violet and Charles are coming to dinner? Or rather, Violet is; Charles is called out again; meningitis or something, Violet telephoned. If you don't feel up to it, it doesn't matter a rap. You can have a tray.'

Alan, half awake, felt a clouded, headachy alarm; he had forgotten. Violet, without Charles to protect her, would be worse than heavy going. Still it was his own fault; Rose asked her sister Violet and her brother-in-law Charles Harper to dinner only because Alan insisted. Rose drew the line at mixing the Harpers with her friends, saying that to bore oneself with one's relatives might be a duty, but to bore one's friends was an imposition. Violet was a perfectly nice woman, younger than Rose, looking indefinably as if she were covered with bows and ruffles, and permanently fussed.

'Of course I'll get up,' Alan said. 'I haven't seen Violet for months.'
Dinner was as dismal as he had foreseen. Rose retired into silence.
It was not her fruitful, talented silence; it was pure inattention. Alan
worked hard, feeling wearier and wearier, and Violet chirped gallantly.
When they moved to the drawing room for coffee, Alan studied the
sisters, seated opposite each other by the fire, and wondered, as often
before, how Mr and Mrs Mackay, a respectable Birmingham solicitor
and his respectable wife, could have produced such different offspring.
Once, trying to pierce the mystery, he asked Rose about her mother and
Rose said, 'Well, you can get some idea of her when you think that she
named her daughters Rose and Violet.'

What little he knew of the Mackay family came from Violet. Violet
had said she couldn't bear to leave Mummy and Daddy but Rose wanted
to go to Brussels to Mademoiselle de Rouvray's finishing school. Rose
was so interested in learning French. Rose's best friend in Brussels was
a girl called Angela Trevor, whom the Mackays had never met, oddly
enough, and when Lady Trevor brought Angela out in London, she
brought Rose out too, which was awfully nice of her, although she,
Violet, would have been terrified of the parties, and what if the young
men didn't dance with one? When Rose was eighteen she eloped with
Lord Radway, such a shock to Mummy, but you had to remember how
young and romantic Rose was. After that, it was all tragedy, according
to Violet, and she never failed to admire Rose's bravery. Daddy and
Mummy died within a year of each other when Rose was only twenty.
It had been too terrible for Rose, widowed so soon, alone in the world
with no one to look after her.

Violet was now complaining of the weather.

'I carry an extra pair of shoes to school for Isabel,' Violet said, 'but
when they go out to play in the morning I'm sure she gets her feet wet
again. It's too desperate, she's in bed half the winter.'

'The way you coddle her and put ideas in her head,' Rose said, 'I'm
surprised she isn't in bed the whole winter.'

'Rose, you know Isabel is terribly delicate. I only wish she were as
strong as your children.'

'My children are strong because that's how they are brought up.'

Alan knew he ought to defend Violet, he was ashamed to abandon
her with that cowed look in her eyes, but why didn't she turn on Rose
herself?

The telephone rang and Rose went to answer it.

'Chloe, how lovely to hear you. No, not at all busy. Oh, how nice . . .
Yes, of course we'd love to . . . Good, at eight on Wednesday . . . Perfect . . . We'll look forward to it.'

Rose returned to the fire in such a smoothed humor that she could ignore her sister's presence. 'Chloe. Apologizing for the short notice. Asked us to dinner on Wednesday. The PM is coming. How very nice of her. We haven't had them here for ages.'

'What is Wednesday?'

'The nineteenth. Oh, darling, don't bother to look at your little book. If we have another engagement, we can easily break it.'

Alan went methodically through his diary and found the right page. 'I can't go,' he said. 'Pity you didn't ask me. It's the night of the Magdalen dinner.'

'Really, Alan. It's nothing but a silly old get-together. You can miss it for once.'

'I've said I'm coming. I always go.'

'This is too ridiculous.'

'I'm sure that Alan —' Violet began in a tense peacemaker's voice.

'It has nothing to do with you, Violet,' Rose said.

Alan would have taken pleasure in knocking the Mackay sisters' heads together. He controlled himself and his face, and said placidly, 'You go, Rose, Chloe can always find an extra man. Tell her it's the night of my college dinner. She'll understand.'

'She will think you are as rude as you are stupid.' Rose was too angry now to care what Violet heard or repeated to her depressing doctor husband.

'Oh, no, she won't,' Alan said, hanging on to his temper. 'Geoffrey wouldn't miss his college dinner for anything. Will you have more coffee, Violet?'

But Violet said she must hurry home and get something hot ready for Charles when he came back. Rose was already turning out the lights in the drawing room. Alan kissed Violet good night at the front door, and Violet pressed his hand in a consoling way, as if there was serious illness in the house. Alan said nothing about next time, we must meet again soon. Violet did not seem to expect it.

Alan put on his dressing gown, dawdled with his hairbrushes, wound his watch, peered at his tongue, took aspirin, disliked himself, and went to his wife's room. Rose, propped up with pillows, snug in a quilted bedjacket, looked, as women do, smaller and younger in bed. She was reading.

Alan stood by the bed and said, 'Well?'

His head and shoulders ached, he felt feverish. He was in a mood to give up, deposit a noncommittal kiss on his wife's forehead, say nothing, and let this undefined quarrel go on until whenever it wore itself out. But he knew he must not; he felt like this too often; it was more than dangerous. Silent criticisms, wordless distastes, little scratchy scenes, lingering quarrels, led finally to the coldness of indifference. They needed to warm each other, they needed to lie in each other's arms and find again what they knew, what was there, what held them together. They needed this badly and now. Somehow they had forgotten to allow time for love.

'Rose?' Alan said.

Rose put down her book and looked at him. He might have been Mrs Zadzicza, waiting for the day's orders.

'You can hardly expect me to be nice to you,' Rose said, 'when you will do nothing to please me.'

'Oh, darling.'

'I care a great deal about Chloe's dinner, and making a scene in front of Violet was inexcusable.'

'Oh, Rose, none of that matters.'

'There's nothing more to say. If you can't see it, you can't see it.'

He was seized with shivering anger. Did badly treated servants feel this way?

'No more carrot,' he said. 'Just the stick.'

'Whatever are you talking about? How disgustingly unattractive.'

'Good night, Rose. Sleep well.'

He was careful not to slam the door. He lay on the not too comfortable bed in his dressing room and told himself that it made very little difference. It was not as if Rose welcomed his attentions at any time; no doubt Rose thought love-making quite useless, or a vulgar self-indulgence, like eating chocolates. Married people, after all, could take things for granted; they had made love often enough to know what it was; a certain amount might be required for health, but why go beyond that?

What, in their lives, was of his choosing; what smallest detail of every day did he order; what claim did he make on this life they shared? When you considered it, it was damned nice of Rose to allow him to waste money and time on tennis. Perhaps tennis was permitted because it kept his figure and Rose believed that looks were a great asset; a thin man presumably went farther than a fat man.

Alan took to his bed and Rose took over. Rose disliked illness and privately thought it a sign of weakness or laziness, but Alan had an authentic fever, although she herself would not have collapsed with only 101°.

At first she was distressed because of the timing, but she began to see advantages. Alan had been in a peculiar state this last week, probably due to coming down with influenza. Alone, she could do his job better than she could with his help. Alan refused to answer the telephone or to see anyone, escaping into detective stories and long, languorous naps. Rose went everywhere, saw everyone; she felt herself superbly on top of the situation.

And Tippy became almost resident. He was the permanent extra man at the luncheon table, at dinner; he replaced Alan, to make numbers even. No one could suggest anything amorous in connection with Tippy; Rose would have loathed the slightest rumor. Tippy was the best possible assistant; he had come to feel that the Empire could hardly survive unless Answell was made Minister of State for Colonial Affairs.

Rose brought the newspapers to Alan's sickbed. 'Hal Thompson's Parliament column. Very nice indeed. And I fancy Lord Hasleton had a word with his dreadful editor. Here's a splendid piece in the *Record*.'

Alan did not care.

Rose reported that Chloe's dinner party had been a great success. 'I had a very good little talk to Chloe after dinner, over nose-powdering. But Geoffrey is so worrying, one cannot tell exactly what he thinks. I wish he and Chloe weren't so horribly unserious. Really, why shouldn't Geoffrey be on your side?'

Alan did not answer because he was not listening.

Rose harried him gently. 'Darling, don't you feel better? How long do you think you'll have to stay in bed?'

'I feel better every day.' Every day he started at the beginning and thought laboriously a little farther.

'What are those things, Rose, that have colored pieces of glass inside them? You turn them and they make one pattern, and you turn them again and they make another.'

'Kaleidoscopes?'

'Yes. That's the way it is.'

'What is?'

'How I see things.'

'Oh. Well, I must hurry to dress. Tippy is taking me to the Ogilvie-Becks' to dinner. And tomorrow Maude is having the Stranges. I'm very pleased, I hardly know them.'

Hugh Strange was Chancellor of the Exchequer. Clearly Rose was not concerned with kaleidoscopes. Why should she be? Changing patterns were not her thing.

When the children came home from kindergarten they sat on the floor outside Alan's dressing-room door and gave him the news of the day. It was understood that germs did not cross thresholds. They spoke a great deal of Tippy. Tippy made a practice of calling on them in the nursery, when he came to have drinks with Rose. He had asked John and Alice to visit him in the country when the weather became possible; he had promised them a ride on a tractor. They called him Lord Tippy, which made Alan laugh; apparently it made Lord Tippinghurst laugh too.

For a week, the children praised Tippy, and Alan came to see Tippy as they did. When John raced up the stairs to show Alan a small well-made tennis racket he had found in the hall, and Alice followed cradling a huge doll, Alan decided Tippy was as nice a man as he knew. He felt guilty and grateful: poor Tippy was enduring all the luncheons and dinners he missed owing to this heaven-sent influenza; dear Tippy loved the children. The one good feature of Rose's assault on the Government was Tippy. They had acquired a friend—not an accomplice, or a tool, or whatever people turned out to be in Rose's schemes—simply a friend.

'I'm going to call her Diana, Lady Tippy,' Alice said, smoothing her doll's rich peroxided hair.

'Lord Tippy likes us best of anyone,' John announced, whooshing his racket in wide, improbable strokes.

'What are you three talking about?' Rose asked. She brought more newspapers, more letters, bulletins from the front for Alan.

'Lord Tippy,' Alice said.

'We must do something for him, Rose. He's been so good to the children.'

'Don't worry about Tippy,' Rose said. 'He's having the time of his life.'

Mrs Braithewaite had a new Messerschmitt insect-car; the police had fined her so steadily for parking offenses that her husband thought it would be a saving to buy this German tricycle which presumably she could leave anywhere without infuriating the authorities. She was driving Lady Harriet home from a cocktail party at Cynthia Delafield's. Their delightful faces beamed in the glass cowling of the car.

'Have you ever tried going *under* a bus?' Lady Harriet asked.

'Not yet,' said Mrs Braithewaite. 'I'm a novice still. Would you like me to drive between those two cars?'

'Do.'

She did. The drivers of the cars observed, far below them, two beautiful women whisking by in this new mechanical joke, and smiled. The road of Mrs Braithewaite and Lady Harriet was always banked with smiles.

'Did you see Rose?' Mrs Braithewaite asked.

'What's come over Rose? She's so frightfully amiable.'

'She must want something,' Mrs Braithewaite said.

'And Tippy. Has Tippy turned into her poodle or what?'

'We always forget that Tippy *is* in the Government all the same.'

'Ah yes. I wonder what Rose is after now?'

'Whatever it is, she'll get it. Isn't this heaven?' Mrs Braithewaite asked, weaving through the traffic like Mignon amongst the eggs.

Geoffrey Ashe Vernham came to say goodbye to his wife every morning before going to his office in Whitehall. He found her in bed, well covered with telephone books, engagement books, newspapers, writing paper, Serbo-Croat grammars, as she was studying that language, and the remains of her latest type of health breakfast. It would seem that Chloe was now living on canary seeds. Her hair was pinned in small circles all over her head and she was experimenting with a new pale-blue face cream.

'What are we doing tonight, Chloe?'

'The pictures. Just us.'

'How very nice.'

'Geoffrey, what do you think of Alan Answell for the Colonies?'

'Needless to say, Tippy has mentioned the matter. What's come over Tippy?'

'Poor Tippy. We all treat him so badly, running for cover whenever we see him. I expect he's lonely. I lunched with Rose again yesterday. That makes the third lesson, I think. I have it all by heart now. Shall I tell you Alan's points?'

'Is it worth it?'

'Do listen, love. Very popular in the House. All his old Oxford chums on the Labour side. Speaks well, or at least easily. Knows the East. Does he, I wonder? But then, who does? Matey with the Colonials in London, you know, goes to their clubs or whatever and gives them chats. And, of course, Rose feeds the important ones regularly in Barton Street. Young. Hard-working. Doesn't smoke or drink, I daresay. Rose tastefully did not remind me that he's Jock's nephew. I can't think of anything else.'

'Hum,' said Geoffrey Ashe Vernham.

'Hum what?'

'It's a filthy job; I can't see why anyone would want it. Doesn't need much brain; the Permanent Under-Secretary does the thinking. Why do you bother?'

'I cannot imagine. It must be Rose. I'm sorry for her. Such a tiring life, always getting somewhere.'

'She makes me nervous. The way she listens to me.'

Chloe laughed. 'Poor Rose. She is rather pathetic.'

'How she would hate you for that.'

'She hates me anyhow. And Alan's a dear, and an old friend.'

'All right. Now I must go.'

'I wonder if Alan's mama will hear of it?' Chloe asked. 'I do adore old Lady Irene. She grows the best delphiniums in England.'

Rose was waiting. She opened the door, took Alan's hand and pulled him into the privacy of his study. She closed the door.

'Alan,' she said. 'Alan. Tippy says the Chief Whip is having dinner with the PM. The PM is deciding it tonight. And Tippy's heard that the PM's PPS says it is bound to be you.'

Her face had never looked like this. Not when she walked from Modesbury church as a bride, nor when the nurse brought in her first-born, nor ever after love. Her face was radiant, marked with joy and tenderness. He discarded the half-formed plans he had been mooning over, he rejected gladly his slow anger against Rose. How could any woman prove her love better than by feeling such happiness for her husband's sake? All he wanted was to keep that light in her eyes for the rest of their life together.

'My darling,' Alan said, and took his wife in his arms. Her kiss had a new warmth. Everything is all right, Alan thought, I've been tired and ill, I've been imagining things. We have all that counts, loving each other. Nothing else matters.

Rose sighed and pulled away from him. 'I'm so excited I don't know what to do. I've chucked luncheon at Cynthia's and dinner at the Hasletons'; we must be at home to hear the great news. Besides I couldn't see anyone, I can hardly sit still. Oh, Alan, isn't it too wonderful? Everyone's on your side, even Geoffrey Ashe Vernham.'

Alan reached for her again but Rose seemed not to notice.

'And it's only the beginning,' Rose went on. 'We're just starting.'

'Beginning of what?' Alan asked, still smiling. How young she looked, how desirable. He wished they were at Le Touquet or in Paris, sensible Latin spots where one did not wait until dark to go to bed.

'The Colonies,' Rose said. 'It's all right for a start, but the Colonies is not one of the really big jobs. I see you in Defence, the Treasury, Foreign Secretary. . . .'

'What?'

'Oh, yes, darling, there's nothing you can't get.'

Alan stopped smiling.

'I thought that the Colonies was what I was especially suited for. I thought it was because I cared very much what happens to those people.'

'Of course, darling, you're absolutely sweet about our little brown brothers,' Rose said gaily, 'and you've worked like a black yourself to learn all about them. It was the obvious starting point, when you came back from the East so full of their troubles. One has to specialize, so as to get a name, in the beginning. After that, it goes by itself.'

'Oh,' Alan said. 'They are rather tiresome, our little brown brothers, aren't they?'

'Well, poor things, they don't count much. Now that India's on its own. We have so few of them left and, on the whole, they're mainly an expense and a nuisance.'

'Right,' Alan said.

'But it will be great fun for a few years. And the gift of gifts, when this is settled, is Tippy.'

'What about Tippy?'

'Well, darling, we won't have Tippy underfoot every minute. I'm so tired of him I could scream. He talks about the children as boringly as Nannie. And his cows. Dear Heaven, what a relief not to have to listen to him any more.'

'The children would miss him a lot, you know.'

'Nonsense. Something else will come along to amuse them. They forget quickly.'

Luncheon was announced. It was the first time they had eaten alone for months. Alan could remember how he had longed for this.

'Why are you looking at me like that?' Rose asked. 'Have some more macaroni.'

Alan excused himself before coffee, saying untruthfully that he had an appointment at the House. Rose kissed him again, with this new fervor. They would hear from Downing Street, she said, probably at about ten o'clock tonight. After dinner, they could wait by the telephone. Alan did not answer.

The pavements seemed stonier than stone, and long. He walked slowly toward the park. He wanted to walk under trees and get his mind clear. For a time he sat on a bench by the Serpentine and went over it all until he was sure of himself. Then he walked back to Westminster. He searched for Tippy and found him gossiping in the passages with a crony from the Lords. He asked Tippy to give him a minute, when convenient, and Tippy dropped his noble friend at once. They went to a corner of the Lords' squalid bar. Alan talked.

'My dear boy,' Tippy kept saying. 'Really, my dear boy.'

After Alan was certain that Tippy had understood him, he thanked Tippy gravely, asked him to dinner tomorrow, and walked home. He went directly to his study and wrote a careful letter, which he then posted at the corner pillar box. When he returned for the second time, he called down the kitchen stairs to ask Mrs Zadzicza where Rose was and learned that she was in the drawing room. Get it over, Alan told himself, knowing that what he felt was fear. The last and lowest emotion, he thought, I have now gone through everything.

'Why are you back so early?' Rose asked. She was at her desk, writing to invite a few chosen friends to celebrate Alan's new position in life; she could send the letters tomorrow.

'I want to talk to you. Sit here by the fire, Rose. It will take quite a time.'

He had not planned what to say and, standing before his wife, Alan found no ready words.

'I don't know how to begin,' he said. 'It's so important.'

'Yes, dear.' Of course this was a great occasion and men always loved to make speeches, given half an excuse.

'There's a farm for sale near Modesbury. Mother wrote to me.' He had not meant to start like this at all. 'It was Saul Marble's, you didn't know him. He only had girls and they're married and don't want it. It's a good farm and by chance has a lovely old house, in a mess now but easy to do over. I want to buy it.'

'Well, really, darling, is it the moment? I don't think we can possibly afford two houses.'

'No, not two. I want to buy it and farm the land and bring up the children there.'

'Alan, what are you saying? Are you ill?'

Rose looked at him with real anxiety, thinking of rest cures. She had never known that flu could affect the nerves or the brain. No one must get word of this apparent breakdown. She would bundle him off to his mother's in the morning, as a start.

'There's been no excuse for how I've lived for ten years,' Alan went on. 'I told myself we were all right, driving ahead like tanks to the Front Bench, because of our motives. Have to be in a position to govern so I can help the people I mind about; my duty to make England the best Colonial power. How everyone must have despised me.'

'Alan, you're not well and you simply don't know what you're saying.'

'I know exactly what I'm saying. I'm sick of myself, sick of it all, and I won't play any more. We're going to have a decent life and bring up our children decently.'

She sat very straight, angry despite herself, although she realized that he was speaking in some sort of delirium.

'I can't imagine what you're talking about,' Rose said. 'And it would be absurd to have a quarrel. I'll get on with my notes, if I may.'

'You may not. I haven't finished. I saw Tippy and told him I would not accept the job and to see that I am not proposed. I wrote to Modesbury resigning my seat. Tomorrow I will put this house in the hands of agents; we will have plenty of money to buy Marble's farm.'

'You've been ill,' Rose said flatly, 'and it has had some strange effect on you. It's only five o'clock. I will telephone Tippy at the House and explain to him; he will do anything I ask. I will telephone old Mr Barth at Modesbury and get that straightened out. You should go either to the country or to a nursing home; we will say you've come down with pneumonia. You will feel quite differently in a few days.'

'No, Rose, it's no good. I've made up my mind.'

At last Rose had to believe him. It took a long minute for the belief to show in her face. Alan was unable to move or speak, watching her face change.

'You fool!' Rose said. 'You disgusting fool! Do you think I've worked for ten years to have it thrown away? For ten years I've arranged everything—everyone knows I got you as far as this. Do you imagine I'll be the wife of a hard-up little farmer? You're a hopeless weakling, you always had that in you. Sentimental about your dreary Colonials, soft and sentimental about the children. Whatever backbone you had, I forced you to have. I've brought us here, and I'd get us to the top; that is what I want and mean to have. If you prefer a wretched second-rate life, you can have it alone.'

'No. Again you are wrong. I believe in the marriage vows. I always have.'

'Do you think I started from nothing, on my own, and did what I've done, to end up like this? Do you think I'll let everyone laugh at me now? Look at Rose, milking cows in Wiltshire. My God,' Rose said slowly, 'I could kill you for this. You miserable, sniveling coward!'

Her mouth held him, that thin line which he knew was truthful at last and never to be forgotten. He had not imagined that any sane person was capable of this passion of hate; but Rose was sane, she understood what she was saying, she meant every word. He could not hope to deceive himself again. Their marriage was nothing; the ten years of it and the children; nothing. A marriage belonged to two people or was nothing. In this room, now, only her hate was alive.

Rose sank back on the sofa and covered her face. Closing her eyes she saw this ruin and saw herself as a colossal fool. A fool conquered by a fool. She could never divorce him: she had no grounds, he was faithful as a dog, no court in England would listen to her. She was helpless; tricked and cheated and finally destroyed.

Alan thought of the children.

'Rose,' he said, 'Rose, we can't ... John ... Alice ...'

Alan's voice roused her. There was no place for despair. All she knew was that she was getting out; she could not endure him. She would not go through life listening to that pleading failure's voice. She would have to move carefully, she would have to think hard and well, above all she must not sink with this sinking ship.

'We have both been terribly hasty,' Rose said. 'And not ourselves. I am sure we can settle everything quite sensibly. Later.'

She was herself again. She knew exactly what she had to do, and she saw how to do it; she also knew where she was going next.

Lady Harriet and Mrs Braithewaite were having tea at the Ritz, after hard shopping.

'Isn't it horrid?' Mrs Braithewaite said mildly, holding up a thin damp sandwich.

'Look at those sweet Central Europeans,' Lady Harriet said, gazing past the potted palms at a group of ladies who had shoved back their nose veils and were wolfing éclairs. 'Like satin-covered beer barrels.'

'Bobby saw Alan at White's.'

'No!'

'Bobby said he looked very fit, if a bit too rural. You know, patches on the elbows. Alan chatted quite happily about cows.'

'Whatever next?'

'They're splendid cows. Tippy's. Tippy gave them because they'd be so nice for the children; he adores those children. Besides the cows are no good to him any more.'

'Do you mean to say Rose has managed to separate Tippy from his cows?'

'And she's made him buy that enormous house of the Percivals' on Halkin Street.'

'Poor Tippy, he always hated London, he only loved his cows.'

'He'll never get out of London now. I hear he looks awful. Tired and jaunty.'

'Really, Rose is the limit,' Lady Harriet said with irritation. 'But why Tippy? That's what I don't see.'

'We keep forgetting about Tippy, you know. He's a perfectly good earl and he's frightfully rich although it never showed much before, and he *is* in the Government.'

'But so horribly old.'

'Not really. About the same age men seem to be nowadays. Chloe's very cross. So unlike her to mind anything, isn't it? But this time she says it's gone beyond a joke. She says Lady Irene is bound to hear of the divorce, now that Rose has married Tippy. She says it's too common, whoever heard of so much marrying.'

Lady Harriet laughed.

'Of course,' said Mrs Braithewaite, 'she always only liked Alan.'

'Well, obviously.'

'Geoffrey says he wishes Rose would try her hand at making the Opposition miserable. He's more cross about Tippy than about Lady Irene. He keeps saying Tippy never harmed a fly, why couldn't Rose leave him alone.'

'Goodness,' said Lady Harriet. 'But the thing is, Rose will make that Percival house awfully attractive and give masses of parties with glorious food and drink and take a great deal of trouble, and people will forget. You know how they do.'

'I imagine Rose thought of that.'

'Anyhow I *am* glad darling Alan got those cows.'

As they left, with sudden inspiration, Lady Harriet smiled and bowed to the Central European ladies among their welter of chocolate-smeared plates. The Central European ladies were flustered, and bowed and smiled back, and whispered to each other that the war had made a great change in the English, poor things, it must have been all the bombing and the bad food, they didn't seem to know how to behave correctly any more, which could not be held against them, they were such a good, simple, friendly people.

*I*N SICKNESS AND IN HEALTH

She had been waiting for him. The door opened gently. There were no sudden movements, no unexpected noise, in this house. She held out her arms and he came across the room and kissed her forehead. He pulled the chair closer to her chaise longue and took her hand in his. She watched him with happy eyes and slightly parted lips. Her asthma is better, he thought. He smiled, hoping there was nothing mechanical or weary about what he felt as a grimace of the mouth.

'I've brought you a present,' he said. It was more of a present than he could afford; Fifth Avenue jewelers were not his style. He took a small velvet box from his pocket and gave it to her.

'Oh,' she said. 'Oh, Ricky.'

It was a pin: three stalks of lily of the valley, with leaves, bound together by a gold band. The leaves were palest green enamel, the flowers white; small pearls imitated dew. He was, himself, sick to death of lilies of the valley, her favorite flower. She tried to fasten the pin to her pretty dotted Swiss negligée, but her hands trembled. A bad sign, he thought. He took the jewel from her and got it more or less properly placed, and she moved her head to see it, and then touched it carefully.

'Our sixteenth,' she said in her low, hesitant voice, the voice that had to be rationed, using the breath that was so costly and difficult to keep in her body. 'I can't believe it. I remember the day we were married as if it were now. Where *have* the years gone? Oh, darling, your beautiful present.'

He knew very well where the years had gone. Doubtless she remembered their wedding day better than he did, since she had so little to remember. He could think of nothing at all to say, so he kissed her hand, and as he bowed his head, she stroked his hair. Then she talked— she saved everything to tell him.

At last she believed she really knew and understood the Bach Concerto in D Minor. She had been playing it over and over and listening with all her attention. And she had read the Chekhov stories he sent her, weren't they sad, weren't they perfect, motionless stories which said everything. The squirrels were now settled down to married life, and Mrs S. was a bustling mother, a competent *Hausfrau*, and Mr S., as anyone could see, was feeling his responsibilities. Three days ago he scampered in through the open French window and studied her room. Soon they would all come. But the robins had left, it was a great loss, probably the squirrels irritated them, being such active, noisy little beasts. Had he ever seen the garden lovelier? Aunt Lucy and Sarine were beside themselves with pleasure over it. Aunt Lucy had given a little bridge party last week, three other ladies, what a twit she had been in, worrying Sarine about the sandwiches and the cake and the cookies, but it was a great success and Aunt Lucy talked of nothing else, she had enough village news to last for half a year. Ted was so good, so constant, so generous of his time, and also encouraging, he was sure she was getting better.

At the name Ted, he listened, hoping to hear something beyond her words. Ted was always good, constant, encouraging, and had been for years. How many? Ten years now. Ted was the ideal doctor, and as much of a fixture as Aunt Lucy, Sarine, and more of a fixture than the squirrels. He saw that she was tiring herself; she had talked enough. It was his turn. Since she never asked about his life, he did not speak of it. Had she simply lost interest; did she fear to know; did she feel she would not understand, as if his life were something lived among foreigners, in a country she had never seen? Besides, what report could he give? I go to the store at nine and leave at five. I sit at my desk and plan layouts, correct copy, write copy. They tell me to push a new line in airplane luggage. They say they want to get rid of last year's fur coats. The china department informs me they have bargain stuff from Copenhagen. Sometimes I smoke and look at the sky. Sometimes I think of a fast selling idea and rush into Blick's office, full of hopped-up, necessary enthusiasm, and pour it out with trimmings, and that way I prove I am a man keen on his work. At five I often walk in the park, walking off the taste of the day, before I go home. What was there to tell? He would speak, as usual, of a play he had seen, a movie, pictures, a record he had bought. It was no use to talk of people; she knew none of them. He saw very few anyhow; they were without meaning to him also. He could not speak of Maggie, who was all, absolutely all, that concerned him.

He heard his voice as a monotone, heavy with boredom. He tried to force color and warmth into the sounds he was making. She listened, fascinated. His voice droned on and on: Arthur Miller, Brando, the gifted young American painter, Perlin, whose pictures of Italy, the Boston Symphony recording of Bartók's ... The insect murmur from the garden matched his words and accompanied them. She lay now in the beginning of shadow, the afternoon was ending. The house was silent around them, although Sarine would be busy in the kitchen and Aunt Lucy was supposedly alive upstairs. This room would make a perfect picture, cool, Degas without ballet girls perhaps. He spoiled it, of course; it was not a room that a man could fit into.

Strange how she never tired of anything; she had kept this soft green wallpaper, printed with delicate clusters of lilies of the valley, for thirteen years. Yet it was so fresh that she must have had her room done several times, always in the same design. Her bed in the corner, disguised as a large divan, was covered with the same rosy damask, the windows were curtained in the same faded rose material. Her writing table, which was an ornament, since she could not sit at it, the tables by her chaise longue, by her bed, the long table against the far wall, were tobacco-brown, lovingly polished pieces of wood made in the eighteenth century by Englishmen who knew their craft; but they were never moved, the order of the room remained the same. And everywhere, for as long as he could remember, there was this luxury of flowers, in bowls, in small porcelain vases, in great glass jars, and always the air held the same light, sweet scent of lilies of the valley. Since nothing else changed, why should she alter the colors and the pattern of her becoming room?

He began to talk of plays he had not seen, discussing the rival reviews, and he studied his wife, thinking that facts were facts and this was indeed their sixteenth wedding anniversary and therefore she was thirty-seven years old and would be thirty-eight in two months, but facts did not obey any known laws in this house. Time was nothing but a theoretical idea here, for she looked as she always had. In a terrible, sinister way, he felt that she grew younger on her chaise longue, year after year. Whereas he grew much older, faster than time, far ahead of time, on the fifteenth floor of Handel's, crouched there in his neat white cell high above Fifth Avenue.

She was beautiful and new and fragile as the spring. Yet how often she had suffocated and fought for air; and while she struggled to breathe, she knew her damaged heart could fail without warning. She lived in horror of death, and the horror grew the longer she waited. Her face should have been drawn and her eyes wild. Instead, her face was smooth and of the clear color of a shell. The curve of her cheek was as touching as it had been when she was a girl. Her eyes had the same look of innocence. Her hair still played that amazing trick of seeming to blow in shadows of curls around her temples and ears. She had always worn her hair long. It was loosely tied back with a narrow satin bow, the color of her eyes. Should there not be gray in that bright brown mane? She was unmarked and unused: her hands, her arms, her lovely breasts, her impossibly small waist, her beautiful legs, her knees—a perfection of the mechanics of bone, all as before, as remembered. Everyone spread and sagged, faded, bloated. His own body repelled him with its new creases and patches of flabbiness. Time scarred the whole human race, except Annette.

He knew, as a wickedness in himself, that he could have cared more, somehow joined in her pain and her terror, if only she showed how her life had hurt her. On the other hand, perhaps it was pure bravery to show nothing. He tried to make himself see that and honor her for it. But he could not quite believe it; he did not know, there was no way of knowing; she would not speak of her illness. He suspected that she had shut her mind, refusing death by refusing to think; he suspected that she stayed young because she would not grow. She lay forever on her chaise longue, or, on the worst days, in her bed, and denied this helpless immobility, denied that anything was different, denied even that he and she were anything but man and wife, as other men, other wives.

He could not imagine what he had found to say; now the words ground to a stop. He was tormented by the need for a cigarette, but naturally he could not smoke here. He felt hot. He would have liked to sleep for twelve hours or go swimming. Annette reached for her handkerchief and he looked furtively at his watch. It was still the fourteenth of April, still the garden crackled and hummed in the late sunlight, and he had delivered his lecture on contemporary art, crawled over that mountain pass of time, in less than a quarter of an hour. He was shaken and sick with something he knew too well, hopelessness, and an anger that had no focus, and pity for them both, and the sense of waste. He could also remember how he had loved her, which was his own pain, altogether different from hers. He remembered the joy and the power, the immense hope of his loving her. It was as if he remembered a happy man and that man was now long dead.

Sarine opened the door without knocking. There would be no intimate scene to disturb, and Mrs Whiteley could not, in any case, raise her voice to call 'Come in.' Sarine brought a tray and laid it on the table by the chaise longue.

'Evening, Mr Richard,' she said, as if she had seen him all day every day, and only missed him since early afternoon.

'How are you, Sarine?'

'Not too bad, Mr Richard. We're all doing fine, aren't we now, Miss Annette?'

She was a tall, ugly, bony, strong, colored woman in her fifties, who smiled for no one except his wife, her Miss Annette. He had thought about Sarine's life often, and with shame. If he could not save himself, he could at least save Sarine. Once, years ago, he offered to finance Sarine's escape. She could find work anywhere. She could live in her own house, he held out Harlem with the greatest doubt, still it seemed better, closer to life, than the virginal dolled-up attic of the white frame house in Grangeville. Sarine was not too old to marry; perhaps too old for children, by then, but not too old for a man. She was healthy, she had a right to live. Sarine apparently was a slave who had nothing to love but her chains. Leave Miss Annette, her little saint, Miss Annette who couldn't do a thing for herself, and was like Sarine's baby? Sarine had never trusted him after that, probably no longer liked him, if ever she had liked him.

'I brought you a cocktail too, Miss Annette.' Sarine poured lemonade from a small glass pitcher into a cocktail glass and gave the glass to Annette who smiled her thanks, that wonderful smile, the smile of a pleased and grateful child. He took bottles from the tray and mixed a Martini. Sarine looked at him, saying silently all she meant to say: Now you be careful, don't you tire our baby, don't you stay more than an hour, don't you say anything to upset her. Then she left them to their ritual.

Usually, he raised his glass and said, 'To you.'

She smiled at him, exactly as she smiled at Sarine, and said, 'To you, darling.'

Today he said, 'To our sixteenth.'

'Yes. Oh, Ricky, Ricky, darling. I have so much to thank you for. Sixteen years. And you've never made me unhappy, never hurt me, never a quarrel. Nothing but your love and your kindness, all that time. I can only thank God for sending you to me.'

He could not answer or look at her. She was used to silence. To drink without smoking was not the same thing, but it helped. He poured another Martini. He asked if he might hear the Bach concerto and she told him where the record was. He listened to the racing intricate music, stopped listening, and drank more Martinis. The sky was greenish blue, with the light going quickly. His allotted hour was finished. He would see her again for a few moments after breakfast and then he would take his train back to New York and this visit, like countless others, would be behind him, and he would organize his mind to forget it.

He kissed her again on the forehead, pressed her hand gently, smiled from the door, called Sarine, and turned and hurried out of the house. He would cross Necher's fields and get into the woods and walk fast along the darkening path until he came to the top of the hill. Then he would sit down and smoke one cigarette and try to think of nothing.

Then he would come back and face the evening meal with Aunt Lucy. He might even run in the woods, although running was only a gesture, only the compulsion of his body, for he never ran as he wanted to, away.

The table was round, so Aunt Lucy could not, properly, sit at the head of it, but she did. He sat at her right, the guest of honor. He always felt a guest in this house, and not a very certain one: any wrong move and Aunt Lucy and Sarine would chuck him out. This was a peculiar way to feel since it was not only his house but he had been born in it, in the bedroom next door, formerly his father's and mother's, now Aunt Lucy's. Of course, when the house became a hospital and shrine, it had changed so much that it no longer resembled the place where he had grown up. His mother ran a feeding station for the Grangeville boys; she felt guilty because she could not give him brothers and sisters to keep him company, and she was always afraid that Richard would be lonely, the only child of middle-aged parents. His mother had not cared how her house looked, or what happened to it, as long as it was filled, positively roaring, with life.

From the beginning, Aunt Lucy, consulting Annette's wishes, sensibly and ruthlessly arranged this old remembered house to fit Annette. They enlarged the real living room downstairs to make Annette's bedroom, because they could move her into the garden from there, and the squirrels could come to call, and she could watch the flowers growing, close at hand. They changed the dining room into a dressing room and bathroom for Annette. They did wonders to the kitchen so that now it had become a noiseless, odorless operating theater. It had to be odorless, because of Annette's asthma. Aunt Lucy made his room, where now they ate at the round table, into a snug, chintzy parlor. Here she could receive her soft-spoken lady friends; the room was not directly above Annette and their footsteps would not disturb her. Here, he had once hung his pennants, his cases of butterflies, his stuffed fish; he had done his homework, thrown his clothes on the floor, slept well and dreamed triumphantly. They kept the tiny guest room, only changing it into a bower of rosebuds and blue lover's knots, and it was known politely as Richard's room. The bathroom was unrecognizably pretty, it had been a bare splashed-up box in his time. In the attic, Sarine was content with her white-painted iron bedstead, her cushioned rocking chair, and her shower bath from Sears Roebuck. Well, why not? he thought. They live here, I don't. It was a little jewel of a house and had cost quite a lot. Luckily, his mother carried a heavy life insurance.

Because they believed these to be his favorite dishes, they always gave him the same dinner, and always, as now, Aunt Lucy said how too bad it was that he had to eat that unhealthy restaurant food in New York when what he needed was this nice home cooking.

Stuffing fried chicken and succotash into his mouth, he began a wordless conversation. Oh, no, Aunt Lucy, you've got it wrong. I eat dinner at home every night. My beloved is interested in cookery as a game, a sport. She has never heard of a balanced diet and probably never will. Last night, for instance, we had a brownish slippery mess which was a mixture of bamboo shoots and almonds and strips of meat said to be duck. You might not believe me, but it was delicious.

Suddenly he noticed the silence. Aunt Lucy, unlike Annette, was not used to silence. He said, 'Well, I have to work, you know.'

'Of course you do, dear boy. And how is everything at the store?'

'About the same.'

She would not ask anything more. The only work she understood was her father's work; he had been the Methodist minister in Petersfield, South Carolina. She thought that was good work. She also had a dim idea of what Judge Mallin, her little sister Bea's husband, Annette's father, had been up to. On the whole, she did not think men's work was any of her business; they worked, as they should, to earn the money to keep their wives. In return, their wives were loving, ornamental, served them excellent food, and made pretty homes for them, as Annette did. Heaven knew it was the least men could do, considering. Richard was very sweet and aware of his duties, but there must have been times. What had he done to use Annette up, in less than four years? She had given Annette to him in perfect health, and when she came back, to bring Annette to this house and nurse her, Annette was a pitiful little white thing, dying before her eyes. Lucy Blair knew exactly what Richard had done, but she would not put it into words in her mind. God had been especially kind to her, granting her Annette to mother, after the child's dear parents died in the Accident. She had this joy without paying any harsh and terrible price. They were all happy women here, and perhaps Richard, who was in a sense guilty, had been God's instrument, and in any case she had long since decided she was not to judge him. Smoothly round, serene-faced, white-haired, Aunt Lucy sat in her rightful place and ate her way daintily through piles of food.

Helping himself to another popover, he said, 'Annette looks fine.'

Aunt Lucy's eyes lighted; now, at last, they were launched on her subject. It is her life's work, he thought, it is reasonable for her to want to talk about nothing else.

'She *is* looking well, isn't she? I'm so glad you said so. I can never be sure if I'm really seeing her, you know, looking at her so hard all the time. Well, we haven't had a bad attack, really not an attack at all since, let me see, it would be February tenth, yes, it was well after you left us the last time.' (Reproach, he thought, and followed his usual technique of continuing to chew.) 'I can't think what happened. There may have been some dust from the garden or maybe she overtired herself.' (How, in God's name? he thought.) 'She just had enough strength to ring the bell by her bed, and Sarine and I flew downstairs and while Sarine held her up and gave her the drops, I telephoned Ted and he got here in no time at all, he must have put his coat over his pajamas, I don't know what. Well, it was terrible for a while; oh that poor angel, that lamb of light, I can never tell you, Richard, what that child is. There she was choking, fighting, you could see the pain she was in, and somehow she managed to smile at us. Ted gave her an injection; I don't know what he does, it's just a miracle; and he saved her again. What would we do without Ted?'

'You didn't write.'

'No, Annette forbade me. She said it was useless to worry you. She thinks of you all the time, Richard. Ted said to me once that he believes what keeps Annette alive is the thought of you and the hope of seeing you again.'

'Did he?'

'Yes, he did. And I said to him, no man ever had a more devoted loving wife than Annette.'

He ate some more; it was wonderful how, if you kept your mouth full, you were excused from speech.

Presently he said, 'Ted is very fond of Annette, isn't he?' It was a daydream he made for himself, in the cell on the fifteenth floor of Handel's store. Ted would come to him, man to man, noble with his sandy crew-cut, and say, 'Rick, I am afraid this will break your heart, but Annette and I . . .'

'He loves her,' Aunt Lucy said, 'the way we all do. If he's told me once, he's told me a thousand times, that she's the bravest, sweetest patient he's ever had.'

'And Annette is very fond of him?'

'Why, you know that, Richard. She's the most grateful person on earth. She even thanks the flowers for growing, she thanks us all for every little thing we do for her. She can't thank Ted enough for his care of her.'

There are also the bills, Rick thought, it is not entirely on this spiritual level of the healer wrestling with death. There are the bills.

'I was wondering,' he said. Now how could he possibly say it? He picked at the apple pie and sloshed the thick cream around his plate.

'Living so much alone, seeing no one, only you and Sarine and Ted, I was wondering if she wouldn't. . . .'

'Richard,' Aunt Lucy said, in a granite voice, 'if you are going to start being jealous of that poor helpless dying angel, it is the ugliest and most unworthy thing I ever heard.'

'Oh, no,' he said. 'Oh, no, you don't understand.'

'I'm sure I don't.'

He gave up; besides it was foolish and hopeless. Ted was thirty-five years old and not crazy and, though unmarried and officially blameless, he was not likely to be a eunuch. No man would start off with a woman in Annette's condition. Not start off, not marry. Probably Ted attended to vital needs in New York or Hartford or Boston. Probably, having seen so many married couples, he was steering clear of the whole business. What did he know about Ted? Nothing, except that he couldn't take him. It was Ted, old Dr Bartlett's sparkling new assistant, who told him, when he came back from the war, about Annette's heart and her asthma, in medical terms which he did not understand, and finished by saying, 'I am afraid that she cannot stand anything, Whiteley, you know what I mean? I am afraid you will have to be a brother and sister, in some ways, from now on. Of course, medicine is not an exact science and there can always be a miraculous change.' No change. Splendid Ted. The perfect doctor. He had learned from Ted the trick of kissing Annette's hand; this did not interfere with her precarious intake of breath.

'I think I'll go for a walk, Aunt Lucy. Delicious dinner. I'll thank Sarine downstairs.'

'You'll be very quiet coming in, won't you, dear?'

Ted was waiting for him in the hall. It was always arranged this way. Ted paid his first call at the Whiteley house whenever Rick came up from New York. This gave Rick plenty of time to catch the 9:40 for the city. Immediately after breakfast, having already thanked Aunt Lucy and Sarine for his visit, Rick went to say goodbye to his wife. She looked as lovely in the morning; she looked as if she had slept better than any other adult on the American continent. He promised to write more. She could not write at all; he got his news from Aunt Lucy. He announced that he would send any good books he read. He kissed her forehead or her cheek, complimented her on her beauty, told her to keep up the good work, and let himself quietly out of the room. For, at just that moment, as he left, there was another expression in her eyes, which he knew well. It was the look, not of a pleased and grateful child, but of a hurt, lost, lonely child, unjustly punished. He never wanted to see that, and during the last four years he had consciously turned his head, to avoid seeing. He would not feel guilty about Maggie. Who on earth had a right to suggest that he was guilty? But he did not wish to see that particular look in his wife's eyes.

When he had closed the door silently behind him, there was Ted. They would now walk down the road, away from the house, smoke, and have a frank chat about Annette's health. And then his train, his train which by now he was longing for with hunger, with passion.

'Well?' Ted said, as always.

'She looks fine, don't you think?'

'Yes, she's doing nicely just now. We had a bad one in February, Miss Blair tell you? It shook Annette a lot. She can't get used to them, poor girl. I don't mean the suffocation. No one ever gets used to that. It's the idea she can't learn to accept.'

'Dying?'

'Well, yes. And each attack brings it nearer, obviously. It's a wonder to me how her heart stands up. She knows that, too. But she can't. . . .'

'I know.'

'I wish there was some way to help her. Spiritually, I mean. It's not my field.'

'Not mine either. A minister, I should think. Have you ever talked to Aunt Lucy?'

'She doesn't want to think about it, any more than Annette.'

'Annette said you thought she was getting better.'

'Better than she was in February. Better than on her worst days. But not better. You know that.'

'Yes.'

'Of course, she's amazingly strong in her will. She may live a very long time. There's nothing new to tell you, Rick.'

'No.'

'Well, I suppose you want to be getting to your train?'

'Yes, I'll have to. Thanks for everything, Ted.'

They were back at the front door. Rick picked up his suitcase and walked quickly down the road. Ted entered the house. Already, walking away, with the house at his back, with the train ahead of him, he could start forgetting. He would not have to come again until her birthday in June.

He kicked open the door, shouting, 'Maggie, Maggie.' She sprang up from a welter of papers, her paint box dropped on the floor; as usual she seemed to have painted herself as well. Holding the bourbon bottles like dumbbells, he hugged her fiercely. She had her arms around his neck, she kissed him. They made sounds as if they had been running toward each other over a great distance.

'Look what I brought you,' he said at last.

'Oh, goody! Oh, wonderful! Let's drink them both tonight, Rick. You've been gone so long.'

'Since yesterday morning.'

'Awful.'

They stood and looked at each other. 'I'm shy,' Maggie said. 'You've been gone so long I don't know how to treat you. What shall we do next?'

'Well, drink.'

'What a good idea.'

She busied herself in the kitchenette, a small hell-hole. There was only the one big room and the bathroom and the kitchenette—they hardly ever lost sight of each other.

'What have you been doing?' he asked, collecting the fallen sheets of drawing paper.

'A bra ad. A beauty. It may be the best bra ad ever done. I think it ought to bring in $500. Here,' she said, showing him her work of art.

'Golly,' he said.

'Why? No, please. Say why. Is it indecent?'

'No, not indecent. But, golly.'

'Good. Then we'll have $500 and we'll take a trip.'

'Where?'

'I don't know. Africa. Chile.'

'What are we having for dinner?'

'Chile. That's why I said it, of course. It's a Chilean dish. It seems to be based on pancakes and fish.'

'Where did you learn about it?' He was always enchanted by this, her monkey curiosity; every day she came home with something added to the glorious optimistic jumble in her mind.

'I have a friend who knows a Chilean. But don't let's eat until late. Your drink.'

He raised his glass. 'To you, Maggie. Maggie darling. And to being home.'

'Yes.' But she was still shy.

'What's been going on, during my long absence?'

'Mark and Jessie were having lunch at my drugstore and when I said I was alone they said they'd come and cheer me up and bring wine, and then somehow Steve and Tommy showed up too, so we ate an immense amount of spaghetti and gallons of ghastly red wine and *discussed*.'

'What?'

'Oh, you know. Discussed. The way they do.'

The way they did, he corrected her silently. She used to have a constant salon, it seemed; her flat here on Thirty-ninth Street was convenient, she was hospitable and lively, people came, bringing contributions to the general welfare, and stayed and stayed and talked and talked. It took a while for them to drift away. She had been twenty-four when he moved in; her friends were her age. It would have been against their principles to remark on this open liaison. But Rick seemed terribly old to them; a man of forty then, he made them nervous; they didn't understand him, or they didn't understand his being so much older. They didn't call him 'sir' because they weren't that kind, but they might have. And he really didn't know what they were talking about, he could not see what excited them so; he could not remember himself at twenty-four, or anyhow he had not been like this. He was a silent spectator; they took his silence for disapproval, whereas it was only uneasiness. Now they came if Maggie asked them, which was rarely; they always appeared, as if by magic, whenever he was away. I have taken her friends too, he thought. What haven't I taken? Four years of her life, half her flat, including her half share of the expenses—there isn't any end to what I won't take from Maggie.

'Drink up,' Maggie said, anxiously. 'I don't like the look in your eye.'

'I was thinking.'

'Yes, I know. I don't like it a bit when you think. Did you order your new suit?'

'Not exactly. No.'

'Oh, why? Did you change your mind? I thought it was lovely, so handsome and practical too. I can't wait to see you in it.'

It was not that he couldn't think of a lie, he had become a talented liar, but he did not wish to lie to Maggie, not ever if he could help it.

'I spent the money on something else.'

'Oh.'

She might well say 'Oh' with that note of shocked disappointment. After all, it was her money too. If he had not saved it to buy a suit, he could have spent it here, on their life; he could have spent it on her. He had thought of himself going without a suit; he had not thought of Maggie, and it now occurred to him that he was down-at-heel, dingy, and that his shabbiness hurt Maggie's pride.

'I hadn't thought,' he said.

'What is it, Rick?'

'I spent it on a pin, a present for Annette. I can't give her anything, except something like that. It was our sixteenth wedding anniversary, you know. I guess I did it out of guilt. Not nice, is it? And I hadn't thought about you.'

'It doesn't matter,' she said, looking crushed. 'It just puts it off. In a few months anyhow, we'll have the money again. Or this bra ad, yes, the bra ad. So it doesn't matter a bit.'

'It does.'

'Please,' she said. 'It's over. Don't let's worry about it. What a damn silly thing to worry about.'

But she did not ask what the pin was like, or how it had been received. She had this in common with Annette; there were things she refused to talk about.

The dishes were stacked and dirty in the kitchenette. Clothes slopped from the chairs onto the floor. Maggie's paint box lay as fallen. The used glasses settled in wet rings on the table, the ashtrays overflowed. They had abandoned everything, suddenly, as if seized by panic. His absence and the reason for it still stood between them. They had to find each other again, they could not afford or endure this strangeness. There was no other way but this, this best and unbelievable, always renewed, always miraculous, gentle, fierce and healing.

'Rick.'

'My dearest?'

'How I love you. Just you. Nobody in the world but you. Good night.'

He held her head against his chest, he held his arm warm around her, and she slept easily. He was too tired to sleep and too happy now; he wanted to stay awake with his happiness. He drifted into familiar fantasy, rearranging the past. They were in Naples. It was a warm spring night, and Maggie and he, standing on the balcony, could smell marvelous things, camellias, magnolias, tuberoses, he was not sure, and below them lay the shining water, and black and high and magical across the bay were the mountains. They had an ice bucket with champagne in the room and the huge Italian *letto matrimoniale*. In the morning they visited the town. He could not imagine Maggie in any sort of uniform, which created a difficulty because how then did she manage to be there? She was there, simply, looking like herself, like a small boy who made a good thing out of selling papers. She didn't look like that, of course; short beaver-fur hair, brown skin, brown bright eyes—did monkeys have happy eyes? no; little girl, very little girl, blown into her clothes somehow, always a belt cinched tight around her middle, always looking wonderful, unexpected, young.

There was Rome; Rome was his favorite place to go on leave with Maggie. Maggie loved Rome. Later they met in Paris. He had to make this up, as he had never been to Paris. His division was the hard-luck kind; they had a long dismal war, from Africa, mountain-climbing desperately and endlessly up Italy, only brought to the center of the world as reinforcements during the Battle of the Bulge. Paris was perfect too, silver and perfect, and Maggie was the toast of the town. They met in London just once. They had a room at Grosvenor House, high above the park. It rained; they stayed in bed most of the time. The war was nothing, it happened in between his leaves with Maggie.

He moved Maggie now, tenderly; rubbed his shoulder, stretched, rolled over on his side and closed his eyes. None of it true, he thought, can't get away with it, can't fool with the past. It's there, you can't change it. It's just there, all the time.

None of it true. On his infrequent leaves he slept. He slept like the dead and the sick. And then got silently, unlaughingly, stonily drunk; and then went back to the regiment. He never had Maggie, he never had any woman. How could he, with his beautiful, beloved young wife dying at home? He had a superstitious terror that if he took a woman, even the ugliest bargain-rate whore, it would kill Annette like lightning. And all he wanted was for Annette to live, only that; let Annette live until he could come home and make her well. He worked, that was what he did in the war. It wasn't so bad; it kept him from thinking. Company commander, battalion commander, second in command of the regiment, never wounded, always there, dependable Rick, not much fun, serious guy, took the war seriously, had some trouble of his own, got the work done. No Maggie, only the joyless years.

Maggie worked steadily at her drawing board for two days. She worked hard because she did everything hard, and she did not mind this job at all; she thought it was a joke, money for jam, drawing these never-never-land women in various ludicrous positions—just now with breasts stuck out, as if they were offering peanuts to elephants—and getting paid for it. She did not worry, she drew; she got paid, maybe not for all of the silly women but for enough of them. She didn't want money except to live, and had no exalted idea of how to live. This time, she wanted money badly.

Her agent had said the Nu-Way people were pleased with her work on the E.Z. Two-Twist Girdle: The Tip-Cup, said her agent, is a big chance for you, you might get a contract. Five hundred dollars now,

Maggie thought, the hell with contracts. She left the wash drawing with her agent's secretary. Then she waited at home for the agent's report. She smoked and roamed about the room and brooded on money.

Couldn't that miserable Dame aux Camélias in the country see for herself how Rick looked? Couldn't she and that household of female hogs cut down a little? What did they live on anyhow, caviar and shredded orchids with cream? Didn't she give a damn, so lost in her successful career of dying, that her legal husband, that self-sacrificing crazy-generous angel and darling, looked like a rug peddler or a bum from under the bridges? Did they ever think about that? How did Rick feel, in those baggy worn-out clothes; what did they think at the office? They probably thought he drank or gambled his money away; maybe they were having conferences about him and saying he looked too awful, it was a disgrace to the store, they'd have to get a sharper-looking fellow for the job. Oh, not that, who cared about that? Him. Him. *Him.* He was beautiful and he was hers and she wanted him to look beautiful and sleek and young, the way he ought to. In dark-gray flannel. She knew exactly how he would look, with his black hair and his black eyebrows and his thin stylish nose and his long, bitter mouth, and then his shape, made for that suit, good shoulders and good legs and not loose and hangy around the waist, the way city men were. *They have to buy it*, Maggie thought, *I want that suit.*

They did buy it too. Her agent telephoned to congratulate her and said that Wallenstein at Nu-Way wanted to talk to her himself, he suggested a conference in his office day after tomorrow at three, Wallenstein thought she had something, very sexy her stuff was, they planned to work her in on their fall line.

Maggie ordered the suit herself, taking no chances. Rick's birthday was not until November, it would have to be a Spring Present. She felt nervous, now that she had given the order. Rick was very touchy. but he couldn't refuse, not when it mattered so much to her. Damn that woman, what did she wear? Balenciaga bedjackets probably. A man who earned thousands a year ought to be able to buy himself as many suits as would hang in a closet, and so he could if he didn't have to support those bloodsuckers in Connecticut.

Rick explained it to her, before he moved in; he wanted her to listen and she did, though she hated it. What it came to, obviously, was that with keeping them all in crepe-de-Chine sheets and larks' tongues and the most expensive medicine they could possibly find, and after paying taxes which needless to say they never considered, he had about $3,000 left for himself. Just enough, Maggie thought, to go on eating so he can go on working, very liberal of them. 'It isn't only that I can't give you anything, Maggie,' he said, 'I can't even keep you. Not even food and rent. Do you see? I'm sixteen years older than you and a pauper. Now what?' She'd told him, with dignity, that if he thought she wanted to be a kept woman, and then she couldn't go on like that, and hurled herself into his arms, crying, and saying she loved him and didn't he love her, and they could get a bigger bed on the installment plan and if he didn't want to live with her she'd just as soon be dead.

'I do not care, for myself,' Maggie said, looking at their room, which was not a very nice room, chewed up, not awfully fresh, mustard-colored on the whole, but theirs, and they were happy in it. That woman, what was she thinking, what was she doing, what did she know, how dared she call that love? He won't take the suit, Maggie thought, he'll look black and angry and hurt and pinched around the nose, he won't take the suit he'll be so beautiful in. Rick, returning, found her in tears on the bed, immediately thought she was ill and felt a cold shaking emptiness in his stomach, held her in his arms, begged her to tell him what had happened, and was so wildly relieved when he heard that he said he was delighted, he would love to have the suit, she was marvelous, he was going to give her a Spring Present too, only never frighten me like that again. Never.

Rick's Spring Present was to be a week-end trip. Long Island somewhere, he thought. Maggie took the matter in hand. Couldn't they go to the shack Mark and Jessie rented in the Adirondacks? Jessie had a toothache so they weren't using it, so much nicer than a hotel.

'We could catch trout and tie a rope around each other and be mountaineers.'

They went. Maggie caught a fish, not a trout, whatever it was. It lay flapping on the bank by the stream, and she was seized with remorse and threw it back into the water, saying she would never eat fish again. They climbed a mountain—Maggie insisted it was a mountain—and made love in a nest of rhododendron bushes at the top. That was all Rick remembered of the mountain.

Little things, Rick told himself, little things, not worth noticing. How could he not notice them? George Gebhardt arrived from Chicago, without warning. He had been Rick's roommate, hundreds of years ago, at Yale. Yale was what his mother saved for, longer and harder than he ever saved for a suit or anything else. George called him at the office, very hearty. George was a successful lawyer, one of the friendly, reassuring type who could not talk to you without laying a hand on your shoulder, arm, or knee. The squeeze-and-pat system of communication. George had been a successful campus politician before. They were oddly assorted roommates.

'I know it's short notice, Rick, but how about having dinner tonight with Ruth and me?'

Leave Maggie? Say what to Maggie?

'I'm terribly sorry, George, if only I'd known you were coming. I'm tied up. It's damn bad luck for me.'

'No, for us. Well, lunch tomorrow?'

'This is awful. I've got a business thing and I can't put it off. How about next week? I seem to have a terrible week right now. Lunch conferences, you know.'

'We're only here three days. I'll try to wire in advance next time. Sudden trip, I didn't know I had to come, myself.'

'What a deal,' Rick said, with too much sincerity. 'Give my love to Ruth, will you?'

That would be one of the last, he thought; not that there had ever been many, and fewer still after the war. He didn't eat lunch any more, better for his figure, foolish waste of money. He could not see George. Not talking about Maggie was like hiding her.

Or was Maggie his excuse? How did I come to this place where I am? Rick wondered. I'm all right, only I want to be left alone. It had something to do with being a failure, of course. He did not mind that either; what he could not stand was acting, dressing it up, keeping the ball in the air. That hopeless talk—how're you, boy; fine fine, how're you; dandy, never better—followed by the determined optimistic brag, the plans, the deals, the triumph, the money. No wonder none of his friends could talk to each other, having to lie all the time, lying to each other and themselves about everything being wonderful, more than they could have hoped. I am not who I wanted to be, Rick thought, and my work is nothing except a pay check; this is a perfectly usual condition; I have Maggie, and I am not obliged to pretend out of office hours. Everyone cannot be Tolstoy or President, Rick told himself, success is the great American error. Maggie is all I have or need or want.

Maggie's sister, the married one from Minneapolis, came to New York with her husband for some reason or other. Maggie's family was not clear to Rick: she had a father and mother, they owned a shoe store, they lived in a small town in Missouri; and she had a brother in San Francisco and the sister in Minneapolis. She never wrote to them or thought about them, as far as Rick knew. She didn't have anything against them; she just wasn't interested. But there was no way to get out of seeing the sister. Maggie explained that to Rick apologetically: she'd meet them at their hotel and have dinner and be home early. She did not say, I'll bring them here for a drink first, so you can all meet. It did not occur to Rick that Maggie was ashamed of her sister in imitation mink and a fancy hat, and ashamed of her brother-in-law and his brassy sales talk. They were not Rick's kind, they would revolt him. She was not ashamed of herself because Rick had chosen her and she was his pupil. She had learned everything she knew from Rick; you could hardly expect to get an education at Buxton High in Missouri.

It had been a specially worthless day at the store. There was nothing to get angry about, there was simply nothing. The day went on and on; by three o'clock he was promising himself Maggie as if he had not seen her for months. He left his office on the dot of five and walked directly home. He made plans for her evening's pleasure. The weather was lovely—couldn't they take a boat somewhere, up the river, or to Staten Island? After all, New York was surrounded by water, not that they benefited from it. Full of these modest hopes, he opened the door and saw at once that something was wrong. Maggie sat still and unoccupied, looking out the window. What you saw from the window was the flat brick front of a dingy hotel across the street: there was no reason ever to look out the window.

'Maggie?'
'Darling?'
'What is it?'
'Well. . . .'

But she could not, or would not, tell him. She launched into an aggrieved recital about her agent and what did he expect and those Nu-Way fiends and their horrid trusses for the female form. He believed none of it. They took the boat to Staten Island and it might as well have been winter or they might as well have stayed at home. As they walked back to the flat from the subway, he began to think that he didn't want to know what was on her mind; he felt menaced.

In bed, in the dark, she curled against him.
'Maggie, tell me now.'
'Kiss me.'
'Now. Tell me.'

She had been feeling odd, she consulted Jessie, and Jessie arranged an appointment with her doctor four days ago. Today she went back, now she knew.

His heart made heavy, sick, thudding sounds.
'But how? But why?' he said. 'After all this time?'

She reminded him of the nest of rhododendron on the mountain—it was the only possible explanation.

In a faraway, brittle voice, Maggie said, 'You don't want it, of course?'

Want it? He couldn't think; he had to catch hold of something first, so he could think at all. Suddenly she rolled away from him, gasping with sobs.

'Can't you say something? You can say something. Anything. I didn't do it on purpose. What do you think? Do you think I planned it so I could trap you? I couldn't help it!'

He caught hold of that, of her, he held her so close that it hurt, saying over and over, 'I love you. I love you, don't cry, something will happen, Maggie, I love you.'

The darkness was a hole to crawl into. Time, he thought, give us time. He felt stupid with tiredness and on the edge of sleep. She was quiet now in his arms. He reminded himself that he must think, and could not. There was no place to begin. From the darkness, he heard his voice, but surely he was thinking, not talking?

'It could kill you,' he said. She moved at his side. 'Aunt Lucy thinks that's what finished Annette. It was in Georgia at boot camp. Annette had a room in a boardinghouse in town, awful, squalid, she couldn't do anything about it, she wasn't a girl who could fix anything. I knew she was delicate, my God, yes, I knew about her asthma all right. I imagined asthma was like hay fever or something, a damned nuisance; I didn't know really. When she told me about the baby, it seemed the most wonderful thing that ever happened. A son, I thought, and she'll have him to look after and keep her happy while I'm away and I'll have them both to come back to. That was what I thought. Divine Providence, everything arranged in the best way you could hope for. She miscarried in the sixth month and nearly died, that's what they wrote me. Her heart, her asthma complicating it, I don't know what. They never bothered to tell me before, the whole bunch of prize fools, that she'd had rheumatic fever when she was eleven and they always knew she had a wacky heart. What do they live by anyhow? I bet her poor doting parents were the worst of the lot. Aunt Lucy treated her like glass, but they never talk about anything they don't like. If I'd known about her heart then.'

In the dark, very gently, Maggie kissed his shoulder.

'And what have you been thinking all this time?' he said. 'I never told you anything. I wanted to keep it away from us so we could live here alone. That's as hopeless as everything else.'

'No, no,' Maggie said vaguely.

'I can't tell you the truth about Annette anyhow, because I don't remember. It doesn't seem true, whatever I say. But I was in love with her, I know that, even if I can't believe it now. I thought she was the most beautiful girl in the world, and much more, not like all the rest of us ordinary mortals. I couldn't get over her marrying me. Who was I? How did I deserve anything so lovely? Then after we were married I moved right into a splendid role, the Tower of Strength. I admired myself very much, I thought I was a Tower of Strength to beat hell. Every day I'd hurry home from work to that apartment we had in the Village and find my beautiful wife sitting in chaos, and then I'd soothe her and comfort her and take over. I was a great one for taking over. But it didn't worry me, it was going to be just a phase. Because very soon now I would be the famous rich great writer, translated into forty languages, and then I'd put my wife on a satin cushion where she could be my inspiration. Naturally, great writers took a while to get recognized—look at their early lives, they all had to work at stupid little jobs, for a start. I was in the tradition, I thought it was perfect, including Annette's helplessness. It makes me sick to think about it.'

'Don't, Rick,' Maggie said.

'I've started, you might as well hear it all. Not that there's much. I haven't had a very varied life. There was joining-up and Georgia, and all that. Then my division went to Africa. I got Aunt Lucy's letter there, in 1943. Annette would never have another child and probably not recover from this one. On and on. I didn't believe her. I thought that she and Sarine were hysterical old women, and doctors are all the same. I thought Annette needed me, just me, once I got back I'd cure her. So I did get back, and even after Ted warned me, I couldn't help myself. I'd been gone for three and a half years. I walked into her room and saw her and picked her up and kissed her, the way a man kisses his wife. She had an attack at once. It was probably excitement but also moving her, kissing her hard. I watched it. She was strangling, she couldn't get enough air to breathe, and what it did to her eyes and her face. I never saw anything worse and I knew it was true then, they were right, I couldn't cure her, nothing could. I left that night, when everything was under control again, and I went to Hartford to a cheesy hotel. I had a fine orgy of drunkenness and despair for about two weeks, and then I went back to work, same old job, waiting for me the way they promised. That was ten years ago. Maybe you never get used to dying yourself but you certainly get used to someone else dying. I haven't any idea what Annette thinks because she hasn't talked to me. She's always the same, sweet and calm and beautiful and delighted to see me and full of little chat about the things she chats about. Of course I've got no reason to worry; I have a good secure job and when I'm too old for it, the store has its own pension scheme. How do people manage?' he said. 'My God, that's what I want to know. How do people manage?'

Maggie took him in her arms and held his head against her breast, making little sounds without words, smoothing his hair, his cheek, rocking him gently against her. She had never imagined that she could help him; he was all her help, her certainty, wiser than she, older, strong, he was the one who would keep her from being a silly, cheap woman with nothing much to do in the world. And she thought he was used to the stale story of Annette, and such a good man that, of course, he would not abandon his invalid wife, but that was all; a duty he fulfilled and did not think about, a habit that cost him more than he could afford, but he was too generous to care. Fool, she told herself, wicked fool; holding him and loving him. She knew better now. She had to save his life. She had to and she would.

Maggie had not foreseen that he would be ashamed of every word he had said, shrugging his shoulders in his office, as if shrinking away from his disgust. Whining, he thought, so sorry for himself, poor little fellow, scrounging sympathy. He could taste it in his mouth. He could not remember when he had loathed himself more. At the end of the day he telephoned Maggie and announced in a flat voice that he had to dine with Blick, and ate at an Automat and went to a movie, hoping she would be asleep by the time he got home.

Maggie settled herself, with a new patience, to say nothing and wait. After days of this, each more leaden and disappointing than the last, she believed she understood him. It was not too bad, the only thing she did not want to lose was Rick.

They stood, wedged in the kitchenette, she washing plates, he drying them, and Maggie said, with extreme casualness, 'Jessie knows a sort of doctor, seems she had a little trouble herself once, I've got the money, from the Nu-Way garter belt. So we don't have to worry about it any more.'

'No. No. *No.*'

'Well, what?' she said, close to tears, her hands limp in the dishpan. 'What, then?'

'Oh, Maggie. Leave these damned dishes. Come here.'

He pulled her onto his lap, in their one creaking, comfortable chair, and said, 'Maggie, what do you want to do? You, yourself?'

'I'm like you. I can't get used to it. I don't know. But if it was just me, Rick, I want to have the baby. We could get an orange crate and fix it a bed here in our room and then there'd be you and me and our little brown baby.'

He laughed. Heaven, she thought, what a long time it's been. He laughed and hugged her and said, 'Naturally. Of course. Of course there's nothing else at all. You and me and our little brown baby in an orange crate.'

They had a Practical Talk. This was Maggie's unfavorite kind of talk but she listened and nodded her head wisely. They would be just as poor; the one thing he could not do was cut off any of the Grangeville supplies. Of course, in time he would get a raise, it was automatic; and in more time, about six or seven years, he would get Blick's job, and the Grangeville needs were stationary, so they could expect to live fairly decently. Yes, yes, Maggie murmured, nodding her head. It would be cruel to break this to Annette on her birthday, so he would have to stay over an extra day, or at least the whole morning, if it was possible to talk to Annette then. On the other hand, what with time and money, it was better not to make a special trip to see her. Yes, yes, Maggie agreed. The only snag was divorce laws—he didn't know about them, and certainly couldn't afford the six weeks and the trip to Reno, but probably they could get a divorce in Connecticut on the grounds of so many years' actual separation. Maggie nodded. She was to be very careful while he was gone; it was these early days that were tricky. Oh, yes, Maggie said, yes indeed.

Now, on the train, he could not plan the sentences he knew he would have to say. There was no picture in his mind of him, standing, sitting, in Annette's room and saying, 'After thirteen years of no marriage, I want my freedom.' He found he had a cracking headache and preferred to think of Maggie's little brown baby, who was as clear to him as if already born, already burbling and waving his legs in the orange crate.

There was a small cake, with white icing and pink sugar roses and one candle to grow on. For him there was a half bottle of champagne, a drink he detested, but it was routine for birthday parties. There was the collection of Emily Dickinson's poems, his present for Annette—no absurd extravagance, this time; he had other obligations. Annette looked at least ten years younger than her age, and especially lovely in a soft blue, ruffled, tucked, gathered robe which Aunt Lucy had made as her birthday gift. Then there was dinner with Aunt Lucy, and a never-ending night, then the usual brisk after-breakfast talk with Ted, who had sent a lavish box of chocolates the day before. With Ted's permission

('She's really much better, give her a kick too, make her realize how
well she is'), he opened Annette's door, thinking that this was perhaps
the last time he would see her and feeling an unsteady lightheaded sense
of relief.

'I've come to talk to you, Annette,' he said. Oh, fool, he obviously
wasn't coming to beat her, and he must find some reasonable voice, not
this croak.

'How lovely, how wonderful. It's the best birthday present of all. I
didn't *know* you could stay over. No one told me. A birthday surprise?'

'Well . . .'

'Pull your chair out of the sun, darling. It's getting so hot. Is it
terribly hot in the city?'

'Quite hot.'

'My darling. I think it's wicked that they won't give you a vacation.
It would be so lovely and restful if only you could come here for two
weeks.'

Ah. Forgot it, he thought, such an old lie that he'd forgotten it. He
spent his annual two weeks with Maggie, mostly at Jones Beach.

None of the beginnings work, he thought. And said, in a perfectly
indecipherable voice, indecipherable even to himself, 'Do you ever think
about us, Annette?'

'Ricky. I think of us all the time.' She smiled, lighted up, shone like
the sun. 'I think of us as a miracle. There isn't anything miraculous
about me loving you. I knew I would all my life, from the first day I
met you. Do you remember, at the Partridges'? I still write, I mean I
dictate, a letter to Aunt Lucy every year, to Sarah Partridge because she
introduced me to you, or you to me, which was it? The miracle is you,
Ricky; you're the miracle.'

He said nothing, and looked at his nails which seemed very far-off
and peculiar, hardly the sort of nails you would expect to see.

'We haven't had the life we meant to have,' she said gently. 'But
think of the people, the poor people, who lose their love, and see it all
as a failure, and have to go through a horrible divorce, and then try to
start again, worn-out and second-hand. My health,' she said, having
difficulty with the word, 'has been a terrible trial, but it hasn't killed
anything. That's what makes it all right, you see, that's what makes
living beautiful for me.'

And how about me, he shouted in his mind, me, Rick, the miracle
man, what is supposed to make life beautiful for me? I am in fine health,
rude health, I haven't got the appetites of a flower or a bird, I am not
safely slowed down on a chaise longue. He hated her. He plainly hated
her. The word 'love' made him sick, made him retch. He must remember

to tell Maggie. I am not going to say I love you, Maggie, because love is a dirty word, it's blackmail, it's the word people use when they mean absolute cannibal possessiveness. And throughout all eternity, I will eat you, you will eat me. Christ. He wanted to shake Annette, hit her, sitting there like a beautiful fresh clean hen on that goddamned egg, her love.

'I get lonely,' he said, flat, like a weather report.

'Dearest. I know, I know. You're never said anything, I knew you always wanted to spare me. I know about loneliness. It's worst at night. I always hope you are asleep, not feeling that.'

Her hand was stretched out to him; he ignored it.

'Do you think about the child, ever?' Now it was like a policeman, impersonal third degree. I didn't give you rheumatic fever, I didn't make your misshapen heart. If you'd had the sense to mention a simple fact like that I'd have damn well seen to it you never got pregnant; you wouldn't have to lie on a chaise longue, at least not all the time; you would long since have been handed over to the care of a better, gentler, richer man, and it wouldn't matter, honey, it wouldn't matter, baby, you'd be surprised; you just need a caretaker-man to love, it doesn't have to be me.

Since she did not answer, he let his nails alone and looked at her. And was horrified to see her eyes, the unjustly punished child, but more, much more and worse: anguish. 'I don't, I swear I don't,' she whispered. 'I did for years, I tried always to hide it. How can they live with me if I am like that, mourning for what I've lost and can never have? I never saw his grave. Did he have a grave? I couldn't ask, I cannot put that on to you and to them, as well, not that too. I don't think of the child any more, I promise you I don't.'

He turned his head and looked at the garden. He would not see her, nor respond to that pain. He would not. Dead. Long dead. There is life to fight for, he thought, not always death, not always what is past, failed, gone. Now, he told himself, now is what matters.

'I would like to have a child.' What a quaint way of saying it. Will you dance the minuet with me? I would like. I must. I will. I am going to. A little brown boy with Maggie's hair and eyes, in an orange crate in our room, next to our bed.

She took in her breath with a hard, grating sound. He rose, ready to get the drops, first emergency treatment, suddenly realizing that he could talk her to death. His hands were sweating.

'Annette!'

But now she turned on him eyes that were alight with wonder, something almost insane, an insanity of hope.

'Adopt a baby?' she said. 'Ricky! Could we? Could we? Would it be fair? I could do so little for it. But Aunt Lucy and Sarine. Here? Here in the garden, playing and laughing in the garden? A very little baby? I could help to bathe it. Would you? It would be ours, it *would* be ours, we'd make it ours. I can still sew, I could sew clothes for it, and later I could teach it to read, I think I could.'

'No,' he said, heavily. He got up from the chair and walked through the open French windows and stood in the garden: the squirrel's tree, the roses growing along the fence, the bird's fountain. Nothing, he thought, she understands nothing; we might be shouting at each other from different planets. Help to bathe it. She isn't guilty, he thought with terrible weariness; she has committed no crime, she doesn't prefer death to life. She is blind and unreal from these years of nothingness, but she isn't guilty. Why can't she die? Fighting to live on a chaise longue, fighting the terrors at night, fighting the need of a child. Why can't she die? Die. God, *make her die.*

He had to go back. He had to finish this, although who knew how it would end? The rocketing hope was gone from her eyes, clouded over with a milky strange fixed look, ready to be fear. If he tormented her long enough, if he confused her so that she did not know what was happening to her and to her tiny world, if he made the walls shake and the garden slant and the sunlight turn gray, she could also take leave of her anchorage, that slight whatever-it-was that kept her bound to this time and this place. Thirteen years was a very long time to wait for death; aside from her heart, there was no telling what state her mind was in; if you hurt it enough, it might give too. Hurry, now, now was the time for the ax and the final blow. However it would end.

'I love,' he began, and saw it happening. Saw the fear, saw her push back against the pillows, recoiling as if he had come toward her with murderous hands, saw the fear slipping too and behind it nothing, her eyes already going dull and empty.

'I love *you*,' he said. 'It's all right, Annette. *I love you.*'

Then he rang for Sarine and pulled open the door, and ran from the house, like an old man, running down the road. They could look after her, it was their job now. They could hardly expect him to give her anything more.

Blick had told him not to come back to the office today. Compassionate leave. Blick was a perfectly decent fellow. They all were. Maybe they hated the job as much as he did, but put on a better show. Maybe they didn't hate the job but that was no reason to despise them. He was not exactly a man who had the right to despise anyone. He would just walk around a bit first, it might be easier later on.

He went up the stairs slowly, wishing there were more of them. Then he opened the door slowly, wishing he had forgotten his key, wishing that Maggie would be out. Maggie was there, and turned to him, her face warm with love and concern and hope, and saw what she saw. He did not have to tell her. He knelt by her chair, smelling paint, and hid his face in her lap.

Grief, he thought, that is what this is: I never knew. No one can live with it. It's beyond caring, beyond hope. A big gray emptiness. We can't, we can't.

Maggie's hand was on his shoulder. He moved, raised his head, and took her hand, which was cold. She was looking out the window. Her face showed nothing.

'Maggie,' he said. 'Maggie, please.'

She turned her head and looked at him.

'Maggie, don't. Maggie, wait. She'll die. She has to die. It can't go on. Maggie, *wait*.'

She did not answer. After a while he got up, his knees hurting and creaking, and sat in the comfortable chair. It grew dark.

In the darkness, across a great distance, he talked to her. His voice seemed to echo, as if he were calling to her on the other side of a canyon.

'Maggie, listen. Turn your face. I beg you to listen.'

She stirred, moved; he saw a pale blur.

'If you think I couldn't because I love Annette, you are wrong. I wished her dead. I prayed for her to die.' He did not know what he expected, perhaps that Maggie would cry out against this crime. He felt it as a crime, and something terrible he would always keep with him, a knowledge of himself that he could not escape. Maggie was silent. Did she not believe him; was she too repelled to speak?

'I could even have done it, I think; I'm not sure, but I think so, said it all, if it had killed her quickly, at once.' Is it true, he asked himself? It may be true. Who am I? 'But not what I saw. What it was going to be. That she'd go on lying there, forever in that room, and mad. Crazy. With those eyes.'

Maggie was doing something. What? Putting her hands over her ears, not to listen, not to hear this horrible stuff? Shaking herself, to shake him off, to writhe away from this whole vile story, from all he had to say and was? He was afraid of everything now. He could hardly understand what he was saying, or his voice. 'You're young. I'm not really old. We'll be free some day, maybe not too long off, but we will be. We can have the baby; we'll be free later. We can count on that, we can, Maggie.'

My God, he thought, my God.

'*No*,' Maggie said, shouting the word across the now enormous room. No. God in heaven, no. Waiting for a funeral, every day, hoping for it with all their strength so they could marry. Dancing on a coffin. I must be mad myself. And besides, it was all very well to live together, you could get away with that, fashion had gone so far, provided you were discreet; but illegitimate children; no one had them, he'd never known anyone; he'd lose his job as soon as they heard; the child would starve; there might even be laws; they'd take the child to an institution. What has happened, Rick thought, I don't even know what I'm thinking.

'I don't care about the rules,' Maggie said harshly. 'Or if it got too tough, we could go to another city and say we were married. If it was only you and me, I wouldn't care. But I'm not going to have a father for my child, on loan. Do you hear? Half there, on loan from a damned ghost who won't die!'

She must have been crying; she made ugly sounds, as if the breath in her throat was metal, and she got up and bumped against the card table and the bookcase and he could hear her heavy on the stairs as she went down to the street.

Later he turned on the lights and went into the kitchenette and opened a can and heated the brownish stuff in a saucepan and sat at the table before the uneaten food, not knowing what he was waiting for.

Blick said to his secretary, 'I think Mr Whiteley's wife must be worse.'
'Poor man.'

Every evening he came home with fear, and found Maggie there, gentle, quiet; they seemed to him like two shadows, performing underwater rites of eating, sleeping, washing, as if they were real people. The fear was so heavy that it ended by numbing him. When he came home now he counted the stairs to their flat, thinking of nothing. The note was on the bed. He walked across the room and picked it up steadily. It was there because it had to be; he had known he would come back one of these days and find it.

> Dear Rick
> I have gone to that doctor of Jessie's who fixes things. After-wards, I am going with Jessie to the Adirondacks for a week or two. It will be nice to lie in the sun. Then I'll come back. I suppose our life will be kind of sad and dull here but maybe that's the way life is, when you get older. Take care of yourself.
> Maggie

He folded the note and put it back on the bed. He took off his hat and sat in Maggie's chair, by the drawing board. Wait, wait, he said to himself. No. Wait for what? He thought of Maggie where she was now, and suddenly he was bent over, breathing through his mouth, struggling against panic and nausea. After a while he went into the dark little bathroom and drank a glass of water and wiped his face with a towel. Then he came back and stood in the center of the room.

Sad and dull. No. No, my darling, it doesn't have to be. There is no law. It depends on the company you keep. It doesn't have to be, it won't be for you, there's plenty of time for you. Annette feeding on him, he feeding on Maggie. Well, no. He could prevent that, anyhow. You just have to be careful of the company you keep, my little one.

He looked at the room: the bed, the drawing board, the scarred old office desk where Maggie hid her disorderly tools and her underclothes, the card table where they ate, the homemade bookcase, the hideous lamp, the radio and record player, bought on the installment plan too. He looked at the floor where the nonexistent orange crate would not stand. He pulled two big suitcases from under the bed and began to pack.

TILL DEATH
US DO PART

The body lay in the next room, under a dirty tablecloth.

The Colonel was in a rage.

'How did he get here?'

'On an ammo truck last night from Batavia, sir.'

Lieutenant Langley felt frightened and heartsick. He hoped this rotten little official scene would soon finish so that he could get away by himself.

'Who gave him his travel orders?'

'I don't know, sir.'

'You didn't check?'

'No, sir.'

'Who gave him permission to go on patrol?'

'Well, sir, he came. I mean, Graham of the *Mail* was coming, and he came along.'

'You realize...'

'Yes, sir,' said Lieutenant Langley, not caring.

'Next of kin?'

'He doesn't seem to have any, sir.'

'His consul, then.'

'Apparently he hasn't got a consul, sir.'

'What's the matter with you, Langley? Stop dithering. You looked for his passport? You must have done something sensible.'

'Yes, sir. It isn't a passport, really. It's rather a long document. It appears to be handmade.'

'What on earth are you talking about?' The Colonel was slowly focusing his rage on Lieutenant Langley. Never noticed the boy before.

'It's different bits of paper, in different languages, with stamps on it, stuck together with Sellotape.'

'Impossible.'

'Yes, sir.'

'We have to do something with him,' the Colonel said. 'In this climate. Who *is* he?'

'He's a war photographer, sir. Quite famous, I believe.'

'What's his name?'

'Tim Bara, sir.'

'What nationality is that?'

'Graham says he made it up.'

'This is the limit!'

'Yes, sir.'

'Did you get the sniper?'

'No, sir.'

'Never!' the Colonel shouted, giving in to his fury with relief. 'Never get the sniper. Never get the one who lays the road mine. The damned little rats don't even notice who they shoot. Perfectly easy to see we're not Dutch.'

'Yes, sir.'

'Send a signal to Batavia.'

Every morning two British jeeps went out on patrol. They drove along the narrow dank mud roads in the jungle. They came back. Sometimes the natives laid a road mine, but they must have been locally manufactured or mildewed Japanese surplus, because there were rarely any fatal results from being blown up. One soldier had lost a leg two weeks ago but that was because his leg got caught under the jeep. Sometimes snipers in the jungle tried a pot shot. The natives were not often accurate with their rifles. You never saw anyone, at any time. There was another patrol, before sunset. It was all irritating, unpleasant and pointless. Graham of the *Mail*, and Cutts of the UP, and Billings of the *Herald* took turns going on the morning patrol, and later pooled the tired story.

The correspondents sat in the press hut, under a palm-leaf roof, while the midday heat rolled in through the open sides, heavy as water, sluggish, numbing. They had looted three long rattan chairs and reclined on these, naked except for khaki shorts, and sweated, and occasionally scratched whatever parts of their bodies itched most at the moment.

Graham, who had been there and seen it and was deeply shaken, said, 'Well, what next?'

'File the story,' Cutts said. 'It's the first story we've had. They'll use it for a change.'

But no one moved; it was too hot to move; there was no hurry anyhow; there seemed to be no hurry left anywhere.

'Bara!' Graham said suddenly. 'Bara, of all people.'

Then he did get up and stumble out of the hut and along the path into the jungle. He could not very well sit there, like a sweating mummy, while tears oozed down his face and Cutts and Billings stared.

Bara and he had been in the back of the second jeep, both suffering from hang-overs, because Bara had arrived the night before with a magical present of two bottles of whisky and a bottle of Dutch gin. Bara was talking, grumpily, and Graham listened, so delighted to be with Bara that he did not mind what this jeep ride was doing to his head and stomach.

'I will return to Singapore tomorrow,' Bara said. 'There are no rattan lice in Singapore. Aside from all that is wrong with them, the Japanese must be also too dirty to live. From every chair and table and bed in Batavia, out come the rattan lice, souvenirs from the Japanese. Look,' he said and opened his shirt to his navel, displaying large red lumps, like hives. 'Look,' he said again and pulled his shorts up to his groin, revealing more of the same red lumps. 'I am like that all over. I am a refugee from rattan lice.'

They bumped a while in silence.

'Trees,' Bara said with digust. 'Since when does somebody want a picture of trees? And such trees. What is the matter with them? Jungle is only interesting in the movies.'

The driver, hoping to make things better, said that the other patrol went over a road mine here a few weeks back. Bara grunted.

'This is a pitiful war,' Bara said. 'War gets worse and worse, people should give the whole thing up. Personally, I will retire. And take photographs of beautiful girls with bosoms. If I never see some ugly men in khaki again, it will be a pleasure.'

But Bara was the most famous war photographer in the world; everyone knew his name and his pictures. Graham had decided last night that their sector was on the way to being a front-page story, since Bara had joined them.

'I have been for ten years at wars,' Bara said. 'Every year my enthusiasm is smaller. Now it is the smallest yet. In a war you must hate somebody or love somebody, you must have a position or you cannot stand what goes on. Here it is impossible. Who can you hate here? That pretty little brown dictator? Well, he is not nice, no, he is a smooth one who went to school from the Japanese. You know what he said last week, when they had their Parteitag in Djokjakarta? He made a big speech, like a real full-size white dictator, but the brown people do not scream "*Heil*", they giggle and clap their little hands when they are excited. So he said, "Indonesians! We must be free! When our great country is free from the cruel, dirty Dutch, you will each have two bicycles!"' Bara laughed. 'It has charm. Yes, now I think of it, I like it.

But no reason for this murder game. Bodies in the Batavia canals. The poor Dutch. They come home from making those Japanese death railways wherever they were, and what do they find? Their wives big and bloated with the hunger sickness and their houseboys after them with a knife. This is not a war, this is a disgust. I cannot even take pictures of it.'

'It's bad,' Graham agreed.

'I tell you what,' Bara said, suddenly cheerful because he had a new better idea. 'Come to Singapore with me. We will eat steaks and have a bath. We will buy beautiful silk shirts. We will make peace.'

'My editor,' Graham said.

'You should never pay attention to editors. I will take one picture of these trees and then I will go. I am anyhow a casualty from rattan lice. You have malaria. It is easy.'

'Yes, I will,' Graham said, raised up from the sweating muck of boredom and futility which was the climate of this war. Bara never went wrong, look at his record; if Bara chucked this war that was because it was a failed, no-good war.

Cutts said Bara was a conceited opera singer; however, he said that after Bara was asleep. And Billings said that most of Bara's pictures were out of focus anyway, Bara was a coony operator who had built up a paying legend around himself. Cutts and Billings were stuck in a palm-leaf hut in the south of Java and their stories appeared on the inside pages if at all, whereas Bara came and went as he chose, obeyed no one, made and spent money like water, and any man would envy his looks.

Cutts and Billings were older than Bara and had bellies and soured expressions. Graham was twenty-four years old, and too tall and reedy, and the army had rejected him because of a perforated eardrum and weak eyes. Bara likes me, Graham thought, or he wouldn't ask me to go to Singapore. Life bloomed, opened, became large and full of promise. Singapore with Bara would be the best thing that had happened to him, and the beginning of much more.

'Stop,' Bara said to the driver, and the driver did.

Bara shouted to the jeep ahead of them, where Lieutenant Langley was, and that jeep stopped too. He and Graham got out and walked down the road and Bara said to the Lieutenant, 'A picture. Posed. Fake. Let the second jeep come up close, not behind you but to the side; get you both in. Bad tactics, no? But to fill the picture. A fine big body of troops.'

The Lieutenant grinned.

Billings had discovered that Lieutenant Langley was an Old Etonian; Billings said that, naturally, if you went to Eton you would be more sensitive than common people. It was known that Lieutenant Langley carried a volume of poetry in his pocket and made no friends. Graham thought the Lieutenant was a decent chap but sad, rotting with sadness and boredom, and lonely. Bara invited the Lieutenant to their poker game last night; Bara plied the Lieutenant with that valuable whisky; Bara told stories all the time, the way he did, about the 'swollen ones' at GHQ in Singapore, the diplomats and their luncheon parties in Batavia, the dance-hall girls in the Chinese quarter of that city, and Langley listened and listened and laughed and laughed. No one had ever seen the Lieutenant behave like this; the Lieutenant's face was changed, the Lieutenant seemed to think life was okay, worth the trouble to live it. Bara could do anything he wanted with the Lieutenant.

'No one may smile at the camera,' Bara said. 'Be fierce. Here we are in the jungle surrounded by a lot of unseen enemy. God. What we have come to. Still, I will make a pretty picture and you can send it to your girls, so that is something.'

The jeeps lined up. Bara walked down the road, calling back that they must look like busy soldiers, for God's sake, this is a real hot action shot, and he fiddled with his camera.

There was the crack of a rifle, muted by the trees, and Bara fell in the road. Langley shouted orders and the men jumped from the jeeps and ploughed into the jungle, shooting off their guns like a Western film. Langley ran to Bara, followed by Graham. He took one look and told Graham for Christ's sake to get the first-aid kit, and then he disappeared into the jungle too, with his pistol. Bellowing about a first-aid kit was hysteria; the sniper had fired from above, the bullet got Bara in the side of the head. Bara was something not to look at, and beyond all aid.

They covered Bara's head with Graham's shirt and bundled the body into the jeep and came back, driving as fast as they could.

Graham now saw where he was, too far into the black skinny trees, and he stopped, suddenly afraid. It was not the jungle they were used to any more; it was something besides a stinking, creeping, itching, sunless trap where they were all caught, for as long as their editors pleased.

'*Bara!*' Graham said aloud. If Bara could get killed, anyone could.

Waking was the nastiest part of the day. It was not only that she felt old and falling apart and had a new ache somewhere. It was the boredom, knowing each morning that the day was another day, and she was bored rigid before she started. Her first thought every morning was of Bara; her second thought was of Bara too but by then she resented him, by then she would like to wring his neck. She was bored because of Bara; she could not get on with living, she was paralyzed, due to waiting for Bara. Five years of it, she thought, I must be crazy. She told herself that constantly, and it had no effect.

These last three months had been the worst, probably because they were the last and the waiting was due to stop. Typical of Bara that he would fly to New York to spend Christmas week with her, and then say he had no money, he was a poor man, a poor man should not marry. But he promised to be back from the East in April; she was to meet him at Wengen. He said there would be morning snow, and he would need it after that Javanese heat, and they would ski. Of course there would be no snow in April; and as usual their money went on air fares. He always had money to travel, never money to settle. No, she thought, irritated, amused and proud, if Bara says there will be snow, there will be snow; he gets what he wants.

She stood up, stretched, felt worse, and went to the door of the flat to collect the mail. Mrs Helen Richards, ad from Mainbocher. Mrs Helen Richards, plea for money from the Harlem Hospital. Mrs Helen Richards, card from the Modern Museum. Mrs Helen Richards, announcement of a meeting of the Civil Liberties Union. Mrs Helen Richards, bill from Saks. Mrs Helen Richards, letter from Louise in Paris. It would not be interesting, Louise was not interesting. She kept up a desultory far-flung correspondence with people who might see Bara from time to time, and report. No letter from Bara, of course. He did not write. He said he could not write, he had never learned except in Hungarian and he had forgotten that. He sent cables, also costing money, and saying nothing: HELLO SCHATZI or IS THE WEATHER NICE? Oh, maddening, Helen Richards said to herself, maddening, maddening. She would lunch with three women; she would dine at the Bakers', with a colorless extra man roped in to complete the table. Her male clientele had diminished to the vanishing point; men did not long to spend money on a girl whose affections were so firmly and publicly fixed.

She picked up the rolled *New York Times*, made coffee in the kitchenette, had a bath, dressed and began the usual morning round of telephoning: hairdresser's appointment, gossip about nothing with Anne Baker, who was obviously talking in her sleep, two duty calls for her colored orphanage. She had ten minutes before going to the Braque show, and must skim the paper, as usual, to catch up on what people would talk about today. In 1941 and 1942, she read the papers with horror and hunger, to see what was happening in the war, to guess what might be happening to Bara. Every day those dull confusing despatches haunted her, for she knew that Bara would be wherever there was danger. She agonized with fear for Bara, and lost weight and got ugly lines in her forehead, until slowly she realized that Bara bore a charmed life, exactly as he said; Bara was invulnerable. She did not have to fear, she only had to wait.

The story was in a box on the front page with a picture. She did not read the words but understood them. It was a picture of Bara she had never seen: he was smiling over his shoulder, and looked tough, sly, unconcerned, a mocking gypsy. She held the paper as if she had grown to it. There was absolute silence in her mind and all around her. Then she began to cry out, hearing her voice, shrill and far off. She cried his name, over and over.

No one came, probably no one heard. The separate lives in the separate cells of that large building avoided touching each other. The wild grief wore itself out; she had thought of nothing and only screamed against the pain which was local and unbearable. Then she stood in the center of her small, elegant living room, among the correct furniture, the right pictures, the new books, and slumped and melted into something shapeless, not recognizable as Helen Richards. The pain had spread and turned into sickness. She walked to her bedroom, seeing nothing, and fell on the bed, and heavy sobbing stunned her, and she slept.

Others had seen Bara's picture and read the brief news report and in their unbelief or sorrow tried to reach the almost-widow. The switch beside her bed was still pressed down, the telephone did not ring. The morning passed. Chrystal, the Harlem girl who came to clean when she felt well enough, did not appear. When Helen Richards woke, she had gone through more time than the morning, a tunnel of time leading into gray no-time. She got up, took off her rumpled clothes, washed, put on a dressing gown and went to the living room. She would now sit down. She would sit down and wait.

The silence of the room began to frighten her, so she found a record and started the gramophone. She scarcely heard the music, but after a moment turned off the machine; it was a Chopin Nocturne and one of Bara's favorites. They had some records like that, he said, in Madrid; they played them when the city was being shelled; it was bombardment music, he said. And whenever he heard that clear mourning music, he went away from her, from here. He had no country: Paris was his city; but Spain seemed to be his home.

Still she kept the record, although jealous of it, and bought more bombardment music, in case he wanted it. Whatever Bara liked, she tried to have on hand: dill pickles, lemon verbena eau de cologne, a Klee drawing, the collected thrillers of Margery Allingham, John Haig pinch-bottle whisky, anything he liked, to lure him, to hold him, to keep him by her a little longer. He always went away; he liked other things in other places; he liked, simply, going away. In five years, how much had she seen him?

They met in the winter of 1941, here in New York, at a cocktail party. It was the usual monkey-house party, with everyone jabbering, twitching, snarling in anxious exhibitionist megalomania. You arrived, babbled in an ever-higher voice to top the other babbling, heard nothing, and left feeling tired and somewhat drunk. But people heard Bara. In a growing circle, there was Bara, gay and rather didactic, talking about London, where none of them had been and none, really, wished to be, owing to the danger and discomfort. Still their hearts beat for London.

'Who is he?'

'Bara. The photographer.'

'Oh, yes.'

Oh, yes, of course. They had seen his pictures, here and there, always more of them, always more prominently displayed, the special feature of whatever magazine they adorned, for the last four or five years. He was a Name. He was someone to meet. She was surprised by his looks; she had not expected him to be so young and also so old; it was puzzling. Naturally he was not American; he had the strangeness of being Central European, added to the strangeness of unsafety. For unsafety was the first thing she felt about him.

She listened and Bara did not sound like any of the returned travel-ers. He spoke of the English with affection, as of equals; he told jokes about their unexcited way of muddling through; he apparently had no tragic or sentimental feelings about England's Ordeal; he also did not seem to be in the least concerned for the outcome. This war, according to Bara, was something you lived through and, after endless mistakes, won.

She could feel the men in the group stiffening. Bara's tone was offensive. He was not bragging, unless it was the act of a braggart to behave as if London was a perfectly normal place to be and live. If he had made a few remarks about the heroism of the English, if he had said, 'God, I don't see how they take it,' the men would have felt better. She stayed and stayed; she was a woman alone and could outsit the competition. She spoke to Bara; looking back, she all but did the Dance of the Seven Veils to attract Bara's attention. He asked her to dinner, which was what she had been striving for, and took her to a Greek place on the West Side.

He would be in New York for five days, he said.

'I am now a big business man,' Bara announced, his mouth full of greasy vine leaves and rice. 'I come for conferences. I go to a big office, high up, everything very expensive, and sit with editors and we have a conference. They talk like generals. I try not to be scared with them, they are so like generals. They also look at maps and they plan the next campaign, so I can take pictures. I say yes yes yes, and ask for more money. You know, with a little face which says: Gentlemen, I am going to be killed to take your pictures while you are going to sit in your fine office. Like that, they cannot refuse me. Look at the money I have,' Bara said, and pulled an enormous gangster's roll from his pocket. 'Did you ever see something like that?' he asked. 'Do you play poker?'

No, she did not play poker, and this saddened him. He explained all about poker. He described it as a wonderful English game, he had only learned it lately, he played it in London with the American correspondents at the Savoy, it was a game so thrilling and so absurd that you might believe it had been invented in Hungary.

He would not talk of the war in England. He said, 'In New York everyone talks of the war. If they are so interested why do they not come to it? Or join it? The English would be very pleased, I am sure. You cannot *talk* about war. Talk about you. That is interesting.'

She needed to fascinate him quickly, because she feared he would leave her after dinner and find men to play poker with so he could use that roll of money.

There was, however, little to tell; she was who she was, and she knew dozens of women exactly like her. She was twenty-eight years old and had been married at twenty-two, divorced at twenty-six; she was childless, lived comfortably on the alimony which her ex-husband could well afford to pay, went to a great many parties, served on the usual number of committees, had a few affairs which she did not mention, planned to marry again, now that she was older and wiser, when the right man came along; she also did not mention that.

The only thing that interested Bara was her alimony. 'Now that,' Bara said, 'is splendid. Where else is it that women have such a fine system? That is clever. Who discovered the idea? If you live to be eighty years old, you will always have the alimony?'

'Yes,' she said, feeling like Shylock or a tart. 'Unless I marry again, and then it stops.'

'Oh, do not be so foolish,' Bara said. 'You have everything for no trouble. Why would anyone marry twice? Once is enough to be married.'

He did not like talking of marriage, evidently, and changed the subject, asking her about New York. This charmed him, he laughed and made foreign clucking sounds, indicative of wonder.

'I love this place,' Bara said. 'When the war is over, I will come here often or for a long time. It is so serious. Everyone shakes your hand so hard as if they mean it. Or hits you on the back as if you are going to the South Pole, immediately, and they wish you luck for the terrible journey. Or they ask you what you think; they do not listen, but they ask you like asking Moses. So serious and so busy. All going somewhere, all doing something. Where is there to go,' Bara asked, 'except here, where one is? And what is anybody doing? Oh, I like it very much. I like to be a Big Business Man. Now, we must find people to play poker or we must go to your house.'

This was not the approach she was used to, by any means. She was conscious of being insulted, but she could not feel that Bara meant to be insulting, and she excused him by telling herself that English was not his language and therefore he could not know how he sounded; and besides she did not want to lose him. If she let him go now, he would meet other people, other women, he would forget her. And she knew also, because she seemed very sure of how Bara behaved, that he would not be angry and rancorous if she dismissed him; he would be good-natured and friendly and not even disappointed. Poker was also a pleasant way to spend the night. She decided to take refuge in a ladylike innocence, and said, 'Yes, do come to my house. It is a much nicer place to sit.'

In the taxi, she could not talk and was seized by panic or shame. She hardly knew this man. She did not want him. He was not tall enough. He looked too queer, in that unlikely brown tweed suit, with those large flossy gold cuff links. His eyes were impersonal and mocking, and she doubted if he remembered her name. What had happened to her? How could she be in this awful position? The word 'cheap' lodged in her mind; it was like a doom; she saw herself starting on an evil path, becoming the sort of solitary woman who went home regularly with strangers, and was known for that.

Bara walked about, fingering things on the tables, and spoke with approval of that splendid invention, alimony. Pouring a drink, with her back turned to him, she found herself in tears. This was not at all her style. She was a cool self-possessed city girl, sure of her looks and her acts; she was not the helpless sort who got run over by life.

Bara recognized her tears as genuine; he must have guessed that she hated to cry. 'What have I done?' he said. 'Please, don't. I do not wish to hurt.'

He made her sit beside him on the sofa in front of the glowing electric apartment-house coals. She blubbed out that he treated her like a whore, she couldn't bear it. He kissed her hands and begged forgiveness. He said, as if talking to himself, 'I am sorry. I do not know much of ladies.'

They would have one drink, he said, to prove there was no sadness between them, and he would go. 'I am only a worthless Hungarian photographer,' he said, smiling at her. 'You will not be upset for such a man? Helen. Now, forget. What shall we talk?'

She asked him to talk about himself, so as to lose this dreadful sense of being a casual pickup.

'In Berlin when I was seventeen,' Bara said, 'I did errands on a bicycle for a shop which sold cameras. Then I went to Paris and became a bad photographer and took pictures when anyone asked me. I did that for a long time. Then I went to Spain and took pictures. Then I went to Czechoslovakia and took pictures. Then I went to Poland and took pictures. Then I went to Finland and took pictures. Then I went to France and took pictures. When the British Army left, I went with them to England and took pictures. Then I came here. Here I am a Big Business Man. Now I will go back to England and take more pictures. That is all. Very interesting, no?'

'No,' she said. 'How old are you?'

'Soon thirty. Old.'

'Are you married?'

'No.'

'Have you ever been in love?'

'Schatzi,' he said, patting her cheek. 'You are beautiful. You are young. You are a good girl. You ask many questions. I have finished my drink. I must go.'

But she would not let him go and presently they went to bed, after all. She could not have imagined what he was as a lover. He was tender and tentative, he was lovingly skilled and grateful. Afterward, she did not feel cheap; she felt that she was someone more than she had known. She was filled with pride, although she could not explain the pride to herself. It seemed to be a quality of her skin, and to have a warmth and a shine.

For five days Bara took her with him where he went, and did what he did to life. The city was another place, it was as if she came to it new, as he was, and discovered it. He made no plans, he roamed. He roamed all day and most of the night, finding people he knew, collecting strangers, eating when hungry, drinking everywhere, talking, talking. In the daytime, often, she had a dream sense of not knowing who she was; she was simply there with Bara, and he treated her as he treated everyone else, like a dear old friend whose name he had failed to hear. She was one of the shifting crowd who sprang into bright hypnotized movement at his passage. At night, late and later and later, they were alone, and love-making became a boon which she conferred with her recent magical power, and Bara was altogether hers.

He gave away wads of money to people who seemed to need it, or he believed they needed it; he lost wads of money at poker; by the end of the five days she was paying for their meals; he had no feeling about money. She made him buy a new suit and abandon forever the strange coffee-colored tweed; she persuaded him to trade in his gigantic cuff links for discreet gold buttons. He was amenable; he had no clear opinion about clothes either and was ready to admit that her ideas were better than his. She dawdled at a nearby soda fountain while he was at his conferences; he did not discuss his work; and although he seemed to know everyone in the world and talked of them with talent, he did not speak of himself. He took for granted that she knew all there was to know, and he did not like questions.

When Bara left, after those five days, she was in love as she had never been nor expected she could be; she thought he was in love with her. She waited for his letters, which did not come. He might have fallen into the sea. But he was very much alive, his pictures proved it; and all travelers returning from England brought tales of him. There was no way to disguise the fact; she had been his five-day New York mistress and was now forgotten.

This broke her heart or her nerve; her friends began to say that Helen was getting pathetic, single women did; in New York you simply had to be couples. She hid and she cried and she studied her face, fearing that she had lost her looks; she felt unwanted and never to be wanted again. Then, from a plain need to survive, she became bitterly angry. Who was he anyhow? A show-off foreigner looking like a Wop when you got down to it, those ghastly clothes, flaunting his war experiences, a cadger, nobody at all. He was nothing more to her than she to him, a passing fancy. She would now fancy whosoever passed.

For four months, she thought, I must have gone to bed with every presentable man in New York who didn't have his wife hanging around his neck. Her friends began to say that Helen was getting hard. Free-handed total sex was not their line; clothes and committees were their occupations. It seemed much worse, remembering it, than it had been at the time; she should have felt depraved but she only felt ashy and none of it mattered, neither before, during, nor after. The men were all right, the regular sort of men she was accustomed to; nothing troublesome happened. But, as revenge, it did not work. A year later, when she finally told Bara, he was sorry for her, not wounded, outraged, diminished, as she had planned. She cried, telling him; how much she had

cried about and with Bara, incredible, dripping tears constantly. Bara
seemed to think it was sad to make love if you did not want to, a waste
of life. She could not explain to him that he ought to be furious, she was
his property, his property had been used by others. He had no feeling
for property. He did not see that anybody belonged to anybody else.

Meantime Bara never wrote; she calmed down; she reverted to her
usual life. She decided that she had forgotten him, he was a finished
memory in the past. But all men wilted and looked half-alive, and New
York was a familiar place and her own, never the city it had been for
five days with Bara. Five days, in 1941, and the rest of the year to
remember him.

Bara came back in 1942 and looked her up at once, as if that was
the natural thing to do. She made a howling scene and it ended by his
comforting her, in tears again, for her own folly.

'But I love you,' she shouted, trying to make the lump recognize
what was at stake here.

'Good, *Schatzi.*'

'Do you love me?' He must understand a few simple words, the way
other people did.

'Very much.'

And the others too, she realized, with lightning jealousy. He loved
women very much. In any spare moment, in any convenient place, he
would take time to glimmer at the nearest attractive girl, with that
brown-eyed tender charm; he would make love deliciously and leave,
forgetful, grateful, loving them all and free as air. His mind was on
something else, his photographs, the state of the world, what happened
to other people, not the women he slept with. She felt helpless, because
she did love him and could not stop. He told no lies, he made no
promises. There was no way to attach him to her.

Bara was worried that year; he stayed in New York for ten days.
He said he could not understand it: it must be the Americans, they were
so efficient, everything had changed, now people were always bothering
him about his papers. He was, in fact, a stateless person and it seemed
a nuisance or more than a nuisance. His worry almost slipped into being
a bore; he harped on papers.

She had the brilliant idea of asking him to marry her; if he married
her, surely he would get a nice green American passport which no one
could question. If he married her, he would leave her anyhow, she knew
that, but he would also come back. For a day, she believed he meant to
accept her offer; he had found it funny. But when she insisted, Bara
said, 'No, schatzi, it is only our little joke. No one marries for papers;
one must not blow up the official people and make them think they are

so important one will marry to please them. No, no,' he had said, finally, cross for the first time, 'I do not marry. I will make them eat my papers, the toads.'

Ten days in 1942. But by then she accepted Bara as her fate, accepted the silence and the absence and the lack of any hope to hold to. She had to have him, he was all she wanted, and she would do the running, the asking, the waiting, for as long as need be. She gave up suffering and started to plan. Her plans worked so well that she arrived in England in 1943, beautifully smart in her Red Cross uniform, and dug herself in at Rainbow Corner in London. Bara, she knew, always came back to London from wherever he went; he came to develop his pictures, read his business cables, rest, bathe, drink, go out with girls, play poker. Not for her the gay mad life of a doughnut girl with combat troops; she had no intention of being lost with some regiment in France or Germany. She would be on hand in London, where Bara could find her, or where she could find Bara, due to careful spying and contacts with the Dorchester and his newspaper friends.

She was a big success at Rainbow Corner, soothing the young home-sick boys, a letter-writer, sister-confessor, chum to all. Those were the great years, or the great days, for Bara never stayed long but came frequently, and gradually he grew used to her, counted on her; in London anyway he belonged to her. London was glorious in itself, London with Bara was very heaven. Although she recognized it as a sin, and sometimes was frightened because of it and expected God's vengeance and prayed to be forgiven, she hoped the war would never end. It was a finer life than she had imagined possible, and people were freer and finer. She understood Bara at last, and knew the air he breathed and needed, she was part of his world. There were, of course, some heroic frauds, the battle-scarred veterans of Grosvenor Square, and there were some shameful profiteering women too; but they did not count, they were lost in the goodness and courage and patience of this place. She realized she had never been happy before, and better still, she had the sense to recognize her happiness now, every minute of it.

It was strange too that she was free of the fear that ate away inside other women. There were girls in Rainbow Corner who were hanging on to their reason and trying to work themselves to death, because of the fear they felt for men they loved. When Bara flew on missions with the bombers over Berlin, when he disappeared at D-Day, when the German attack in the Ardennes started and everyone grew bleary with confusion and dread, she did not fear, she waited for Bara's return. He must have bewitched her into such confidence; it never left her, she never doubted.

When Bara came to London, he seemed to throw off his memories with his dirty clothes. Sometimes he was very tired; then he bathed and slept alone, until he could join her in his London mood, recklessly gay, funny, often drunk but never heavy, motionless drunk, more and more excited, moving faster and faster with more and more people, gobbling up time, and she hurtling along beside him.

She tried to make Bara tell her of the places he had been and what he had seen. He would show her his photographs, but with indifference. Once, when she was tearful again because he shut her out so completely from his work, he said: 'It is how it is, schatzi. The ones who are there know how it is. No one else will ever know. Not from pictures or anything they read or anything they hear. I am only a visitor, I do not know too. I go for a while. I run around with my camera. Then, when I have enough, I come back, to this fine hotel, the bathtub, you, all the whisky I can put inside my stomach. I have a privileged position. It is not the same. I also do not know.'

On one of his visits, in the quietness before dawn, in their snug blacked-out hotel room, after love, when he was leaning on his elbow admiring her by the light of the weak bedside lamp, she felt sure enough of her power to say, 'Shall we get married after the war, Bara?'

'Who can say? Maybe so. You have a lovely body. Like a racehorse. Lovely, lovely.' He stroked her flank, the long good line from her hip to her knee. 'After the war, I am going to see horse races. I have never done it. I did not think of it. It is something I have missed. That will be fine, we will go to all the races. The horses must be beautiful to watch.'

It was not much to hold to, but she held. Maybe so, indeed, she would tell herself, exulting. He will see, he will see.

When Bara was away, she tried to find Lep, who was always hard to find and often at the fighting war too. Bara and Lep worked as partners, covering the war for several magazines and papers in England and America; they divided the stories but Bara did not like Lep to go to the worst places; he had some anxious feeling about Lep's eyes and his huge horn-rimmed spectacles. If he protected anyone in the world, it was Lep. She was jealous of Lep, and knew this to be futile as well as dangerous; should she parade her jealousy and force choices, Bara would take Lep. Everyone was Bara's friend; for a struggling woman, it was scarcely desirable that her man appealed to such an unlimited number of people. But Bara loved Lep; he needed Lep as he needed no one else; Lep was the one fixed point in his life.

She could not understand about Lep, except that he had known Bara longer than anyone else, since Bara was a boy in Paris. But they seemed an improbable pair. Bara was so dashing in his special gypsy way, loved by women, welcomed by men, a life-giver, the sort of person people claimed to know when they didn't, made up stories about, quoted, were proud to be seen with, happy to be used by. And Lep looked something like an owl and something like a panda and something like a head of Buddha, quiet to the verge of invisibility, a man who smiled slowly and rarely laughed, a serious man given to serious obscure friends like archaeologists and doctors and musicians in Philharmonic orchestras, a small gentle man with a domed forehead over his vast spectacles, not at all a man for war, a professor, who astonishingly enough was only two years older than Bara and often seemed old enough to be Bara's father.

She did not know whether Lep approved of her, though he treated her with perfect courtesy, but he was like that, formal and polite to everyone. Sometimes, when she was privately seething about Lep's power over Bara, she decided that Lep treated her as if she were Number One wife in a harem. He had seen others come and go, no doubt, and considered her no better and no worse than her predecessors. Sometimes she thought Lep was sorry for her, knowing how she loved Bara and how that was like loving water in a sieve. But when Bara was away, she searched for Lep, to speak of Bara, and it was generally a waste of time, Lep being as secretive about Bara as about himself.

Bara had told her, after persistent questioning, that Lep was a Pole; they had met in Paris in 1931. She knew Bara's name was an invention, he had dreamed it up as an actor or a writer might choose a name that would be easy to say and remember. She had never heard Bara's real name, and it did not interest her; Bara suited him, one could not think of him as anything else. Lep, on the other hand, simply shortened Lepczinski into Lepson. He called himself Paul Lepson, and people who did not know him addressed him as Paul. Lep was a Jew, obviously, but this was a fact of no importance. Knowing Lep, one could not understand why it made any difference if people were Jews or Gentiles. Bara said that Lep was the finest photographer alive, an artist, not a hit-and-run man with a camera like himself. Bara's pictures were the famous ones; everyone wanted Bara's work if they could get it; yet Bara only valued his pictures if Lep did; Lep was his final judge. His final judge in everything, she thought, for if Bara made the decisions in his flashing way, Lep had the right of veto, which he exerted quietly, hardly bothering to explain himself. Was Lep so clever, she asked, did he know so much about selling pictures and what editors wanted and all the tricks of their trade? No, nothing, Bara said, but if Lep did not want to do something, then it should not be done; if Lep did not like something, then it was not to be liked. She foresaw that she would never get Bara without Lep; she tried to win Lep to her side.

Memory was what you made it, memory was a comfortable accomplice, and if she preferred to remember that she had been happy every minute in London, that was all right, but not true. There was one night when she and Lep and Bara went out with Bara's chosen drinking companion, the writer Bob Martinelli, and some other men whose names and faces were long dimmed, and the usual assortment of chicks that Martinelli collected and favored. They were at a night club near the Dorchester, where Martinelli and Bara were treated as reigning monarchs, and the girls were all over them. She held herself subtly apart from these girls, who were usually a mysterious class of English, not ladies, not tarts, floating husbandless creatures who seemed only to exist for the night when Martinelli called them into being. Yet she was careful not to criticize them after her one mistake in that line. Bara turned on her, when she objected to some pink-haired, overdressed, too-adoring doll and asked whether Helen had ever tried working nine to ten hours a day in a small-arms factory. That night, Bara was dancing with one of the ladies, a brunette who hoped to look like Rita Hayworth, and apparently danced out into the dark, not to return. Lep was there, Lep would take her home, in case Bara stopped to worry about such ways and means. Jealousy was a disease, certainly, and who had never suffered from it could not speak of it. She got away quickly; she had kept herself under control before the others, she was not going to take pity from those good-time girls. In the taxi, she wept like a madwoman, the terrible crazy tears when you wanted to do murder and die, the shameful tears of the woman spurned. In his way, Lep tried to help her.

'It is strange of Bara,' Lep said. 'I do not know how it goes in his mind. He had such suffering from jealousy when he was young, I should think he would never wish to give that misery to someone else. But perhaps he suffered so much that it is all gone from him, and he cannot understand jealousy any more, he has burned it away.'

'Why was he ever jealous?' she asked, at once envying and hating the woman who could make Bara miserable.

'For Suzy.'

'Suzy?'

'His wife,' Lep said, surprised now. 'Did you not know?'

'He's married?' She was shocked out of crying, the Rita Hayworth type did not exist. It came to her that Bara could easily have a wife somewhere, whom he would have forgotten too.

'No. Suzy is dead. Many years.'

'When was he married?'

'In the past,' Lep said, 'when he was seventeen.'

The relief of it. The way her lungs filled with relief. A long-ago boy-and-girl marriage, to someone dead, long dead.

'I am sorry I have spoken of this,' Lep said. 'Since Bara did not speak of it. Perhaps he thought you knew. It is not a secret, it is only so old now. But still, it is wrong to go into the heart troubles of other people. I was upset. Somebody crying is always upsetting. Also, Helen, now that I am acting as your uncle, I will tell you something. Do not make a fuss about tonight. With Bara it is no use. He will not do anything because he is supposed to. No, I think I will be a real uncle, poor Helen. You will not like it. I think you are in a strange place with strange people. It is not good for you. Bara does not belong living in a home. You belong living in a home. Women do, I think.'

She paid no attention to that, naturally, and Lep did not expect her to. He did not have to tell her about Bara, she knew from experience.

Jealousy, she thought, I had it like malaria. How could she help it? What else could you feel if you wanted a man for yourself, and everyone stole bits of him, and you knew you never owned him anyhow? That was how it was really, a seesaw fever down into ugly slit-eye, sick jealousy, and up into joy. Nothing between them; there were no easy stretches of time with Bara when you simply felt calm and safe.

She had reason enough to be jealous of all the women who looked at Bara, or the ones Bara turned his head to see, but she admitted she was losing her grip when she took against the hideous Dorchester chambermaid just because the creature worshipped Bara and Bara gave her unsuitable presents, like perfume and cheap jewelry. However, the jealousy ranged further and wider; it knew no limits; sometimes she could not even name what she was jealous of.

There was Bob Martinelli. She behaved, although cautiously, as if she found Martinelli a bore and an embarrassment. Why should he insist on being a GI and such a GI, dressed in shrunken khaki blotting paper, with his overseas cap resting on his ears? Everyone in New York knew he was a famous young novelist; surely people like that were morally obliged to be officers. And they were Americans in England, after all, and some sort of loyalty was required; did Bara think it right of Martinelli to mock his Army job in front of the English? Martinelli was in some special London outfit, all of them movie and literary celebrities, where he wrote training or propaganda pamphlets. He said his *chef d'oeuvre* was one which explained to incoming GIs that they should hate the Krauts, not the Limeys. On and on she went, nibbling at Martinelli, and

Bara, if he said anything, only said, 'He has much talent.' Much talent: was she jealous of that, knowing how Bara felt about talent and knowing she had none herself?

No, it was not that; it was because Bara laughed with Martinelli, always, in a way he did not laugh with her. It was secret-society mirth, she thought, they had only to say a word, or a half sentence which she could not understand, and the rocketing, united laughter was there. Bara got in touch with Martinelli the minute he came back to London; she knew he had called Martinelli because laughter was what happened first.

But there was more, and she could not unravel her reactions. Martinelli was insolent to Bara; he took liberties she would not have dared to take. If she needled and teased and pried at Bara, as Martinelli did, Bara would study her, with one black eyebrow raised and a small smile, and presently he would find a quieter woman who did not bother him so much. Besides that, she resented Martinelli's impertinence. Bara was in every way Martinelli's superior; she was also jealous for Bara's position and reputation and personality. God, what else had she been able to think up?

Martinelli, speaking slowly because he was rather drunk, his normal state, had said, 'I do not say you are a fake, Bara. I will fight any man who says you are a fake. I only say you are a liar.'

She was furious but Bara looked interested and said, 'So?'

'No man is as complete as you seem. Every man has contradictions. There is the other side of the coin. Where is yours, Bara, old boy? Stand up and show your other side. Stop lying to us all the time, Bara, old boy, old boy.'

Drunken oaf, she thought, but Bara was amused.

Then Bara started worrying about Martinelli and that made her more jealous.

'He must go to France,' Bara said. 'He is too good a writer to make himself crippled, staying in London, not learning what he needs.'

'What is the difference?' she asked. 'He's a great big conceited boy now; he can look after himself.'

'It is every difference,' Bara said. 'He has real talent. And he is my friend.'

After D-Day, Martinelli decided to leave his desk in the Haymarket and volunteer for the infantry in France. She concealed her pleasure in this turn of events. He arrived at a night club where they were waiting for him, and as usual Bara seemed happier the minute Martinelli, a slovenly khaki gorilla, hove into view.

'Got to go home early and pack,' Martinelli said. 'The Army only moves at dawn. I'm going to some nearby top-secret Nissen huts, so they can be sure I know how to salute and about-face properly, before they send me to France.'

'Good,' Bara said.

'You better be right, Bara. This is your doing. Why do I listen to you? Who are you, what are you? That's what I've been trying to find out all this time.'

Bara had a system for answering questions, even Martinelli's, with nothing more than a cheerful, if Sphinxlike, smile.

That night before he left, very drunk now, Martinelli said, 'Well, pal, I'm glad to have met you. You might say I'm gladder to have met you than anybody I can think of. I'm about ready to admit you aren't even a liar. Maybe you're just a freak. God bless you, freak.'

She sighed contentedly in the taxi Bara had managed to snag, though she knew Bara already missed Martinelli. Never mind. Farewell, Martinelli, one less to be jealous of.

But it did not end with people she could watch and listen to; she succeeded in suffering about total strangers. She was hopelessly jealous of a woman she had never seen whom Bara and Lep called Marushka, though her name was Mary Hallett and she was as American as Helen Richards. Bara said that Marushka should have been Russian since she had a pre-Soviet Russian soul, so fierce, so illogical, so elevated, so absurd.

Bara came back from Italy one winter, all the dates and times were jumbled together in her mind, and told Lep he had seen Marushka at Cassino. They both laughed with pleasure whenever they said Marushka's name, which was enough to make the woman detestable.

'How is she?' Lep asked. 'I think I will go to see her too.'

'Fine,' Bara said. 'Fine, fine. She is very angry. Angry to pop. She is angry with the Italian campaign. She thinks someone should be shot for it. Churchill? Roosevelt? She says mountains, what a clever idea, they take one mountain with terrible casualties and everyone freezing to death—and what is it? Another mountain stands right in front. The Germans go back slowly, with plenty of time, planting mine fields as if planting daisies, and then our people come along and walk on them. She is bursting with angriness.'

Lep smiled, as if he had heard something splendid about his favorite child.

'I see she is happy,' Lep said.

'This year she is thin,' Bara remarked. 'And coughs all the time and blows her nose. Italy is much the best place in this war. Very nice and mixed up, nobody cares about papers except the Americans. You stay away from the Americans and no one asks for your papers. You can move like in a good war. Marushka is with some English tank people now, excellent people, very crazy. She says the Goums are interesting, also the Gurkhas; she says the Poles are almost like Spain. She sent you her love.'

Several times, Mary Hallett had been in London and Bara slipped off to see her alone, never for long and never at suspect hours of the night; but he did not suggest that she should meet this wonder friend, whom he and Lep cherished.

Once, beside herself with jealousy, in that state when you do not care what damage you do and cannot stop yourself from speaking, she accused Bara of being in love with Mary Hallett.

'Marushka?' he asked, looking at her as if she were a new type of insect. 'Marushka is my brother. Or my sister. My sister *and* brother. Do you think I am in love with Lep, too?'

She questioned Lep, when Bara was away, the jealousy still poisoning her. Lep, usually so remote, so patient, lost his temper.

'Do not be so silly, Helen,' he said. 'Do not be so bloody stupid silly. You have what you have with Bara. Leave Marushka alone.'

As if the damned woman was some sort of holy figure, not to be talked about by mere mortals, she thought, and went on hating Mary Hallett in silence.

But there was the joy. How memory tricked you, first making it all smooth and bright, then dumping you into a sort of mud of failure and resentment. She had lived the joy and it was true and lasting. Little hints and gestures gave her confidence in the future, as when Bara sent word, God knows how, from France, telling Lep to get Helen safely into the country because he had heard of the buzz bombs falling on London. She would not go, of course; could not, anyhow, because of her job, but would not have run even if she were free. Though he wanted to protect her, Bara would not feel the same afterward if she failed to be as steady as the ordinary Londoners. But he cared, he worried; it was all she wanted. And she began, finally, to wish the war over so that they could marry. She knew she would be able to lead Bara to that decision, after all these years.

Then it was over, taking one's breath away because, though they had been expecting it for weeks, they could not believe it had come at last. Bara arrived, late in the evening of VE-Day, from Germany. She did not recognize him; he had never looked or acted like this. He came from Buchenwald, he said, he had been there for several days. And he had got out on a plane carrying wounded, crouched on the shelf behind the pilot; he had taken up the room, he had bullied and begged and lied to get out. Suddenly he could not stand that country for another hour;

he thought he would go mad and kill Germans, any Germans, if he did not leave. He would never go back there, in his whole life, and he prayed to God that fire and plague would sweep Germany and destroy them all and turn their land black and that there should be no Germany on the face of the earth.

They did not join the river of people flowing through the streets of London that night, under the shining forgotten street lamps. She sat on the edge of the bed in their room and hugged herself because she was getting colder and colder, cold into her bones, and Bara was locked in the bathroom, making terrible sounds, sobbing, cursing, sobbing again. They never spoke of it. She could not understand it or forget. The sense of Bara's apartness was what made her shiver in the dark room. She only knew of Bara what she had seen with her own eyes, and how much was that; and for how many days, in four and a half years, had she seen him?

There was a curious coma after VE-Day, when no one knew what to do. Lep said it was as if a film suddenly stopped and everyone was stuck in that pose, some with their feet in the air, some scratching their noses, some with their mouths open to eat or sing. Bara said, perfectly seriously, that it was going to be very hard to get used to peace. Meanwhile they must go to the Pacific, of course; the war would finally end there and they must take their last pictures in Tokyo. This made her cry with despair. She had imagined Bara and herself in a registry office, giving the promises, signing the papers, within a few weeks of peace. What did Japan have to do with them? Europe was their war and it was won. The other would take care of itself. Inspired, she pointed out to Bara that it was an all-American show in the Pacific, and think of the trouble he would have with his papers. Lep, surprisingly, agreed.

Lep said there was no hurry, watch it for a while, and in fact their first occupation should be to get real papers like everybody else. Perhaps they could become British. Bara said that he liked the English better than anybody in war, but did not know how he would like them in peace. Before the Big War, he often wished to kick them in the bottom. He had come to London at the time of Munich and remembered it. When they want to, he said, the English can be self-contented wood-heads, talking in that awful voice as if everybody else has bad manners and gets too excited and they are so correct they do not need to argue. They can be very irritating in peacetime. Lep asked since when was anybody good the whole time, and besides one was not supposed to be in love with papers, one was supposed to have them, genuine ones that bureaucrats would enjoy.

Instead of going to the Pacific, she and Bara went to Portugal for a week, the Red Cross graciously giving her leave. That week, now, was impossible to remember in detail because happiness worked like drunkenness, or like being blinded by sun. They went to a marvelous beach resort near Lisbon and lolled on the sand and ate until they were sick. Bara gambled in a casino, discovering, to her anxiety, roulette, which he said was neck and neck with poker. They made love in a pine wood, and in a brass bed that was trimmed with ribbons. She was sure Bara loved her. It would have been impossible for her to love him so entirely if she were doing it alone.

While they were in Portugal, the war ended in Japan. Bara celebrated that victory in a normal way, getting drunk on champagne, and she celebrated with private intensity, because now Tokyo was ruled out.

Then they came back to London and the Red Cross shipped her home. She seemed wrapped up and strangled in red tape which required her to leave. She waited in New York, desperate, feeling like a ghost come back from the living to the dead. She hated New York and everyone she knew there. She wept for London, as much as for Bara. He was taking pictures in Yugoslavia, Greece, France, Italy. He did write to her occasionally, short illiterate notes, almost like time tables.

She could not get back to him; it was no joke about papers, as she now saw. The State Department was determined not to let US citizens travel; the very wish to travel seemed a crime. Her spirits flagged and failed, she reconverted herself dismally to peacetime life, to everything she had known before. Waiting, waiting.

Then Bara arrived for Christmas, the first Christmas after the war, a great time, although she would rather have celebrated in London, as she respected bombed cities more than unbombed cities. Bara was quieter, older, and everyone was not his friend; he often spoke sharply and left parties because he was disgusted. She nagged him, there was no other word, to marry her. Nagged and wheedled and argued and pleaded. Bara answered her gently. It was not easy, he said, to swallow nearly ten years of war; it took a little time. A man should be settled in everything before he married; otherwise it was not fair. He must get some nationality, as a start, and arrange his work so that he would always have money. Also, she had only known him in war, and it would be better if she waited and saw whether, in peace, she felt the same way. She did not believe there was a word of truth in this. Bara did not plan and worry, Bara lived in the moment; if he wanted to marry, he would do it as he did everything else, like diving joyfully off the top of a building. When he went back to London, she had not given up, because she could not; there was no other way to use her life except to want Bara. But she began to resign herself to a lifetime of waiting.

Bara wrote, in January, saying that he was leaving the next day for Java. Distance was also an enemy, and not having him even farther away was worse than not having him across the Atlantic. She was slow to finish the letter, because Java discouraged her so much, but at the end Bara asked her to meet him in Switzerland in April. 'Then we will decide,' he wrote. Her hope, an insane plant, suddenly sprang up and grew. Only until April; there was an end to waiting. *Decide*, she said to herself, oh, the lovely word. For he would decide to take her and keep her, he would now, at last; she knew it as she knew that she must breathe to live. All she need do was stay quiet, and have faith, and wait for three months to pass. After that, she would have to do nothing except follow Bara around the earth, and suffer and be happy and his wife.

The room was dark. Time had changed its whole quality and did not touch her. She felt neither hungry nor thirsty, and though she had sat, unmoving, with her hands in her lap, for whatever hours passed, she did not feel her body as cramped and tired. If Bara had a mother, she could go to his mother now and sit with her, in another dark room; it would be a comfort to stay with someone else who was waiting for nothing. But there was no one, she could find no one in this city where so many people thought they were Bara's friends. This was the first night, and afterward there would be all the other nights. No one knew him, no one would know how to mourn him. He had left her alone, even in this.

Except Lep. Somewhere Lep was in this darkness too. Lep knew, as she did, what it meant to have Bara gone from the world.

She would talk to Lep, she could not manage alone. She got up, slow and steady and doped with silence, and went to her desk. She took a sheet of paper and dated it carefully and wrote, 'Dear Lep.'

Then the trance broke. She was back in life, which was full of loss and pain, and her breath hurting in her throat and her eyes burning with tears, and there was nothing to think, only this torture to live in. She beat on her desk with her fists, pounding the desk as if it were a wall, a barrier, something to smash. 'How could he?' she kept saying. 'How could he? How could he?'

The room was neat, though cluttered. Lep had asked the lift boy and the floor-waiter, Albert, to range Bara's assortment of old suitcases, rusty footlockers, and cardboard boxes, his collected life work, along the wall under the window. Lep sat at the table and methodically sorted photographs. His eyes felt hot and painful and he tried to ease them, foolishly, by cleaning his glasses. There was no order whatever in Bara's luggage; he had not expected it. Occasionally, Bara made the supreme effort of putting a rubber band around a wad of prints. The rubber bands were old and many had broken. Bara took pictures as if a camera was a gun. Bara shot everything that moved, and later dumped the duplicates into any receptacle which would hold them. Whereas Lep preferred to take careful pictures of buildings, old buildings which, God willing, nothing would ever move. His own photographs were classified in a special filing cabinet which stood beside the armoire. If he died, no one would have anything to do.

Lep did not allow himself to think about Bara's pictures, he was simply separating them by countries, by years. Later he would make a selection, and publish the best in a book. Whatever happened to the book now, it would be saved in libraries, and in time the right people would find it. Due to the mess the photographs were in, this cataloguing used his whole mind, and at night his tired eyes put him to sleep.

Hearing a knock at the door, Lep said, '*Entrez!*' It would be Albert again, the old nuisance, with his theories about keeping the strength up by constant eating. He turned with a smile for Albert and saw little Gaston, the lift boy, gazing at him with mournful eyes and offering a telegram on a salver. They all looked at him in this way, a band of kindly *de-coeur-avec-vous* cows, and it embarrassed him. He had begun to feel important, a celebrity, a man you looked at in silence with special eyes. He did not crave fame for any reason and surely not as an object of universal pity.

He thanked Gaston and took the telegram, noticing at the same time how cold he was. A kerosene stove, Lep thought, in case there existed any kerosene in Paris.

The telegram said: COME TO LONDON OR I WILL COME TO YOU EVERY-THING IS HOPELESS EVERYWHERE WHAT AN UGLY WORLD IN DESPAIR HALLETT.

This made Lep smile; dear Marushka. He would cable her to come here, he did not want to interrupt the job of sorting Bara's photographs. But he remembered Marushka on the subject of this room. The Hotel Belvoir, according to Marushka, was a fit home for lepers or rats who could do no better. She had started protesting when they first found this place and chose it for permanent headquarters in 1938. She said they were certifiable when they raced back to it, as soon as Paris was liberated. Lep considered the long gray velvet curtains rigid with old dust, the neuter hotel furniture which stood about in positions of maximum inconvenience; he admitted that the lace counterpane was grimy, the rug spotted; and the room was freezing. Marushka once bought them a huge plant with shiny leaves, but no one remembered to water it and it stayed on, shriveled and brown, and she said if it was possible for their room to be more hideous they had now accomplished that, with a dead plant for sole adornment. He thought, on the whole, he had better go to London.

Lep summoned Albert and ordered sandwiches and coffee and tried to invent a plan for consoling Marushka. It would not be easy. There must be several hundred people throughout the world who sorrowed for Bara's death, but surely none of them would be in despair because they had lost the one person they always quarreled with. The fierce childishness of Bara's and Marushka's quarrels had entertained Lep for the last eight years; he was sorry he had missed the beginning of hostilities in Madrid. Sooner or later, wherever they were—Prague, Helsinki, Warsaw, Barcelona, Rome, and any points between—Bara and Marushka could be seen walking on opposite sides of the street, their faces creased in frowns, Bara scuffing his feet like a furious ten-year-old, Marushka striding ahead in black indignation, both silent, although occasionally shouting 'Shut up!' across the road.

Albert brought a tray; Lep said that he would eat in bed as it was warmer. He climbed in, fully dressed; Albert clicked his tongue over the disaster of life in Paris; Lep said pleasantly that soon they would all learn to eat with gloves on, and Albert left him to his sandwiches.

They were of course quarreling about the very nature of the world and man, although they never saw that, and believed they were fighting each other's idiotic points of view. Bara said that Marushka was more stupid than a herd of mules; she traveled over the earth, she looked, she questioned, she read, she wrote articles on the miseries that afflicted mankind, and she would not accept what she had learned. She wanted to change things for the better, she demanded action and salvation. She had eyes in her head, did she not? What had she ever seen changed for the better? She suffered from a major tic about injustice. Without effort, you could see nothing but examples of injustice twenty-four hours a day, every day of your life. Yet each time Marushka's attention was called to injustice, she behaved as if this were the first one and here and now it had to be stopped.

Marushka loved humanity, Bara said, but people made her nervous. Bara thought humanity was lost, it never had a chance from the day it started, but there were still people, and one at a time you could perhaps for a few hours make their lives easier. No one sane would attempt more, because it was useless. Marushka was not sane. She was always driving people to do something this minute on behalf of other people. The fact that she never succeeded did not teach her to keep quiet, resign herself to the human condition, enjoy herself as much as possible, and spread a little enjoyment wherever she could, one at a time. No, no. If she could not save all the children in Spain, all the refugees in Czechoslovakia, the entire Finnish nation, she was not only in despair, she also blamed Bara who would not join her frantic efforts to bully generals, statesmen, presidents, archbishops, editors, and God knows what, to rescue the human race. Then they walked on different sides of the street.

Marushka said that Bara was lazy, cynical and selfish: how dare he, being so privileged, accept the evil fortune of others as if it were an act of God, when it was nothing but an act of man and as such could and must be corrected? If everybody was like Bara, which thank heaven they were not, the world would be an even worse place than it already was. A human being had to be responsible. Look at those people, Marushka would say in a tearful fury, showing what was indeed one of the many scenes from hell, the Prague railway station packed with refugees, blank-faced and sodden in fatigue and fear, look at them, do you think it is enough to go around giving away your money and your cigarettes and taking pictures of babies and flattering their mothers, do you think that's the way to help them? Yes, Bara said, because it is the only way, so now run off and exhort Masaryk and anyone else you can find, and I will bet you five hundred dollars the people will still be sitting in this railway station and sooner or later the Nazis will get them.

Yet they agreed like turtledoves, Bara and Marushka, on politics. They were always on the same side, they despised or approved the same public figures. The difference was that Bara thought in the end nothing would change, and Marushka lived in hope of the future. Marushka had only to say the word 'future' for them to start a fight. But privately, Bara admired Marushka's tireless battle against the facts, the real world, the truth about life. And privately Marushka knew that Bara was more effective than she; he did heal, he did make people briefly happier, easier; and though it was not much it was better than what she accomplished, which was nothing. And maybe, if your life was being smashed by uncontrollable general cruelty, it was a rare memory, Bara passing with his smile and a pocketful of hard candies and cigarettes. Meanwhile, no one else had ever dared to criticize Bara when Marushka was present.

There came a time, though, when Bara felt as Marushka did, or understood her point. By way of his parish priest, the Vatican, the International Red Cross, however these bits of news were passed through and around warring nations, Bara had learned that his father, arrested in some vengeance or roundup of the Germans, had died in a concentration camp. Bara heard later that his mother, hungry and old and alone, killed herself in their village. His brother disappeared in Russia, drafted into an army and fighting for a cause that he hated. Probably because he had to, Bara closed this information in his mind and managed to hide from it. He thought of his family as dead, and refused to think about the manner of their dying. There was nothing he could do; rage would not raise the dead. But when he saw Buchenwald, when he saw the lumber piles of naked starved bodies, and the tiled gas chamber, and the faces of the hardly human survivors, Bara also saw his father there. Bara came to Paris, a week after the war's end, to find Marushka. He needed Marushka. He needed to share his hate—long, deep, never-to-be-forgotten hate—with Marushka.

Marushka's one private war aim was to see the gates of all concentration camps opened. Bara had taken it as a sign of growing reason in her that she expected nothing else from the Allied victory. So, pursuing her war aim, she made her way to the gradually liberated concentration camps. She had gone like a sleepwalker from one to the other, the nightmare travels through Belsen, Buchenwald, Dachau. Of course she never imagined what these places would be like; no one could possibly imagine. And no one who had not seen them with his own eyes would ever again be able to imagine it. Marushka then returned to Paris. She no longer believed in the perfectibility of man, nor in the future; she believed that man was fatally diseased, and there was neither safety nor hope in the world, because what was possible for any men was possible for all men and at any time.

They found her in bed in the dingy Hotel du Pré on the Left Bank. She was frightening to see, and babbled about the number of sacks of human ash to be used for fertilizer which you could hope to get in a good day's work at the crematorium, and the month's quota of female hair for mattresses which kept very steady, year after year, and how it was surprising the amount of gold you could collect from teeth, which of course had to be removed before the crematorium but would that be after the gas chamber or before? It was an awful two weeks. He did not know which of them was in a worse state, and could help neither.

Bara was the first to return to his normal behavior, at least; but Marushka seemed permanently changed. Bara then began to mutter to himself, as he did when he was upset. In all the languages he used, intermingled and inaccurate, Bara kept saying that he didn't like it, it was not well with Marushka, she was not angry, she was probably very sick, she did not scold, she did not have a daily disgust about how the world went. He was distressed because Marushka stopped reading the papers and instead read an English writer called Trollope and announced she was going to buy a small house and settle in London, the English were decent people if anybody was, and she thought the best thing was to have a few friends and not move much. Bara tried constantly to rouse

her, and even went to London to work Marushka up on behalf of Java
and make her come with him and save the Javanese or the Dutch, he
was not sure which. But she said No, she had been to the Orient, it was
incurable, the heartlessness of the rulers and the hunger of the ruled
were equal plagues, there were too many people, they had lived in misery
forever and always would.

Well, Lep said to himself, I have certainly not thought of the right
way to go about consoling Marushka.

Still, he must try to comfort Marushka as he was trying to comfort
himself. The system was not entirely successful but it was the best he
could manage. The basic idea was to forget oneself, and the hollowness
of life without Bara in it, and think instead of Bara. Since Bara was
dead, and beyond recall, one might at least see that Bara could afford
to die. If you thought of that very hard, it helped. It was the only help
now, and he concentrated on it, telling himself that Bara had missed
nothing. He was a full man, a complete man, he had had everything. It
was greedy to expect to have everything twice, and besides it was impossible. Only the very rich in life could afford to die; the rest have to go on
scratching away, year after year, as if they were trying to open a steel
safe with their fingernails, to get at what they know is there but unreach-
able. Surely Marushka would see this.

But then again, perhaps Marushka would not. However, since she
respected work above all else, she would agree that Bara's work was
complete. For ten years he had shown everyone who cared to look the
exact face of our time. No one could have done it better, on film, for no
one had his eye, his nerve, his speed and his understanding. You could
find fault with his technique, but even Marushka would not consider
that. Bara was always there, where you had to be. Was he not? Think
of the pictures, Marushka.

Remember when he parachuted in, with the Americans, on D-Day?
What a record that was of the pure madness of man. I will never forget
those pictures: the faces of the men as they shuffled toward the open
door of the plane, clenched, staring, drugged faces, drugged with the
effort of will and the fear; those lumpish spinning bundles which were
human beings, caught in the slipstream in the upper air; the one picture
of a man like a pencil, dropping straight to his death, with his parachute
unopened, straight too, a lean rag in the sky above him; the man floating
down, so gently, with the lovely big silk umbrella swaying over his head,
and he with the twist of unbearable pain on his face, shot in the guts,
like a slow pigeon; the parachutes settling on that flooded marsh, tomb-
stones for those drowned under them; the man strangled in a tree, hung
by his own twined parachute cords; and those who somehow, despite

the madness, landed, were alive and whole, pulled along the ground by their parachutes, untangling themselves, looking about them with set eyes, ready to go, going toward the unseen enemy and the machine guns. My God, how I admired those pictures. Not only for what they told but for the discipline it needed to take any pictures at all. You know yourself, Marushka, that a writer can have what emotions he wishes or cannot avoid, at the time of getting his material; later he can sit down for a while and bring order out of what he saw and remembers. But for the photographer there is no time; there is only that one instant; he cannot afford any emotions for himself. Of course Bara was a brave man, of the best kind there is, the kind that sees and feels and imagines and understands, and issues to himself the command: be still.

The pictures, Lep thought, looking across the room at the littered table, looking at the chewed-up collection of boxes under the window. Marushka, do you remember the early ones from Madrid? Do you remember the trucks they loaded full of children, as if children were cattle or perhaps only packages, to send them from the city to safety? Do you remember those thin numbed faces, those eyes, and some, the little ones, with mouths torn apart in crying? Do you remember the hands of the mothers, the small black-looking women who all seemed old, shawled, mourners reaching up hopeless hands to the tailboards of the loaded trucks, and the one mother who would not let go and was dragged behind as the truck drove off? I remember.

And the army coming back in Czechoslovakia, after Munich, all the vehicles, even the tanks, so gay with fresh leafy branches and flowers, the army so clean and neat, the vehicles so good and well-oiled and new, and the people lining the roads in silence, weeping. And Finland: I had only to see those pictures to know how cold it was, how the cold was the murderer and the enemy and would kill the Russians too.

Bara was always there, always seeing what had to be seen, always understanding what it meant, fast, fast, and with himself under control or forgotten, doing his work. Great work, Marushka. He made a massive portrait of war, ten years long the portrait was, our new kind of war, which spares no one. That is work enough for any man. That is work to rest on.

But how right, how good, and what a pleasure that Bara also earned fame and all its trimmings. Marushka was conventional in odd ways and tended to think fame was only valuable if you got it a hundred years after your death. She suspected immediate success, it did unattractive things to people, and at one point she said that Bara was becoming a caricature of himself. That was not true. It amused Bara to act the way people expected him to act and besides it was a form of privacy, like wearing clothes.

Marushka did not object to Bara poor, but she complained steadily about Bara rich. This happened after his first trip to New York when Bara returned covered with money. Why shouldn't the dear fellow hurl money around like a child gone crazy in a snowdrift? Why shouldn't he pour money on any deserving or undeserving character he met, lose money, borrow money, and deck himself out in all those comical gold gadgets, cigarette cases and cuff links and remarkable clips to hold down his tie? Marushka had not lived for three years in a Berlin cellar, and dreamed of food, and never escaped from a landscape of pavements. Nor had she finally, after how much desperate underpaid work in Paris, achieved a full stomach and an overcoat and a second pair of shoes. Bara endured poverty as lightheartedly as anyone could, and when he had money refused to take it seriously. What fools we should have felt now if Bara owned savings in a bank.

And it was absurd of Marushka to act as if a Protective League was needed for the girls, to save them from Bara's marauding. Bara did not seek the girls, they sought him. It began some six months after Suzy's death when Gertrude, Bara's well-known Tunisian tart, annexed him. Bara had not thought of himself as a man who would appeal to women; he was quite frightened of Gertrude as a matter of fact, although delighted with this new sport. Bara clung to tarts, or tarts to Bara, because he liked them, they were as unattached as he was. He was astonished when a non-tart made advances, and after that he was launched on amateurs. True, he had more girls than most men: is that a sin? The girls would be the first to give Bara testimonials; he was kind and cheerful and generous. Do women often get that much from men? There had to be the banquet of girls and the careless money in his life, Marushka, don't you see? He needed the balance of lightness. Of course he was never serious about them, as you so often said. How could he be? He used up his whole life's supply of seriousness on Suzy.

Lep rose and put his tray outside the door in the hall. He ought to telephone the concierge and arrange for a plane ticket to London. But he felt sleepy, after eating, and besides he was too cold to decide anything. I am a sort of pudding, Lep thought gloomily, Bara dragged me after him, a pudding in human form. Bara always made the quick decisions, wangled the transport, attended to the ceaseless kitchen of life. If Marushka had not been so busy quarreling with Bara, she would have noticed her friend Lep, a really good subject for exhortation. Perhaps I am just lazy, Lep thought, or perhaps cowardly; in either case he would now slip back into bed, the only comfortable place to be, smoke, doze a bit, and presently no doubt a decision would have made itself.

How pretty they were, Lep thought, closing his eyes and digging his shoulders into the pillows. Oh, Marushka, if you could have seen them. They were sitting outside the Café des Artisans, a cheap café across the street and down from the D — kome, and it was April. They each had their feet up on another chair, thus exposing to the world big holes in their shoes. Suzy wore a beret on the side of her head in the style of the young Garbo. She had long straight green-yellow hair and a wicked little face like a fox that is going to play a joke on you. She was very small and very thin, and she always seemed to be waiting to guess what she was going to do next. Bara was like a tough boy from the South, and wearing a nice Apache expression, a baby scowl full of thought and importance. I was walking around Paris because I had only been there three weeks, taking pictures of the beautiful buildings and the bridges and doorways. I had graduated to this exciting amusement; some people are never young. I was the sort of child who plays chess at six, and it was always like that. Then I was an old man of twenty-two, in love with monuments.

I looked at them and I wanted to dance in the street and make singing sounds. I even wanted to take a picture of them, and I did, my first picture of people. They looked the way I would have wanted to be if I had ever been young, and also they looked like all the books I had read about youth in Paris. I knew at once that they were lovers and could not pay their rent, and it was perfect.

Bara did not like it that I took a picture and he got up and said 'Hey!' in a menacing manner. If Suzy was around, and anything happened, you always had to explain to Bara that it was in favor of Suzy, not against her, before he would stop wanting to fight. For himself he had no such *amour propre* but he was very particular about Suzy. That was how we met. They had friends, they had been in Paris nearly six months. They had a friend called Bhurlipan who worked in the Hammam on the rue Lafayette; he said he was an Assyrian and in any case wore a beard. There were two young Americans, a girl and a boy, giants, who were actually going to an Institute to learn how to design wallpaper. And two baby Dutch Communists, from the Sorbonne. And a Frenchman named Louis, who had an obscure job at the Agence Havas. It was a splendid world, it suited them. I was so excited, I cannot tell you. I followed them everywhere, thinking that this was life at last. Their life, of course, not mine; I went to the Ecole des Langues Orientales because my family in

Poland still had money then, and I always studied, I did not know anything else to do.

They did my living for me; it was an excellent arrangement. I could not understand Bara and Suzy for a long time, because I kept putting them into something I had read. They were both nineteen then, almost twenty, and they had been married for two years; you must admit that is like a book. They were married in Berlin because their landlady said they could not live in her room as they were immoral, and they could not afford two rooms. The minute Bara was married, it became the most important truth in his life: he was a husband and Suzy was his wife. Suzy loved Bara, but to her, marriage was an administrative detail. This was a great disagreement between them. The only one, but you can see it might be grave. Suzy took pictures for a fashion magazine, not a good fashion magazine, and Bara worked for a photographic agency called Clix, and they barely managed to eat, but they were used to that and they never quarreled about money and all the things they did not have. They quarreled about marriage.

Suzy thought going to bed was like eating ice cream or dancing or the movies. If she wanted to, and found a man who pleased her, she did. You could never tell when it was going to happen. Then she would come home to their room, in a high gray house behind the Gare Montparnasse, innocent and carefree, having already forgotten the man. Bara sometimes beat her; I can tell you I was shocked, I only knew such behavior in books, naturally. He beat her sometimes, he pleaded with her, he was known to weep in despair. Suzy could not see what Bara was making all this fuss about: she said that any other woman would be very angry with him and even call him a bully.

But this is only something of their life, not the main thing at all. It makes a confusion really, Lep thought, deciding Marushka would not understand and judge Suzy harshly and jump to the wrong conclusion that Bara and Suzy were unhappy together.

How could he describe to Marushka those years in Paris, from 1931 until Bara and Suzy went to the war in Spain, late in the summer of 1936? They were the golden age of man, but did not sound remarkable if one started to talk about them. If you talked about them, it would seem that their lives had been small and hampered if not strangled, by poverty, and their pleasures the pitiful makeshifts of the poor.

He understood how Bara loved Suzy, or understood as much as an outsider could. They even looked alike, Lep insisted, trying to explain it to Marushka. They had the same laugh, they laughed at the same time. They watched everything, they saw everything, they saw it together at the same moment and in the same way. They were proud people. No, how could one say any of it? And they were never afraid of life; they wrestled with it, they did not believe they could be beaten. The first time Bara sold a picture with his name on it, and got extra money, he bought Suzy a beautiful leather belt with a silver buckle. Suzy needed almost everything except a beautiful leather belt, but she loved it, especially the silver buckle.

I explain badly, Lep thought, and started again, looking for the acts, the words, the events that would convince Marushka. Bara thought Suzy more beautiful than any woman in the world, but that was usual for men in love. Was his carefulness usual? Bara knew how Suzy felt; he knew if she was cold or tired or disgusted with her day's work or longing for something beyond their reach, like a trip to the seashore. Somehow, in some form, Bara managed to get for Suzy what she needed, or to console her if he really could do nothing. Yet it was not all Bara's gift. It was not one of those sad loves, offered by an obsessed man to an indifferent woman. Bara would never have believed in himself and in life, as he did, but for Suzy's faith. Bara could not be less than daring and talented and gay and open-handed, because that was how Suzy saw him.

When Hitler took Germany, or rather when the Germans took Hitler, Bara remembered that Suzy had been born a Jew. This was not a visible fact nor a relevant fact until Hitler produced his race sickness and the Germans were gladly infected. Suzy was Hungarian too, legally registered as Fruzsina Goldenstück, a name far too ugly for her, and since Bara was called Dezsö Afpád Nagyvazsonyi, which no one could pronounce, they agreed to adopt quick homemade names which would suit them when they were rich and famous. So they became Tim Bara and Suzy Dann, and they forgot the matter.

Hitler, through Suzy, taught Bara politics and widened the world so that all of it concerned him, whereas before he was only concerned with what he could see in the lens of his camera. This insane monster, Hitler, threatened Suzy; Bara saw that plainly. The indecency and the cruelty and the shamefulness of threatening Suzy spread into the general crime of threatening the world. Bara was very angry, in those days, Marushka; that was before he had lost his anger. He hated the Nazis as much as he loved Suzy, and he suffered in Paris because there was nothing he could do to defeat the Nazis and thus remove the danger to Suzy and the world.

When the war started in Spain, Bara knew at once that Spain was the place for all free men to fight Hitler, the Nazis, and the corrupt ideas which the Nazi imitators also practiced. He did not expect to fight, since he had never held a rifle; he expected to take pictures which would force everyone to see what there was to fight. You remember, in those days, people still spoke of the trains running on time in Italy, and said that poor degenerate France needed a strong man like Hitler, and now there was Franco, instantly hailed as a Christian gentleman. Bara went to Spain to save Suzy first and the human race also, and Suzy went along because she always went where Bara was; they could not imagine spending a whole day apart from each other.

They loved Spain, they were very happy. They loved the Spanish and the land and all the other passionate foreigners who had dropped everything to go to Spain and fight for the rights and dignity of man. Everyone was poor and friends; the early months in Spain must have been like a love affair on a national scale. And everyone was full of hope. Here, in this most beautiful country, among these noble people, the evil of the world would be defeated. There were also many jokes; it seems to have been an intimate war. But you know about Spain, Marushka; it is the home of your heart, not mine. I only know from Bara.

At the same time, though it was all thrilling, heroic, active and full of laughter, it was also serious, and something happened to Suzy. Bara did not know what it was, nor do I, but I imagine Suzy saw women grieving for their dead husbands, and she began to accept marriage as an act of faith. I sympathize with Suzy's earlier point of view; two people could not have belonged more to each other than she and Bara, and I do not attach all that importance to the sex act. But that was not Bara's idea, and in Spain, who knows why, Suzy finally agreed with him; there were no other men. They worked together, and Suzy's pictures were better than Bara's; she was a more careful technician. He was terribly proud of her pictures. I am quite sure it did not occur to either of them that in a war you can get killed.

I ought to get up, Lep said to himself, I ought to open the window and clear out the smoke, I ought to speak to the concierge, I ought to look at the clock. What a curious couple they would make, he and Marushka, sitting in Marushka's new house which he had not seen, talking of love. Bara described Marushka's new house as the last and worst of all Marushka's follies. When Bara was pleased with Marushka he thought of her as a tiger, when cross he thought of her as a mule; now, being cross, he said Marushka's house was like stabling a mule in a candy box. Marushka constantly shoved ash trays at you and screamed if you put a glass down on a table. It was all pink and blue, and Marushka must have gone insane, and where would it end? So they would sit in Maruskha's candy box and talk of love, they who knew nothing of it.

But that was the point, and though it was the blind leading the blind, he must make Marushka see. Because Bara did know about love he was complete; Suzy was Bara's real fortune and strength.

Bara and Suzy came back to Paris for two days in the late autumn to buy a stock of films and canned food and soap. They were like young eagles, except that eagles are ugly birds, soaring in this new brilliant clean air of Spain. I have never seen two people so happy; it is not often that the inside and the outside climate fit together. But think of it, they loved each other and they loved the world they lived in; they were working in partnership as they always planned to do, they were absolutely joined, and joined for something, not against something, which is a luxury of soul you cannot fail to appreciate, Marushka.

I remember no battles unless I have been there, and then I usually remember the scenery and not the place name or the date. Could it have been the Battle of Brihuega, Marushka? It was before you came to Spain so perhaps you do not know, but that is no matter. Suzy was hanging onto the side of a car, taking pictures; Bara was somewhere farther ahead on the road. I imagine it was one of those typical clogged war roads where everyone is mindless and the only idea they all have is to move, although no one knows exactly why or where. It must have been even more disorganized than most war roads are, because Spain must have been an even more disorganized war. Fascist planes came over to machine-gun the road; Bara said they were Heinkels. Naturally they machine-gunned the road; there was no protection against them. Those who had rifles fired into the sky, which is useless but helps the person who has the rifle. A machine-gun bullet entered Suzy's back and cut down into her body and she fell off the car and a soldier, passing, moved her to the side of the road so she would not be run over, but that was all he could do.

You remember the mysterious way news travels in combat, Marushka. Bara heard the rumor that a woman was hit, and by that system he had of always knowing about Suzy, he knew it was Suzy, so he ran down the road and found her. For the next four hours, in that traffic jam, he tried to move Suzy toward help, an ambulance or a doctor or a dressing station, but since the whole battle was in motion, he could find nothing. You can imagine her pain, pressed into crumpled positions, shaken on the bad road, lifted to another vehicle that was going faster, you can imagine it. She went off her head, and did not know where she was or recognize anyone. She called and called for Bara, although he was right beside her. At last he took her to a field, farther on, to let her die quietly. She died calling for him. I think that was what he could not endure. He could not make Suzy understand that he was with her.

He came back to Paris soon after that and I will not talk about it because I do not want to remember. Everyone must grow up sooner or later or do something that functions in the same way as growing up, but everyone does not have to do it in a week, and also not at the age of twenty-five. Bara and Suzy had been married for eight years when she was killed. Eight years is a long time but especially if you are young, then it is almost all of your life. In one week, Bara buried Suzy so deep that no one else would ever find her, and he would never lose her. Bara was not an introspective or an intellectual or a religious man; I do not know if being any of those would help a man to accept what he had to accept, but in any case Bara was obliged to invent his own method. It was painful to watch. You met him in Madrid a few months after this, and you have always told me how gay Bara was, how funny, and also that you learned by accident of his wife's death because he never spoke of it.

He did not share Suzy with anyone, not even with me. I stayed in Paris, and as Bara's work sold more and more, I became his Paris errand boy, and slowly he made me into a professional photographer and his partner, which was a lucky thing because money stopped coming from Poland. I mourned Suzy by myself; I was careful not to speak of her to Bara. A man does not want someone to pick sympathetically at a great wound that runs through his whole body.

Bara lost his anger. I have lost mine too, although differently, and I understand how that works. He could be sickened by what he saw, but that is not the same. To be angry, you must have hope. He had nothing more to be angry about for himself, he did not care. But Suzy was his world and he saw her as the world, and he felt that always, everywhere, and for all time, it was like him and Suzy: men were permanently engaged in losing what they loved, and destroying what others loved, and there was no help for this, it was the nature of man and the real shape of history. I believe in buildings, as you know, and I would point out that some of the fine work of man lasted, and Bara would say that it lasted until it was hit by a bomb or someone blew it up otherwise, but he did not deny the fine work of men, nor think it useless; he thought it a necessary bravery. If you lived in a desert you had various choices; you could kill yourself or go mad or plant flowers. It was only planting flowers in a desert, and the flowers neither changed the desert nor had much chance to survive, but the act of planting was good, because bravery was good. Bravery, Bara came to see, was really a form of consideration; if you were brave, you did not frighten the others who had plenty to be frightened about.

I am not saying this is a correct view of life, since I have no idea what the correct view might be, if there is one. But of course, Bara was a happy man, which makes a big contradiction and can hardly be explained. He did not lose what he loved. He had love and he never lost it. He always loved Suzy.

Bara refused to make plans; you know that from much irritating experience, Marushka. If you asked him at seven to meet you for dinner at eight he would probably not come because he disliked being trapped in agreements. I am sure he did not plan how he would live without Suzy, nor how he would feel. I am sure it happened as it did without effort, because he could do nothing else.

He did not share his work with any woman; Suzy had been his partner. I was no rival to Suzy, I stole nothing from her. I think Bara's work was a monument to Suzy although he would have been amazed to hear that. I think he had to be so good because Suzy believed him good, and I think he was showing the world, in that long record he made, in thousands of pictures, what kind of a world it was which killed Suzy.

Fame did not hurt Bara, no matter how much you liked to tease him about it, Marushka. He took it as an accident, which perhaps all fame is, and he used it. If Suzy had been alive they would have laughed and marveled and profiteered together. Alone, it was something he had which opened doors and made it easier for him to get around. No wonder he was idiotically careless of the money which fame brought; he had no one to spend it on. Do you suppose money mattered to him when he had never had it for Suzy?

You will remind me of Bara's girls, but that is nonsense. Nothing Bara did or said or gave to any girl touched Suzy, or the place where Suzy lived in him. He too enjoyed the sex act as ice cream, movies, dancing; with Suzy, and only with Suzy, it was the act of love. That American girl worries me still; she was so nice a girl and she could not be discouraged from wanting Bara as her own. I am sure Bara drifted, trying not to hurt her, and so no doubt hurt her more. But he could not oblige Helen by marrying her, he never could have. He was married, he had a wife, and he was faithful to her. If you love a woman entirely, you cannot help it if she is dead.

How do we know it was not right for Bara to die, now, a complete man? How do we know what would have happened to him in time? He might have grown tired in his heart, the way people do, and failed in his love, and given over to blurring and compromise until he became like the rest of us. As poor as we are, Marushka. On the other hand, he might have lived to be eighty, and done more fine work and shone his light for us, and kept Suzy with him always, stronger and stronger, like a private love of God if you believe in God. We cannot be sure of anything.

No, this is ridiculous, Lep said to himself, I am going to get up, it is not as cold as I think. I will fly to London today. We will sit in Marushka's new house, but I will not talk of Suzy. Bara never spoke of her; why should I give away his secrets now that he is dead? Besides, it would probably not help Marushka anyhow. I will go to her and be very stern, as Bara used to be, and talk to her like Bara. Stop it, Marushka, stop it now. Is this the proper way to behave? For shame. What are you doing at that Wailing Wall? The only thing to do, as long as you are alive, is live.

A PROMISING
CAREER

Andrew Lingard came to kiss his wife good morning and good-bye; he was off as usual to the British Museum Reading Room. The mornings, at home in Connaught Square, were made hideous by the telephone bell. Lotte Lingard had a full-time job; she arranged lives. For her friends and their friends and for passing waifs and strays, she found dwellings, doctors, publishers, plumbers, servants, holiday resorts, whatever was in short supply. She advised, consoled, scolded, encouraged, as required. This large voluntary business was mainly transacted on the telephone and though Mrs Lingard claimed to detest every minute of it the telephone never stopped ringing and she was unable to refuse its demands. She was now speaking to one of her troubled clients; Andrew Lingard moved the breakfast tray from the foot of the bed, shoved aside the daily litter of newspapers and letters, and sat down to wait.

'Very worrying, I know. But you mustn't get in a flap. Talk to Dr Hermann at Wigmore 4067. He's an excellent man. Yes, do that. I'll call you later to hear what he says. Yes. Yes.'

Lotte hung up, as was her style, without farewells and cutting off the thanks at the other end, and said, 'Good morning, darling. I have a note from Claud. Too disappointing. He's not coming to us for Christmas.'

Lotte's Christmas house parties in Oxfordshire were of extreme importance to her. It might be, Andrew thought, that, being childless, she hungered for a band of sprightly middle-aged orphans to mother during this children's festival. Claud Roylands had been a member of her Christmas group for at least ten years, perhaps longer.

Andrew Lingard, mildly surprised, said, 'That's a break with tradition.'

'I don't know what we'll do without him. I count on Claud. It won't seem a proper Christmas.'

'Poor Lotte. Why isn't he coming? You'll find someone else.'

'I'd like to know where. London isn't creeping with attractive unattached men. He's going ski-ing.'

Claud, the indispensable bachelor, brilliant at paper games, uproarious in charades, sensible and even witty over port, attentive to the charmed ladies, and Lotte's favorite chum. Was it possible that he liked Claud less because Lotte liked him more? Not worth troubling about. What a rut they were in; imagine fretting over Christmas guests. Too easy, too safe, too comfortable: exactly the life that ninety-odd per cent of the world dreamed of and longed for and would never get.

'What are we doing tonight, Lotte?'

'Dining at the Lowthers'.'

'Fun?'

'I shouldn't imagine so, darling. Oh, I will miss Claud.'

'I'll think of someone. I'll comb the clubs. Now I must run along to the Sumerian Kings.'

He kissed his wife on the forehead; the telephone rang again.

Claud Roylands, driving to London where he should not be going, tried to tell himself that he felt elated, daring and happy. It was term time and no headmaster, let alone the headmaster of a school like Newhall, left his post while the premises were full of boys between the ages of thirteen and eighteen, any of whom were potentially capable of arson, suicide, poliomyelitis or other outrages. Adorable little Kate, so yielding in all else, failed to realize that the Captain of the *Queen Elizabeth* had nothing on him in the way of responsibility. The Captain might not need to spend every waking minute on the bridge but he was certainly obliged to remain on board somewhere.

Claud had announced to Richard Mitchell, his senior housemaster, that he was taking the evening off to hear Menuhin at the Festival Hall. Music, or perhaps an evening preview at the Tate, were just barely suitable excuses for a night out. He had never told such footling lies until he met Kate in September, at Lotte's memorable dinner party. During term, only a declaration of war and a general mobilization would remove him from the cluster of Georgian brick buildings and the elevated penitentiary life for which Newhall was famous. He knew his duty; he also knew that doing this duty well was the first step towards higher duties.

He could not risk it any more; Kate would have to understand. One night he had driven to town allegedly to see a mammoth Picasso show; Kate had sent him an invitation which he displayed for some days on the chimney-piece in his study. One night, so he said to Mitchell, a governessy-gossipy man, he had been tempted by the chance to hear *Die Walküre.* Tonight Bartók; Kate was instructed to procure a program for him, in case anyone wanted to discuss the concert at school, but mainly so that he could drop the program casually on the table where his staff found cigarettes and sherry when they came to consult or natter before dinner.

Life of crime; he made an effort to feel elated, daring and happy again. A life of crime was delightful and safe enough in the holidays, and after all he had four months a year to be merrily criminal. But in term, no. Third and last escapade, he promised himself. It was flattering, it was even intoxicating, that Kate could not live without the sight, sound and touch of him; now she must control herself until Christmas. And her daily letters, in her distinctive hand, had become a problem; she would have to buy ordinary envelopes and type the address, or cut down on her declarations of love. She didn't *see*; she had never lived in a large public school. It's somewhere between the priesthood and the army, he began telling Kate—he often reasoned with her silently in his mind— I am not a free agent, I am Caesar's wife. I am morally and physically accountable for six hundred mothers' darlings. Can you imagine what would happen if—but he dismissed this trend of thought, it was too appalling.

Blinded by oncoming headlights, Claud swerved his car off the hard surface and slithered for a minute on the muddy verge. This shook him and he drove more slowly. November, three hours on greasy roads to London, not home again until four in the morning, and the stiff day to follow. Usually Claud felt that being forty-three was tough, alert youth; now he felt the dismal limitations of middle age. It is not only a question of practical sense, he explained to Kate, it is also a question of what I can handle. Running Newhall is hard work. His voice whined a little in his head. Anti-aphrodisiac work, he added, to make the point clear.

After Christmas, when she had done her Yuletide bit by her two small sons and her husband, they could elope for nearly a month to an obscure Swiss ski resort, the type of place where they would meet no one they knew. Meantime Kate must accept the facts of his position. She was as trusting, generous and natural as a child; his job was to teach her gently the ways of the world. He meant to begin tonight. He had been the sort of bachelor who was never short of women and never short of society. He had been cool and greedy and always in charge. He had lost his head over Kate; high time to get his head back. How Kate managed to deceive her husband, Francis, was beyond him, but women were astonishingly able, as he knew from wide experience with married ladies.

At any rate, once this odious drive was finished, he would be rewarded with ease and comfort. He kept a superior suite of sitting-room, bedroom and bath in a house in Charles Street, which his old batman Hodges, the owner and proprietor of the establishment, called chambers for gentlemen. Hodges had done well out of the war; a rare range of people emerged better off after the late conflict. Claud presumed that Hodges had learned a few tricks from the clever Yanks; it was generally understood that the GIs made fortunes through brilliant black-market operations. Hodges could be counted on to remain wooden-faced, blind and respectful, calling Claud 'Major' and attending to his every need.

Kate would be waiting beside the fire which Hodges had lit; there would be flowers bought by Hodges, and ice next to the cocktail shaker; when Claud rang, Hodges would bring a delicious supper and champagne in a bucket. This love affair might be dangerous but it was not squalid. Kate would be dressed in a sleek evening gown—such a change from the tweeds or the long-sleeved grisly afternoon dresses of the housemasters' wives—and her hair would be foaming around her head, and her soft irregular mouth would be raised to him. He drove faster.

Entering Hyde Park, he began to look at the bright side. He gave thanks, as usual, to his dear old grandmother who had left him six hundred a year; no one could call this riches but it made all the difference, the small luxuries, the holidays abroad. And he did not complain of his salary; a single man, unburdened by a wife and offspring who grew out of their clothes and required endless dentistry, lived very well and could save money too. He was indeed fortunate, his material wants satisfied, engaged in work of his choice with the future open and promising, and a beautiful mistress to complete contentment. Let it last, Claud prayed while moving at the prescribed twenty miles an hour through the park, let it last.

He opened the door to his rooms, with his key, and there was Kate, as imagined. She wore, aside from a midnight-blue velvet dress, her special expression, eager and shy, offering him everything yet waiting for his signal. He stretched out his hands and she came to him; she was engulfed in his arms. Claud was a very tall man, strongly built, stooping slightly out of consideration for others who had to look up to him. With Kate, who was tiny, he felt notably powerful and protective.

'Darling,' Kate murmured. Her voice was always a murmur, a little breathless, a little uncertain; it was absolutely unlike the hundreds of voices he heard at school. 'Darling, darling. It's been a lifetime.'

He kissed her, at length. Ready for the next move, Claud said that he would have a bath and change quickly; could she make cocktails meanwhile. He kept evening clothes in the bedroom cupboard; when he returned to the sitting-room, he had left the worries of Newhall with his discarded suit. Kate mixed perfect cocktails, very dry, very cold. After the second Martini, after her tender enquiries about his work, his health, his state of mind, she looked at him with her large pleading eyes and remarked that Francis had gone to live at his club.

Claud felt cold all over. He put his glass on the table by his chair and lit a cigarette, controlling panic. Kate sensed this fear. She realized that a man of forty-three, with Claud's eminent attractions, had remained a bachelor only because he insisted on doing so. He would be terrified of traps. She had no intention of terrifying him.

'Of course, it has nothing to do with us,' Kate said. 'Obviously. No one knows anything about us, darling, and no one will. We're entirely our own business. Francis and I had a bang-up row, that's all. He'd just announced that he was again going off for a golfing week-end at Sunningdale, never thinking of me or the children, and never giving me a chance to fix any plans for my own amusement. I said I wouldn't stand for it, so he said he'd move to the club until I came round, and I said if he did he could stay there for good. I do feel sorry for him, he's such a bore; but his club is full of bores and he'll be far happier with them. And I must say it's heaven at home now. I think the boys are relieved too, no Daddy to bellow at them about nothing; and the servants are on air. I've been hoping for years that Francis would walk out, and I really think he stayed because of the cook and his chair that he's so used to.'

'Yes.'

'My dearest funny one.' Kate snuggled beside him on the sofa. 'You're feeling responsible, aren't you? Please don't. I knew our marriage was hopeless long before I ever saw you. I knew it almost from the beginning. I've been wanting to end it for ages, only I didn't know how to. But Francis did it all; perhaps he's just as pleased as I am. See? Now don't think about it any more. Couldn't we have supper? Aren't you starving, after that ghastly drive?'

Hodges brought them soup in little French lidded casseroles, and smoked trout and a cold bird; the champagne was always excellent. Soothed by this unacademic fare, Claud explained his situation at Newhall, the impossibility of any more nights out during term, the dubiousness of daily letters unless she could disguise the envelopes. Kate was penitent, blaming herself for selfishness. She must try to love him less; she must never be a burden. With her small pliable body pressed against his side, her hair on his cheek, her dove murmurs in his ear, Claud did not want her restrained, so he took back everything he'd said and guided her to the bedroom. Later, Claud wondered how he could face the five weeks until Christmas without her; he also thought what a colossal fool Francis Patchin was to prefer golf at Sunningdale to this.

Claud felt driven. There had been an outbreak of measles in the Fourth Form. It was too horrible to contemplate the infirmary full of spotty boys during the Christmas hols; whom could he delegate to stay and preside; would the Matron of Tong House be enough or would parents expect at least a master, if not himself? Also Backer must be a miserable Latin teacher; it was unlikely that eighty per cent of the boys taking Sixth Form Latin should fail their end-of-term tests; stupid they might be, but not stupid in such overwhelming numbers. Added to which, the chapel roof had sprung a leak.

And here was Kate's letter. He read it again. He began to scratch his cheek nervously. Four weeks without Kate had indeed made him nervous, which was unusual; he was accustomed to his life, a balance between the monastic and the voluptuous. He had been aching for Kate; he had slept badly.

Now she wrote to say that since Francis remained at his club, and had never been any sort of baby-sitter at best, she had no one to look after the children during the holidays. She could see no solution except to bring them to Switzerland, where they would not be in the way, really, darling; they'd stay at the kiddies' ski school and on the nursery slopes all day, and go early to bed. She need only lunch with them. Claud could come separately and they would meet with cries of astonished surprise at the Hotel-Pension Vanetta. In fact, the children might be the best possible camouflage; and anyhow she did not know what else she could do. Of course, if Claud thought this depressing she would understand, and they would have to forgo their lovely Christmas treat together. But by spring, she would surely discover some way to take care of the children; perhaps she and Claud could go to Greece in April.

April, Claud groaned. He was momentarily furious with Kate. She ought to have been more competent; her involved life, not his, was ruining their plans. Best to cut the losses now; write and say that he thought this outing with infants unsuitable; go off elsewhere by himself and find another lady to share the cold starry nights; or easier still, and always delightful, go to the Lingards in Oxfordshire.

He knew, now clawing his cheek with irritation, that he would do no such thing. It was Kate he wanted, and only Kate; for four weeks his imagination had fed on her. He must accept her children, and with good grace too. If Kate realized how tired he was of children.

The last week of term, which was a triannual nightmare and not improved by the prospect of two small boys cluttering up his love affair, unexpectedly took on sunrise hues of hope. Claud was waited upon by two imposing gentlemen, one a general in mufti, the other a youngish bishop in gaiters. They were emissaries from the Board of Governors of Rotherham, and they said they had come to sound out Mr Roylands. They had also come to inspect Mr Roylands, which they did not say but Claud knew. What they saw was encouraging: a big man with a bony clever face and a virile broken nose, very good clothes just properly rumpled, a deferential manner based on complete assurance, who plied them with excellent Amontillado and Turkish cigarettes.

Swearing Claud to secrecy, they announced that the venerable and learned Dr Mortimer, headmaster of Rotherham, intended to retire in the course of the coming summer. Mr Roylands was extremely young, by the standards of Rotherham, but his unusual talents were known. Would he, in case the post was offered him, feel inclined to accept?

It was all vague and discreet; Claud's reply was equally so; they understood each other. He would leap at Rotherham, though leaping with dignity. Newhall was a first-class school, but Rotherham was one of the Famous Four. Newhall, in time, Claud hoped, would lead to his real ambition; Rotherham was the sure stepping-stone. There was a long line of precedent; in fact, Mr Anthony Hailey, Dr Mortimer's predecessor, had moved onward and upward from Rotherham to be Master of Clare.

A Cambridge college was Claud's final cherished goal, and always had been. As an undergraduate, he raised his eyes to the High Table, night after night, and saw himself sitting in the Warden's chair. He took a First in both parts of the History Tripos, knowing exactly why he needed this laudable degree; it was a passport to the desired place. The war interrupted his progress for seven years, but he did not regret the war, since he had survived it. The war gave him invaluable experience of administration, on every level, from an infantry company to staff planning.

Perhaps because of his military record, to say nothing of his Cambridge degree and the publication of a stylishly written, scholarly book on the taxation system of the Hapsburgs, he had been called to Newhall as the youngest headmaster that stern institution had ever employed. With Rotherham as his next prize, he might really achieve a Cambridge college before he was fifty. And then he would be where he wanted to be, in that beautiful damp grey and gold city, associating with his peers and guiding, from a benign distance, the destinies of young men.

By the time Claud reached Laroche-sur-Sion and the Hotel-Pension Vanetta, he had forgotten the inconvenience of the Patchin children, and was thinking only of Rotherham and Cambridge, and the delight of sharing his secret and his dream with Kate. It was an indisputable fact that children go to bed at eight o'clock and are seen no more. Kate, who preceded him, had written to describe his room: the most glorious view of mountains, a balcony for breakfast and a marvellous double bed.

For three days, Claud sat alone at lunch in the poky spotless Vanetta dining-room, while Kate and John, aged eleven, and Martin, aged nine, made merry at a table by the window in the sun. On the fourth day, he joined them. The children did not actually call him Uncle Claud but that became his position, just short of parental. Though he believed boys were pestilential and he only approved of adult young, he found these two delightful; they looked like Kate, not like their squarish red-faced father. No doubt before boys went away to school they were nicer. Besides, by training and temperament, Claud could not keep his hands off growing minds. He hardly noticed when he began discussing John's talents and Martin's minor failings with Kate, at dinner; he hardly realized that these dreaded children were fastening to him like affectionate little lichens. He was absurdly anxious for John to do well at ski school and pass his test and win his Bronze Medal.

Kate was ravishing in ski pants. She seemed now, against the background of white mountains, a deliciously curved, pink-cheeked, windblown girl of twenty, not a thirty-six-year-old mother of two. They skied all day, Claud in the lead. When the trail passed through pine woods and was briefly private, he stopped, turned, and despite the encumbrance of skis managed to kiss Kate who tasted like an icy apple. He felt wonderfully well and lighthearted; he was charmed to be in love outdoors and in the day-time.

And Kate understood and applauded his ambitions. With brandy glasses cupped in their hands, they talked by the hour about Rotherham, planning, imagining. Kate assured him that he would be installed in Cambridge within five years. She urged him now to get to work on the book he had only dallied with, another stylishly written, scholarly volume, this time on the progressive breakdown of government in Paris during the siege of 1870. She listened, thrilled, to his talk of those terrible famine-stricken days; he had never realized how absorbing he could make history.

Kate saw herself at Cambridge in the Master's Lodgings, giving tea to besotted undergraduates, worshipped by older, discreeter dons, bathed in the flashing light of various skilful minds. She owed this gilded vision to novels, for she knew nothing of the academic life. She had attended a mediocre Swiss finishing school. Her sons were still in the placid infantile stage of primary education. And thirteen years with Francis

Patchin, a stockbroker, had taught her only to loathe golf, musical comedies and fast bridge, and Francis' circle who indulged in all of these. Andrew Lingard had been her first introduction to the intellectual man and she found him fascinating if a trifle forbidding; he was of course much older than Claud and she presumed grander, as he had been a don or a professor or something, at Oxford, and universities were statelier than schools. Still, he and Claud lived in a magical free world, unlike stockbrokers. They said whatever came into their heads and all of it was new to her; they took enormous vacations and traveled everywhere and knew everything about the places they visited; they joked at the moments when Francis stood to attention: they seemed not to recognize all Francis' sacred subjects: the Royal Family, the Empire, the Conservative Party, Eton, the Bank of England, there was no end to it.

To Claud, Cambridge might mean homecoming; for her, it would be release from slavery, a dull life in a dull Victorian house with the predictable years stretching ahead. Claud was not her first affair in the long flat time of her marriage, but he was her first serious hope, therefore her first serious love. She thought it a miracle to have found what she needed, when she was thirty-six, and nearly past the time of finding anything; and she was desperate with fear. She might lose Claud, she was never sure of him; at any moment he was free to disappear. There had been no pledges; and even pledges could be broken.

In one way, at least, Kate knew her power. At night, she flitted over the scrubbed boards of the Vanetta corridor, opened Claud's door silently, and slid into the large double bed. Here, he belonged to her. Here, she gave him what he fiercely wanted. Claud, who was accustomed to success with women, had never counted himself accomplished to this degree. Kate was a genuinely ravenous lover. Sometimes, when she left him to tiptoe back to her own room, Claud felt drained and dimly frightened. But the fresh, natural, laughing girl on the ski slopes next day reassured him. Kate knew all this too, and was aware of the danger of surfeit.

John did pass his test, and Claud, now almost in the role of proud father, paid five francs for the gimcrack little bronze pin and fastened it to John's windbreaker. John threw his arms around Claud's neck and kissed him. This had never happened to Claud before, and though he made some joking deprecating remark, he was amazed to feel tears in his eyes. You could decently have tears in your eyes outdoors, on account of the cold and the wind. He suggested to Kate that they ought to dine with the children, a celebration party for John, who would be allowed a glass of white wine with water in it. John had decided to become a ski instructor when he grew up.

At dinner that night, Martin's face suddenly crumpled and Kate asked what had happened.

'I don't want to go home,' Martin said. 'It's much nicer here with you and him. I want to stay here always.'

'Now sweetie,' Kate said, 'don't be silly. You have to go to school and Mr Roylands has to work and I have to run the house.'

'Why couldn't I go to school here? Why couldn't you run a house here?'

'Daddy,' Kate began.

'Is Daddy coming back?' Martin asked, with obvious alarm.

'Eat your dinner, Martin.'

'Couldn't we come again in the spring?' John said. John, being older, was more practical. 'You'd come, wouldn't you, Mr Roylands? For the spring hols. You would, wouldn't you?'

'Darling,' Kate said hurriedly, 'spring's a long way off. Let's not make plans.'

When the children had gone to bed, Kate said, 'Poor Francis, he never won such a vote of confidence.'

'Nice boys.'

'They adore you. Just like their mother.'

'Sweet little poppet. It has been fun, hasn't it?'

'Bliss, Claud. Pure bliss.'

They decided to go home on the same train; no one would be meeting them; no one would notice. After the children were tucked in, they could have a last night together in Claud's compartment.

Lotte seemed to be snarling into the telephone. Whatever next, Andrew wondered. How can they keep it up, day after day?

'Probably they just ran into each other there. It's exactly the sort of quiet inexpensive place Claud would choose. They're all very old friends. I'm sure you've got it wrong, Mavis, you're too romantic.'

Lotte hung up and glared at Andrew, though meaning nothing personal by this; she was glaring at her distant telephone partner.

'He's mad,' Lotte said.

'Who?'

'Claud. Barking mad. Imagine going off to Switzerland with Kate Patchin and her two boys. He's old enough to know that you're *always* seen, no matter where you go. I believe that a loving chum would be passing through if one was having a walk-out on the Maldive Islands. And Claud cannot afford that sort of thing.'

'Ah.'

'That was Mavis Lowther. I admit it's particularly hard luck on

Claud. Not everyone gets caught by a champion gossip. She says she went over to some Swiss place from Crans, where they were staying, because she'd heard it was less spoiled than Crans and far cheaper and she wanted to look into it for next year. And what did she see but Claud behaving like husband and father to Kate and her children. So that's why he chucked us. I introduced them, in the autumn. It didn't occur to me. What is going on with Kate and Francis?'

'Who knows? Francis seems to be living at his club.'

'I always thought Claud's most astounding talent was the way he managed his private life. Naturally, one didn't imagine he'd taken vows of chastity, but no one ever *knew* anything. If Francis and Kate are getting a divorce, it really is the limit for Claud to be playing about.'

Between the newspapers and verbal reports on the telephone, Lotte was apt to be distraught in the mornings. Andrew thought how attractive she looked—rosy without make-up, her leonine hair brushed carelessly—and how interesting it would be to come in one morning and find her languid, inviting, not bustling with concern over something or other.

'You smoke too much,' Andrew said.

So Claud was off to the races with little Kate Patchin. Any man could see that Kate was succulent and far from tethered to Francis. Easy to look at, less easy to talk to; women should read more. Kate seemed astonishingly ignorant, even for a pretty woman; perhaps stockbrokers led sheltered lives. Careless of Claud to be seen *en famille* like that; why hadn't he taken them ski-ing in Poland? Very good ski-ing and surely no Mavis Lowthers in the Carpathian mountains. We academic men, Andrew thought, knowing the straight and narrow path prescribed for his profession, having trod it warily all his life.

What a relief to be retired; what a relief to spend the mornings in the Reading Room, the afternoons at his desk, no more undergraduates, no more colleagues; the daily society of the dear old Sumerian Kings and the ritual round of London cocktail and dinner parties. Yet suddenly he envied Claud, which was odd, since he did not wish to be Claud nor possess Kate. Eaten with ambition and sex, Andrew thought, lucky Claud; still goaded by the illusion that there's some place to go and that he will get there. Claud would be thirteen or fourteen years younger than he; the vital difference, the enviable difference between folly and peace.

It might have been more interesting or more intense if we'd needed money, Andrew reflected; always too safe. Did that explain Lotte? Was she so violently involved in everything because their safety saddened or sickened her? Had she been Claud's mistress at some past moment?

Possibly. In twenty-seven years of marriage, Lotte could not have avoided all whims and excursions, any more than he had; it was not the sort of thing they would ever discuss.

Not bored; content. In the long-dead world where he had passed his life, as student, professor and now chronicler, did they know about contentment and boredom? Historians missed this point; he must try to find the answer. Did Ur-Nammu, first King of the Third Dynasty of Ur, twenty-one hundred years before Christ, ever ask himself whether there was any valid reason for getting out of bed? Fierce, busy, insatiable men who died young and had therefore less time to waste, or perhaps it was only distance that made them so much more alive.

'What are we doing tonight, Lotte?'

'Dining at the Haverhills'.'

'Fun?'

'I shouldn't think so, darling. What can we do about Claud?'

'Nothing.'

'He ought to be warned.'

'Not by me. The rumor is that he's going to get Rotherham.'

'No!'

'Mortimer's gaga. He's even forgotten his Greek, which was all he ever knew. He spills on his shirt at the Athenaeum.'

'But then we must warn Claud. It's too important.'

'His life.'

'You're heartless, Andrew. You will *not* take responsibility. Claud's our friend.'

'I must go, love. I'm late.'

Richard Mitchell, smoking an evil pipe in the drab Newhall common room, said to Ralph Backer, 'What's on the Head's mind?'

Backer shrugged. 'New plans for Sixth Form Latin.' New plans for Backer was more like it. Backer, unsurprised but none the less dismayed, foresaw his future: a second-rate school next, teaching Latin just as badly for a reduced salary; in due time a third-rate school, and near penury. He knew he was a failure as a schoolmaster, but he could do nothing else.

'When Dr Saunders was Head here, before your day, Backer, he never left the school in term. He used to say that anything, no matter how minor, which concerned the school concerned him; we were encouraged to drop in at any time. He never even stayed away for the whole hols. He took a great interest in the grounds. The rose garden behind the library was all his doing.'

'Really?'

'Poor old man. He must be writhing in his grave.'

'Really?'

'It is of course a rare novelty to serve under a headmaster who commutes to London.'

'Oh, not that bad surely?'

'I have counted six absences this term. And we are only in February. I wonder what the Governors think.'

How would they know, unless Mitchell told them? But then, if you wanted to tattle, how would you go about it? Which of those pompous old boys was nanny for the headmaster, or were they all? So Roylands was a slave too. What a trade or career or profession. There were people who had incomes, without teaching Latin, and no wives; there were free men somewhere in the world. He could weep to imagine it. A thousand quid a year, and a bachelor; the Himalayas, the Amazon, anywhere that wasn't a school. What did Roylands do in London? Drink? Gamble? The man wasn't fool enough to get involved with a woman, not after he'd avoided all that so cleverly.

Backer sighed. 'Have you ever imagined what you'd have done if you hadn't been a schoolmaster, Mitchell?'

'Certainly not.'

Well, Mitchell was the true type anyhow, wizened old maid with the soul of an alarm clock. And Roylands gave one splendid sherry, even as he readied the axe. But you didn't feel that Roylands liked axing; nor did you feel that Roylands thought Latin a matter of grave moral importance. He simply thought those accursed Sixth Formers had to know enough Latin to pass their exams and someone had to teach it to them.

'A teacher must be a dedicated man,' Mitchell said. 'The public schools are the very backbone of England.'

I'd rather be a bachelor like Roylands and have a fast sports car and go to London or the Himalayas. Backer looked at his watch. 'Virgil again,' he said.

'I don't know what to do,' Kate said. She lay in the curve of Claud's arm; she was particularly touching in a pseudo-Victorian high-necked dressing-gown. They had come back to the sitting-room and the dying fire, for a last cigarette, a last murmuring talk, before they dressed and sallied out into the dark night. Claud would call a taxi for her, but not accompany her to the door, in case any of Hodges' other gentlemen should be late about. When she had safely disappeared, he would get into his car, parked in the next street, and begin that exhausting drive back to school.

Claud did not know what to do either. He felt put upon, so many problems. His own were bad enough for he knew how perilous it was to keep coming to London, and especially now that Rotherham was nearly his; of all times, this was the moment to be above reproach and to hold one's breath. But he could not stay away from Kate, and he could not blame her for this. She did not insist or demand; she only made herself more alluring than flesh and blood could resist. Why should he also have to handle her problems? Worse still, he was jealous. Before, he had felt a condescending tolerance for husbands. They had nothing to do with him and, as far as he could see, very little to do with their wives. Now the thought of Francis returning, and probably claiming his conjugal rights, made him almost sick with revulsion and anger. Why couldn't Francis live quietly at his club and shut up; the arrangement had been perfectly satisfactory.

'He was really quite pathetic. He apologized and said he'd been very wrong to leave, and I was right about Sunningdale, and he hadn't looked after me enough and he missed the children and wouldn't I start again. All marriages went a little stale and needed a jolt to set them off and he'd had the jolt. He looked at me like a loving dog. I felt too cruel. What shall I do when he comes tomorrow, darling? Tell me what to say.'

'I can't, Kate. You'll have to say whatever you feel.'

She did not stiffen, except in her mind. She continued to lie softly in his arms, and to show him a sad little lost face. Was he never going to speak? Did he intend to go on like this for ever, this shaming hole-and-corner business? Did he think he could keep her indefinitely, without offering marriage? Certainly she didn't want Francis, not at all, but if she turned him away now, and Claud failed to fill the vacant place, she might end up a woman alone, with two small boys. She was not a girl and most men were already married. Naturally. People married in their twenties, not in their forties. Or else they were pansies. It was frightening.

Besides, Francis had made an ominous remark about money, not repeated to Claud. He said that it was his home after all, he did pay for it. Meaning that he wouldn't continue to pay for what he did not enjoy. And she had no money; terrifying fact, hateful fact; her mother lived in the south of France but not on the fashionable sea, in the hills above Le Lavandou, using up her dead father's life insurance. Doctors were never rich, unless made peers and employed by Royalty. One hundred a year of her own, from an unremembered aunt; money for taxis and cinemas and hairdressers at best; not even that.

'I simply don't know what to do,' Kate whispered, and meant it.

'Oh God, it's one o'clock.'

'Darling, how dreadful. We must hurry.'

Was he getting tired; these awful cold drives to and from Newhall? More trouble than it's worth? I'll have to let Francis come home, Kate decided, I can't take the chance. She thought of Francis, installed again in his chair, saying the things he did, and occasionally, horribly, on the way upstairs to bed, asking, 'Well, old girl?'

'Torture,' Lotte Lingard said. 'Pure torture.' She sat at her dressing-table and removed mascara adroitly with cold cream.

Andrew sprawled on her chaise longue, watching.

'The ones we give are just as numbing as the ones we go to.' Lotte was now brushing her hair as if she hated it. 'I think of St Simon Stylites on his pillar in the desert, with envy. Why can't we meet someone new and different, at least? I feel we've been saying and hearing the same things for fifty years.'

'What I can't understand is why everyone talks of Claud and Kate all the time. Is it a very dull season for scandal in London?'

'In our set anyhow. Probably actresses and painters and dashing people like that are having a high old time.'

'The tone of moral indignation amazes me. You'd think Claud was on his way to Wormwood Scrubs for embezzlement.'

'Claud's an absolute fool.'

'Jealousy. We're all getting elderly and staid, so everyone's jealous of the rutting stag and the female with the musky odor of sex.'

'How you talk, Andrew.'

Andrew Lingard laughed. 'It isn't likely that the Rotherham Board of Governors goes to the Four Hundred or wherever it was that people saw Claud and Kate dancing in such close harmony. You're right, Lotte. Dinner parties are hell.'

'When will Claud know whether he's got Rotherham or not?'

'He has got it.'

'Well, I ask you. How idiotic can a man be? Why doesn't he take out some other girls? Nobody minds promiscuity. Besides, what *is* it all about? Mavis Lowther told me that Francis has gone home.'

'Poor Francis.'

'Why?'

'As a general rule, Lotte, men dislike being well publicized cuckolds. It upsets them.'

'You don't suppose Francis knows, do you? I'm sure he's the one person between here and Highgate who's never heard a word.'

'If true, that's just as well for Claud.'

'That's what I've been trying to explain to you. Claud cannot afford trouble. He's such a fool. Also his manners are disgusting. Ever since he's taken up with Kate, he's simply dropped us. Dropped everyone, I imagine. But it's a lamentable way to treat old friends.'

Her feelings are hurt, Andrew thought; what does Claud mean to her? He yawned and stretched and pulled himself up from the low chaise longue.

'You're lovely to look at, Lotte, with or without mascara. Compared to you, Kate Patchin's a poor mousy little thing.'

Lotte stared at her husband's face, reflected in the dressing-table mirror. Suddenly, she felt a hundred years old.

The children were hardy and leapt in and out of the sea, but Kate found it too cold and instead lounged on the beach or in a deck chair on her balcony, slowly turning a delicious golden colour. Claud had chosen Santa Margherita. It was not the most discreet place he could have found for the spring holidays but Kate did not mind, although she pretended concern. Other people had also thought of the Ligurian coast in April, people they knew; they were well and truly marked as lovers by now. To be well and truly marked had been Kate's aim, but it did not seem to work: Claud felt no more compromised than he had during the discreet period. Apparently, now that he had Rotherham in his pocket, he considered himself invulnerable.

Claud was sweet to the boys, but took them for granted; took her for granted; took everything for granted. He spoke at length of the future, and there was no mention of her in it. Except for her role in his holidays. He had suggested that they (family life, not he and she, but they, his accepted, no doubt unexciting, little group) could go to Sweden in the summer; travel broadens the mind; so good for the children. She did not feel like a wife, she felt like the accompanying governess.

It had slowed down. It had become routine. Love-making was still as triumphant as ever, but not as copious. Claud would announce that they'd had a tiring day, and that was that. One more year, Kate thought, if as long as a year; then he'll find someone new, someone thrilling. And why not? He was in the splendid male position of having his cake and eating it too.

Kate rolled over on her back and shut her eyes against the sun. Claud was writing letters in his room; he had written no letters in Switzerland, he couldn't spare a minute away from her. John and Martin splashed and shouted.

And Francis, Francis for ever. For a while, she had been glad of Francis' return; Claud was jealous. Claud had forgotten that he could not decently leave Newhall at night, in term; he came to London at least once a week and studied her anxiously, to see whether Francis had been at her. He took her dancing, he took her to the theatre; he was in competition with Francis, who never took her anywhere, if Claud only knew. What a pleasurable winter it had been. But she had reassured Claud too successfully. A mistake. A lie too, of course; men were fantastic. How did Claud imagine she could stave Francis off? Francis had his small appetite, and his marital rights, and he wrote the cheques.

Francis was blind and dull and manageable. Francis was also deeply conventional and believed in private property. Francis hated to be laughed at; he was at his tiresome worst when intoning about dignity. If a man had few ideas, he clung even more tenaciously to them. Francis would not tolerate Claud; Francis would not be a worldly complaisant husband. Francis would throw her out and clamor for a divorce. But Francis would never know, and no one would tell him. Luckily. Or was it luckily?

At lunch, Claud announced that he was writing to Lotte Lingard; a letter from her had arrived in the morning post and it was so amusing that it compelled an immediate answer.

The children asked to be excused, having finished their sweet. Claud and Kate lingered over coffee, free to talk.

'You gave Lotte your address?'

'Yes. Why not? She doesn't know I'm not alone. I went to see her for a minute before we left. She's really the best company in London.'

Kate said nothing. She saw Lotte Lingard in her mind—tall, fair, crisp, mocking, at home in her beautiful house, at home in the world; that hateful object, an attractive older woman, how old, forty-eight, fifty, older than Claud; an ageing woman who lured younger men because she carried some shine from that unknown lost world of before the war.

'It seems that Andrew's finished his book on the Sumerian Kings. I bet it'll make a stir, too; Andrew's quite brilliant. You know he had the Banwel Chair of Ancient History at Oxford when he was only thirty-seven? Lotte says Andrew goes about like a man exiled from his country, and all his friends dead. She says she can't stand the gloom and every time she suggests a lovely new subject to Andrew, he looks at her as if he were going to be sick. So she's decided that what Andrew needs is a swing round the Middle East, to cheer him up and give him some ideas. They're going to start at Rome. I suggested stopping here on the way, to see me.'

'But you can't let her!'

'No,' Claud said, and he seemed surprised and puzzled. 'No I can't, can I?'

If he dared, Kate thought, in fury, he'd ask me to take the children off somewhere and hide, so he could chat with his adored Lotte for a few days.

'Lotte's got everything,' Kate said in unguarded bitterness. 'Her own money, and Andrew's as well. She's perfectly free. Andrew's so polite and detached. She probably has a string of lovers.'

'Not that I've heard of. Obviously she wouldn't tell me, or anyone. But I've known Lotte for years and haven't seen any signs. I doubt very much whether Lotte would go in for that sort of thing.'

Damn him, Kate thought, oh no, Lotte wouldn't stoop to that sort of thing. He is just as sickeningly conventional as Francis at heart; two kinds of women. He despises me now that he's got me.

'Lotte has all the admirers she needs,' Claud went on. 'She's such a treat to talk to. And she's a glorious traveling companion. I went to Jugoslavia with her one summer; I've never laughed so much. Besides, Andrew's a charming man; they're devoted to each other.'

I'll get up and leave, Kate told herself. All he's saying is that I bore him and am no better than a tart.

'There's that girl again,' Claud said, brightening. 'She always wears white. I saw her on the beach yesterday in a white bathing suit.'

An Italian girl, or perhaps she was French, had come into the dining-room; she could not have been more than twenty-five, with smooth black hair and brown glistening skin, and clearly she had nothing on under the white dress, cheap copy of Brigitte Bardot, her body rolling like a boat on a choppy sea. This was the real blow, the real warning; Claud looked at other women, and with what eyes. He wanted to eat that girl; unfaithful in thought if not more, missing Lotte Lingard, leching after strange Italians.

'Let's take a nap,' Kate suggested, in a small choked voice.

'You have a lie-down, darling. I'll finish my letters. We might walk after tea.'

This last summer term at Newhall was like the memory of itself, golden and peaceful, veiled in nostalgic tenderness. He liked everyone, boys and masters, he saw their oddities and found them endearing. Every day was a last day, and appreciated as endings are. In his seven years at Newhall, his work had never gone so easily nor could he remember any summer when the school looked so handsome, when the weather stayed blazing clear. He enjoyed the comfortable sorrow of leaving, and the comfortable excitement of foreseeing an even richer life ahead.

Also he felt much better since he had stopped going to London every week. The winter term now seemed a delirium of haste and effort; those fearful dark drives to and from town, and anxieties that he could hardly understand, they appeared so unnecessary. Kate was adorable as always. The fact remained that one grew accustomed to women. Delectable and essential as women were, one needed something else, something more. One did tire of that inevitable you-and-me conversation, the basis of all love affairs. Except for rare eccentrics, like Lotte Lingard, one could not talk to women, a lack which always made itself obvious after the first fine fever had worn off. And in any case he would see Kate in the summer, a month in Sweden with the children; most agreeable and quite enough. For the other three weeks of the holidays he had invited himself to the Lingards' in Oxfordshire; how amazing that he had forgotten and forgone the pleasure of that entrancing house for a whole year. The Lingards were returning from their swing round Andrew's historical haunts and would be full of the gossip he loved best, gossip of the distant past and the ancient dead.

On the whole, he preferred this soothing phase of a love affair. Desperation did not become a man of his age. He welcomed the prospect of passion sinking into happy habit. With luck, he might have formed an attachment that would last. He could imagine himself grey-haired and serenely linked to a charming lady of a certain age, his mistress of fifteen years' standing, their relationship accepted by the world and sanctified by time.

The sun shone. The Newhall eleven was doing beautifully and Dr Saunders' rose garden had never before produced such dazzling blooms.

Lotte said, 'Well, thank heaven, Claud is over his madness. I am so relieved. Nothing will happen now. I was terribly worried about him. I saw him making a mess of his life.'

'Why?'

'Why what?'

'How do you know he's over his madness?'

'He wants to spend nearly half his hols with us. A man doesn't take that much time away from his beloved if he's in a state of slathering lust.'

'Poor Kate.'

'Nonsense.'

'You never liked Kate, did you?'

'I don't trust soft helpless women. Women aren't really soft and helpless inside, ever. They can't be; they wouldn't survive. The velvety stuff is fraudulent—it reminds me of those flowers that eat insects.'

'You're a hard woman, Lotte.'

'In a long life, Andrew darling, I have observed that men would always rather be lied to. Not being lied to they consider hard. If it would amuse you, I could try being soft and helpless. I know how it's done.'

'God forbid.'

'Anyhow, I am relieved about Claud.'

'Why do you care so much?'

'It's a habit. I always care about old friends. Come on, darling, the donkeys have been waiting for an hour. Goodness, I'll be glad when we're through with Turkey. The country's all right but the citizenry gives me the shivers.'

Kate had read the note ten times. She knew this was the turning point. Either she fought now, or she was lost. She understood everything Claud had not said: I still find your body attractive but not overwhelmingly so, and I have always cared about talk which you do not adequately provide; now we will settle into a nice friendly affair, at my convenience. In fact his note simply stated that a month in Sweden would be ideal, and fine for the boys, but more was rather a strain in hotels and he had promised the Lingards ... he suggested that they leave for Sweden on 28 July and he would plan to be back in Oxfordshire on 28 August.

For a time, they would drift pleasantly on. Then, one day, somewhere, Claud would see a girl, a woman, and he would leave her evasively, and plunge again into the sort of passion she knew him capable of. And she would stay with Francis and she was not getting younger and she wanted Claud and she wanted the life Claud was going to lead. She needed him, she had fixed her hope on him.

It was now or never, and it was a fearful risk. It might end in disaster. Or it might end where she meant it to end, in the Kensington Registry Office. Her hands sweated; she loathed taking chances. But who wouldn't loathe taking a life-or-death chance?

Come, come, mustn't exaggerate; nervous women are deplorable. It would work exactly as she foresaw; Francis, red-faced and furious, roaring into her room with a letter in his hands demanding an explanation. She would tell him, sadly, that she could not deny it, she had wanted to explain long before but found no way, she was desperately sorry, people were not in control of their fates. She was helpless against love. Francis would stamp and shout. She would probably cry. It would last a long time, and presently he would be calm if bitter; and they would make arrangements for the divorce. Brighton and a prostitute, she thought, that was the usual gentlemanly way to handle these matters.

Kate rented the typewriter and bought the paper and envelopes at a stationery shop far from her neighborhood, typed the letter slowly, and posted it to Francis from a pillar-box in the Strand. She thought how useful detective stories were; anyone could learn the techniques of crime. Then she took to her bed, being ill with fear.

Claud had been extremely short with the bowler-hatted chap who would not state his business. He said that he did not receive visitors except by appointment, and kindly be quick about whatever it was. The chap stared at him with tapioca eyes and asked his name, which enraged Claud; obviously the brute knew his name, or why be there?

'I'm Mr Roylands, of course.'

'Mr Claud Roylands?'

'Naturally.' Great temptation to kick the fellow, a type who positively asked to be kicked.

The man shoved a long legal-looking envelope in his hands, displayed masses of bad teeth in a smile, and departed.

Claud had now read the contents of the envelope. He locked his study door and fell into an armchair. Suddenly he leaned over and hung his head between his knees. He'd felt he was about to faint.

It can't be true, Claud told himself, it can't be true. I'm dreaming this, it couldn't happen to me.

In a little while, when he dared, perhaps after a swig of brandy, he would have to read that vile paper again.

He did and it said the same thing. It said that Francis Michael Patchin was suing his wife, Katherine Trent Patchin, for divorce on the grounds of adultery and naming Claud Roylands as co-respondent.

This happened to other people. One read their embarrassing stories in the *Express*. One did not know them; one imagined them as wildly silly and careless and certainly common. Occasionally a clergyman was caught; one supposed the poor oaf to be so inexperienced that he would get caught; one also knew he'd had it. Clergymen, like schoolmasters and judges, must be virtuous; at least, their names could never appear scandalously in the press.

I'll fight it, Claud thought, but this was futile bluster and he knew it. Francis Patchin might be a bore but he was a businessman and a successful one, not an imbecile, not a baby. He would never have started such a suit unless he had proof. Proof, good God, there was proof everywhere.

If only Lotte and Andrew were back, he could talk to them; they'd tell him what to do. What could they tell him? What could anyone tell him? There was no way out of this.

Unless Kate could persuade Francis to drop the case? Was that possible? Could you change your mind in law? Probably; the state wasn't involved; adultery was not a criminal offence.

He asked the operator for Kate's number. Kate's voice, simply saying 'Hello,' sounded out of control. He arranged to meet her tonight at Charles Street and rang off quickly.

Later in the day Mitchell said to Backer, 'What's happened to the Head? He looks frightfully ill. I went to discuss the arrangements in chapel for Speech Day and he seemed deaf, or feverish. He kept saying, "Yes, yes." Most peculiar.'

Backer thought perhaps the Head was suffering from a hangover. Lucky man. Free. Could do what he liked. Drink all night if he wanted to. Had the money for it, and no wife to spy and nag.

'Probably he's got a lot on his mind,' Backer said.

'The cad! The swine! He put a detective on me, that's what he must have done.' Kate had been in floods of tears; now she was striding around the Charles Street sitting-room, like a red-eyed crazed kitten. She was repeating herself. She was terrified. 'Not a word! Not a word! He moved his clothes when I was out; he went to his club; he didn't say anything. Then that horrible creature came and gave me an envelope. The children! Imagine what it will be like for them! He didn't think of anything except his own damned vanity. And revenging himself. I am the children's mother, after all.'

'It is quite disastrous for me, too,' Claud observed.

'Oh, darling, forgive me! Of course it is. Wicked! Cruel! But it's so different for a man.'

'How?' Claud asked coldly.

'Well, it doesn't really matter what a man does. I mean, people don't mind.'

'I can quite see that no one minds what a stockbroker does, for instance. They mind very much about schoolmasters, I assure you.'

'But it isn't your fault.'

'Oh, Kate.' He gave it up. She understood nothing. He could only try to save them now, though she did not realize what was at stake.

'It seems to me that our one chance is for you to persuade Francis to drop the suit. It will be frightful for us, naturally; we would have to stop seeing each other. We couldn't take any more risks with Francis, now that we know what he's like. After a time, when it's all quieted down, you could reason with him and try to arrange a sensible divorce or a legal separation. But now we must avoid this ghastly scandal, which will ruin us all. You'll have to make Francis believe that you lost your head for a bit over me, and regret it, and want to go on with him. There's no other way out that I can see.'

Kate was not pretending panic; she had not realized, until she saw it in that fatal legal language, what she had done. She had not imagined that it would look as ugly and naked as it did, nor how dangerous it could be. I only wanted to make sure of Claud, she thought, not this. This was Francis' fault. And more terrifying even than the hideous legal menace was Claud's voice and what he was saying. He had not rushed to take her in his arms; he had not comforted her and implored her to be calm, scandal lasted a mere day in the papers, no one would remember, besides millions of people were divorced; and what difference would this miserable incident make in their lives, when she was safely Mrs Claud Roylands?

Kate burst into tears again, racked genuine sobs.

Claud, beside himself with nerves and fear, did take her in his arms and try to quiet her. He had thought Kate more intelligent than this. She was blindly concerned with her own name, with the disgrace for the children; she seemed not to notice what it meant to him. The children would survive all right; they would not even know about this disgusting divorce until they were older; Kate might have to send them to boarding school in Switzerland for a bit, that was all. As for Kate herself, a touch of scandal made a woman more fascinating. He was the real loser, the unique victim; he was the only one who faced catastrophe.

'I tried,' Kate said. 'I thought of that at once. I called Francis at his office. He said he would not see me now or ever in his life, except once more, in court. You've no idea. He hates me. He said that if I called him again he would tell his secretary not to put me through. He said he would return any letters unopened. He said he was going to teach us both to make a fool of an honest man. You don't know. It made my blood run cold.'

This had the truthful ring of the funeral bell. Yes. That was how Francis would feel and how he would behave. There was no escape. Nothing to do now except wait for the dreadful day; the horror of hearing their lives described before a judge (bored? contemptuous?) in open court, of being stared at, photographed coming out to the street, or did that only happen to film stars and peers? But the headmaster of Newhall was quite a tasty bit, as good as a sinning clergyman probably.

Claud knew what he had to do, now; not for Kate, not for the children, but for the rules of the game. It might mitigate the offence in the eyes of future Boards of Governors. In any case, it was the inevitable gesture.

'Of course, Kate,' Claud said, 'when this is over, we'll get married.'

'Darling!' Kate burrowed against his chest and wept with relief. Not the happiest proposal, surely, but it would all be finished soon, and then they would marry and forget this awful beginning, and Claud would love her again, and they'd have the wonderful life she had dreamed of. Claud had been born and educated to be a gentleman. He kissed his future wife.

It would be wiser to write to the Rotherham governing body at once, before there was any publicity. If he could write an inspired letter, neither admitting nor denying, but somehow deprecating the whole mess, somehow reducing its importance, they just might, just barely might decide to overlook a divorce. After all, times have changed. Claud spent three nights making draft after draft of the letter. At last he thought he had the right tone; he offered his resignation in the most correct manner but implied the doubt that men of the world would accept a resignation for such insignificant reasons. Then he tried not to hope too hard, knowing that there was scarcely any hope at all.

The Board of Governors, by the hand of their chairman, replied immediately; their letter was neither censorious nor indignant, but it did point out that the traditions of Rotherham precluded etc. On the whole, Claud decided, they were nice not to mention the trouble he'd given them, for where would they find a qualified, unsmirched headmaster, at this late date?

The Newhall Board of Governors had scrambled round on short notice and dug up a man to replace Claud; between themselves they thought that Roylands was something of an opportunist, as well as damned inconsiderate, and Claud knew this. He was in no position to ask to remain; besides, what would they do with Lockwood whom they had already engaged? However, he could inform them that, owing to certain circumstances, he was at liberty; he could hint. This letter was answered too, with exemplary speed, and the answer was far more devastating than Claud had foreseen. The Board of Governors said that, in view of the unfortunate personal difficulties of Mr Roylands, it would perhaps be better if Mr Roylands left Newhall before Speech Day and before his name was mentioned in the newspapers. His presence would be rather awkward in the chapel, at Speech Day, as Mr Roylands of course remembered the very firm opinions of the Right Reverend R. W. W. Prebble, who was the preacher. Any excuse Mr Roylands saw fit to give for his early departure would be acceptable; in the interval Mr Richard Mitchell, Senior Housemaster, could carry on the headmaster's duties which at the end of the summer term were largely ceremonial and social.

. . .

'Oh my poor Claud,' Lotte said. She was all but wringing her hands. 'How perfectly frightful. You'll come to us at once, of course; we're going to the country next week. But that's not the answer, is it? I must consult Andrew. He's amazingly practical about anything connected with teaching.'

'If you would, Lotte.'

'But of course. Whatever we can do. I couldn't feel more terribly about this. Still, you will have Kate, darling, and there's a lot to be said for marriage once you get used to it. You do love her; the future isn't coal-black. And I always thought Rotherham was the stuffiest school in England.'

Claud tried to smile; Lotte found the smile heartbreaking. But when they were married, he might fall in love with Kate; men were remarkable beasts; ownership cheered them up; they were much more apt to be devoted after the wedding ceremony than before. Still what a fool Claud had been; why oh why sleep with a married woman when London was full of spirited ladies who were either already divorced or too sharp to tie themselves down? Sex, Lotte thought, it's about on a par with cancer.

'How is Kate?' Lotte found it difficult to get the words out. She had taken against the Patchins, man and wife. Inconceivable that a woman could live with a man for years and not know what sort of man he was; therefore Kate, whom she had never thought brilliant, was a criminal moron; one did not commit adultery if one had a husband who would behave like Francis Patchin. As for Francis, she would never have him in the house again. He seemed more like a police spy than a normal human being; imagine actually naming who your wife went to bed with, it passed belief.

'She's terribly cut up, poor little thing. She blames herself; I do my best to comfort her. She's far more distressed than I am about Rotherham. From the moment this started, I knew I'd lost Rotherham and you have to accept facts. But Kate keeps talking about it, and about Cambridge, saying how horrible it is, everything gone, all her fault, what are we to do? I'm afraid she'll make herself ill. It will be a blessing when the whole wretched business is over and we can get married and settle quietly to something.'

Claud was looking at her drawing-room as if it were the last time he'd ever see it. Does he imagine he won't be asked anywhere, Lotte wondered; does he see himself stoned in the streets? Poor Claud.

'Have a drink, darling, do mix us both whoppers. I swear to you that when this is over, it won't be so bad. Honestly. I know scores of people who've had the most uproarious divorces. Think of Helena Partridge, good heavens; as I remember she was divorced because of a Negro boxer. And Peter Graham was divorced for being a pansy in the park. I mean to say, it doesn't matter a bit, anywhere except in schools.' 'But I still have to earn my daily bread, Lotte. And Kate's too, now. And I am a schoolmaster.' 'I'll talk to Andrew. He'll think of something.'

'What's up?' Backer said to Mitchell. 'I just saw the Head. Leaving. Without saying good-bye to anyone. Leaving, just like that. He told me his mother was ill. I didn't know he had a mother.'

'No.'

'What is it, Mitchell? Who's going to carry on?'

'I am assuming the headmaster's duties until the end of term.'

'You know something.'

'Well, yes, actually I do. But I am not in a position to speak.'

'Trouble?'

'Yes. Oh, yes indeed.'

There was a pause, while Mitchell smoked and looked creamy with satisfaction. Reluctantly, wretchedly, Backer asked, 'A woman?'

'I can't say more. You'll learn everything soon enough.'

'Oh hell,' Backer said. 'Oh *hell*.'

'Andrew, do stop *chewing* your soup and say something helpful.'

'My dear girl, I cannot change the mores and prejudices of English schools, even to please you.'

'But what did they say?'

'They said, simply, that they had no vacancy. It might be true.'

'Can't you write to someone else?'

'Lotte, be sensible. That's three refusals. Even if I do the asking for Claud, it's no good for him to be offered round and turned down. I tell you, he won't get a post now, not anywhere. In time, when everyone's forgotten all this, perhaps in ten years, it may be possible. But for the moment, he simply hasn't a chance. Bullying me isn't going to improve matters.'

'What then? What then? It's too awful.'

'I know the Minister of Education in Ghana. He was a student of mine. Keen Egyptologist. I could write to him. I believe he's having a hellish time with the schools out there. I shouldn't think they minded about scandals, and they do need teachers. Personally I deplore the idea of spoiling the lives of those healthy happy black people with education.'

'Ghana? Oh, Andrew. What's Ghana like?'
'Hot, I should imagine.'

Since Katherine Trent Patchin and Claud Roylands were not contesting the divorce suit brought by Francis Michael Patchin, because they could not, they were not required to appear in court. They were represented by lawyers and the judge was very brisk, being unimpressed by Mr Patchin who seemed a vindictive man and inconsistent as well. Mrs Patchin could scarcely be the Whore of Babylon if Mr Patchin was quite willing to leave his children with her except at those times, during their vacations, when he chose to see them. Three lines in *The Times* announced the divorce; the *Express* gave the affair a paragraph on the justifiable grounds that adulterous headmasters were unusual news.

The wedding took place at the local Registry Office and was outstandingly gloomy. Kate clung to Claud's arm, looking pale and ill and scarcely able to stand. Claud looked grave and heroic. Wilted flowers, in ugly baskets, remained from some of the previous conveyor-belt ceremonies; the official, in hair oil and striped trousers, handed Claud the ring on the green receipt for the licence fee. Claud and Kate were going to the Lingards' in Oxfordshire for a week's honeymoon, while Francis had a farewell visit with the children.

Lotte and Andrew, the witnesses to the depressing ceremony, waved the newly married couple off, saying that they'd see them at the boat in ten days. Then the Lingards went to walk in Kensington Gardens, silent with melancholy, until Lotte remarked that it was really much easier to stay married to the same person. Andrew pressed her hand. She observed also that churches were much nicer, weren't they, and although vicars had every known sort of accent they never spoke genteel cockney and somehow the marriage vows coming out in that voice made one feel quite sick. Andrew urged her not to fret; it was all right; Kate adored Claud and personally he thought it exciting to go to Ghana, a whole new world; he wished he had done something dashing like that when he was a young man.

He was troubled by a brief conversation he had had with Kate. Kate had urged him to keep on trying to find a school in England for Claud, she had suggested various schools which were out of the question, not that any school was obtainable now. She said that nowadays no one went on and on about divorces, they were routine, she was sure Andrew would manage to get them home within a year. Andrew produced soothing sounds since there was nothing he could say, and pitied Claud. After all, you spent a startlingly small amount of time making love during any given twenty-four hours; but a quite amazing amount of time was spent seeing your wife, listening to her, talking to her, a wife was nearly always around. And a wife who could not get the basic facts of life straight would be a severe trial.

Andrew did not mention this to Lotte who was upset enough.

There was a nagging small rain. The ship looked shabby and smelled of damp. One could imagine what the food would be like. Time did not move. Claud had opened a bottle of champagne and they drank it in the uncomfortable cabin and tried to talk. At last they heard the welcome and long-awaited order for visitors to go ashore. From the pier Lotte and Andrew watched the ship slowly pushing through the molasses water.

'Lotte, they can't see you any more. Stop waving. Lotte, you're crying. For heaven's sake.'

'Shipped to Devil's Island. Or felons to Australia.'

'Lotte! Here, take my handkerchief. Thank God it's all over. If this had gone on another week, I think you'd have had a nervous collapse.'

'People are bloody. That's what they are. Claud had tons of friends. And Kate has been feeding people at her house for years. Not a soul to see them off. No letters. No telegrams. No flowers. People are pigs. They're bored with anyone who's in trouble.'

'There was a telegram from a man named Backer. A master at Newhall. Claud showed it to me. He seemed terribly pleased. Lotte, don't start crying again. Come on, we'll miss the train.'

'The children are so *little*.'

'Now, darling, do look on the bright side. Kate was very lucky to get them; by rights, Francis could have kept them if he'd wanted to, and then she'd have been miserable. And it's a good thing they're little. They'll find it all a lark and they'll get used to Ghana that much more easily.'

'I think Claud's being wonderful. Looking after Kate and the children, being so sweet to them. Not caring about himself at all.'

'Kate still seems rather dazed. But I must admit she's most appealing with that pale bewildered look.'

'I wouldn't think the world well lost for Kate. But then, I'm not a man.'

Andrew handed the letter back to his wife.

'You're sitting on the *New Statesman*, Andrew.'

'Sorry.' He got up from the littered bed and fished out the crumpled magazine.

'Lotte, do you ever pay the bills or do they simply get lost in this mess?'

'Certainly I pay them when I have time. It's a good letter, isn't it?'

'I'm revising my opinion of Claud.'

'How?'

'I've always liked him, in a way. Still, I can't say I thought much of him. Charming fellow, but too ambitious by half.'

'Weren't you ever ambitious, Andrew?'

'I don't think so. Not much. But perhaps only because I didn't need to be. You're right, it's not fair to criticize Claud for ambition.'

'He longed for a Cambridge college. He dreamed of it. He never wanted anything else.'

'Yes. Well, that's why I'm revising my opinion. I think he's behaving splendidly. He'd always work, but he seems really to be putting his back into it. It's quite admirable to write so cheerfully; not false enthusiasm or disguised self-pity, either. And he couldn't be nicer about Kate and the children. You'd imagine he'd planned it this way and got his heart's desire. Somebody else's children, after all, and a rather obligatory marriage. I'm beginning to like Claud a lot.'

'I wish I knew what Kate thought. But she never was a real friend of mine. There's no reason for her to write.'

'Uxorious,' Lotte said, 'positively uxorious. Too comic. Here, Andrew, read it.'

'He writes a lot, doesn't he?'

'Well, I suppose it's too soon for him to have picked up any intimate chums among those nice black people.'

Andrew read the letter, slowly smiling.

In a reciting voice, Lotte began: 'Talented Kate has made the house perfect. It sounds heavenly, doesn't it, Andrew; something between Somerset Maugham and those Southern mansions in *Gone with the Wind*. Angelic Kate is charming to the Ghanaian ladies. What do you think? The School Board or the Mothers' Union? I imagine a lot of very stout black ladies, in bright tight shiny dresses, balancing teacups. Oh, I wish I could see it. Clever Kate helps me with my book. The Siege book? I'm so glad he's writing again. And the children are splendid and dark brown, almost native colour, and loving their new school. Really, isn't it all too marvelous?'

'He does say that Kate suffers from the climate.'

'I know. Isn't it too drearily English to complain of sun?'

'I have a letter too.'

'You are mean, Andrew. I show you everything.'

'I didn't think you'd be interested. It's a business letter. I can't quite understand Claud's position but he seems to be rising like a rocket. Apparently he's planning all the history studies now. He wants my help on working up a basic course in Ancient History. I don't know anything about secondary-school teaching, but I'll find someone who does. Perhaps Claud will be the Chancellor of their University College one day. Unless it's too big a handicap being white.'

'Astonishing. Wonderful. The inscrutable ways of Providence.'

'It looks like that.'

'Darling, let's smash all precedents and go out to lunch. That new Chinese restaurant in Kensington High Street. I want to celebrate. I feel so happy about Claud.'

'Andrew!'

'Lotte dear, I'm working. I thought it was a law that I'm not to be interrupted in the afternoon.'

'This is *so* important. Please leave those wretched Assyrians for a minute. I've seen Kate.'

'Sit down, Lotte.'

'I'm not off my head. I tell you, I've seen Kate.'

'Kate's in Ghana.'

'She is not; she's in Harrod's.'

'Oh.'

'She wasn't a bit pleased to run into me, either. She made a huge speech about her health; the heat was killing her; her liver is seriously damaged, I don't know what else. There can't be a word of truth in it. She looks lovely, much better than she ever did here. Sunburned and fresh, not at all liverish. Then she went on and on about Ghana, horror stories. Finally I managed to get a word in and I asked after Claud. She called him "poor Claud". She expects he'll be back on home leave in about a year. She's left Claud. I know it.'

'Oh, no.'

'She brought the children with her too. Doesn't that prove it? If she was only coming home to see doctors, she wouldn't drag the children along.'

'Bad.'

'We were standing in the bank part. You know, where all the old ladies rest from shopping; where you meet people. I saw a good-looking man, about forty, making those sort of signs to Kate. Evidently she'd staved him off while she was talking to me.'

'Only a year. It does seem very hard.'

'It's abominable. Abominable.'

'Don't cry, Lotte.'

'I'd like to kill her.'

'But Claud's doing so well, Lotte. Even if she has bolted, he'll manage. It must be marvelous work. All new; he's practically inventing it. A man can live on work.'

'I think of his college in Cambridge.'

'Are you receiving callers?'

'Come in, love. Isn't it a beautiful morning? We must leave for the country this week. I can't bear to waste such weather in London.'

'I have bad news, Lotte.'

'No.'

'A letter from Nii Jawso Obuasi.'

'*Who?*'

'My ex-student. The Minister of Education in Ghana.'

'Oh.'

'It's very nice. It couldn't be nicer. He writes more as a former undergraduate than as a member of the Cabinet. He speaks of Claud with admiration and affection. They are all so grateful to Claud for his fine work, etc. He turns to me because I recommended Claud in the first place, and he knows I'm an old friend of Claud's. He wants my advice. The plain fact, Lotte, is that Claud's taken to drink.'

'Oh, *no.*'

'Yes. Too much disappointment. More than he could handle, I imagine.'

'We must help, Andrew. What can we do? Write? Warn him? We could fly out to see him.'

'We'll do anything you like, Lotte. But I doubt if it will be much use. We can't change his life for him.'

And I envied him, Andrew thought, and I regretted our safety and I defined contentment as boredom. Lord forgive me; I'm only a foolish man of fifty-seven and I haven't learned enough. I imagined Lotte had been his mistress whereas Lotte's just old-fashioned; she takes friendship seriously.

He walked over to the bed and lifted his wife's hand and kissed it. He gave her his handkerchief.

In a muffled and despairing voice, Lotte said, 'There must be something to do. It's too unfair. No justice, no justice. I can't bear it.'

'We're not really in charge, Lotte darling. We're not in charge of anything much.'

He patted her shoulder and admired and pitied her. So laudable to grapple tirelessly with life, attempting to force it to behave for the best;

and so idiotic. History was the sure refuge; everything had already happened; one could not break one's heart with the effort to impose a shape or perform a rescue. And yet, who was to say that Claud, drinking himself into the gutter in Ghana, had lost his future? Claud might become a much better man than he would have been, swollen with achieved ambitions—and he might learn more. How would the black people treat him when they no longer felt any respect for him, or any awe? Perhaps the colour barrier would be melted by gin, perhaps they would act naturally with Claud and Claud would have in return the gift of real understanding. And was it such a tragedy to lose Kate; was it ever a tragedy to lose the woman who could be lost?

'It may not be as bad as you think, Lotte.'

'I have to help him. I will help him.'

Lotte blew her nose and looked grim. He knew she was turning over schemes in her mind for the rehabilitation of Claud. Dear Lotte, who would not learn. Poor Claud, who was learning. And what about him, Andrew, the lucky man always safely above the battle? The telephone rang. Andrew sighed.

Lotte answered, listened, frowned and said, 'No, Ernestine, she'll never find anything for that rent in the central parts of London. I think Swiss Cottage or Wimbledon would be the best bet. What's her telephone number? How old is Mrs Brady? Seventy-two? It's shameful the way people don't make proper provision for their servants in their wills. Yes, I'll see what I can do.'

Business as usual, Andrew thought, and smiled at his wife's intent face and closed the door quietly behind him. He was already late for the British Museum Reading Room.

THE CLEVER ONE

He was a clever one. He understood this world and this life. The notion of good or bad luck was for idlers, fools; he knew the exact price of success. He had the useful conceit of believing that he could learn everything, and for his purposes he was right. He never tired and he never wasted time. He was a cold man, and untroubled by the consequences: loneliness was his natural condition. He was not handsome and had no wish to be, since only dreamers wish to change what cannot be changed. He made the best of a short squarish body, an alert but unmemorable face, a general lack of color, by keeping himself neat, clean, taut. The effect was satisfactory, probably more so than positive good looks, as men resent beauty in other men, and women do not require it.

It took him a long time to realize that being liked was almost essential. He discovered this finally in America but could not quite get the knack of it.

His paternal grandmother chanced to be born a gentile and brought up an earnest Lutheran. She was an orphan servant girl with nothing to offer a man except her health and devotion, and she was fortunate to marry a reliable young Jew and the security of his small grocery shop. The young Jew had been attracted by her fair hair and her placid outlook. The fair hair, diluted, reached her grandson as a mouse tone; the Lutheran features were forceful enough to transmit to him a mediocre Nordic nose.

At the age of ten, after thorough reasoning, he became an agnostic. At the age of twelve he was starrily converted to the Roman Catholic church because of an excellent Jesuit school in which he planned to study. His parents attended synagogue only on the occasions of Rosh Hashana and Yom Kippur, and did not bother their son in the arrangement of his life. He was grateful to his father for having progressed from the grocery shop to a medium-sized wholesale grocery business; the boy was well educated owing to this advance. Since he had not chosen his parents, he felt no obligation to the race he inherited. The whole tedious question of tribal prejudice, Jews being as disagreeable about gentiles as the other way round, bored him. He was alone, joined to no camp, tied by no passions; he did not wish to be hampered. He decided to leave Vienna, his native city, while he was a student at the University. Austria was powerless and poor; furthermore, in Vienna, he was limited by the social position of a medium-sized wholesale grocer. Class was another boring handicap which he had no intention of accepting. He studied law in Paris, adopted French citizenship, selected a fashionable lawyer for his master, met one after the other according to plan the valuable people, and saw ahead an assured future.

He married, adroitly, the daughter of a Jewish family so old and so aristocratic that it had ceased to be anything but itself: a name which opened all doors. This family had been rich for too many generations. Finally the stock disintegrated into pure charm and civilization, with a resultant loss of practical sense. By now the family, though still living in its ancient house, amongst admirable furniture and fine pictures, was relatively short of cash. The girl's parents welcomed the sober, able, well-bred young lawyer; they were worried about Angèle who was quite an expense to them, and flighty. The girl herself was sick of being a chaperoned *jeune fille*, and of wearing dismal *jeune fille* clothes. Marriage brought Angèle acquisitions, but perhaps she most enjoyed her new visiting cards which announced to the world that she was at last a full-fledged woman called Madame Théodore Ascher.

Madame Ascher's parents gave her lovely bits and pieces to furnish her home; she devised an imposing *mise en scène* for her husband, a flat on the Avenue Bosquet which looked richer than they were. Théodore and Angèle had been living there for three years, with all prospects more and more golden and a child on the way, when Hitler was elected Reichskanzler in 1933. Théodore was twenty-nine years old, Angèle twenty-two. Théodore was a close student of politics; he seldom made mistakes because he probed the records of the men in power, in all countries, as if he were an historian and a private detective, and based his conclusions on the lowest possible estimate of human character and behavior. In 1934 Théodore moved his family, wife and six-month-old son, Gabriel—Madame Ascher's choice of name—to London. Hitler had now become Reichsfuehrer, dictator of Germany. In the event of war, the English alone could be counted on to defend themselves. Their history of racial tolerance was laudable—for though Théodore did not consider himself a Jew, he was aware that the Nazis would hold no similar view. And besides there was the Channel.

At thirty, Théodore Ascher anglicized his name by dropping the c, and having noted that the English went in for nicknames and abbreviations, he became Theo, which seemed more suitable to this environment. He started as a law student all over again, joined Gray's Inn, and prepared himself to be an English barrister in wig and gown. He learned English law and the English language in two years, while Angèle pined for Paris, for friends, for fun.

Angèle was small and very pretty in a saucer-eyed way that would not last, light-hearted, addicted to daydreams and the hope of surprises. She had told herself she was in love with Théodore, as she had to imagine this in order to marry him. But after the first tremendous pleasure of no longer being a virgin, and the satisfaction of managing her own house, and painting her eyelids blue, and buying clothes freed from her mother's veto, she found that Théodore was not lovable. He did not have time for love and saw no purpose in it.

Théodore was a blameless husband and as generous with money as he could afford to be. He left Angèle in full charge of her domain but she did not feel liberated, she felt abandoned; he would not listen to her conversation about cooks and curtains. He made love often and well and apparently forgot what he had been doing the minute it was finished. And nothing was allowed to interfere with his work, or the schedule of daily living he had planned for himself. Angèle tried to quarrel with him about friends. No one could quarrel with him. He did not enjoy people for themselves; if he took the trouble and endured the expense of entertaining, he insisted that the effort be worthwhile. Angèle wanted to laugh; she wanted to gossip; she wanted to share in many lives. Théodore said that she could ask her friends, within reason, to lunch and to tea, if he was not at home. When she made a scene, he read the paper.

Life with Théodore in Paris had been rigid enough, but Angèle could escape to her parents' house, to pre-marriage friends, and her younger sister was still there to giggle and shop with, discreetly flirting as they went. London, however, was too much. Angèle spoke correct governess-taught English and to her the English were a nation of male and female governesses. The sky depressed her; she thought the city ugly. And Théodore now did nothing except work, eat sparingly, and make love in his effective but brisk way.

Just after Théodore was called to the bar, Angèle said she ought really to take Gabriel home on a visit to the grandparents. She needed a vast amount of luggage for this brief outing but as she explained, and as Théodore knew, she was dependent on clothes. From Paris, three weeks later, she wrote to say that she was never coming back; marriage had been a disappointment; she was sure Théodore would not miss her;

she would keep Gabriel, please; and Théodore should divorce her at his convenience.

Théodore's pride was hurt but not for long. He reasoned that pride, largely indistinguishable from vanity, was a luxury he could dispense with. Though fond of Angèle and used to her, he saw that she would not fit in to English life. She was a nice silly girl and he condoned her desertion without pain after a month. As for Gabriel, of course she could keep the child; what would he do with a baby; he was not interested in children anyhow. He arranged, gallantly, to have Angèle divorce him in Paris, where it was a quicker and cheaper operation.

Angèle had originally suggested, then implored, then nagged Théodore to smoke or drink or both. She assumed that a little vice would soften him, and modify the dreaded regularity of his timetable. He observed that these indulgences were deleterious to health, and costly; his nerves were steady without tobacco and he needed no alcohol to stimulate him. From this total sobriety Angèle, and everyone else, wrongly concluded that Théodore was a man of almost repulsive virtue. In fact, Théodore was a sensualist, although one who always controlled his tastes and pleasures in favour of his career. He had never been faithful to Angèle.

In Paris and then in London he kept a small flat, rented under another name, which was as essential to him as his home and his office. He experimented in women, much as if he were trying out different patent medicines. For ideal comfort, he wanted a steady mistress, he begrudged the hours spent on repeated pursuits. He was charmed by English women; he enjoyed their toughness, their interest in men's talk; and though he hardly grasped them, he admired the crisp sound of English jokes. He also liked the contrast between the coolness of the woman in public and the violence of the woman in bed.

Shortly after Angèle's desertion he met a married woman of thirty-five who owned a smart decorating shop. Théodore chose her at once for the rôle of permanent mistress. She taught him how to dress, for he now understood that Austrian and French men's clothing were equally lamentable. She taught him all she knew of furniture, pictures, china, glass, silver, fabrics, colours, and their proper combinations. She taught him how to drink enough for sociability, and how to be knowledgeable about drink for others. She taught him the importance of food. She taught him to recognize jokes and when to smile and when to laugh at them, even if he could not make them himself; indeed, she warned Théodore against trying, because his efforts were of the kind that stunned others to silence. A ready listener, she pointed out, was rare and always appreciated. If he laughed at bad jokes, no harm was done; the bad-joke-maker would be gratified. She improved his accent and enlarged his vocabulary.

The lady, Mrs Mayne, was more than pleased with the arrangement. She was a passionate, adequately educated, matter-of-fact woman and Theo's temperament matched her own. If she had ordered him to measure she could scarcely have expected a better lover. She liked her husband and meant to stay with him; their married life was agreeable. Billy Mayne was an amusing creature too, and they had their friends in common. But she was not a designer of interiors for nothing; it was far more fun to decorate a man than a house. She was also amazed to meet a man without vanity. Theo released her from the perpetual feminine tedium of coddling masculine sensibilities. He practically made notes of her rebukes; he never sulked; he learned and learned. And pleasured her mightily but did not vaunt his special triumph. She knew that his discretion was as great as her own. Theo would not embarrass her at any time, in any way. Finally, she taught this model lover how to choose attractive gifts for a lady, which he did gladly, not parting with a penny more than he could spare.

Théodore was perfectly happy in London. He had no friends but did not notice their absence. He imagined that the coldness he inspired was the well-known English reserve, and approved of it. He revelled in the manners of his associates and acquaintances; the fact that the English never raised their voices proved that they never had to. Life obeyed them, they were certain of themselves, always in control. Scrupulously honest in his work, Théodore had been contemptuous of the taint of connivance and disingenuousness which cheapened legal circles in Paris. The impeccable honor of English judges, the polite fair play of the courts, all the intellectual elegance which rich, powerful and proud men can afford, thrilled him. He knew that he was in the right place.

Theo Asher became a successful barrister with unnatural speed. The Silks, the King's Counsel, had discovered in him a man who worked as no native-born legal dog's-body could be expected to do. Asher prepared their briefs; they shone; but Asher was also well paid, establishing his name and learning more law. Théodore decided he would take silk himself after the minimum ten-year period as a junior barrister. He was so enamored of England that he planned to make a sufficient fortune, as a lawyer, then aspire to the less remunerative glory of the bench. He was not sure that a naturalized subject of the King could achieve the judge's red robe, but he would find out in due course, and meanwhile not set his mind dangerously on a hope, but only beguile himself with a possible picture of the future. There was plenty of time.

Théodore's confidence in the English had lulled his vigilance. He felt that he could safely leave the conduct of public affairs to the House of Commons. He cultivated his garden until Mr Chamberlain returned from Munich, waving his umbrella, and announced defeat to the cheering nation which hailed him as a hero and savior. For the first time in his life, Théodore came near to despair. He realized that he had been in love with England, and he suffered as a man bitterly deceived. He said nothing of this. Caution returned with his misery. Love had lured him into acting the fool; but he was not incurably idiotic like the English, who went on behaving as if 'peace in our time' was a solid promise. Théodore had been ready to fight alongside the English, they for England and he for English law, but since they believed this monstrous fraud with his umbrella, he could not afford to wait until they woke up to the true facts. It might well be too late, by then. English phlegm seemed positively suicidal.

At this point, groping his way out of loss and pain, emotions unknown to him, Théodore remembered Mr Harold Rudge. As the junior to the famous KC, Mr Desmond Locke, Théodore had worked on a complicated tax case which involved a great American automobile manufacturer, who also owned factories in England. Mr Harold Rudge, a Wall Street lawyer, arrived in London to help and advise his English colleague and protect his American client. Mr Rudge gave off such a smell of wealth that he stank in the nostrils of Mr Desmond Locke, who was rich enough by English standards. Mr Rudge, on his side, disliked England, and most especially disliked English KCs with their airy pose of amateurism. He did not consider the law to be a gentlemen's club; he regarded it as Big Business for very shrewd men. Mr Locke and Mr Rudge, in their different manners, bored each other to fury. But Mr Rudge thought the young barrister, Mr Locke's slave, who did all the work and had all the brain, an excellent chap; Asher was sensible and professional, serious and accurate, and always appreciative of Mr Rudge's little jokes. Of course Asher was not English, which explained it. A shame to waste such gifts and such energy in this piffling country. Before he returned to New York, Mr Rudge suggested that Théodore should come to them in America, where the future lay; Mr Rudge would see to it that his path was made easy. Théodore had been grateful, charmed, and forgot Mr Rudge. Now he remembered, and wrote.

He said nothing of Munich or his disillusion with the English; he simply said that he thought the future was wider and grander for a young man in America. Mr Rudge answered his letter.

Before leaving for his new country, Théodore sent a long warning to his former parents-in-law. He explained, in detail, the menace that hung over them; he begged them to take all the money they had and could raise, at once, to Switzerland; and there to reside. He assured them that war was coming and they would not be spared. He spoke of Gabriel, their grandson, who could be well educated in Switzerland, and also survive. He used every tone and every argument he could think of, to convince Angèle's parents, who were easy-going, and not notably intelligent, of the necessity of this move. He could do nothing more.

Several years earlier, he had written a similar letter to his own parents in Vienna, imploring them to flee with their two unmarried daughters to the same safe country for the same sound reasons. Not being as wise as Théodore, they could not believe his ugly predictions. It was some time since he had heard from Vienna, and Théodore thought of his family as dead. He preferred to think of them as dead perhaps a decade ago, dead peacefully. If they were in fact not already dead, they soon would be and he did not wish to imagine the conditions of their dying. He could not help those who would not help themselves; at least he had tried.

Théodore calculated that America would either stay out of the coming war, or enter it and win it; he did not see America as being overrun. But whereas he had been ready to fight for English law, he was not enthusiastic about fighting for America, an inconceivable, not especially sympathetic country. As for fighting Hitler, the many politicians and other public figures who had admired Hitler, aided him or appeased him had a more commanding obligation than he. Since they, surely, would do nothing at all dangerous, Théodore did not feel impelled to a greater heroism than theirs. Considering his possible future as an unwilling soldier, he went to his doctor for a physical check-up. He said that he was thirty-four years old and wondered whether his body was still good enough to serve England.

The doctor, touched by the patriotism of a foreigner, but also deploring this gloomy continental outlook (for had not Mr Chamberlain said?) examined Théodore carefully. He told Théodore with regret that his feet were a bit flat—which no one would have guessed in the splendid Lobb shoes that Mrs Mayne had advised. The spectacles Théodore used for reading law texts also debarred him from the service. He could neither march nor see to shoot, according to army specifications. The doctor and Théodore parted in an atmosphere of manly sadness and Théodore was relieved to know that, once in America, he would not at any later date be sent out of it, wearing khaki.

With Mr Rudge's cordial invitation in his pocket, Théodore booked a first-class passage to New York on the *Mauretania*, four months after Mr Chamberlain promised peace. Théodore sold his possessions and the lease of his two flats, and bade a grateful farewell to Mrs Mayne, who knew his real reason for going and thought him absurdly alarmist but in the end, she felt, Central Europeans did have a curious streak of hysteria.

The *Mauretania* was a pleasure to Théodore, who had never traveled in this style before and could hardly feel like a lone, lorn immigrant in the midst of so much gilt and brocade and obsequious service. He had used his four preparatory months to read at length about America, but could make no clear picture from the books and was on the whole alarmed by what he read. He dismissed the United States from his mind and concentrated on life aboard. His attention was drawn at once to Isabella Trapani, whose table in the dining saloon and whose deck chair were near his own. Not every man would have noticed Isabella, few men had. She was twenty-seven years old and unmarried, with her mother at her side, and her habitual expression was a dark threatening frown. She wore superb jewels and costly clothes which lacked all chic; and several times Théodore had surprised her looking at people with hope in her eyes, belying the frown. He decided that this young woman scowled from anxiety and disappointment, and since he was quite right he soon made friends with her.

Isabella, he discovered, though certainly old enough to be a woman was a child. She was a beautifully trained child, having at her command four languages including English, all the suitable sports, the expensive education which fosters the appreciation of expensive things, gracious manners. She also hungered to give love and to be loved but so far had only dared to use her emotions on her family—father and mother and a younger brother. She was surrounded by the various suffocating fears that imprison the rich, and are inevitably inflicted on their children; from the infantile fear of robbers to the mature fear of fortune hunters, Isabella had been taught them all. Being sensitive, she shed the meanest of these suspicions but was left with her paralyzing shyness. Since her adored mother was prettier than she, she felt herself hideous, and the shyness grew and the frown deepened and aside from the more obvious profiteers, no man approached.

Théodore set about easing Isabella's shyness. He told her that she was *jolie-laide*, which is much better than being plain *laide*, as she imagined; he happened to be speaking the truth. Having learned a great deal of feminine lore, first glumly from observing Angèle, and then with care at Mrs Mayne's orders, he could discuss with Isabella the way she wore her hair, made up her face, and dressed. He encouraged her, he guided her, and by the end of the six-day voyage, she did indeed look a different person. The frown was now intermittent, and Théodore always chided her for it; her hair was newly arranged, her make-up brighter and more dashing, and by some alchemy of cinching in waists and lowering necklines, accomplished by her maid, Isabella's clothes started to look smart and even alluring. She could not wait to reach New York, and shop from scratch.

Théodore considered Signora Trapani a fool; imagine handling the girl so that she was headed, but for Théodore, straight into spinsterhood. On the other hand, Théodore felt nothing but respect for Signor Trapani. Isabella, trusting by nature, lonely, unaccustomed to sympathetic listeners, had told Theo their plans, the reasons for this journey. Signor Trapani, Théodore recognized, was a vigilant man like himself.

The Trapanis, Isabella confided, were Jewish by blood though in no other way; emancipated, rich, long established in Rome, they were indistinguishable in life and appearance from most other well-born Romans who are often endowed with bony antique noses and curling black hair. Then came Mussolini; then, gradually, and really due to that German brute Hitler, there began to be anti-Semitic talk. Signor Trapani was as much of a Fascist as the times required; and owing to his immense wealth and influential acquaintances, he felt safe but continued to keep his eyes open. Keeping his eyes very wide open during these difficult years, he had slowly and silently moved most of his fortune to the United States and to Switzerland. He settled his son, who was chiefly dedicated to fast cars and race horses, in a minor position in a Chicago brokerage firm. This also provided an excuse for Signor Trapani to ship valuable pictures to America; the mother and daughter were traveling with more of them in the hold, as well as some rare furniture. In the last year, safety rapidly vanishing, Signor Trapani had given out that he was old and tired, missed his son, thought the family should be together, the boy needed parental supervision. He put his huge palazzo on the market; after all, he explained to friends and associates, Isabella would soon be married, the boy was only interested in his new career, the Roman house was too big for him and his wife alone. He was now winding up his business, a private bank. In three months Signor Trapani would join his family. He knew exactly what was going to happen to Europe and to Jews, even to the richest of them, with the best Fascist connections. He thought of buying an estate in California, where the son would be content with cars and horses while Isabella, doomed in her father's eyes to a single life, could at least enjoy the sunshine.

Théodore noted and approved; he would get on easily with Signor Trapani. He also began to have a feeling almost like tenderness for Isabella. Having been so long a pupil himself, he found it exhilarating to be a teacher, and to have as pupil a woman in whose eyes he could do no wrong. Angèle had fallen into complaints and tempers and mockery, as the years passed; Mrs Mayne had simply bossed him and wasted no strength on consideration. Isabella worshipped. It was a comfortable change. Her money did not diminish her appeal. And in America, as Théodore had read, a wife was regarded as a social necessity. It was not respectable to be without one. Promising to call Isabella at the Plaza Hotel, Théodore decided that as soon as he understood America sufficiently, and knew the shape of his work, he would give some thought to the matter of Isabella and matrimony.

The only fantasy Théodore allowed himself was a certain interior freedom with words. At night, he circled in thought around his life, looking at it, describing and evaluating it. Intoxicated by New York, he let the words run loose and large in his mind. He had loved England as a man loves a lady; now, he thought exultantly, he was in love with America as a man is in love with a whore. Daily, the lady of England drifted farther away, became smaller, older and grayer: charming of course, perhaps somewhat pitiful too. Meantime here was this red-blooded fierce beckoning whore, America, and he was made for her; but no sane man forgets that a whore is a whore. He takes all he can get and gives as little as possible.

Further: he was a leopard, born and raised in a zoo, who had suddenly been returned to his native jungle and knew it was home. The jungle teemed with other leopards; he saw them everywhere. He liked that. He had company. These men understood the system as he did: vigilance and work.

Théodore realized that he must immediately lose his English intonation; he could see how it enraged Americans. He practised morning, noon and night to develop the universal sloppiness of pronunciation. He could not change his voice, which was the average educated non-nasal European voice, and he could not forget grammar, his having been founded on Latin and being a part of him, inseparable as his hair. Americans would permit a foreigner to speak correct English in a pleasant voice, as long as he did not have an English accent. Théodore sounded, within two months, much like an Ivy League American, but not offensively so.

He had settled in a good unpretentious hotel, in the East Sixties, while deciding on his permanent home. He chose a small apartment on Park Avenue; the address was a trifle further up the street than the best addresses; still it was Park Avenue, and again it would be unwise to seem rich too quickly. Americans preferred foreigners to make their money in America, and thus declare themselves beneficiaries of the American way of life. He suggested to Isabella that she should furnish this apartment; taste was part of her training. Théodore could have done it himself, after Mrs Mayne, but did not care to waste the time. Isabella was ecstatic to have a job, and fascinated to consider costs. It made everything more like a game, one took pride in doing so handsomely on a prudent budget.

At first unconsciously, soon consciously, Isabella arranged the flat as her future home. She also enroled in a cookery class, on the sly. She intended to marry Théodore and she was elated at the prospect of being helpmate to a struggling young lawyer. The day the apartment was finished, Isabella gave Theo a house-warming party in it, just the two of them. The dubious meal was her own handiwork. She proposed to Théodore, who accepted her, subject to her father's approval.

Isabella said that she did not mind whether her family agreed or not; Theo was all she loved. Théodore protested against her coldness of heart. Surely she would not want to hurt those who so cherished her and for whom she felt such deep affection. They would never be happy together, under a parental curse. No, no, wait until Signor Trapani arrives, said Théodore, and then we will talk. He was certain of the favorable outcome and he was not in a hurry to marry, for he had a lot on his plate already.

It turned out, as twice before, that Théodore would have to become a law student again. He wondered ironically if any other man had sat as often in as many classrooms. But he congratulated himself on not needing a new language as well; and though American law was different it was not entirely dissimilar to what he had learned in England. He calculated that he could pass his New York State Bar examinations in a year. Mr Rudge had promised Theo a job in his office at a munificent salary.

Mr Rudge's firm was called Galway, Hickham, Rudge and Myrtle, and before involving himself too much with Mr Rudge, Théodore made enquiries. It appeared that Mr Rudge's firm was one of the three largest and richest on Wall Street, entirely satisfactory to Théodore. What he neglected to learn, because the question did not arise, was that Galway, Hickham, Rudge and Myrtle had never employed a Jew. It was a point of pride in this city which pullulated with expert Jewish lawyers; Galway, Hickham, Rudge and Myrtle clients avoided all dealings with what they regarded as a tricky inimical race. Mr Rudge did not dream that Theo Asher, conservatively and expensively tailored, reserved, courteous to a fault, unexcitable and in every respect properly unremarkable, was a Jew.

Mr Rudge admired the way Theo buckled down to his studies, without a word of complaint though it was hard for an accomplished lawyer to start over and memorize the school nonsense which good lawyers had long since forgotten. He approved Theo's choice of residence, and his staid new black car; he applauded Theo for ridding himself of that la-di-da English accent; he observed that Theo was correctly adapting himself to American manners. Théodore was entranced by the American leopards' camouflage: the easy back-slapping, handshaking, patting; the extraordinarily informal speech; the recommended golf; the ritual though rationed occasions for complaining of last night's snootful, or skinful—never the truth, in Théodore's case, but a popular lie, proof of goodfellowship, even leopards should relax. He learned and learned, with no teacher this time, using his eyes and ears.

Signor Trapani arrived in New York and took to Théodore on sight. Since his son was little better than a Roman princeling, he was delighted to add a man of his own kind to the family. He considered the law as good a profession as banking, closely allied; he would have been offended by a son-in-law in trade. He also enquired about Galway, Hickham, Rudge and Myrtle, and was pleased by the answers. He told his wife, still so pretty, always so stupid, that no one who worked as Theo did was a fortune hunter. Isabella was lucky, considering her age and how sexless and dowdy she had been until she met Theo, to snare this young man. They could marry at any time. Signor Trapani had a private conference with Theo, which assured Theo of an unimagined financial security. Théodore was dignified; he thanked the older man, but said that he could support Isabella decently as soon as he was allowed to practise law. Signor Trapani agreed but saw no cause for the young couple to deprive themselves in their earliest, happiest years. A lavish settlement was made.

Angèle and Théodore had been married in the *mairie* of the Sixth Arrondissement, godlessly. Isabella and Theo were married in the Church of St Vincent Ferrer. They had both been baptized in that faith which especially values its converts. Isabella was radiant, beneath her veil, and Theo, in a grey stock and cutaway, was visibly but composedly grateful for his blessings.

Mr Rudge, from his aisle seat, studied the bride and her father as they passed, and later paid absorbed attention to Signora Trapani and son Carlo. From their looks, one might almost think they were Jewish, which was a pity. Of course Italians did resemble Jews, but the girl's appearance would not be helpful to Theo in New York. Mr Rudge had visited Italy once and thought it even worse than England. Ideally, he would never treat with anyone except Americans, inside America. Theo had spoken, in a vague gentlemanly way, of his new in-laws; Mr Rudge understood that the Trapanis were an old, distinguished and very rich family.

Mrs Rudge, who cried at weddings, was enraptured by the light that flashed from the bride's eyes when the groom slipped the ring on her finger. Taking his cue from Mrs Rudge, Mr Rudge decided that Isabella was a nice, loving girl, despite her unfortunate nose; but Mr Rudge could see that a European like Theo, coming to America for the first time, might feel a little lost and lonely and perhaps more comfortable with a European wife, being used to that type of thing. One could hardly urge one's future employee to wait for marriage until he found a fine American girl.

The honeymoon, lasting a week, proceeded as Théodore had foreseen. The bride was frightened, given to sudden tears, then grateful, dazzled, adoring. The groom was kind, patient, dominant, successful. Théodore was happy to return to New York and his studies.

Isabella settled dotingly into her new life. She was satisfied if she could sit at night in the room where Théodore bowed over his books. She pretended to sew or knit or read, but all she really did was steal glances at Theo, not enough to upset him or disturb his concentration, but enough to feed the happiness within her. Signora Trapani felt that her daughter lived like a peasant. On the rare occasions when Theo thought it useful to ask someone to dinner, a cook was hired; otherwise Isabella, gleaming with pride, combated the kitchen stove. A charwoman appeared for a few hours each morning, but Isabella liked to tie her hair up in a scarf and potter with silver polish and the vacuum cleaner.

Signor Trapani, who was as sharp as Théodore and as prompt to learn, understood why Theo did not touch the marriage settlement. Mr Rudge would have suspected too much unearned increment, a man should make his own way. Mr Rudge had not pampered his daughter and son-in-law. In order to keep Signora Trapani quiet, Signor Trapani took her and Carlo, who was tired of office hours and no longer useful as a decoy, to Santa Barbara, where he began to build a Palladian house. Théodore was relieved to see them go. It was his desire to become one hundred per cent American and stay like that for ever. The senior Trapanis and Carlo were hopelessly European, a damaging background but not harmful if out of sight.

In September 1939, Poland was invaded and war was declared, as Théodore had expected. Isabella wept, but learning joyfully at almost the same time that she was pregnant, she could not keep her mind on the world's sorrow. Théodore wrote once more to Angèle's family in Paris. They answered haughtily that they had confidence in the Maginot

Line and General Gamelin, and reminded Théodore that he was in no position to dictate to them.

In May 1940, Isabella presented Theo with a daughter, named Louise after her mother. At the same time the British Army withdrew from the Continent at Dunkirk. Théodore, having passed his Bar examinations without difficulty, and by now at work in Mr Rudge's office, followed the distant war as if it were a giant bullfight, certain that in the end the bull would be killed. Isabella cooed over her baby. Mr Rudge fumed at the American laws which prevented Theo from becoming a United States citizen for seven long probationary years. Théodore, aimed in the right direction, was content to be an increasingly well-paid back-room boy in Mr Rudge's firm, a consultant, an associate. He knew he would make himself indispensable. Meantime, if you had a big safe country to sit in, technicalities like citizenship were not necessary.

Pearl Harbor came as a sickening shock to America, but not to Théodore. What shocked him was the incompetence of the American military command. Why on earth, while their diplomats prodded and threatened, did they collect their fleet and their planes in one vulnerable area? He was also shaken by the American panic, a feature of local life he had had no previous chance to observe. It worried him, but he assured himself that a country so large, so rich and so remote could afford a certain amount of unseemly foolishness.

Two days after Pearl Harbor, Théodore informed Mr Rudge that he was going to enlist. It was not essential to be a citizen in order to fight for the nation. Mr Rudge pressed Theo's hand. Théodore was promptly rejected because of his feet and eyes, and branded 4F for the duration. Mr Rudge, although aflame with patriotism and moral indignation against the treacherous yellow men, realized that big war meant big business and there would be a heavy demand for lawyers. He was thankful, secretly, that poor Theo had not made the grade; he would keep Theo's valuable assistance when most of the other young lawyers in the office had marched off to desk jobs at 90 Church Street, and Pensacola, and San Diego. He did not fail to note that Theo had been the first one in the firm to offer his services to the flag.

Théodore urged Isabella to join the Red Cross and the ladies who nobly made surgical dressings. She devoted much time to the Red Cross, as Théodore had judged that they could safely move up in the world and they now lived in eight rooms, instead of in three, on the best stretch of Park Avenue, and employed a refugee English nanny for Louise, a bad-tempered cook, and disdainful maid. Isabella was not as happy with this grandeur but would not have dreamed of opposing her personal preferences to Theo's career. She packed gauze squares and chatted as well as she could, having no talent for chat, and retreated whenever possible into loving daydreams about Theo and Louise. She also fought, in herself, an unvoiced jealousy; she was ashamed of her nature, and blamed herself for base suspicions.

No one, except the sirens who visited him there, knew of Théodore's delightfully appointed apartment on East 38th Street. For a year, occupied with his studies and the excitement of learning American life, Théodore had been faithful to Isabella, whom he valued but who inevitably bored him, as slaves are apt to do. He was not taken by American women as he had been by English women, although he found them instructive. American women were fantastically garrulous about their own concerns and demanded every attention from a man, including frequent declarations of love. Still, they were beautiful and he needed variety. He realized that permanence is not a quality of American life; his mistresses, if they lasted at all, lasted about six months, when a mutual fatigue usually set in. The termination was sometimes recriminatory, which Théodore detested, but by straining his patience he could often manage serene endings with a piece of jewellery thrown in.

The war stayed, as Théodore had imagined it would, far from America, and while an American tendency to dramatize American sacrifices and hardships irritated Théodore, it did not incommode him. He knew when he was well off, even if the Americans did not. In 1943, a letter shattered this order and security. It was sent from London and bore the insignia of the Free French. Théodore was astonished that the Free French should know his name and address, but was dazed when he read what they had to say. It appeared that Madame Angèle Mondore—by French usage, Angèle's correct nomenclature after divorce—had been tortured to death in a Gestapo cellar in Paris, without betraying a single name, a single fact to the enemy. She was posthumously awarded the Cross of Lorraine and the George Cross; she was a heroine of France whose work in the Resistance had been fearless and efficient. The King recognized her services in helping shot-down British airmen to escape. France and England honored and mourned her. Monsieur Asher would want to know about his son, which information Madame Mondore had passed on to her chiefs in London. At the time she undertook her dangerous work Madame Mondore sent her child, Gabriel, to the south of France in the care of an old family servant, one Thérèse Bouchet; this woman would pass the boy off as her grandson. Madame Bouchet was indisputably gentile and of humble origin; it was presumed that the boy was still living in her village, near Aix-en-Provence, as an Aryan peasant. Madame Mondore's parents and her sister had been rounded up, in one of the earlier Jewish mass deportations. Nothing was known of them and regrettably they must be considered extinct, together with millions of their co-religionnaires.

Théodore read this letter several times, forming the words with his lips; he was unable to absorb their meaning. Angèle? Angèle the frivolous and vain; brainless, one would really say, interested in nothing except clothes and fun. Angèle, a heroine of France, dead by torture? Angèle ready and able to die for an idea, an ideal? It was impossible to imagine or understand. As for his son, Théodore did not see what could be done, the Germans occupied all of France. After the war, he would try to find the boy. Angèle had been, he thought, remarkably clever about the child, if remarkably reckless about herself. He was sorry for the old ones, her parents, and for that silly *jeune fille*, her sister, but they had been warned in time and had rejected wisdom; foolish people could not expect to survive in this world.

The letter from London, which was too alien to take root in Théodore's imagination, affected Isabella like a wound and a revelation. It not only took root, it took charge of her mind. Never having been taught, never having seen living examples of the moral sense, she suddenly learned from a dead woman, whom she had accepted, on Théodore's estimate, as a shallow nonentity. Theo was now proved wrong and wrong in some profound way. If Angèle had within her such power, such courage and such faithfulness, she must always have had it; only Theo could neither see it nor foster it.

Even now, when she was dead, Theo did not realize what Angèle had been and what she had done. But Isabella felt that Angèle had died for her; she was heavily burdened with this death and this debt. Extending her thought slowly, alone, in silence, Isabella became unbearably involved in all the dying, for ever indebted, and disgusted with herself, with Theo and with their snug selfish life. Isabella vowed that she would find Angèle's son and she would protect this child always, as the only repayment she could make to Angèle. For the unknown others, Isabella did not know what to do, but she would no longer ignore them. If she could not help, she could at least try in spirit to share their sufferings.

Hitherto Isabella had regarded reading as an excuse to sit with Theo, or as an occupation for one sick in bed. Now she devoured the terrible literature of oppression that grew with and because of Hitler, year by year more detailed and appalling. She fed her new conscience on records of imprisonment, heroism, despair, faith and death. She followed with passion the fresh reports, in newspapers and magazines, of those lately escaped from Nazi rule. Théodore was impatient of this morbid desire to understand what they had so wisely avoided. Isabella continued to read. She built up, at last, a personality separate from Theo and increasingly hostile to him.

One night, during the dark winter of 1944 when the Germans had unaccountably struck back, and even distant America felt a chill of fear, Isabella spoke to Théodore as she never had before. She was frowning, in the old nearly forgotten manner. She suggested that Theo should do something besides make money. They had far too much money already. There must be work of a more humane kind, work which gave, which helped. Théodore, incensed by Isabella's criticism, pointed out coldly that he assisted and supported the law, which helped everyone; without law there was no civilization and no safety. The Nazis were surely proof enough of what happened to the world when law was lost. He could be doing no finer work.

Isabella still frowned but was unable to argue cogently. She recognized that she could not make Theo understand her or her disquiet, her sorrow, her guilt. In a different way, she came to agree with Angèle's verdict. Theo was not lovable. Isabella now needed to admire the moral man in order to love, and Theo, climbing the American ladder of success, was not admirable to her, he was only successful.

Isabella seemed surprisingly competent as well as insistent; Théodore was pleased by this unsuspected angle of her character. Using the Red Cross as if by right, and without any suggestion of shyness in her dealings, Isabella located Gabriel. Through an Army desk colonel, she managed to send food and clothing to the child, money to Madame Bouchet. Newly liberated France had no organized postal system, but Isabella wrote and received letters from Gabriel by commandeering another American officer for the purpose. Her love for this unseen, eleven-year-old boy grew; he sounded hardy, honest and generous. He knew of his mother's death. Isabella began to think of him as her son, and to dream.

Théodore might have guessed the shape of her dreams if he had bothered to notice what Isabella was reading now; a mixed bag, Thoreau and the New Testament, and unbound, closely printed documents from the Department of Agriculture, expounding the best means to keep and increase chickens and bees, the recommended care of cows. Isabella knew what she wanted to do after the war, and the war was dragging to its murderous close. On the other hand, of her own free will, she had made binding promises in the Church of St Vincent Ferrer, and she did not see how she could break them, and still be the sort of person she wanted to be, the sort of person who was fit for Gabriel and, as she hoped, a better example to Louise than she had been before.

Théodore, living beside this changed woman, was too busy to consider Isabella. He knew Isabella; she had her niche in his life and there he left her. The office claimed most of Théodore's attention. Mr Rudge, supported by a troop of rich loyal clients, had decided to leave the ancient firm and set up for himself. He had been go-getting for Galway, Hickham, Rudge and Myrtle long enough and would now devote his efforts to enriching a smaller group of partners. He invited Theo Asher to depart with him, saying that as soon as Theo became an American citizen, in a matter of months now, the new firm would be complete and the engraved letterhead would read: Rudge, Bascomb and Asher. Théodore had the greatest confidence in Mr Rudge's ability to attract clients, as Mr Rudge had the greatest confidence in Théodore's ability to find the useful legal answers. Théodore accepted the offer and the honor; even in his luxurious night-time imaginings, he had not aspired to rise so high in such a rush.

The victory over all foes, jack-booted and yellow-skinned, was celebrated with frenzy. Very soon, Isabella thought, she would be free to go towards the life she dreamed of, were it not for her binding promises. Theo had given her no cause to leave him; the promises did not allow for altered emotions, higher hopes, finer resolves: the promises said plainly that you had made your bed and must lie in it. Her depression was so strong and so apparent that Théodore suggested a psychiatrist; he had known few American women who did not use one; psychiatry seemed to be a general prophylactic in New York life. Isabella refused, and suffered, and was suddenly saved.

Théodore had lately acquired a new mistress, whose golden, long-legged beauty was as outstanding as her stupidity. He did not like stupid women, but many were available and he had little leisure to search for the desired creature who would have the body and the coloring as well as the mind to please him. The present incumbent, a model called Veronica, telephoned to his house to put off a rendezvous with Theo. She saw no danger in this; after all, men met women constantly for drinks in New York; she did not intend to declare over the telephone that she had lovely carnal relations with Theo. She had also understood from Theo that he and his wife were friends but no more, and led their own lives in mutual tolerance. Théodore found that this sort of cover-story was useful with American women, though he could not imagine why.

Isabella answered the telephone. Immediately upon hearing Veronica's voice, she operated with such cunning as she could scarcely credit, changed her accent and became a slow but responsible Italian maid who always wrote down messages for the master. Miss Veronica Hastings, she wrote, would be unable to meet Mr Asher today, being prevented by a business appointment, but would meet him at the same time tomorrow. Where must he go, Isabella asked, in her dim-witted accent. Don't bother, Miss Hastings said impatiently, he knows where.

Isabella, who would have died of grief three years earlier upon receiving such news and understanding its whole meaning, felt now nothing but a large, weary relief. Theo had broken the promises; she was absolved.

That night Théodore came home cross, since he had had no word from Miss Hastings, and found Isabella, calm, steely sure, and final. Miss Hastings, Isabella announced, could not be the first infidelity; obviously Theo kept a *garçonnière* and had an established *cinq à sept* pattern of life. She did not upbraid Theo, she simply stated that she was leaving him. Théodore, shaken by the suddenness of this attack, tried blandishments; he might as well have gone at granite with a toothpick. He was genuinely upset: one divorce was routine, two divorces might be regarded as scandalous by Rudge, Bascomb and Asher-to-be. Isabella said she had no desire to marry again, a legal separation would suit her unless Theo later changed his mind, as she predicted he would. In which case, the divorce would be forthcoming.

Angered by this fool of a woman, who made a fuss like a real American over adultery, Théodore asked her intentions about money. He hoped to alarm Isabella, knowing that she hated talking or thinking of money; she could afford a fastidiousness which was not possible to most of mankind. Isabella, without hesitation, said that she would take half of the marriage settlement, and certain pictures—presents from her father—which she specially cared for. This was so pleasant an outcome that Théodore could not complain. He had invested the dowry during the war; he had nearly trebled its original value. He would be left without a wife and a few pictures, but with a fortune. As for Louise, who was to be Isabella's total property, he saw the child seldom, usually on Sunday mornings when she interfered with his reading the papers; he thought her pretty, spoiled and a bore like all small children.

Isabella made one last condition. Gabriel was to be hers, too. She would adopt him legally. Théodore was amazed at this singular wish and finding it odd, therefore suspect, demurred. Isabella said, in that event, she would sue Theo for divorce on the grounds of repeated adultery; she did not think his partners would like it. Théodore weighed her threat against the pointlessness of clinging to a stranger who would be a nuisance to bring up, and agreed to all Isabella's terms. However, uncertain of the reaction of the US Bureau of Immigration and Naturalization to himself suddenly wifeless, Théodore demanded that Isabella wait for her freedom until January. She might overlook her own safety, he argued, but could not reject, for her children, the protection of a good passport. On the appointed day Theo and Isabella Asher stood side by side beneath an American flag and swore undying loyalty to their new country and eternal hostility to its foes. Théodore immediately became the third partner in his firm and set about drawing up the Asher separation papers, while Isabella dealt with the steamship company.

The senior Trapanis were dismayed to hear of Isabella's decision but she was thirty-four years old, rich in her own right, and there was no way to dissuade her. They had not felt at home in America, and now that the war was well over, they were returning to delicious Rome. Never bombed, except on the poor outskirts which did not count, and with the black market working at a high pitch of efficiency, Rome was what they yearned for; the Palladian villa in Santa Barbara was exile. Signor Trapani intended to buy back his old palazzo and spend his declining years in familiar pleasures.

But Isabella was not coming with them. She meant to take the two children to Calabria, where she would buy land and farm it. She wanted the children to grow up in a simple world, become—she hoped—plain honest people, attached to the reality of the seasons and to the satisfaction of working with their hands. She knew that Gabriel would love this and she counted on Gabriel to teach Louise.

Théodore, mulling it over, concluded that he had had peculiar wives: one of them apparently wished to be a martyr, the second was getting ready to be a saint. He did not ask himself troublesome questions about these mutinous women. Some women were more sensible than others; he happened to have fallen on women who were not sensible. Neurotics, he thought, having picked up many helpful words in New York.

Mr Rudge was paternally gentle. Théodore had given him to understand that Isabella was not happy in America; even though honored by American citizenship, she preferred Europe. He realized this would be the unforgivable sin in Mr Rudge's eyes. Mr Rudge did not actually say that he considered Theo better off without such an ungrateful wife, but that was what he thought. He urged Theo to get out more in the world; you never knew what valuable contacts you would make, even while only relaxing in New York. A man in Theo's position, partner in such a firm as theirs, should see and be seen; he should have a full social life.

To Mrs Rudge, Mr Rudge praised Theo's fortitude; Theo did not take to drink nor wear a mournful face as a lesser man might. With Theo, Mr Rudge said, the firm always came first. Mrs Rudge had certain reservations but did not voice them; she never contradicted Mr Rudge, having long ago discovered this effective method for getting her own way. She thought Theo a cold fish, and Isabella amply justified in leaving him. Mr Rudge was also partly a cold fish, under his genial manner; the rest of him was pure baby. Mrs Rudge, who often traveled alone, leaving Mr Rudge to a contented bachelor summer of golf and business friends in Connecticut, knew Italy and loved it. She envied Isabella's being able to walk away from a dull man and live in a sunny fascinating country.

Theo became that nearly extinct and highly desirable object, an extra man. He was in great demand, though he was not regarded as a trophy by any means, but accepted and used as a properly dressed and sufficiently conscientious guest. Théodore rapidly divided New York social life into its various categories. He decided that aside from a few hermetic circles—possibly the academic, the clerical, and the moribund old-family set—New York was a vast nomad camp, in which all roamed freely, depending on appearances and responsible for nothing else. Success of some kind was vital but success came and went, faces changed. Théodore realized how Isabella, with her shyness or detachment or formality or combination of these, had hampered him. He felt light and merry as a rich bachelor of forty-two, with his triumphant career like a rock to stand on, and the whole city to hunt in.

Théodore met Mrs Fairleigh at a large untidy publisher's cocktail party. Cocktail parties were recognized hunting grounds, and he attended them frequently, bellowing and elbowing with the rest, never even slightly drunk, and always alert. He saw a fashionably emaciated blonde woman, with high cheekbones and Paris clothes, dominating a circle of men who laughed loudly at her remarks and did not disguise the greed in their eyes. Théodore arranged an introduction quickly and, in the usual jovial American way, the lady was told not only his name but his standing. Asher of Rudge, Bascomb and Asher, his affable acquaintance said, youngest partner in the youngest, smartest firm on Wall Street; you want to treat him with respect, he'll probably end on the Supreme Court. It was not entirely surprising that Mrs Fairleigh consented to dine with Théodore, after the party.

Unerringly, Théodore took Mrs Fairleigh to the most expensive restaurant in New York where, equally unerringly, she knew the head waiter, that certain proof of social position. She ordered the most expensive dishes on the menu and toyed with them. One glance at her marvellous narrow American hips showed that she did not eat. Languidly, and as if she talked to amuse herself, too confident, too popular to trouble with her host's reactions, she told Théodore a little of her past.

She was a widow. Charles Fairleigh had gone down with his destroyer in the Battle of Leyte. She was new to New York, having come here from their plantation in South Carolina, after Charles's death, too sad then to stay on alone with her memories. She married when she was a mere child, eighteen and all innocence, and lived with Charles on his family's land, which he loved as people only love the place where their ancestors have been born. Vistas of magnolia and cotton, hereditary black servants, Greek pillars, thoroughbred horses were opened before Théodore's attentive eyes.

Her own family, originally from Virginia, had pioneered West; she was brought up on those endless acres in Texas. More vistas, wilder but grand, occasionally dotted with the spires of oil derricks, were displayed. Her marriage with Charles had been an idyll of bliss; she asked nothing more, not even to travel; she had scarcely felt the sorrow of having no children, so complete was their love. Théodore was made effectively jealous of Charles Fairleigh, a god in beauty, a faultless gentleman, an athlete, a scholar, a landowner who never needed to struggle for money and fame as New Yorkers were obliged to do. When she was twenty-eight, after ten years of this joy, Charles was killed. There were no Fairleighs left in the world and she was the last of the Mertons. Théodore, quickly doing mental arithmetic based on the Battle of Leyte, figured that Mrs Fairleigh, so elegant, so assured, so authentically American of the highest class, was now thirty years old.

Anne Fairleigh had been born Anna Wolski forty-one years before her dinner with Théodore, on the Polish West Side of Chicago. She was the fourth of eight children whose father, a Polish bricklayer, drank heavily from general disgust and whose Irish mother whined, prayed, and neglected her offspring because she was understandably defeated by life. Anna Wolski took her last entirely honest look at the world when she was sixteen; she saw nothing but squalor, failure and cruelty, and she decided to get out of this and stay out of it for ever. She disappeared, which troubled her parents very little, and hitch-hiked to San Francisco. Her equipment for the future was her appearance, not beauty but a certain style of bone, unyielding determination, quickness of mind and a thorough understanding of the average sensual man.

Her early years were as hard as they were unlovely. She did not seem to be progressing far from the horror of her family's home. She made many mistakes and suffered for them; she also learned from these mistakes but immediately erased the memory of the sources of her knowledge. She became a gifted mythomane, developing her version of her life as she went, and believing it, no matter how often the story changed. She achieved no real security until she was twenty-one, when she found a single protector. This man, a fairly well-to-do insurance salesman, set her up in a small furnished flat, and Anna Wolski, now known as Anne Johnson, saw the beginning of a pattern to life, the road—at present only a path—to success. San Francisco was not the place to stay; it had been a rigorous school from which she graduated to Los Angeles.

She moved slowly, with forethought, from city to city, always advancing her position, always altering her story. The quality of her protectors improved; their wealth also increased. Anne invested her wages on good instruction, and used her income for expensive clothes and a veneer of education. She was aiming at New York but did not intend to establish herself there prematurely. Her special talent lay in being able to plan and carry out her plans without ever telling herself or anyone else the truth. From the age of twenty-five, she had used the framework of widowhood; the war came as a boon, providing her with a dead hero as the mythical husband. By the time Anne Fairleigh reached New York she was financially sound, secure in her chosen personality, and fixed on her present name and her alleged background. Her past was too far away and too far down to endanger her. She eschewed Southerners, by instinct, without the inconvenience of giving herself a factual reason. Southerners were easy enough to avoid because of their accent.

Mrs Fairleigh, two stages earlier in her career, had made the useful discovery that rich, very important politicians were the best kind of protectors for her needs. Politicians were discreet if they wished to keep their jobs, which they all did. Voters did not approve of sexual scandals on the part of their elected representatives. The lower cheaper class of politician might go in for call girls; the breed Mrs Fairleigh cultivated wanted a permanent, charming, ready woman, a well-furnished apartment, good food and drink and a chance to indulge themselves, in talk and in bed, without the ever-present menace of publicity.

For the last two years, Mrs Fairleigh had been kept, in her handsome East River apartment, by a distinguished senator. He came to New York as often as he could but it was not too often for Mrs Fairleigh, and the allowance he paid was so sizeable that she could live in the manner she required and save money as well. Whenever the senator notified her of his next visit, Mrs Fairleigh informed her acquaintances and her telephone-answering service that she was leaving town—a week-end in the country, a short jaunt to Palm Beach, a beauty cure in Maine, or a flying trip home to South Carolina. Mrs Fairleigh and her senator had never been seen together in public, which was what they both wanted.

Mrs Fairleigh took a lover from time to time, for appearances and for pleasure, and prettily accepted, at the end of the brief affair, his heart's tribute in jewels or furs. These gentlemen were also discreet, but not so discreet as the senator. Mrs Fairleigh counted on this. It would not do for an unattached woman in New York to get the reputation of blameless virtue; she might be considered to have queer tastes or to be frigid. People vaguely knew that Anne Fairleigh, a natural woman with natural needs, tried on occasion to fall in love once more, but in vain; she was deeply inconsolable for her dead Charles, though not tiresome about it.

But Mrs Fairleigh was now forty-one, a fact—perhaps the only one—she did admit to herself. She had begun to consider the greater security of the alimony racket as practised with such noteworthy results by the legalized girls. She dreaded marriage and the prospect of the same man always around the house, but she realized that she might have to come to it.

Théodore escorted Mrs Fairleigh respectfully, at her wish, to the opera, the theatre, art galleries. At the opera Mrs Fairleigh bowed to old women with large busts and large diamonds, seated regally in the boxes. She told Theo their names, stately names; sometimes the old women returned the bow, sometimes ignored it. Anne, gently smiling, explained that the dear old lady was blind as a bat and too vain to use even lorgnettes. At the theatre Mrs Fairleigh chatted wittily in the foyer, during intermissions, with that flashing group whom Théodore knew from the gossip columns: café society, it was called. At the art galleries, exotic and, Théodore presumed, artistic people hung on her words, exclaiming at the divine rightness of her comments. Théodore had never felt himself to be glamorous and had not so regarded his women: Mrs Mayne, though a lady and highly intelligent, was a bit horsy-looking and did not move with this aplomb through the encompassing scene. Angèle and Isabella, well brought up and of good family, were mouse-like muted creatures compared to Anne. Théodore was filled with pride to be Mrs Fairleigh's escort, and with desire to possess such a prize. Having served his term as the man who held open doors, walked behind, paid, he decided that the time was ripe to lead Mrs Fairleigh, whom he coveted as he coveted America itself, to his 38th Street apartment. He arranged to meet her there for a drink and go on to dinner.

Mrs Fairleigh took one cool look at his establishment and remarked that it might almost have a neon sign over the door, saying: Love Nest. She let Théodore understand she was not used to this sort of thing and did not care for it. He had made a mistake, she implied, due to not being a native-born American; one did not ask a lady to this type of dwelling. Since she was there, she would have a glass of white wine; she trusted that at least he kept suitable wine in this unsuitable place, and then they would dine. The assumption was that the apartment, and Théodore's intentions in bringing her there, would not be mentioned again.

Théodore, who had never been obliged or inclined to court a woman, bowed to this new task with enthusiasm. He felt more and more American every day; the strong, successful man, helplessly dependent on the imperious whims of an American beauty. Mrs Fairleigh, shrewdly judging his character, made him work hard and gave no rewards. Meantime she enquired into his financial position and prospects, and decided Theo would do. He was a bore, but one could not expect too much in a husband. Testing her strength, she announced that she was unable to take a serious view of a man who indulged in the vulgarity of passing affairs, and the furtiveness of an extra flat. Théodore gave up 38th Street. Mrs Fairleigh smiled sweetly and soon had him in a state of sexual desperation. He proposed marriage; nothing else would procure Mrs Fairleigh, though he feared even that would not suffice. Mrs Fairleigh remarked that bigamy was a crime in the United States. Théodore, urgent and wild, began cabling Isabella for release. Presently he flew to Mexico, which seemed the most respectable of the quick divorce mills, and there hungered for Mrs Fairleigh's imagined body, and telephoned to her hourly in terror that she would change her mind.

The third Mrs Asher gave a smart reception at her East River flat, following the civil marriage, and moved to Theo's Park Avenue home. The wedding night was ample repayment for all torments and delays; Anne, when she thought it worthwhile, was an inspired courtesan. Théodore could find no name to give this bright, glowing, general sense of happiness he felt; gradually, and rather ruefully, he recognized that he was in love.

Anne had expected obedience but not Theo's boyish, even childish adoration. She used it ruthlessly. She told Theo that one simply could not live on Park Avenue, look at the sort of people who cluttered the street; and besides she was not accustomed to flats, she hated their horrid communal quality; she had only lived in that pitiful box on the East River because she was alone. They must have a proper house, and she had found just what she wanted on East 73rd Street, between Park and Lexington Avenue, an address that one need not be ashamed of. Théodore was dazzled; he had not realized that Park Avenue was common and he had certainly not considered Mrs Fairleigh's flat, with wide windows looking on the river, a pitiful box.

The new house was like nothing Théodore had known before. Angèle and Isabella, he now saw, had a limited, drab conception of how to live. Anne, his beautiful American Anne, went in for opulence, grandeur; she made a home fit for a genuine American millionaire. In this splendor, Anne became an indefatigable hostess.

Anne Asher's mythomania extended to others, when convenient, so that Théodore believed his house was filled with a throng of Texas oil kings, airplane magnates, gray eminences in politics, famous scientists, stars of the theater, the assorted brilliance of literature and art, and finally, most rarefied of all, the well-born idle rich. Theo thrilled to see Anne queening it over these gatherings. She was so elegant, so witty, so sure, and received homage as her due: his wife. The bills were stupendous but Théodore would not have dared mention this to Anne, knowing her scorn of the careful, the less than aristocratic.

He worked longer and harder, because he needed all the money he could get; it seemed that in America, unlike Europe, wives kept their own fortunes for themselves. He had considered himself abundantly wealthy with over a million dollars as his share of Isabella's swollen dowry. But, as Anne dipped her lovely hands deeply into it, this once massive capital appeared to him only a frail barrier against poverty. For himself, he did not mind but could not bear the thought that Anne might one day be deprived of the unlimited riches she was born to. He struggled to earn more money, while Anne spent it. The law, which had been his single love, was superseded by Anne; he saw the sad irony in being forced to devote his whole time to the office when at last he had learned the value of leisure, idle hours with his ravishing wife.

For a year, Théodore would have said he was the happiest man in New York. He had made two mistaken marriages but had finally found the woman beyond dreams, the passionate, miraculous lover, the sharp intelligence, and the unceasing glamor. Presently Mrs Asher concluded that a wife need not labor as strenuously as a non-wife in pleasing a man; she had never been attracted to Theo, he was not at all her type, her taste being for very tall fairish confident rather brutal men, and she began to withhold herself. There had to be some advantages to marriage, she reflected, besides a house and a certain position; one of them might be the comfort of sleeping alone, well smeared with face cream. Théodore suffered, pleaded, humiliated himself. When she considered it necessary, because Theo was a good provider and as such should be kept, Anne acceded to his demands and inflamed his ardor so that he continued to beg.

Mr Rudge thought that Theo was looking worn; but of course a man did have to amuse a brilliant woman like Anne Asher; he could not hope to sit peacefully at home with slippers and a glass of bourbon, after office hours, and go to bed early. Anne would want to be everywhere, see everything, know everyone; and Mr Rudge, who had received charming attention from Anne, did not blame Theo for burning the candle at both ends. Theo's work was always first-class; it was Theo who was becoming a bit seedy.

Anne employed on Mr Rudge alluring glances from under her lashes, listened to him with graceful concentration, took his arm confidingly, fussed and smiled; but she did not trouble much about Mrs Rudge. She knew the power of women; only some women, like Mrs Rudge, failed to use it and were therefore negligible factors in life. Mrs Rudge, blue-haired and benign, given to guide-book reminiscences of her European tours and accounts of the awful antics of her grandchildren, simply watched. She was amused to see Theo, the cold fish, so ridiculously taken in; Mr Rudge's submission to Anne did not matter. Mr Rudge was perfectly safe and perfectly innocent with women; she expected him to be asinine about Anne.

One evening Anne showed Théodore a small gold powder box from Cartier's; she was constantly showing him new and costly purchases, seeking and getting his praise for her bargains. Anne already had several precious powder boxes but Théodore did not remind her of this fact. The box in her hand was made of woven gold strips, so pretty and so practical, she said, for the country, or the morning; she disliked jewelled ones, except after six. Théodore, who only wanted to go to bed with his wife, dutifully admired her box; it might make her happy and therefore compliant.

The next night the Rudges dined with the Ashers, just the four of them, like family Mr Rudge said. Some time during the evening, Anne brought out her gold box, to dab powder on her nose, a much nicer nose than Isabella's, Mr Rudge reflected. Mrs Rudge, observing the box, said she had been tempted to get one herself when she saw them on the counter at Merkel's. Merkel's, Anne exclaimed, oh don't tell me they've already copied Cartier's; it is really too bad; Cartier's ought to protect one. Théodore, who happened to be looking at Mrs Rudge, saw—with amazement—the expression in her eyes, which was brief but clear mockery. He was furious at this unspoken insult to Anne; he decided Mrs Rudge was a jealous old woman, a cat, and he longed to avenge her silent slur on his darling.

Théodore suggested to Anne, while he was watching her undress for bed, a privilege he was sometimes allowed if allowed no further, that she should have her gold box valued for insurance. She had already done so. And what did the insurance people say? Anne stared at Theo and replied, off-handedly, that they valued it as Cartier's did, at four hundred dollars. Why did Theo ask? Well, Mrs Rudge had seemed to imagine it was a cheap thing from a department store and he would like to set her straight. Anne laughed at him; so absurd, noticing what Mrs Rudge thought, what possible difference did it make; did he think it would be better for them to go about with price tags on their clothing, and perhaps even scattered over the house? Théodore was ashamed, at once and as intended, of the coarseness of his reactions.

At Anne's large cocktail parties, the guests often failed to greet or thank their host or even meet him, in case Anne was too busy with her duties for introductions. Théodore was usually late, in any case, tied to his money-making; and Anne told him that it was unnecessary to speak to her when he arrived; the best thing he could do was to make himself useful. She hired waiters for these frequent, stunningly noisy events, but Théodore understood that in America a husband was a sort of extra, honored butler. To be useful meant to roam about and ask people if they had enough to drink. Sometimes the guests looked quite surprised to hear this question from a rather small, weary stranger; but it hardly matters who gives you more drink so long as you get it. Théodore told himself, at these affairs, that he was like the husband of the star on a successful opening night; all the men in the room envied him because he alone owned the lady, all the women envied the lady her beauty, her charm, and her array of admirers. He kept hoping that one day he would feel entirely American, as much at home in his own house as others were, as easy, bright and talkative as everyone else.

Mooning around the outskirts of one of these crowds, Théodore came on a couple standing, with half-full glasses, before Anne's fine blue-and-green, wind-wild Van Gogh. The man, Théodore noted, had floating chiffon hair which could not be dyed, surely, but glinted with gold. The lady was middle-aged and forcefully tweedy, an unusual combination in Anne's women guests, and the blond old-young man treated her with deference. Théodore, waiting for an opportunity to offer drink, dawdled beside them.

The man, in a curious, giggling, lisping voice, remarked to the lady, whom he called darling, that he knew she'd be too amused which was why he'd brought her. Isn't it killing, he enquired, indicating the picture with his glass, what did Anne think she was doing, hanging such a weird fake as if it were the real thing; either she was full of wit or full of brass, but do admit darling, it is a treat. The lady looked at the picture sourly, and in a careless way glanced at the jammed room. She observed that the owner of this place might have wit or brass, what she certainly did not have was taste. Come, come, said the man, chirruping like a bird and mewing like a cat, taste indeed, we cannot all be born on Beacon Hill, don't be so cruel. Taste, the lady asserted, could be learned by anyone who was not so bone-rotten with vulgarity as to be permanently blind. The man took this as a personal reflection, and pouted. The lady announced that she was going, she had had enough of this monkey house. She clumped off and the man, remaining alone, stamped his foot.

Théodore, horrified and angry but uncertain how to handle such a fantastic situation, approached the man. He stated that he was Theo Asher, and when this remark had no effect, he added that he was Anne's husband. Indifferently, the golden-haired one replied that this was no doubt very nice for him. Théodore was silenced for an instant; he recognized the correct, abrupt New York manner but he himself was clumsily incapable of keeping up with it. He then said, pleasantly, that he had noticed his guest admiring Anne's Van Gogh; her grandfather had bought it from the brother of the painter, soon after the painter's death, it was one of the best examples of the artist's style. The guest stared at Théodore with slowly brightening eyes; then he bleated out a high sudden laugh, patted Théodore's shoulder and walked away.

When the party was over and Anne was resting on a sofa with her feet up, Théodore described those two and said that he thought Anne should not ask them again, they were disagreeable and malicious. Anne did not enquire what gave Theo such an idea, but observed that there had been a hundred people in the house this evening; Theo was surely not naïve enough to imagine anyone had a hundred loving chums in New York? Really, he must try to understand New York and life in America better. The man with the glinting hair was Tony Lent, she explained, the most successful interior decorator in town; the woman with the pot hat was a rich old body from Boston, one of those tiresome but grand Brodericks, a client of Tony's whom Tony had brought along in order to impress her. Théodore would not have hurt Anne for anything so he did not repeat what he had overheard; he only insisted doggedly that he preferred not to have Mr Lent and Mrs Broderick in the house. Anne yawned. But she had made careful note, and determined never to include that treacherous little fairy among her guests again; as for Mrs Broderick, she was unlikely to reappear.

Always eager to please Anne, Théodore brought back from his office one day a Southern gentleman, a newspaper owner in those distant regions, who was a client of Rudge, Bascomb and Asher. Théodore was delighted with himself; he had scooped up a tycoon on his own. In the taxi, he told his guest, with simple boastfulness, of his wife's previous life as a great lady in South Carolina.

The two men found Mrs Asher at home, in a long revealing gown, reading and drinking by the fire. Mr McIntyre, from Charleston, thought she made a mighty pretty picture; Southern ladies always looked and behaved much more like women than those hard bossy Northern creatures. But it appeared that Mrs Asher had been so softly dressed and so softly reclining because of a headache; she had not expected company; she excused herself almost at once, having given Mr McIntyre time only to say that he surely thought he knew every living soul in South Carolina but he just could not rightly place the Fairleighs. He was disappointed by the lady's quick departure, as was Théodore, who explained that his wife suffered from migraine.

Anne dined on a tray; Théodore came to kiss her good night and enquire after her health, which had seemed to worsen since marriage, she was often indisposed. Anne received him with fury; how dared he bring home, without her permission, ghastly stage Southerners? Such a man would never have crossed their threshold in South Carolina. Obviously Theo knew nothing about Americans, and despite her efforts was unable to learn. She had been shocked, she would not allow this sort of thing. He was not to lower the tone of her house through his own utter lack of perception. Théodore apologized; Mr Rudge treated Mr McIntyre with marked respect; Mr McIntyre owned many newspapers. Newspapers, Anne said with contempt, of course, that upstart trade. Theo would in future kindly keep his business acquaintances in his office where they belonged.

The Southerners and indeed Northerners whom Mrs Asher liked were friends of dearest Charles's. Charles seemed to have been a man literally inundated with close friends; many of the gentlemen he had known, as a boy, came to spend the afternoon with Mrs Asher and were often there when Theo returned gray-faced from corporate mergers or estate taxes. They were all good-looking men too, self-assured and unhurried, not slaves to Wall Street as he was. Anne said they were darling silly boys, really, who never had wanted to work, except at polo or pigeon shooting; satisfied to be nothing but gentlemen, she explained to Theo, it was an unheard-of condition in pushing, *arriviste* New York. Théodore was jealous of them all. On one occasion, his wife, adorably kissing him behind the ear and rumpling his hair, said that he was a sweet old fool, imagine being jealous of Charles's friends, they were brothers to her, he wouldn't be jealous of brothers, would he? The jealousy was repressed and persisted.

There was one man called Bobby Winhope whom Théodore loathed. He loathed Winhope's cold insolent blue eyes, his six feet two of lounging height, his drawling voice, a drawl that was almost a sneer. He above all loathed the proprietary way in which this fellow treated Anne. And Théodore figured that he had provided enough whisky for Bobby Winhope to set up a saloon. But Anne, timidly reproached for the too frequent presence of Mr Winhope, was very angry, and Théodore paid for it by long solitary nights. Bobby had been Charles's most intimate friend; they had a lifetime of memories in common. Theo had not bought her, nor could he hope to eradicate her happy past.

Briefly, Théodore's many small scars were healed, briefly Anne was very much his, tender, welcoming, even interested in his work. He could ask favors, such as dining alone with her and going to bed, together, at a reasonable hour. He could, with due warning and after cross-examination, bring home his office acquaintances for drinks. Anne took a lot of trouble for a few weeks, then sweetly asked a favor of her own. She had seen a divine cottage on Long Island, near Southampton, an absolute dream. Its price was a joke, the owners had divorced and were as anxious to be rid of the house as of each other. Only ninety thousand dollars and ideal; Theo could come every week-end in the summer. And as Theo knew, her headaches were getting worse all the time, unbearable really; she could not stand the air or the pace of New York. She longed to garden again; she was a country girl at heart; it was her dearest wish to make a quiet cosy nest, for the two of them, by the sea. Théodore bought the house.

Anne spent most of her time there; of course she had to, although it was desperately lonely during the week without Theo, but she was arranging the cottage, extraordinary what discomforts and uglinesses other people could put up with. The bills were again stupendous. Théodore forgot the bills, every week-end, when he found Anne so fresh, so contented and so actively grateful to him for his present.

Summer came; the big house in New York was sad all week and the air-conditioning gave him colds. Théodore felt ill, but was afraid to consult a doctor; a doctor would surely prescribe rest. Anne obviously needed her own car in the country, and had bought a little Jaguar two-seater with pigskin upholstery. Theo, she said, must keep his car, for driving down to her on week-ends. But he must not, she said, with loving pats and pouts, use the car to take pretty girls out on week-day evenings, when his wife was far away. Théodore would not have considered this and was anyhow too tired. He dreaded the long hot traffic-choked drive to and from the country.

Nearing his Long Island estate one Friday evening in August, drooping with fatigue, Théodore saw a low white convertible, with the top down and in it, loose and easy at the wheel and not a bit fatigued, Bobby Winhope. In a few more minutes they might have met in the drive that led to Anne's dream cottage, with its black-and-white marble floors and its swimming-pool, which replaced the untidy sea. Théodore kissed his wife, who looked radiant in a pink linen boy's suit from Hattie Carnegie's. He remarked that he had just passed Winhope on the road. Oh yes, Anne said, Bobby stopped in for tea; he'd been at the Gershways playing polo all week. Going back to New York on Friday, Théodore mused. Anne stiffened and said that Bobby was driving to Connecticut, he was bored with the Gershways; now Theo, run along and have a bath and change, you look hot and citified. But Théodore was too tired; he lay on the bed in his dark room, leaving the door slightly open so that he could start getting ready when he heard Anne come upstairs. He might have fifteen minutes of rest, before dinner.

Through this door, lying in the dark, Théodore heard Anne's voice, but it was not a voice he had ever heard before; it made a shrill muted hissing sound. She was saying, in this incredible tone, that she had ordered the guest room to be cleaned before five. The voice that answered belonged to Lydia, the maid, and was also unimaginable, impudent, coarse. Lydia observed that she had plenty of other things to do and she forgot. Still hissing, Anne said that Lydia forgot too much; she could pack her bag and leave early tomorrow. Some things, Lydia said, she did not forget; she would have a little talk with Mr Asher before she left. Anne's voice changed; it was ice now, and ice with a menace. Anne stated that if Lydia tried anything of the sort, Anne would see that she went to jail; she was not, as Lydia could guess, bluffing; the Commissioner was a close friend. Lydia mumbled that she hadn't meant anything. Anne said that she should hope not, but in view of this unpleasantness, Lydia would leave now, at once, tonight.

Théodore, already dull with exhaustion, could not understand what he had heard, but was distressed especially by the remembered sound of Anne's voice. Then Anne went to her room, and he silently shut his door, bathed and dressed. Anne was waiting for him in her simple country sitting-room which she had done up in pale green satin and Venetian mirrors. She gave Theo a mint julep, her favorite drink she always said, and apologized for a delay in dinner. That miserable Lydia, Anne explained, had been offered a better-paid job and elected to give notice just like that, probably having arranged for her boy friend to pick her up. Servants were the absolute limit nowadays, if one didn't want to be in a constant temper the only thing to do was ignore them. They'd have rather a picnic, serving themselves, until she found a new maid; she was only sorry this had to happen just when Theo came, so uncomfortable for him.

After dinner, for once, Théodore did not yearn, wait, hope, wonder, hint, plead. He said that he felt ill and was going straight to bed. Lying under the monogrammed *crêpe de Chine* sheet, Théodore began to think, not in the orderly way he was trained to, but in flashes of pain. His head was filled with nails, coals; he could not think properly. He kept clenching and unclenching his hands. Finally he reminded himself, with an effort of will, that he was a lawyer; and what a lawyer had to have, always, was proof.

Proof was shamefully easy to get. Théodore took Anne's forgotten gold powder box to the insurance valuer, feeling like a criminal and with a ready story: if Anne had in fact presented the box and it was genuine, he would apologize and say he had muddled her instructions. The expert assured Mr Asher that it must be some other box that needed valuing; this was gilded tin, though of course ordinary inexpert men did not know about such matters; when new, the box might have cost twenty-five dollars. Théodore explained that he was hopelessly ignorant; he would get the matter straight and send back the right box. And he wondered how much tin he had paid for as if it were gold, while—he could only presume—Mrs Asher banked the difference in her own account. Or, more likely, in another account, in a different bank, under an assumed name. If the fake gold box was a sample of Anne's usual procedure, she must have laid by quite a tidy sum.

Then Théodore brought the blue-and-green Van Gogh to a famous art dealer, saying that a friend was determined to buy it but he wanted to make sure of the picture's proper value. The art dealer was more suave than the insurance expert; he imagined that the unfortunate Mr Asher had paid a whopping amount for this grotesque copy, believing himself to be a smart chap who could pick up Van Goghs on the cheap. The art dealer launched into a tirade against immoral copyists and the crooks who sold their product; Théodore knew the verdict long before the gentleman with the magnifying glass had got round to saying how sorry he was, Mr Asher had been robbed.

Now Théodore, whose firm occasionally handled divorces for important clients, called in a private detective. This man's solid record of discretion was in the firm's files. Théodore met the detective, Mr Joseph Birch, at a bar; and though his face was expressionless and his voice dry and exact, Théodore felt faint as he talked. Mr Birch understood perfectly and quickly, and spared Mr Asher the miserable necessity for going into detail. He noted Mr Bobby Winhope's address in New York and Mrs Asher's address on Long Island, and asked for a picture of Mrs Asher; he would dig up a photograph of Mr Winhope on his own.

Théodore telephoned Anne to say that he could not come for the week-end; too much work; she commiserated with Theo and also with her poor self, abandoned in the country. But Mr Birch had returned, in a mere four days, to opine that there was a pretty clear pattern—Mr Birch managed an impersonal jargon to save everyone's feelings. Mr Winhope regularly spent three week-days and nights on Long Island;

at Mr Winhope's flat in New York the doorman, lightly bribed, recognized Mrs Asher's picture. She had visited Mr Winhope frequently during the last year though she was not, the doorman announced without an extra bribe, the only one.

Instinct or legal training or both forced Théodore to go on, pry further, know all. He avoided Anne, always using work as an excuse, and though Anne tenderly and pitifully complained over the telephone she did not suggest joining her husband in New York, since he could not come to Long Island. Mr Birch was gone longer, and his expenses mounted; he was traveling widely, it would seem; he was also employing sub-agents; there was a great deal to learn, and one fact led inevitably to another. By the third week in September the dossier was complete, documented, bulging with affidavits.

Théodore no longer looked taut and fit; he looked wizened, grey, with haggard eyes, and nearer to sixty than to a vigorous forty-seven. His only shield against despair was more and more work. He knew what he had to do, and as the sleepless nights passed he went over this forthcoming scene, with disgust. But even worse was what he imagined: did everyone know what he alone, the foreigner, easily willingly deeply fooled, had never guessed? Was he a laughing-stock in his world?

He could still use his bruised mind; the instinct of self-preservation had not been destroyed. He realized, after thought, that his firm was a kind of protection. If everyone had known what he now knew, Mr Rudge would have known it too, or soon learned; and Mr Rudge, not from friendship but for the honor of the firm, would have warned him. Warned him or managed to get rid of him; some action would have been taken. As for the others, those specious characters whom he had entertained as if they were the fine flower of America, presumably they were getting by with murder or petty larceny too; they might be congratulating themselves on having gulled Anne. The tweedy woman with the pot hat had not been deceived; the man with golden hair evidently enjoyed frauds, being one himself. Théodore decided that there was no intolerable public exposure to fear. Mr Birch, aware of the buttered side of his bread, could be relied on for silence.

Théodore paid all outstanding bills and cancelled all charge accounts; he instructed his bank that his deposits would now only diminish when he signed cheques, no other signature was valid. He went through the house, first with a hired maid, then with a hired packer, and collected every one of Mrs Asher's pre-marriage belongings, both the fake and the authentic; but nothing that he had given Mrs Asher was included. The boxes were shipped to storage; the suitcases and trunks were shipped to the St Regis hotel, to await the arrival of Mrs Theo Asher on the afternoon of September 28th. Théodore consulted a less elevated legal firm than his own and arranged, with the local lawyer clearly briefed in advance, a Reno divorce, the grounds for which were incompatibility. There was to be no alimony. Mr Asher would pay costs.

When all was in readiness, Théodore telephoned to Anne. He wanted to see her on the afternoon of September 28th at six o'clock at home on a matter of urgent business. Anne resisted, saying that he really might come to her, it was exhausting and bad for her headaches to rush in and out of New York like that, and she had a dinner engagement in the country. Théodore answered with unprecedented coldness that she would have to cancel her engagement and he would meet her as he said, at the hour he had named. He then hung up, wondering whether Anne would obey, and guessing that she would, since he had never taken such a tone before, and she would be curious if not unquiet.

Théodore prepared his case as thoroughly as if he were going to argue before the Supreme Court; he knew each statement, each proof, by heart; the part of his mind which was in charge of the indictment had frozen hard around the facts. But there was more in his mind, weakness, folly, he thought, unnerving him. He knew that he was ready to forgive, to start again, to clean up this vile mess of cheating and betrayal, and love his wife, if only she would change. Why hadn't she trusted him, Théodore asked himself in anguish, when he so trusted her? Then, being honest, he answered himself that Anne could not have trusted him before marriage; he would have fled in terror from her past. But after marriage, when he had come to know her and value her, Anne could have spoken, and he would have seen her past as tragic, driven, and Anne—he could see it so now, late at night, alone—as a brave woman who had fought fiercely with her only weapons, in order to survive. He understood the struggle for survival, he would have given her credit for courage and brain, he would have helped destroy every odious trace, in a way she did not know how to do. He would have protected her final victory

This was madness: struggle, courage and victory indeed; the woman was vicious all through. Remember Winhope, and others besides Winhope, before Winhope—Mr Birch had been meticulous—but after Théodore. Théodore could have forgotten the forgotten men who had paid for Mrs Fairleigh's long journey from the Chicago slums to the East River apartment; he could not forget the unnecessary men whom Mrs Fairleigh had enjoyed even when she was safe, married, living in her own splendid house with a husband who footed her insane bills gladly. Enjoyed, Théodore said to himself, and pictures flooded his mind; he knew that body; he knew every sound, gesture, movement, every seduction, every trick. He could only assume that he knew the sham—convincing as it was—not the genuine passion: Anne would have saved that for lovers of choice. On Théodore she had used the imitation, the accustomed professional wiles. He sweated with rage, with shame, with jealousy, with actual nausea, as he thought of this. He could see Winhope, in his drawing-room, drinking his whisky, smiling at him with condescension and treating his wife as Winhope property, which she was, which she was. Forgive her? He would kill her.

And yet, hating Anne, and eaten with the cancers of jealousy and shame, and knowing, to the penny, how she had misused him, worn him out as a slave to her extravagance, cheated him like a common thief when it suited her, still he desired her, still perhaps loved her, and still saw the life they could have had, the life he had dreamed they were sometimes having: the imagined, rich, triumphant American life.

At a quarter past six on the afternoon of September 28th, Anne Asher arrived at her front door, in a temper. Théodore, hearing her key in the lock, opened the door. He had sent the servants away. He ushered his wife into the drawing-room and gave her a chair, as though she were a new but not significant client, come to talk in his office. With frigid courtesy, he offered her a drink which Anne took as if from the butler. Théodore told her, politely but sternly, to keep quiet and listen until he was finished. Then he unraveled her life, as he had planned, from Anna Wolski to Anne Asher, forgetting nothing. While he spoke he waited, and waited with longing, for her to stop him, to throw herself in his arms and beg forgiveness and swear reform, and cry out that she had been wicked and a fool but loved him and wanted another chance, she could not lose him. He waited in vain; and hid his sickness of heart and his final despair. At last, each devious knot undone, her life like a soiled string stretched straight before them, Théodore indicated his briefcase, beside his chair, and announced that it was filled with sworn testimony to each of his statements: the case was proved to satisfy any court in the land.

There was a brief silence, while Anne's mouth slowly curved into a sneer of pure hate. Her eyes matched her mouth. Then, in a voice that she had long left behind, in a harder life with uglier people, she drawled that she might have known what to expect from a Jew.

Théodore did not betray himself; he was disciplined to the core of his being. He had neither vaunted nor concealed his heritage. He regarded Hitler as a criminal madman and murderer, and if he had not foreseen the shape of history he would be dead with millions of his race; but that was a different matter. In New York, he had come to realize that Jewish blood, though not expiated in gas chambers, was a grievous inconvenience, and since no one questioned him, he kept his mouth shut. Only fools created difficulties for themselves, when difficulties could be so easily avoided. No country was perfect, no country lived up to its professed virtues, and though he mocked the disparity between America's basic tenet that all men are born equal and its actual reading of this law, he did not trouble himself, being no reformer; he accepted reality and adapted himself to it. But it would seem that a proved whore and thief, if a native Aryan American, could despise a Jew; what he had been born was a greater disgrace than what she had made of herself. Théodore sat still and apparently calm, waiting for more.

It came. Anne, speaking in that voice which might, he thought, be her true voice at last, suggested that Mr Rudge would be astonished to hear that his youngest senior partner was nothing but a little kike; and she would take great satisfaction in telling Mr Rudge. Perhaps right now, over the telephone.

Théodore remained silent. Anne, hating this man as she had hated no other, this sneaking, snooping, miserly Jew, boasted that Theo was not the only one who could pry where he wasn't wanted; she had long since suspected his secret, she had long since taken measures to be sure of him if he ever turned tricky, the way one of his race could be counted on to do, sooner or later. She had her proofs too, and meant to use them.

No, Théodore said, quietly, she would say nothing, to Mr Rudge or to anyone else, not now or ever. She would do exactly as he ordered and in the manner he prescribed. If she failed to do so, he would divorce her, using all the material in his briefcase, every single item would be brought out as testimony in court. Divorce cases, he observed, were reported in full in American papers; it would make an interesting story. But if, after the conventional discreet divorce which he had arranged, Anne should at any future time feel tempted by spite, he must remind her that he retained the documents relative to her past and they would afford those helpful vultures, the gossip columnists, a tasty libel-free tale. He explained the disposition of Anne's goods and chattels; she would find at the St Regis a letter with directions and her plane tickets for Reno. He gave Anne ten minutes to consider and reach her decision.

Anne made herself another drink. Sipping it, she said she might also have known that a Jew would always win on a dirty deal. However, she would be safe from him and his filthy ways in the future: his silence about her was as necessary as her silence about him. She did not enlarge on what Théodore had to conceal about Anna Wolski; she had already started to forget it. She announced that she would resume with pleasure her own honorable name of Fairleigh after the divorce. Well, nothing gained, nothing lost, Anne remarked, but added with malice that this was not entirely correct; there might be a few trifling hundred thousands salted away, during the past few deplorable years, which Theo would never get his hands on. She walked to the front door, opened it and left without a backward look or word of farewell.

Théodore climbed the stairs, holding to the banister railing. He went to his bathroom and stood in the dark, mindless, not knowing why he had come. Then he turned on the glaring neon light over the mirror and gazed at his face. He saw a man with grey hair, beaten eyes, sagging cheeks, a man who was sick and old and afraid. He put his hands over this stranger's face and wept.

Théodore sold the house on East 73rd Street and the palatial cottage on Long Island. He moved back to Park Avenue, to a small flat like the one he rented when he first came to New York. He furnished it himself, according to what he had learned from Mrs Mayne and Angèle and Isabella. It did not matter how it looked to anyone else; it was his own place; he did not intend to bring guests to it; he would not have known whom to bring. He was only safe in the oasis of the law, in his office and the extension of his office, the rooms where he ate at night and slept. Slowly he started to recoup and reinvest the money he salvaged after Anne's thieving and squandering.

His children wrote regularly and dutifully from Italy; Théodore could not understand their letters. The children were not of course responsible for this lunacy, but Isabella must be completely deranged. It appeared that insects, fungi, floods, droughts and other scourges beset their hectares in Calabria, and that the children thought this normal and interesting, and were full of idiotic prophecies about better times ahead. Why Isabella should elect to keep them slaving away without purpose was beyond him. His answering letters dwindled to a paragraph of enquiry about health; he sent presents on birthdays and at Christmas. Isabella did not write.

Mrs Fairleigh resumed her quiet arrangement with the senator and continued to be seen, attentively escorted by various other gentlemen, in the most expensive restaurants and night clubs and at the larger parties.

Théodore now did nothing except work, a relentless marathon race without end. He knew that he was a success in his profession; he knew that he would become a very rich man.

Mrs Rudge, comfortable and ample in a flowered morning coat, spoke to her husband over the breakfast table. This was their only certain time for conversation, and generally Mrs Rudge used these precious moments to discuss their two children and their five grandchildren. Today she remarked that Theo, who had been commanded to dine with them the night before, lived like a hermit since his divorce, looked ill, depressed, needed cheering-up and a nice vacation, didn't Harold agree? Mr Rudge was surprised by Mrs Rudge's concern. He answered with an astuteness which in turn surprised Mrs Rudge; he had never thought Mrs Rudge liked Theo, why was she now troubling herself over Theo's state of mind and health? Mrs Rudge couldn't exactly say, but Theo seemed changed somehow, gentler, quite pitiful really, she was sorry for him. Mr Rudge nodded and made the sounds he made when thinking. No, he wouldn't say pitiful, but changed, yes. The other men in the office had noticed it too; they appeared to like Theo more. Perhaps Theo had been rather stand-offish and formal and European. Theo was warmer, that's what it was, warmer, more human, but then how could he help it, America affected everyone sooner or later, it was a warm humanizing country.

Mrs Rudge was not so sure what had influenced Theo but kept her suspicions to herself. She did not argue with Mr Rudge; she only maintained that however Theo was or whatever had happened to him, he did need a nice vacation.

THE FALL AND RISE
OF MRS HAPGOOD

Mrs Hapgood, a woman noted for her sense of order, drove aimlessly through the Loire valley. From time to time she wept at the wheel. The Loire valley might have been made for Mrs Hapgood since its order verges on the sublime. When not blinded by tears or by that clenching of the ego which also blinds, Mrs Hapgood was able to see the castles on their spread lawns, the river running silver between sandbanks and willows, the forests. This beauty affected some unused part of her anatomy, neither her brain nor what she would have called her heart. She supposed that the emotion which then invaded her must be joy.

Mrs Hapgood had never travelled unaccompanied and without a plan. Mrs Hapgood was fifty-one years of age and tortured by growing pains.

After two cathedral towns and three days of motorized wandering, she realized that she did not cross the Channel on the Lydd-Le Touquet air ferry to observe the marvel that is France in late September. She had come to look at herself. She needed to understand. Blaming one's parents seemed to be the accepted modern excuse for private failure. Mrs Hapgood had no wish to blame her father and mother; she had loved them alive; she loved them dead. It was a disgusting trick to charge up your mistakes, your weakness, your defeat to other human beings who were people like yourself, older at the time. Mrs Hapgood could recall her doubts with her own children who were now grown and almost certainly misshaped through her devoted efforts. She did not want to blame and run away; she wanted to dig in and find answers.

They should not have named me Faith, Mrs Hapgood thought. Nonsense. Don't try to wriggle your way out. They did not mean to force upon her a name, with all the power of a name, which she made her own or made herself to fit. Was there ever an odalisque, a ballet dancer, a simple slut named Faith? Her parents had been married for six years, hoping and one assumed trying, before she was born; the reward of faith and so called.

She pulled up in a village and went to a restaurant that had flowers in window boxes and on each table a checked table-cloth. The Auberge de la Vierge Folle, an obvious tourist trap, provided miserable hors d'oeuvres and a heavy omelette, but she drank Pouilly Fumé, and lapsed thankfully into muzziness. It was a rest and a new experience to become tipsy twice a day on the unshared bottle of wine. Remembering the road, Mrs Hapgood went to the ladies' room. Here she met herself in the mirror above the washbasin. She expected to look drunk but she did not. She considered her face with a fury somewhat diluted by wine. Nothing much was exempt from that fury; it burned inside her like rags. What's to be done, she said to her face. Off with it. Too late and ridiculous to change her name, but a different face would help. If you resembled yourself as little as possible, you might come to feel like someone else. I look like a Roman matron, Mrs Hapgood thought, hold myself like Queen Mary and am repellent. She hurried to her car; she felt shielded inside it, and when thinking hurt too much she could turn for consolation to the natural world.

The road ambled into a wood. The trees grew, as they do in France, close, slender, straight, feathery; and green underwater light moved through them. Mrs Hapgood decided to sleep beneath these trees, suddenly hungering for the smell of earth, the silence, and to lie looking up at leaves. She climbed down the bank at the roadside and followed a path, no doubt made by fishermen on their way to a stream that twisted off from the Loire. Within ten steps, Mrs Hapgood saw that the human race had come here before her and she hated them, the whole careless lot, which excreted dirty paper and tins and bottles, and had no grace. Raging and sickened, she began to collect this muck; she would burn it or bury it. Was there nothing on earth that people could leave alone and give a chance for perfection?

In the midst of this remarkable service, the cleaning of an unknown French wood somewhere on the south bank of the Loire, Mrs Hapgood woke to what she was doing. It's madness, she thought, it's beyond my control; I must feel that I am appointed to put things right. I must believe that I always know what is right. Mrs Hapgood dropped a sodden yellow newspaper and an oily sardine tin and washed her hands in the stream. By an act of will, discounting typhoid, she cupped her hands and drank. That was a weak start towards accepting the disorder she now felt to be universal, the very climate of the world.

Mrs Hapgood searched until she found a glade which was not decorated with the litter of civilization; she lay on the ground and watched the leaves floating like coral plants in the sea. She fitted this grass bed and it fitted her, she felt light and loose, welcoming, bathed in air, blissful, mindless on the edge of sleep. Her brain did its mole work while she slept. She woke with a plan. She would experiment recklessly on her body and deal with her soul later. As for her soul, since it was rotten with bitterness, she would be lucky if she could lose it.

Mrs Hapgood took the best suite in the best hotel in Tours, and was elated by her extravagance. She would dine in her sitting-room and guzzle champagne, a drink with a halo of the dissolute about it. I'm rich, Mrs Hapgood told herself for the first time in her life. All things being relative, she was rich, not like Greeks, South Americans and film stars but jolly rich, anyway. Money, up to now, had been used with taste and decorum, to pay for a decorous tasteful way of life. It was also to be given to those who lacked it, to worthy causes, and handed on to one's children. What idiocy; money should be squandered.

The warm blue-black evening lured people to the streets. They walked under plane trees in the French public postures of love, they drank at cafés, they gossiped, played dominoes, promenaded in their cars. They gave the impression of living with complete satisfaction in that evening and no other. Mrs Hapgood window-shopped and studied her fellow men. I am going to learn, thought Mrs Hapgood, I am going to learn everything. Mrs Hapgood is dead, or always was; I will start again where I never had the sense to begin.

But it was not as simple as that; wounds did not heal so fast. Mrs Hapgood woke in her imitation Louis Quinze bedroom, tears on her cheeks and pain in her throat, and for a moment did not know where she was but only knew who she was: lost and bereft and with unbearable time ahead.

Some of the habits of a lifetime were valuable, among them the fine old English tendency to tell oneself to buck up and get on with it. Mrs Hapgood set off for the *salon de coiffure* chosen on last night's prowl. In two hours the star hairdresser would deign to cut, dye and arrange her hair. Idling past the plate-glass shop fronts, Mrs Hapgood brooded on her appearance. She had never dyed her hair. She had always worn it long and pinned up in the same style. Peering in a window, she saw reflected a broad forehead, dog-honest brown eyes, too flared nostrils, too wide a mouth, too square teeth but at least good and white. She could not see but knew the twin lines between her eyebrows, stigma of the worrying woman, and the faint sag under her chin. Turning sidewise, she examined her body. Tall, slim, and well-made, discreet, unexciting, it was exactly the body to carry her face. She looked after herself as scrupulously as she looked after her house. No man, even in France where it was a national sport, would pause in the street and admire her. They were not meant to. The men she knew were supposed to like her, find her agreeable to talk to, good-humored, a thoroughly nice woman. The men she knew did like her. And perhaps, Mrs Hapgood thought, faltering in the sunlight, they were sorry for me too.

I shall have it dyed dark red, Mrs Hapgood decided, and buy a whole new wardrobe of dashing French clothes. She would now sit in a café, read the Tours paper, and wait for her forthcoming rebirth. From having had no time in her London life she now had time as if it were given to her in big lumps labeled hours. She had finished the paper; the hair-dresser would still be back-combing immense heads. When she was a girl, her hair had been the same, hadn't it, though less tidy? She could no longer see that girl but knew she had been searching for her role, like all the young. Miss Faith Kendall's manners were so good that she searched sensibly, causing no uproar. She wanted to become a painter, not the way you wanted to breathe, not the way a real painter must be a painter. So she went to the Slade, a handsome girl, reserved rather than shy, and already set in her ways.

Mrs Hapgood remembered the students she had ruled out, on sight. She withdrew quietly from what did not suit her. And although she could learn with her fingers, she could not learn with her spirit. She understood quickly that she would never be an artist but this did not crush her because Daddy, a famous collector of books, introduced her to publishers who commissioned illustrations. She was clever at making pretty pictures, for children, which were full of flowers and animals with cuddly bodies and sweet faces. At an earlier date young ladies did embroidery, or painted teacups. She had learned enough at the Slade to become absorbed by the techinques of painting, to go to exhibitions, and thus she met her lover, one of three young men who were having their first show at the Shipman Gallery.

She was a virgin of twenty-two. She had been surrounded by men of all kinds and ages, converging on the Kendall house in St Leonard's Terrace because they cared for books. Not feeling neglected or spinsterish, she was companionable with men, and serene. Sex, Mrs Hapgood said to herself, couldn't someone have invented a more imposing word for what probably rules human life? She wouldn't put it past herself to have ignored the fact because the word was so distasteful, with a mixed sound of adolescent smut and science. After all, she had been brought up on words.

She should order more coffee, or how about cognac; one had to look as if one was doing something. I am doing nothing and I have nothing on earth to do, Mrs Hapgood thought, and the smoldering fury returned. A waiter brought a narrow glass of brandy. Spirits at quarter before

eleven in the morning tasted medicinal. All right then, she told herself,
sharpened by the fury, it is fairly clear. Either you were backward on
sex by nature, or so conditioned that you thought sex and love were
quite separate. Sex was an ugly word whereas love was a splendid one,
so you chose love. Ass, Mrs Hapgood informed herself and swallowed
the rest of her drink, imbecile, idiot.

Heated by anger and cognac, she rushed along the street to the
hairdresser's. Monsieur Gilbert was now ready. Mrs Hapgood felt she
was mad to entrust herself to a clown with a Napoleonic fringe and
effeminate gestures. The scissors, which now appeared to be surgical
instruments, were brought out. The operation took place with deadly
speed. There were then suffocating smells, grayish pastes, a girl half-
way between a chemist and a witch doctor hovering over her with gloved
hands, until finally her hair was being washed. Mrs Hapgood's eyes
ached; she craved fresh air. The other women, seated along the length
of the wall mirror, were hideous and frightening, all with heads like
spun sugar candy, all worshipping themselves in gluttonous narcissism.
The hair dryer was a boon, a windy cave where she could hide and
forget that she had plunged into this insanity.

Under the dryer, Mrs Hapgood thought of Mark, her lover. He was
twenty-four and a real painter, at least judging by the will and the
obsession. It was too soon to judge by anything else. He had come to
the Shipman Gallery to hang about, to look at his work and at anyone
who was also looking at his work. He was in that shaken, hopeful,
vulnerable state of the person who first exposes his being to the gaze of
strangers. Faith Kendall was examining a red and orange and mustard
and black landscape of factories when she felt a presence beside her. She
spoke of the picture to the young man not knowing he was Mark Tyne,
the artist himself. She spoke nicely, the young man was alight with
gratitude, they went out to have coffee. And so it started.

She had no sense of guilt, because her motives were so elevated. Mrs
Hapgood groaned and stirred and a hairpin pressed into her scalp. If
only she had been haunted by guilt and wallowing in sex, if only, if only.
After the beginning, which was painful and awkward, for Mark was
not an experienced lover, she could not say that she liked or disliked the
sexual act. She liked being tender, she liked knowing that this too was
part of her usefulness to Mark, she liked (it had to be admitted, it had
to be seen at last) feeling noble. For surely hers was a most disinterested
love; she asked and took nothing, except the pleasure of being essential
to a man in need. Drivel. Only essential because she cleaned and mended
and cooked, coming from her own spick-and-span studio to his cold,

grubby one; she listened; she soon managed the business end which was mild enough but a nightmare to Mark; she ran errands; she made no scenes.

Apparently no one guessed that Faith Kendall had a lover. She made no effort to conceal passion; the passion, not being in her, did not show. Mark could appear when he wanted to, at her parents' parties, and be accepted as another young man of talent; the house was full of them. Seen together, she and Mark gave the impression of being good friends, alike in their age, tastes, work. There was no gossip. She was protected by her fatal niceness.

And she was so different from the girls Mark's friends went to bed with that she had a special standing in Mark's set. The young men and their sloppy young women treated her like Mark's sister. She was faithful, of course, no other idea crossed her mind. She would not have dreamed of touching Mark in public, or of using endearments. Whereas the sloppy girls, rotating among Mark's chums, carried on with incredible wildness, shouted, wept, got drunk, kissed, flaunted black eyes. Miss Faith Kendall believed they had read of this style and were showing off, pretending to be bohemian as they imagined painters and their bedfellows were in Paris. Mark and she were made of finer clay; they meant something real to each other.

She was pleased when Mark's need for sex seemed to diminish; this proved the pure spiritual quality of their love. Dear God, Mrs Hapgood said to herself under the roaring hair dryer. I must have thought I was Florence Nightingale. That was all glorious up to the day she entered Mark's studio, with a bag of groceries, to find one of the sloppy girls frantically pulling on her clothes, and Mark sheepish and scared under the rumpled blankets. She sailed out, blazing like a fireship. She never came back, she never again saw Mark, she never shed a tear. Mark had desecrated everything they had, he was contemptible, he was to be rooted out and utterly forgotten. She did not belong with such people, they had nothing to do with her.

Mrs Hapgood realized that the wind had died in the cave and a sleek young woman was joggling her elbow. She was in a mauve-and-gilt Tours hairdressing salon, with dried sausages stuck on her head, and this stranger must not see that she had been weeping for an innocent, goodhearted prig of a girl. The sleek young woman remarked that Madame had had a nice nap. Monsieur Gilbert sent his apologies; he had not correctly gauged the time but the shop was being kept open for Madame. Monsieur Gilbert suggested that Madame have a facial and cosmetic treatment while he lunched. Mrs Hapgood felt that she had been in these airless premises for weeks but could not very well wander about Tours covered with curlers.

All these years, she had been embarrassed by the way her sex crowded in beauty shops, thus admitting that they were in constant pursuit of men. No woman who had any self-respect pursued men. You were yourself, and yourself should be enough to assure the love of one man and the regard of others. It had not occurred to Mrs Hapgood that women might enjoy hairdressers the way men enjoy their clubs. One was spoiled and pampered, wrapped in a lavender blanket, while skilful hands delectably massaged one's face and throat and the back of one's neck. If I could begin again with my daughter, Mrs Hapgood thought, I'd take her to a hairdresser at the age of ten. But Caroline was twenty-one, a devoted wife and mother in Greenwich, Connecticut, and the chances were that she was as reliable, proud and sensible as her idiot mama. Mrs Hapgood must have drowsed for the sleek young woman was saying, open your eyes, now part your lips. With brushes, salves, and pencils, Mrs Hapgood's face was deftly disguised. Monsieur Gilbert thrust his head in the door and announced that he was at Madame's service.

Mrs Hapgood was stunned by the sight of herself. *Très joli*, Mrs Hapgood murmured, but even her voice sounded queer. Her eyes did not look a bit honest, they looked much bigger, much darker, quite nasty, she added with delight. And her eyebrows were plucked, curving, and seemed to be raised in invitation. Her grey-brown hair had emerged a warm auburn, with golden wire glints. She looked ten years younger and hardly her idea of a lady. She thought herself dazzling and was afraid to move. If she moved, it would all blow away; it was too miraculous to last.

For a week, Mrs Hapgood revelled in an orgy of shopping. In her other life, she would have judged this concentration on herself to be cheap and ludicrous. Now, by the hour, she stood before mirrors and watched an Englishwoman, whose ideal had been correct unobtrusiveness, change into a Frenchwoman whose ideal was to be seen. At night in her suite, Mrs Hapgood drank wine and tried on her trousseau.

And men did admire her in the street. When Mrs Hapgood realized this she was overcome with gratitude and would have thanked the casual admirer if she had known how. She glanced at men too, under her mascaraed eyelashes, but uncertainly. What if this quick exchange led to some sort of commitment? She moved in a fever of self-consciousness, as if she were naked and yet, for the first time, dressed.

Mrs Hapgood woke one morning sufficiently healed to remember her former life without anguish. She had two children, one in America, one eccentrically acting in a stock company in Australia, and a husband in London. Common courtesy, to say nothing of maternal duties, required that she send an address to her husband. The suite in Tours had staled; she studied her Michelin and located a château, converted into a four-star hotel, a few miles from the city. The château-hotel reserved rooms by telephone. Mrs Hapgood cabled her position on the globe to London, and drove to the Château de Varincourt.

Varincourt stretched along a slight rise, flanked by candle-snuffer turrets. Its terrace overlooked a long formal garden, with *jets d'eau* in marble basins, and statues. Acres of combed woods and meadows, tamed streams, surrounded the great house. She would be content not to budge from her rooms; she could amuse herself indefinitely by slinking before the looking glass, or posing in the beautiful rosewood chairs. Why ever return to her high, quiet house in Hanover Terrace? Why not take to wine, shopping, daydreaming and self-love at Varincourt? This might not be happiness but it was the absence of pain.

She walked down the waterfall of steps to the garden. The beauty of the world gave her that new sudden sensation of joy. The ground was light under her feet and she light upon it: a voice that was not hers or anyone's sang within her; she did not have to think; she saw, she praised. At the far end of this planned harmony, Mrs Hapgood stopped at a marble bench to smoke and rejoice. From nowhere and without reason, the misery she was running from settled on her like a sickness. She stumbled back into it, a convalescent more wretched because of the relapse. Time, she thought, soothe yourself with time. Time heals nothing really, it only dims facts. In time, one can even become bored with pain.

Robert Hapgood came to the Kendall house, as so many had before him, because he was a genuine reader, and her father liked the way he read and what he read. At twenty-seven, no woman could be excused for remaining a dolt of a girl. Robert was not a dolt of a boy; he was thirty-nine years old and, she now supposed, he was in a panic. Nobody would ever have associated the word panic with Robert. He was, he still is, Mrs Hapgood reminded herself, a fine figure of a man. Foreigners think of all Englishmen of a certain class looking like that; it is almost a cliché for an English gentleman to be tall, lean with a carved, expressionless face, beautifully cut unmussable hair, beautifully cut unmussable clothes, a rolled umbrella, and sure manners. Robert Hapgood paid tactful court to the daughter of the house; he had decided that she was just what he needed in the way of a wife.

The daughter of the house was equally unflustered. Star-crossed lovers, according to the books, run a high temperature compounded of destiny, doom, thunder, lightning and rapture. Faith Kendall and Robert Hapgood had so few problems that they might have married within a week of their first meeting. They married within three months, as if obeying an unwritten law about time limits for contracting matrimony. Faith, who knew nothing of love, believed herself blessedly in love. But what was Robert thinking?

During their courtship Robert told her about himself and his life. After Winchester and Magdalen, Robert had wanted to be an archaeologist but sadly renounced desire for duty. His duty was the old, rich, solemn pharmaceutical firm of Hapgood and Ardley, founded God knows when. Robert was the only son and did not place his wish to be an archaeologist above his father's wish for a successor. He became an amateur archaeologist and a respected businessman. She had pitied Robert's loss of his chosen career, and revered the selflessness which made him value his father more than himself. Because she felt Robert to be so good, so uncomplaining but so disappointed, she had lavished an extra concern on him; it was tragic for a man not to use his talents as he wanted.

Now her angle of vision had changed. Did people ever give up what they really wanted? Those numberless women who had rejected careers as concert pianists in favour of wifehood and never forgot their sacrifice were more apt to be cowards than concert pianists. When you set out, alone, you were up against competition and doubt; you might turn out to be nobody, not a wife nor a concert pianist. You threw away security for hope; but those who were driven by hope did not stop to add and subtract; they could not help themselves; they did what they had to do, undaunted by final results. If Robert had had the conviction and courage he would have been an archaeologist and poor; archaeologists do not earn millions, and papa would think archaeology a wilful waste of time. Robert would have had to make his way in a world where he had no connections, and no name to help him. It was peculiar too that Robert was such a success in business; people did not usually do well at what they despised.

In their first year of marriage, Robert had taken his wife Faith on an archaeological outing: Roman ruins. She'd failed him there all right; old stones and rain, and nothing came alive to her; she didn't happen to like the Romans anyhow. Robert had laughed and said he would spare her archaeology. Ashamed of being so unresponsive, she encouraged Robert to travel alone, to feed his imagination on this mysterious longing to find the past underground. Especially she sent him away when the children were young and required summers by the sea or in the mountains, depending on what doctor had said what. Robert was too old or too intellectual to be the sort of father who enjoyed rolling around like teddy bears with his offspring. She packed Robert's bags, gave him her blessing, and carted the children off in loving solitary boredom.

But Robert had not waited thirty-nine years before selecting the one and only wife. Surprisingly, since he was such a restrained man, he had married at the age of twenty-two, fresh out of Oxford. It would have been unusual and thrilling if he'd married a gipsy or a beautiful orphan housemaid but he married that season's most popular debutante, called Clarissa. Faith the fiancée had asked to see photographs of this wife, and had been generous in her praise of a beauty which did not in the least appeal. Clarissa looked like what she was: a born flirt. She was small, blonde, and fluffy; she adored to dance; one could picture her raising great blue eyes to the tail-coated partner; one fancied a lisp. Robert Hapgood had married from passion, trying quickly to seize this slippery light-hearted bundle of sex appeal and keep it for himself. Having never liked anything as much as the mass flirting at balls, Clarissa went right on with balls, varied by night clubs. She did not want to dance with Robert; on the contrary she encouraged a changing guard of conquests, while Robert watched and swallowed jealousy like an acid, in silence.

After five years of this life, Clarissa agreed to have a child. Robert had wanted a child all along, not from frustrated paternal emotions but in the hope that a child would sober Clarissa, and keep her home a bit and off the accursed dance floors, out of the arms of other men. Clarissa did not want a child, but her friends were having them, it was the done thing. People might believe she couldn't bear a child and was not completely a woman. So she did have the child and it killed her; and Robert was tucked away in a sanatorium, while his father feared that his son, his heir and the future head of the firm had lost his mind at the age of twenty-seven.

How much of this did I know from the beginning? Mrs Hapgood asked herself; how much did I weave together, as the years passed? She would have ignored a great deal. She would, for instance, have ignored the fierce joy Robert must have felt, sometimes, or he could not have kept going through five such alien years, and he would not have broken to pieces at the end. And after that, Robert told her, he took occasional mistresses. This did not surprise or shock young Faith Kendall, bride-to-be. The man had been alone, a widower, for twelve years. He was not a monk. She imagined these ladies, all faceless and wraithlike, to have been passing trained nurses, attending to male wants. They were now obliterated; Robert had come to her, his home. The loneliness of his life, as misinterpreted by her, was one of her strongest reasons for loving him. She meant to make him happy; she meant him never to suffer again. Robert would find in her the safety and the care he had missed.

God help me, Mrs Hapgood thought, lighting the sixth cigarette from the stub of the fifth, he was only in a panic. After thirty-nine comes forty; forty is the terrifying age for everyone, men and women. Forty is when you feel the winds of decay waiting to blow like hell and death. By fifty, you are used to it; forty is the watershed. Most people do produce children, therefore nearly everybody believes they must be essential to life. Robert was a kind, charming father and fond of his children. He was relieved that they were successfully grown (no twisted limbs, no perversions, no prison sentences) and off and away.

His life appeared to be a model of order, divided between the claims of duty and the satisfactions of the mind. But underneath this conventional superstructure, there must have been a perilous disorder he couldn't escape and desired and dreaded. No doubt Robert chose her so definitely and so fast because he needed her; she was to serve as a guardian. Perhaps Robert hated being at the mercy of his sexual clamor but knew that he was as caught as a secret drinker, full of firm resolves, and always again shutting the door and reaching for the bottle. And there she was, the answer, not a cure but a rock-like nanny to look after him. Mrs Hapgood, perfect in a Chanel suit, so beautifully made-up that even sunlight did not spoil the work of art, put her hands over her eyes and saw herself as square, ugly, frozen and cheated to death.

She felt a shadow blotting out the sun before she knew a man had cast the shadow. For one hallucinated instant, she thought Robert was standing before her. Not Robert, just another tall Englishman. No, not just another tall Englishman either; a remarkably tall one, and remarkably ugly. It came as a surprise that a face so poorly put together—the eyes too small and too far apart, the nose too flat, the mouth too big— could be interesting and even reassuring. But there was something wrong with this man; he was unnaturally intent, yet withdrawn. She must herself be far gone on an uncharted direction since she had not found it embarrassing to stare in silence at the stranger, and to accept his thoughtful study of her.

'I'm glad you came,' he said. 'I've been here a week. It's like an elaborate stage set and it needed a beautiful woman to give it life.'

She had been mistaken again; there was nothing remarkable about him except impertinence. She could not fault his clothes, nor his voice. His haircut was dubious but might be the product of a Tours barber rather than uncertain taste. Mrs Hapgood guessed that he had not gone to quite the right school and no generations of right schools marched behind him. A gentleman, it would seem, was restrained by many subtle brakes; a not altogether gentleman was one who did not sense the varied brakes or when to apply them. Mrs Hapgood deplored her instinctive system of weights and measures, but also deplored the man's vulgar opening gambit.

'You probably think this trouble you're in has spoiled your looks,' the man went on. 'It hasn't.'

Mrs Hapgood was too startled to answer and after consideration realized she could think of nothing to say. He sat beside her, uninvited, and offered a cigarette before he noticed that she held one in her hand.

'You're not ill,' the man remarked, glancing at her through thinning smoke. 'You're just desperate. I'm one up on you. I'm ill *and* desperate.'

He smiled and his face briefly became open and gay.

'I'm sorry,' Mrs Hapgood said, and meant it.

'Well, I'm sorry for you too, so that's a help. It's such a trap to be only sorry for oneself.'

Mrs Hapgood thought, quite clearly, I am not going to speak unless I want to. I am through with being the kind of woman who can always make dinner-table chat to the man on the right, then to the man on the left. This man apparently did not mind silence.

He had been looking up the vista of lawn and geometrical water and now said, 'No one thought of family life in any part of that house. They cared about style not emotion. Self-assured, cold fish. I daresay they saved themselves a lot of bother by regarding the heart as an organ for pumping blood. Shall we walk? The woods are better than this.'

The woods were perfect and no one dropped in them the plastic, paper, metal and glass excreta of modern man. Mrs Hapgood began to feel rest warming her, like a hot drink.

'Are you tired?' the man asked.

'No.'

'Are you less desperate?'

'Yes.'

'It was only a crisis,' he assured her. 'It comes and goes like that. You get used to it.'

Mrs Hapgood stopped, stricken.

'I can't,' she said. 'That's just it. I can't get used to it.'

He looked at her for a moment in his too intent way.

'I'm glad you're here by yourself, for my sake, but I see that's wrong for you. Please don't feel so alone. Help is at hand.'

He leapt the barriers of reserve with outlandish ease; the men she knew did not talk like this. But she was moved by the large kind creature, who had appeared literally out of the blue, and wished to comfort her. She was not spoiled, she realized; if you do not allow yourself to be helpless, no one helps you. Robert admired her fortitude and she had not known how much she needed, instead, protecting arms.

'It is not a sin,' the man said gently, 'sometimes to tire of standing on one's own two feet. You might try leaning a bit.'

She heard his voice rather than his words and, raising her head, thought that the pupils of his eyes had widened and were drawing her in, and that she too had made some sort of declaration in silence. She did not understand where they were going nor why they had mysteriously started to go there, but the pace was too fast.

'I think I'll turn back now,' Mrs Hapgood said.

'Yes.'

They walked through the delicate ferny trees to the formal garden. At the second mirror pool, he said, 'My name's Philip Naisby.'

'Faith Hapgood,' she said and laughed.

'One does have to know names.'

He left her at the door of the château saying, 'Don't worry, you know. Don't be afraid. It's absolutely no use.'

Mrs Hapgood decided not to go down to dinner. She could not imagine where to begin again with this curious stranger; she could not see herself bowing as she passed to her own table; she cringed from the idea that he might think he ought to sit with her. She could not plan any way to behave with him, and was sure that she would feel like a teen-age ninny when next they met. She examined herself in the silver-framed glass on the dressing table and saw what he saw: that brand-new face, designed to attract men. The brand-new face had served its purpose, and she was bewildered by the result.

It was an unfair hardship that books had deserted her. Mrs Hapgood had read her way through the bad patches of two pregnancies, through the threatening emptiness of war, through all the minor nerve strains of daily life; and now she could not read. She concluded that in her state of mind she could not expect to feed on her usual diet, but Colette might fill the bill, Colette exhaling sex like a perfumed locomotive; or thrillers which were cross-word puzzles with a plot. She had bought stacks of both and both were useless. She might paint again; tomorrow she would go to Tours, acquire more clothes and some tubes of gouache. She could keep herself busy making pretty-pretty portraits of Varincourt. Meanwhile there was tonight.

The game of dress-up would have to do and unexpectedly this amused Mrs Hapgood. She ordered food, in order to preserve appearances, and wine which she wanted. She would clothe herself in a black net and lace negligée. Only a peroxide blonde, kept by a plump tycoon from a small northern city, could wear such vamp stuff seriously. She had become adept at make-up; once you stopped thinking about your face and considered the object before you as canvas, it was simple to paint it. She rimmed and slanted her eyes with black crayon, she widened her mouth and coloured it purplish red. To complete the masquerade, she clamped on paste ear-rings, emeralds, diamonds, turquoises in hunks big enough for a *nouveau riche* maharanee.

Mrs Hapgood drank the first comforting glass of wine and told herself that she was waiting for her lover, an evil irresistible man, for whom she had no feeling except lust. Amateur theatricals, Mrs Hapgood decided, are really quite absorbing. The telephone rang. It would be Philip Naisby; she could not speak to him normally when she was deep in this fool's charade. The telephone rang again. Mrs Hapgood hurriedly wiped off lipstick on the napkin, and answered in a muted voice. It was not Philip Naisby; it was her husband.

Robert sounded as close as if he spoke from the next room.

'Faith, where were you? I've been out of my mind. How could you do this? You might have had an accident with the car, you might have been lying in some filthy hospital in France. I had no idea how to reach you. Where are you?'

'I'm here,' Mrs Hapgood said. 'You know the address and the telephone number. I am quite all right and of course I didn't have an accident.'

'Oh, Faith.' It was a groan of helplessness. What is he unhappy about, Mrs Hapgood wondered, the upset in routine?

'You can tell people that I haven't been well, the doctor prescribed sun and rest. It's a plausible explanation.' If a snake could talk, Mrs Hapgood thought, that's the way it would sound.

'I don't give a curse for people. Faith, how can you? It's you I care about. What's happening to you?'

'I'm very well.'

'For God's sake, come home. Darling, Faith darling. Or let me join you. Listen to me. I implore you.'

'No.'

'Faith, I swear to you.'

'Don't swear anything, Robert. I shall be here for some time. You know where to reach me if there's an emergency and I don't want to talk to you now.'

'Will you write to me?' His voice was an old man's, beaten and exhausted. What excuse did he have to feel like that? How dared he ask for pity?

'No,' she said. 'Good night.'

She lay on the swansdown bed, trembling in a chill of revulsion. She hated them both; she hated the whole banal situation; she hated the past. It would be a piece of luck to have died before one reached this loathsome end that didn't even have the dignity of being an end. How I wish he could have seen me, Mrs Hapgood thought. Telephones with eyes. How I wish he could have seen me, painted and dressed like a tart, and believed that I had gone to bed with taxi drivers and Negro drummers and pick-ups from every street, had taken to drugs and drink, become a public spectacle. How I wish his pride could have been torn to dirty shreds like mine.

She was sweating and thought she was going to faint or be sick. She was badly frightened. She was getting worse, not better. She had been careful of hate; she had held it off rigidly. She told herself she would not hate because hate was unjust and senseless; if there was blame, then blame never fell on one person alone. The only hope of health was to understand, to define cause and effect, to discover a cure. Hate sickened the hater, not the hated one. Forgive, she thought, forgive what cannot be helped. But she could not forgive herself; and she could not forgive Robert. If this stone of condemnation stayed inside her, so hard she could feel it beneath her breastbone, she and Robert were meaningless. There was nothing to return to.

Take off your fancy dress, Mrs Hapgood told herself, drink more wine, and try again. It was a help to be so tired; it calmed you. You could not dramatize yourself when all you really wanted was someone to rub your back and turn out the light.

There was no question of finding where she went wrong; she had gone wrong from the beginning. But that, honestly, was not her fault, unless she could blame herself for her nature. She could detest her nature, now; but her nature had been as straightforward as oatmeal. Since she knew no other nature, she could not be accused of failing to see what inadequate nourishment oatmeal was.

They were married in her parents' house. The Kendalls were agnostics who treated all religions with respect. Robert was Church of England, taking for granted a creed he never thought about. Faith had told Robert, the minute he began to court her, about Mark; she had asked Robert if he thought it dishonest to wear a white wedding dress. Robert kissed her, smiled with the sweetness she loved, said she was adorable and would look entrancing in white.

Robert, so wise, so experienced, took her to Ravello for the honeymoon. His soulful bride would not have done well in Paris or Rome or Venice or Madrid; she was carried up to a quiet romantic place above the Mediterranean, in April of 1938. There were wild freesias on the hillsides. Robert taught her what Mark had not. She worshipped Robert and believed that their soft delight was all; she believed this was the entire magic between men and women, of which she had read with so little comprehension. And as she loved to look at Robert and to look after him, and to lie in his arms at night, she knew, without a shadow of doubt, that they had the ideal marriage, the union of body and soul. Honeymoons are a special phase and meant to be unique in kind. It did not alarm her that daily life provided no freesias on hillsides, no mornings lying late abed, no moonlit walks ending in the gentle fulfilling embrace.

They were not moral imbeciles, and knew very well that the world was sliding faster every month to death and destruction. But people always live their lives because they have to, as long as they are able, and Faith, alight with her peaceful love, bustled through London furnishing the house in Hanover Terrace which Robert had given her as a wedding present. She had barely finished this, not really finished it, before she became pregnant. For three months she was nauseated and disgusted with herself for such weakness, and often tearful, while Robert was a ministering angel. Then she burgeoned into glowing health and was as proud as if she were the first woman to accomplish this vital task, and Robert showered her with presents and compliments.

Meantime, with her willing consent, Robert clung to some of the habits of his bachelorhood; on certain afternoons he played bridge late at one of his clubs, on certain nights he dined with men. She wanted to take nothing away from him, but only to add and to fill the empty spaces. He also went on business trips and short archaeological outings. She was not lonely or idle; she had the house, such a trial it always had been, so much of it, so essential that every nook and cranny be perfection, and her family and her friends, and in the summer of 1939, their son Jonathan. If she did not brag openly, she gave off an offensive braggart smell; she was the luckiest happiest married woman she knew.

The war, wrenching half the human race apart, left them together in their own house. Robert was forty, too old and too valuable for marching and firing guns. Robert was needed in a ministry, engaged in providing them with whatever they had; orange juice for babies, Spam as a treat, sandy bread for everyone. She immediately joined the Women's Voluntary Service; it was the best she could do to combine her duty to her fellow men and to her infant child and her overworked husband.

There was no one left to help in the big house except her old nanny, who was too decrepit for war work but not too decrepit for Jonathan. Mrs Hapgood moved them all down to the ground floor and basement. Then, hating herself for hating it, she turned over the drawing-room floor and the first bedroom floor to three Jewish refugee families; in due course the top two storeys went to the Free French who lived there in jammed profusion. And all the time, all those years, through the tragedies and horrors, she suffered because her home had become a shambles; and never admitted this to anyone.

On the contrary, she was steadfastly civil and as kind as she could be to the strangers who destroyed the neatness, the cleanliness that seemed to be either an incurable craving of her nature, or an incurable deformation of her soul. But deep and hidden inside her was a core of mean-mindedness, mean-spiritedness. She longed for this ghastly war to end so that she could be freed of the resident horde, smooth and scrub her home and her life back to its narrow happiness. She wanted to be snug with Robert and the children; she wanted to be the loved centre of a private cosmos. Naturally, when peace came, she would accept the outside duties of privileged women, the orphanage board, the hospital board; she had to preserve that virtuous image of herself. Lying to herself about motives, she would attend the committee meetings, paying a small tribute to some god who must be placated. It would be dangerous to ignore the needs of others; vengeance might fall; her own needs might be jeopardized.

I think I am one of the nastiest people I ever knew, Mrs Hapgood told herself. I wonder how many women are exactly like me. England must be creeping with nasty, good women.

They had conceived their second child during the blitz, on a night when the sky was crashing down and there seemed no reason to expect morning. It was their personal, and very likely their last, act of defiance against cruelty and hate and madness. They could do nothing except affirm their belief in love; or that, at any rate, was what Mrs Hapgood thought at the time. As for Robert, she could no longer imagine what he had thought at any time. By the spring of 1941, Mrs Hapgood was bulging out of her green WVS uniform; but wore it and worked in it as long as she possibly could. Then Caroline was born, and the war went on and on.

The war had dulled love, but of that she could truthfullly say she had never complained. To be dulled was the least the war could do. She understood a great deal about the abomination of this war, the Jews on the floor above knew, the Free French in the attic had different knowledge. She would not now make herself out as inhuman. She might be a nasty woman, enamored of her virtue, but she was not a monster. She had noted the dullness, yet she had never once considered boredom between them. If Robert seemed bored at any period during the twenty-four years of their marriage, she attributed this to his work. After he retired from the panelled office on Wigmore Street, she attributed it to lack of work.

Peace of course did not come to Europe, as the history books affirm, on May 8, 1945. It came slowly, bit by bit, day after day, for years. Mrs Hapgood doubted if it had ever come. But Faith Hapgood did not want to think of the human condition; she wanted to rebuild her home. She was as single-minded as a bird carrying twigs. She did not fiddle paint on the black market or buy extra ration coupons from the poor; she slaved, within the law, to make the frame in which her family could again live the good life. Of course, Mrs Hapgood thought, pulling up the satin quilt to keep out the cold which no satin quilt would warm, there may be the simplest possible explanation for everything. I may just be stupid. Nothing more complicated than that.

One could not say when peace really came, or what they called peace; it might have been when the house fronts of London began to be painted one after the other, so that people walked in the city, revived, as if each house was a bright spring crocus. Gradually, and deeply shocked by the news, Mrs Hapgood learned that masses of people had enjoyed the war like billy-o. The little island had been submerged by legions of glamorous, unattached, randy men, with solitary women waiting for them. One had drunk oneself silly because tomorrow we die or do some dismal job all over again; and if you could find anything to spend money on, why not spend it? Dazedly, in retrospect, Mrs Hapgood saw London as a darkened chamber of orgies, filled with rutting animals having the time of their lives. Mrs Hapgood felt very queer and perplexed and out of all this. If she and Robert had been separated they would have agonized about each other's safety, prayed for the day of reunion, and been faithful. There was no other way to be.

Many couples could not join again, after the war; too much time and too many bodies had come between them. But now, more and more, infidelity appeared to be general and freely discussed at dinner tables, with wit and relish. She had never heard such conversations in her parents' house; before the war her married friends, men or women, had not suggested that they passed their spare time with extramarital bedfellows. Mrs Hapgood was not the sort of woman who goes about crying shame; she was also uninvolved. It did not concern her and Robert. She loved Robert; Robert loved her; they were faithful without effort, as they breathed. She could only assume that they were set apart, especially blessed, unlike weaker mortals; their marriage had been made in heaven. For her and Robert there was the problem which faced every living thing, and was not to be feared or bemoaned, but accepted; one of them would die first, one of them would have to live on a while longer.

Oh give it up, Mrs Hapgood told herself, aren't you satisfied to have a broken heart? Do you like using a hammer to make sure? At any rate, she had thought her way out of hate into this horizonless sea of sadness. She might drown in the sadness but that was an improvement over going crazy with hate. She went to her sitting-room, collected the untouched plates, and dumped the food in the toilet; the hotel people must not get the notion that she was either daft or a drunkard. She was staggering with weariness. The swansdown bed engulfed her.

Philip Naisby was not at lunch. Mrs Hapgood thought he must be avoiding her, uneasy as she was; and this made her uneasier. But the sky was the same gauzy blue, the trees were swollen green bouquets, the air tasted of sun and smelled of burning leaves, and she went into the woods, searching for that joy which came, when it did, like the gift of grace. She found Philip Naisby drinking from a bottle with his back against a tree and the remains of a picnic lunch gathered together on a pullover.

'I looked for you,' he said, not moving. 'Too good a day to eat at a table. Where were you?'

'In Tours.'

He had a habit, which would have alarmed her before and now amused her, of staring long and in silence.

'At the hairdresser's,' he said. 'You look edible. That's how you look. French-style edible. Do sit down.'

She obeyed, wondering what this unpredictable man would think up next in the way of quick intimacy.

'I've had a revelation,' he said. 'About half an hour ago. It came to me, the way great inspirations must, I suppose. I feel like a chap who has suddenly seen how to make a toothpaste from electrons which will cure tuberculosis. Would you like a swig from my bottle?'

She drank awkwardly but happily, dribbling a bit. The Kendall children had not been taught to drink from bottles.

'Do you want to know about my revelation?'

'I do indeed.'

'It's this. Why not have fun?'

She choked with laughter, and blew out wine like an atomizer.

'It's no laughing matter. I bet you hadn't thought of it. It's terribly important. Do you have much fun? It's a talent or an art or a state of soul that people like us have nearly lost. We do pleasant things, don't we? We either don't enjoy them a bit or tell ourselves we do. We say to each other, I had a lovely time, such a nice evening and etc., etc. That isn't fun. That's routine boredom. We don't know anything better to do so we go on doing what is certified as agreeable. I hate the theatre and am always going to plays. I hate dinner parties. I hate golf. I hate the awful holidays I take every year. I hate all the agreeable things I do. So then I was visited by this revelation. Why not have fun?'

'Oh, yes,' Mrs Hapgood said. 'Why not? If it's possible.'

'What do you really like to do?'

She felt as if he had knocked her wind out. The truth was that she did not really like to do anything, not the way he meant. Then why stay alive? Just to do what you were expected to? Just to crawl comfortably through a lot of nothing?

'Lately,' she said, 'only in the last week or so, I've started to like buying clothes and going to the hairdresser.'

'Bravo.'

'Don't mock. I know it's poor stuff.'

'It isn't poor stuff. It's fine. Did you know it was fun at the time?'

'Yes, after the first leap. Only I don't imagine it would go on being fun for ever, once I got used to it, or if that was all.'

'No. Speaking as one who has practically forgotten what fun is, I would think there ought to be a big variety of it.'

'I bought dozens of tubes of gouache today.'

'You're way ahead of me. It's fun for you to paint?'

'I paint like a Victorian maiden,' Mrs Hapgood said harshly. 'That's not fun. It's a refined amusement. It must be fun to hurl cans of paint on a huge canvas and roller skate on it and sweep it with a broom and wallow in colour and confusion and not give a damn.'

'We might try that. I'm ready for anything. Do you like to sightsee?'

'It depends.'

'Ah, you've done a good deal of the right sort, have you? Well, we can only experiment, we are beginners after all. We might paint the little, balmier local châteaux, the while being potted on white wine.'

'You're a painter?'

'No. I'm an architect. And I would love to watch you buying dresses. I've never gone into a dress shop with a woman in my life. Having thought such an occupation was reserved for fairies or Frenchmen.'

'All right, we'll do both. Goodness, I feel cheerful.'

'You will be happy to know that I have another bottle of wine stashed away in the stream, keeping cool. Wait a minute.'

He returned with a dripping bottle, pulled the cork expertly, settled back in his place and said, 'Here, put your head against my shoulder. It's more comfortable since I'm taking up most of the tree. Heel-taps for me. New bottle for you. As a start.'

It's so easy, Mrs Hapgood thought, it's so marvelously easy; if only it need never stop. But they would get cold or stiff, it would grow dark, there was always a later, you always had to go on.

'I was in hospital for three weeks,' Philip Naisby remarked, as though talking to himself or the surrounding greenery. 'Luckily they did not net me, because they didn't know there was anything wrong with my head. Luckily I had something wrong with my body, gallstones; an operation. The patient, cured of what is making him turn green and vomit, by surgical intervention, is now pronounced whole and well but needs to recuperate. A sunny quiet place, a careful diet, no drink for a time, dear boy. In a few weeks you'll be as fit as a fiddle, and happy as a bird dog, back at your work. I was very clever to keep them from knowing that you can't take gallstones out of the brain.'

Well, Mrs Hapgood thought, I am not alone; but I never imagined I was. In her case, there was the rankling humiliation of knowing that millions had been and were and would be in exactly the same trouble; you were a type, not a person; you could take no comfort from an exceptional disaster; you were ashamed because your type was so common. And still it remained your own trouble.

'Did I hear you right?' Philip Naisby asked. 'Did you say you had just started to have fun at dressmakers' and hairdressers'?'

'Yes.'

'But how interesting. Why should something you've always done suddenly become fun?'

'Not always done. Never done. I got my clothes from the same place, when needed, about as exciting as buying potatoes or soap. And I did not go to hairdressers.'

'You mean you've invented yourself in a week?'

'Yes.' And he would not have dreamed of suggesting that the other Mrs Hapgood rest her head on his shoulder and drink from a bottle.

'Of course you weren't a hunch-backed crone. But what did you look like? I can't imagine you any other way.'

'I looked clean and respectable.'

'You are funny. Do you think you look unwashed and criminal now? You look edible, I told you. Does it make you feel different? I mean, changing the outside? Does it work for the inside?'

'Sometimes.'

'How?'

'Sometimes,' Mrs Hapgood said shyly, aghast at the way she was talking to this man, but why should it matter what she said, 'I feel like an apprentice loose woman.'

He gave a shout of laughter and seized her in his arms, bottle and all.

'Oh I do like you, I really like you. The apprentice part has such charm.'

He let her go; she felt wonderful, slightly tipsy, and young and quite small and appealing.

'I was married to a natural, real, you might almost say professional loose woman for ten years,' Philip Naisby announced. 'And I promise you the genuine article is the biggest bore going.'

Mrs Hapgood was instantly sobered; this began to look like a lunatic game of musical chairs.

'Did it hurt,' she asked, 'when you found out?'

'So long ago and I found out at once. Yes. I suppose it did—cheap sort of hurt, really. Getting your vanity and your so-called ideals and what-not kicked in. After that, no. I married too late, not until the war was over. She was eighteen years younger, you'd have to be a certified loony to start off like that. Very pretty, helpless; I saw myself as the strong protector. Makes me quite sick to remember myself; I must have worn such a fatuous expression.'

'Don't tell me if it makes you sick.'

'No, I rather like it. I've never told anyone. One doesn't care to go around whining because one's wife's in bed with any man when she has fifteen minutes to spare. If I'd had proper guts or sense I'd have walked out at the beginning. But the funny thing was that Molly actually was helpless, she never got anywhere with her fornications; she was always dumped; she made a mess of it, and was frightened and needed me to clean up after her. But finally she managed better and hooked a man four times richer than me and was off like the wind.'

'A relief then?' Mrs Hapgood asked softly. He did look ill, pale, and though his arms, seizing her in that unexpected hug, were strong, they felt thin as rope.

'Oh yes, though the end was the limit of shoddiness. Solicitors with lists: that chair is mine, that table is yours. I gave her the whole lot naturally; I meant to, or chuck it in the street. Can you believe that people haggle over bits and pieces when they're getting divorced? As if they wanted to hang on to a smell of corpses? I moved to the Connaught. She never went near the Connaught; her notion of an old folks' hostelry. Wonderful to live in a hotel room that doesn't mean anything and doesn't resemble you or anyone else. Then I moved to the hospital. Then back to the Connaught. Then here. Clean as a whistle; free as air.'

'That's the reason for the gallstones that can't be removed, isn't it?' Mrs Hapgood asked. Any question was indelicate and perhaps worse, unkind; but she needed to know, for herself.

'What? My ex-wife? My ten years of living with a well-brought-up nympho? The divorce with its chic commercial angle? Perhaps. In part. Though I was only sickened by the style of the divorce; I certainly didn't regret her. No, it must be much more than Molly and older and more important to me. Otherwise, they'd have dissolved, wouldn't they?'

'I don't know. I don't know anything.'

'Never mind. Neither do I. I've been using you, Faith. It's as revolting as being sick in someone's lap.'

'Oh don't,' Mrs Hapgood cried. 'Don't talk like that. We haven't before. Don't let's start.'

'Good.' He took the bottle from her, looked at her hand carefully, and kissed it. 'Good. Agreed. Is your bottom getting cold? Shall we go to Azay-le-Rideau for tea? That château's a dream. The work of a woman really, though her husband gets official credit. I've never been able to discover whether she was happy in it but then history leaves out all the important stuff.'

He had flown to Paris and taken the train to Tours; they would use Mrs Hapgood's Lancia. He insisted on driving, saying that it was a blow to his virility to be chauffeured by a woman and besides nine men out of ten drove better than women. Mrs Hapgood adored being treated like this; she was only too glad to surrender the wheel and her competence. Robert disliked driving, therefore she drove him, proud as usual of her ability to manage.

They did not talk on the narrow backroad, they watched the green world, and Mrs Hapgood marveled at the ease of this silence. Even alone with Robert, on their occasional trips, there had been conversation, or rather little bubbles of talk. 'Do look at that! Oh how pretty! I think it's the next road to the right. No more than thirty kilometers now. Goodness, the way these foreigners drive . . .' Contact nattering, effortless but perpetual, to stave off what? Silence which wouldn't have been easy, but empty? She was the prime source of the natter. Making her little chat and therefore dragging replies from Robert, had she spoiled every journey, washed off glamor with commonplaces, prevented rest, given emotion no chance to grow? She was always in charge, that was it, she was always keeping something going. What a horrible woman; she would have loathed herself if she had met herself. Robert's courtesy must have been like reinforced steel, something he used as armor. He must often have been half crazed by ennui. He should have screamed at her, beaten her, commanded her to stop being the perfect wife, and become a woman.

Mrs Hapgood shivered.

Without taking his eyes from the road, Philip Naisby said, 'What's the matter?'

'I was thinking of myself.'

'You couldn't possibly be that hateful.'

'You know nothing about me.'

'Not about your life. I don't think I want to. It's idiotic as I'm well aware, but I couldn't help being jealous of the man who's made you wretched.'

'How did you guess it was a man?'

He swerved his head quickly, to smile at her. 'You do surprise me. The things you say. You don't imagine I thought you were in despair over the Cold War? How did I know it was a man? Because you're very much a woman; what else could it be?'

'You don't know me,' she repeated.

'Objection. I know how you are now and though you say you've made over your outside in a week, no one can do that with the inside. And how you are is not hateful.'

'Now?' she asked stupidly. 'But how am I?' For she did not know; she was only beginning to see what she had been, and presumably therefore was, since she agreed that you could not dye your soul like your hair.

'You're touching. And badly hurt and lonely and you'll never get beyond the apprentice stage as a loose woman and you have no idea how fascinating your face is. That wonderful French make-up, so smooth and seductive and worldly, with everything you think and feel flashing across it as if you were about fifteen years old, and out on your own for the first time.'

Mrs Hapgood turned away, staring at the deep green ribbon of the Indre. He was sorry for her. This was the best she could do, eye shadow and uplift brassière and auburn mane and all.

'Listen to me, Faith. Left to myself, I would pull on the brake, block the road, and kiss you. The only reason I don't is because it's too soon. You wouldn't believe me.'

'No, I wouldn't.'

'Well, wait and see. And don't shiver again and stop giving yourself hell. We're almost there.'

They walked arm in arm across the little wooden bridge and before them rose the château, sun-warmed stone, fragile, feminine, built to last for ever and to lighten the heart. Near by a German couple listened earnestly to a box-like machine which lectured them on the history of the castle.

'For a hundred francs,' Philip Naisby said, 'all the essential facts in any language except Japanese. And you can't go in without the guide, in a herd, so one can't go in. But the best is those inspired windows with the stairs moving up behind them. And the views all round from the garden.'

He led her by the hand along a graveled path to a bench under a gigantic copper beech tree. Mrs Hapgood sighed; there were no words for such loveliness. The château changed from each side, and around it flowed a narrow river soft with water grass. The great and noble woman, who had created this beauty, must have planted the trees too, so old, so adroitly placed. But this is peace, Mrs Hapgood thought, to be filled with gratitude, filled full and no room for anything else.

'Philip,' she said, 'thank you,' and saw that his face was numb in sadness.

'I can't get over it,' he said. 'You can drive anywhere in Europe and find beautiful houses; it would take a lifetime to see them all, none alike, but all with the quality of magic. And look at us and what we do. A man is a genius nowadays if he whomps up a new way to stick chromium or bronze on another concrete-and-glass box. I'm a successful architect, Faith. We are ruining the looks of the world and the world begins to look the same everywhere and people are pleased with our work and pay us huge fees instead of hanging us to lamp-posts. Our minds must be like little plastic slugs.'

She could not encourage him because she abhorred every similar towering hive that reared above the London sky-line.

'It's the time we live in,' Mrs Hapgood said. 'Too many people, everything costs so much, speed, machinery.'

'My only hope is that everything we build will fall down, which it probably will, from general shoddiness. And that later, some day, there'll be a race of men with real minds again and what they build will be beautiful and last.'

'You hate your work, Philip?'

'I was very ambitious when I was young. I've done nothing in my life except work, and supervise a certain number of hellishly noisy guns in the war. I am nearly forty-nine years old. Barring the holocaust or being run over by a bus, I shall probably live for twenty more years. I have to do something, and I don't know anything else to do. I'd be satisfied to copy the fine work of the dead, if anyone wanted it, or could use it. But you know that doesn't turn out either. With all our tools and techniques, when we copy it looks shoddy too. It must come from within.'

I am older than he is, Mrs Hapgood thought, and felt a hot blush creeping up her neck, as if she had been caught in a shameful theft. It was awful, something she'd read about; the unattached predatory female hunting the younger male. She had not hunted; it was not true.

'There must be a solution,' Mrs Hapgood mumbled, not sure whether she meant for them or for modern architecture.

'Yes, there must be. Only if there was, you'd think someone would have found it by now, wouldn't you? Come on, my beauty, we'll walk around the far side and then go and have tea.'

By the time they returned to Varincourt, the sky was the color of water sapphires, with a few fresh diamond stars. At the door, Mrs Hapgood said, 'Philip, I've had fun today. Really. It *was* a revelation.'

'When will you be down for dinner?'

'I won't. I mean to dine in my sitting-room.'

'Oh,' he said, hurt at once. 'Too much of a good thing? Afraid it might go on too long?'

'No. Please don't look like that. It's only that I'm taking fun seriously, I want to practise. You see, my sitting-room is absurd and I never lived in anything like it, brocade and satin and rosewood and gilt and acajou and heaven knows what else. And I had a rush of negligées to the head, a few days ago; I've got five. I thought it would be fun to wear one and dine in that foolish room and take time to remember the day.'

'Darling Faith,' he said. 'You do that. Have that fun. What colour is the negligée?'

'For tonight, yellow. It matches the curtains.'

He laughed. 'Will you meet me in the morning? On the terrace at ten? That isn't too early?'

'At ten. Sleep well, Philip.'

The yellow negligée did not look like the kept peroxide blonde; it was edible, Philip's word. Mrs Hapgood drank a large martini, reclining on the chaise longue, and read *Le Retour de Chéri*. Colette's novels, modified and translated for private use, might serve as text-books. Mrs Hapgood appreciated the taste of her food, and was relieved by this sign of health. She carried her wineglass back to the chaise longue and told the day over to herself, like telling beads. She was actually sleepy, and she went to bed feeling desirable, freed from barbiturates, and now she would curl up and go bye-bye like a baby.

She must have slept and been wakened by a dream, but it did not seem like a dream; it reminded her of those terrifying moments in a children's pantomime when, in a burst of sulphurous smoke, the ogre or the witch is revealed, grinning. 'No,' she said out loud. 'No!' She turned on the light and ran to the bathroom to find the bottle with red pills, the other bottle with black and green pills. She had no idea whether that mixture went together or how much of it was dangerous, and she did not care. She had to sleep, quickly; if there had been a doctor to call and beg for an injection that would knock her out like a felled ox, she would have done that. She could not go through it again.

Her hands were clenched at her side and she thought, it can't last long, the pills will work.

It was late afternoon, perhaps five-thirty, when Gertrude, the maid, looking alarmed, said there was a call for Madam from Connecticut. Across the sea came Caroline's voice, tearful, hiccuping, turning to Mummy in her terror. The baby Jimmy had an appalling fever, something too awful, she wasn't sure, 103 or 104, and they'd taken him to a hospital and there he was, in a cot all by himself, little and purple and breathing so you couldn't listen, and maybe it was polio. The doctors didn't know. 'Mummy, Mummy,' the terrified voice pleaded over that improbable distance. Mummy always fixed everything, Mummy arranged, Mummy could be counted on; but could not, of course, save the life of a nine-month-old baby thousands of miles away.

Mrs Hapgood had held on to her own voice with steely discipline; she had soothed; she had talked of the way babies ran sudden meaningless fevers; it had happened with Caroline herself, with Jonathan. Caroline must have confidence in the doctors, they were known to be brilliant in America, Bill was with her, now she should have a drink—some brandy—and something to eat, and then rest, Bill would stay beside her, Matron would find a place; she must not give in to panic and despair; it would all certainly come right; Mummy was sure of that. The crying girl did quiet down; she thanked her mother; Mrs Hapgood asked for the telephone number of the hospital and said she would call back in a few hours when she expected to hear good news. Mrs Hapgood hung up; her hands were shaking. She must get hold of Robert; she needed Robert; he would tell her what to do. Probably she should catch a plane for New York tonight.

It was Robert's bridge afternoon at his club. Mrs Hapgood had never disturbed him there; men went to clubs in order not to be disturbed by their wives. She rang the club. The porter said Mr Hapgood was not in. Had he come and gone? No, he had not been there at all. Robert rented a little office, near the British Museum; it was, as they both knew, only an excuse to be out of the house. She understood that a man who had gone to work all his life would feel lost and old and lonely, sitting at home day after day. Robert was writing a monograph on Roman ruins; he kept his papers there. She called that number; no answer. Then, frantic, she began calling his friends; he might have varied his routine for some reason; he might be with one of them or they might know where to find him. She tried four, none of them had seen him, none could guess his whereabouts. They were odd in the way they answered her, flustered, and foolishly insisted that of course Robert was at his club, the porter was a well-known moron.

She felt hot and sticky as with fever; she had a bath, she dressed early for dinner—they dressed every night, as a reaction from the scruffiness of the war years. She could not read or think; she smoked, and at last, punctually, he was always punctual to the minute, Robert came home at quarter-past seven.

She ran down the stairs from the drawing-room.

'Robert! Oh Robert, where were you? I tried the club . . .'

'My dear, what's wrong? I should have told you, I simply forgot. I promised to go to old John Withers this afternoon, he's not well, poor chap, and rather dismal.'

She had called John Withers, she had spoken to him, he was perfectly well and had neither seen nor expected her husband. It was as fast as that, as fast as if Robert had shot her between the eyes, with a small-caliber bullet, leaving an almost invisible hole, no bleeding, while the bullet lodged in the brain. She turned white and staggered against the hall table.

Robert caught her in his arms, saying, 'Faith, what is it? What's happened?'

'Caroline,' she said. She felt calm and quite dead. 'She called from Greenwich. The baby is very ill; they fear polio; she was beside herself. Do you think I ought to take the night plane for New York?'

'Oh, my darling,' Robert said. 'How awful for you, when did you hear? Five-thirty? And alone all this time not knowing where to reach me. Poor little Caroline. No, don't take the plane tonight. We'll call her in an hour or so to see what's happened and then decide. If you get the morning plane, you'll still be there in the morning, the difference in time. Come upstairs and have a drink. You look ill yourself.'

He made her a stiff martini, kissed her forehead, said it couldn't be polio, it simply couldn't; surely the child had been vaccinated. It was just one of those ghastly fevers that babies did get. Remember Jonathan? Remember Caroline? If she would forgive him a moment, he'd rush up and change. He invariably changed in fifteen minutes; he did everything with economy and order. He was an organized man.

He returned to find his wife staring into the fire; he had never seen her like this. He remembered her nerve as unbreakable through every crisis, private and public. Probably she was shattered now because there was nothing to do. Faith was always one to take decisive action.

They hardly spoke at dinner, Robert feeling that babble would only scratch against her nerves and it was useless to go on and on about the Salk vaccine and how over-anxious Caroline was, as they knew. Mrs Hapgood excused herself and said she would wait in the drawing-room for coffee; the smell of food affected her badly. Robert rose and held open the door; he had never failed in any slightest gesture of courtesy. It would be best to give her a little time to herself. Faith would hate his seeing her undone; she was a proud woman. It was the worst coincidence that this had to happen on a Tuesday when he was, as always, with Paula. Dreadful for Faith to have worried alone, those extra hours.

He thanked God that it wasn't Faith who was frightfully, possibly mortally ill. Faith was the solid earth he stood on, though he had never understood what he gave her in return. An ordinary woman would feel repaid in terms of the usual female bargain; a beautiful house, plenty of money, nice children, a kind husband. Faith would have been the same in a slum; her only use for money was to make his life easy. She loved her children, but he knew he came first. Meantime, he did not know whether to wait here on a Chippendale chair or run up the stairs and take her in his arms. He did not know what to give his wife who was at last in need.

Robert found her again, listless by the fire; Gertrude brought the coffee tray, muttered good night, and creaked off towards the basement. Gertrude the maid and Sarah the cook were the lone survivors of the war, but with this reduced domestic staff, and relays of chars, Faith kept their big house in its usual untroubled order, and dominated life so that it was as steady as it had been in his youth. Paula never stopped having maddening difficulties with servants, with tradesmen, her bank, her car; she was in a perpetual fluttered distress. He did nothing for Faith because Faith did for them both, but he tackled Paula's problems, soothed the sweet, clinging creature, and felt he was the man in charge. Faith was too intelligent for that feminine nonsense.

More alarmed than he realized by the air of catastrophe in this house where everything ran according to schedule, he said, 'Thank God, you're all right.'

Faith gave up staring at the small logs on the hearth. She turned her head slowly and looked at him. Her eyes frightened him; they were almost black and frozen. She had looked at him with unwavering affection for twenty-four years.

'You never go to your club on Tuesdays,' Faith said.

He sat down quickly, in the deep chair across from her.

'Nor do you dine with men on Thursday. Nor go on business trips and archaeology jaunts alone.'

Her voice was as impersonal and as cold as the voice of the judge, summing up: the sentence would clearly be death.

'And this has been going on from the beginning of our marriage, this has always been so.'

'Faith,' he began. It was senseless to lie to her; besides he had no practice in lying. Since she did not lie, he could count on her not suspecting him of untruth. What could he say that she would understand, and that would not wound her intolerably? The truth was very simple; he was a sensual man with a taste for small, highly-sexed women. Seven days a week, year after year, they would be hell; he had gone through that hell once. He was not all of a piece, as few men were; perhaps he was more orderly than most men, who took their pleasure as offered by chance. He could not say to Faith, I love you more than any woman on earth but you are not much interested in sex, and I am, and whether that's a filthy disease or a normal itch, I know myself and have come to terms with what I am. My terms are discreet regular infidelity. He did not like chopping and changing, with the possibility of some angered woman causing a scandal. Paula had lasted for seven years and become more like a muddled nuisance of a second wife than a mistress, but was passionate and a habit of his flesh. How could he explain such things to Faith? When he knew that Faith gave him her whole life, how could he say it wasn't quite enough?

There was no decent excuse, and it was grotesque to apologize or beg forgiveness. A plea for another chance is feeble stuff after twenty-four years. And if God himself had not intervened, to send Caroline's baby a fever on Tuesday, Faith would never have known. They would have lived together, both fully satisfied, though in different ways and for different reasons, until their deaths.

He could not raise his eyes; he sat in silence and studied his hands, opening and closing the fingers.

'Will you put in the call to Greenwich now?' Mrs Hapgood said.

He was glad to sit at the table in the corner with his back to her. He was too shocked by the suddenness of this disaster to be able to think; he was unaccustomed to suddenness. The call came through in minutes; he spoke to Caroline who was still tearful but now with relief. Mrs Hapgood spoke to Caroline. The baby's fever had dropped; the doctors were convinced it was not polio; a virus, there were so many viruses. Bill had been an angel, she could not have lived through it without Bill. Mrs Hapgood sent all three her love, coupled with more reassurance, and said she would telephone again tomorrow; she would want to hear that Caroline had got some sleep.

Mrs Hapgood hung up, rose and left the room. Robert Hapgood, stunned, sat alone by the fire. He poured himself coffee, now lukewarm. It will have to come right, he thought stupidly, it will have to. I'll talk to her in the morning. He had the night to find the words that would keep Faith with him. He could not lose Faith. He had not been able to live with her alone but he could not live at all without her. She would have to understand. Women did. It's merely sex, he thought, I must make her see. It isn't something that matters to her.

Behind the locked door of her bedroom, Mrs Hapgood looked at the ruin of her life. Lies, Mrs Hapgood thought, built on a lie, lived as a lie; the only man I ever loved is a liar and I have been a dupe for my entire adult life. The past was wiped out; there was nothing left in it to believe. Her reason to live had never existed. To Robert she must have seemed a fool, to everyone else a joke. She had imagined herself uniquely loved, and surrounded by friends. She had been used as a domestic animal, and surrounded by conspirators.

The bullet in her brain dislodged or moved; shock was turning into pain like fire. Year after year, and from the very beginning, after the honeymoon, he had given to other women what he let her believe was hers alone. Nothing had been hers. She had lived in a solitary self-made dream, while Robert kept his secrets and encouraged her childish fantasy, and lied and lied and lied. What sort of man would treat a woman like that; robbing the blind is the lowest crime.

Twice a week and all the other times, the business trips, the archaeology—oh archaeology indeed, do you take pretty ladies to dusty sites and ask them to sit on a wheelbarrow while you sift dirt; you take them to luxury hotels and send your wife a postcard or a note, saying you are stopping overnight in Rome, Athens, Istanbul, and not to worry about the lack of mail, there is no postal service in the wilderness. Did he go to them on his regular Tuesdays and Thursdays, panting with desire, and was he so calm, so courteous, so kind in the intervening days because he was indifferent to her; she hardly disturbed him, she did not count. If twice a week you expended all the passion in your body and your heart, you might well be glad of a rest between. What did they do together, how did they talk, what did the women look like, and how was Robert with them, this stranger whom she fancied she knew as well as herself, what did he change into; what did he give them that he had stolen from her?

But he made love to me, she thought, to me too, all these years. She circled her room, bumping into furniture, for now she saw herself in his arms, grateful, quiet, satisfied; and he so gentle. Bored, perhaps sickened; but doing his duty. The evil of it, the rottenness; how could he, why not have lied better so that he need never touch her? He could have spared her that. He did not want her and gave only what he felt he had to; he wanted the other bodies, he gave them himself. His duty and yes, it must have tired or repelled him more as the years wore on, for he had been saying—and she had laughed at him, with love—that he was growing older; their nights together became gradually less and less frequent.

Now she was tearing off her clothes; her skin was covered with fungus; she was suffocated by a vile smell; all the bodies had smeared off on her, all the tastes and odors, the hands, the lips, the cries. She stumbled into the bathroom but it took too long to fill the tub. She stood in the steam, and scrubbed herself wildly with the hard long-handled brush. She washed her hair with hands like claws; there was soap in her eyes, her mouth, there could not be enough soap. Dripping and crazy, she began on her teeth, scouring them again and again. In the washstand mirror, she saw a naked madwoman, scratched around the throat and breast. She leaned against the porcelain bowl and wept; it sounded like someone retching, unable to stop.

She was in her room, wrapped in a towel, shivering. She must stay quiet for, somewhere, only waiting to edge closer, were thoughts she knew to be the end of sanity; kill Robert, kill herself. Quiet, she told herself, holding her breath. In this quiet, she began to hear whispers; they came from the cornice, from the chimney, from behind the chest of drawers. She spun around trying to see the noise; not whispering, not words; light, glacial laughter. Mrs Hapgood put her hands over her ears. They had been laughing at her for years, years; and at last they didn't care, let her listen, let her know. Robert's laughter was there too, with all the others.

She must have blacked out, a piece of time was gone. Naked and very cold, she lay sprawled across the marriage bed. She pulled herself off it, hating it, hating all memory; and knew what she had to do. Leave. Go away at once. Never see Robert again, or listen to more lies. She heard Robert clearly, saying as he had thousands of times: 'I love you.' Of all lies, the most obscene. She was stiff and fumbling with cold but managed to dress and throw clothes in a suitcase. In her neatly pigeon-holed desk, she found her passport, car papers, traveller's cheques, the hoard of cash always on hand for emergencies that had never arisen. She had wasted herself on order, which she believed was needed and wanted; this very order made it easy to escape.

Mrs Hapgood opened the long chintz curtains and saw weak gray dawn light over Regent's Park. The whole world looked dirty.

Philip Naisby was comfortably settled on his spine, with his feet on the balustrade, basking in the sun. He rose when he heard Mrs Hapgood's heels on the marble pavement. Standing over her, holding both her hands, he said, 'Bad night?'

Mrs Hapgood nodded.

'Yes, I see. Very bad. I must find a way to stop it.'

'What?'

'Giving yourself hell. Well, on this splendid day, the ticket is the healthy outdoors. Where are your paints?'

'In my room.'

'Run off and get them. You have enough paper for us both? I'll collect the rest of the paraphernalia. You might change into something sturdier. We'll be sitting on grass most of the time. Meet you at the car in fifteen minutes.'

A Tours saleslady had lured her into trying on tight green trousers; Mrs Hapgood was struck by how good her legs were, so clothed. The former Mrs Hapgood never wore trousers; it was a compelling reason to wear them now. She gathered up paints and brushes and drawing pad, and hurried to join Philip, feeling uncertain. She might seem many things to him but must not seem a middle-aged woman, trying to look young.

Philip Naisby finished stowing gear in the back of the car, turned, grinned all over his face and said, 'You can't think what you're like. Surprise after surprise. Now you've become a perfect lady beatnik. Have you got five sets of these too?'

'No.'

'We'll get them. Pile in, dear girl. Our equipment is rather improvised; dinner plates for palettes, a milk jug for water, butter knives for palette knives, and two trays to balance the paper on. We'll make out. Shall we go back to Azay-le-Rideau?'

They agreed that the best view of the château was from under their beech tree, two angles and the loop of the stream; besides it was more private there. They distributed themselves on the grass; tubes of gouache were opened, squeezed, mislaid, searched for, where's the lemon yellow, have you got the viridian? They became absorbed. They forgot they were playing, two grown-ups busy with brushes to fill time, to ward off the real fear of not knowing what to do with themselves or their lives. The light was fading and the air felt cold when they exchanged their finished sketches, not minding a bit that the work was so poor, they had the good day as a clear gain.

Driving back to Varincourt, Philip said, 'I don't want to end like yesterday. I want you to put on a negligée and ask me to dine in your sitting-room. I want to keep you from another bad night, if I can.'

Mrs Hapgood thought this out slowly. Not looking at him, she said, 'You mean you want to sleep with me?'

'Yes, Faith. Very much. Terribly.'

'I'm no good at it,' Mrs Hapgood said in a flat, final voice.

'How do you know?'

'It has been proved to me, over a long period.'

'I don't set myself up as an authority; far from it. But speaking purely on a theoretical basis, I'd say people were good at it or not depending on how interested they were in each other. I am not talking about athletes or confirmed exhibitionists.'

'I don't know anything, except what I told you. I am.' Mrs Hapgood said, taking a deep breath to steady her voice, 'a failure in bed.'

'Faith, let me come. You can kick me out after dinner if you like. I won't make a fuss. I've got the bare minimum of vanity left.'

She did not want to refuse him; she would have given him any pleasure she could. But this was a question of nerve, and she had lost hers for ever.

'What do you drink as a start?' Philip Naisby asked.

'Martinis.'

'I shall order a quart to be sent to your sitting-room and be there at eight.'

So that was that, unless she was prepared to hurt him; and she was sure he was a man of his word.

'You're beautiful,' Philip Naisby said, as if he had been asked to make a vital decision and had made it. The patter of the practised hostess deserted her, she told herself furiously that she was behaving like a sixteen-year-old virgin on the brink of seduction.

'I see what you mean about this room. It is a nest, isn't it? Mine's solemn, Empire, with much cerise satin and gold bees. May I have a drink?'

Mrs Hapgood was relieved; something to do; a use for her hands. Then, unless her vocal cords were paralyzed, she could ask if the martini was cold enough or dry enough.

'Look what I brought.' Philip showed her a small transistor radio. 'We can listen to the news of the gay mad world, to tide us over your nervousness. Or if it would help, I'm quite prepared to play Snap or Crazy Eights.'

Mrs Hapgood realized that she had not thought of the wide world, and its illimitable woes, since that night in Hanover Terrace; and had read one newspaper, without noticing what she read. Her condition could only be described as egomania. God in heaven, she thought, one would imagine I was in some danger which imperilled life generally; or dying of a disease that could spread and kill thousands. Who *do* I think I am? A special case, the first special case, with special permission to nab suffering as my private province.

'Turn it on, Philip.'

With his back to her, he made a performance of twiddling the dials. He had to conceal his face but could not stop smiling from pleasure and tenderness. Faith, whom he judged to be a bit over forty, was now shy enough to faint, frightened stiff, ashamed of these girlish emotions and deeply appealing because of them. Or perhaps only to him; perhaps you had to be formed by a trollop to be so moved by a chaste woman.

The waiter knocked, wheeled in a table laden with silver covers, served, hovered, popped about like a Punch and Judy show, and leered at them amiably. Given half a chance, Philip thought with irritation, the fellow would bless the nuptial couch. He didn't want to lure Faith to bed because he'd been on short rations or because it was ridiculous to be in France with an attractive woman and not go to bed. He wanted something enormous which he had long since renounced as being beyond his scope.

'Shall we ask Ivor Novello to clear, Faith?'

'Yes.'

They were alone. Mrs Hapgood bustled with the coffee pot and Philip Naisby, thanking heaven for his luck, found a program of Chopin on the radio. If Chopin would not help, nothing would. Words, at this moment, were as dangerous as moving a person with broken bones.

The lovely music, falling clear like separate drops of water, provided an excuse to hide; she could close her eyes. Quietly, Philip Naisby turned off lights until the room was dim. What is the matter with me, Mrs Hapgood wondered. To be so shy was neurotic, or perhaps the inevitable result of faithfulness. She could not conceive the act of love, it plainly terrified her, with anyone but Robert. Philip would find her inadequate, he would be disappointed, but certainly kind and polite. In a day or two, not wanting to repeat failure and embarrassed by the situation, he would leave. One could hardly say that this was comparable to leaping off the Matterhorn, yet that was how she felt about it. But why? Fear was unbearable, not understanding the reasons for it doubled fear. She might actually be peculiar in the head. Not like other women. Abnormal. Better to leap off the Matterhorn.

'Philip, shall we go to bed?'

'No, darling. You haven't finished your brandy. Come here beside me.' He was lying on the chaise longue, he made room for her. 'This is Rubinstein we're listening to; it would be churlish to walk out on him.' She did as told; and was eased by his arm around her.

A high Frenchwoman's voice announced, 'Vous avez écouté...' Philip switched off the radio.

'You're half asleep, darling,' he said. 'Go to bed and I'll tuck you in.'

He would not oblige her to speak or make impossible decisions; he would leave on his own. Mrs Hapgood undressed quickly, nestled into safety with the covers up to her chin, and called him. He came at once, and sat beside her. Something in his face forced her to touch his hand, which was cold; he was trembling. Could a man be as shy as she, and as uncertain? She knew only the energetic boy, Mark, and the accomplished adult, Robert. She could not fit a shy man into her notions of sex and instantly saw the cold hand and the trembling as something else: Philip did not want her, he had got himself into a wretched position and was shaken with nerves; he longed to kiss her forehead and escape.

The fury, that she believed burnt out, blazed against him, against Robert, against all men. She would not be treated as a poor creature who could evoke affection but no more. Men were lusting after women all over the world, she was as good as the next woman, they were to lust after her. She too had demands to make, men were not the only ones with their everlasting physiological needs. She had another need and it was not to be denied; she would teach him and Robert and their whole greedy cruel sex; she would get what she wanted.

She reached up her arms and pulled Philip down to her; she managed to slide out of her nightgown. He was gasping with surprise, perhaps only surprise so far, but she had other plans. Vénus toute entière—her prey would learn. Fury inspired her, nothing else counted. Unknown and untried weapons had been given to her from nowhere and she used them, mindlessly. She meant to be devoured by a man whom she had driven to frenzy; and she was.

She lay quietly, gloating over her power, while Philip slept as if drugged. Her anger was gone; she could hardly remember it because she had won. Robert was proved wrong. She was free of that deadly vision of herself, Robert's vision: the virtuous wife, a rôle, not a woman. Robert, clearly, had everything wrong and he had been her teacher; he kept her in kindergarten since that was where he wanted her and she, cowardly or complacent, had been quite happy to stay for ever in the kiddies' class, memorizing her few lessons. One of the lessons would be that now she should be writhing with shame, having conducted herself like a wanton, and this sleeping man would no longer respect her. Where did these notions begin? She had not invented them. Handed down, no doubt, from kindergarten to kindergarten; how much kinder to bind feet rather than emotions. It did not matter a hoot whether Philip Naisby respected her or not. People like her were choked to death on respect, their own and that of others. As for shame, she was ashamed of the former Mrs Hapgood, a blind dullard. She had started to like this new Mrs Hapgood, who fought for her life like a sane animal that wants to survive.

I must sleep, Mrs Hapgood thought, I must look well tomorrow. Tomorrow she would be desired again, and tomorrow and tomorrow, if she had anything to do with it. She intended to leave the kindergarten and advance into the elementary grades, at least. I am as good as the next woman, Mrs Hapgood told herself, and triumph tasted like cream.

Before dawn, Philip waked her. Later he opened the curtains, letting in the first light, and came back to bed to study her face.

'How could you have said you were a failure? You must have detested your husband.'

Mrs Hapgood said nothing.

'I'm afraid of some words,' Philip went on. 'Mainly the word "love". The way it's bandied about has rather spoiled it.'

'Ah yes. For me too.'

'Well then, I won't say it, darling. I'll prove it, if you'll let me.'

He decided to dress and creep back to his room before the servants got up.

'You wouldn't like to be beamed on by the staff in the morning, would you? And if I stayed, I might not be able to leave you alone.'

She was asleep when Philip had closed the sitting-room door.

The telephone bell jerked Mrs Hapgood awake; the sudden noise hurt her like toothache. Robert again. She could not speak to him. The telephone went on ringing. Damn and blast Robert; what did he want of her? The bell trilled and trilled. Get it over with, Robert could not harm her now. She was greeted by a voice she scarcely recognized, Philip's, altogether changed. He had become an importunate young man in love.

'Faith, I have a plan. May I come to your room?'

'Not yet, darling, please. In half an hour.'

'I don't know how I'll wait. All right.'

She had done this, Faith the good gray mare, the reliable wife, mother, committee-woman; she had altered a man so much in one night that he sounded new.

Philip took her in his arms; 'Darling, do agree. Promise you'll agree.'

'To what, Philip?'

'My plan. I want us to go to Tours and spend the day buying clothes. Lots more of your elegant beatnik things; and one dress at least that's chosen with me and only to be worn for me. You can't think how much it means. I was too poor and too busy to be romantic when I was young; you must let me be, now. And tomorrow we'll leave.'

'Why? Where?'

'So we can live in the same room. That's why. I don't want you out of my sight. And where, to the Gorges du Tarn. I've never been to that part of France. Have you?'

'No.'

'You see. Everything first, for us together. I looked it up and there's a château with one more star than this. We can use it as our base and drive around; it must be marvellous country.'

She was thinking quickly; one room was a grave risk. Her mind moved in an accustomed groove: ways and means. She could wake before him and tiptoe to the bathroom, scrub off yesterday's mask, paint on a new one, slide back into bed and be discovered looking like an artificial flower. While Philip shaved, she could worm into what was accurately called the foundation garment. Glamor, obviously, depended on absences; no wonder mistresses had a better time of it than wives. You could not act and lie and scheme, interminably: fatigue would set in. But for a few weeks ...

'I agree.'

'Darling.'

'Give me time for breakfast.'

'I'll talk to the hotel people.'

Philip insisted on paying for all the tight trousers and bulky sweaters, and for the dress he had chosen. He said she looked like the chatelaine of Azay-le-Rideau; it was a medieval gown. Mrs Hapgood protested; she was scandalized; one did not accept gifts from men. She saw her mistake immediately, and withdrew the protests. Of course Philip must pay; he must feel her dependent and somehow owned, it was what he wanted. To buy a woman's clothes was partially to buy her, but then a man took care of his property, did he not? Honorable and exact, she had used her own small income for her clothes; it was unfair to waste Robert's money on her personal necessities. She objected if Robert spent too much on presents for Christmas and her birthday. No doubt Robert showered gifts on the other women, and luxuriated in being generous, appreciated, and an owner.

Dressing in the curtained cubicle of the last shop, Mrs Hapgood marveled at herself. The crookeder she became, and the more she enjoyed it, the better she understood Robert. She would end by blaming herself entirely for Robert's betrayal. Who could be expected to live, without rest or relief, in the company of a Girl Guide? On the other hand, Mrs Hapgood thought as she combed her hair, though she might understand and therefore forgive she would never touch Robert again.

This château, as towering and solid as a fortress, was the color of sunbaked earth. Built on the floor of the gorge, it guarded the foaming river. Inside, it was superb five star. Philip had taken a suite; they would often dine alone. There was a double bed. Philip explained that he had always wanted to stay the whole night with a cherished woman; by implication his wife Molly did not care for the arrangement. Mrs Hapgood neglected to say that, except when forced to it during the war, she and Robert had separate rooms.

They ranged the countryside from Avignon to Lascaux. She was carried on a cushion, and wondered why she had thought herself obliged to carry everyone on her shoulders. She felt spoiled and irresponsible, with no wish to be otherwise. All day and all night, Philip vindicated her. She had no place to live except in her body, and she knew that she could not live with the idea of her body Robert had forced on her; unwanted, ageing, sexless, a marital burden. Robert had done more than cheat her of love and time. He had destroyed her identity. Now Philip gave it back; make-up, make-believe and all, she existed as a woman in the eyes of a man.

There were difficulties: never to be seen as your unadorned self required much fast footwork, and concentration. And Philip was untidy; she cursed herself for minding the muddled bathroom, the clothes thrown in corners, the extraordinary places he found to put out cigarettes. Mrs Hapgood decided that two weeks of this bliss would be all she could bear. After that, she would need more sleep, and time to be herself with a washed face and a neat room.

'The first grey day,' Philip said. They were walking down a side road near Uzès. 'We must talk about what next, Faith.'

She waited.

'I want you to marry me.'

She stopped and kissed him. A few weeks ago, she would have spoken the truth, the whole truth and nothing but the truth. The truth was that she had been married enough for one lifetime. Being a wife was a condition of soul, a state of mind, irrespective of the man you married. Philip's wife would have a different life from Robert's wife, but remain a wife; like Frederick the Great's mule, which attended all the wars and remained a mule. She was heartily sick of being a wife. Philip must not be wounded with the truth; she had also learned that lies could be kind.

'My dearest Philip, if I were childless, I would.'

'I was afraid you'd say that.' He had known she would selflessly think of her children first. And he could not urge her into an English divorce, which still lay like scum on his mind. If he had been younger, he would have fought for his heart's desire; instead he bowed to the facts of obligation and age. There was nothing else to do. Why make her unhappy by useless pleading?

'Winter's coming, Philip. You have your work. I can't live in châteaux for ever. We must go back.'

'But Faith, not really. I mean we're not going to separate. We can't. You don't want that, do you?'

'No.'

'All right; I'll manage. You can tell your husband or not, as you choose, but we'll have our time together, as much time as you'll give me.'

'I'll tell him, of course.'

He would find a flat in London; she would live officially with her husband. Appearances would be preserved. Since that was all he could have, he would settle for it and be grateful. He knew he could trust Faith. If she loved him, she would never share herself with anyone else.

Mrs Hapgood counted the hours now, and became sadder as the miles passed. Finally she calculated that from the moment he had blotted out the sun in the garden near the Loire to this instant when he placed her luggage by the front door in Hanover Terrace, she had known Philip Naisby for seventeen days, four and a half hours. He had flagged a taxi, shifted his bags from the Lancia and was driving away. She turned, wanting to run after him, crying 'Wait. Stop. Take me back to France. It isn't enough. It isn't nearly enough.'

Mrs Hapgood rang the bell. Robert had been informed of her return, by telegram. She had left her house key in her room, nearly a month ago, never meaning to use it again.

The telegram said, 'Returning Thursday afternoon.' Afternoons were long and indefinite, any time between two and six. Mr Hapgood was ready at two, fortified by tranquillizers. He feared seeing those frozen black eyes and hearing the voice of the judge. But this was childish cowardice; he deserved his sentence and though it would be hell, he accepted it in advance, as much of it and for as long as Faith decreed. He could survive that; all that mattered was to get Faith back.

At two-thirty he began to play solitaire in his study. He laid out the cards like a machine, made the correct moves, kept winning. The tranquillizers were wearing thin. He knew he did not think any more; thinking would be progress, a scheme for the future. All he did was rehearse remembered scenes, whine and justify, flail himself, and hide from facts with all his might.

When Faith did not come down to breakfast, that fatal Wednesday, he had fallen into panic. She was never late and rarely ill; if she was, she concealed it as long as possible, gave him full warning so that he would not worry, and maintained the stiff upper lip throughout. This morning he had a vision of such horror that he could not move from the table: he saw Faith dead by her own hand on the floor of her room. He managed then to get up the stairs, though his legs seemed unable to support him and he was pulling himself by the handrail. He expected to find her door locked. It was open and Faith was gone. There was no note and her room seemed as tidy as usual. He searched the house, more and more idiotically; he remembered looking in the hall coat cupboard. He had not spoken, the silence itself was part of the nightmare. At last he thought of the garage. Faith had taken her car. He started a new panic; she would drive crazily, she would kill herself on the roads.

He waited all that day and all night near the telephone; he could hear an official voice asking if he were Mr Robert Hapgood, and the flat official words announcing death. He got slowly and ineffectually drunk. At some moments he allowed himself hope; the telephone would ring and it would be Faith. He had invented a story for the servants; Mrs Hapgood was called away to help an ailing friend. If they believed it, good; if not, what matter? The story was only an invention for himself, so that he would not have to talk.

The next day he went to Paula. He could not endure the house and the silence and the fear. He babbled like a lost child. The conversation, if those disconnected bleats could be so named, must have been a revelation to Paula. He had given her to believe, over the years, that he and Faith had an old companionable marriage, rather like a pair of Chelsea pensioners sharing a house; they were too grown-up, responsible and conventional ever to break this bond. Paula was permitted to see herself as the essential woman, the source of joy.

Paula was sweet; she kept him with her; they made love. He telephoned his house to give Paula's number; he was to be notified of messages. He drank a great deal. Paula treated him like an invalid, using sex as the basic medicine. He must have been in a stupor and glad of it; any escape from thought was welcome. That lasted for two days and nights.

Slowly he realized that Paula, who never stopped reassuring him about Faith's safety, believed that Faith had left him for good. Paula knew very well that Robert could not live alone. When he became convinced that Faith would not return, Robert, the man-who-needed-women, would marry her. Faith's disappearance gave Paula the idea. Or perhaps Paula, who was no longer a girl—forty-three now—and tired of coping as much as she did, yearned for two strong arms and a bank account at her permanent service. Perhaps the scheme had lain in her mind from the beginning; she had waited all this time for her chance. He felt a trap, which he had built for seven years, closing. He thought of Clarissa and a life he had barely survived.

He had emerged rational from the sanatorium, but tottery. In the years after Clarissa's death, he never loosened his grip on order. Growing surer of himself, he began to take small regular doses of his required drug; the type of woman who satisfied his type of sensuality. The moment a woman made demands, exceeding the dosage he had set himself, he broke off; he fled; he lived at his club, the image of a self-contained celibate, until he could afford another risk. It was a bad life, always threatened because he saw that he could not trust himself. He needed someone else to trust, someone so reliable and so entire that he would be protected. He did not consider his case to be unique or even interesting; a small thing but his own. He was not ashamed to admit to himself that he must find help.

There was no dearth of trustworthy women; he met them as the wives of his friends, at dinner parties, wherever he turned. At least they looked and sounded trustworthy. The fault lay in him. Though the small voracious sirens were doom, he could not imagine life with their opposite, he dreaded boredom. Until the day he saw Faith, a tall hand-some girl with the face of an intelligent child. She was so guileless that she took his breath away; she said what she thought and she thought for herself; she was utterly trustworthy and utterly trusting. He did not know, when he married her, whether he felt love or awe; he knew from the first instant that he needed her.

Without guessing what she was doing, Faith removed danger and fear, by existing. He did not have to rely on himself, he could rely on Faith. He came to think well of himself because she loved him; she would not love a worthless man. She gave him such a sense of wholeness that he dared to be all of himself. Faith sustained a decent, useful man and that was what he counted on, with gratitude, with love. Inside him, never dying, lived a little ravenous animal which romped with equal animals for a few hours on Tuesdays and Thursdays. He had found real pleasure in making love to Faith; it was the pleasure of giving candy to a beloved child. You would not cram a beloved child with candy until it was sick. Faith did not belong in the disorderly world of physical passion. She was his wife.

When he realized that Paula meant to take him from Faith, he made excuses to go home. The servants would need money, he should attend to his correspondence, and heaven knew what trouble would again blow up with Caroline. For another two days he composed the letter to Paula; he must have written it ten times. She was not the guilty party, and he did not want to hurt her. In plain words, he would have said that he had lived quite a lot with Paula for seven years, adding up journeys and London hours, and she had satisfied certain needs and he felt more than lust for her, fondness, a kind of harassed, pitying responsibility. But the part-time pleasures of seven years were possible because he had Faith to return to, Faith his wife. Without Faith, Paula became a menace. He disguised the plain words and sent them to Paula with an enormous sheaf of roses; he also deposited an enormous cheque in her bank. He reproached himself for allowing this liaison to go on so long that the end was unavoidably surgical. He discovered to his amazement that Paula was gone with the roses and the cheque. Had he ruined his life for so little?

Four o'clock and the cards in neat rows on the table. Perhaps Faith would not come after all; a last-minute revulsion. He must not be drunk or just tipsy when she arrived, if she arrived; but he had to have a drink. What now? Television, the easy dope of the masses. He did not see the small figures prancing before him, but there was noise in the room, voices or music. His eyes fixed on the screen, he drank whisky in sips to make it last.

By the time Faith cabled her address in France he was near the end of his rope; knowing the worst would be better than knowing nothing. When he telephoned to that château-hotel, he had been crushed by Faith's icy self-possession; if she had cursed him, he would have felt safer. Did she mean to discard him, without another word, like a piece of soiled clothing? As he remembered from so long ago, that was the way she had treated her one lover. She was capable of it and she had the right; her standards were intolerably high, but she lived by them. He knew that pleading with Faith by telephone or pursuing her would be futile; she would only despise him more. He had abased himself to

Clarissa, interminably and always in vain; he would not repeat that pattern with Faith. A man who had lost his pride was altogether lost. Why in God's name did Caroline have to ring up on a Tuesday?

He only knew how to plan for himself the stolen times; he was helpless without Faith's brisk presence to make days seem sensible, and give them a beginning, a middle and an end. He could not go back to Paula, she frightened him since he had seen that cunning look on her face and besides he could hardly, so soon, swallow his farewell note, his cheque and his roses. It would be possible to find another Paula but the thought of the preliminaries daunted him: the luncheons, the dinners, the blandishments, memorizing a whole new set of tastes and habits. And another Paula, without Faith to shield him, would also become a trap in due course. But he yearned for all he had found in all the eager bodies. There was no other way to escape time.

Walking home from his club where he now dined with exhausted amiability at the long table, Mr Hapgood noticed a girl in Baker Street. She was being very careful to stay within the letter of the law on soliciting. She looked young; prostitutes used to be sad old things. They were growing fresher and smarter every year, no doubt this was more atomic-age progress. Since his undergraduate days, when he was both drunk and showing off, Mr Hapgood had not dealt with a tart. Feeling ashamed and nervous, but also desperate and indifferent to consequences, Mr Hapgood spoke to her and went to her room. The room depressed him, with its spotted taffeta bedspread and dirty curtains.

The girl was a surprise; she had a nice voice, high cheekbones in a pretty, thin face, her hair was soft and fell to her shoulders. He saw himself as the classical dirty old man and was smitten with conscience; she was much too young, it was dreadful that a child had to earn her living this way. He questioned the girl, kindly. She had little sympathy for the guilts of men and answered that as far as she knew she was the third generation in this line of business and considered herself good at her work. Did he want it or not? If not, she couldn't afford to sit here chatting. Mr Hapgood was offended and had given offence; he hesitated. The girl decided to take matters into her own hands, and undressed. Her body was slim and smooth, young as she was, intoxicatingly young. Mr Hapgood was caught, and glad of it.

Moreover the girl was good at her work, as she had said. And safe; she would not expect anything except a certain amount of cash. But her room still depressed Mr Hapgood. He gave her more money and told her to take a suite at the Henley House near Marble Arch; he would be along. He did go along, obsessively in fact; she made him believe that he was special in her experience of lovers. He spent most of a week with her but Faith's voice, ice-cold all the way from France, echoed louder and louder in his mind until the girl was no use to him, and he no use to her. He wrote down her telephone number. If his life ever came right again, he might like to have it.

After that, he waited. It seemed months now. He waited and grew older; hopelessness is ageing. He did not expect Faith to come back, or only come back to arrange for divorce. He could not imagine the future because there was none. He walked in Regent's Park; sometimes he sat at the desk in his rented office, sometimes in his study. He drifted to cinemas, he watched the television. Time was unending and stationary. And ironical punishment had been meted out. Faith cast him off, with loathing, because he could not stay away from women; now that Faith was gone, and would not return, he had lost the wish and ability for women.

Gertrude opened the door and paused, waiting for the strange lady to speak.

'Here I am, Gertrude.'

'Madam! It's you! I'd never have known you. You look so *young*.'

'Oh, good.' Gertrude hauled suitcases across the sill. 'I've had rather a shopping and beautifying spree in France. It seemed time for a change.'

'Wait till Sarah sees you, Madam. She won't believe it. Why, Madam, you look like a film star.'

Gertrude and Sarah would have talked to each other, but to no one else. 'Madam looks like a film star.' All well. Film stars were fine.

Behind his study door, Robert heard his wife's voice but stayed where he was, not wanting to meet her until Gertrude had gone. The door opened and a fashionable foreigner said, 'Hello, Robert.'

He had often thought his wife beautiful, though her looks were like the weather report: variable. Now she was striking; *la femme mûre* of French novels, the ripened woman combining experience and artifice. He knew Faith's habitual expression: eyes concerned, mouth rather severe, a slight frown: the trustworthy child doing her best. He had killed that child, and there was no trace of the body. Until that moment, he did not feel he had committed a crime, but only a terrible folly. He went to his wife, with grief on his face, meaning to take her in his arms.

She avoided him so swiftly that the gesture could be ignored. She sat in the chair by the fire and asked for a drink.

'Ghastly day,' Mrs Hapgood remarked. 'The French are too lucky in their weather.'

Robert fortunately had turned to the drink tray, and would not see how shaken she was. His colour was normally ruddy; now his skin had gone blotched and grayish. He stooped. She had scarcely noticed change in Robert over the years; he always seemed to her what he had been when they met, a strong, erect, handsome man. Couldn't he even call a doctor without her? She wanted to scold Robert angrily for not taking care of himself. Unconsciously she balled her hands into fists, while she swallowed back inexplicable tears.

'Here you are, my dear.'

He had no right to that voice, either. How dared he sound so tired and so humble? He was putting on another fancy dress to deceive her. She would not be deceived. She had finished with Faith the fool. He would find her a hard woman now. Robert groaned a little as he lowered himself into a chair. Oh no, it was too much; did he expect her to believe this role of the poor abandoned husband, worn from suffering? What about his lady love or loves? Freed of his wife, he could spend every night with them. Perhaps that accounted for his sorry state.

'Robert, I must talk to you. I'll make it as short as I can and we need never discuss this again. I have a lover. If you agree, I'll live here and we will behave towards others as we always have. I'm sure you'll find it a relief to have our position clear. If you don't accept this arrangement, we must separate, but I hope not. For people of our age, public admissions of failure seem quite lamentable.'

'I don't want to live without you.'

'Then you agree to my terms?'

'What else can I do?'

'I'll unpack now. Dinner at eight, as usual?'

She sat beside him when they dined alone; the length of the table made her feel like a board meeting, not privacy with her husband. Gertrude had set the table in the accustomed way. Now his wife sat at his right and made dinner party conversation. He felt he was dreaming; he was the victim of mixed identities, Faith thought he was John Withers or Tommy Burke or any one of dozens of men she was used to chatting with. She spoke of the cave paintings at Lascaux, there was in particular a frieze of five reindeer swimming which stunned the imagination. The line of the paintings reminded her of Picasso. She had been to Rocamadour, an ancient city of pilgrimage plastered against the stone face of a cliff. How was his monograph getting on? Had he seen any new plays? Robert began to hear her low pleasant voice from a distance; he was slipping away from himself; he must be losing his mind.

Mrs Hapgood rang for coffee, saying that it was kinder to spare Gertrude the stairs, she should have thought of this long ago. There would now be no need to settle over coffee cups in the drawing-room. After coffee, she excused herself; she was weary from the day's travel.

Robert moved to his study, to drink brandy alone and stare at the red coals.

He was tired too, but not in a way that sleep would remedy. He must hang on, he knew how to hang on. Had he not gone to the same office for thirty-nine years, without ever wanting to go there? A man who could do that could discipline himself to any form of endurance. If I were a good man, Mr Hapgood thought, I would set her free. She ought not to live the standard double life, it's against her nature. But he was not a good man, he had never thought he was; he wanted Faith because he wanted to live; and he would hang on.

As he climbed the stairs he told himself to be a sensible chap, keep a perspective after all, his problem would solve itself; soon Faith could wheel him round the Rose Garden in the mornings and read to him a bit in the afternoons and tuck him up and join her lover; the ideal marriage. Passing Faith's closed door he heard her voice; it did not sound like dinner-party conversation. He stopped, not meaning to spy, but held by the sound.

'Do you miss me?' Faith was saying in a tone he knew well but had never heard from Faith.

There was a pause.

'Yes, darling,' Faith said. And again, 'Yes.'

He was seized with jealousy as by an attack of nausea. He stumbled down the hall to his room and kicked the door shut to close out Faith playing up, like any woman, to the vanity of a man.

Philip Naisby had rented a furnished flat in Grosvenor Square. The owner of this flat, an American lady, was off on a cruise: Mrs Hapgood guessed her to be a divorcée in early middle age with an eye out for men. Faith and he would search until they found a suitable home, and together collect all the bits and pieces to make it theirs. He could hardly wait for the antique shops, and the earnest discussion of colours and cloth. He saw himself shopping with Faith, as her husband.

She met Philip every day. He was as ardent as ever. Mrs Hapgood often envied Molly who lusted so readily and often; why didn't science find a way to even up the score in people, think of all the real trouble that would save. Philip called for her at the hairdresser's, went with her to buy clothes, still engrossed in his portion of ownership. They dined at small restaurants from Kensington to Soho, where they were not likely to meet acquaintances. Philip was not fretted by jealousy of Robert. He trusted Faith without question.

More and more often, Mrs Hapgood had to bite back cross words; Philip should not take her arm so possessively, in the street; he ought to have more discretion everywhere. It was a question of taste, he did not know exactly how far to go and when to stop. These unwritten rules would not have been floating in the atmosphere of a genteel chartered accountant's home in Leeds, where Philip had grown up. Then Mrs Hapgood would turn on herself in remorse. How dared she prefer formal false manners to a loving heart? She did however, very delicately, mention Philip's haircut; it was not becoming, she said, and as she admired his forehead and the shape of the back of his head, she hoped he would change his barber. Philip was delighted by her noticing and caring and hurried to obey.

Philip said he was excited by his work, after years of futility, because he could discuss it with her. She did her best to visualize a huge building from a piece of drawing paper, and disliked this aspect of her rôle. It felt too much like a wife. His numerous presents embarrassed her, her room was like a florist's shop. He revelled in having her to love. Yet how could he be so contented in this schizophrenic life? Was the real penalty for growing up the knowledge that you were alone? Two halves do not make a whole. One is by oneself, for ever incomplete. Probably all adults arrived, one way or another, at this busy emptiness. Her life had always been busy; she had escaped knowing how empty it was. A fortunate woman, Mrs Hapgood reminded herself, who belonged in that tiny percentage of the world's population called privileged. Sometimes, driving between Hanover Terrace and Grosvenor Square, Mrs Hapgood had such a sense of dislocation that she thought she might forget her own name.

Now she took her breakfast in bed, arranged to be out for lunch, and at home to dine only if there were guests. It was painful to see Robert alone, they had nothing to say to each other. More people were invited for drinks or dinner; Robert put up a good front. If an old friend was clumsy enough to remark on his seediness, Robert said he'd had the flu and still wasn't feeling quite right. Everyone said that Mrs Hapgood had never looked better. The women, she guessed, believed she had gone to Paris for a face-lift; the men cheerily supposed she had taken a lover. She was uncomfortable in a new atmosphere of cattiness and conjecture.

At whatever hour she came home or left, Robert was there. He was polite, detached, he avoided her too. She was alarmed for his health and urged him to get some exercise. Robert answered that she was not to trouble herself. Exasperated by an unfair guilt, she asked him why he didn't visit his ladies. He could at least keep up his regular Tuesdays and Thursdays. Robert said there were no ladies. This made her angry; of course he hadn't altered his way of life after all these years; why should he still lie to her? She laughed at him in disbelief. He accepted the laughter in silence. She hated this small scene and blamed herself for provoking it. Robert repeated obstinately, 'None'.

Mrs Hapgood visited her doctor, keeping the visit a secret from both Robert and Philip. She slept so badly and woke in such weariness that she thought perhaps she was anaemic, could the doctor suggest something, a friend had told her about magic pills which made you feel lively. Now she took capsules for sleep, and others to revive, and still more to brighten her mood.

None of the pills worked like magic; Mrs Hapgood was dead tired coming home from Philip Naisby's bed at one in the morning. They ought to put in a lift, the stairs were too long for this middle-aged household. The drawing-room door was shut but light shone under it. Really, the carelessness; they expected her to look after every detail. She opened the door, reaching for the light switch, and stopped. Robert sat by the cold fire, with his face in his hands, crying. She had never imagined that this man could cry; she felt she was watching Robert bleed to death.

'Robert!'

He jerked aside from her voice, turning his back. He drew in his breath as a cough. Fumbling in the pocket of his dressing gown he said, 'Go away, Faith.'

'No.' She sat beside him on the sofa and put her arm around his shoulders. They were too thin. She had been trying to save herself, that was all; trying to make some sort of a life instead of none. Why did she have such power to give pain, if she'd had no power to give pleasure?

'Robert, tell me what to do.'

He held himself stiffly and used his handkerchief with his left hand. 'What's the use? Go away, Faith. Leave me alone.'

'I won't.'

He had his voice under control now but would not look at her.

'Self-pity,' he said. 'I was indulging in a little fit of self-pity. Pay no attention.'

'Please, Robert.'

'It's too late. If I touch your hand by accident, you shy away. You can't bear to see me; I revolt you. I hoped you might change, with time. But you won't. I'm not blaming you, Faith. I was never worth very much and I'm not worth anything now. But I can't go on with it. I'm leaving.'

'Where?'

'I don't know and it doesn't matter.'

No, she thought, not like this. She understood nothing. Perhaps she was the habit of a lifetime and Robert was a man of habit. No more than that. Her job was simple; she had to console Robert for breaking her heart. If he went away, he would leave her the memory of a thin old man crying alone; and she would die of it.

'I won't let you go.'

'I am going, Faith. Tomorrow early. There's only one thing I must say to you before, and you won't believe it. I love you.'

What did anyone mean by that word? For all she knew, what she felt now might be love: this resignation. She saw herself carefully building up Robert's health and confidence. He would become again the strong erect handsome man. Once his life was certain, and he at home in his skin, he would go searching for his ladies, as he had to. I'm too tired, Mrs Hapgood thought. What he really wanted was the usual, the impossible: turn the clock back. He wanted Faith ignorant as before, reliable, concentrated on him, loving but managerial; he wanted his modest, grateful wife in the marriage bed. And what if she couldn't? What if a clock inside her had stopped? She longed to postpone all this, at least until she'd had eight hours of sleep. There was no time because Robert had no time.

'It's very late, Robert. Come to bed.'

They went arm in arm up the stairs, she kissed him lightly at her door. It was their old ritual for the uncounted nights of love. Undressing in his room, Mr Hapgood told himself that he had begged for charity and charity would be given him. He was without a shred of pride. Pride, he imagined, was the last emotion you bothered with when drowning. He had hung on as he meant to; he had told himself he would win because he must. He was speaking the truth when he said there were no other women; he had decided superstitiously that one self-indulgent gesture would lose Faith. And now, when he had finally given up hope, obstinacy and discipline were rewarded. She was going to take him back; his life would come right again.

He knew Faith better than anyone, far better than her lover could; Faith had discarded her lover with three words: 'Come to bed.' Faith was incapable of the lies which kept a lover and a husband both contented. Did he have the right to grab Faith's offer? Her lover might be the man he failed to be and make Faith happy. No, he refused to believe it. He had the right to Faith because he'd loved her for twenty-four years. He would take better care of her, much better care. Never hurt her again. I promise, he thought, and stopped. Had he suddenly found reasons to trust himself? Not that he knew of. An untrustworthy man could at least be honest, and make no promises.

He was as nervous as a boy. He could no longer enter this door, sure of the woman waiting for him. He did not know how to behave, and surprised himself by knocking timidly. There was no answer. He opened the door into a dim room. Dressing-table lights shone on a mirror where he saw reflected a temptress in a black net nightgown and barbaric jewelled ear-rings.

'We make too much fuss,' Mrs Hapgood said, smiling. 'It's quite ridiculous. We are scarcely tragic figures, and you wouldn't say this act was a sacrament, would you, Robert? There's been much too much fuss. My fault. I had absurd old-fashioned ideas. Do you like my new nightdress?'

He stared at her, unable to fit that voice, those words, the luxurious vulgar get-up in this dignified room where his wife had always lived. Was this how she showed herself to her lover; did she pose before a glass, languidly brushing her hair? She must have dyed it that colour for just such lighting: it glowed, it poured and floated; her raised arm raised her breast and the black gown hid and did not hide; what sort of man had taught her? He wanted to kill her and he was afraid of her and that smile, it had turned into a memory of mockery. She was not watching him in the mirror, she seemed absorbed by her face, which knew too much. He was cold with fury; how dared she invite him here, her husband, and treat him as one of the queue? He had come to her with love, and with hope, and she would bestow her favors whenever she got through brushing her hair. After all the misery, he was not as important as her beauty treatment.

Mrs Hapgood turned off the lights on the dressing table, rose and said pleasantly, 'Come to bed, Robert.' She might have been saying 'Have another drink.' It seemed to him that she moved with studied and disgusting grace, her body white beneath the smoky black stuff; at the bed, in a slow practised gesture, she lifted the gown over her head. She slid under the sheets; and looked at him. Why didn't she laugh? She had played her hand to perfection; vengeance is mine, saith the wronged wife; reducing him first to tears and then to impotence.

'I no longer want to,' Robert said.

'Your manners, darling.'

The quirk of the eyebrow, the little pout, mockery like a blow in the face. He stormed out of the room, slamming the door so that pictures rattled on the wall.

Mrs Hapgood sighed, leaned back against the pillows, and said aloud, 'Shock treatment.'

She sighed again, got up and went to the bathroom. With a mouthful of toothpaste she mumbled suddenly, 'I've had enough, I've had *enough*.' She took two sleeping pills and hurled herself into bed.

Mr Hapgood went downstairs to collect the whisky decanter and siphon, returned to his room, made a drink the color of strong tea, and began a tiger pace from wall to wall. His interior monologues normally rolled on in contained sentences. Now words raged and yelled in his mind.

Ruining my life, for nothing, nothing, good husband, good father, shaming me, acting like a whore, who is the man, some low type to make it worse, teaching her low tricks, only behaved all these years because I had the whip hand, never give a woman an inch, should have thrown her out the minute she said, took it all like a little gent, never give them an inch, how they make you pay, crawl, beg, laugh at you, do you like my new nightdress, talked me into retiring and walked off, not one cursed thing to do all day, what did she care, oh no, better be distinguished archaeologist, forty years too late, what does she know about the American take-over bid, who fought it off, now they've lost Pinner and Strauss best research scientists in the business, Tomlinson can't do the job I did, she never respected my work, would Jonathan soil his hands making money, not my son, rather bounce around a stage, fat allowance, she fixed that, stupid children, mummy's kiddies, she didn't want to go on trips did she, stay with kiddies, doctors say this doctors say that, any other woman would have seen, she was perfectly satisfied wasn't she, never heard any complaints, the way she said Darling, Robert darling afterwards, all right perhaps slacked off a bit, women don't feel same needs, lost the feeling anyhow growing older, not like Paula, Paula used her imagination, no imagination that's what, wonderful noble Faith and no imagination, then blow up, ruin life, laugh at me, haven't worked all my life to be made a fool of, people talking, of course why not, like to choke her, make her eat those earrings, tear up nightgown, beg me to come to bed, forbid it, forbid every bit of it, behave decently, behave like my wife or get out, took enough nonsense, made me miserable, made me impotent, never happened before, worst thing ever happens to a man, did it on purpose, not allow it, won't, stop, *damn her stop it all*.

Mr Hapgood swallowed the last half of his fourth drink in great gulps, threw the glass into the fireplace, and strode down the hall. Knock like a polite little gent indeed, he said to himself, and wrenched open the door to his wife's room as by right. The dark slowed him, he had to grope, having forgotten the light switch on the wall. This fumbling progress stoked his anger, it looked uncertain, like a blind old man. *Not* blind, *not* old, the enraged shouting voice said inside him, where's the bed, room as big as Victoria, damn silly, put her in a coat cupboard, teach her to behave, show her who runs this place, where is that bloody bed? He tripped against it and sat down harder than he intended; even things conspired to humiliate him. He found his wife's shoulder which was unnervingly warm and soft, and shook it, saying, 'Faith! Wake up! Wake up at once!' He managed to switch on the bedside lamp; it was the one light in the room he knew from old usage.

He hoped her eyes would look frightened. He wanted her to cower before his wrath and weep and implore forgiveness. Her eyes looked unnaturally dark, drugged, and unsurprised.

'This cannot go on,' he said. 'I will not have it, do you hear? We're going to live the way we always did. I won't have it! You must stop, at once. Do you hear me? I won't allow it!'

But what did she smell of? A scent he could not remember, and large sleepy mascaraed eyes went on staring at him, in silence. As if she were accustomed to being waked in the night by a man, and was ready for his demands. Mr Hapgood, tormented, half drunk, helpless before this silence and these eyes, plunged his hands in her hair, meaning to bang sense into her head or tear that dyed mane out by its roots. Instead he found himself kissing her but not the way he had ever kissed Faith his wife; brutally, with fury flowing from him, in a desire to hurt until she cried for pity. And more, more, this was not nearly enough, treat her the way she looked, treat her the way she deserved; rape, he thought while he could still think anything.

The whisky was burned out of him. Now Faith had the whip hand, for ever. He'd shown her what he had always kept secret, though he had never dreamed he could take a woman with hate, wanting to harm her. You might beat your wife, if provoked beyond endurance, but not rape her. It had happened so fast, he had not planned it, he was dazed, but something else alarmed him. The victim of assault fought back; any woman would try to protect herself against any man, even her husband, if he came at her like a beast. But Faith had not resisted, she had been an accomplice, his rage mounted because she was willing and knowing, prepared for whatever a man did, indecent like any other woman. No, it couldn't be. He must talk to her, say something; she must say something. They were all twisted, he had to know who she was, he had to find order again. He wanted her to revile him; he wanted to apologize humbly; he would understand then; the world would be right side up.

'Faith,' he whispered. There was no answer and he realized they were in a dark room. He reached for the lamp and it was gone; had he knocked it over and broken it, good God, in Faith's room, in Faith's bed? He must have been mad. There was another lamp on her side on that table; he felt his way around the edges of the bed and touched the switch. 'Faith,' he began. She was asleep, with a faint smile on her lips. She looked amused.

Mr Hapgood telephoned to the girl whose name was, embarrassingly, Lili Marlene. That placed her, a war baby, twenty years old, younger than his admirable tiresome daughter. He called the girl Lily which was grotesque too but less so. She would gladly meet him at the Marble Arch Lyons, her days were of course quite free. Mr Hapgood plied her with cream cakes, five-pound notes and plans. He knew exactly what he wanted; he was sick of trouble. He wanted a talented young woman, ready to hand, and well pleased by an improvement over her previous living and working conditions. It was to be an orderly business arrangement. Lily should find a comfortable clean flat near Paddington, he had not forgotten her room, and abandon her trade and reserve herself for him. Lily, though tough and young enough to face hardship cheerfully, was almost tearful with gratitude. Winter was the worst time for a girl and this winter was the worst she could remember. Mr Hapgood said she looked tired, perhaps she needed a tonic. Did she have a doctor? Well then, go to him and get a complete check-up. Lily understood but did not laugh at the nice old boy, her benefactor. She only hoped the deal would last, anyway until spring.

Mr Hapgood rode in the park on a pale winter morning, and took stock. Faith was extraordinary. She had never mentioned that night, she appeared to have forgotten it. And it was not repeated; he would run no further risks. There was much to be said for a purely companionable marriage. Most men his age had probably long since stopped sleeping with their wives; connubial bliss belonged to young couples. Custom and security were bound to stale sex. Affection remained. He had to admit that Faith looked after him with devoted concern. Since she had talked him into real tennis and riding again, his skin shone with health, his muscles were in splendid condition, he was the same man he'd always been, as good as new. It was unbalanced and unnecessary to get all knotted up in emotions.

Besides he was now more interested in his plan for the future than in any women. Women were essential but a man needed a purpose in life. He had planted a word here, a word there, nothing actionable, nothing even very definite; he knew how words divided and multiplied. If his scheme ripened as it showed signs of doing, the shares of Hapgood and Ardley, solid as the Bank of England, would drop a fraction, the Board would be in a fine stew, they would force Tomlinson to resign and plead with him until he consented to go back where he wanted to be, at his own wide mahogany desk in his own paneled office. Having had two years to taste the horrors of leisure, he could scarcely wait for the day. But he was waiting like a spider, Mr Hapgood thought with satisfaction. He would return Pinner and Strauss to the fold, they were ready to come. He had met them casually a few times and sounded them; they were used to the old firm and unhappy with their new employers. Pinner was now fascinated by alopecia; if by accident he discovered a cure for baldness that would be as world-shaking as a cure for cancer, and far more lucrative.

Mr Hapgood had a sudden vision of Pinner who was small, rumpled and myopic, staring at a billiard ball head which was slowly sprouting stalks of hair. He whooped with laughter. A pot-faced nanny, and her pramload of two tiny tots wearing white gloves, stared at him. Mr Hapgood gently kicked his horse's flank and braced himself for a short canter.

At Christmas, they telephoned to the children. Jonathan had left Australia for Texas; he was now attached to a stock company in one of those unlikely cities whose name one had never heard. Jonathan spoke of Broadway, so near and yet so far; Caroline spoke of the baby and her husband. Mr and Mrs Hapgood sounded exactly like Daddy and Mummy. Mr Hapgood thought how much funnier the conversation would be if they could see their mother, dressed in tight green trousers and a big loose sweater, like the Chelsea girls.

Mr and Mrs Hapgood had decided to make nothing of Christmas; they would eat a simple luncheon as on any other day. Beside his plate Mr Hapgood found a neatly wrapped package containing a black morocco wallet with his initials small and discreet in gold. Mrs Hapgood opened a box, done up in festive shop paper, and lifted out a handsome crocodile handbag. They thanked each other with polite enthusiasm. There had been many previous wallets and handbags. He was dining with Lily, she with Philip. Lily had bought a Christmas pudding at Lyons'; Philip a turkey at Fortnum's.

In the basement, Gertrude and Sarah huddled by the Christmas tree, which Mrs Hapgood had thoughtfully provided, watched televison and wept for the old days.

Rain beat against the windows but the curtains were drawn. Mrs Hapgood sat by the fire, knitting, while delicious smells crept from the kitchen. Philip adored to cook, another revelation. His idea of the perfect evening was this: happy experimenting on the stove, the beloved woman safe by the hearth, opera on gramophone records, a pipe, and then bed. Poor soul, Mrs Hapgood thought, he should have married the right little wife years ago, and sired a brood of children doing their homework all over the floor. He was made for profound domesticity.

And Robert whistled through the days, back at the hated office which it now seemed he doted on; back with some desirable lady because he would not have been so pink and pleased, otherwise; and nicely tended by Faith who kept his house and clothes and engagements in order. Would she ever finish this ludicrous pullover? Philip could buy fifty of them but became starry-eyed at the sight of her knitting away. Here she was, an adulteress enjoying all the delights of home, with the gray cold sky to wake to, and the same streets, and the endlessness of it. What a relief to earn your living; what liberty to go off to work every day. How had she endured her life all these years, how had she survived the boredom of being a woman?

I loathe London, Mrs Hapgood thought and was astonished. She had taken it for granted that she lived in London, always had and always would. At least she had staved off furnishing a house with Philip, she dragged out fussy objections to every place he showed her. The lucky divorcée stayed far from this sickening climate; Grosvenor Square remained their nest. It had come to feel like a dear wee villa in East Grinstead. Philip emerged from the kitchen, promising her a surprise, a soufflé he had invented while talking with that clod McGruder about the design for his factory.

'Darling, isn't this fun?' Philip said. 'Remember when I produced my revolutionary theory, long ago in France? Why not have fun? Remember? I never dreamed it would be possible, night after night.'

Mrs Hapgood smiled sweetly over the blue-gray wool. Soon she would reach the armholes, unimaginable fun. She had another memory of long ago in France; joy, not fun. It had come to her briefly, an intoxication of spirit that swept away the rubbish of one's insignificant life and left one bodiless, part of the beautiful world, filled with thanksgiving. That could not be searched for but might be found; it needed a high bright sky, a wide land, it needed solitude. She had not been ungrateful but too trapped in her tiny miseries to appreciate the magic enough. She would give anything to get it back, if only for an instant, if only once.

'I haven't made you a drink,' Philip said. 'Forgive me, darling. I'm becoming a neglectful—' He had been about to say 'husband', frowned, and said 'brute'.

Mrs Hapgood continued to smile sweetly, thinking of solitude and joy.

'Is Mr Hapgood at home?'
'No, I'm sorry he isn't.'
'When will he be back?'
'I'm afraid I don't know.'
'It's very urgent.'

Things were hotting up for Robert if his ladylove called his house and treated his wife like a secretary. This high typically English voice must belong to his ladylove; who else would dare that owning manner?

'Have you tried his office?' Mrs Hapgood asked mildly.
'Yes.'
'His club?'
'Yes.'

It had taken her twenty-four years to intrude on his club; life was not as serene for Robert now.

'He's bound to be back later,' Mrs Hapgood said. 'Can I leave a message?'
'Please tell him to ring Mrs Clark the minute he comes in.'
'Right.'
'Thank you,' the voice said, as an afterthought.

Mrs Hapgood was even more amused by the consternation in Robert's face when she delivered her message. He stammered, so unlike Robert, hurried to his study to telephone and had no time for a bath before rushing out again. Mrs Hapgood was enjoying a night off. Philip had to attend a meeting which fortunately would last very late. She sipped vodka by the drawing-room fire, to the tune of the seven o'clock news, while Mr Hapgood fidgeted in a taxi, wondering what was wrong with Paula now, and preparing his alibi.

He had finally nerved himself to see Paula again, he had jumped through the necessary hoops for her vanity's sake, and settled her back into his life. Clandestine sex lost its lure if nobody cared what you did. Lily was convenient, docile and excitingly young, but permitted. Not that he had spoken to Faith about her, but Faith did not mind where he went or when, and in those circumstances Lily became a bit of a bore. Paula would be hysterical with jealousy over another woman, and though Paula's conversation could not be described as brilliant, still she could talk. And he was used to her and he liked to have a base. The trouble with Paula was that she tended towards unforeseen disasters of a minor nature, and obviously she was deep in some irritating mess or she would not have called his house. They were dining together; she might have waited a few extra hours before sounding the alert. He had dropped in on Lily without warning; he'd had a sudden urge to keep his eye on her and not always give her advance notice of his visits.

Mrs Hapgood dined off a tray in the drawing-room, relieved that she did not have to flatter Sarah about the food nor eat more than she wanted, as encouragement. The peaceful evening stretched ahead. She had no idea what to do with it. She could feel her boredom as if she had been sewn in a sack, unable to move or breathe. How was it possible to be suffocated and maddened and numbed, all at once? Come, Mrs Hapgood said to herself, hysteria is the limit. Tonight's no worse than any other.

What had she done with herself before, at least on the solitary Tuesdays and Thursdays? Bustled, Mrs Hapgood decided, that's what I did with my whole life. Was that all women ever did? They craved to be needed, it was the reason for their being. She couldn't complain; she was needed by two men, not just one as the law allows. Needed as an answering service for mistresses, as a knitter. No, they loved her, they would both say so, Robert in an old-shoe tone, Philip with rapture. She didn't believe in love, or not in any she'd been linked with; and it tasted like salt unless you were in love too. Tied in a sack and eating salt; a really gay design for living.

But I loved Robert, she protested, I know I did, he was the meaning of existence. How could that strip away as unimportantly as dead skin after sunburn? What if she had never loved Robert but loved a man she created, a fine graven image, whom she called Robert? Think of the qualities and emotions she had dressed him in, so that he looked just right for her taste. It wasn't his fault that she had worn pink magnifying glasses. Nothing pink and nothing magnified remained; Robert was an ordinary man, healthy and happy in his average shabby, average respectable life. She took no further interest in him. And she had never loved Philip; she had loved the services rendered, pulling her out of a swamp of self-hate and sexlessness, by force of adoration. The job was done. If Philip wasn't half-witted, he would soon recognize her uselessness, too.

Zero, Mrs Hapgood thought, and I'm stuck with zero for all eternity or at least as far as the eye can reach. The only part of any day she really liked was sleep, get out, get away, be quit of the two men who loved her.

Meanwhile, what should she do with this evening? If you fell into bed at nine you waked at four, despite barbiturates, and that was hardly a good plan. Baudelaire, she remembered, was a great hand at ennui; it might be nice to join a fellow sufferer. Mrs Hapgood went directly to the proper shelf, for all these shelves were ranged in alphabetical order by category and author. How hopeless to run one's life as tidily as one's house, a husband and lover, each in his proper alphabetical place with no hint of confusion and nothing to search for.

She glanced over the rows of well dusted leather backs and disliked everything in her life including her possessions. Baudelaire, Boccaccio, Coleridge, Cummings. Mrs Hapgood stopped in surprise. Her father had given her this book, specially bound as a token of his admiration for the author, and been disappointed because her ungracious comment was to sniff at the whimsical punctuation. She might now try to do better by her father's memory. Ah yes, she would love to lay a wreath, in the form of improved manners and greater comprehension, on the memory of that charming man who had never bored her.

Mrs Hapgood turned the pages, still annoyed at words printed together, unreasonable parentheses, commas breaking into the middle of syllables, rashes of unlikely capital letters. She was not reading, she was disapproving and ashamed of her narrowness, until suddenly she was reading and holding her breath, and reading again, and light flooded her and she understood and believed. She heard herself laughing aloud. Had her father, so long ago, meant her to get that casual message of courage and good cheer? This glorious poet, this splendid Mr Cummings, simply told her what she had forgotten or doubted: there is no end to life until you die.

Mrs Hapgood said the words over softly.

> 'why then to Hell with that: the other; this,
>   since the thing perhaps is
> to eat flowers and not to be afraid.'

'Yes,' Mrs Hapgood announced to the long correct room, 'Yes. *Yes.*'

She needed music and would have liked fireworks too. The gramophone records were also catalogued. She chose Rachmaninoff's 'Rhapsody on a Theme of Paganini,' remembering only the fine racing notes of the beginning; Rhapsody anyway suited her exactly. Hugging the book—her bright sword, her passport—she telephoned to the kitchen and startled Sarah and Gertrude, who had washed up and snuggled down for a happy time with 'Emergency Ward', and ordered champagne. A bottle was always kept cold because Robert occasionally liked a glass before dinner. She tuned the gramophone until the music roared like an army with banners, and toasted her reflection in the mirror above the mantelpiece. And presently Mrs Hapgood, drunk on joy not wine, whirled along the silvery-gray Wilton carpet, dancing to hope and Rachmaninoff. The tiny percentage of the world's population called privileged had this one great privilege: they made their own prison sacks, but could also cut their way out. The words repeated and repeated in her mind, set to music, they fitted any music, and set to the releasing laughter that felt like freedom itself: To eat flowers and not to be afraid.

Robert came home early after an abominable evening with Paula. She had talked at length, revoltingly, of a cyst in some part of her anatomy which he did not wish to know about in medical terms. Her doctor said it was nothing, Paula would only spend two days in the nursing home, and she carried on as if menaced by imminent death. Faith, at any rate, looked happy; no wonder, she had arranged everything to suit herself. He meant to go straight to bed after a grumpy good night but Faith said, 'Sit down, Robert.' By God, if there was more woman trouble, he'd give up, take the veil or rather the cowl, renounce the whole wearying lot of them. But Faith did not seem primed for nagging, she was radiant, as a matter of fact, and considerately brought him a drink.

'Robert, tomorrow I am going to turn this house over to an estate agent. To sell it.'

'What?'

'It's mine. You gave it to me as a wedding present. I shall keep the proceeds. That's all I'll want. And then I'm clearing off, for good.'

'You *bitch*,' Robert said with utter conviction, and for the second time in his life threw a glass into a fireplace.

Mrs Hapgood decided she could not face Philip. She wrote an affectionate letter, giving detailed advice on what sort of woman to marry and how many children to have, and urging haste.

The house was known as La Fidelidad, a picturesque but reassuring name. The servants addressed Mrs Hapgood as Señora Fidela, much prettier than Faith but the same idea. She had found an old rambling ruin, repaired it, added to it, and installed an amount and quality of plumbing which awed the natives. There were fourteen bedrooms, all beautifully and luxuriously furnished, each with its bathroom made diverting by Spanish tiles. Mrs Hapgood left untouched the jasmine and bougainvillaea which cloaked the walls, the roses that grew like weeds, the cypress alley leading to the door, and the surrounding acres of eucalyptus and cork and live oak and olive. Since times were so good, she planned to put in a swimming pool next winter. People had grown too soft for the unpredictable sea, and liked having cold drink within easy reach. La Fidelidad was the smallest, most expensive and successful hotel on the Spanish coast. For fifteen guineas a day, the guests gratefully accepted Señora Fidela's hospitality, while being very careful not to put a foot wrong. The rooms were booked a year in advance.

Jonathan and Caroline had reacted to the news of their parents' divorce much as Mrs Hapgood expected. They were sorry but unaffected; it was as if Mummy and Daddy had got arthritis, painful, though not fatal, the kind of disease that the old suffer from. They were both charmed at the prospect of visiting Mummy in Spain, whenever they could make time in their busy lives. And of course they'd want to see Daddy in his new home in Wilton Crescent.

The guests at La Fidelidad speculated about Señora Fidela in cautious whispers. The Americans told their wives that she was still quite a dish, the English thought her most attractive. Señora Fidela was graciousness itself, but not very approachable. It was rumored that she walked alone on the beach, at odd hours, just after dawn, just before nightfall. To meet a lover? They could not understand why she didn't marry.

Everyone had been delighted to have Mr Robert back where he belonged, and they stayed delighted. He could truthfully pride himself on knowing how to handle people. And what an ass he had been for years, decades, telling himself that he despised this work and dreaded this office; probably he had made that mistake because of hating his father. He loved the work, he basked in his office. Every morning he walked to Wigmore Street elated by thoughts of the day's struggles and decisions. His father would never have believed what National Health had done to the English, they consumed drugs like candy, and there was no end in sight. The modern world produced more cures every day, and more diseases; he was in an expanding industry, full of risks, rewards and cut-throat competition. And there he meant to remain until he died.

Lili Marlene, exhausted by housework and regular hours, had flown the coop taking his presents and a certain number of movable furnishings; but he kept the flat for a more suitable girl, Gloria, older, twenty-two, who was soft and light-hearted and a delight when he could wangle the time. He had married Paula as he had to, after so many years, and he did need a wife and an established routine. He thought of Faith, with resentment, when Paula mislaid her car keys, overdrew her account, muddled their engagements, or when Gertrude and Sarah, in tears, threatened to leave because Madam made them so nervy, always changing her mind.

Philip Naisby, in a fever of bitterness, returned to his old barber and told him to straighten out that pansy haircut. Gloomily and with ever greater success, he went on spoiling the London skyline. At a symposium organized by the *Observer*, he met a young woman named Agnes, who was secretary of the Hampstead League to Preserve Fine Buildings. He discussed 'Irresponsibility in Town Planning', to applause, and Agnes came to thank and praise him afterwards. They were married in a month. Agnes was unremarkably pretty, devoted, and sensible. She presented him with three sons, very quickly; he preferred daughters. Agnes was everything a wife should be and whenever Philip began to feel he could not stand it he would think of the nymphomaniac Molly and Faith the faithless, and remember to count his blessings.

On the Mountain

There was much talk when Jane and Mary Ann Jenkins came home to Mount Kilimanjaro. Mary Ann had been gone for only two years in an American city no one ever heard of, called Cleveland; but Jane was away for twelve long years, cutting a swath in Europe, so the locals understood. Gone into the wide world, far from this mountain, to make their fortunes, and returned to the ancestral hotel with no fortune and unmarried, both of them.

All the Europeans knew the Jenkins family and all had something to say about the surprise reappearance of the Jenkins daughters. In Moshi, they talked at the hotel bar, the post office, the best general store, the petrol station, the bank; up and down the mountain, they talked in the farmers' homes when the ladies had a bridge afternoon, at Sunday lunch parties, in matrimonial beds. Henry McIntyre, who'd farmed coffee on Kilimanjaro longer than living memory, delivered the majority verdict: 'Those poor gormless girls have made a proper balls of it.'

His wife said, 'Girls?' lifting her eyebrows.

Jane was thirty-two and Mary Ann thirty.

Everybody sensed defeat, the end of great expectations. Bob and Dorothy Jenkins, the parents, were overjoyed. They had no idea that people were talking about their children.

But everyone agreed that Bob and Dorothy were getting on and it was only right for the girls to come back and give them a hand. The older generation remembered when Bob and Dorothy showed up, thirty-five years ago, and bought land on a dirt road, back of beyond on the east side of the mountain, to start a hotel. The neighboring farmers thought they were mad. Who would come to it and why? The hotel was nothing but an overgrown log cabin in those days, with five bedrooms the size of broom cupboards. Bob and Dorothy named the place Travelers' Rest, and were undaunted.

There were thirty bedrooms now. The log cabin had expanded into a long central building, two stories high, still faced with split logs, that was its charm, that and the great wistaria circling the verandah pillars by the main door, and the golden spray and the mat of ficus leaves and bougainvillaea against the dark wood. Inside there was a fine bar and stone fireplaces and a lounge with comfortable chairs and writing tables and a dining room tricked out in daffodil yellow cloths and napkins. The bedrooms above were chintz-draped, with plenty of first-class tiled bathrooms.

Eight bungalows, four on each side, stretched in a semicircle from the main hotel: sitting room, bedroom, bath and a little verandah for private drinking before lunch, too cold in the evening. The bungalows were the last word with Swedish type furniture, Dorothy had said, and curtains and upholstery of bright jagged modern designs. The swimming pool was an ornamental blue lake set in the lawn; no one but tourists would be fool enough to plunge into that ice water. Behind the bungalows nearest the entrance drive, they built a tennis court for the young. Land Rovers were on hire. All of this was buried in a garden like a huge flower bed. Old Bob was a true gardener, he'd suffered when he had to cut down trees for the new construction. Anything grew with so much rain and mist and unlimited water in the mountain streams.

No one was disagreeable about the Jenkins' success. They had earned it. Everybody knew what a sweat it was to make a business thrive in Tanganyika, now Tanzania. The *watu*, the Africans. You had to be on your toes twenty-four hours a day: they forgot everything; they broke everything; they were naturally unreliable and mindless; you couldn't begin to imagine what idiocy they would invent next. Specially in a hotel where foreigners didn't understand and expected slap-up service. Dorothy was after them day and night, checking, instructing. And Bob was a darling. Everyone loved Bob.

All the resident Europeans found a chance to take a good look at the prodigal daughters. Everyone was curious about the changes wrought by time and absence. Jane had been a dewy English rose, with golden hair and big blue eyes, spoiled rotten by her parents. The dew had definitely dried off, which gave satisfaction; Jane had been too fond of herself, too pleased with her appearance, though no one could say she was by any means a hag now. Mary Ann looked pretty much the same. She didn't look like her parents, any more than Jane did. Jane the beauty. Mary Ann, officially the homely one. Mary Ann was all shades of brown and average features. Jane had the tall lean elegant body of a fashion model; Mary Ann was short, with a bosom and hips and a waist. No man thereabouts had ever laid a hand on either of them. It had always been an unspoken sour assumption that the Jenkins girls were waiting for a better bet: Kilimanjaro and environs were not good enough for them.

America had improved Mary Ann. She didn't dress as sloppily. Before her Cleveland adventure, Mary Ann cut her hair with a nail scissors and wore any old trousers, or dresses like flowered chair covers in the evening. Now she did things to her hair, sometimes piling it on top of her head, sometimes wearing it in that odd younger generation way, as if you'd got out of bed and forgot to brush it, hanging down all over the place; sometimes in a pony-tail with a scarf knotted and floating behind. And miniskirts and well-fitting slacks and pullovers that enhanced her breasts. American clothes. Clothes were reported to be very cheap in America.

Aside from losing dewiness, Jane seemed to have picked up an extra dose of the haughties in Europe. From the way she behaved, they were all *watu* to her now.

'I like how they talk,' said a newcomer, the young bank manager in Moshi, who weekended at Travelers' Rest, and enjoyed the company and the tennis. Moshi was a dead little town, the week was long and lonely. 'Where did they get that accent?'

'Chagga,' Henry McIntyre explained. 'Chagga English. They spoke Chagga first, running around with the kids in the servants' lines and the village up there. Considering how they grew up, it's funny to hear Jane now. She sounds like a typical old colonialist Memsaab. God knows the *watu* drive you batty but there's no malice in them, poor sods. No reason for Jane to go on as if they were monsters. Half the *watu* in the Jenkins hotel have been there all Jane's life; she used to play with a lot of them. Though I will say she bossed the hide off them, even as a child.'

Mr and Mrs Jenkins beamed, Bob from behind his gold-rimmed spectacles, Dorothy from her sharp darting black eyes. They beamed and relaxed, glad to see the girls taking over. It was the girls' hotel, they had made it only to give to their girls. Dorothy, who seemed never to have sat down since the moment the hotel opened, now often took her ease by the big fireplace in the lounge or in a woven plastic chair on the verandah. And Bob, who had grown stooped and half bald on this mountainside, looked younger from happiness in having his daughters home.

Bob and Dorothy agreed that the girls shared out the work wisely. Mary Ann supervised the staff, the supplies and the office. Jane attended to the guests. Jane had real poise and style after her years in Europe; the guests were charmed by her; and she'd become a linguist too. Very important now that they got so many nationalities on these tours. Jane handled them beautifully, speaking French and Italian. The guests were thrilled to hear that their daughter was a celebrity, the famous singer Janina, resting after triumphs in the capitals of Europe. Jane knew the amount of French and Italian needed in a hotel; she'd used those words, living in hotels. The guests sometimes wondered who the little dark girl was, rushing about in the background.

At the age of seven and a half, Mary Ann's eyes were opened painfully and permanently. They had returned for their first Christmas holiday from boarding school, Jane from Tanamuru Girls School, the most expensive establishment for young ladies in Kenya, and Mary Ann from a modest little place near Arusha, practically next door.

Jane said, 'How's your school?'

'Very nice.'

'I'm *so* glad.'

It was like being hit in the face. Mary Ann could not have put it into words; she was not skilful with words at thirty, let alone at seven and a half. But she knew by Jane's smile and voice and the look in her eyes: the golden-haired princess was graciously condescending to the peasant. That was how Jane saw them and meant them to be. From that day, Mary Ann ceased to follow and adore her older sister.

She wanted to strike back; she wanted to hurt Jane. She hid a small harmless snake in Jane's underwear drawer and Jane, screaming with terror, was petted and stroked and kissed and cuddled by Mummy and allowed to sleep in the parents' room until the fear passed. She broke Jane's favorite doll, claiming an accident, and Daddy bought Jane a new and better doll. Mary Ann realized then that she was not clever enough to fight Jane. Her parents didn't love her, they had found her in a basket, she was not their child, she would run away and live in the forest like Mowgli. Mary Ann was unhappy for the whole month.

But since Mary Ann was born to be cheerful she gave up worrying about Jane and ignored her, which was easy to do as Jane spent less and less time at home. Bob and Dorothy paid more attention to little Mary Ann, thinking she would be sad without her sister. Mary Ann rejoiced to be alone with her parents and back on the mountain, where she always wanted to be.

'Jane's so popular,' Dorothy would say with pride and some sorrow. Jane wrote about the wonderful time she was having at Ol Ilyopita with Cynthia Lavering, at her family's enormous farm in Kenya; Sir George and Lady Lavering, Jane noted. She had been to the Nairobi races in the Hallams' box with Stefanella Hallam; Mr Hallam owned the best race horses in Africa, Jane explained.

'Jane's making fine friends,' Bob Jenkins would say, awed that his daughter bloomed in the fashionable society of Kenya where he would have felt out of place and miserable.

Bragging, Mary Ann thought, big fat show-off: a hideous offence. But who cared, the more Jane stayed away from Kilimanjaro the better. They would never guess how Jane sucked up to Cynthia and Stefi, the richest, grandest, prettiest girls in school, and how brutally they mocked and rejected her. Nor how she had wooed their mothers, at a school festivity, clinging wistfully to the great ladies until the mothers gave the desired invitations and ordered their daughters to be civil. There were no further visits in those realms of splendor, as Cynthia and Stefi turned sullen and unmanageable; but Jane continued to write to her parents about the Laverings and the Hallams, while accepting third and fourth best offers of hospitality. She hated Cynthia and Stefi who made her beg for what should be hers by right. And she was determined that one day she would be where she belonged, at the very top, looking down.

Bob and Dorothy were to blame, of course, aside from the mysteries of genes and chromosomes. They had read no books on child psychology or any other psychology and believed in their simple old-fashioned way that love was the best guide in rearing the young.

'You're my little princess,' Bob would say, holding Jane's hand, parading her through the lounge for all to admire.

'You look like a little princess,' Dorothy would say, smoothing a new dress, giving an extra brush stroke to shining yellow hair.

To Mary Ann, Bob would say, 'Be my good little girl and bring home a fine report this term.'

And Dorothy would say, 'Tidy your room, darling, don't dawdle, there's my good little girl.'

So they bent their twigs, as parents do, with the best intentions. Jane had to conclude she was a princess in exile since princesses do not stem from pub-keepers with 'The customer is always right' as their royal motto. Mary Ann had to conclude that being a good girl was the highest aim in life, or despise her parents as fools. The Jenkins' friends and neighbors agreed unanimously that Bob and Dorothy were making a perfect mess of Jane though Mary Ann was a dear little thing.

Jane was a beauty, no getting around that fact. Mary Ann accepted that fact as she accepted Jane's cast-off, cut-down clothing. It was pointless to resent being plain and plain girls automatically got second best in everything. While Jane took singing lessons in London, she learned shorthand and typing in Mombasa because her parents needed a competent secretary. If Jane wanted to dazzle London, let the silly bitch go to it; her life was here on the mountain, helping to run the hotel. Everyone couldn't be beautiful; she was happy as she was. Jane, for all her looks and privileges and the blind adulation of her parents, never seemed happy.

When she returned from the secretarial college and worked with them every day as an equal, Mary Ann finally understood her parents and forgave them. They were loving and humble and very much ugly ducklings and, for no explicable reason, after six years of marriage when hope was gone, they had produced this swan, Jane. Mary Ann realized that Jane was the achievement of their lives, not the hotel. It had never occurred to them that building a hotel 7,000 feet up Kilimanjaro, out of sight of the famous sugar loaf top, on a bad road, was an act of folly. Ignorant and confident, they had built and worked, built more and worked more; the hotel, filling no previously felt want, was a success from the beginning.

But Jane was a dispensation from heaven, a miracle. Merely by looking at a photograph of Jane they felt singled out for divine favor. Mary Ann, small and cosy and dark, was what they might have expected: an ordinary person like themselves, to be loved, not worshipped.

Neither of the girls talked to each other or their parents or anyone else about their years away from Kilimanjaro. Jane buried memory under layers of pride. Pride had kept her going and pride reminded her that she was Janina, temporarily resting at her family's stylish hotel in East Africa until her agent proposed a worthwhile engagement. But waking at night from a bad blurred dream, she could not forget the last memory. The Savoy, in Harrogate: the too large chilly provincial dining room and the terrible band and the clients, often gathered in determinedly hearty conventions, middle-aged, middle-class, safely accompanied by their wives. She had finished her number, microphone returned to Sammy, the band leader, herself slipping behind the curtain to her dressing room, when she was stopped by a voice from the past.

'Hello, love. Don't you recognize old friends?'

He was fatter and more common but also richer; he looked oiled with prosperity. Jeff Parks, her secretly married husband of less than a year; a man, scarcely a man then, who had walked out on her when she was twenty-one. She remembered every instant of that final scene and every word. He'd said, 'You're as cold and limp in bed as a slab of plaice. And you better live in Africa where you've got all those blacks to do the work, no man wants to come home to a pigsty and feed off tinned beans. And besides that, Goldilocks, you'll never be Lena Horne, never, got it? You'll never never never make the Savoy.' Then he left, and his face was alight with relief and gaiety as he closed the door behind him.

Now he said, 'Congratulations, Goldilocks. You made it after all. The Savoy.'

Jane fled from him; she did not cry then, as she had not cried when she was twenty-one. She stood in this bleak cubicle where no artist could ever have received baskets of flowers, throngs of admirers, flattering telegrams, and stared at her face. Her eyes looked crazy with fear. She left a note for the manager, mentioning a cable from home, packed her bags and caught the night train for London. She kept the taxi while she cashed a cheque at the London bank where, year after year, Bob and Dorothy deposited her allowance; it was the least they could do to help their gifted child, all alone in the costly cities of Europe. Then she drove to the airport and waited until she could get a seat on a plane for Dar-es-Salaam.

The road had been long and stony and cold: singing in coffee bars on the King's Road, and later in shabby nightclubs in Soho, snubbing men, after Jeff Parks, not wanting them anyway, wanting only her name, Janina, on billboards, in newspapers, on records, engagements in great hotels, the stage, films: fame. Then the Left Bank in Paris, a series of basement *boîtes*, hateful people to work with and the male customers assuming that a girl nightclub singer was also a whore. And always the dead time, between jobs, resting in smelly hotels, listening to her gramophone, practising before the mirror, patting her face with creams and astringents, brushing her hair, exercising her body, fighting off loneliness and doubt and four walls. Until Rome.

In Rome, there was Luigi, three years younger though she never told him, and beautiful with tight black curls and a glorious profile and satiny olive skin and eyes to drown in and a soft voice murmuring praise and tenderness. He worked as a salesman in a men's shop on the Via Francescina; he was poor but superbly dressed, they made a stunning couple as they walked arm in arm along the Via Veneto. Her allowance and salary were enough for them both.

With his touch, Luigi woke the frozen sleeping princess at last. She had not imagined that life held such wild happiness; her singing showed it. Five months of unclouded delight. She felt young and carefree, protected, truly loved, a woman fulfilled. The solitude and ugliness of the past vanished; she had Luigi, the golden present in this magical city, the glowing future. One night Luigi came to the Club Aphrodite glum and Luigi was never glum, always gay, warm, proud of her, passionate. He said he'd lost his job but did not say the boss called him a lazy bum who better find a rich old American to keep him like all the other lazy bums. He was sick of Rome, Luigi said, noisy shoving people; everything cost too much. He was going back to his paese, anyway he'd been getting angry letters from his mother, telling him his duty was to return, his wife was about to drop another *bambino*. The third, Luigi said, making a face, shrugging his shoulders.

Jane believed that Luigi had not offered her marriage because he was poor; she understood all the aspects of pride. He had explained that he was learning the business from the bottom; his uncle planned to set him up in a shop of his own. When Luigi had his shop, Jane knew he would speak. Her relentless endurance and ambition seemed absurd now, except as a means to this end. Her career had been a trick of destiny to lead her to Rome and Luigi. What was the lonely dream of fame compared to the joy of being Luigi's wife? It was only a matter of time, a little waiting, but enchanted waiting, until Luigi's male pride was soothed by the possession of his own shop. They had invented the name together: Palm Beach. Jane wondered whether she could work with him, be near him by day as well as night, or would a woman's presence lower the tone of the most elegant men's boutique in Rome? She would learn to cook and to sew; she meant to serve Luigi tenderly, ardently, in every way, with her whole heart.

Jane's arm moved by itself. She hit Luigi hard, swinging her handbag like a club. He clutched his cheek, glared at her with fury, and ran from her dressing room. Jane locked the door and wept, for the first time, until she felt cold, faint, blinded and choked by tears, too weak to move. A broken heart was a real thing, a knife pain in the chest. And in the mind, black despair. There was no one in the world to turn to; she was alone with this anguish, she was freezing to death from loneliness.

But no one must ever know, no one, ever. She could not live if people mocked her, laughing behind her back, the proud English Janina fooled by the first Italian who laid her. She would wait here until everyone had gone so that no one should see her ravaged face. A terrible word hovered, pushing itself forward to be heard. *Failure.* There were no tears left, only this sensation of creeping cold, in the airless dressing room on a summer night. Wait, Jane told herself, wait, wait. The couch with the bumpy springs smelled of mildew, the worn green damask was greasy from many other heads.

Later, singing those ritual words—'Doan evah leave me . . . why ya treat me so mean . . . youah mah man, I need ya honey, I need ya lovah . . .'—there was meaning and emotion in her voice. But now she hated Rome too, hated every beautiful young man with tight black curls, and the streets were full of them. She welcomed a stout middle-aged English gent who said he was in Rome on holiday, the manager of the Savoy, in Harrogate, and a lovely English girl like her didn't belong here with all these slimy Wops, she ought to come home, his clientele wasn't an ogling bunch of lechers, they were good solid English people.

Mary Ann had less to remember and no special reason to forget. There had been eight years of work in the hotel, lifting some of the burden from her parents' shoulders. When she felt she could steal time for herself, she was off up the mountain, passing the Chagga village where she chatted with old friends, into the damp jungly world of the rain forest. She had learned little at school but Miss Peabody, beloved maths teacher, happened to be an amateur botanist and Mary Ann had acquired curiosity and excitement from her. Before that, Mary Ann treated the natural world as Africans usually do: fauna were a nuisance or a menace or something to eat; flora were uninteresting unless edible or saleable. Bob called this botanizing Mary Ann's hobby and was glad the child had an amusement. Mary Ann became extraordinarily knowledgeable, an untutored scientist.

Mary Ann was too busy to think about men and, considering herself plain as a plate, she did not imagine that men would ever think about her. Sometimes, playing with African babies, she was shaken by the lack of her own; but then the hotel wrapped her in its coiling demands, and time passed. Until Mr and Mrs Niedermeyer arrived as guests and took a tremendous shine to her and finally proposed that Mary Ann return with them to Cleveland.

'It's perfectly lovely here,' Mrs Niedermeyer said to Dorothy, 'I can't imagine a lovelier place to live. But don't you think the child should see more of the world and meet more people? I won't make her work too hard, I promise; she'll have plenty of time for parties and fun and young men.' Mrs Niedermeyer had in mind her favourite nephew, thirty-one and single, and though the comparison was disloyal she found Mary Ann sweeter and gentler than the girls she knew around Cleveland; and romantic too, with that little brown face and funny accent and demure manner. If only Jack fell in love with her, everyone would be settled and happy.

Working as Mrs Niedermeyer's secretary was a rest cure after the hotel. Mary Ann had plenty of time and money. She had refused to accept any allowance from her parents, but Mrs Niedermeyer paid her well. With the aid of her new enthusiastic Cleveland girl-friends, she bought clothes and tried out hairdressers. Jack taught her to play bridge and dance. She was surrounded by talkative cordial girls and by Jack, teacher, guide, protector. He was a cautious young stockbroker and took a year to decide he was in love with Mary Ann and was dumbfounded when she thanked him and said No, with a look in her eyes like one who has accidentally hurt an animal, like knocking over a dog in the road. Jack then knew he was passionately in love with Mary Ann. Mrs Niedermeyer had kept her Fred waiting too; she realized Mary Ann was not playing with Jack, the child was truly uncertain.

Jack offered Mary Ann everything and more to come. How could she explain that she didn't want everything; she didn't know that she wanted anything. It seemed to her that she already had too much; why did she need eight lipsticks for instance? Principally, she could not say to Jack or any of these generous American friends that Cleveland and surroundings produced something like a stone in her stomach, a solid heaviness of depression. She never woke with a singing heart because she knew what lay around her, a vast lake full of filth, an ugly sprawling city, a slum for both rich and poor, a flat weak countryside with spindly trees. She hungered for the air and silence and space of Africa and the great untamed mountain. At first snow had fascinated her; then she watched it turn to yellow slush and she thought it was hell. She had a fur coat, a present from Mrs Niedermeyer, and was cold all winter and in the summer felt she would suffocate. Air-conditioning stopped up her nose. Jack persisted with patience and unflagging will. Competition, Mrs Niedermeyer thought, the breath of life of all of them, even if the competition is only a girl saying no.

Mary Ann reasoned with herself. Who did she think she was, a beauty like Jane, with a queue of suitors to pick and choose from? Jack was the first man to want her and would certainly be the last. He was kindness itself and good-looking though she could never exactly remember his face when she was alone. But marriage was long, look at Daddy and Mummy, forever long, sleeping in the same room. When Jack kissed her she felt embarrassed; he talked a lot and laughed a lot and that was nice but she could not keep her mind on what he said. Perhaps if you weren't attractive to men, it worked the other way too, so you weren't very attracted to them.

Finally, because everyone seemed to accuse her, silently and sadly and somehow justly, of meanness, Mary Ann agreed to be engaged, but a long engagement; she had saved money to see the Far West, already glimpsed in the Moshi cinema, and she also wanted to visit her parents. Jack kissed her with unusual force and gave her a handsome diamond ring which she did not wear unless she was with him, for fear of losing it. Her innocence was her armor. Jack would have been more assertive sexually with a more experienced American girl. He was a bit frustrated but also pleased, as if he'd netted a rare bird of an almost extinct species. Mary Ann set off on bus and train to see America.

She kept thinking it was awfully small. Perhaps it wasn't but the cars and buses and trains and planes and roads made it feel crowded or used up; and there were signs of people everywhere, interminable muck, though when she reached the west and the mountains, it felt better, if not as splendid as in the films. She thought the California desert was like parts of Africa she didn't know, for she hardly knew Africa either, like the country around Lake Rudolf. She went walking, she was always searching for a chance to walk where there were no cars. The desert grew a rich crop of empty beer cans and bottles, and sometimes great mounds of used tyres, and dirty papers and plastic containers blew in the hot wind. She dared not tell Jack that she couldn't face it, so said she was now going home to visit her parents and wrote to him, sick with guilt, on the airplane, explaining that she could never make him happy and would he please forgive and forget. He would find his ring in the top right-hand drawer of the desk in Mrs Niedermeyer's guest room.

Her parents misunderstood Mary Ann's misery when she first returned, guessing at blighted love. They were glad when she revived which she did within four months upon receiving a letter, at once perky and hostile, from Mrs Niedermeyer announcing Jack's marriage to a girl born in Cleveland, someone he'd always known, a fine old family. Now, at thirty, Mary Ann knew that she would never marry. But the mountain was there, a gold mine for a botanist except that she never had a minute to herself.

If she'd known Jane was coming home, she might have stayed in Cleveland and married Jack. Daddy and Mummy were crackers; what did they mean dumping the whole hotel on her shoulders as if doing her a favor? Daddy and Mummy sat around boring the guests and making asses of themselves, boasting about Jane, you'd think Jane was Marlene Dietrich. Jane did nothing. She idled in her room with green cement on her face to ward off wrinkles and listened to her gramophone, wah-wah-wah bellowing about love like a sick cow. Or she floated among the guests being lordly or drove to Nairobi to chat up travel agents. What did Daddy and Mummy *mean?* Room boys, waiters, gardeners, kitchen staff, drivers, desk and office clerks, fifty-nine Africans and one Asian, and she alone was supposed to keep them all up to tourist standards. She was so tired and worried she felt sick. She was just about ready to give Jane a piece of her mind. High time someone took Jane down; she'd been conceited enough before she went to Europe and now she was worse. And Amir had gone on leave so there were the accounts as well; too much, too damn much, more than flesh and blood could stand.

Mary Ann had never before given Jane a piece of her mind. Jane stamped into the office where Mary Ann was bowed over a ledger, saying, 'There's an African drinking at the bar.'

Mary Ann went on, moving her lips, adding the long line of figures.

'Since when,' Jane said furiously, 'do Africans drink at our bar?'

'Since Independence,' Mary Ann said, still adding.

'It's the limit. Why do we put up with it?'

Mary Ann laid a ruler to mark her place and made a note. Then she turned to Jane. 'He's the MP for this district. A very nice man and an honest one. He even insists on paying for his beer. We're lucky he likes to stop in here when he's visiting his people.'

'Lucky?' Jane said with scorn. 'We certainly don't want African good will and a ghastly lot of African guests.'

'You fool,' Mary Ann said, 'We want African good will like mad. Haven't you heard about Independence? What do you keep under your peroxided hair? We're visitors here. It's not our colony, it's their country. If we insult Africans, we're out. Deported. They can do it and they do.'

'I never heard such rot. I'd rather sell the hotel than crawl to Africans.'

'Would you? Have you got a buyer? My God, how stupid can you be?'

Jane was too stunned by this turning worm to answer properly. Instead she said, 'I'm sure Daddy's put money aside.'

'Think again. They've ploughed the profits back so they could make a big fancy hotel for us, to keep us in our old age. Were you rude to him?'

'He smiled at me,' Jane said, furious again. 'I didn't say anything but I imagine he got the message.'

'Oh for God's sake. Now I'll have to go and try to make up for you. You tiresome dangerous half-wit.'

Jane brooded and fumed and sulked and, for once, her parents backed Mary Ann.

'We've had very few African guests,' Bob said. 'Mostly Ministers. Decent well-behaved chaps. Africans don't really like it here and it's quite expensive for them. But of course we do our best to make them happy if they come; we must, Jane. It's different from when you were a child. They don't want the hotel and they know we're useful for the tourist trade. But believe me, if we offended them, they wouldn't worry about anything practical, they'd kick us out.'

From spite, to show up Mary Ann and her parents, Jane unleashed all her charms and wiles on the next African guest. He was the new African, a young bureaucrat in a gray flannel suit. He came from the coast; there were ancient mixtures of Arab in his blood; he had a sharp nose and carved lips and a beautifully muscled slender tall body. With white skin, he would have resembled a Greek god as portrayed in the statues in the Rome museums which Jane had never visited. His name was Paul Nbaigu, a Christian like the Jenkins. He had a bureaucrat's job in the Ministry of Co-operatives and a European's taste for bathrooms and respectfully served food. Instead of staying with the African manager of a Co-op, he chose to do his inspector's round from Travelers' Rest. At the bar, where he was quietly drinking whisky and soda, splurging his pay on European pleasures, Jane joined him, introduced herself and smiled her best, sad, alluring, professional singer's smile. She might have been moaning more of the ritual blues' words: why doan yah luv me like yah useta do.

Jane suggested sharing his table at dinner, more spiteful bravado: let her family see what crawling to Africans looked like. Paul Nbaigu could not refuse but failed to appear honored. Jane began to notice him.

'Where did you learn English?' Jane asked. 'You speak it perfectly.'

'Here and there. And at Makerere University.'

She could hardly inquire where he'd learned his table manners which were faultless. He began to notice Jane too, in particular the way she treated the waiter, not seeing the man, giving orders contemptuously. A small flame started to burn in the mind of Mr Nbaigu, who did not love white people though he did not specially love black people either.

'Where did you learn Swahili?' he asked.

'I was born here.'

'Upcountry Swahili,' Mr Nbaigu said mildly. 'On the coast, we rather make fun of it.'

He was not easy to talk to but Jane had never talked with an educated African before, nor talked with any of them since childhood when she ruled as queen of the infant population in the nearby Chagga village. And talk was not really the point. All during dinner—roast lamb, mint sauce, potatoes, cauliflower, treacle tart, good plain English cooking, Dorothy's pride and speciality—Jane felt an alarming sensation, as if waves of electricity flowed from this handsome composed African and rippled over her body. She was babbling like a nervous girl by the time muddy coffee was served. Mr Nbaigu excused himself, saying he had work to do. Jane swaggered across the dining room to her family's table.

'Well?' she said. 'Making Africans happy, Daddy, buttering up our bosses.'

Bob nodded and continued to chew treacle tart. Dorothy's hands trembled but she said nothing.

'He's not one of our better bosses,' Mary Ann remarked.

'And how do you know?' Jane asked.

'I've friends, Chaggas. They don't like the way he stays here and pops in on them, all neat and citified, and asks a few questions and gives a few orders, and hurries off. They think he cares about his job for himself, not for them.'

'You've certainly got your finger on the pulse of the nation. Why don't you become a Tanzanian citizen so you can really shove in and run things? Does he come often?'

'Every few months,' Bob said. 'He's got Meru district too, probably more. Mary Ann's right; he's not popular with the African farmers. A proper bureaucrat, same breed all over the world. Funny how quick the Africans have picked that up. They've taken to government paperwork like ducks to water.'

Dorothy still did not speak; Mary Ann was too angry to look at her sister. Jane's little exhibition had hurt the parents. They were incurably old colonialists, not the wicked ogres of propaganda either, kinder and more responsible employers than Africans were, ready to expend time and thought and money to help any Africans in their neighborhood who needed help. Mary Ann knew of all the loans, all the transport to hospital, all the home doctoring, all the advising: calls for aid heeded by day and night over the years. Like good officers, they cared for and liked their troops. But there it was: Africans were Other Ranks. By law, Africans were now equal. Laws had not changed emotions. And the sight of a white woman with a black man roused emotions which Mary Ann did not understand, but knew her parents were feeling now.

Clearly, Jane had been teaching the family a lesson: do not criticize Jane, however gently. They were helpless, and Mary Ann wished Jane would turn into Janina again and depart before boredom and frustration made her sharpen her claws on the old people.

Jane dreamed of the black man several times and woke afraid. Erotic dreams, ugly dreams. She cursed Luigi and knew with fear that Luigi had left her with more than a broken heart and that she was starving and she was also getting older and perhaps she would starve to death, taking a long time over it, a long empty man-less time. She went to Nairobi more often; she sat at the pavement tables of the Thorn Tree café looking at men, to see if she could find someone she wanted. No one. East Africa appeared to be overrun by middle-aged tourists wearing paunches and peculiar clothes, rumpled garments from where they came or instant comical safari kit. Or there were very young men, young as puppies, with masses of hair and occasionally beards to make them sweat more, with shorts little better than fig leaves and strong brown hairy legs. She wanted someone as beautiful as Luigi and far more trustworthy;

an Anglo-Saxon of thirty-odd, perfectly groomed, perfectly made, and single.

Paul Nbaigu returned sooner than usual; something was wrong with the coffee plants on a co-operative farm, a bug, a fungus. The farmers were anxious, he had to report. Jane joined him again at the bar but now she was hesitant, not graciously condescending, and he was worried for he knew nothing about his job except how to fill and file all the mimeographed forms. They talked little, locked in their separate trouble, but the waves of electricity flowed even more strongly over Jane, concentrating, it seemed, where Luigi had most expertly caressed her body.

She was staring at Paul Nbaigu, hypnotized, when he turned to her and something unknown happened; she felt herself drawn into his eyes as if they had widened like black caves and she was physically pulled into them. At the same moment, mindlessly, she knew that electricity now moved both ways, that he too felt this hot demanding warmth on his body. She blinked, to break the spell; and they looked at each other, startled, sharing absolute knowledge without words.

Jane did not suggest joining Paul Nbaigu for dinner but sat with her family, lost to everything except the sensation of spinning in a whirlpool, voiceless with terror, and compelled by inescapable force to the dark sucking center.

'Aren't you hungry, darling?' Bob asked.

'No, Daddy.' Surprised she could speak and surprised by that voice, someone else's Her own voice was screaming silently, No! No! No! to another question.

'You don't look well, Jane,' Dorothy said. 'You haven't forgotten to take your Nivaquine? They say there's a lot of malaria in Nairobi now. There never used to be, before, but everything's so changed.'

Mary Ann was silent too, though eating heartily. An Englishman had arrived that afternoon, in a scarred Land Rover, and asked a magical question: what was the best way from here into the rain forest? She told him, longing to ask why, and he obliged without questioning. 'I'm a botanist,' he said, and was amazed by the delighted warmth of her smile. Now Mary Ann was debating whether she could seek him out, after dinner, without seeming pushy; wondering, beyond that, if he would let her go along some time to watch and learn.

Mary Ann was settled in the lounge, chatting to a tall skinny Englishman, whose neck was also tall and skinny and badly reddened by sun, obviously a newcomer getting his first dose of the climate, with a skin all wrong for it. Jane pretended to be casual about the guests' register: Paul Nbaigu was in room 24. Second floor of the main building, and there was no reason for her to go up the wide wooden stairs. The family lived in a log cabin of their own, like the bungalows only larger and set back in a private garden west of the hotel buildings. Mr and Mrs Jenkins would circulate a bit, asking the guests pleasant questions about their day, available for complaints or requests, and then take a torch to light their way home. Mary Ann seemed glued where she was, hanging on the Englishman's words. Jane roamed through the bar and lounge and stepped out to the verandah, useful at night for brief stargazing if cloud permitted or it wasn't raining; in all cases too cold to linger. Paul Nbaigu must be in his room.

She felt now like a sleepwalker at the edge of the whirlpool, dreaming her helplessness and the force that pulled her. She had stopped thinking of her parents, Mary Ann or any inquisitive guests; she was not thinking at all; she was moving slowly towards the powerful drowning center. She did not knock at the door of room 24; she turned the knob and entered. He was waiting for her.

He locked the door and turned off the light; a gleam came from the lighted bathroom. He took her face in his hands and kissed her once, but kissing was not what they needed. In silence, in the shadowed room, they got rid of their clothes, pulling them off and dropping them on the floor. Then he held her, close against him, the whole length of their bodies pressed hard together. He groaned softly, softer than a whisper. She felt deaf and blind; all sensation was direct and overwhelming through the skin. He lifted her and laid her on the bed. They made no sound, and muffled the final wrenching cries against each other's bodies.

Much later, Paul Nbaigu looked at the luminous dial of his watch. 'Go now,' he said. Jane obeyed, collecting her clothes from the floor and dressing herself without care. The man lay silent on the bed. When she had her hand on the doorknob, he said, 'Tomorrow.' No other words had been spoken. She moved as secretly as a hunting cat and was not seen or heard on the way to the Jenkins bungalow. The family was asleep; in the morning they would not question her. Adults could not live together if they spent their time questioning. Presumably she had stayed in the lounge, perhaps playing bridge.

Mary Ann found the day difficult. The cook had forgotten suddenly and entirely how to make apple pie. This sort of amnesia was frequent and why not? Africans never ate the European food, had no idea how it should taste and merely remembered—except for lapses—how to cook it and how it was supposed to look when done. Five houseboys sent word they were at death's door having got drunk on village homebrew the night before; the hotel was full. Three Land Rovers were out of commission just when everyone seemed bent on making the cold bumpy trip to the Bismarck Hut to watch the sun rise or set over the vast gleaming top of the mountain. Several guests had objected to their bar bills which were inaccurate. The barman, who wrote the chits, had in his eyes a look which Mary Ann knew well; he was withdrawn into the dream world that Europeans cannot penetrate or imagine; all his outside actions were meaningless, he was living elsewhere. Routine, nothing special, nothing to get fussed about. But today Mary Ann was absorbed by what Tom Withers, the botanist, had said last night; she was repeating it to herself; she needed time to sort it out.

He explained himself, he thought simply and clearly, and left Mary Ann baffled.

'I've got a grant for a year,' Dr Withers said. 'Another scientific carpet-bagger. If it keeps up like this, there'll be more scientists than business men here, all carpet-bagging like crazy. Poor Africa. Anyway I comfort myself that I'm harmless, don't cost anyone here a penny and won't destroy anything. It's my sabbatical, I'm a botany don in a university you'll not have heard of, and I've got this grant to work up a survey of the plant ecology of the montane rain forest. Best luck that ever happened to me. I've always wanted to come to Africa but lacked the lolly, of course.'

What could it all mean?

Then they talked about the rain forest; slowly, it seemed that Mary Ann was doing the talking. He listened and said, seriously. 'Look, this is damned unfair. You should have the grant and make the survey and get the recognition. It's your bailiwick and you know it like the back of your hand. Let's do it together, you sign the work too; I'll see you get paid, if need be I'll split the grant. It can't cost much to live here, specially as I'll be camping.'

'Oh no,' Mary Ann said, 'Oh no.'

'Why not?'

'I wouldn't dream of it; besides there's the hotel. My parents have practically turned it over to us, you see.'

'Well, if you can't take time off for fieldwork during the week, I can bring samples and consult you, and you could surely get away on Sundays. I mean it, I want to work with you. It's purely selfish of me, you could save me all sorts of time and keep me from making dumb mistakes.'

Heaven, Mary Ann thought. For the first time in her life, something she wanted to do with all her heart. Not work at all, plain bliss. He was called Doctor, she found out, because he was a Ph.D.; and don meant professor, far better than dear long-lost Miss Peabody.

She was not going to lose this chance. If the hotel fell apart that might make Daddy and Mummy see how lunatic they were, she didn't care, Jane wasn't the only one who had the right to a life of her own. And Dr Withers did indeed need her badly. Mary Ann thought he was wonderfully sporting and eager but not very practical. She hired a safari servant, despite his protests ('I can cook and look after myself, I'm not used to servants'). But camping, Mary Ann explained, was an occupation in itself: gathering firewood and making fires, boiling water, washing up, washing clothes, even if he cooked for himself which was a good idea; and besides someone had to help him in the forest. No, it would be unwise to set up his tent actually in the rain forest, too damp and gloomy, but she knew a sort of glade by a stream where she'd always thought she'd like to stay.

In the late afternoon, between tea and dinner when not much could happen at the hotel, Mary Ann drove up the track and bumped across country to Dr Withers' site, a grassy slope shaded by wild fig and mvule and podo trees, with a stream between high banks, the water creaming around boulders and smooth over brown pebbles. She counted a day ruined if she could not come; her heart lifted when she saw the neat camp. The big tent that was Tom's home and office, Koroga's small tent, the thatched cookhouse lean-to with firewood stacked to keep dry, the careful circle of stones around the charred camp fire, the tarpaulin-screened latrine, the unscreened shower bucket hanging from a branch.

Tom learned a little Swahili before he came; Koroga knew some English after three years at a mission school but Tom had asked Mary Ann to translate in Chagga his one firm order. 'I didn't come here to spoil the ecology,' Tom said. 'Please explain to Koroga that we'll leave no muck behind us, we'll keep this place clean, we bury or burn. I never saw anywhere more beautiful and we won't pollute the stream either, we share the latrine. Get that across to Koroga like a darling. I'll raise the roof if I see one tin thrown in the bushes.'

Tom and Koroga were always there, back from cutting their way through the forest, collecting samples. The big plastic bags full of the day's haul lay beside the table where Tom sorted the samples and wrote his observations in the field notebooks. Plant presses were drying on two charcoal braziers. If Koroga was not washing or ironing their clothes, he might be practising with obvious delight his new skill of mounting samples with Bexol. Tom said that Koroga's hands, with the dried bits of leaf and flower and that oil can of plastic glue, were more adept than his; just as he said the accuracy of Mary Ann's line drawings in Indian ink made his look like baby bungling. 'What would I do without you both?' Tom asked. She adored the feeling of this place, three workers in the vineyards of science.

She had returned Tom's paint-box and delivered a water-colour sketch and her information on the habits and habitat of a plant with a narrow pointed leaf and three-petalled lavender flower when Tom suddenly put his arm around her and laughed and said, 'You know what you are? You're the most wonderful odd little creature who ever lived.' And kissed the top of her head. That made Mary Ann shy, but the next day he had forgotten his outburst and was asking about a spidery moss. Mary Ann found it intoxicating and incredible that a professor should make notes on what she said.

Jane had become less of a nuisance. She went off to Dar where she said there were many travel agents, as yet unapproached; and then to Arusha, another haven for travel agents. When at home, Jane seemed detached and rather sleepy. She made no further exhibitions with Paul Nbaigu, who stayed at the hotel more often now; and Mary Ann thought it a good thing that Jane spent so little time with the guests, not having been sure that the guests were as charmed by Jane's queenly intrusions as Daddy believed.

Paul Nbaigu had never had a white woman before. He imagined them cold and proud and thought probably their skin would be clammy, fish-belly white. Jane must be in a class by herself. She was the most passionate and insatiable woman in his wide experience. Sometimes he felt they were eating each other, swallowing each other whole, not just copulating. There was none of the teasing and joking you got with African girls; Jane looked at him, he looked at her, they didn't need more to set them on fire. He hated to admit any of the backwardness of his people but a lot of African girls were still circumcised and you never knew how much they were fooling you and how much they felt. With Jane, you knew. And he had tested her good and proper, he wasn't taking any Memsaab stuff, he made jolly sure she worshipped every inch of his black skin. Beautiful, my God, she was beautiful, and the easy stylish way she wore those clothes that came from Paris and Rome and London. All for him, all to himself, and no other black man before him.

On the other hand, he had to be careful. He did not mean to risk his job for her. A few top African people had European wives, but they were the old boys, in at the start. He doubted whether even a European mistress would be wise nowadays. He intended to end up a Cabinet Minister and saw no reason why not. Though he lusted for her, simply thinking about her made him sweat, he was going to tell Jane she had to stop following him around. She wasn't exactly invisible and he wasn't unknown, being an official; and it began to look dicey the way she was in Dar or Arusha when he was, and he couldn't chance coming to

Travelers' Rest so often either. The local Co-ops might begin to wonder why he showed up all the time and make inquiries at the Ministry in Dar and nothing good would come of that.

When he explained to Jane, she beat against his chest with her fists and cried out with such anguish that he clamped his hand over her mouth. Then she wept in shuddering sobs, the way his womenfolk wept at a death. Nothing would calm her except his body, and he had a frightening vision of an octopus, strong white writhing arms holding him, crushing him. Later he said it again, coldly, 'The way I want or not at all.' Then, curiously, 'Don't you ever think about your family? What if they got wind of this? They wouldn't be very happy.'

'I don't care, I don't care. I don't care about anything except you.'

'You care about me, pretty Jane, from the waist down. If you really cared about me, you'd care about my career too.'

'Oh, career! Don't be ridiculous! What sort of career is there in a stupid little tinpot African country?'

It was the turning point. He did not desire her less but saw her now as the enemy, like all whites, in her heart despising his country and his people and thus himself and his hopes. To Jane, they were servants, people without faces, meant to take orders. She would obey him, Paul decided, and she would eat dirt and like it, and then finally she would beg forgiveness for insulting his nation. Jane followed him to Dar once more. Paul had never told her where he lived. Before, he had come discreetly to her hotel room late at night. This time Paul refused to see her and she had the sense—not because of her family or her reputation but from her knowledge of Paul—not to pursue him to his office or waylay him outside the Ministry door.

Jane returned to Kilimanjaro and waited, suffering the agony of withdrawal symptoms. Dorothy wanted to call the doctor in Moshi but Jane said she was only tired, for God's sake leave me alone, let me rest in bed, send trays from time to time and please please please will everyone get the hell out and stay out. Mary Ann was too involved with botany and Tom Withers to pay much attention. 'Temperament,' Mary Ann said. 'After all, she's the famous singer, Janina.' The parents were distressed by both their girls: one seemed to be hysterically ailing and the other seemed heartlessly indifferent.

Mary Ann was concerned about Tom. February was supposed to be a dry month but instead was one long drip; the man had lived in his tent for six weeks and would soon be growing moss, not studying it. He would turn against the place; he would want to move; Mary Ann could not bear the thought. No, of course not, Tom was a scientist with work to do, and she had never seen a man so concentrated and so disciplined.

She had also never seen a man so constantly exuberantly happy. Until the last few weeks. Now something was the matter. Perhaps he only needed a break, a rest, and surely he would enjoy a hot bath. She suggested that he weekend at the hotel.

'Darling Mary Ann,' said Tom. 'It's a beauty hotel but it's expensive as it has a right to be. And my branch of science is not spoiled with money. I've got to stretch that grant a good long way. Besides, this home you chose for me is the best I've ever had. The richest man in England would envy me; imagine having trout out of your own stream for breakfast.'

So Koroga was poaching upstream with poison in the time-honoured Chagga way. Mary Ann gave Koroga a sharp look, Koroga smiled innocently, and Mary Ann decided to forget it. In fact, good for Koroga if trout at breakfast made Tom happy.

'I consider that I am living in the lap of luxury,' said Dr Withers who meant it but also pined for a hot bath and something longer, wider and softer than his canvas cot.

'You had a very expensive room. We've got much cheaper ones. Though I wish you'd come as my parents' guest. We invite friends all the time.'

This was not true and would have resulted in early bankruptcy. Mary Ann knew Tom would not accept that invitation but she could quickly whip the price card off the room door, and there would be no problem with her parents in making special arrangements about his bill.

'We'll see, and thank you,' Dr Withers said. 'We really ought to set up as a permanent team. You know everything and I can look up the names. Now help me place this uninspiring growth. It's Haloragidaceae, the water milfoil family, of which there are eight genera and . . .'

'How much is your grant?' Mary Ann asked sternly, because she was so afraid of offending him.

'£2,500. Sounds a lot but the Land Rover and the camping stuff and air fares all come out of it. I told you my branch of science isn't overwhelmed with money. If I could find a poisonous grass or a flower that killed on touch, and think of a way to plant them wherever our rulers dreamed up an enemy, I'd get a grant of millions. But nobody, I promise you, gives a hoot for botany except some scientists and little old ladies who like to press wild flowers.'

'And me,' Mary Ann said.

'Yes, and you, bless you.'

'Please come to the hotel for the weekend.'

'Mary Ann, I should tell you that I'm married.'

She hoped and prayed that her face showed nothing, not knowing until this minute that there would be anything to show. Now she knew, and it was heavy sad knowledge.

'I don't see how that affects having a bath,' she said.

'No. But it affects me. You see, I'm in love with you. And I don't know what to do. I'm thirty-six and badly married and I have two children and no money to mention and I clamber around the forest all day thinking of you and when you'll come and when I'm not doing that I think about Adele and how frightful it will be to go home to her and then I think about Billy and Mike.'

She took his hand, a big freckled hand with good Kilimanjaro earth under the finger nails. Heavy and sad for him too.

'We have a year,' Mary Ann said. 'No, but more than ten months.'

'It's not enough. I want to spend the rest of my life with you in Africa. Adele is brainless, that's not a crime, maybe not even a handicap. It's her emotions I can't stand. They're all small and competitive and ungenerous. If I walk out, she'd get the boys and I couldn't leave them to be brought up by her; it would be like crippling them. What can I do?'

'Nothing,' Mary Ann said, and felt deep lines forming on her face: old age and loneliness.

'Mary Ann darling, I never stopped to ask if you care at all for me.'

'Yes,' she said. 'I didn't know it until now. I thought it was only botany.'

He laughed and leaned awkwardly across from his camp stool and awkwardly kissed her.

'Oh hell, I must get a sofa up here so at least I can put my arms around you. You darling delicious little brown girl, to think I've made you unhappy too.'

'But will you come for the weekend?'

'Yes. We mustn't waste a minute. And who knows, I might get a brainwave and figure out how to manage life. I can't say I've ever managed anything to date except plant life. Would you mind standing up and then I'll bend down and kiss you without falling off my stool?'

Even that was awkward, due to his extreme height and her lack of it, but gentle and tender and satisfactory to them both.

Paul Nbaigu made no plans but felt himself guided: the words and the acts came of themselves. He was in fact possessed. Cruelty, the power to inflict pain, possessed his mind. Jane's crime—contempt, insult—merged with all the other white man's crimes. She was linked to the outrage of South Africa and Rhodesia and Mozambique; to every offence he had endured before Independence when he was a native in a British colony; to the sneering European professors who sent him away from Makerere after only one year. He hated Jane's white skin for he knew he longed to be white like her, European, rich and traveled and well-dressed and arrogant like her. Insanely, he was revenging all his people by scourging one white woman. He was reckless now, he could not resist the joy of his power. Each humiliation that Jane accepted inspired him with a wild urge to impose worse humiliations. He forgot his precautions about his job. He came to Travelers' Rest every weekend, leaving his work unfinished elsewhere to get the time, turning in hastily invented reports and forged forms to hide dereliction of duty. His salary would not cover this weekly extravagance. It was a special pleasure that Jane had to pay for the room where he made her suffer.

He was not waiting when Jane came to his room now; he was reading.

'Hungry, pretty Jane?' he whispered, since he still had some caution left, enough to know that Mr Jenkins would bar him from the hotel forever if Jane's visits were heard. Jane dreaded that whispering taunting voice, and every word it spoke. She dared not answer back, if she could have imagined any answer, because she knew the certain punishment; Paul would withhold what she craved.

'Take your clothes off,' he whispered, 'and wait until I'm ready.'

And she did, again, as often before, numb with shame, silent, tears sliding down her cheeks. It excited him unbearably to find her aching and arched to his touch, her face wet with this proof of her servitude. He resented his own need, as avid as hers though different. He would only be master when he could play with her and use her and feel nothing.

'What a bore,' he whispered, 'I think I'll take a rest,' knowing he had left her at the peak of that slow undulating yearning climb.

'Paul, Paul, please, please, please.'

'No.' He removed her desperate hands and felt her by his side, shivering like a dog.

'Stop crying,' he whispered. 'You're losing your looks. You go on like this and you'll be so ugly even a white man won't have you. All right. Come here.'

The sob of relief, of gratitude, was delicious but never enough, for he wanted her too; he had not entirely won yet.

He invented games. 'We're going to be two nice simple Africans, pretty Jane. You're a Chagga woman with a big round ass and a bundle of *kuni* on your head and I'm a big sweaty fellow in from the fields, just passing by and thinking what a nice quick fuck you'd make.'

'*No.*'

'No?' he whispered, mocking.

'Yes.'

'That's better.'

Her mind was empty except for a ceaseless incantation: come to me, come to me, come to me. By the end of each Sunday they were exhausted from cruelty given and received and from the gluttony of their bodies. The servants knew. Jane had not realized at first what was happening. Imperious as always with them, she ordered Jagi, a houseboy, to empty ashtrays in the lounge, remarking that he was lazy and stupid not to do it without being told. Instead of mumbling some excuse, the man smiled broadly and picked up an ashtray with insolent languor. Jane went to Mary Ann demanding that Jagi be sacked for cheekiness and incompetence. Mary Ann, counting groceries in a storeroom, said wearily, 'It's not your job to supervise staff, Jane, I wish you wouldn't meddle.'

'Is it all right with you if the lounge looks like an African beer parlor?'

It was too much trouble to explain to Jane the routine of the hotel; one houseboy was not detailed to lurk in wait for every stubbed cigarette end, there were regular hours when the waiters tidied up. This was not Jagi's task and Jagi was a perfectly efficient room boy and perfectly polite. Mary Ann knew Jane's manner to the staff and assumed Jagi had simply been fed up and showed it.

'Jagi's been here fourteen years,' Mary Ann said. 'You can't just sack people offhand any more. They have rights based on years of employment. There'd be a huge to-do with the labor office, the whole staff might walk out, and even if we won, there'd be a mountain of bonus pay. For heaven's sake, Jane, calm down and leave the Africans to me.'

After that it was like a nightmare, when one dreamed of running into endless closed doors but now it was endless knowing smiles; every African on the place had that smile, only for her, and only when she was alone, whether she gave them an order or not. The smiles were an extension of Paul's horrible whispers. Jane stayed in her room most of the day and surprised the family by saying that she could not stand the scruffy way Josphat cleaned the bungalow and the body odor he left behind him; she would look after her own room from now on. Since the parents and Mary Ann were seldom in their bungalow, they did not notice the obsessional way Jane took baths, four and five times a day, scrubbing herself with a loofah, muttering frantic promises: I won't, I won't, not ever again ... Nor, of course, did they notice when she took to drink.

The week, waiting for known misery, became unendurable. Jane could not free her mind of its sickening memories nor could she bear the shame of wanting Paul still. As she was safe from the Africans' smiles with the guests around her, she began to sit at the bar, drinking with them before dinner. When one group left for the dining room, Jane joined another group and so became drunk for the first time in her life. Bob saw this at once and spoke to her gently.

'Jane darling, at this altitude drink goes straight to the head and I think you've had a wee one too many. You don't know about whisky, little girl. It's nice of you to keep the guests company but you'll be safer with tomato juice. I'm afraid you're going to have a bad headache or tummy-ache tomorrow.'

Jane realized that drink had blurred everything, the rooms around her and the people in them, and the agony in her mind and the burning in her body; all had become wavy and far off, not really attached to her; and sleep came as immediate merciful darkness. She had heard the guests talking about drink; Americans especially were partial to vodka.

'Doesn't smell on your breath,' one said.

'Doesn't really taste on your tongue either,' said another. 'But it does the job all right.'

In the middle of the afternoon, in the deserted lounge, Jane risked the barman's inevitable smile and sent him off with a load of soft drinks to the Jenkins bungalow. She then stole a bottle of vodka, slipping it into a large embroidery bag brought along for the purpose. She did not think of driving to Moshi to buy a supply, nor imagine any consequences. That afternoon, alone in her room, Jane drank vodka until the walls began to tilt; the bed swayed and circled when she reached it; she was asleep, dead drunk, when Dorothy came to call her for dinner. Dorothy ordered a tray with a thermos of soup and cold meat and salad to take back to the bungalow later.

'I'm terribly worried about Jane,' Dorothy said. She could talk freely because Mary Ann was dining at another table with her botanist, Dr Withers.

'She looks so dragged down,' Dorothy said. 'It's not fever, I don't think, but something's very wrong. Intestinal parasites maybe? Only I don't see how, with the kitchen so clean; unless she picked up a bug in Dar or Nairobi or somewhere. She won't listen to me. She won't see Dr Ramtullah. I'm really terribly anxious, Bob.'

'Yes, Dorry, I know. I'm worried about Mary Ann too. The child's tired, that's what. It's too much for her; she's practically running the hotel single-handed. Jane's been wonderful with the travel agents but there's nothing more for her to do, and jollying the guests isn't a very interesting job. Probably poor Jane is bored sick, she's used to a much gayer life than we have here. Sometimes I wish we didn't have to charge so much, we'd get younger people; you know they're mostly pretty well along, the ones who come here. Oh my, I'm afraid we retired a bit too soon, Dorry girl.'

'What shall we do, Bob?'

'Well, you're so tactful, love, couldn't you offer to take some of the staff work off Mary Ann; perhaps the kitchen department as a start? I'll tell her I'm tired of sitting around and say I'd like to get back to the office, I think that would ease her quite a lot. And slowly we'll nudge our way in again. But Jane, well, what can we do? You know it's possible after all the time she's been away that the altitude upsets her. Could we suggest she go to the coast for a long holiday? There's that club at Kilifi, I heard it's very attractive and all the smart people from Kenya go there and overseas visitors; it might cheer her up. Then we'll have to see. If she wants to go back to Europe, Dorry, of course we'll help her.'

Dorothy smiled sadly. 'It was lovely while it lasted,' she said.

'Children aren't born to help parents, Dorry dear, we know that, it's the other way around. One day the girls will have their own children to look after.' But as he said it, he saw Dorry's face and knew his own would have the same hurt look of revelation. He couldn't believe it, Dorry couldn't believe it: their babies, born on this mountain, the golden-haired little nymph and the funny little brown muffin, were women in their thirties. It was late, almost too late: no sign of husbands, no sign of grandchildren. Two grown women, their daughters, both looking ill, both stuck here with no future except more of the same, a future like their parents' past.

'I wish to God we'd never built this whacking place,' Bob said with passion. 'I wish we'd saved every penny of the profits and put it in a bank in Switzerland so we could get up and go, now, all of us, to where the girls have a better chance.'

'No, my dear,' Dorothy said and took his hand. 'You mustn't talk like that. We've had a wonderful life here and the girls have a fine business to inherit. You mustn't forget how happy we all were when they were growing up. It's just a bad piece of time now, troubled like, but it will pass, you'll see. I won't have you regretting what we've worked so hard for. It isn't right. Now smile at me and tomorrow we'll begin fixing everything just as you said.'

Mary Ann found out about Jane's drinking in an obvious way: there was a discrepancy in supplies, so much liquor accounted for and so much more gone. In the wine cellar, the vodka was fourteen bottles short. Mugo had been with them as long as Mary Ann could remember; he must have lost his mind to start pinching one kind of drink and in such quantity, and what on earth was he doing with it? He didn't drink himself; Mary Ann could not imagine the mountain Chaggas paying large sums for foreign booze when they got tight as owls on their own homebrew; did he sell it in Moshi? She chose a time when no one was at the bar and, hating to, accused Mugo of theft. He looked shocked and said with dignity, in Swahili, 'I thought you knew, Memsaab Mariani. Memsaab Janny took those bottles, all the time, she takes them to her room and drinks them. Ask Josphat how he finds them in the dustbin behind your house.'

Mary Ann begged his pardon and asked him not to speak of this to anyone.

'Everyone knows,' Mugo said, 'except your father and mother and the European guests.'

Mary Ann felt her cheeks flaming, but managed to say quietly, 'All right, Mugo, and so it must remain.'

Now what? It was too much; it was more than she could take. She walked out into the garden, pretending to inspect the farthest wall where bougainvillaea splashed great sprays of scarlet and orange and yellow. She had problems of her own, secrets of her own, and felt like a trapped rat desperately trying to find a way out. She had sensed a peculiar atmosphere among the hotel Africans, something strange which she could not identify or understand, but clearly this was it.

The eldest daughter of the house was a thief and a drunk. Mary Ann knew the Africans well, knew their laughter, their mockery, even the most loyal would be pleased to see the mighty *wazungu* fallen, silly sinners like themselves. Word would spread up and down the mountain. How could they hope to keep order in the hotel with the Africans privately laughing at this splendid joke? Especially as it was Jane, who treated them as if she were the Queen of Heaven and they were insects beneath her feet? We've come back to ruin our parents, Mary Ann thought with despair, ruin all their work and spoil their lives. In return for love and kindness, this was what their daughters were giving them: disgrace.

It was a perfect April day, with huge white iceberg clouds floating over a bright blue sky. Pansies, calla lilies, lupins, roses, geraniums, larkspur, violets, in sun and shade flowers gleamed as if lacquered. The air was rackety with birdsong, and Mary Ann wished she were dead.

She would have to take the only action she could think of. The parents were in Moshi, luckily, ordering supplies; Mary Ann had agreed to relinquish some of her duties, not saying it was about time, before she collapsed from running the hotel on her own. And Jane, of course, would be in her room where Mary Ann never went, and Jane was, listening to a successful rival on her gramophone, and drunk though not helplessly so, having learned the dosage of vodka required to dull life but not knock her off her feet. Jane made no attempt to hide the bottle. Mary Ann said, 'You have to stop, Jane, or you have to go away. Better if you did both. The *watu* all know you're stealing and drinking by yourself. It's a matter of time before Daddy and Mummy find out, and they must not ever. Daddy wants you to take a holiday at the coast and God knows why you refused. We can't run the hotel if the Africans laugh at us, you know that, you can't have forgotten everything you knew before you went away.'

'Finished?' Jane said.

'Yes.' Mary Ann wanted to hit her; that maddening smile, that special Jane smile, condescending to lesser mortals.

'You doan know the half of it, dearie.'

Mary Ann shuddered with distaste.

'I know enough. Jane, go to Kenya, the coast, I'll see you get plenty of money. You can drink yourself blind, for all I care, just so you don't do it here. Jane, please.'

'Good lil Mary Ann, goody goody lil Mary Ann. Jane's the baddy; Mary Anne's the goody. I'm staying right here. Got my reasons. Got *a* reason.'

'I'll see you get no more drink, I'll find a way, I promise you.'

'Can't stop me driving to Moshi. Buy a crate. Too lazy before but not much trouble.'

'Jane, I beg you, think of Daddy and Mummy, don't you care about anyone in the world but yourself?'

'*Yes!*' Jane shouted. 'Now get out!'

It was a dim last hope and Mary Ann controlled her voice.

'Listen to me, Jane. You're destroying your looks. I had no idea why and Mummy thinks you're ill. Your face is puffy and the skin isn't marvelous the way it was. Your eyes have veins in them. You can't want to spoil all that, you must take care of yourself, you're a great beauty. If you go on like this, you'll be ugly.'

'So I've been told,' Jane said drearily. 'Now get out, will you?'

It was early to drive up the road through the powdery red dust, but Mary Ann decided she had to get away to the peace of Tom's camp. Perhaps she had been right in the beginning when she said she thought she'd loved only botany; she loved this work and admired it, the slow and thorough completion of a task.

She brooded vaguely on Koroga whose family she knew; they were ordinary mountain people and lived in the usual welter of babies, chickens, rags, pots, rubbish. Koroga was a nice boy, perhaps twenty years old, willing to work as a casual laborer on the coffee or pyrethrum farms if he got the chance and also willing to lounge around the village. Koroga was now changed beyond recognition. Had he been infected by Tom's example? Or was it the way Tom treated Koroga, with courtesy and confidence, rather as if Koroga were a student, sharing this project, eager to learn skills and accept responsibility?

Not knowing Africans, Tom found nothing remarkable in Koroga's recent conversion to tidiness and reliability. Mary Ann had meant to warn Tom that the *watu* got uncontrollably bored from time to time and disappeared for a beer party and dance, or disappeared into their special dream state and forgot all duties. It could be disastrous with no evil intent; Koroga might let the plant presses burn from absentmindedness. Koroga instead had become a devoted assistant. He only stopped work when Tom asked him to; then they drank beer and talked together companionably about the animals Tom had so far failed to meet in the forest. Koroga would be heartbroken when Tom left the mountain. Pure luck. Well, someone had to be lucky around here.

Oh yes, Tom was happy as a lark. He was thrilled by the work and by its progress. He loved Mary Ann. He hadn't a problem in the world; England, Adele, the boys, the future were blotted out as irrelevant to the exciting present. Mary Ann steered around a deep pothole and told herself that she must not, she absolutely must not take against Tom. No one was guilty; inexperience could not be a sin though it was obviously a hell of a disadvantage.

Tom had been stunned when he realized Mary Ann was a virgin. Well, why not, a virgin of thirty must be a peculiar event; spinster was probably a better word than virgin. He was far from happy then, on the contrary, almost tearful, blaming himself, begging her forgiveness, wretched with the certainty he had hurt her, which he had, though she could not see it mattered so much, it was by no means a fatal wound. She'd had no time to consider how she felt about her initiation into the rites of love, being too busy consoling Tom. It turned out that whereas he was her first man, she was his second woman. He had married at twenty-four, a gawky shy studious young man, a virgin himself, and been faithful not from love but because he had neither opportunity nor confidence to stray. His field had always been botany, not sex.

Innocence protected them both. Mary Ann went openly to Tom's room when he came to the hotel, and no one remarked on it. They ate at a separate table, obviously wrapped up in each other's talk, and no one gossiped. Sometimes, in the late afternoon, they wandered off into the forest and Tom, overcome by the sylvan idyll aspect, made love to her, and no African spied on them. Hiding nothing, no one seemed to notice there was anything to hide. They were accepted as a pair of botanists, not a pair of lovers.

Meanwhile, inexperience was the enemy. Though Mary Ann was a virgin, Tom assumed she knew the drill on birth control since she did not mention the matter. Adele had managed all that side. Mary Ann was waiting for guidance, to be told what to do next. So no one did anything and the result was known now only to Mary Ann, and known by instinct; she was sick in the mornings, she felt sick and weak all day, her body had never failed her before and now it was a burden. All she really wanted to do was lie on her bed and feel awful and drizzle tears.

It seemed a fearful price to pay for an act which wasn't important to her. In fairness, Tom ought to be sick and sick with anxiety, since he was the one who took such pleasure in love-making. No, she told herself, stop it. Perhaps sex wasn't all that important for women anyway but afterwards was lovely, snug and cherished in his arms, feeling herself special because apparently she was unique and wonderful though she could not imagine why. But now, now: what in God's name should she do now? Not tell Tom at any rate because there was nothing he could do. He might have erased Adele and the boys from his mind but Mary Ann had not.

There were old women on the mountain and Mary Ann knew all about them in theory. They brewed up weird disgusting things and girls drank the brew and aborted, or so the Africans said. She had known of this since childhood, as she knew so much, without relating it to herself; African ways, African troubles, part of her knowledge but nothing to do with her. She had friends among the Africans, she could be led to one of the old women, probably what worked on an African girl would work on her, or kill her as the case might be, you'd not know without trying. But she wanted to have this child, for herself. Tom would go away and right now she didn't mind, feeling too sick and harassed to care for the cause of her misery. But she wanted a child to love and look after in the long years when she was going to be older and older, struggling with the hotel, alone on this mountain.

The problem was her parents and how not to shame them, for they would be horrified and she understood that. Europeans got married; Africans rollicked around lustfully and had babies all over the lot: two different worlds. She was cleverer each day with little lies. She agreed with Dorothy that she wasn't well and drove to Moshi allegedly to consult Dr Ramtullah and returned saying a liver upset had been diagnosed, and produced a bottle of vitamins with the label washed off as her prescription. She could only be in the second month, and must have a ghastly physique to be sick so soon, but nothing would show for some time. She had planned it all and now Jane threatened her plans.

She intended to plead exhaustion to the parents, knowing they would insist on a rest. She meant to go to the Seychelles, where she knew no one and no one from here ever went, and from there write that she had found a baby she meant to adopt as she longed for a child but would never marry. And have the baby in the Asian hospital in Mombasa, and return with it, fudging dates as best she could, recognizing that she and the baby would be trapped in the lies to spare her parents. Perhaps it wasn't a brilliant scheme but she could think of nothing better. And now there was Jane, who wouldn't go away and wouldn't stop guzzling, and Mary Ann could not leave her parents alone with that blowsy selfish bitch, for Jane would break their hearts.

That was the difference; Mary Ann might disgrace them which was bad enough, but Jane was the one who could break their hearts. It's cruelty to children, Mary Ann said in her mind, pleading with Jane, can't you see? They're as simple and trusting as children inside themselves; wrinkles and gray hair are just on the outside. Jane wouldn't see so it was up to her to protect them. She had become older or wiser or tougher than they were. They lived by the rules they'd been taught by their own simple God-fearing parents. Right and wrong and no complications. They wouldn't understand anything, they'd look stricken and curl up and die of broken hearts.

If only she could spill all this on Tom but what was the use? He couldn't help with Jane and if she told him about herself he'd just be harassed and unhappy too. She was a woman of thirty, supposedly in her right mind, and the man hadn't raped her, and she had to take the consequences of her acts and cope with Jane somehow and she also had to stop this loathsome habit of dripping tears all the time.

Tom was drawing a heart-shaped leaf with a flower like a green and red caterpillar but put aside his work as the Land Rover drove up the track. He said at once, 'Darling, you look ill and sad, what's happened?'

'Nothing. Just a bum day at the hotel, I think I ate something funny, nothing really. What's that?'

'You mean to say you've never seen it before?'

'Never.'

Tom seized her in his arms, lifted her in the air, and whirled around before the tent, shouting, 'Oh, Linnaeus, here I come! I've discovered a new species!'

'Put me down, idiot,' Mary Ann said. 'New to me. I don't know every foot of the forest.'

'Well yes, but it is wonderful, I can't believe it. It's Piperaceae but I can't find a description of anything like this species in my books. I'll have it checked at the Herbarium in Nairobi and at Kew, if they don't know it, and no doubt it will turn out to be as common as dandelions. But it is exciting, isn't it? Koroga and I set off very early and ploughed on, north-west, much farther than we've gone before and this proves I must move camp and tackle a whole other area.'

That too, Mary Ann thought, now she would not have the relief of the afternoons, the satisfaction of sharing this work to take her mind off the miserable troubles at home.

'Mary Ann, dearest love, you're crying! Oh no, don't. I'm not going miles away, do you think I'd leave you, I couldn't, I need you every way. Just a few miles, we'll figure it out together, it might mean a little longer drive but I'll never get out of range.'

'I'm being silly. We could drive around on Sunday with Koroga and see what's the best next site.'

So they sat side by side on camp stools and Tom gave her his treasure and said, 'You make a drawing of it, darling, you're much better than I am,' and she took up the fine pointed pen while he sorted and noted the rest of the day's samples and her stomach did not feel queasy and her headache went away and she forgot Jane.

All week, Paul Nbaigu had been planning this, he could think of nothing else, he was in a fever to get back to Jane and arrived earlier than usual on Friday evening. That night in his dark room he was kind; the terrible whispers ceased; he made no degrading demands. After months of torment Jane was allowed to take her ecstasy freely and again and again. Pain washed from her mind and body; she felt beautiful once more; she would stop drinking. Sensing the return of her power as the desired object, she was sure she could persuade Paul to let her rent a flat in Dar; night after night like this, all she wanted on earth.

When Paul suggested that she come with him tomorrow, as he had to visit a nearby coffee Co-op briefly, and then they could drive up the mountain and find a moss bed for their purpose, Jane believed her long torture was finished. Something had poisoned Paul, he was a mysterious animal, perhaps he had been gripped by an evil spell cast on him with burning herbs and bits of feather and skin and incantations. She had watched these dread performances as a child, hidden with African children who were deeply frightened while she was only watching. What Africans believed came true. Cobras, Jane thought vaguely, a curse of cobras and now he was released because her magic was stronger.

Paul gave instructions before Jane left his room. 'Walk down the road away from the hotel, I'll pick you up out of sight of here around nine.' Jane was very gay in the car, surprised at how exciting it was to sit near him and move over the daylight world. She could not take her eyes from his profile nor stop thinking of what it would be like under the great trees with sun seeping through to make gold patterns on his smooth black skin.

'Be quick,' Jane said. Paul had parked his car on a track by the coffee bushes, far from the Co-op buildings and the farmers' huts. Paul grinned at her. And he was quick, but not as she'd expected. Jane was smoking and dreaming about Dar, they'd find deserted stretches of beach where they could swim naked and make love in the warm sand, when she heard an African girl giggling. Even as a child, Jane had detested African girls, complete imbeciles the whole lot, giggling and teetering around on their ungainly big bare feet, and she was annoyed at this intrusion on her fantasy, the white beach, the black body, the aquamarine water.

But the giggling was near and insistent, to the left, in the low coffee bushes, and Jane turned her head, meaning to say crossly, *wacha kelele*, shut up, when she saw Paul. Paul with a little African girl of fourteen or fifteen, giggling her head off, all teeth and wide fascinated eyes and sharp little tits and a neat hard little bottom under her cotton dress, but nothing else under it most obviously. Paul pulling the little African girl by the hand, wheedling, and the little African girl slowly coming closer, giggling less, closer, closer, under the covering bushes but clearly in view from the track, the car; and the girl crouching on all fours, with Paul lifting up her dress and Paul kneeling, his hands holding, reaching, and then and then. Jane watched as she was meant to do until she yanked open the car door and stumbled to the side of the road and retched. She could hear the giggling, renewed now, and a slap like a friendly hand on a hard little bottom, and Paul's voice, amiable and brisk, telling the girl to be off, she was a good little piece, he'd see her again soon.

Jane got back in the car, stone cold, with that bile taste in her mouth. Paul came out on the track, ahead of her, casually doing up his trousers, and looked around, pretending to search for the car and then sauntered towards her. Opening the door on his side he said, 'Funny, I thought I'd left the car up that way.'

'You did not,' Jane said.

He turned expertly and headed out towards the main dirt road but not before he had studied her face, which was white and set and haggard, a ruin of a middle-aged woman. Smiling, Paul said, 'Oh you saw? Jealous, pretty Jane? That's a sweet age for a girl. The kid's been following me around for weeks. I couldn't resist giving her a bit of what she wanted. I like to oblige the ladies.'

'You filthy pig.'

Not taking his eyes from the road, Paul hit her back-handed across the mouth. But he was smiling again, his voice calm and pleasant, when he said, 'Okay, get out here, mustn't be seen driving in together. I'm feeling a bit tired, I'll be taking a nap after lunch if you want me.'

'No.'

'Suit yourself. Now or never, as they say.'

He had passed beyond all caution. After lunch, when the corridors were full of guests going to their rooms, when the servants were all over the place, bringing down luggage, readying rooms for new arrivals: his recklessness added to the excitement, because now he knew he was winning. He only had to prove it finally; if Jane would take this and still come to him, he knew he would feel nothing and be absolute master, despising her far more than she had dared despise his country, his people, himself.

And she did come, reckless too or beyond thought. Jane understood the threat, it was always the same. Now or never. Hating Paul and hating herself, but going to that room because she could not endure the never, knowing herself diseased in mind and body, mad, or under his spell. Paul had paid the witchdoctor, he had watched the medicine mixed on the fire, listened to the incantations to enslave her and drive her insane, it didn't matter, she could not stop herself, she was blind to the startled glances of the servants and only habit made her close the door quickly before any passing guest saw a splendid black body naked on the white sheets.

'Ah, you've come,' Paul whispered, triumphant because her face was no longer beautiful but somehow shriveled, haunted, with crazy staring eyes. He was well satisfied by the juicy little farm girl and Jane was no one to rouse a man today but there was the last step, to play with her and use her and prove to himself that he felt nothing.

'I forgot how nice that African way is,' Paul whispered. 'All this time fooling around with a Memsaab but I find I like it, maybe best of all. Hurry, take your clothes off, I have to get back to work. You know what to do; you saw.'

Tears burned her eyes, her head hung down like an animal being beaten to death, and yet still her body ached and yearned and welcomed and clutched and dissolved. Paul stood up, naked and strong before her, revenged on all of them, proud, certain of himself forever. Jane had fallen back on her heels, lifting eyes that had gone dark and blank. There was no pride left in her.

'Now apologize,' Paul commanded.

'What?'

'You heard me, apologize.'

'I apologize.'

'*No*,' he said furiously, 'Apologize for what you said.'

'Said?' Jane repeated. 'What did I say?'

'You said this was a stupid little tinpot African country.'

Slowly, groping for sense and memory, Jane remembered, long ago, that first lesson in misery when Paul told her she must wait his convenience, the first time he had threatened punishment. What he wanted or not at all. Slowly, she recited those words in her mind: stupid little tinpot African country, and suddenly she seemed to understand.

'That was why?' Jane cried. 'Just for that? That was why all along?'

Paul nodded. 'And now you will apologize.'

At first Jane hiccoughed and gasped out words, hard to hear, then he got them patchily, through a choked mixture of sobs and wrenching laughter. 'Poor little ... black boy ... Jane ... hurt his ... feelings.' She was rocking back and forth on the floor, the laughter swelling to screams, broken by sobs, her eyes closed with the tears pushing out from under the lashes. 'Poor little ... black boy. ...'

Paul stared at her in terror, paralyzed for the moment by this hideous noise and the sight of her and by that pitying contempt; poor little black boy ... hurt his feelings. ... Then instinct took over, flight, as fast as he could move and as far from here as he could get. He tore into his clothes and slammed the door behind him and raced down the passage, down the stairs, across the empty reception hall to his car, and was driving at speed towards the hotel gates when Jagi came into Paul's room. Jagi flung a blanket over Jane's nakedness and ran for Mary Ann.

'Someone sick,' Jagi said to guests peering out from their rooms, alarmed by the muffled but incredible sounds, was it pain, or drunken laughter, what was it? 'Sorry,' Jagi threw back to them. 'Someone sick. All right soon.' Mary Ann followed Jagi up the stairs, walking as fast as a run. She had no idea what had happened but slapped Jane's face hard and repeatedly, told Jagi to fetch a pail and threw cold water on Jane again and again. The insane sounds stopped and Jane sat on the floor, huddled in the wet blanket, silent, staring at the wall.

Mary Ann gave orders. Jagi was to get a driver to bring a covered Land Rover to the back door, and leave it; Jagi was to make sure the upper hall was empty and that the parents were not anywhere around; then Jagi was to help her take Jane down the back stairs to the car and come with her to Moshi. Mary Ann managed to get Jane's dress on, but nothing more; she wrapped Jane in a dry blanket and waited until Jagi gave the all clear. Jagi half carried, half dragged Jane to the car, sitting on the rear seat with her as Mary Ann instructed. He stayed with Jane, who was limp and still staring at nothing, while Mary Ann hurried into Dr Ramtullah's office and made the clerk understand he must interrupt the doctor, it was an emergency. Dr Ramtullah followed in his car to the hospital; Jane was put in a private room; Dr Ramtullah injected a strong sedative.

'Now,' said Dr Ramtullah, standing in the corridor outside the closed door.

'I think a nervous breakdown,' Mary Ann said. 'She was hysterical, laughing and crying. I must tell you, Dr Ramtullah, that Jane's been drinking for several months. A lot. Probably because it was a great blow to give up her career and come home; she must have been brooding.' As she spoke, Mary Ann realized this would be the story for the parents, with the drink part excepted, and for guests or friends or anyone who inquired or had to be told. The Africans in the hotel would know, that could not be helped and did not matter, as long as the parents never found out.

'Miss Mary Ann,' Dr Ramtullah said. 'I am keeping Miss Jane here until she is being calm and rested, but then you should be taking her to Nairobi. I am writing to my colleague Dr Kleber, he will be treating her. Here we are not having facilities for such a case. Miss Jane is needing treatment, do not think she is well again in one week, no, from hysteria and alcohol it is longer than that.'

'Oh yes, I agree, Dr Ramtullah. I'll take her to Nairobi as soon as possible, that's much the best. But would it be all right if I told my parents they mustn't come to see Jane? She might be upset or they might.'

'That is very wise, Miss Jane must be having complete rest. You will be telephoning me, I will inform of everything.'

In the Land Rover, driving back slowly to the hotel, Mary Ann said: 'Jagi, what driver brought this Land Rover round?'

'Moses.'

'Did you say anything to him?'

'No, Memsaab Mariani, only to bring the car.'

'And when you were looking around the back stairs and the hall, did you talk to any of the staff?'

'No.'

'Then you and I are the only ones who know about this, Jagi.'

'Yes, Memsaab Mariani.'

'No one else must ever know, Jagi. If anyone does know, it will be because you have spoken. I do not ask this for Memsaab Janny, but for my father and mother. They have been friends of your family for a long time, Jagi. I remember when your sister Nyamburu pierced her foot on a nail my mother took her to hospital and looked after her and her foot was very big with poison coming from it and she would have died if my mother had not helped. Do you remember, Jagi?'

'Yes, Memsaab Mariani.'

'Then it will be a secret between us. Tell me, whose room was Memsaab Janny in?'

'Paul Nbaigu,' Jagi said promptly. 'That *maridadi* Swahili from Dar. It was the first time Memsaab Janny went to his room before night.'

Mary Ann hung on to the wheel. Her hands felt weak, she was afraid her unstable body might do something violent like vomit or faint. There must not be a car accident. She stopped the Land Rover at the side of the road, the motor idling, and leaned her forehead against the steering wheel. If I'm not careful, she thought, I'll start screaming and crying hysterically myself. So it was not Jane's drinking, not nearly that and all the Africans knew. Jane, who was so beastly to the *watu*, Jane of all women. It's ended now; I'll get her to Nairobi and then back to Europe; I'll do murder to keep this from Daddy and Mummy.

Jagi had waited silently, behaving as if he were not there. Mary Ann straightened up and took deep breaths, testing herself. It was safe to drive on and safe to speak. She couldn't lose her grip again until she had cleared away this awful mess and sent Jane far far from Kilimanjaro.

'Jagi, I want you to pack Mr Nbaigu's things and bring them to me, when no one is in the office. He will not be staying at the hotel again.'

'Good,' Jagi said. Well, that was one help; evidently the hotel Africans didn't like Mr Nbaigu any more than the Chagga coffee farmers did.

Bob and Dorothy were beside themselves with anxiety but Mary Ann kept reassuring them, Dr Ramtullah reported that Jane was resting calmly, there was nothing at all to worry about. Believing Mary Ann's story without question, Bob and Dorothy blamed themselves bitterly for having accepted Jane's sacrifice; were it not for them, she would be singing in Europe instead of recovering from a nervous collapse in Moshi. They failed to notice the pinched, drawn face of their younger daughter. Dorothy said, 'If Dr Ramtullah thinks it's better for you to look after Jane, darling, please forget about the hotel; Daddy and I can handle everything. You just take care of Jane.'

Mary Ann stole enough time to help Tom find a new camp site. Tom was glowing with joy because the Herbarium in Nairobi seemed to think he had come up with a new species of Piperaceae, though they were sending the sample to Kew Gardens for a final opinion. Immortality within his grasp: his name attached to a plant. He was also tense with hope because he had finally had a brainwave about how to manage life, yet did not tell Mary Ann lest his scheme turn out a disappointment. He felt crafty and unclean but supposed that if you managed life a certain amount of cunning and dirt rubbed off on you.

He had written two letters, the first to the head of his department, with some colour photos, some drawings, and many notes included. He said that this montane rain forest was an unspoiled marvel and deserved more than a year's study; he would like an extra year, he felt sure he could guarantee then a definitive survey of the plant ecology. Would Dr Harvey put in a word for him with the Murchison Foundation, suggesting an extension of his grant? Obviously this work would redound to the credit of their department and their university (ah, the slyness when you began to manipulate events). There was a financial problem because he realized the university could not pay his salary after the end of the sabbatical year; he would therefore need more assistance to support his family in England, but less money out here. And naturally all this depended on Dr Harvey keeping his place open, in case Dr Harvey agreed on the value of his Kilimanjaro research. Pompous old Harvey, Tom Withers thought, and a fine pompous letter to match.

The second letter went to his wife Adele and jumped the gun. In it, he announced that he would be staying an extra year on the mountain to complete his study and would of course make the best financial arrangements he could for her and the children, but an extension of his grant would not equal his regular salary. This letter caused him some anxiety. If Adele rang Dr Harvey to protest or gum the works, she would learn he was lying in his teeth but he decided Adele was too brainless to be as crafty as he had become.

He expected Adele to have a fit, not because her beloved husband was missed and longed for, but because a woman needs a man around the house for odd jobs and because of the promised money shortage. Adele was neither bad-looking nor old, thirty-two now, and just the sort of woman to mate with a chap who sold insurance or frigidaires or cars, a steady small businessman type, interested as she was in boring useful gadgets and what the neighbors thought and what the neighbors owned.

As for the boys, he could not be certain of Adele's emotions except that the boys were her property, which was the tricky angle, for she was a great believer in property. On the other hand, they got on her nerves; she was the kind of mother who shouted and administered slaps and complained of the endless work of rearing the young. Dr Withers could not believe that his wife loved anyone though admitting that, since he was not a mother, he had no way of knowing how maternal instincts worked when the crunch came.

He was banking on Adele to look out for another bread-winner and man about the house, and then to realize that two lively untidy little boys might discourage a future second husband. At aged eight and five Billy and Mike were too young to be harmed by their mother's lack of intelligence and by the meanness of her standards and ambitions, though they could, he reflected sadly, be having a pretty dull cramped year now. But if only Adele left him, Billy and Mike would have Mary Ann for a mother and then choirs of angels would sing and all would be beer and skittles.

He had sent the letters ten days ago. Dr Withers would not permit himself to fret about the answers, having determined that three weeks was the correct waiting period. Meanwhile he had this new section of the forest to explore and Mary Ann was overburdened with her overpainted, overdressed sister who seemed to have developed a nervous breakdown from frustrated vanity.

In the parents' car, driving to Nairobi, Jane was sullen.

'This is all absolute nonsense,' she said.

'Dr Ramtullah doesn't think so,' Mary Ann said, 'and you're under doctor's orders.'

'If you imagine I'm going to hang around the Nairobi hospital for months, you're mad.'

'Until the doctors say it's all right to leave, that's all. What do you plan to do afterwards?'

Mary Ann chanced looking sideways at her sister. Jane was thin and pale and a tightness around the mouth showed the bitter shape of things to come and her hair lay flat and lifeless on her head. At Mary Ann's question, there had been a sudden involuntary sagging of shoulders and face, a sigh or a groan repressed. Then Jane lifted her head and Mary Ann had to admire her. Everything was wrong with Jane, she was an appalling person, but now when she was wrecked, Jane's conceit began to look like pride and took on the quality of bravery.

'I'll go to Europe, of course,' Jane said, head high. 'I was a fool to come home, Daddy and Mummy aren't doddering, they can run the hotel perfectly well without my help. I'm through with Africa. It's the dreariest backward nothing place there is.'

Jagi told Mary Ann when she got home, exhausted from the long drive, that Paul Nbaigu had come to the hotel and been informed by Kibia at the desk that there were no vacant rooms and when he asked for Memsaab Janny Kibia said that Memsaab Janny had gone to Nairobi and was not returning to Kilimanjaro. Thank God for that, Mary Ann thought, no scene, no argument for the parents to hear. She spoke to

Kibia saying that he must remember, if Mr Nbaigu came again in a couple of months as he had before, there were never any vacant rooms since Mr Nbaigu was not the sort of guest they wanted.

'He will not be coming back,' Kibia assured her. 'I hear from a man in the Co-op office he lost his job.'

Not only Jane had seen Paul Nbaigu and the giggling little African girl. Two old women, weeding invisibly and silently under nearby coffee bushes, had seen and heard. They told the girl's father, who beat the child until she could neither sit nor stand, and they told the manager of the Co-op. He in turn informed Paul Nbaigu's boss at the Ministry in Dar. The farm people were furious; it was a grave affront and an indecency. This city African, not of their tribe, came to them in his fancy clothes, speaking his fancy Swahili, and debauched one of their girls for his morning entertainment.

Paul's boss called him in and said Paul was the biggest damn fool he ever met in his life, if Paul was so randy why not hire a tart in Moshi, and Paul was sacked on the spot. The boss wanted no scandal which would reflect on his section. Both Paul and his superior knew Paul was finished in government work. Mr Mabari would not stick his neck out by covering for Paul or slipping him into another department. Mr Mabari, to keep this dirty little scandal from his own administrative record, said he would accept Paul's resignation and if Paul could get a job in private industry he would write a non-committal recommendation.

Paul knew there was no appeal, and besides he would be well advised to go quickly and quietly for they might look more closely into his behavior if he made a fuss, and thus learn of the cheating on time and work. The top boss of all would be outraged enough by the story of the Chagga girl, and unforgiving about dishonesty towards the government.

Paul walked through Dar, red-eyed with hate and shaking with panic. Jane, he muttered to himself, walking on the hot pavements, past the Asian shops, past the reek of dried fish by the market, on the dirt lane that led to the small house with its flaking white-washed plaster where four African families lived. Back to the stinking rooms shared with his mother and younger sisters. Jane did it; Jane had picked up his life and smashed it. He was twenty-five and all he had worked for and dreamed of was lost. The years at a mission school when he was such a Christ-loving book-bound kid he wouldn't even listen to a dirty joke for fear the missionaries would guess and he would lose what he lived for: the scholarship to Makerere. Slave jobs in vacations, 'Carry the basket, Memsaab?', 'Paper, Bwana?', a kid anybody could kick around for a few shillings. And finally Makerere, the dream come true.

Maybe he had been a little wild, how could he help it, it was the first time in his life that he had what he wanted, God he was so happy, free, somebody, wearing a short red academic gown in hall, living like a European, maybe he didn't study enough, they could have given him a second chance. Europeans feared an African with spunk, they couldn't wait to chuck him out. And how he had grovelled and scraped to get a desk job in the Ministry, where boredom was like pain until, only a year ago, he started to climb, with a car, off on the roads, an official, the liaison between Dar and the upcountry peasants. The months at Makerere and this year, out of twenty-five years; less than two years of the kind of life he had longed for and worked for and suffered for. *Jane did it.*

He banged through the room where his mother as usual was washing other people's clothes, shouting at her that he'd been fired, thrown out, ruined, all because of a lying ugly whore.

'Don't shout at me,' his mother said. She was a fat strong-willed woman, long since abandoned by Paul's father, who had raised six children and took no nonsense from any of them. Paul was the clever one, and also the worthless one. Her pride in his looks, education, success, had withered into doubt. If a man was no good inside himself all the fine clothes and fine ways would not hide it forever. 'And don't shout about that woman whoever she is. A man who lets a woman mess up his life can blame himself. You won't find me crying for you. And you better get a job fast, boy, because Mama isn't going to feed you.'

No. He would not plod from office to office, where signs on the doors said: *Hakuna Kazi*—there is no work. And wait and beg and gratefully, if he was lucky, take a little clerk's job under some unschooled African or sharp Asian, with a serene white man far off in an air-conditioned office, like a king ruling them all. Jane would pay; Jane would provide the work and good work, clean work, pleasant, well-paid work. There was plenty he could do in that grand hotel of hers. And if she didn't feel like it, he knew how to get his way. He'd tell her stupid cheerful old Daddy what kind of daughter Jane was, he'd tell the whole hotel full of rich *wazungu* coming to his country to have a nice time looking at animals and mountains, he'd make such a bad noise they'd hear it all over Tanzania. But now he had no car; the car belonged to the job, not to him. His hate for Jane festered like an infected wound during the ten-hour jolting ride in a bus, surrounded by Africans smelling of dirt and poverty, laughing and babbling like idiots mile after mile.

He felt fouled when he got off that rickety bus in Moshi, stinking like all the other passengers, his clothes rumpled and sweaty, and now he had to take another bus up the winding mountain road and walk through the dust. He had come to this hotel before in a car, as well put together as a European, stopping always in a Moshi petrol station first to groom himself in the lavatory, changing his shirt and suit if need be. He arrived as an equal with the guests or better because he was a government man and they were only foreign tourists and if any of them stepped out of line they could be deported; he, Paul, could report them, he had power and they had none. Now he came on foot, tired, soiled, an African out of work, like any of his people, the poor and faceless, and he felt with shame that he belonged at the back door, not in the reception hall. The cold hostility of Kibia at the desk, the flat unsmiling stares of the hotel servants, finished him.

He was defenceless among enemies and afraid. If he made a noise here, Mr Jenkins would call the police. The Europeans always won. They had the money and the real power and they thought ahead and were quiet as snakes and knew what they were doing, and his people were slaves who would serve them, even against their own kind. He walked back down the drive to wait at the lower bus stop. He didn't walk, he shuffled. The strength was gone from the magnificent body which had been his certain source of pride.

Counting every shilling now, Paul spent the night in a cheap African hotel in Moshi. He lay on the lumpy kapok mattress on the iron cot and heard through the slat walls the disgusting sounds of his people, loudly attending to the night's business: peeing, belching, drinking, laughing, talking at the top of their lungs, fornicating, snoring, to the tune of whiney Indian music and solemn news broadcasts on their transistor radios. He felt imprisoned, a man alone, everything lost except his one possession: hatred. Hatred for Jane, for white people everywhere, men and women alike: this passion clamped over his mind forever

He wanted to kill them, he had no other desire. All that sleepless night he thought of this: kill them, any of them, all of them. By morning he had thought of a way, without going to jail, and rose with gummed hot eyes and a sour taste in his mouth but no longer ashamed of his filth and stench and his loss of place in the world. He had a new nobler place: he would make his way to the southern frontier and join a camp of Freedom Fighters and sooner or later it would be given to him: the chance to kill white people. He could not reach Jane but there were others, and he knew what he wanted, he would not forget or waver. He would be the sword of vengeance and they would come to fear him before he was through.

Mary Ann brought the two letters, since Tom used the hotel as his mail address, but he would not read them while she was there lest they be dusty answers and he had to conceal defeat. However Dr Withers could not conceal his distraction and Mary Ann, puzzled and rather hurt, left early. Presently Koroga thought his Bwana must be drunk for he was laughing and talking in a loud voice. 'God bless us every one!' Dr Withers said, hugging himself and laughing like a lunatic. 'Oh too good to be true! Too good to be true!' This called for a celebration; first of all he would have a large whisky, normally rationed because of expense, and read both letters again. Tomorrow he would drive to Moshi and on the way invite Mary Ann to a dinner party for two. He wanted special luxuries for the feast: a tin of pâté, a cake, and a bottle of wine. Could he wait until tomorrow night or should he ask her for lunch? No, dinner, so she wouldn't have to hurry back to that cannibal hotel which ate her alive, but would have hours for talking and planning.

Adele had never given him a gift like this; he could almost hear her high complaining voice as he read. He savored the typical longed-for abuse. Tom, not she, had destroyed this marriage; she knew her duty but Tom felt no obligation to anyone except himself. Did he expect her to sit alone in England another whole hard year, coping with the boys by herself, with not even enough money? She had kept her vows faithfully, but now considered herself free. Unlike Tom, who traipsed off whenever he got a chance—remember Wales, Switzerland, and every weekend he could manage, if he couldn't go farther, he'd leave her for Kew Gardens—there was a reliable steady man in Reading, Mr Billingsley, who owned a large furniture store.

She had met Mr Billingsley some months ago when she went in to price a little table. Mr Billingsley was a widower, childless, somewhat older than herself, with a very good position and lovely taste and manners, and she was no longer going to reject his attentions. She knew Mr Billingsley wanted to marry her and she warned Tom that she intended immediately to consult a solicitor about the divorce laws. As for Billy and Mike, Mr Billingsley had a beautiful home and naturally cared a great deal for furniture and was unused to children, and Tom would absolutely have to take his share of responsibility, she could not be expected to assume the entire burden of bringing up the boys.

Dr Withers kissed this letter reverently, and treated himself to another whisky. Damn the expense. Life was a bowl of cherries. The future shone with a rosy sunrise glow. And Dr Harvey was a dear man, not a pompous bore, who said he fully agreed with Dr Withers' assessment of the importance of the Kilimanjaro rain forest, and had written the Murchison people for an appointment and would urge the extension of the grant next week in London. Dr Withers kissed that letter too. What the hell, kissing letters might turn out to be some sort of juju, bringing massive good luck to the kisser.

Mary Ann felt a rush of tenderness for this tall gawky man, with the flop of blondish hair on his forehead and the peeling nose. He had put a jam jar full of wild orchids on the table beside a candle in a beer bottle. He pushed in her camp stool as if he were a footman in a palace, and would tell her nothing until after the first glass of somewhat vinegary wine. Then he talked a blue streak, laughing so much with happiness that Mary Ann hardly took it in. Tom began again, and she understood: he had managed life, he had planned and taken steps and succeeded; he might be inexperienced but this showed he was far from incompetent. 'Crafty,' he kept saying. 'You'll have to watch me carefully, I may turn into a prize crook.'

He came to kneel by her stool, with his arms around her. 'Darling Mary Ann, if all goes well and believe me I'll help it along with both hands, we ought to be free to marry in a very few months. And I feel in my bones that old Harvey will nag the Murchison people into another year. You'll love Billy and Mike, I promise you, and think what it will mean for them to camp on this mountain. We'll have a little village of our own, our tent and theirs and a work tent and an eating tent, oh God in heaven I can hardly wait.'

To his dismay, Mary Ann burst into tears. He couldn't believe it, he could hardly breathe. Not a bowl of cherries, no sunrise rosy future? He was speechless before these incredible daunting tears.

'It won't be soon enough,' Mary Ann said, wiping her cheeks with a paper napkin.

'What?'

So Mary Ann explained that, perhaps not in the eyes of God or man but for practical purposes anyway, they were married already and though she hadn't seen a doctor she calculated she was about three months pregnant.

'My love,' Dr Withers said. 'And you never told me, you carried all that worry around alone? Don't you trust me?'

'I didn't want to make you unhappy.'

'You mean, just be unhappy by yourself? Mary Ann, you're going to have to stop being heroic and looking after everybody else. Darling, don't you want the baby?'

'I want it more than anything in the world.'

'Oh thank God for that. Now everything's fine, no problems, joy on all sides. We'll have *another* tent, a tiny baby-size tent. It's really too good to be true. How do you feel?'

'Sick mostly. But I think a bit better now and pretty much all right by evening.'

'Oh my angel, angel, how *could* you not have told me?'

'Tom, there are problems. Even if we could get married tomorrow which we can't. I don't know how to keep it from my parents; I mean, that we didn't wait.'

'My knees hurt,' Dr Withers said, 'and I still haven't got that sofa. You'll have to stand up.'

He took her in his arms lovingly, and said to the top of her brown head, 'Mary Ann, couldn't we tell them the truth? It's not such a terrible thing, the truth. We love each other and we'll love the baby and there's nothing ugly about how nature works and this is late in the twentieth century and people don't fall over dead from shock any more when men and women make love without benefit of clergy.'

'I don't know,' Mary Ann murmured against his khaki shirt.

'I do. Leave it to me. You're not to worry about a thing. We'll have a whale of a time on this mountain, and you'll have a perfect baby with two ready-made older brothers and we'll all live happily under canvas forever after or anyhow quite a while. You'll see. I'll manage. Crafty Tom.'

She pulled away from him and looked up that great distance into his face. 'I'll tell you one thing you'll never manage,' Mary Ann said earnestly. 'If you want to marry someone else later on you'll never manage to get my baby away from me.'

By the light of the bonfire Koroga had made, by the light of the kerosene lamp hanging on a pole before the tent, Tom had a vision of how the little brown girl would look when she was old: a little brown woman, square in build, with a very firm chin and a warrior's eyes if anything menaced her loved ones, a tough determined hard-working and fiercely protective little old lady.

He laughed with delight and seized her and hugged her. 'Nothing on earth would make me come between you and your baby. I'm not crazy. I know a lioness when I see one.'

'Drive home with me,' Mary Ann said. 'And use Jane's room tonight. You can manage Daddy and Mummy in the morning. I do leave it to you.'

There was much talk when Jane and Mary Ann Jenkins left home on Mount Kilimanjaro. All the Europeans had something to say about the surprise departure of the Jenkins girls. In Moshi, they talked at the hotel bar, the post office, the best general store, the petrol station, the bank; up and down the mountain they talked in the farmers' homes when the ladies had a bridge afternoon, at Sunday lunch parties, in matrimonial beds. The young bank manager wished to God these bloody farmers would stop using his bank as a club and stop being such bloody gossips.

He was browned off with Africa and would willingly have exchanged his three servants and spacious bungalow for a dingy bedsitter in Earls Court.

Here they were, the regular gang, Henry McIntyre, Arthur Wells, Peter Kinlock, come to collect payday cash for their *watu* and, lucky for them, a farmer from Meru, Ralph Harrison, come to look enviously at McIntyre's coffee beans and give them all a chance to chew over their bloody gossip again. You'd think this bloody mountain was the only inhabited place on earth and the Jenkins girls the only two living females.

The man from Meru remarked, 'I hear the Jenkins girls have flown the coop. Here today, gone tomorrow,'

The young bank manager groaned silently and waited for the chorus.

'Well, yes,' Henry McIntyre said. 'Jane's gone back to England and good riddance if you ask me. I had a feeling that girl could cause old Bob trouble with the *watu*, she didn't have the hang of Independence. But Mary Ann's around, on safari somewhere on the other side of the mountain.'

'According to the *watu*,' said Arthur Wells, 'Jane was whisked off because she'd been hitting the bottle. Houseboy to cook, they didn't know I could hear them, that's the way to pick up the straight gen.'

'I heard worse than that,' Peter Kinlock said. 'Some sort of nasty little African sex deal on one of the Chagga Co-ops, an African got sacked for it, but it seems Jane knew about it for some reason. Tricky thing to be mixed up with. I bet Bob rushed her out for fear the DC would want to ask questions.'

This was new news and Henry McIntyre disapproved of it. 'You can't believe everything the *watu* say. You know how they are, talk, talk, talk their silly heads off. Half the time they're making it up.'

'You know,' Arthur Wells began, as if he hadn't broached the subject often before. 'I'm surprised Dorothy hasn't raised a row about Mary Ann going off with that scientist fella. Dorothy's so prissy you'd think she was running a nunnery not a hotel.'

'Well, for God's sake, Mary Ann's in her thirties. About time she went off with a man.' For once the young bank manager thought Peter Kinlock normally intelligent. 'I've met that scientist fella, can't remember his name. Seemed a nice enough chap, not much to say for himself, but you've got to admit it takes some guts to camp for months on the mountain. He's not like the tourists who have a heart attack if everything isn't just so.'

While the gentlemen were in Moshi attending to business, Mrs McIntyre was giving a bridge afternoon for Mrs Harrison from Meru. Mrs McIntyre said firmly, 'I hope it's so. Best thing that could happen to Mary Ann and best thing that could happen to Bob and Dorothy if they have any sense.'

'But they're not married, dear,' Mrs Wells said.

Mrs Kinlock said, 'I heard he was getting a divorce, didn't you?'

Mrs McIntyre was senior lady on the mountain and talked when and as she chose. 'Dorothy told me Jane had gone into partnership with a man in London, they're setting up a boutique. Obviously Jane nicked them for the capital. Dorothy couldn't have been more pleased. Really, she and Bob are ludicrous. You'd imagine Jane was about eighteen and Helen of Troy and all the men were panting after her. Dorothy practically said she felt Jane would be safer in a dress shop than on the stage.'

'I didn't notice any men swooning with love for Jane at the hotel,' Mrs Kinlock said. 'She's as cold as an iceberg. Probably wouldn't let a man get near her in case he mussed her hair.'

Mrs Harrison of Meru had been excluded from this purely Kilimanjaro chat, but she had general ideas to contribute. 'You can't count on children for anything any more. I keep warning Ralph that young William will never come home from university and take over our farm. I tell you, we're the last of the settlers.'

'And no doubt one day we'll all end up stabbed to death with pangas,' Mrs McIntyre said.

The ladies laughed merrily.

Bob and Dorothy were happy to be back at work. They agreed that it wasn't very interesting to live in a hotel unless you managed the place, and they had been silly to think they were getting old, people in their sixties weren't old; they must have been suffering an attack of laziness. Again Dorothy raced around, peering, checking, instructing, and Bob returned to the office, the accounts, the bills, the correspondence, and all the new complicated paper work which the government piled on. They did not admit it to each other, but they felt that the hotel ran more smoothly under their supervision, they'd noticed odd looks and odd behavior in the staff but everyone seemed settled down now, the way they'd always been.

Dorothy was fondly re-reading a postcard, Changing of the Guard at Buckingham Palace on one side and Jane's scrawl on the other. 'Opening great success. Clothes much more fun than singing. Teddy's so talented angelic like younger brother, Love J.'

'More tea, Bob dear? Isn't it wonderful how Jane's fallen on her feet? She's such a clever girl. I always knew she'd be all right. Never caused us a day's trouble.'

'Now, Dorry love.'

'I hate to think anyone can talk about one of our daughters. Yes, I know Tom's a good man and they'll be married but even so, I hate to think what people are saying about Mary Ann.'

'I don't expect they're saying much. People have plenty of worries of their own. And what we don't hear can't hurt us, can it, Dorry? Come on, cheer up, love. You know we've been hoping and longing for a grandchild. You know we have. Think how lucky we are, we've waited for years and now we only have to wait a few more months.'

By the sea

Begin at the beginning. I overheard people at the next table. Two couples, Australians or New Zealanders, I think, those accents. At breakfast in the dining room. The dining room is too big. They were talking about carmine bee-eaters. Swarms, thousands of tiny red birds, flying in to trees at the head of a creek. Making a tremendous row, thousands of them, settling for the night or squabbling over insects or whatever. Wasn't it amazing, one woman said. And the creek looks so romantic, so African. The lunch at the something Club is much better than here, a man said. Oh the whole place is much better, the woman said, I mean it looks like real Africa, that palm thatch roof and the mud-brick bungalows, I wish we'd known about it before, instead of staying here. I don't consider this place exactly hell, the man said, and they laughed. Why not hire a car again today, the other man said. One of those darling pink-and-white baby jeeps, the dark-haired woman said, probably his wife. I'll never forget those tiny red birds, the first woman said, *millions* of them.

I imagined a cloud of rosy hummingbirds moving over the sky, then breaking up, and the trees would seem to blossom with fluttering red flowers. It sounded lovely, like nothing I'd ever seen or could really imagine. They looked happy, the two couples, with their new sunburns, one of the big men had a peeling nose. They were enjoying themselves, having fun on their holiday. Everyone here in this luxury hotel is a tourist, it's a holiday place but not all the faces look happy. Of course I haven't spoken to anyone, I wouldn't know how to start, but I watched the other guests, at the Olympic-size pool mainly. It's rather like going to the movies alone.

I was quite wrong to believe that flying off to Africa was extraordinary and a dashing thing to do. Every nationality is here, treating Africa as just another tourist resort, French people, Germans, Italians, some cruise ship Americans, all kinds of British Commonwealth, and three pairs of giggly Japanese. At the pool, the Japanese ladies wear big boudoir caps of lace and ribbons and mannish striped swim suits on their short mannish bodies.

My favorites are gone now, they only stayed five days, I'm certain they weren't tourists like the rest of us though it's odd to think of any white people living in this part of the world. Really living, not here on a trip. I watched them whenever I could: a sturdy sunbaked small woman and a tall thin man, tomato-coloured with a ferocious burn which didn't seem to bother him, and two tow-headed lively boys, about eight and ten years old I'd guess, and a fearless brown baby in an infant's lifejacket. They took turns teaching the baby to swim. It was their best game, obviously they all doted on the baby. The baby was wonderful, serene and confident, not the least disturbed by being hauled and pushed by so many hands. That family looked as if they were always happy. I hoped they'd speak to me but they didn't, nor to anyone else, they were complete together.

Perhaps I was beginning to get a bit sad from watching, the single person alone here, otherwise I might not have thought about the carmine bee-eaters, charmed by the name. I realized how dull I am, I never find anything special to do. There were only a few days left and I hadn't budged from the hotel. Not that I hadn't been content with the white sand beach to walk on, and the warm sea, and the splendid pool when the tide is out, and the colors and the soft air and the sky.

After breakfast I went to the woman at the desk, the one who arranges things, car hires and visits to the game parks, and spoke of the carmine bee-eaters. She knew all about them. She suggested driving to the something Club for lunch and a swim and renting a boat to go up the creek at four in the afternoon. No, it wasn't really a Club, that just meant they could keep Africans out, no problem for Europeans. It was the season for the birds, apparently they weren't a year-long sight, only now for a month or so they came in hordes to this grove of trees. Did I have a driving licence? She could give me a nice small white Peugeot and if I started at eleven I'd be there by noon. You turn left when you leave the hotel grounds and go straight to the bridge and turn right until you see the Club sign on the right just before Kilifi creek. You can't miss it, there's only one road.

I've never driven a Peugeot but it works like any other car. Alone on an African road, I felt different. For two weeks I'd felt that I was coming alive. What do I mean? Perhaps it's very simple: physical well-being. I was at home in my body again. Glad to wake to the morning sun, golden warm but not hot because a breeze blows steadily from the sea. The breeze is called the monsoon, I learned, surprised since I thought the monsoon was some ghastly wind that happened in India. My skin felt smooth and fresh as if I was breathing all over, taking in bright air through my whole body. I slept without dreams to remember and woke to look at this beautiful world. All I could see of it from my balcony or walking on the beach. Certainly not a varied view of Africa but enough; the dazzling blue and gold and the brilliant night sky. The colors change hour by hour.

It wasn't necessary to think or feel or plan. Planning to fill time is what I always have to do. In these weeks, there wasn't any time, just the days with nothing to mark them, slow and easy and gone before I'd noticed. Time is terrible if you know there's nothing ahead but more and more time. Perhaps that's what I mean. I forgot time, I was free of it.

On the road, away from the sea, hot wind blew through the car windows. I decided it smelled of Africa, not that I know how Africa smells. This wasn't like the scented air around the hotel with its sloping gardens, the flowers, the flowering trees. Because of this new smell I felt daring, unlike myself who am not daring. All alone in darkest Africa, setting out on an adventure. There wasn't much to see at first, or nothing you could call particularly African. The backs of hotels and a grimy gray factory with chimneys and a few petrol stations. The sense of Africa was emptiness, almost no cars and empty space between these uninteresting buildings. Then there was a toll bridge over a wide river or inlet and after that, idiotically, I began to think I was Livingstone and Stanley, driving along a good tarmac road at fifty miles an hour to lunch at a club for Europeans.

The trees were strange, none recognizable, surely none planted by man. Wild trees. Despite the car noise and the wind noise, I felt the silence. A huge silence over a huge land. I couldn't see any distance into the huge land, only feel it going on forever. I passed an African village by the roadside, mud huts with pebbles stuck in the mud (why? for ornament?) and thatched roofs. African women wearing printed cotton cloths wrapped around them, African men with white skull caps and gowns like nineteenth-century nightshirts, jolly naked children. It was very picturesque and very poor.

The idea came to me that I could make a life like this, not all the time naturally, but as something to look forward to. Every year, I could do this. Go away to some unknown place and stop being me, lose my life, live by looking. It would be a way out, or part of a way out. I must have been mad, grabbing at hope after two weeks of feeling peaceful and half an hour on an African road.

On both sides of the road were fields growing great cactus plants of some kind, like giant cabbages, with spikes that looked murderous. The ground was dry as brown cement. The cactuses grew in long straight rows. How could anyone get near those dangerous spikes to cultivate them or cut them or whatever they did? Anyway there was no sign of people. The cactus fields ended in a band of trees, very thick, tangled, a piece of jungle which scared me into thinking of poison snakes and spiders and malaria. The monsoon does not reach this burned earth, the handsome European hotels on the coast have nothing to do with what belongs here. I hoped the something Club would show up soon and began to have more natural emotions, natural to me: no cars, no people, no houses, the immense silent sunstruck land, I shouldn't pretend to be adventurous and sure of myself, an experienced traveler.

It was foolish to be alarmed by the dark trees because they were a patch not a forest and the road went straight on between flat unused ground; long yellowish grass, stubby grayish bushes, unused, unlived in, much of Africa must be like this, not desert but no water, you couldn't say it's ugly but miles and miles of such emptiness would be sinister. I wasn't thinking, or telling myself hopeful stories about future journeys, I was just driving in my usual way, eyes on the road, when suddenly, from nowhere, up from the ground, suddenly, suddenly, suddenly a child leapt running. Directly in front of me, directly in front across the road, running. A second. One second. I saw his face, his profile, running . . .

A sound wrenched out of her, not from her throat, from deep inside, loud, a long rasped groan, a sound like 'NO' but not clearly a word. Mrs Jamieson did not hear it. She pressed her hands over her eyes, grinding out a picture she must not see. There were flashes of red and yellow under the pressing hands. The pain in her head that never stopped flared into defined points on the temples and at the base of her skull. She lay on the bed, rigid, watching the lights behind her eyelids, the pain numbing her mind. Then she walked to the bathroom, unsteadily, and turned on the cold shower.

She stood under the spray, holding up her long hair, gabbling to herself about the water: that's nice, nice cold water, that's nice, that's better. She dried herself, gabbling now about the thick green towels which matched the green tiles and walls of the bathroom. You'd never expect such a perfect bathroom in Africa. You'd never expect such a lovely room. Think about the room. One wall of glass, opening to the balcony. Long yellow curtains like the bedspread. White leather chairs or whatever looks like leather. Marble floor or whatever looks like marble. Big built-in cupboards, big built-in dressing table. Good lamps with plain white shades. White walls. So cool and clean and light and pretty. One painting, local work obviously, tacked on to show you where you are, an African maiden with a collar of silver rings giving her a giraffe neck, and bare breasts. All right now. Breathe quietly. Two aspirins. Ice from the Thermos.

Ice cubes in a hand towel made a wet cold bag which she held against the bluish lump on her right temple, then against the unbruised left temple where the pain was worse. Raising her hair, she passed the melting ice bag across the back of her neck. The condition of her head was a fact to be ignored. The cavity inside her skull felt filled with a single hot stone, too large for the encircling bone. When the regular pain altered into pulsing jabs she sweated and was rocked by nausea so she handled this inconvenience with aspirin and ice. It did not concern her.

The mirror over the wash basin covered the wall. Another long mirror covered the bathroom door. She could not avoid seeing all of herself. She looked at her face which was unchanged except for the colored swelling on her temple. She couldn't remember when she had stopped caring about her face. Probably when she knew she was old. Long ago. Being old did not depend on your looks or on a number of years, it was a truth you knew about yourself. Forty-three last week; she had forgotten her birthday here in those timeless days which seemed long ago too.

When she was a child her parents must have told her, or let her understand, that she was pretty so she took her face for granted, but there was something wrong with it now. It was frightening. Her forehead. The dark blonde hair grew in a central point and on the sides the hair grew closely as if glued to the skin: a broad low forehead. And it was completely unlined. Nothing had happened to her forehead, nothing showed. It looked blind or worse: insane. As if it were detached from her, from life, existing alone untouched by all events, any feeling. She was wearing somebody else's forehead.

The ice had melted and there was no more in the thermos jug. She drank thirstily the last of the cold water. Food? When had she eaten? Dial 4 for room service. Ice water, iced tea, chicken sandwiches. No, the effort of speaking was too great. And she would have to find her dressing gown. Her body must be hidden from questions. Like curious sleeves, purple, yellow and green bruises from shoulders to elbows; like a splotchy belt, bruises across the pelvis and back; like torn dark stockings, the discolorations on her legs. Unimportant. She put on her nightgown and went to lie on the bed.

Two days now? Three? Some day she would leave this room. It didn't matter. Time was different again. Not what she had known for so long, a ceaseless chore to attend to every day. Not like the magical drifting time of those two weeks. Time had no shape at all and she was not responsible for it. It went on, it was no business of hers.

She could tell the hours by the light flowing through the balcony window, from the silver shades of early morning to the straight white glare of noon through a slowly cooling gold to the sudden sunset. Late afternoon now, still hot on the beach. The first day here she discovered a sunset rite. A flock of green birds, miniature parrots, green with red trimmings, flew together, disorderly and playful and loud. They were evidently coming home. Home was a tree taller than the hotel, rising above her room on the top floor, to the right of her balcony. The trunk and branches were yellow, the leaves like ferns. She asked the name of the tree from the young Englishman at the front desk, an assistant manager keeping his eye on things. Fever tree, he said. She thought the name was disagreeable for the home of the sunset parrots.

Craning over the balcony she had seen the afterglow of the sun, orange and pink and streaks of pale green. Not the actual sunset, out of sight behind the hotel in a distant part of Africa far from this marvelous coast where tourists like herself were safe and snug in a tourists' Africa. By day, according to the tide, the sea looked like a map, areas of green jade and aquamarine and sapphire, a jewel map. As the sun went down, the sea darkened to purple, then to pewter while the sky briefly glowed into deep blue, glass with light behind it. You had to be quick to grasp this moment before the white line of the reef vanished and it was soft black night, but shining and crowded with stars.

These wonders continued. She had only to walk a few steps from bed to balcony to see them again but they were meaningless to her now. She must lie here and get it straight. That was all she had to do.

Begin at the beginning. It was November but already the Christmas frenzy was in the air. The year had been endless yet suddenly Christmas came round again. All my life Christmas was us together on the farm at Derry Bridge, my parents and I, then Richard after we married, and finally our son, our own private world, a special time when we had nothing to do except be happy, loving each other. The last Christmas at Derry Bridge there was only Richard and me and it doesn't count, it wasn't Christmas, bleak days while Richard talked, droned on and on, and I listened or didn't bother to listen.

He said that he had always been in third place, coming after my parents, and then definitely in fourth place since I loved Andy more than anyone in the world. I had never thought of it like this, I thought one loved different people differently, but when he said that, I agreed he must be right because I had no love left in me, not for Richard or myself or anything. He had waited through the months of my depression and hoped I'd recover and adjust—his voice droning that odious word— but he felt he was living in a cemetery. I was tending graves, and he couldn't stand it. He loved his son with his whole heart, but one had to accept what couldn't be changed, and he was not ready to die at forty-five, he meant to go on, he had to, and how was he supposed to make a life with a woman who had turned into a ghost, or a sleepwalker, who wasn't really here. I didn't care, that was all I felt. I remember his voice álmost crying and almost shouting at me. Don't you think it's terrible to declare bankruptcy after eighteen years of marriage? No. The most terrible had happened, the death of an eight-year-old boy from leukaemia. What else was terrible after that?

I asked Richard to sell the farm as I would never come here again, and attend to all the other arrangements. Of course he should live, he is a successful lawyer absorbed in his work. I'll find something to do, I said, but all I want for now is to be left alone.

People say such crazy things, intended as comfort. You have the happy years to remember, they say. No one would urge a starving man to remember the fine big meals he'd had in the past. I don't understand what is expected of me. It's as if there was a fixed ration of grief and when you've used that up, you are obliged to be cheerful and act as if nothing had happened, life is back to normal again. If you grieve too much, they call in the doctors and there's the hospital, grief is a sickness, you must be cured. The funny part was all the anxious consoling words about our divorce. I was permitted an extra ration of grief when I felt nothing.

Like everyone else, Marian was distressed by the divorce. My college room-mate, always a kind bossy girl who knew exactly what to do next. She married a young English barrister about the same time I married Richard, and by now her husband is important in politics and Marian is gloriously active in London and Wiltshire being the perfect wife for a British MP. Last spring, Marian wrote that a change would do me good. Why not move to London for a while? Why not? Anyway my departure relieved poor Richard, who had a bad conscience for no reason. It's not his fault, nor even mine, if I'm queer and can't forget the face of my little boy, if I can't stop longing for my father and mother just because they're dead.

Marian took over my life, she's an organizer, a planner, she believes there's an answer to everything. She found a pleasant furnished flat and introduced me to her friends and to charity jobs, looking after lonely poor old women three afternoons a week and shoving a book trolley through hospital wards two afternoons a week. Marian thinks it noble of me to give up all my afternoons, not knowing that I'm a fraud, I have nothing to give.

Marian's answer to everything is to keep busy and no doubt she's right. If you're busy busy busy you haven't much room to think of the past and the future. My future is time, years of it, like this. I don't know any answers so I accepted Marian's: all you have to do is fill fourteen hours a day and never wonder why. When I felt sick of acting like a nice cheerful woman, I hid in my flat and doped myself on reading and the TV and nobody asked questions, I was left alone. I was getting on pretty well, I was managing, but I couldn't face Christmas.

It's just a day, it has to pass, the loudspeaker carols don't blare on forever, besides I must get used to living through Christmas. Instead I walked around London in the winter darkness thinking: there's no place to go. No one. Then I heard myself saying it out loud. A woman with an armload of parcels in Christmas wrappings stared at me. I began to run.

Soon it will be the blue hour that doesn't last an hour. Time to switch on the lamp by my bed. It would be stupid to lie in the dark trying to get it all straight. I woke last night in the dark, when the sleeping pills wore off, and was terrified, not knowing where I was or how or why. Absurd that even turning on the light, the smallest decision, requires will. Oh God why am I so thirsty? Tired. From what? Lying on a bed. I have no right to be tired.

The hotel called a doctor. I had a confused impression that my room was full of peering people, maids, waiters, the doctor, a woman who turned out to be the housekeeper. The doctor had cool hands and prodded me everywhere and took my head in his hands, twisting it. He kept asking, does this hurt? He studied my eyes with a pencil torch. He said a very serious shock, you're incredibly lucky not to, complete rest, aspirin, Valium and sleeping pills. I didn't feel dazed, only exhausted. I needed to ask him something. The people seemed to crowd and stare. I said I wanted to see him alone. He said 'What?' and leaned closer so I realized I was whispering. I didn't have any voice which was peculiar and silly, why should my voice fail? He waved the people out and I asked him what I had to know. He frowned, looking annoyed or puzzled, and said, 'Yes, of course.' As if it was an absurd question. After that, the housekeeper, Miss Grant, came in several times.

She is stocky with short stiff gray hair and tense eyes. She must be worried, harassed, so much to remember and supervise in this large hotel. The African waiters and maids are young, with laughing faces. Towels and ashtrays and wastebaskets can't be vital matters to them so

Miss Grant has to remember. She is very kind. 'Are you all right, dear? Is there anything you want?' She ordered food that I didn't want and cold drinks, fruit juices and iced tea and thermos ice jugs that I did. She opened the door with her key and let in the waiter, she told the maid to be quick and not make any noise to disturb me.

And was sorry for me, constantly sorry for me. 'You poor dear, so wretched for you on your holiday.' As soon as I understood that sympathy, I couldn't stand it. Aside from being wrong, I was afraid I might start feeling sorry for myself and then I'd hate myself and nothing would ever get straight in my mind. It would be wicked if I offended Miss Grant, though I put it as unnecessary to visit me any more since she has so much work and I am quite all right now, I'd ring for whatever I needed, but I really meant leave me alone, you're a danger to me. She couldn't have guessed that. No, she seemed relieved; of course she is overworked and I am another worrying responsibility. She said, 'Are you sure, dear?' I am trying to become sure, that is what I am doing.

Let's see. I can ring room service and wedge open the door with a book and cover myself with the sheet so I won't have to find my dressing gown or stand around while the waiter is here. Room service? How prompt they are. Right away, Madam. The book. All ready. I'll close my eyes and rest until the waiter arrives.

She slept instantly. All day, unaware, she slid into and out of these lapses of consciousness. She woke to see a tall young black waiter, tray in hand, by her bedside.

'You better, Memsaab?' A wide smile, uneasy.

'Yes thank you.'

But he couldn't figure out what to do with the tray. She couldn't figure out what to do with the tray. He stood there, holding it with one hand, looking at her flat on the bed while she looked at him. She thought: I don't know what to do. I'm going to cry because I don't know what to do. I can't tell him, I can't think. I'm going to cry over a tray, not knowing where to put it. I'm going to cry over a tray and I can't stop. He must go. Tell him to go. Tell him to stop standing there. Don't look at me. He must go. I can't help it, I can't stop, I can't.

The waiter turned and laid the tray on the long empty dressing table. He brought the square stool, padded in imitation white leather, to the bed. He deposited the tray on the stool and straightened up, beaming. A triumph of intelligence and competence. She was breathing with difficulty through a tight throat, against pressure in her chest.

'I come later, Memsaab?'

'No thank you. Tomorrow.'

Her voice was a whisper again. Draught from the open balcony slammed the door hard behind the waiter. She lay, unmoving, and got her breath back, refusing to think of that insane panic over a tray. Iced tea filled a parched hollow, even inside her head felt cooler. She munched small chicken sandwiches, determined to eat them all.

I was hungry. I have hardly eaten these days. I must eat regularly and tomorrow I'll get up and go on the beach. Lying here and not eating is ridiculous. My head is simply bruised and bruises take time to heal or evaporate or whatever bruises do. In a few days I'll be quite all right and then I'll leave. The fever tree assistant manager will fix everything. This is ridiculous, lying in bed, weak from hunger.

That's what I needed, just a little food. I'm much better, I'll finish now, I'll get it all clear. But what baffles me is the advertisements on the back page of *The Times*. Holiday in the Sunny Caribbean. A Villa on Glamorous Corfu. Ski in Andorra. Cruise to the Canary Islands. Cheap Flights to Johannesburg, Singapore, Hongkong. That page fascinated me from my very first day in London. Births and deaths on the left, then all the personal ads, people wanting to sell pianos or sending mysterious messages to each other, and even announcements about how much money the lately deceased had left behind and would their nearest kin apply to the Treasury. The right-hand columns are travel bargains.

I read that page every morning, it was like a very odd fascinating gossip column, reading about unknown people being born and dying, and places I'd never been or wanted to be. So why, one morning, did I get the idea of going on a trip alone, and staying in a hotel alone which I've never done, and on a continent I've never dreamed of seeing? What drove me to this lunatic scheme? I told myself that I was yearning for hot sun, I needed a change from the dismal wet gray London winter.

Agnes Markham asked me for Christmas dinner. The Denbeighs invited me to stay in Dorset. New friends, inherited from Marian. And of course Marian, looking worried, begged me to come down to Wiltshire. I am lucky to have kind friends. I know that, I'm always grateful, I don't earn the kindness by being clever or amusing or interesting. I'm an extra woman. At Christmas, family people are specially sorry for extra people. They think they can take you into their home and make you feel you belong in their family. They don't understand this is the most dreadful of all. They don't understand that you cannot bear it. I have learned how to be an extra woman if no one fusses, if I am left alone to manage the way I have learned. Perhaps other extra people are happy to be asked to join in someone else's Christmas.

And I am afraid of being a burden, of people saying to each other, 'Poor Diana, she's alone, we must do something about Diana.' On the worst days, I imagine voices talking about me with pity, and also boredom. A duty, a burden. I fear that. But even more I fear I will not always be able to behave properly. Cheerfully. It is essential to behave cheerfully.

I lied to everyone, saying more or less the same thing. 'How lovely, thank you so much, what fun it would be, but I'm meeting American chums in Switzerland, ski-ing for a few weeks.' Nobody could check on this harmless lie and nobody would. The English don't pry, that's one of their best points. Marian was delighted, I could see she felt I'd cheered up wonderfully if I was planning to go off on a ski party. I didn't want to speak of Africa, explanations, comments, excitement. Switzerland is usual but it would sound very eccentric to say I'd read an advertisement on the back page of *The Times* and was launching myself alone into the blue. I meant to sneak off quietly and come back quietly. No one knows where I am. I am lying on a bed in a luxury hotel by the Indian Ocean and I don't understand why.

But I do understand. Sun was an excuse. I was swamped in loneliness, drowning, it gets worse all the time, not better the way people tell you. I ran away as far as I could, running from everyone and everything that reminds me of Christmas when I had a child and a family. I knew it would be easier alone in a place so strange that I'd be a stranger to myself. Why do I have to go on acting like a normal woman? 'Adjusted' is the word. Why do I have to get up and wash and work at my time-filling jobs and shop for food and telephone about repairing the fridge or the TV and buy clothes and pay bills and chat with friends and smile and pretend to care when I don't care about anything on earth? Why can't I scream and scream and scream I hate it all, I don't want to be here, I want to die, *leave me alone*.

No. NO. Peering people. Doctors. The hospital. Be quiet. Be orderly. Calm. Now I have to start again, I've made it harder for myself. Marian will be astonished when I tell her how I planned my trip and kept it as a surprise for when I got back. The night flight was appalling, wedged between two men, cramped, I was so worn out that Nairobi was just blinding sun and the smell of the warm wind and a blank wait in the airport. Another plane, yellow empty land, blue gray hills, too tired to look, and the airport here, jungle trees, terribly hot, the hotel car, the hotel room and sleep.

Then it worked better than I'd dared imagine. I didn't mind being a lone woman, the hotel didn't make me nervous, I was invisible anyway.

I'm the invisible age, too old for flirtations around the pool, too young to be motherly, a nice old lady that people talk to. It was fine, wasn't it, and so clever to have thought of this, and so energetic to pull it off.

One morning I decided to make a short trip to see some birds I'd heard about and lunch at another smaller hotel. I felt the car plunging into the ditch, a split second, not enough time to think, and I was knocked unconscious. When I came to I was in the passenger seat covered with dust and dry grass. Facing back the way I'd come which was impossible but it seems the car turned over on its top and then rolled back on its wheels. Someone told the police and they told me. The windscreen didn't shatter. A freak accident. There are millions of road accidents every year all over the world. I never had an accident before but millions of people have an accident the first time. It was just another road accident. That's all it was. That's absolutely all it was and now I've got it straight and tomorrow I'll talk to the assistant manager about a plane to London.

The two African policemen wore gray uniform shirts and shorts and long black knee socks and black boots and they were very kind, driving me back in their Land Rover, and they saw my filthy dress, my hair half down, my general condition I suppose, and said very kindly, don't worry, everything's all right, you just relax. Everything's all right. I started to laugh, my face cracked across the middle, and they said now now there's nothing to cry about and I thought how weird that laughing looks like crying in Africa.

Stop, please stop, please, stop, *stop!* What? Am I talking out loud again? That sound, I can't bear it, that sound like a sick kitten mewing. No, no, it's not here, it's all right, there's only the sea. I fell asleep. I had a dream, very bad, but I don't remember it. I heard the sound in my sleep. So hot, stifling, what's the matter with the wind? My pillow's soaking and my nightgown. Fell asleep, forgot to turn on the light, stupid. Turn on the light; what time is it? Now my watch isn't working. Maybe it's midnight, that would be a piece of luck, the night half gone. If I'm always going to hear that sound in my sleep, I'll go mad. Be quiet. Listen to the sea.

Slap, thud, pause, slap, thud, pause. Small waves, the ocean held back by the reef. The long shallow beach, white sand churned into the small waves, but the water is transparent. You can see the bottom as you wade in, and warm as a bath until you swim far out and then it's cool and silky. I never saw or felt such water; bliss. There's no wind at all and the insects are quiet. Do they go to sleep at night? Is that possible?

They're always here, unseen, never still; I imagine hundreds of millions of them, making a high crackling buzzing whine all over Africa.

I could go out on the balcony, it would be cooler there. But the truth is the night sky frightens me, it's too big with more stars than anywhere else, enormous and far away and silent. I don't think people were meant to live on this huge empty land under this huge sky. I feel I'm lost, nowhere, nothing to hold to, the truth is it's terrifying to be alone beneath that enormous beautiful black sky.

What am I going to do, lie here bathed in sweat, and wait for morning? And count over the different pains in my body and have a nice slobbering cry because I hurt so much? I wish I were like Marian. She'd make a plan. She'd know what to do next.

'May I come in, Mrs Jamieson?'

This is the limit. Why can anyone get a key to open my door?

'Who is it?'

'Dr Burke. May I come in?'

The young doctor, with red hair and a dark beard, the one the hotel sent for. He ought to shave that beard; perhaps he wears it to look older.

'What time is it, Dr Burke?'

'Nearly seven. I thought I'd pop in on my way home to see how you're getting on. Miss Grant reported at noon that you were resting nicely. That's the best treatment. You had a mammoth shake-up yesterday.'

'*Yesterday?* How long have I been here?'

'In Kenya?'

'No, no, here, now, in bed.'

'Why, since yesterday afternoon.'

'I thought I'd been here for days, two or three days.'

'There's nothing like a big bang on the head to muddle one. How does your head feel?'

I'll tell you how it feels. Right now it feels as if steel clamps were fastened on my head above my ears, and a loop of steel joined them across the back of my skull, low down, and the clamps and the loop are being tightened and tightened until they'll squeeze my head so the top bursts open. This is brand new, I didn't know there was such a style of headache.

'Not too bad.'

'And the bruises?'

Any movement hurts. However I lie hurts. I feel as if I'd been beaten all over with a bicycle chain. That's how the bruises are. 'A bit stiff. What's happened to the wind?'

'It always drops at sunset and sunrise. Hadn't you noticed? This is the hottest time of year, the monsoon's changing. Shall I close the balcony door and turn on the air-conditioner?'

'Please, no.' I want to hear the sea, it keeps out that other sound. Now thermometer and pulse and the doctor look on his face, studying, puzzling, calculating. There's something I have to ask him, and I dread the words. He's got his pencil torch, to peer at my eyes.

'Dr Burke.' My voice has failed again, it comes out as a whisper. I seem to have no control over my voice. 'Can an unconscious body make a sound?'

'Yes, of course, Mrs Jamieson. You asked that yesterday.'

So it wasn't pain. Thank God it wasn't pain.

'I heard a sound after the accident. Like . . . like a whimper.'

He's watching, he knows that's a lie, but I can't say how it really was, I can't speak.

'Yes, I guessed something of the sort. Not a whimper. What you heard was the last automatic exhalation of air from the lungs.'

My eyes feel they're being burned. I try not to understand what he's said. Because then it's true, what I didn't know or didn't dare to know. Afterwards, sitting in the car in the ditch with the sun beating down, the road was empty. The little body on the road, nearer to the right than the middle, and the sun and that sound in the silence. I could not move and there was dust over my eyes, or in the air, I saw through a haze. Africans came from nowhere, from the empty land, and lined the road close to the child's body, but none stepped out on to the road. Women wailed, a wild up and down wailing that didn't break the silence. No one came near me. I was miles away, not there or anywhere. Nothing happened; nothing changed. I thought I would stay there always, alone with the little curled-up body.

The police spoke to me but I couldn't answer. I didn't watch what they were doing, I closed my eyes and saw the same thing: the empty road and the child and me, alone. The police helped me into their Land Rover; in back were children, I didn't see them but I knew there were children and on the floor something, a bundle. I didn't look or hear. Everything was very slow, under the sun, the light and heat of the sun were part of it and it would never end. I was in an office on a chair by a desk and a young black policeman was talking but I don't know what he said. He took my bag which he must have found in the car and copied things from my passport and driver's licence.

I was trying to explain to myself what happened but I couldn't because what happened was not believable. I don't know if I was talking to myself or out loud. The same words went on, over and over, in my mind. I was driving on the left the way you do in this country and a child ran out from the left from nowhere and I swerved as hard as I could to the right to get away from him and I heard a soft plop, like a cloth flapping against the car behind me, and I saw the ditch and then I saw nothing until.

The policeman took my arm to move me from the chair and led me to the Land Rover and helped me in and it was all very slow, with the sun beating down, but I didn't feel pain in my head or body and I didn't see anything except the empty road and the child and I didn't hear anything except that sound. But I must have known he was dead only I didn't ask and no one told me. Now I know he is dead, a beautiful little brown boy, not black, dark brown, six years old I think, naked to the waist, running like a deer, running faster than I could get away from him.

'But I didn't run over him. I know that. I swear I didn't run over him. How can he be dead?'

'Apparently he slammed head-on against the rear fender of your car. Broke his neck instantly. He can't have seen anything or known anything, otherwise he'd have stopped. You mustn't think of it, Mrs Jamieson. It wasn't in any way your fault.'

'If I'd pulled the wheel one second faster.'

'From what the police say, impossible in that distance. Mrs Jamieson, listen to me. You did all anyone could do and more than most would. It's a miracle your neck wasn't broken too.'

'I'm alive. And he's dead. A child.'

'You don't know this country, Mrs Jamieson, and I do. I was born here. Believe me, if the Africans out there thought it was your fault they'd have torn you apart before the police got to you, and disappeared back into the bush. And I might add the police wouldn't have been all that amiable.'

'He's dead.'

'And so are any number of children every day of the week on the roads here, and even in the towns. They rush out without looking and get killed. It's the parents' fault. They don't teach their children, they don't train them, they don't keep track of them. They're ignorant and irresponsible. They're entirely to blame for this sort of needless accident.'

'The mother? Blame the mother?'

'Yes indeed. No one else. It's her duty to explain to her children about traffic. Yours wasn't the first car ever to pass on that road. They've had years to learn and they don't bother. Children have no business playing alongside a highway. The mother is at fault. It happens all the time and still they don't look after their children properly.'

He's insane. I don't want him near me. *Blame the mother?* A woman from a poor mud village. What does he know about the mother? I know. I know she's looking at her child and saying *why*, screaming *why*, until there's nothing else in the world but that, why, *why* is my child dead? She'll hold his body in her arms and try to make it come back to life and then she'll start to die too, and she'll go on dying and she'll never remember when he was beautiful and ran like a deer, she'll only remember him as he looked dead. She'll remember that always, she'll have lost all the happiness of him because she can't forget the last, the worst.

'Mrs Jamieson, please stop crying. You must, really. You're tormenting yourself and making yourself ill. It isn't doing your head any good. You want to get well and go home, don't you? I'm giving you a stronger sedative for tonight and I want you to swallow these pills now. I'll be back in the morning.'

Leave me alone. Go away. Don't talk to me. How can you blame the mother, you're insane, you're inhuman, you don't understand anything. All right, I'll swallow the pills, I don't care what I do, only go away.

'Goodnight, Mrs Jamieson. Take these capsules later. You must get a good night's rest. You'll feel better in the morning. You're still badly shocked but I can assure you there's nothing wrong, no damage that won't heal naturally.'

No damage. Bruises and a headache. And knowing that if I'd been one second faster, the one second when I saw the child directly in front of me, the stunned one second when I shouted NO, the paralyzed one second of horror. Why couldn't I have died? Always someone else, but not me. Maybe wherever I go someone will die. Maybe I bring death.

'You've had a nice nap, dear?'

Everyone has a key. Anyone can come into my room. As long as I lie here I can't stop them. It's Miss Grant, I thought she understood I wanted to be left alone.

'Dr Burke told me you were hot and uncomfortable. Shall we freshen up a bit? Could you take a shower while I change your bed? Here, let me give you a hand.'

I feel dull and heavy. It's too much trouble to argue. She's treating me the way they do in hospital, as if you're frail and half-witted. Ah yes, the shower is nice, I'd like to stand here under the cool water until morning.

'I found a clean nightdress. Is that all right, dear? We'll have this one laundered and ready tomorrow. Now your bed's all fixed. There you are. Dr Burke says you don't like air-conditioning. Neither do I. The wind's coming up again, it'll soon be nice and cool.'

She is kind and it's much better like this, in dry smooth sheets. If I could read, time would pass quicker. This day has lasted several days already.

'May I sit down a minute, dear?'

'Yes of course, Miss Grant. Thank you for making my bed.'

She seems nervous, or is that the way she always is, the strain of her job?

'Mrs Jamieson, Dr Burke thinks it would be better if you went to Nairobi as soon as you feel able to move.'

'Nairobi? What for? I'll fly back to London.'

'Well, there may be a delay. And Dr Burke thinks Nairobi would be better, where your Embassy is, so they can look after you.'

'The Embassy? Why should the Embassy be expected to?'

'Oh, they will. We've spoken to the Duty Officer. He's very nice. He suggested it might be a good thing if some relative came out to keep you company. We could send a cable or telephone for you.'

What is she talking about? She doesn't make sense.

'Miss Grant, I'm filled with some dope Dr Burke gave me so my brain isn't working. I don't follow you. I'm a grown woman, I'll simply get on a plane and fly back to London. All this about Embassies and relatives is ridiculous.'

'You see the point is, dear, you can't right away. The police have your passport. Don't worry, no one's going to charge you with anything. But there are formalities, paperwork, and I'm afraid Africans are frightfully slow.'

The police?

'Really don't worry, Mrs Jamieson. The police spoke to Mr Hammond yesterday. He's our assistant manager. The manager, Mr Burckhardt from Switzerland, is in Nairobi for a meeting. The police explained to Mr Hammond what happened and they were very sympathetic about you. But Africans love paperwork and they're not much good at it. It's such an awful stupid story.'

'What is?'

'According to the police, the boy's sisters were in the ditch on the other side of the road.'

'There wasn't anyone anywhere. And I didn't see any ditches.'

'No, you wouldn't, they're so overgrown. Old drainage ditches. It looks as if the bush grows right up to the tarmac. But they're quite deep, well, you know that, you poor dear. Naturally you wouldn't see children down below the road level, hidden in that long grass. Anyway the two girls called to their brother to run across quick before the car came.'

'There weren't any other cars, ahead of me or behind.'

'I know, that's what makes it so stupid. The boy only had to wait a second and you'd have passed and the road was clear. But evidently he heard his sisters and just jumped up and ran without looking.'

I cannot endure it. I cannot. It's as if there was some crazy cruel plan, tied to one second in time, for no reason, for nothing. It could just as easily not have happened. But it did, that will never change. It did.

'Are you all right, Mrs Jamieson?'

'The sisters, where are they?'

'At home, I suppose. The police said they deserved a good beating. They were older, they didn't have to be so stupid.'

I hope they're not old enough to understand. I hope they can forget. Because if they were somewhere in the ditch, they'd have seen what I didn't, the instant when the boy and the car, and they'd have heard that sound. I don't know how long I was unconscious so I don't know how long that sound went on. I heard it twice. Or three times? I'll never be able to forget it. But no one was there, no one on the road. Then they were hiding. Afraid. Afraid of death that came when they were only playing.

'Mrs Jamieson, here, have a drink of water, please. I shouldn't have told you all this. You look terribly pale. My dear, it's been a dreadful shock for you but it's different for these people. They have so many children, one a year, they die as easily as they're born and the women just go on making more. They don't feel about life the way we do.'

They're trying to tell me a black woman doesn't love her children. A woman loves her child, I know, I'm the one who knows. Nobody understands anything except that black woman, that mother, and me. We're the only ones who know.

'If the police want to arrest me, I'll stay here.'

'Mrs Jamieson! Don't say such a thing! There's no question of arrest, merely delay. And you'd be much happier with someone to keep you company. Your husband perhaps?'

'I haven't got a husband.' She looks scandalized, poor plain Miss Grant, I want to laugh. I shouldn't laugh, there's nothing to laugh about but I can't help it. Now she looks frightened. Why? Does she think Richard's dead too and I'm laughing? Oh God what a mess, I'll have to explain, more talk, I'm too tired to talk.

'It's all right, Miss Grant, really, he's not dead. He's fine, really. He's married again to a much younger woman and she's pregnant so he'll have another son. People thought I was upset about the divorce but I wasn't. Honestly. There wasn't anything left to be married for.'

Why on earth is she patting my hand and saying, 'There, there.' I've got hiccups from laughing. Her face was so funny at first but it isn't now. I don't want to be a nuisance, she's an overworked middle-aged woman and it's night and she ought to be in her own room with her shoes off.

'Miss Grant, you've been working all day. You needn't stay here. You must be tired.'

'No dear, I'd rather stay with you a while. Could you eat something?'

'No thank you.'

'How about ice cream? And a pitcher of fruit juice? They make a very nice mixture of fresh pineapple and lime and a little mango.'

'That sounds lovely. And then you can go, I'll be all right.'

Dial 4 for room service. Miss Grant speaks Swahili and her voice is brisk and stern, talking to Africans.

'Now then, Mrs Jamieson, let's see who could come out and be with you. Perhaps your mother?'

'My mother is dead. Is your mother alive?'

'No.'

She doesn't know about being a mother, but she knows about being without a mother. It's natural, it's inevitable, parents die before their children, it happens to everyone. If something happens to everyone it's not special and you mustn't show what you feel because you embarrass others, you're a grown woman, not a defenceless child. Long ago, people wore mourning for a year. They were allowed a year at least. But we go faster, we have no time to mourn, mourning is shameful.

All your life there is someone to talk to and be heard. One person is never indifferent; one person is always there and looks at you as no one else ever can; you are not alone. Richard said we were unusually close, my mother and I, but, Diana, you knew it had to happen one day. Oh yes, I knew, it was the only thing I feared, I feared it from childhood. Knowing something will happen does not prepare you for how it is when it actually happens.

I understood I should not speak of this and besides the one person I could tell was her, and she was dead. The roof and the walls and the warmth inside are gone. It's up to you, there's no one between you and all the space, all the space of the world. A husband is a man of your own age, he has his own fears and needs and loneliness, and he can't hear everything, even when you don't speak. Richard disliked his mother and his father died when he was a boy. Richard tried not to be impatient with me but he wanted me to hurry and get used to the fact that I would never see her again. Not even in dreams. My dreams are filled with strangers.

But Andy was there, my son Andrew, six years old and discovering each day as if it were a new country. I knew that though I had lost my safety I must provide the same safety for him. That's the order of life, obviously. You don't tell a child that you are homesick and heartsick and weak, you tell a child comforting lies for both of you, and you try to become yourself the necessary roof and walls. I am glad my mother did not see Andy die.

'Did you love your mother, Miss Grant?'

'Yes.'

For a moment, we look at each other, not like a responsible housekeeper and a problem tourist, but like two extra women. Someone banged on the door.

Miss Grant says crossly, 'That idiot, Juma.' The moment is over. I want Miss Grant to go, I can't talk any longer. The same young waiter comes in but his face is different, not lit up by the wide grin that I remember, and he seems even more awkward with the tray. Miss Grant snaps at him in Swahili and he shuffles to the dressing table stool and brings it, with the tray, to my bed. Miss Grant must have put the used tray outside. More Swahili and he is gone, letting the door slam. Miss Grant makes a little annoyed click and shakes her head.

'Juma? Is that his name? He was here before. He seems very friendly and obliging.'

'He's not bright but he's a nice enough boy, though he was better when he began here, last year. Now he keeps bad company, one of the handymen, a coast Arab, a real trouble-maker, but the union loves trouble-makers so we daren't sack him. Oh well, anyway I'm pleased that Juma's been giving you decent service. They've sent three kinds of ice cream. I recommend the coffee, if you like that flavor.'

I mean to eat so she will be reassured and leave me. I pull myself up to a sitting position and let out a snivelly moan before I can stop it. Moving my head suddenly tightened that clamp arrangement.

Miss Grant cries, 'You're in pain. It's too miserable for you.'

And I say angrily, 'I am not. Nothing has happened to me. Can't you see? No bones broken, no vital organs crushed, nothing, nothing, nothing.'

In silence, but hurt, Miss Grant hands me a glass bowl of coffee ice cream. She only intends to be kind and has again thought of the helpful gesture. The ice cream is cold in my mouth, cold going down my throat, the coldness soothes my damned head. I am ashamed to feel pain, I have no right. I eat ice cream and try to think of a way to apologize to Miss Grant but I can't concentrate and find the words.

'All I ever wanted was what the African women have, a baby every year. That's all I ever really wanted.' I don't know whether I was thinking that or saying it out loud. Either Dr Burke's pills or the bang on my head are making me worse, more confused. I must have been thinking it because Miss Grant says nothing, though she observes me warily, but perhaps that is due to my rudeness. Rudeness is a great offence to the English, another point in their favor.

'This is delicious, Miss Grant. I'll finish it slowly and drink the fruit juice but please don't wait. You've done everything for me. I'm very grateful and you must go now, you need your rest too.'

'Are you sure, dear?'

'Quite sure.' Poor creature, what a burden I've been. Why did she come in the first place when I told her I was all right yesterday, no, today, but hours and hours and hours ago. She has left a glass filled with fruit juice and ice cubes so I won't have to lift the pitcher. Considerate Miss Grant. The stuff is too sweet, I'll suck the ice cubes and plod on with the ice cream and then I'll go to the bathroom and brush my teeth and swallow these new red and green capsules and get rid of this horrible day.

It's true about only always wanting what African women have, a baby each year. Through my whole childhood, I told myself a long continuous story about Diana and her six babies. I invented those six when I was practically a baby myself. An only child is supposed to crave brothers and sisters, but not me, I was perfectly happy having my parents to myself and my own six babies, three boys and three girls, roly-poly butter balls all the same age, dressed alike in bright coloured caps and mittens and zip-up woolly suits. I played with them, gave them baths, fed them and instructed them in good behavior. Since I didn't know how babies were made, there was no provision for a Daddy. Besides I had the best Daddy in the world already, he served for my babies too.

When I got the hang of things, my six babies changed into the most ordinary female dream. I would grow up and marry a gentle good man and have four children, one each year, and live happily ever after. My friends at school weren't interested in babies and in college everyone was thinking of some sort of career, thinking and worrying. I had no worries, I knew what I wanted and never doubted I would get it; I never really abandoned my childhood fantasy.

In due course, as expected, with no effort on my part, the gentle good man appeared and we fell in love and married. All I had to do was wait for the tumbling laughing babies. Instead of them, I had miscarriages. Three. They would have broken my heart except for my mother. I couldn't have survived without her. The great hope and then the failure and hope lost in a hospital bed, sick in my body and my mind, and all the doctors I consulted and the waiting to try again and fail again. She knew I had to have a child, she gave me courage, telling me it had been just as difficult for her, she promised I would succeed with patience. How I needed her and how I leaned on her. And on the loving steadiness of my father. He understood too. Poor Richard. But Richard had his work, he had a meaning for his life and for me there was only one.

With patience for seven years, and seven months in bed and a Caesarian, I got Andy. My first born and my last, the doctors said, and I didn't mind at all. Thirty-two isn't exactly a young mother but I felt something I'd never known in my life before. I think it was joy, I didn't know anyone could feel such rejoicing. From the moment I saw my son. He was beautiful and perfect, he was everything I wanted. I couldn't have loved another child as much, it was right to have only Andy. And I thought now it's come true at last and we'll live happily ever after.

Why not? Why shouldn't we? What did I know of unhappiness except for three miscarriages? I didn't spend all the time between those failures in abject gloom. In between times, Richard and I enjoyed ourselves like any lucky young married couple. Christmas and summer at Derry Bridge with my father and mother were always heaven. Why not expect to live happily ever after if you've been as happy as a cabbage all your life aside from three temporary setbacks? And I was happy when I had my son in a way I can no longer believe or remember. I've often wondered if I am being punished because I had too much, when life is so terrible for millions upon millions of people. But punished by whom? And is happiness a sin?

October is a beautiful month, the red and yellow leaves and the special clean blue of the sky, but it's sad too, the beautiful ending of the year. I've always wanted to hold the days back in October, make them stretch, before November and winter set in. November is an ugly month. Ugly, ugly, hated. On weekends that October, Andy and I used to play explorers in the woods at Derry Bridge, or on our bikes on the dirt back roads, meeting imaginary animals, climbing trees to spy out unknown territory, but Andy tired quickly which he'd never done. I worried and he loathed being worried over and anyway I had trained myself since his infancy not to be a smothering Mum. He'd become a great reader and I thought perhaps he was in one of the many mysterious phases of growing, and books seemed more manly than make-believe games with Mummy.

Then one morning in New York my little boy crept into my bed and said he felt sick, he had a sore throat, it hurt to swallow. I took his temperature, 103, and called the doctor in panic. The doctor came within an hour and didn't do much that I could see. He checked Andy's temperature, gently poked places below his waist, studied his skin and inside his mouth, and telephoned for an ambulance. They knew right away, though they made all the tests before they told me. My brain froze. I heard but could not believe or accept the words. Acute leukaemia on a fulminating course. Those words. From nowhere, from nothing, for no reason.

I had a bed in Andy's hospital room, I never left him, I sat beside him and watched while he shook with chills and poured sweat as the fever rose and dropped and always rose again. I could never take him in my arms, that was my torment. I felt him so alone, I wanted desperately to hold him so he would know I was close, but the pain in his bones had started and the slightest pressure on his chest and ribs caused him anguish. I could only hold his hand, kiss his hands, kiss his forehead lightly lightly, I felt everything in him was breaking. Needles in his arms, transfusions, antibiotics; he cried from all the different pains, he vomited and cried. He cried weakly, hopelessly. He couldn't understand what had happened to him, of course. He must have thought no one heard his weeping because no one came to save him.

Was consciousness worse than delirium? How can I know? Burning with fever, my little boy raved in fear about animals which he'd always loved. He had a mission in life already; when he grew up he planned to take the animals in Central Park Zoo back to their homes where they belonged so they could be free and happy among their relatives. Delirious from fever, he saw his friends, the animals, as monsters threatening him. It was too cruel that he should lose his friends.

When his temperature dropped and his mind cleared, he would beg me to make this agony stop. His voice always fainter, Mummy make it stop. And then he gave up, I had failed him. His eyes were dark and despairing; I had failed him. I wanted him to die, to escape the murderous fever and pain in his child's bones, I sat by him day and night, helpless, watching him die, in nineteen days, in November. His face wasn't his face, wasted, old and lonely. Because I couldn't make it stop, I couldn't take the pain for myself, he suffered alone. There was nothing left of Andy that was like him except his shaggy yellow hair. I held his little wrecked body in my arms and died too. I went away into the darkness where Andy had gone.

Why did they give me shock treatment and force me to come back where there was nothing to come back to except the memory of his face, his eyes, begging me? It is useless to weep though it goes on all the time, like internal bleeding; she'll learn that too, that other woman, that African mother. She'll hate me as I hate the disease that took Andy from me and she'll never know how gladly I'd have died instead.

The land was gray and flat and wide, nothing grew on the hard ash-colored ground. The road was a lighter gray, narrow, cutting straight through the vast distance of the land to the horizon. The sky was gray too, paler than the road. There was no movement anywhere, the air silent. Far away at first, then nearer, she saw gray figures on the road. She did not move, nor did they, yet they grew in size so that she recognized them. Her throat ached with the need to cry out, she felt the tears on her cheeks, but she could not speak or move.

Her mother was bending over a little curled-up body on the gray road. The body looked shapeless, a small bundle of gray rags. Her mother's face was gaunt, shrunken, not her face in life, her face in death. Her eyes, which had been a shining cornflower blue, were black and dull. She did not touch the child's body. She was dressed in rags with her arms showing stick-thin through the dirty gray cloth. She was on her knees, staring dry-eyed at the bundle on the road.

The child's face was hidden, the only color in the grayness of the world was his shaggy yellow hair. Softly, from somewhere inside the little hump of rags, a sound came out, a single mewing sound like a sick kitten, a hurt kitten. It came again louder. Her mother did not touch the child, or hear, her mother's face was unchanged, fixed in exhaustion and defeat. The sound came again and now louder and louder, a cry of fatal pain, an agonized cry for help.

She struggled to move, she had to run to them, she wrenched and tore against some unseen force that held her, she tried to scream to stop the sound, to scream for them to wait, stop, wait, *Mother help him*, I am coming, I am coming to you, only wait! Shouting, sobbing, but could not move. . . .

'Wake, Memsaab! You wake! No sleep!' A hot damp hand pushed her shoulder. She looked up, through half closed eyes, stunned by the dream and barbiturates, dazzled by the lamplight, to see the face of the young waiter close to her. She smelled him, a foul heavy odor of sweat. She saw the road and her mother and the child, helpless, and understood the waiter was holding her so she could not run to them. She shrank away from him, from his red-veined eyes, and his black sweating face, she had to get away from him and run.

Ali thought of this. Ali was born in Mombasa, a sharp city boy, not an ignorant bush fellow. Ali made him say it four times so he would remember. Get the key from the night houseboy on the floor below. Tell him you have to pick up a tray. Not *her* tray, *a tray*. Tell the woman you are the cousin of the boy's father. She killed the boy. She must give you one thousand shillings for the father. She is rich. But Ali did not say the woman would be twisting like a snake on her bed and crying strange words and that her eyes would look as if she was crazy from *bhang*.

'I am cousin of father of that boy. You kill that boy. You give one thousand shillings for father.' He was whispering but the whisper shocked him, it was as loud as the steam whistle at the cement factory. He stank of fear, he couldn't remember whether Ali said one thousand or ten thousand. It was not easy, as Ali said. It was bad. She would call him a liar and Memsaab Grant would come and know he was lying. The police. He wanted to run from this room but was too full of fear. And the woman watched him with those crazy eyes, she wouldn't let him go, she was watching him.

'You give me money. Ten thousand shillings. You kill that boy.'

'No!' She slipped her shoulder free of his hand and rolled off the bed, crouching on the other side by the open balcony door.

He could not remember how to say the words Ali told him, father, cousin, shillings, only 'You kill that boy.'

She was crying the strange words of her sleep. 'No, I didn't! Mother knows, she knows, *don't run wait Andy!* I didn't, I didn't!'

They would hear her, they would all come, and the police would beat him until he was covered with blood. He had to stop her, sweat poured from his face, from his armpits, his clothes were wet and cold, he was wild with fear. He had forgotten all the other words, he moved around the bed, to reach her, to stop her making that bad bad noise, whispering insanely, 'You kill that boy, you kill that boy.'

The woman screamed 'NO!', and ran so fast he barely saw her in the dim light, ran out to the balcony, ran. Far below, in that same instant he heard something, nothing, not as much as the sound of the waves. He stood, shaking, his hands over his mouth to shut in the terror. Shaking, he backed slowly to the door. The door, the door. With one hand still holding the terror inside, he opened the door and began to run. He threw the key away on the stairs and ran down five flights to the big empty dark dining room.

Less than an hour after sunrise, Miss Grant and Dr Burke stood on the path along the north side of the hotel. The air was sweet with the scent of frangipani and jasmine and mimosa, birds sang, the morning breeze ruffled the leaves of the fever tree. Dr Burke had signed the form; while the balance of her mind was disturbed. The police had come and gone. Nothing marked the place except a mashed oleander bush and some stains on the coral rock bordering the path. Miss Grant looked as old as she was, without make-up in an orange kimono. Dr Burke had grabbed the nearest clothing, bathing trunks, beach sandals, a T-shirt. He felt hollow, sick from discouragement. He tilted his head to study the balconies above him. All the wide glass panels were closed, the curtains drawn.

'Lucky they like air-conditioning,' he said.

'Most of them would have been on the terrace on the other side. There was a dance last night.'

'Lucky none of them are early risers.'

Miss Grant could not take her eyes from the oleander bush and the coral rocks.

'Bad for tourism,' Dr Burke said bitterly. 'Mustn't upset the tourists. Our great national industry.'

'To think I was the last person to see her,' Miss Grant said. 'I could so easily have stayed. I'll never forgive myself.'

'You? I could just as easily have sent a night nurse and a day nurse or put her in the hospital whether she liked it or not. I knew she was over-emotional about that damned stupid accident but she wasn't concussed, she wasn't off her head. In God's name, how could anyone guess? Oh, Mary, it's so *useless*. Why can't these bloody morons keep their kids off the roads!'

'I'd better get dressed before they start coming down for breakfast.' She couldn't afford to let go, the working day began at seven thirty when the dining room opened. Not now, later. And how would she handle the memory of the path and the broken body? Miss Grant took Dr Burke's arm for company, for comfort; she was shivering.

'Poor woman,' Miss Grant said. 'Poor woman. She should never have come to Africa.'

In the Highlands

When Luke Hardy took to the bottle, everyone understood.

His wife, Sue, the very picture of health, had keeled over dead while cutting roses in her garden. People heard it was a clot, something like that, one of those things. Luke and Sue were childless; for twenty-six years they lived on Fairview Farm in perfect love. Discussing this sad and sudden death at the Karula Sports Club, a woman said nobody would think to look at them that Luke and Sue were in fact Tristan and Yseult. Not to look at: both short, gray-haired, sun-wrinkled, in their fifties, one lean, one plump. The neighbors, English farmers and their wives from thirty miles around Karula, drove to Fairview to pay condolence visits. They were greeted at the door by Luke's head houseboy who thanked them politely and made excuses for the Bwana. Luke Hardy could not disguise his pain and knew how embarrassing grief is to others.

Luke buried his wife, without benefit of clergy, on a high ridge at the southern perimeter of his farm. They had agreed that the view here was their favorite though it was hard to choose one beauty from so much beauty. After that Luke sat on his verandah, with another spectacular view before him, and started to drink. Fairview Farm went slowly down the drain.

Luke thought a man could drink himself to death at speed but the process proved remarkably long-drawn-out. He applied himself to the task for one year and two months. The head man and the cook stopped coming to the verandah for instructions since the Bwana received them with glassy indifference. Between them they ran the farm and the house to the extent that anything ran. When sober enough, Luke filled time by picking through his collection of books bought at sales after other funerals or when people moved away from the Highlands. The complete works of Robert Louis Stevenson, the complete works of Thomas Carlyle, H. G. Wells' *Outline of History*, Zane Grey, the collected poetry of

Robert Browning, Conan Doyle, Agatha Christie, the Koran, Baroness d'Orczy, Jane Austen, on and on, all without interest.

One morning in January, shortly after dawn, Luke was drinking tea laced with whisky while reading Roget's *Thesaurus* when disgust overcame him. He had been insulting Sue. Together they carved Fairview from the bush, with no money behind them. Together they made it a happy prosperous farm, never rich but comfortable for them and their *watu*. He didn't have it in him to carry on the work alone but that was no reason to destroy it. Sue would never have thrown away the effort of his lifetime.

Luke got up and shouted for Kimoi, the head houseboy, a man almost as old as he. He wanted a fire built in the boiler outside the bathroom, he was going to wash and shave and eat breakfast and drink much coffee and write a letter which the driver should take to Karula immediately. Kimoi laughed like a lunatic, stoking the boiler. The Bwana had decided not to die. Actually the Bwana had decided to postpone dying; there was business to settle first.

Fortified by coffee, Luke printed the advertisement since his handwriting was none too steady.

BEAUTIFUL FARM FOR SALE. ROTTEN CONDITION DUE TO NEGLECT. FIFTEEN THOUSAND ACRES. UNLIMITED WATER FROM BEST SPRING IN THE HIGHLANDS. TWO THOUSAND HEAD NOTHING SPECIAL CATTLE. DAIRY RANCHING. USED TO AVERAGE FIFTEEN GALLONS CREAM DAILY BUT LESS NOW. ROOF LEAKS OTHERWISE HOUSE SOLID. WILL SELL REASONABLE PRICE TO BUYER I LIKE. DONT WRITE INSPECT IN PERSON. ASK DIRECTIONS KARULA GENERAL STORE LUKE HARDY. FAIRVIEW FARM KARULA.

He read this over and thought it an exact statement of the facts. He addressed an envelope to the *Kenya Weekly News*, a periodical subscribed to by all serious cow men.

The neighbors saw the advertisement and wondered to each other how drunk Luke had been when he dreamed it up. It was a real come-on, it made your mouth water; rotten condition, nothing special cows, leaking roof: you could scarcely wait to snap up such a bargain. But anyway, if Luke was making jokes in the *Kenya Weekly News*, he must feel better and would reappear in Karula and start living a normal life.

Luke suffered for a week, watered his whisky, sipped all day instead of swigging, and bellowed orders. The work section of the farm was hopeless but he could spruce up his house and garden for the stream of prospective buyers. The four indoor servants swept, scrubbed, polished, aired everything in sight. Not bad, Luke thought, seeing for the first time in over a year the familiar furnishings. Big red cedar chairs and sofas, with wide arms for drinks and books, and lumpy cretonne cushions; big square tables and straight chairs to match; worn impala and zebra skins on the plank floors; faded brown rep curtains; pressure lamps; book cases; stone fireplace with the obligatory trumpeting elephant in oils above. The two bedrooms were as plain and satisfying. A local carpenter had made it all for the young Hardys, and made it to last.

The garden shamed Luke. How could he have forsaken what Sue slaved over and cherished? The magnolias were dead and the roses and all the soft pretty flowers in the borders around the house. Oleanders and hibiscus survived, as did the podo and pepper trees, the jacaranda and wild fig which framed the view. Luckily golden shower and bougainvillaea and jasmine still bloomed on the rough stone walls of the house. The lawn looked like a hayfield; Sue would have hated that. Luke told the *watu* to slash the grass; useless to pretend he hadn't let his place fall into ruin.

Every day Luke was shaved, clean, as near sober as possible and waiting. No cars bumped the twenty-three miles over ruts and potholes from Karula to Fairview. Luke couldn't believe it; his feelings were hurt. He was more than half drunk and entirely hostile when a Dodge pick-up turned from the public road into the long driveway. Luke heard the car but did not move. He meant to tell the bastard that Fairview was no longer for sale. In the usual Kenya farm style, the driveway ended at the kitchen door. Kimoi led the visitor around the house to the verandah. Luke had not expected to see a boy; this one wouldn't be a buyer, probably the young dolt ran out of petrol.

'Mr Hardy?'

'Yes.'

'My name's Ian Paynter. I saw your advertisement in the *Kenya Weekly News.*'

'Took your time, didn't you?'

'I'm sorry, sir. I only saw it this morning.'

Luke unbent. 'Sit down. Come to look it over for your father?'

'No, sir.' Luke couldn't understand the expression on the boy's face.

'You're getting married?' After all he bought this land when he was a boy, with Sue.

'No, sir.' My God, Luke thought, what have we here? The chap certainly wasn't making conversation easy. Well then, let's not talk. Silence did not appear to worry the Paynter fella. The Paynter fella sat upright and tense on one of the old verandah chairs which were not built for that position and stared at the view. He must be six feet two and weighed nothing at all. This wasn't the slenderness of youth, this was more like emaciation. Sick for a long time, TB maybe. He had the sort of face young Englishmen have, public school voice, perfectly ordinary young chap, except he didn't seem capable of speech.

Out of this puzzling silence, Ian Paynter said, 'If your farm isn't already sold, sir, I'd like to buy it.'

'You haven't seen it, man, what are you talking about?'

'I've seen this.' Ian Paynter made a small gesture towards the view.

'How old are you?'

'Twenty-five.'

'You're too young to live here alone. The nearest neighbors are five miles away, people called Gale, and I don't much care for them. The ones I like most, the Gordons, live 15 miles the other side of Karula. It's lonely. You'd go crackers. Besides the farm is a mess. You'd have to work your balls off. What do you know about farming anyway? How long have you been out here?'

'A year. I was second assistant to the dairy manager at Ol Ilyopita.'

'George Lavering's place. That's a Rolls Royce compared to here.'

'Mr Hardy,' the boy turned to him and smiled for the first time. The smile came as a shock, revealing a complete set of outsize lustrous false teeth. 'I hope you will sell me your farm. It's exactly what I want.'

Luke Hardy told himself he was a stupid old sot and deserved a kick up the ass. 'How long have you been out here?' What sort of question was that? The boy had been in the war, of course; just demobbed before arriving last January. More likely he'd just got out of hospital, ghastly gut wound judging by his skin and bone looks, no doubt infection, poisoned blood, something did in his teeth too. And the nervy way he held himself and the trouble he had to force out a few words at a time, probably recovering from shell shock, plenty of chaps were shaky afterwards, Luke thought, confusing his distant war with the war he had missed, that ended a year and a half ago.

'I'm going to bed,' Luke announced. It was four o'clock on a glittering afternoon. 'Kimoi will look after you. Stay the night. See you in the morning. Talk then.'

Ian Paynter sat alone on the verandah, first refusing Kimoi's offer of tea, then the offer of drink as sunset colors streaked the sky. He was thinking of Fairview and its sozzled owner, Mr Luke Hardy. How can I make him sell it? I must have it, it's the only thing I want. But I can't go through all the talk, I can't explain. Why in God's name do people ask questions?

No, I'm not looking at your farm for my father; my father is dead, so is my mother, so is my sister Lucy; everyone's dead except me. It was the war, you see, Mr Hardy. My sister Lucy was seventeen and riding in a lorry with a lot of other girls to a dance at some American airforce base near Aylesbury where we lived. The lorry skidded in the black-out and overturned and Lucy and one other girl were killed. My mother went to London for the day to shop or maybe have some fun, a matinée with friends and tea at Claridge's, and a buzzbomb hit a building and a piece of masonry smashed her skull. My father had a heart attack when he heard, quite natural after two such accidents wouldn't you think, and that weakened him so he died of pneumonia. All this happened in England while I was in Oflag XV B outside Hannover.

No, I'm not getting married, Mr Hardy. I went straight from Marlborough into the Army and straight from the Army into Oflag XV B, Dunkirk till the end, five years. Not much chance to meet girls. I'm not interested, I never got the hang of them and it's too late now. I loved three people and they're dead and that's the end of it. No, Mr Hardy, I won't be lonely. If you'd spent five years in a room with nine other men, and shared one and a quarter acres inside barbed wire with three hundred men, you'd see that being alone in a lot of space is my idea of heaven. I don't want people. I don't know how to talk to them any more, I kind of gave it up in those five years. I found the best way to keep from going round the bend was not to listen or talk or think or feel, you might say I went to sleep for the duration.

Perhaps I'll get over it in time, I mean be able to natter about nothing like other people, but I can't cope now. I learned that in Aylesbury when I was sent home after we were liberated. Not to our house, I couldn't look at it, I stayed with the Mayfields, Paynter and Mayfield, solicitors, third generation of both families. God how everyone talked, day and night, squawking like parrots, I didn't understand any of it. Civilian life in the war. I didn't understand the soldiers either, when Tom and Larry Mayfield got demobbed and came back. They used to be my best friends. Larry was a gunner, Tom was in the tanks. They talked and laughed until I thought the windows would break. Their war sounded like one glorious leave in Naples and Rome and Brussels and Paris, getting drunk and jokes and girls.

I suppose I wouldn't be here if I hadn't overheard Larry talking to his mother. He said he and Tom were going to visit pals from their outfits because the house was too gloomy with old Ian creeping around like a ghost. I didn't mind leaving, I was glad to, I hated it in Aylesbury where I'd always been happy, people being sorry for me and nagging about my teeth until finally I got these awful choppers which are worse. I remembered some men in the Oflag talking about Kenya, starting a new life there after the war. They said it was big and empty. So I told Mr Mayfield I wanted to go to Kenya and he wangled a job with Sir George Lavering through the old boy network. I didn't imagine I'd like farming but I had to do something and live somewhere. The point is, Mr Hardy, what I've been getting at, is that I like farming better than anything I've ever done, it's wonderful for me, I couldn't begin to tell you how wonderful because now I've got an interest in life, I've got something to think about.

You needn't worry that I won't have enough money to pay for Fairview. I have plenty, being the sole inheritor and our house was pretty valuable and had some good things in it and that's all sold too. I can give you a cheque in the morning, only for God's sake don't ask questions, just leave me alone and sell me the place. I know it's right for me, I know it, and I don't care what shape your farm is in, I haven't anything else to do with my life except work.

Kimoi called him for dinner. The cook had said he wasn't going to wait all night until the strange Bwana tired of sitting on the verandah in the dark. Ian came blinking into the big room, dazzled by the pressure lamp over the dining table. The fire was lit, the table set with sticks of celery and raw carrot in a glass jug, a lump of home-made butter, a home-made loaf on a board, a soup tureen, and a quart bottle of cold beer. Roast beef and roast potatoes, cauliflower, peas and baked apples with thick cream followed. Ian ate like a man starved. He thought this the finest room and the finest food in Kenya. It was extraordinary how contented he felt here in the easy quiet.

At Ol Ilyopita, there were too many people, the European staff, all public school to suit Lady Lavering, all friends, all given to evening drinks and dining in each other's houses. They were jubilant because the war was over, they were alive and where they wanted to be, on the biggest grandest farm in Kenya with agreeable jobs and super perks including polo ponies, two tennis courts, a swimming pool and Lady L's sumptuous parties. They enjoyed themselves at the top of their lungs. Ian was painfully conscious of being a transplanted ghost. They knew Ian had had a beastly war, the worst, and no wonder the poor chap was a bit touched in the head. They treated him with tact like a cripple. Ian saw the reasonableness of their attitude but he hated it. He was not a cripple to himself. He didn't dislike them, he didn't dislike anyone; he simply could not fit in.

His immediate boss, Johnny Leitch, thought well of Ian, who worked hard and was eager to learn but also clearly odd man out in the general chumminess. When Ian thanked him for his teaching and gave notice, saying he meant to buy a small farm, Johnny Leitch said, 'There's no better way to learn than trying it on your own. You can use your digs here as a base if you want, while you're looking around.' The trouble was that Ian had no idea how to look round and was too proud to admit himself helpless from the start. Johnny Leitch showed him the advertisement in the *Kenya Weekly News*, roaring with laughter.

'Luke Hardy's a card, a real old settler. He must have been pissed to the eyes when he sent that in. It's pretty country near Karula. Well, there's your farm, Ian. Whatever you do you couldn't make it worse.'

Ian asked for leave to visit Fairview Farm at once.

Lying in Luke Hardy's guest room bed, Ian thought about accidents. From what little he knew of life, he had decided the whole thing was purely accidental. God was not up there with his eye on the sparrow, busily planning for one and all. There was no plan. People believed they could direct their lives but in fact they were tossed around by accidents. Accidents wiped out his private world and his future, fourth generation in his father's firm and in his father's house. He had not considered that there might also be good accidents, but there were. The first was coming to Africa, the second was coming to Fairview Farm. He began to allow himself hope.

By habit, Ian was up and dressed with the sun. So was Luke Hardy, apparently sober though with slitted eyes and a hoarse voice.

'Show you the early milking,' Luke said. 'Take your car if that's all right, mine's at the workshop.' Where, he did not add, it had been as long as he could remember, perishing of old age and disuse.

In the cool first light, the scene looked so crazy that Ian had to swallow back laughter. Inside a rough circle, fenced with whistling thorn, half naked barefoot Africans sat on stools, sunk in cow dung, and milked the herd while shouting conversation and laughing their heads off. An ox cart dragged milk cans to a dilapidated shed where other talkative Africans worked hand separators. Ian wondered if you could get fatal diseases from germ-laden cream. The *watu* were plainly astonished to see Luke and greeted him with beaming smiles.

'Haven't been down here much lately,' Luke muttered. 'Might as well stop in at the office.'

Farther along the track, the office occupied one small section of a modest building, cracked cement walls, broken window panes, corroded tin roof. A big African stood in the office door trying to make himself heard above the uproar of a milling jolly mob.

'Simuni,' Luke said. 'Head man. Assigns jobs.'

Here, Luke received an ovation. The mob swirled around him, grinning and shouting *Jambo, Bwana, habari*. Luke looked embarrassed.

He told Simuni to move them off, he wanted to show this Bwana the farm map. Inside the office was a chaos of cobwebs, cigarette butts in dirty tins, loose papers, papers stuck on spikes, ledgers jumbled on shelves and spilled on the floor. The farm map, tacked to the wall, was yellow and fly-speckled. Luke began to explain it and gave up; the map was long out of date.

'Africans aren't much good at paperwork,' he said, defensively. 'But Simuni is a good man, trustworthy, doesn't drink.'

He indicated the open door to the next room; Ian glanced in. This was the farm storeroom. Ian could not imagine how the *watu* ever found anything from salt sacks to nails in such total disorder. Luke was sitting in the Dodge with the scowl of a man ready to pick a fight. He couldn't pick a fight with Paynter who gave him no excuse, no hint of criticism.

'Don't bother to stop,' Luke said as they passed the workshop, which appeared to be a scrap iron dump where three merry Africans prodded in the motor of an antique Bedford lorry.

Luke perked up at the spring. Thick trees, tangled with wild flowering vines, surrounded a large deep transparent pool. The bottom was flat gray pebbles and white sand. The water moved slightly in the current from an unseen source. Ian didn't know what he had expected to see but nothing as lovely as this. A rusty intake pipe and a collapsing pump shed failed to spoil the magic of the place.

'It's really a small version of that spring they've got at Tsavo, Mzima, you know?' Luke said. 'And that supplies all of Mombasa. You can do anything if you've got enough water, water is the most important thing you can have.' Luke seemed to be encouraging himself rather than Ian.

Ian said, 'Yes,' and stood entranced.

Luke sighed. 'Better finish it, take you to the African lines.'

Ian had thought everything a marvelous joke except the spring which was simply marvelous. How or why this farm worked was a mystery, but it did work; the proof being that it fed Luke and his *watu*. But the African lines were not funny. Rondavels with flaking walls and soggy ruined thatch dotted a large dust patch that stank of garbage and human excrement. Naked black children swarmed around like benign bees, pushing each other to reach Luke. *Bwana, Bwana*, they shrieked, beside themselves with pleasure. Ian noted their protuberant bellies, their filth, flies nestled in the corners of eyes, noses running yellow slime, scabs and sores. Women, with colorless lengths of cloth wrapped above their breasts, scratched at maize plants, hung rags of clothing to dry on bushes, squatted by blackened cook pots. They too laughed and yelled fond greetings. Mr Hardy had no right to the *watu*'s affection when he let them live like animals.

Driving back to the house, Luke said angrily, 'It wasn't always like this. I wrote in the paper the place was in rotten condition. I told you it was a mess.'

Ian said, 'I don't mind working my balls off.'

Luke did not speak at breakfast and pushed food away while Ian consumed papaw, fried ham and eggs, toast, lime marmalade and coffee with the thick cream that was Luke's livelihood. Luke left him at the table and took a weak whisky and water to the verandah. Ian was not sure whether he should follow; he knew that the morning tour had upset Luke. He could not know that Luke was communing with Sue, blaming himself bitterly.

'I don't see where you put it,' Luke called from the verandah. 'Eating like that and looking like a beanpole. Come on out if you're finished.'

Ian was chary of smiles, not wanting to expose those tombstone choppers. But in this fresh clear light, the view was so heart-lifting that he smiled all over his face. Africa lay before him and not a human habitation in sight. The land was lion color shading off to blue green in the distance. It surged upward to trees on the high range in the south, descended in plateaux below him to rise slowly again to a far mountain rim, dropped sharply to a screen of woods on the north.

Moved to speech for once, Ian said, 'I think this must be the most beautiful place in the world.'

Luke grunted. 'Want to see more or have you had enough?'

'I'd like to see everything.'

The farm roads were rivers of dust, a foot deep, more than a foot. The Dodge churned up blinding clouds of it. Hidden beneath the dust, rocks jarred the axles violently. More fences lay draggled on the ground than stood firm on their posts. Unless the dust blew back and obscured the view, everywhere Ian looked was wonder and delight.

Luke had said the bulls were pastured in the southern section. They passed a Masai herder in a squashed felt hat and ancient army overcoat. Luke told Ian to stop. The Masai wore his huge pierced earlobes neatly draped over the tops of his ears, and delicate bead bracelets on his delicate wrists. Luke asked about the bulls; the Masai, pleased to see Luke like all the other farm people, said he knew where the heifers were.

'Go on, we'll find them,' Luke said. 'The herders are Masai. They live in their dung huts off there, south east. Give them some blankets and an old army overcoat from time to time, sack a man if he loses cattle, otherwise leave them alone, that's my system. They've got their own ways.'

'The others?' Ian asked. If you talked you got a mouthful of dust.

'Kipsigis. Good chaps. The house servants are Luos. There's not a single bloody-minded bastard on my farm,' Luke said, again defensive.

On a hill where Luke got out to scan his property for the invisible bulls, Ian inspected a round brick reservoir. The trough that circled it was filled with sludgy water, as much muck as water. He climbed on the trough to peer over the top. The water smelled like a sewer; he thought it might be a graveyard for vultures, bats, snakes if they could make the trip. Obviously no one had emptied and cleaned the tank in living memory.

Luke watched Ian's face for a sign of contempt but there was none. 'I have four of those on the farm,' Luke said. 'They need whitewash with a lot of lime and copper sulphate.'

Ian nodded.

'I can't locate the bulls but there's a nice view at the south if you want to see it.'

After a particularly rough jolt on a buried rock, Luke said, 'Had a bad war, did you?'

Ian was driving slowly, now, with concern for his car, the best he could get, second-hand, 28,000 miles on the meter; had to wait your turn for new vehicles. 'I only had a few days of war, after that I was a POW in Germany.'

'The whole time?'

'Yes'

He steeled himself for more questions and for sympathy and blessed Luke for shutting up. The track corkscrewed towards the tree line. The pick-up was about ready to boil.

'Do your parents approve this scheme?' Luke said. 'You buying a farm out here on your own?'

Ian gritted his porcelain teeth; Luke saw the tight muscles in his cheek.

'My parents are dead.' God damn it to hell, why does he ask questions? What business is it of his? Say you'll sell me the farm or say you won't. I'm not here to tell you my life story, I'm here to buy or get out.

'Stop,' Luke said, unnecessarily as the track ended at the trees.

Luke led him to the edge of the ridge.

'It's a pretty good view in my opinion,' Luke said.

Eagles must see the earth like this. Africa went on for ever, in waves of mountains. Ian felt the sky as a presence, alive like the land, another continent spread over them in endless layers of shining blue. He had no words for any of the beauty of this farm, least of all for this.

'Yes, it is,' Ian said.

Luke walked a few yards into the lion grass, where he bent to wrench out handfuls of the tough golden stalks. He beckoned to Ian. At his side, Ian read the headstone, unevenly carved by someone who was not a stonecutter. Susan Elizabeth Grant Hardy, beloved wife of . . .

'I'm not asking you to do anything about it,' Luke said. 'Not keep the bush cut back or anything. I'm just asking you to see it's never disturbed.'

Ian realized that Mr Hardy had finally made up his mind to sell him Fairview.

At lunch, Ian said, 'I'll collect my kit at Ol Ilyopita and be here late tomorrow morning, if that's all right.'

'You haven't asked the price, son. You'll lose your shirt if this is the way you do business.'

Ian permitted himself a guarded smile so as not to flash the full repellent display at Luke.

'How do you know I won't want a hundred thousand pounds?'

Ian let his smile rip; to hell with the teeth.

'I know,' he said.

Luke was on the verandah, with a noticeably darker glass in hand. After seeing the headstone on the mountain, Ian understood why Luke drank and why he abandoned his farm. No drink was available in Oflag XV B but he had wished to die when he lost his family, and he had abandoned his own home without once visiting it again; the emptiness was unbearable. If he were as old as Luke, he wouldn't trouble to live either.

'You must have nipped right along,' Luke said. 'How's your Swahili? Want a noggin before lunch?'

'Beer, please. I think I can make out.' In his spare time, when the other young gentlemen employees at Ol Ilyopita were whooping it up, he memorized word lists, wrote out exercises, and when alone with Africans he practised. Upcountry Swahili was a patois that even a language dummy like him could learn.

'Good. Seems better to me if you potter around on your own. I've told Simuni you're the new Bwana. Get the feel of it, talk to the *watu*. I'll be leaving in a week.'

Ian felt a flutter of panic. 'A week, sir?'

'No sense hanging about. We'll have to go to Karula, tomorrow or the day after. Show you the ropes, introduce you around. The station where you'll ship your cream. The post office, you can take over my box. The general store, I've got to pay my bill, you open an account. The bank, we have a little business at the bank, don't we? Sign a deed, get a big fat cheque from you. And the Sports Club. Means two tennis courts.'

'I don't play tennis,' Ian lied. Oh no, people, natter and merriment, all the dumb misery of it.

'Nobody does except the kids when they come back on holiday. The courts look like the craters of the moon. People stop in for a drink after they've finished their errands; gives them energy to drive home for lunch. Meet the neighbors.'

'I'd rather not, sir.'

'What do you mean? Of course you have to meet the neighbors, not all of them, just whoever is in town. You can't skulk into Fairview like a criminal. People would think there's something wrong with you. It's getting much too civilized here but even so neighbors depend on each other in a pinch. And you'll need advice, Paynter. They're experienced farmers.'

Ian decided not to think about it, and was glad to have a free run of the farm. He couldn't very well pry and probe, with Luke distressed beside him.

'Is it all right if I start after lunch, sir?'

'The *watu* knock off at two-thirty; six-thirty to two-thirty, straight eight hours. We better eat. Kimoi, *chakula*!'

Ian had a long talk with Simuni, inquiring what rules and routine had governed this farm before Bwana Looki retired to the verandah and the booze. It was clear enough that anarchy now reigned. He feared the *watu* would resent him as an interloper but Simuni was helpful and friendly, another reason to be grateful to Luke, who must have spoken on his behalf. When Simuni left for the shameful African lines, Ian started to clear the chaos in the office. He returned to the house at six; Luke was in bed. For two days, with excitement, Ian roamed over the farm and made notes on the order of reconstruction. Aside from Luke's splendid house, everything had to be torn down. A new corrugated tin roof and a few coats of white paint would fix the house. But what if Luke took the furniture with him?

Ian did not know how to approach this matter. 'Unless you want all the furniture,' he began.

Luke, as usual, was drinking his lunch.

'All thrown in, lock, stock and barrel, including one shotgun and one rifle. I won't want any of it at the coast. You'll have plenty to do without furnishing a house. That's woman's work.'

'Thank you very much, sir.' He was overjoyed and hoped Luke could feel his gratitude since he was unable to express it. The atmosphere of the house depended on Luke's excellent things; the house would lose its quality if stripped of them. But now he had to tackle a tricky question and he dreaded offending Luke. 'I thought of doing some building.'

'I daresay.'

'Could you recommend anyone?'

'Going to call in an outside construction man, are you? I made it with my own *watu*.' Then, remembering the condition of Fairview, Luke was ashamed of his boasting tone. 'George Stevens in Nakuru. He doesn't soil his hands but he has tough Sikh foremen. Be sure you get a definite contract on costs in advance. Otherwise you'll find they've put up a latrine and charged you for the Taj Mahal.'

Latrines happened to be one of Ian's major priorities.

They proceeded to Karula in convoy, Luke ahead in his old Austin, Ian close behind ready to push when the Austin stalled on the boulders and gullies in the road. Luke was taking the Austin to the garage, to charge the battery, tune up the engine, get the old bus fit for the trip to Mombasa. Ian thought with anxiety of Luke in that decrepit car on the long hard journey to the coast. The garage was not reassuring. Behind the petrol pump, vehicles in various states of dismemberment were parked in the workshop, an expanse of oil-stained cement floor under a tin roof supported on flimsy posts. Africans battered away at these cars, shouting comments and advice. Two brave men worked in a pit edged with old railroad tracks to prevent the truck above from sliding down on them. A fat Sikh, the owner, bounced from his box-like office to welcome Luke with protracted handshaking.

'Yes, yes, Bwana Looki, leave all to me, fine as new, day after tomorrow,' said the Sikh whom Ian instantly classed as a prize liar in a trade renowned for lying.

Ian had not paid attention to Karula when passing through but Luke now took him round as if they were sightseeing an important city. The station provided no amenities for travelers but was better equipped for freight, the large godown being at present loud with caged chickens and smelling strongly of *posho* and kerosene. The post office and the bank on the main road, though toy-size, were the only stone buildings. Wooden one-room African dukas and beer parlors lined the two short dusty side streets. The general store looked palatial by contrast, a long narrow shed, painted yellow, with five smeared windows letting in light on a range of merchandise from patent medicines through food stuffs and toys to hardware. The proprietor received them in his office, beneath a photograph of the Aga Khan, and assured Ian it would be his greatest joy to serve him. The remainder of Karula was a sprawl of African shanties and an open fly-ridden market where women sat on the ground by mats displaying small heaps of vegetables and nameless African herbs. Ian saw no cause for Luke to fret about an excess of civilization. Luke had left the serious business at the bank until last. He was easing Ian into urban life gently. Though silent as always, Ian behaved all right when presented to the station master and the post master and Ram Singh at the garage and Jivangee at the general store. But Ian froze with Jim Barnes at Barclays. Perhaps the boy became paralyzed only in the company of whites. Jim Barnes was visibly put off by Ian's manner. Luke talked to cover Ian's stony silence. Ian had not bothered to ask and Luke had not bothered to say how much he wanted for the sale. Hearing now Luke's price for Fairview and everything in it, Ian was distraught. When papers had been signed and witnessed and the cheque written, Luke, in a temper, hurried Ian out.

'Honestly, Paynter, what bites you?'

'I couldn't say anything in there, Mr Hardy, but it isn't right. It's too little, you're giving me Fairview, I can't take it, I'm not poor, I can afford a decent price.' To date, Luke had not heard Ian speak so long or so fast. He put his hand on Ian's arm, smiling at the unhappy young face above him.

'Listen, son. I know what I'm doing. I don't need more, I haven't anyone to leave it to. I want you to spend your money on Fairview, see? That's all I care about.'

'I will, sir, but all the same this isn't right.'

'It is. Now forget it, will you? We're off to the Club.'

Luke was thinking that Paynter was a good boy, a nice boy, yet with a screw loose somewhere. What ought to have scared Paynter, taking over a large gang of unknown *watu*, didn't ruffle him but the prospect of meeting a few pleasant neighbors, people of his own kind, obviously scared him stiff. Could Paynter manage Fairview if he had such wacky nerves?

Ian expected the Sports Club to be elegant on the Lavering style and filled with the sleek types who frequented the Laverings. The Karula Sports Club was a tatty little cement building, masked by handsome trees. Mottled brown linoleum covered the floor. A bar, flanked by doors labelled Memsaabs, Bwanas, stretched along one wall. A tinted photograph of the King and a Union Jack had been nailed rather crookedly above the bar. Small wood tables, stained by glass rings and cigarette burns, and kitchen chairs completed the furnishing. Ten people, five of each sex, were comfortably knocking back beer, gin and orange squash in this room where none of them would be caught dead at home in England. They rose, when they saw Luke, and fell upon him with kisses, handshakes, back-slapping and cries of rejoicing. 'Darling Lukie, *what* a treat!' 'Lukie dear, you've *made* the day!' 'How are you, old boy, wonderful to see you!' 'You're looking fine, Luke, perfectly fine.'

But he wasn't, of course. Luke was the other kind of drunk, the sort that stops eating and shrivels and grows gray-faced and trembly. They were all much more effusive than was their habit, being shocked to find Luke so sick and so old. When they had quieted, Luke made introductions. 'This is Ian Paynter who's just bought Fairview. Mr and Mrs Ethridge. Mr and Mrs Gale. Mr and Mrs Gordon. Mr and Mrs Farrell. Mr and Mrs Brand.' They smiled and shook hands and said cordial things like 'We must get in touch . . . come to lunch soon . . . let us know if there's anything we can do to help.' But they were not interested. They hovered around Luke, who was dismayed to be the center of attraction. Months of solitude at Fairview had unsuited him for so many voices, so much carry-on. He understood Ian better. Promising falsely to see everyone before he left Karula, tell them his plans, hear the news, yes, sure, I'll appear on the doorstep, Luke extricated himself with Ian in tow.

Safe in the Dodge, Luke took a crumpled handkerchief from the pocket of his crumpled khaki shorts and wiped his forehead. Ian's guarded though knowing smile annoyed him. 'The secretary will send you a membership form and a chit for your dues.'

'Actually, Mr Hardy, I don't want to join.'

'Of course you'll join. If we didn't all pay our dues, how do you think the Club could keep going?'

This was the authentic voice of the old colonialist. The Club must be kept going, not only to satisfy an inborn English need for clubs but as a symbol of Empire. Ian didn't give a hoot; he would pay his dues, since that was the drill, and never set foot in the place again.

'I'd be glad to drive you, sir.'

'No, thanks, I'll go with the lorry.'

'Won't you be awfully early?'

The lorry left at eight in the morning to haul cream churns to the station.

'I have things to attend to,' Luke said. 'And you ought not to waste time. Get on with your job. You'll probably have questions you want to ask before I leave.'

The lorry was as decrepit as the old Austin. Everything about Fairview amazed Ian. Logically, the farm should have ground to a halt long ago.

Luke bought tickets for his cook, Joseph, and Kimoi at the station; they were to sit in the crowded train for most of a day and all of a night but that wouldn't depress them; the train was as good as a beer parlor. What depressed them was the coast, alien territory, alien tribes, but they did not consider refusing to accompany their Bwana into exile.

Luke fumed around Karula in a rage; Ram Singh the old shit didn't have the Austin ready. He had planned a morning call on Helen Gordon and was so late now he could barely make it before lunch.

'About time goddamnit,' Luke said and headed for the Gordons' farm which was called Mastings, a meaningless name, because Charles Gordon's family place in England was called Mastings, also a meaningless name.

Charles Gordon fell in love with Africa while on a shooting safari. To emigrate, he required a wife whom he quickly found, a pretty fair-haired girl, the belle of the previous London season. The parents of the bridal couple regarded this African venture as a foolish fling and expected their children home within months, or else Helen without Charles. The Gordons had now lived in the Highlands for fourteen years. Africa gave Charles everything he really cared about, from trout fishing to stalking elephant. Farming provided camouflage for the sporting life. He talked as if he was a burdened earnest farmer but old Roy Dobson, sixteen years his senior and hired as manager from the beginning, ran the farm. Old Roy, Charles was apt to say, is a priceless chap, one of the best, with the implication that old Roy was not quite one of us.

Helen Gordon liked Roy Dobson more than any man around Karula. Roy had started her on gardening, taught and encouraged her. She built her life on her garden; she was inseparable from it now that Charles had torn her children from her bosom and shipped them home to England. Charles was in a fever lest the war go on so long that his two sons would miss a proper education.

Despite the difference in age, Sue Hardy and Helen Gordon had been close loving friends, bound by their passion for making the earth bloom. Luke turned naturally to Helen for help. He found her, as always, grubbing in the garden, her face streaked with dirt where she had pushed back her sweat-damp hair, her old trousers mud-caked fore and aft.

'Luke! If I hug you, I'll get you filthy, but at least a kiss.'

'You're a pretty girl, Helen.'

'Hardly a pretty girl, darling, not at thirty-four. Lukie, come with me at once. I have to show you my latest. I've made a bosky dell, all spring flowers. In January, that's what I like, so dotty.'

She led him under trellises, down terraces, across immaculate lawns past glowing borders, to a far corner of the garden.

'Charles is furious, he says I'm wasting his precious water. Do you like it? Isn't it a dream? Though I must admit using a sausage tree and mwangwas for shade rather spoils the Old England effect.'

The bosky dell was a small natural bowl with a cunningly contrived imitation natural pool in the center. Fringing the pool and scattered up the grassy slopes, iris and daffodils, freesia and jonquils, violets, narcissus, fairy bells grew in lovely confusion, as if growing wild. The light fell softly, broken by the African trees.

'Your year's work, Helen? It is a dream.'

'I've sweated blood on moss but I don't think it's going to take. Now come and sit down, behold my rustic bench. I had the carpenter make it as I thought this would be the perfect place for reading poetry, not that I ever sit or read poetry. Tell me your news.'

'I wanted to talk to you about Ian Paynter.'

'The gangly young man you brought to the Club. What's that tic on his face?'

'Tic?'

'Yes, you know the way he keeps loosening and widening his lips.'

Luke laughed. 'I hadn't noticed but I reckon it's his party smile, to stop from showing his teeth.'

'Why, for heaven's sake?'

'They're the size of horse teeth and false. He ought to sue his dentist. Poor chap. I expect his went rotten in that Hun prison camp.'

'Lukie, explain.'

'They shouldn't make war with boys,' Luke said in sudden fierce anger. 'They ought to call up old men like me; let the old men fight their bloody wars. I figure the Huns had Paynter in jail from the age of eighteen to twenty-three, think of it, Helen, the best years of a young man's life when he's just got out from under school and family and feeling his oats, everything is new and exciting, and he can't wait to start. Why not wreck the old men, we've nothing to lose.'

'They did it to your generation too,' Helen said gently.

'Perhaps that's why I feel so sorry for young Paynter. I was lucky, I got in and got out quick.' Second Lieutenant Hardy invalided out with a cushy wound, leaving his right arm permanently shorter and bent and scarred from shoulder to elbow as though by a lion's claw, which didn't hamper him at all. He wore long sleeves. He hadn't missed his youth and the cocky fun of it.

'Anyway, Helen, I wanted to ask you to keep an eye on him.'

'Of course, Lukie. I'll have him to lunch at once, Charles will take him off on his killing sprees.'

'No, no, absolutely not. No parties, no fuss. He'll do best on his own at Fairview. Five years like that is enough to bust anyone up but I think there's more.' Luke stopped, feeling he was about to betray a confidence, Ian's voice when he said his parents were dead. 'The point is, he's a bit strange and I don't want people gossiping about him. I know how it gets in a place like this, people start talking and then everyone begins to look at you as if you're queer or contagious.'

'Lukie, you sound positively paternal. He must be a very nice young man. What would you like me to do?'

'Put in a word for him. That's all. See he doesn't get a bad name. And spread the idea that he's been ill or something, hasn't got his strength back, doesn't want a shower of invitations.'

'I'll do my best. Oh Lord, we must run. Charles will give you a drink while I tidy. I've never grasped why Charles foams at the mouth if he's kept waiting for his food.'

The sitting room at Mastings bore no resemblance to Fairview. Chippendale and Queen Anne, family possessions from home, Persian carpets, old Dutch still-lives of dewy fruit, old English rural scenes, flower-filled vases everywhere. Charles Gordon looked at Luke with pity and comprehension and splashed in a drop of soda to dilute the whisky for the sake of good form.

'I cannot understand why Helen is alway late,' Charles said. 'Though I suppose I should be thankful she doesn't have her meals sent down to the garden. Have you seen her latest? Pretty soon there won't be water for the stock.'

'How are your boreholes?' Luke needed to drink quietly, and knew Charles enjoyed holding forth on boreholes. Helen interrupted an account of Charles' recent excavations.

'Here I am,' Helen said. 'Bring your drink, Lukie. I always drink steadily right through lunch.' Iced tea but it looked enough like whisky to avoid shaming dear Luke, and the houseboy filled glasses without being told.

'We've been talking about Ian Paynter, Charles.'

'Well, Luke, I hope you got a good price for Fairview since you wanted to sell it, but my God what a monkey the *watu* will make of that young chap. You know how sly they are. They'll see he's green as grass and pull all their tricks on him.'

'He seems to do all right with them.'

'Naturally, at the beginning. He's the new Bwana. But in a couple of weeks, they'll be coming to him for money, moaning about funerals, sick *totos*, I can hear it now, and then asking for leave, more funerals, more sick *totos*. They'll drive him up the wall. A young chap with no experience can't run a farm like Fairview. They come out from home thinking there's nothing to it but we jolly well know better.'

Helen smiled; her great big booby couldn't run a chicken coop without Roy's guiding hand. Luke drank.

'I give him a year,' Charles said, interested now in a plate full of delicious lasagne verde. Except for tardiness at meals, Helen was a highly satisfactory wife. She had taught herself to cook and then taught that surly old ape in the kitchen. 'One year,' Charles said, chewing contentedly. 'Then he'll go broke and Fairview will be on the market again.'

Helen saw that this wounded and worried Luke. 'Come off it, Charles,' she said abruptly. 'You met the man once for a minute. How do you know he won't turn out to be the best farmer in the whole Karula district?'

Luke gazed at her with affection and began on his third whisky. She thought it wise to give Ian Paynter a rest. Charles might decide to put on his farmer act and list all the ways Ian Paynter could mishandle Fairview.

'What are your plans, Lukie? Where are you going?'

'I'll stay with Billy Blake, you remember him, he used to farm on the Kinangop. Moved to the coast about four years ago, high blood pressure, some place the other side of Kilifi creek. He'll lend me a bed until I find a furnished house.'

'But Lukie, nothing grows at the awful coast. Nothing except bananas and mangoes. You'll die of boredom. What will you do?'

'Drink,' Luke said. 'With a clear conscience.'

Joseph and Kimoi had been driven off in the lorry with their iron cots, bedding, pots and pans and cardboard suitcases loaded behind. They looked like men on the way to prison. Luke was leaving two servants for Ian. Mwangi, Luke explained, was as good a cook as old Joseph but Joseph's jealousy held him down to assistant and substitute when Joseph was on leave. Kimoi trained Beda and Beda was a perfectly capable houseboy. In case Ian wanted more servants; Ian interrupted to say he would never need more. Now Luke was ready to depart. He took only four worn suitcases as salvage from his entire adult life. Ian felt like bursting into tears which would disgrace him, Luke, Marlborough and the British Empire. Mwangi and Beda stood at the kitchen door weeping without shame.

Luke had not foreseen the anguish of this moment. It was as if Sue died a second time. He wanted to hurry away from the sight of Fairview and the pain of homesickness. Ian closed the door of the old Austin.

'Thank you for everything, sir,'

'Take care of the place, Paynter. Take care of it and find someone responsible to leave it to.'

'Leave it to?'

'You aren't immortal, you know. A place like this,' Luke said, with difficulty, 'a place like this deserves looking after.'

The Austin backfired and creaked down the drive. Ian watched its dust trail rising into the tall double row of eucalyptus that Luke and Sue had planted long ago. He watched until he could see no further sign of Luke. Depressed and aimless, he wandered on to the verandah, thinking he would take a look at his property before facing the tedious chore of sorting out the office. Some kind of miracle happened there in the morning sun. He saw no visions, heard no divine voice. The miracle was how he suddenly felt so happy, happier than he'd ever hoped to be again. He had a reason for living: fifty African families and land and stock and a house and garden to look after. And there was this wonderful feeling in him, like coming home.

The *watu* were bewildered by their new master, Bwana Panda. They had never seen a European, naked to the waist, sweating as they did, wield a pick and shovel alongside them. Bwanas kept clean and gave orders. They had never seen anyone, black or white, enjoying work like this Bwana. If he wasn't racing over the farm, pitching in on all the jobs, he was racing to Nakuru. Each time he went, more lorries full of cement timber roofing piping bricks fencewire machinery arrived at the farm, as well as more outside workmen to be hounded by that Sikh boss. There was no peace; everyone was running around as if in the middle of a forest fire.

When it rained for a week in March, the *watu* counted on a rest. Nobody wanted to get soaked and chilled, you couldn't be expected to work in the rain. Bwana Panda worked in the rain, soaked and chilled, driving them and himself. What's a little water, he said; dig drainage ditches along the roads while the ground is loose, pry out the rocks, get trenches ready for new piping, put up fence posts. Hurry, hurry, hurry. This wasn't the life they had known.

But Bwana Panda was not a bad man, by which they meant bad-tempered, their only standard for judging Europeans. He never shouted at them. Ian knew from the Oflag how it eats into a man's soul to be shouted at and unable to shout back. The *watu* gave him a nickname, as they did to all Europeans. They called him Soft Voice. It was a compliment.

Though Soft Voice was constantly crazily on the move, the *watu* had seen him stop his small truck and stand beside it for a moment in silence. They discussed this act and agreed that Soft Voice was praying. His God commanded him to stop anywhere, any time, and stare at Africa, praying. Ian looked at the land, mile after empty beautiful mile, stretched out to the smooth receding mountains and said to himself: I'm free, *I'm free.*

The African bush telegraph operated with its usual efficiency. Karula was also an information centre. Ram Singh at the garage and Jivangee at the general store were subtle gossips with connections in Nakuru. There was a steady flow of news about Ian and Fairview Farm. Paynter had built new large rondavels for his *watu* and piped in water to standing taps. Every rondavel had a latrine. Moreover, Paynter gave his *watu* domestic furnishings, iron cots and kapok mattresses, wood tables and chairs, buckets and cook pots, blankets and coarse towels, and a regular ration of blue soap. He had dressed the laborers in new overalls and wellingtons and thrown in yards of cloth for the women and children. This was unheard of, a dangerous precedent. If you spoiled the *watu,* they asked for more and worked less.

Reports filtered in about projects for a stone dairy with a sixteen unit milking parlour and milking machines to run off a new generator, a new pump and pump house at the spring, a rebuilt and richly equipped workshop, a new office and a storeroom like the Nakuru Star Hardware Emporium, the Public Works bulldozer to clear new farm tracks, and miles of fencing. Drivers from other farms saw the new Fairview Chevrolet lorry at the station and Ram Singh said Bwana Panetah had put his name down for a new Ford pick-up to haul his endless purchases from Nakuru. Everyone knew that Paynter was spending money like water and getting little back. Gopal the station master confided to Mark Ethridge, whence the word went round, that Bwana Panetah was shipping less cream than Bwana Looki had in his declining years. Anybody could tart up a farm but that was not the same as making it pay. Charles Gordon's opinion became general: Paynter would go bankrupt within a year and Fairview be back on the market.

No one had the straight gen from the horse's mouth because Ian only went to Karula early on Friday mornings to collect cash for payday and his mail. If any of the farmers met him, by chance, Ian answered questions in monosyllables. Sam Brand observed that Paynter always behaved like a man in need of a pee, twitching and wriggling until he could get away. The Memsaabs said that if Ian happened to spot one of them in the distance, he fled. This terror or distaste caused Rose Farrell to ask Maggie Ethridge if she thought Ian was queer.

They were shopping in the general store.

'Just a minute,' Mrs Ethridge said, checking her list. 'Don't tell me you're out of Gentlemen's Relish again, Mr Jivanjee. Oh well, never mind. How do you mean, Rose? Queer-homo or plain queer?'

'I don't know. I can't decide.'

Dick Gale, gnawed by curiosity, dropped in at Fairview Farm uninvited. He did not find Ian, which was all to the good. Beda said the Bwana was cleaning a reservoir. 'Himself?' Mr Gale asked. Beda said oh yes, Bwana Panda worked with the men on everything. 'He comes to this house at night, seven o'clock, eight o'clock, eat, sleep, wake up, go, work, come back eat quick, go, work, come back, eat quick, go, work. Not like Bwana Looki.' Dick Gale had a snoop round and a chat with Simuni who looked harassed.

Mr Gale's audience at the Sports Club next day was spellbound. 'The man's off his rocker. Can you believe it, Simuni told me he's putting up a pig palace and he doesn't own a single sow. There's an army of builders swarming over Fairview, but the same old mingy herd, from what I could see. Luke was always a lazy farmer, but Paynter must be mad. His *watu* seem pretty fed up, I mean no one works like that, fourteen hours a day.'

'He's a boor,' Mrs Farrell said. 'Sending everyone the same note— so sorry, I have to be in Nakuru. As if Nakuru was Calcutta. A child of two would have better manners. He won't be invited to our house again.'

'I bet George Stevens is swindling the pants off him,' Charles Gordon said with some satisfaction. 'If he asked advice, any of us could save him a lot of money and mistakes.'

Ah Lukie, Helen Gordon thought, they're all miffed, the men and the women, because your Paynter boy doesn't want them or need them. How can I keep my promise to speak up for him?

'I think he looks like Gary Cooper,' Helen said out of the blue.

This was greeted with shouts of laughter.

'I do,' Helen insisted. 'Nice and shy and with a golden heart, like Gary Cooper. He never says anything but Yes Ma'am or No Sir and everyone suspects him because he's a loner but in the end he gets the girl and they make him Sheriff. Come on, Charles, we'll be late for lunch.'

They were wafted out on waves of merriment which was better than pointless spite. How well Luke understood the neighbors or perhaps the human species though, apart from elephants, the animal species didn't seem full of Christian charity either. She longed to get back to her garden.

. . .

The Africans kept headline news to themselves. Though tireless chatterers, they could be secretive when they wished. All the *watu* around Karula knew that Bwana Panda had quelled a mutiny six months after he took over Fairview.

At first, Ian's *watu* could hardly believe their good luck. Fine houses, more goods and chattels than ever owned before, clothes, double rations of tea and sugar and *posho, kuni* and charcoal, and those large bars of soap. Soft Voice even laid out a big new *shamba* for the women, and gave them seed. Instead of scratching at a few plants of their own, they were to cultivate the *shamba* in turn and share the produce. The women were doubtful of this innovation until the *shamba* sprouted a glut of cabbages and beans, potatoes and tomatoes, maize and onions, more than enough for all. The men were paid regularly once a week instead of irregularly maybe once a month. Soft Voice evidently had a soft heart.

The *watu* were happy until Soft Voice expected them to earn his gifts. After hours, Soft Voice wanted them to tear down their old houses; for what reason; they had moved to new quarters. Soft Voice ordered this same kind of useless work all over the farm. They were sick of hearing Soft Voice say '*Safi*', clean—clean this, clean that, make it clean, keep it clean. Every week, he inspected their village, sharp-eyed for *takataka*, dirty papers, empty bottles, and stern about latrines. Bwana Looki was easy-going; he let them live as they liked. Simuni was their proper overseer; Bwana Looki didn't interfere with Simuni; he also let them work as they liked.

They took their comforts for granted now and told each other life was better in the old days when a man had time to down tools and rest and laugh with his friends. They began to dawdle and loaf and malinger. They were sullen and complaining. Ian saw this at once with despair.

At the Lavering estate as a newcomer to Kenya, Ian was quickly taught the European doctrine on Africans. The *watu* were lazy and filthy and ungrateful. It was senseless to try to change them or improve their lives. This didn't mean the *watu* were wicked, it simply meant that they were shiftless children and should be treated accordingly with a firm hand. Left to themselves they would do nothing except get drunk and screw their women. Firmness was all they understood.

Ian rejected this doctrine. He had been treated as inferior; flea-ridden, half starved, dirty, ragged and helpless while his jailers were clean, well-fed and powerful. All men were not equal, of course, but all men had a right to respect. He meant to trust his *watu*, assure their needs, and explain the purpose of their work. He talked to every man on every job, pointing out that their joint task was to make Fairview efficient. Dirt and disorder were not efficient. When the farm operated as he planned and showed a profit, their wages would rise. He should have saved his breath. The *watu* were determined to prove the European doctrine correct.

Ian knew what he had to do and he hated it. Make examples, he thought with bitterness, like the goddamned despicable bloody Germans. In one week Ian sacked a Masai herder who had neglected to report a sick cow, three men who were smoking and telling stories instead of cleaning a reservoir, and the gardener who was watering Ian's roses in the heat of the day. Ian gave them all twenty-four hours to get off the farm. The *watu* were impressed, and especially by the way Soft Voice shouted at the gardener. His face was pale with rage, he swore at the man.

No one heard what went on at the Masai encampment but in the African lines there was female wailing. The wives knew they would never live so well on any other farm. A revolt against the men flared among the women. They screamed and nagged; if their men were *bure* and *shenzi* and lost their jobs, they would leave them. Punishment worked like a charm.

It worked on Ian like an illness. He slept badly and lost his appetite. He couldn't rest, he walked up and down, sitting room to verandah, back and forth, trying to understand why he had come to this ugly relation with the *watu*. He had to talk to someone or jump out of his skin so he wrote a letter to Luke which he knew he would tear up. Dear Mr Hardy; I thought I got on well with the *watu*, I liked them and I thought they liked me. I know I'm a deadweight with other people and I even know what they think of me because I overheard that too, Mrs Mayfield telling Larry I had an inferiority complex from being a POW. Out here I didn't care what people thought, I could keep out of their way and I felt easy with the *watu* and I was happy because I'd found the right life for me. I wanted them to live and work in decent conditions and I wanted Fairview to look the way it should. That's all I've been working for. You've got to admit Fairview was a shambles and the *watu* lived in a pigsty. But they loved you and now they treat me as if I wanted to cheat them instead of help them and I feel they hate me. They've made me see I can't get on with anyone. I'm a misfit wherever I am.

He tore the letter up; apart from being shameful, a good cry on Mr Hardy's shoulder would not help. The full truth was worse. The *watu* could defeat him. The *watu* could drive him from his home. If the only way to run Fairview Farm was by bullying and fear, he couldn't do it. He couldn't live like that.

Cold and unsmiling, Ian went on with the work; no more jolly chat, no more stripping off his shirt to give a hand and an example. Simuni received flat orders; inspecting the jobs from his pick-up, Ian made flat corrections. The *watu* were subdued; everyone worked as directed. Ian wondered how long he could stand this atmosphere, harsh master, obedient slaves. Slowly, the climate of the farm changed. The *watu* worked without that air of cringing; they smiled and greeted him amiably. *Jambo Bwana, habari.* Ian assumed they had made their choice: work and be rewarded, otherwise get kicked off the farm. He was wrong. They had simply become accustomed to the new regime and the new Bwana who would tolerate no nonsense and now kept his distance as a Bwana should. Fairview hummed along cheerfully, Bwana Looki and the old ways forgotten.

Ian still liked the *watu* but they had disappointed him. They did not respond to trust, they responded to a firm hand. A firm hand need not be cruel. He could live on these terms, accepting the barriers set up by the *watu*. He felt lonelier but compensated by the work; week by week he saw his dreams for Fairview coming true.

He dealt with the men all day long and could not have worked with them except on terms of liking, however altered. He saw the women once a week and they repelled him with their shrieking laughter and their hideous bodies, black blubber swelling out to huge bottoms. But these repellent women produced the best *totos* he had ever seen, round-eyed, chubby, fur-topped, fending for themselves as soon as they could waddle. In childhood, they grew thin and swift and lovely as gazelles. More food, good housing, soap, enforced hygiene had transformed these *totos*. The *totos* loved the new Bwana. When Ian inspected the African lines, they rushed to meet him. He brought them toffees, he let them clamber over him, patting and hugging, he played with them, he carried the smallest in his arms. With them there were no barriers.

The *watu* were amazed by the Bwana's devotion to their children. They mulled over this clear but mysterious fact and decided that Soft Voice felt about their *totos* as he felt about his roses. No one understood his feeling for the roses either.

Ian had made a trip to Nairobi to buy the plants at a nursery. The names meant nothing to him, Golden Dawn, President Hoover, Madame Butterfly, Picture: they were roses and roses had been his mother's favorite. Ian's roses were set out in two rectangular beds, like infantry platoons, on the rough lawn in front of his verandah. To protect them from the sun, they were hidden under little thatch roofs with straw packed around their roots. Perhaps they didn't look like much but they were there and occasionally Ian cut a few and put them in a beer mug in his sitting room. The roses mattered to him. His mother was buried in the churchyard in Aylesbury. He felt that his roses kept something of her alive and with him.

Coming out of the post office, Ian saw Helen Gordon in tears by the wall of mail boxes. He could not pass without a word yet could not think what word to say to an unknown woman in unknown trouble. He stood near her, silent and awkward until she looked up. 'It's Luke. He's dead. Read it.' She gave Ian a telegram. LUKE DIED LAST NIGHT IN HIS SLEEP DOCTOR SAYS HEART ATTACK HE LOOKED PEACEFUL WHAT SHALL I DO BLAKE Ian felt a pain that was as sharp as it was unexpected, for himself not Luke. He had written to Luke a week ago inviting him to Fairview to see how he had spent his money, how he had kept his promise. In the year of work, he imagined Luke approving, he counted on that, he wanted desperately to show what he had done and talk about it and be praised. Now there was no one who would care. He had thought of Luke as somehow his partner and his friend because they both loved Fairview.

'I can't bear to think of Lukie dying there alone,' Helen said.

'He wouldn't mind that. He couldn't bear living alone.'

Helen brushed at her tears, too absorbed in grief to notice that Ian had spoken to her for the first time.

'But he had so many friends, we all loved him.'

'It's not the same thing.' He had friends too, long ago in Aylesbury. If only he could have shown Luke Fairview, if only that, just once, for both their sakes.

'This Mr Blake,' Ian said. 'Does he mean what to do with the body?'

Helen flinched. 'Yes, I suppose so.'

'He ought to be buried at Fairview, beside his wife. He ought to have the same headstone, only saying beloved husband of, instead of beloved wife.'

'You really are a very nice man just as Luke said.'

Instantly Ian was thrown back into himself and became a mumbler, anxious to flee.

'I'll have the place ready. And I'd like to pay for it all, whatever there is. I owe Mr Hardy a lot.'

Four days later the funeral cortège arrived at Fairview, six cars and the coffin in the Gordon pick-up. Helen made a blanket of rose geraniums to cover the coffin. The pick-up looked like a florist's van with all the sheafs and wreaths and bouquets contributed by the neighbors. The neighbors had doubled up, since you wanted company badly when going to a funeral. Beda faced this crowd and delivered his speech in agitated English.

'Bwana Panda say you follow his driver, please come after here for food and drinking. Bwana Panda sorry he must go Nakuru.'

Mrs Ethridge laughed.

Mrs Gale said, 'I don't think it's funny.'

Mrs Farrell said, 'I think it's the absolute limit.'

Helen Gordon slipped away from the indignation meeting. Walking around the house, she saw that Ian had obviously planted the seeds in the borders packet by packet. Pansies grew beside hollyhock, lavender next to dahlias, asters clumped by gladioli. The lawn was coarse Kikuyu grass but well mowed with the hideous rose beds in the centre. Poor old boy, Helen thought, he's tried hard. Sue would think it touching, the feeling was right even if the result was an eyesore. Helen returned to hear Sam Brand saying, 'Look, he didn't invite us to a party. He offered a place to bury Luke so let's get on with it, shall we?'

They piled into the cars, following Ian's pick-up. Ian had detailed two men, in clean overalls, with ropes and shovels for the manual labor. On the way to the gravesite everyone craned and peered, rather shamefaced, to see what Ian had been doing out here alone. They pulled themselves together on the mountain, forgetting Ian, while Sam Brand read parts of the funeral service. Though Luke was not a churchgoer or believer, they had agreed he wouldn't mind if they left out the Resurrection and so on, and kept the factual bits about being born of a woman cometh up and is cut down.

No one stopped at the house for food and drink. The Farrells and the Brands and the Gordons were silent driving back to Karula in the Gordons' estate car. Helen prepared to give them hell if they began to complain of Ian's manners. Luke's little burial ground was turfed and fenced in, with morning glories twining around the white slats of the fence. As a gardener, she knew this work was recent and she knew whose work it was.

Charles Gordon broke the silence. 'Whatever one thinks about him, I have to hand it to Paynter. He's made Fairview better than it ever was. He's really done a bang-up job. Luke would appreciate that.'

These were lush years for the farmers in Kenya. Britain needed all the food it could get; the African weather did nothing drastic; no epidemics of disease or insects blighted the animals or the crops. The farms boomed, none more than Fairview. Ian sold off the lacklustre cattle inherited from Luke and bought pedigreed Friesian bulls to serve his high grade shorthorn cows. Now he had two lorries making two daily trips to Karula station, hauling whole milk as well as cream. He filled what Dick Gale had called his pig palace with large white sows and shipped baconers to the Uplands factory. He acquired sheep because he liked the look of them nibbling away on the slopes north of his house, but soon the sheep proved so fertile that he was sending lambs to the Nairobi market. His own vegetable garden and chickens also overproduced and Mr Jivangee at the general store was pleased to take the surplus. The *watu* were not slow to see that profits for Fairview meant profit for them, as their wages rose; they settled down into a reliable work force.

Fairview was coining money. Ian did not care about money; he would have been satisfied if the farm broke even. But money was the sure proof of success and he coveted success for Fairview. This success had a soothing effect on Ian. He gained weight and forgot his teeth for weeks at a time until he forgot them entirely. Though not by nature a roistering type, he smiled when he wanted to. He felt equal to other men, in work at least. He could talk farming with confidence and knew that his peers, the Karula farmers, accepted him as one of them. He was still clumsy with the Memsaabs but no longer bolted on sight and managed polite if brief conversations. The Memsaabs were used to him and besides had him taped ever since Simon Farrell said that Paynter couldn't help it if he was a misogynist. 'I never believed they really existed,' Simon Farrell said. 'But obviously that's what Paynter is. Poor fellow, he doesn't know what he's missing.' There was nothing personal in being a misogynist so the Memsaabs stopped scolding about Ian's manners.

Ian celebrated his twenty-ninth birthday with an extra whisky. He lay on the sofa by the fire, balancing the glass on his stomach, and thought of Fairview. Five years ago he had been a hopeless ghost in Aylesbury. Now he was a man with a mission and the mission filled his days and would fill the rest of his life. Time didn't cure the old sorrow that remained like an ache in his bones. When he imagined his parents and Lucy here with him, he was close to tears; his father taking over the business end, proud as he was to see this small industry galloping along; his mother making a beautiful garden; Lucy gay and noisy in the house, riding beside him in the pick-up, loving the land, mad about the *totos*. It was useless to cry for what might have been. He missed three people, no others could take their place. Without them, he knew he would always be alone but alone in this peaceful room on this marvelous farm. That was the way accident had shaped his life. He didn't have the happiness he would have chosen; he had a different happiness and enough to keep him going.

·   ·   ·

Except for Ian, all the Europeans knew that Miss Grace Davis had arrived in Karula. Miss Davis came from England to teach spelling, grammar, penmanship, composition and reading to small girls at a small boarding school, Heather Hill, outside the town. Advanced news of a young woman fresh from a fashionable school at home secretly worried most of the Memsaabs. They foresaw a peach complexion, the latest hair-do, and the sort of smart clothes bought in a city for country wear. Africa was unfair to European women, as the Memsaabs frequently said. The sun struck straight down from the equatorial sky and ruined their skin. The men's faces were like cordoba leather, which was becoming, but the Memsaabs finally looked like withered apples or, if they fled the sun, gray-white mushrooms. Their figures did not survive too well either, growing stout like Mrs Ethridge or skinny like Mrs Gale. The exceptions were Helen Gordon who exercised by gardening and preserved her skin by magic, and Rose Farrell who exercised relentlessly in her bedroom, watched her diet, creamed her face and bought the best clothes she could find in the best shops in Nairobi, but was the most worried Memsaab in the area due to Simon's wandering eye.

Women who feel they have lost or are losing their looks tend to be nervous about their husbands. Miss Davis posed no threat to anyone and was therefore an instant hit with the Memsaabs. She was invited to all the farms and to the Karula Sports Club; she met everyone, she went everywhere. The Memsaabs were bursting with cordiality. Almost at once they seemed to know the story of Miss Davis' life. She had been engaged to a wonderful man, a bomber or fighter pilot, in the RAF or the American Airforce, who was shot down in flames over Berlin or Hamburg or some other place. The wives passed this sad tale on to the husbands.

'You must be getting barmy, Rose,' Simon Farrell said. 'Do you mean to tell me that any pilot, and they were the glamor boys and in a hurry too, would go for those specs, that awful crinkly mud-colored hair, and that body? I can't look at her without thinking of a Dover sole.'

'Eight years ago, perhaps ten years, she might have been very pretty,' Rose said, delighted.

'Balls. All you can say about her face is that she has the usual number of features and none are actually deformed.'

Mark Ethridge said, 'Well, Maggie, since men are known to copulate with sheep, I am ready to believe anything. Though I'd rather have a nice warm soft sheep than Miss Davis any day.'

The wives soon tired of Miss Davis. She had an affected voice, she was so ladylike you wanted to kick her, and she gushed. 'Drowns you in syrup,' Mrs Gale observed. Miss Davis, they agreed, was a typical spinster schoolmistress and fine for the children but they had done their duty and that was that.

During her popular period, Miss Davis met Ian Paynter at the Karula Sports Club. She had no idea that this was a unique occasion. It was a Friday before Christmas and Ian had been doing business with Simon Farrell in the bank, relative to a sale of heifers. Simon Farrell said, 'Come and have a drink at the club, Ian, Christmas cheer and all that.' When Ian began to mutter excuses, Simon Farrell said crossly, 'Oh stop being such a blushing violet, nobody's going to eat you.' Ian's war victim act had gone on long enough; Ian was a mental hypochondriac. Simon Farrell had had a whizz of a war, chasing the Wops out of Ethiopia, but thought that good or bad wars were ancient history.

Goaded and indignant, Ian followed in his brand new cherished Land Rover, a Christmas present to himself. The club room looked even nastier decorated with artificial holly and mistletoe. Miss Davis was sitting with Mrs Farrell. Pink gin for Mrs Farrell, orange squash for Miss Davis. Miss Davis wore a blue linen dress and looked like a hospital nurse in uniform. As a favor to Helen Gordon, Mrs Farrell had collected Miss Davis at Heather Hill, which was on her way to Karula. Mrs Farrell was now thinking that the claims of friendship and motherhood were both excessive. She was bored rigid by Miss Davis. She had been buttering up Miss Davis on behalf of Jenny, her ten-year-old daughter, but this was her last effort and Helen Gordon could jolly well drive an extra eight miles in future.

As soon as she saw the men, Mrs Farrell said, 'Simon, you have time for a very quick one, you know I've got a mob of little girls to lunch.' Before Simon could protest, his wife gave him a fierce wink. She was in such a hurry to leave that she didn't remark on Ian's presence. 'You'll take care of Miss Davis until Helen gets here, won't you, Ian?' Mrs Farrell said, beating a fast retreat.

This was much worse than Ian had expected. He could already feel the silence that would lie between him and a woman he had never even seen before. He asked if she'd have another drink and Miss Davis thanked him for more orange squash while he downed a strong gin and french. But then, to his amazement, there were no silences; Miss Davis chattered and he only had to say Yes or No, and with two big gins under his belt and this easy conversation he found he was quite enjoying himself. Miss Davis had ascertained cleverly that there was no Mrs Paynter. Just as cleverly, she led Ian to invite her for lunch at his farm the next day. Ian gathered that this was how Miss Davis lived; on weekends and during holidays she lunched around the countryside.

When Helen Gordon arrived to pick up Miss Davis, she couldn't believe her eyes. 'Why, Ian,' she said in a wondering voice and Ian immediately became all stumbling feet and stammers. On the way back to Mastings, Helen Gordon said, 'You're a wizard, Miss Davis. You must be the first woman Ian's ever talked to. He's so shy it's like a disease. The men say he's perfectly normal with them, but he has St Vitus' dance with the ladies. I think he's sweet though I can hardly get a word out of him. Oh, he's about twenty-nine or thirty. Yes, he lives alone at Fairview and he's made it clear to all of us that the last thing he wants is company. He's in love with his farm, he doesn't need anything else, and I'm convinced he's going to be the best farmer around Karula. A born bachelor, I'd say; what Charles calls more steer than bull.'

With her eyes on the road, Helen didn't see the prim tightening of Miss Davis' mouth. How long can I dish up this babble, Helen thought, and how on earth will we get through lunch?

'Not that he's unattractive,' Helen went on. 'Except for those teeth. No, his family doesn't come out to visit. I don't know anything about them but Lady Lavering is such a cracking snob that she wouldn't let old George hire anyone who hadn't been properly vetted. Oh yes, Ian worked for the Laverings before he settled here.'

Miss Davis was restfully silent during lunch. Helen sent Miss Davis back to Heather Hill with the driver; one personally escorted trip was all politeness required.

'You see, Charles, you didn't have to raise such a hellish row. It wasn't that bad. Poor thing, I do feel sorry for her, she's so wildly unappealing.'

Ian was stunned by his invitation. In almost four years, four years next month, he hadn't asked anybody to Fairview, and was greatly relieved when the Memsaabs stopped inviting him. Miss Davis seemed to think that he would naturally have people for lunch and this assumption was flattering though he couldn't explain why. Miss Davis' lack of looks was an advantage. Ian didn't see her as a woman. She was a nice person who gave him the happy impression of being easy to talk to. He didn't know about women or think about them; they did not exist in his life.

All the twenty-three bumping miles home, Ian fretted over food. What to give Miss Davis? He was both nervous and elated. He never planned meals, that was Mwangi's business; but for this special event he would make suggestions. Friendly, nice, about his age; roast chicken with bread sauce, mashed potatoes, peas, Brussels sprouts, tinned fruit salad with cream and a bunch of roses on the table.

Grace Davis had always harbored great expectations. The mystery was why, exactly, on what basis, for what reason she entertained so many hopes for so long. Her father had risen from a shoe clerk, bowed forever over female feet, to part owner and still active salesman in a small shoe store in Lincoln. Her mother, by temperament a mouse, became a mouse ravaged by childbearing and housework. Her three sisters and two brothers, as plain as she was, had burrowed warm holes in the world. Grace despised them all.

She chose to be a teacher since not much training was required and a teacher was several cuts above trade, especially her father's trade. Grace learned enough to teach young children, whom she did not care for; more importantly, she learned a refined accent and finicky manners. Her origins had nothing to do with her. She felt herself born to be a lady, her hands alone proved it; the hands of an aristocrat.

Grace was just twenty-two when the war began. For a girl whose sole ambition was to marry a gentleman, the war came as a boon. Aside from all else, war is a giant game of musical chairs. Men are seized from their homes and shunted around the world, men without women. In England, plain girls were finding mates right and left among displaced Poles, Dutchmen, Frenchmen, Americans. Lonely men without women were not a bit sure they would have time to seek their true loves. Grace could not understand why she was passed over.

She had been rejected by the FANYs because of her near-sighted eyes. Her occupation as a teacher saved her from factory work. She volunteered for every job that brought her close to men; the canteen at the station, the NAAFI club, the local hospitality committee. She struggled to be where she could be met, appreciated, invited out, proposed to. But she was never invited out, let alone proposed to.

She did not deceive herself that she was pretty, but girls less pretty were walking out on a soldier's arm, or better still on an officer's arm. She was not misshapen, she was not old, heaven knew she was eager to please. Perhaps determination to get a wedding ring and no nonsense beforehand is something men can sense or smell; and if the virtuous girl isn't much to look at, why waste time trying to beat down her defences? Perhaps the men of all nations could not take Grace's refinement. Perhaps it was her voice. Even when Grace was using it hopefully to charm and compliment, her voice had a thin built-in whine.

There had never been a hero fiancé, shot down in flames above a German city. Leaving Lincoln, after the war, twenty-eight years old and bitterly conscious of spinsterhood, Grace invented the fiancé, Robert, over bedtime cocoa with the geography and history mistress at a girls' boarding school near Southampton. She was terrified by her story after it emerged in dim outline; she lay awake that night wondering if it could be checked and she prosecuted for libel, defamation of character, false pretences. The story remained fixed in its bare form of love requited and death the tragic end. Grace took strength from this myth and soon believed it. She had been loved; a blissful married future in America was destroyed by anti-aircraft fire.

St Mary's, outside Southampton, was no academic or social pinnacle but for a while it seemed perfection to Grace. She had left for ever the insufferable vulgarity of her home. Next to the games mistress, Grace was the youngest teacher in the school. After a few years, she saw her elders as crotchety old maids, and her future like theirs. Knitting, tea parties, sensible brogues. When Grace read the advertisement in the personal column of *The Times*, offering a post for a qualified English mistress in Kenya, she wrote a letter of application that night and held her breath in hope.

St Mary's didn't teach much but it was a cosy little school and the old maids were fond of their girls. As a teacher, Miss Davis' work could not be faulted; but the children hated her. She discouraged them and disciplined them with sarcasm; she was unsmiling. Even by St Mary's standards, it was alarming to see how badly the girls got on in Miss Davis' classes; and more alarming, for Miss Heyworth the headmistress, to see the mulish faces of the girls after an hour with Miss Davis. Miss Heyworth dreaded scenes or any trouble. She had reached the hand-wringing stage over her nightly camomile tea. 'I can't sack her, Hetty,' Miss Heyworth said to Miss Burton, her second in command. 'I have no grounds. What if she kicks up a rumpus? What am I to do? She makes the girls miserable; it's all wrong.' Miss Heyworth wrote a fulsome recommendation and thanked the Lord for providing Heather Hill in Kenya.

The Misses Ferne, who owned and ran Heather Hill, were astounded and delighted to receive the letter from Miss Davis. They knew that anyone who could read and write was adequate but the parents of their pupils insisted on trained teachers from England. One letter to an academic employment agency in London had brought a lowering answer: salary too small, and where was Karula, and what was the scholarship rating of Heather Hill? In desperation, the Misses Ferne launched their need like a bottle on the sea, addressed to *The Times*. And got Miss Davis, whose photograph looked suitable, and whose present employer recommended her warmly. Miss Davis explained that she was leaving the congenial environment of St Mary's because she must live in a warmer climate; she'd had serious problems with her chest the last three winters.

Beneath that healthy but flat chest, excitement began to bubble. Miss Davis was careful of money, a prudent saver. She splurged now on clothes: nothing in her life or the English weather had previously called for cotton frocks in lovely pastel colors, and two evening gowns, one of blue taffeta, one of yellow chiffon. These alluring garments were for the ship and though Miss Davis adored them she felt uncomfortably naked with her white thin arms and so much of her bosom exposed. She sailed early in September, to be ready for the October term; and was giddy with hope as she walked up the gangway of the B.I. liner.

The ship added tightness to Miss Davis' narrow lips. There were deck games and dances and card parties, but the shipboard company divided into two worlds: welded old couples and the flirting young. The purser danced with Miss Davis once and was seen wiping his forehead afterwards. Miss Davis dressed proudly for dinner every night, alternating between hard blue and vicious yellow, and sat alone to drink coffee and listen to the band in the lounge. Every night she wept in her inside stateroom. Some of the old couples made friendly gestures and were rebuffed; Grace Davis was afraid of age now.

Karula was like the ship. There seemed to be no single people of either sex except the five spinster teachers at Heather Hill and boys and girls too young for wedlock. Evidently people could not live alone in this vast silent country; any partner was better than none. The African day was beautiful and sparkling and so was the night, but the night oppressed. The Africans shut themselves in their huts, closing doors and windows and sleeping in a huddled consoling fug. The Europeans shut themselves in their houses with the lamps lit and played their gramophones and talked or quarreled or read together, holding the night at bay.

Miss Davis, lunching around the countryside, decided that even those couples who snarled at each other were as tightly attached as Siamese twins. At any rate, the climate was an improvement over Lincoln or Southampton, and a teacher here was not treated as a genteel hired hand but as a member of the community in equal social standing.

Ian Paynter did not appear as an answer to prayer because Miss Davis did not go in for such revealing prayers. She told herself that Ian was a dear and dreadfully lonely and she must do everything she could to be kind to him. She was thirty-three years old, with hope still, hope again, hope undefeated despite all the years of failure.

Miss Davis began to exclaim the minute they turned into the driveway under the arching eucalyptus.

'But it's heavenly!' Miss Davis said. 'It's much the most beautiful farm I've seen!'

'The view!' Miss Davis said.

'The roses!' Miss Davis said.

'What a divine house!' Miss Davis said. 'It's so full of *character!*'

'Goodness, you've done wonders!' Miss Davis said. 'In less than four years, all this! It must be a model farm, isn't it?'

'Do you mean to say you plan such superb menus yourself?' Miss Davis said. 'I always thought men living alone didn't mind what they ate. Too delicious, I haven't had anything like it since I came to Kenya. Well, I would love some more; I'm making an absolute pig of myself but I can't help it.'

'Oh it all looks so different!' Miss Davis said. 'I didn't see how people could bear to put the Africans in those terrible dirty huts. But yours really look pretty enough to live in oneself.'

'They're positively edible, those babies,' Miss Davis said. 'Such dear little funny black faces. And the way they follow you around! They *worship* you!'

Ian asked Miss Davis to come again on Sunday next week, if it wouldn't bore her. He'd like to show her his cattle, his *shambas*, his pigs and chickens and workshop and dairy. Friendly, nice, about his age; and so easy to talk to. Miss Davis decided to invest most of her remaining savings in a second-hand car. With her own car she could drop in from time to time for tea; much nicer when you didn't have to arrange about transport. She bought the car within a week at Nakuru, an old Morris which listed slightly to the right.

'Poor little Morrie,' Miss Davis said. 'It's got a limp from climbing all these hills.' Ian thought that funny, the sort of thing Lucy might say.

Ian would come home, soaked by the erratic rain of that winter, to find Miss Davis curled up on the sofa, saying, 'I hope you don't mind. It was so gloomy at school. I thought I'd just drive up and beg a cup of tea.'

'I'm delighted,' he said, meaning it. 'Give me a minute to change.' He shouted to Beda to bring tea and raced through his bath and thought how agreeable this was, someone to talk to at the end of the afternoon. He couldn't of course knock off work so early as a regular thing. Normally he would dash in for tea and dry clothes and dash out again to oversee the last milking and catch up on paperwork. But as a surprise and special treat, Grace's visits were lovely and it was sporting of her to make the trip in such weather.

Sunday had become a fixed engagement; Ian never knew how but certainly didn't object.

'See you next Sunday,' Miss Davis would call gaily as she drove off in her Morris. Once, Miss Davis suggested staying on for dinner but Ian would not hear of it. If your car broke down at night on the appalling roads, either you were a competent mechanic or you slept on the back seat. It took Miss Davis three months to steer Ian into an invitation for the weekend: arrive Saturday afternoon and have the whole of Sunday to themselves. If she wouldn't mind the walk, Ian said, he knew a pretty spot at the top of the farm for a picnic. Ian did not consider gossip, being pure in heart. Miss Davis had already considered and devised a plausible lie about meeting friends from England at the Lake Hotel in Naivasha.

Any risk was worth it. Ian must become used to seeing her at all hours, dependent on her presence in his house. Miss Davis was not in a hurry. Her contract with the Misses Ferne ran until the end of the school year late in June, and it was only April now. Besides Ian never went to Nairobi or Mombasa or anywhere that he might meet other women.

Mrs Ethridge had a chat with Mrs Farrell in front of the post office, among the dusty farm cars and the shoving Africans.

'Seems Miss Davis has got off with Ian Paynter,' Mrs Ethridge said. 'Can you beat it?'

'Poor brute,' Mrs Farrell said.

Mrs Ethridge giggled. 'Mark says it gives him a cold sweat even to think of Miss Davis in bed.'

'Bed's not everything,' said Mrs Farrell, who had surmounted Simon's various infidelities.

Mrs Ethridge was prematurely gray and overweight and drank too much but she knew what she liked. 'Maybe not everything,' said Mrs Ethridge. 'But quite a lot.'

At the petrol pump, Mark Ethridge had a thoughtful discussion with Charles Gordon about tyres, then gave him the latest bulletin on Miss Davis and Ian Paynter.

'My God,' said Charles Gordon. 'He must be barking mad.'

'He's got his head screwed on right when it comes to farming. But if he falls for that piece of old rope I'll think he's the biggest clot from here to the Zambezi.'

'He's an odd chap, isn't he?' Charles Gordon said. 'I don't mean queer or anything like that, but you know what I mean.'

For many reasons Grace did not speak of her life, past or present. Instead she listened. Ian saw that he had hungered for company without knowing it. He was starved for praise, starved for concern, and needed to talk about Fairview as a lover needs to talk. With Grace, he felt almost as if he were talking to his mother again, sure that she wanted to hear, was never bored, and shared his enthusiasm. Words poured from him, he could tell Grace all he had done and all he planned to do. As soon as the profits justified it, he meant to clear a thousand acres for arable land; he foresaw waving wheat fields, barley, oats, lucerne, his pasture enriched by sowing better grasses. He dreamed aloud of overhead irrigation. He showed her, as if showing art works, the catalog pictures of combine harvesters, tractors, seed drills, road scrapers. Grace applauded his past achievements and his future schemes and said he was wonderful, wonderful, wonderful. Ian ate it up.

At first, he refused Grace's generous offers of assistance. She was run ragged during the week at school and deserved a rest at Fairview. But he was always behind on paperwork and Grace said she loved helping him with the cattle records and the muster roll books and the accounts. Coming from the same background as Ian's in a small English town, Grace said, she had always thought of farmers teetering on the edge of bankruptcy but here they were, with their heads together over the big dining table, seeing in clear figures just how well Fairview paid.

Ian never spoke to Grace of Oflag XV B. He blotted out that memory except when it overwhelmed him in nightmares. On the third of the now regular weekend visits, he told Grace about his family. Grace said nothing but put her hand on his and Ian saw tears in her eyes. Then she said quietly, 'I am alone too.' That was another bond of another kind. Hard enough for him, a man, how much worse for a woman, with no one to care for her, no home as a refuge. That night Ian began to feel pity for Grace and the tenderness of pity.

Yet it did not occur to Ian to think of Grace as a woman who could be a wife. He thought of Grace with gratitude as his friend, someone like him too old for that romantic part of life and uninterested as he was. They were lucky to have found this companionship; they were both content in it. Years ago as a schoolboy before the war, Ian had imagined that he would meet a beautiful Aylesbury girl one day and fall in love with her and marry her in the same church where his parents were married; a nice boy's standard dream of the future. It had not been an urgent dream and was long forgotten, lost with the rest of his past.

The precepts of his school and family on the subject of sex were daunting; Ian had no urge to go forth and sin. He was a virgin when he joined up and on the rare days of leave from his training camp he went safely home. In France there was neither time nor opportunity for an experience which he didn't anyway crave. He still had a known future then which included the beautiful Aylesbury girl, virgin like himself.

After that there was Oflag XV B. The other nine men in his room were married or engaged; they wrote their weekly permitted letter card to these girls, they read their mail in longing silence. They talked of their wives and fiancées but not of sex, perhaps from discretion, perhaps from being too hungry to yearn beyond food. Something that had not waked in Ian stayed dormant. He wasn't suppressing desires, he did not feel them. And when all the people he loved died, the concept of loving died too. He was still a virgin, without sexual curiosity or need. The idea of marriage never crossed his mind.

The idea of marriage never left Grace's mind. Sex was the horrid part and she avoided thinking of it. She saw marriage as wifeliness and constantly demonstrated her talent in this role. She sewed buttons on Ian's shirts and darned his socks. On Saturday afternoons she made goodies for Ian, crusted apple pies and sponge cakes and oatmeal cookies and caramel custards. She bought Mr Jivangee's best fake cut-glass flower vases and filled the house with bouquets from Ian's garden. She tidied his clothes in drawers and cupboards and arranged his bills and accounts and records in admirable order. Ian said, 'I don't know what I'd do without you.' Grace held her breath, but nothing came of it.

Stretched on separate sofas after Sunday lunch, digesting and reading, Grace murmured, 'Oh how I wish I could stay here always.'

'I wish you could,' Ian said absently and turned a page.

It was now May.

By June, Grace had dark circles under her nearsighted eyes. Her voice not only whined but lashed at the unfortunate girls in her charge. She was smoking heavily and often had to clasp her hands to hide their trembling. The Misses Ferne, though fluttery and not very bright, had observed exactly what Miss Heyworth observed before them. They might not be able to lure another trained teacher from England but a pleasant amateur from Kenya would be better than Miss Davis. Their Kenya girls were more high-spirited than the inmates of St Mary's had been. They protested to their parents.

'She's an old cow,' Jenny Farrell informed her mother. 'No, she's a damn old bitch, that's what she is.'

Grace knew that her next year's contract should already have been discussed. She also knew that the Memsaabs had been watching her throw her cap, as if it were a hand grenade, at Ian Paynter. She felt rejected, mocked, isolated and terrified; and time was running out. All or nothing, this Saturday night.

Ian's best hour was before dinner over drinks; he became annoyingly sleepy afterwards, having been up and on the go from five thirty in the morning. Grace had taken on the service of drinks and learned to swallow gin without making a face when Ian remarked that he wished she'd join him, he felt like an old boozer drinking alone. Two whiskies were Ian's evening ration. Grace said she was a bit weary, let's have another. Ian's drinks were strong while hers were mainly water. Grace had worked on her face and hair and left off her spectacles. She was wearing a new long loose housecoat from the Asian tailor in Karula.

'I've got to make up my mind,' Grace said.

Ian looked interested.

'I don't think I can bear another year at Heather Hill. All work and almost no pay and it's so frightfully boring.'

Ian now looked sympathetic.

'I've had a good offer from Roedean. I have to let them know this week. Of course one dreads the English weather but on the other hand.'

'Oh no,' Ian said, startled.

'Well, what shall I do?' Grace peered across at the man who was a brown blur on the opposite sofa.

'You can't go,' Ian said.

'You'd miss me?'

'Grace, you know I would. I can't imagine . . .'

'All I've cared about was the time with you. Working with you, trying to help you, being here with you.'

Ian looked touched. Grace waited. In vain. She didn't know what she felt: despair, fury, for God's sake the man was like an ox, slow, slow, slow, didn't anything jell in his brain; she wanted to weep and hit him.

'I can't throw up a good job in England. I really can't. I have to think of the future. Unless . . .'

'Unless?' Ian asked.

'Unless *you* were my job.' Grace was now peering at her hands, clenched in her lap and trembling uncontrollably.

'You mean?' Ian said; actually he did not understand.

'We've been like partners for a long time,' Grace murmured. 'I hope you've been as happy as I . . . you see, Ian,' and here it was, all or nothing. 'I love you.'

The silence seemed to Grace endless, hours of it. She dared not raise her eyes, besides she could not have seen Ian's expression unless she put on her spectacles.

'I can't believe it,' Ian said at last. Impossible to decipher his voice; it sounded dazed.

Silence again. Grace felt cold and on the verge of hysteria; her head ached.

'You mean you'd stay with me, live with me here?' Still that bewildered tone.

Grace nodded, unable to speak.

'We're not young.' A note of doubt had crept in.

'Two people alone,' Grace said hurriedly. 'Keeping each other company always.'

Another silence. The pain in her head was blinding; her hands were ice cold but wet.

'We could get married!' Ian said with an air of discovery. 'Between us, we'd make Fairview the best farm in Kenya!'

Now Grace raised her head, smiling tenderly.

'Married!' Ian cried and bounded across the room to kneel by her sofa. 'Grace, what a brilliant idea, I'd never have thought of it.'

Ian took one of her ice cold hands and kissed it. He did not think of kissing her on the mouth; he had never kissed Lucy or his mother like that. Grace rested her other freezing hand on Ian's hair, blinking away tears due as much to relief as to migraine. Close beside her, Ian was no longer a brown blur but his features remained indistinct. Grace could imagine him as she had so often imagined the man that never was, the passionate pilot on his knees begging and imploring her to become his wife . . .

Ian ate while Grace talked ways and means. The church at Nakuru, so much nicer than the tin-roofed cement chapel in Karula. Let's see, we'll invite the Misses Ferne of course and the Gordons and the Ethridges and the Farrells and the Gales and the Brands and the Parkinsons and the Barnes and the Ogilvies and . . . The wedding breakfast at the Nakuru Hotel, surely they can manage a proper cake. Immediately after the end of term, first week in July would be best. Lovely if Ian had a ring of his mother's, did he, such a joy to wear his ring, she could hardly wait to tell everyone, wasn't it thrilling. Ian smiled and nodded; he seemed to have no opinions of his own.

Grace sent notes announcing the engagement and the wedding date. She added that Ian would have written too but you know how he works himself to the bone, scarcely a minute to breathe.

Rose Farrell showed this letter to her husband at lunch. 'I thought you said he was a misogynist?'

'Well, my God, if this doesn't prove it, what does? No normal man would regard Miss Davis as a woman.'

Helen Gordon said, 'Oh Charles, do you think Eddy and Alan will suddenly tell us they're going to marry some absolutely horrendous girl?'

'Considering that Eddy is in his first year at Eton and Alan's still in preparatory school, I hardly see the need to have a fit now. I'm not going to spoil my dinner just because Ian Paynter is off his chump.'

Mrs Gale said, 'Do you suppose she'll want to be neighborly, Dick? Popping in for a cuppa and a nice matronly chat? I'd go out of my mind.'

Mark Ethridge said, 'My heart bleeds for that poor sod and I don't care to talk about it.'

'Better to marry than to burn,' Sam Brand said, 'if I am quoting St Paul correctly. In some cases, any fool would choose burning.'

When the great day came, the farmers grumbled furiously about dressing up and besides it was as jolly as going to a hanging. The wives would not hear of defections. The prevailing sentiment seemed to be that they had to rally round Ian in his hour of need but at the same time Ian wanted his head examined. The congregation, assembled in town suits and hats, listened with varying expressions to that noteworthy phrase in the marriage ceremony: with my body I thee worship. At the Nakuru Hotel, toasts were drunk with grim cheerfulness. The champagne was not very good and also not very cold. The hotel dining room smelled of hotel cooking. Everyone ate cake and spoke heartily to the bride and groom, and in lowered tones to each other.

Rose Farrell sauntered over to Helen Gordon and said, 'Your hat's even worse than mine, I'm pleased to see. Wouldn't it be a good thing if the new Mrs Paynter had a dear friend to advise her never never to wear yellow?'

'I think we should all stop being mean. She looks radiantly happy. Really. And happiness improves people. Who knows, it may be a wonderful marriage.'

Mark Ethridge joined them. 'I've done my best with this champagne but it isn't having any effect. The bridegroom looks to me as if he'd been poleaxed. And he hasn't said a word from beginning to end except "I do".'

Coming in on this remark, Mrs Gale said, 'The bride makes up for that. If only they could change around like Jack Sprat and his wife, if you see what I mean.'

Helen said, 'We must break this up. Come on now, shoulder to the wheel. Let's try to make it merrier for Ian.'

As soon as was decent, the entire company returned to Karula. A pouring unseasonal rain had not helped and Grace was cross about damage to her new shoes, dress and hat, but Ian was delighted, thinking of his pasture. The rain was really the best part of the day. There had been no question of a honeymoon; Ian could not possibly leave Fairview.

Ian had told Beda to make up the guest room and shift his clothes, so the drawers and cupboards in the master bedroom would be empty for the Memsaab. Naturally he gave Grace the best room. He had hardly seen Grace since the night they agreed to marry. She said the end of term was hectic and she had all her packing to do and she had the sense to keep to herself the fuss of the wedding preparations and her intense elation. To Ian, this marriage was a sensible arrangement for them to work together at Fairview, companions as before. But Grace had been unlike herself at the awful wedding party, clinging to his arm, holding his hand, smiling at him in a new embarrassing way; and he had also been shaken by the same words in the marriage service that so impressed the congregation. Now while Grace unpacked, he lounged around the house disoriented and filled with foreboding. Surely Grace did not expect ... they should have discussed this before.

After a light supper, the newlyweds said in the same breath, 'You must be dead tired,' and laughed a little and went to bed, with perfect accord, in separate rooms. That's all right then, Ian thought. He rather missed waking to the view from the front bedroom but would soon get used to the change.

For a week, Grace was busy dominating Mwangi and Beda. In a week they knew who was boss. But Grace started to worry because Ian showed no intention of claiming his marital rights and she wondered whether an unconsummated marriage was actually legal. She remembered something about Roman Catholics, a wisp of information from a newspaper: unconsummated marriages could be annulled, something like that. Inwardly shuddering, she held Ian's hand as they reached her bedroom door.

'Ian dear?' A rising note, a smile, a special look.

Ian got the message. He couldn't speak and his stomach clenched in nausea. Too late now to say this was no part of the agreement. Grace would be mortally hurt if he refused and how could he when there she was, gleaming at him? He undressed slowly and went to her room, well buttoned and tied in his pyjamas, to find Grace well covered in her nightdress. He turned down the pressure lamp and slid into his own bed which felt strange and hostile, with a rigid woman filling half the space. The disastrous failure left them both hot from shame and limp from fatigue. Grace blamed Ian silently and with fury. It was a man's place to know how to handle this. Of course a man should keep himself pure for his wife, just as a girl should for her husband, but that was meant for young people and a man of Ian's age ought somewhere to have learned whatever you had to know. She dreaded the next attempt but instinct told her that she must persevere, in her own best interests.

The second attempt was even worse, since both now knew what indignities to expect. Ian rose in the dark room from the disordered bed. He wanted a bath and a strong drink, he wanted to be a hundred miles from here. But more than anything else he wanted never to go through this again as long as he lived. He didn't care what Grace felt.

'I'm sorry, Grace. There's been a bad misunderstanding and it's my fault. I should have said something before. But this isn't on, I'm very sorry. You are of course free to get a divorce. I only wish I'd had better sense sooner and I apologize.'

Grace, though numb with disgust over the proceedings, was galvanized by the word 'divorce'. She sat up in bed, collecting her wits quickly, and said, 'Oh Ian dear, what a stupid muddle. I thought *you* wanted it. I'm so sorry, do forgive me. You know what I love is living here and being with you and working with you. I don't want anything else ever. Divorce, my goodness what an idea. We're going to be happy exactly the way we were before.'

So that took care of that, except for hidden and confused emotions. Grace hoarded her contempt for Ian, he wasn't a real man; a real man would have known how to take her in his arms and teach her love. Deep beneath this righteous sense of being cheated lay doubt too painful for words. No man had wanted her; perhaps another woman would have known how to teach Ian. Ian was relieved by the way Grace ignored what had happened. But he felt a lingering sadness: if he had grown up normally, slowly—he knew he was slow—learning about girls through Lucy's friends, he might have met the beautiful Aylesbury girl, at the right age, and loved her entirely as a man loved a woman.

Now that this sordid mess was disposed of, Grace got down to the real business of life.

'Ian, I'll have to do the house over from top to bottom.'

Ian was drinking beer in one of the old comfortable chairs on the verandah, waiting for lunch. The glass wobbled in his hand.

'But Grace, you said . . .' He remembered all she had said, she never stopped saying it's such a *homey* house, it's so right for this country, it's so welcoming, so lived-in, it has such character.

'Oh of course, Ian, it was fine for a man living alone. But not for a married couple. You don't suppose Mrs Gordon or Mrs Farrell live in such a primitive place. I assure you they have civilized houses like a country house in England.'

He didn't want an English country house and he was shattered. But the house was the Memsaab's province and he couldn't deprive Grace of any more rights.

'I'll need money,' Grace said. She meant to sound casual and sounded mistreated. This was a test point.

'That's all right, I'll fix it at the bank, a joint account. You know as much about the farm finances as I do. You know what the farm needs. Otherwise you can do what you like.'

Grace was his wife and he wanted her to be happy. Grace was now free to shop in Nakuru and Nairobi, hire workmen, boss and buy. Unfortunately she seemed more exhausted and outdone than happy.

'My God, how can they be such fools!' Grace cried, showing Ian a chest of drawers that was painted shut. 'You have to stand over them every second and even so they can't do anything properly.'

'Look at these curtains!' Grace cried, showing Ian curtains that hung eight inches from the floor. 'The Asians are as hopeless as the Africans. I told Patel the exact measurements six times if I told him once.'

'You won't believe it!' Grace cried. 'I've been to Karula again to that idiot carpenter. Never ready, never ready. The idiot just smiles and says *"bado"*. I could choke him.'

'I will *not* accept these sofa covers!' Grace cried. 'Lalji will have to do them again, that's all.'

'It's enough to drive you crazy!' Grace cried. 'No one in this country can get *anything* right.'

Ian said mildly, 'I think everything looks fine, Grace,' and she flew at him.

'It does *not*. It's disgraceful. You're far too soft. I will not pay for such shoddy work.'

Grace's trials and tribulations were the stuff of all conversation. Ian began to cringe from her voice, the drilling quality of the whine. The poor girl was strained, of course; she wasn't used to Africa; she wanted everything to be like England which was impossible. She'd learn to make-do as everyone did and stop fussing. Beda looked hunted, cleaning up after the untidy workmen with the Memsaab snapping at his heels. Ian prayed the house would soon be finished to Grace's satisfaction.

You couldn't sit here or touch there and the rooms smelled of paint and were cluttered with the new bits and pieces Grace bought. He used to put his drink on the wide arm of a wooden chair or on the floor but those big chairs were gone and a spindly table stood by an upholstered settee and he'd been ticked off sharply after he knocked the table over twice. He had to think carefully and move carefully lest he damage Grace's handiwork.

At last the house was done, not to Grace's satisfaction, but near enough; or perhaps she was worn out and defeated. Ian said he thought the bright yellow brocade curtains in the sitting room were very pretty and so were the chintz slip covers of parakeets and hibiscus flowers. Grace was sweet to get the mail-order shower stall for him and the large cupboard for his bedroom. He did not say that the room looked absurd, like a nursery, with the old brown wood furniture painted red and curtains of gambolling red and white lambs. He didn't care. He only wanted peace and an end to Grace's nervy complaints.

'Well, it's a home,' Grace said, surveying her achievement. 'We don't have to be ashamed of it at any rate.'

Ashamed? He felt as hurt as if Grace had insulted an old friend. Though Grace said this stuff was only fit to burn, he saved all Luke's things in a partitioned section of the workshop out of respect for Luke and the past. You didn't throw on the junk heap furniture that had served well for more than thirty years. Perhaps Luke's house was unsuitable for a married couple but that was no reason to speak of it with contempt.

Grace quickly defined her share of the work. She was responsible for whatever concerned money and for the house. She attended diligently to bills, statements, and accounts ledgers in her bedroom at an ample new desk. Nothing would persuade her to work in the farm office, surrounded by Africans. Of necessity she had to deal with Mwangi and Beda, who at least understood English, but there she drew the line. Ian must absolutely forbid Africans to come to the back door when they wanted home doctoring; tell them to go to the office with their loathsome ailments. Healthy Africans smelled bad enough, sick Africans smelled to high heaven. Ian's suggestion that she take over the inspection of the African lines was grotesque. Poke at their huts and latrines and garbage dumps, with African brats swarming over her? And she wasn't going to let Ian bore her blind with tales of pregnant cows and the foibles of his generator. Farming was Ian's job and deadly, except that it paid.

Grace was now ready to entertain.

'I have so much hospitality to repay, Ian. I'll invite people here on Sundays. They'll love seeing my house.'

'If that's what you want, Grace, but I'm no use at parties.'

'You just pass round the drinks. The women do the talking anyway.'

Grace did the talking. Ian hoped the Gordons and the Farrells were interested to hear the story of every nail, tin of paint, yard of cloth, for they were treated to a play by play account of Grace's struggle against the stupidity and incompetence of Africans, not that Asians were a great deal better. The party broke up right after coffee, with Grace saying, 'Surely you're staying for tea?' She had baked a special cake; when she was a teacher, lunching around the countryside, she always stayed for tea.

'I have to keep an eye on the new gardener,' Mrs Gordon murmured. 'He drowns things.'

'Trouble with the main pump,' Mr Gordon said, backing her up. 'You're damned lucky with your spring, Ian. My boreholes are a curse.'

'I must get home to Jenny,' Mrs Farrell said, 'I promised to give tea to a horde of her chums.'

Mr Farrell was past speech. Grace and Ian waved goodbye and Grace led the way back to the verandah where she flopped into a new canvas chair, looking sulky.

'That was very pleasant,' Ian said tentatively. At least the ordeal was behind him.

'I thought I'd die with shame over Beda.'

'Why? What did he do?'

'Didn't you see the way he stacked plates, like in a cheap cafe? And the way he passed the pineapple flan on the wrong side to Mrs Gordon and Mrs Farrell?'

'Did he?'

'And he looks so disgusting. Mrs Gordon's houseboy wears a hat, you know, one of those Arab things, and a white jacket. Beda looked as if he'd slept in his clothes, not even clean, and he keeps grinning at one's guests as if they were *his* friends.'

The whine was razor sharp. Ian's heart sank. Beda had worked here for almost fifteen years. Beda's great quality was cheerfulness.

'You could buy him a tarboosh and a jacket,' Ian said.

'He'll never learn. He's got bad habits, he's sloppy and lazy and that grin is just plain cheeky.'

Ian surprised himself by a life-saving idea. 'Why don't you get another houseboy, for serving at table? With two of us and the house so new and everything, we really need an extra servant. Beda can go on with the cleaning and you find someone to train for parties.'

'They're backward apes, these upcountry natives. Perhaps I could find a boy in Nairobi.'

So Beda was safe and the first of a series of houseboys, with red tarboosh and white jacket, entered the Paynters' lives. They came and went, not pleasing Grace, but changing the atmosphere of the home.

They quarreled with either Beda or Mwangi, they upset the fixed routine by which Africans do their work and which makes their work bearable. Beda's grin disappeared.

All the Sunday luncheons were the same; Grace talked and everyone left promptly after coffee. In return for hospitality, they were asked to other people's Sunday luncheons though these were smaller affairs, just themsleves and their hosts, with the hostess saying she'd not been able to lay hands on a soul, people were at the coast or fretting over farm problems or playing polo or off on safari or ill. Gradually no one was free to come to Fairview Farm on Sundays; nor were there invitations to leave Fairview Farm.

Ian felt this creeping ostracism as an absence of pain. It was disloyal to be embarrassed by your wife. He was ashamed of Grace and for her, and ashamed to be ashamed. He couldn't understand the change that had come over her, from the contented friend before marriage to this restless garrulous woman. Driving around the farm, Ian no longer stopped to look with a lifted heart at the shape and sweep of the land. He was curt with the *watu*, grown nervy from life with Grace and his failure to understand her. More and more, Ian remembered his mother and father, their smiling affection, their gaiety together, an unspoken tenderness that spread around them and made their home serene. His mother had been a beautiful Aylesbury girl.

Grace saw the melting away of invitations as proof of jealousy and her triumph. The Paynter farm was the most successful, the Paynter house the most elegant: the neighbors were green with envy. She didn't like them anyway, she had only wanted to exhibit her surroundings and herself as Memsaab.

Grace now turned her attention to the garden. People talked about Helen Gordon's garden as if gardening were some sort of art but Grace believed Helen Gordon had fooled them from pure vanity, it was her way of showing off. All you had to do was tell the gardener what you wanted. Grace set out to reform the borders around the house, the vines on the walls, and the pots and hanging baskets on the verandah. Ian left before Grace got up in the morning, returned for a quick breakfast and a quick lunch, come back at dark, and resolutely ignored signs of destruction. One day he arrived for lunch and saw the rose beds dug up. Sun poured down on the exposed roots. The roses looked like a massacre.

Holding himself very still, Ian said, 'What are you doing, Grace?'

'They're too silly planted out like that,' Grace said. 'Like a public park. I'm going to move them into the borders.'

'You should have asked me.'

'Now, Ian,' Grace said, her voice raising to its steeliest whine. 'I wish you wouldn't interfere. I don't tell you how to manage the cows.'

'They will die,' Ian said.

'Nonsense.'

Ian did not wait to hear more. He drove the Land Rover recklessly, jarring along the roads with dust like a comet's tail behind. He had no idea where he was going, he wasn't thinking, he saw nothing except the uprooted roses. He waked from this vision when he found he was in Nakuru, running out of petrol. With the tank filled, Ian sat in the car until the African attendant asked him to move, another Bwana was waiting. He didn't know what he wanted, except to be away from Grace. South of Nakuru, the great lake offered sanctuary. He drove as far as the narrowing track allowed and left the Land Rover. On foot, in silence, Africa was given back to him.

Through the fever trees, he saw grazing zebra and tommy. A tiny dikdik leapt away almost under his feet. Above him, a tribe of vervet monkeys rollicked. Walking carefully, he came to the lake edge but his presence disturbed a legion of flamingos who rose, like a pink scarf thrown against the sky, and settled to feed farther along the shore. He sat cross-legged and still, watching ibis and egret and heron and hearing the lovely babble of birds. Where the land curved into the flat water to the north, giraffes were nibbling at the tops of acacias.

The land around the lake was not as beautiful as his land, too enclosed in rocky jagged hillsides. But it enclosed wonders, flashes of color in the trees, tits and starlings and hoopoes and sunbirds, the pink fields of flamingos, a sudden glimpse of curved horns and the sheen of impala. He hadn't lost the capacity for joy, because he felt it now as a sense of thanksgiving. If only he could stay forever, cross-legged and marveling, at the edge of Lake Nakuru.

He hardly remembered his mother's face; she had blue eyes and smooth hair, a gentle mirage, not a face. But he remembered her voice and it sounded like music in his mind, always low, soft, loving. His mother and roses. The roses he had planted and grown and cherished. His mother and his roses. After eight months of marriage, Ian knew he had made a fatal mistake and was imprisoned in it. Of his own accord, like a man doomed, he had destroyed his freedom and built his private Oflag. He thought of himself with despair. He was a misfit and a failure. But Fairview Farm was not a failure. He had a purpose in life, quite apart from the catastrophe of his marriage. For the sake of his farm, he would protect himself in the old known way. He would detach himself from Grace as he had learned to detach himself from Oflag XV B.

Grace was waiting, with anxiety under her anger.

'What on earth is the matter with you, Ian?' But already he had started to be deaf to that voice. 'Behaving like a baby in a tantrum! I never heard of such nonsense! What do you suppose the servants think? The Bwana rushing out of the house without luncheon. Coming back late for dinner. All because of a few roses. I won't stand for such behavior!'

Ian ate without speaking. Grace's complaints and arguments beat against his silence and ceased. She was afraid now though she could not name her fear. Divorce? On what grounds? Rose beds? It was laughable, it was ridiculous. If Ian wanted to sulk, she would show him who could sulk longer. Her mouth narrowed; she tossed her head; her spectacles flashed in the light of the pressure lamp hanging above the table. Ian ignored these signs of temper; he was thinking methodically of a better way to sterilize his ten gallon churns.

Grace soon decided the gardener was a moron. She told him what to do, using Beda as interpreter, and he made a complete mess. The wretched flowers wilted and died or looked even scruffier in their new arrangement. She lost interest before she had time to tamper with the vines on the house or the flowering shrubs or finish the borders. Half the borders remained as Ian had planted them; half, with bald patches, showed Grace's intervention. The gardener went on with the watering and mowed the grass. Whatever Grace had not killed survived as before. There were no more roses.

The Mau Mau Rebellion, the Emergency, which caused such horror throughout Kenya, proved a blessing to the Paynters.

Grace had never let a day pass without stating, in detail, how Africans got on her nerves. Now irritation turned into terror. The Africans were mad, were monsters, they were murdering Europeans like savages, cutting off heads, hands, one dared not think of it. She demanded police dogs to guard the house at night. Ian refused. Alsatians had patrolled the high barbed wire fences of Oflag XV B. Grace whined and whined, beside herself with fear. Ian was out of his mind, she kept saying, they could be killed in their beds; they must have bars on the windows. She could have bars on the windows of her room; Ian would not allow any other windows to be barred, none that he saw. And there were no weapons, Grace shrilled, did he want her to be hacked to pieces?

'You can take the shotgun to your room at night.'

'I don't know how to use it,' Grace wailed.

'You don't have to know. Just raise it and pull the trigger. Deadly at close range. Be careful you don't fire it by mistake at Beda when he's bringing your morning tea.'

Grace wept. She was supremely ugly when she wept.

Ian said, 'Grace, go to Nairobi, for God's sake. Stay in a hotel with a lot of other people. There's no danger there, none here really, but you can't go on like this. Stay in Nairobi until it quiets down.'

'What about the book-keeping?' Grace said.

Ian laughed then, merrily, showing all his false teeth.

Grace found a gem of a hotel, the Dorset, the nearest thing to a Bayswater Residential. Altogether charming, she wrote Ian, such an attractive room with ornamental iron grille work on the windows, and two comfy chairs and a small table if she wanted to take tea by herself, and a very pretty color scheme, cherry pink and baby blue and a bit of mauve. The permanent guests were delightful, well bred, mostly retired or civil servants. They sat at their own tables in the spotless dining room and were served by trained respectful servants, but talked to each other cosily from table to table.

She had met an angelic older woman, Mrs Milbank, widow of one of the top men in Mackenzie King, and a Miss Greene who was Secretary at the hospital and a Miss Ball who worked in a government office; they made a bridge four. She had taken up needlepoint and was stitching away on darling patterns for footstools at Fairview. The shops were lovely, all the little things one needed, and a tiny bookstore with a lending library, the latest novels from England. Sometimes she went with Mrs Milbank to the pictures in the afternoon though she wouldn't budge at night but the hotel was very gay and lively, always someone to talk or to play cards with. She hoped Ian wasn't too lonely and advised him to be careful.

Ian was not careful. If his *watu* went crazy and decided to slit his throat, then they would. He saw no reason for them to do so and certainly wasn't going to take precautions. He hated the whole thing, he wanted no part of it and he wasn't on anybody's side except the victims. After there had been enough killing all round, enough Oflags for Africans, enough general misery and waste and ruin, the British politicians would give the African politicians whatever they asked for; it worked like that every time. He detested the lot of them but since he could do nothing to save this beautiful country he meant to withdraw and save Fairview.

When a young British officer from the Kenya Police Reserve came to Fairview for a routine check on African staff, Ian went to meet him before he could get out of his car. Ian said stiffly, 'There are no Kikuyu on this farm. I vouch for the others. They've worked here for years, they're family men, not lunatics. My herders and I are all over the place all the time, we'd know if any strangers moved in. Besides this isn't Mau Mau territory. We won't have any trouble at Fairview and the best way to see that the work goes on sensibly is to leave us alone.'

He didn't offer a drink or future hospitality, like all the other farmers who welcomed their compatriots and their protection. The young officer, much put out by Ian's manner, made inquiries and learned that Ian was known locally as an odd fellow and a hermit by choice. No doubt, the young officer said, he'll be more cordial if the Mau Mau attack him, more cordial or dead.

Ian's *watu* were terrified by the news that flowed over the bush telegraph. Mau Mau murder victims were mostly African; European soldiers took Africans away and locked them in camps for no reason; there were rumors of torture. They knew Ian had protected them. Ian thought he was probably being foolish but it seemed as if the *watu* were now at last as fond of him as they had been of Luke.

In Karula on Fridays, Ian listened with sorrow to his neighbors telling each other horror stories. Simon Farrell had shipped his wife and daughter home to England. The Ethridges barricaded themselves at night in the style Grace had wanted. Helen Gordon said she wasn't going to abandon her garden just because some insane Kikuyus were drinking blood and swearing oaths. All carried handguns in their cars and slept with them at their bedsides. The farmers pointed out that war was straightforward, why didn't the bastards fight honestly, this way was indecent, you didn't know who the enemy was or where, any African could be a killer. Even your own servants after all you'd done for them. Obviously no one was happy.

Except Ian. Since Grace had gone he was happy again, a free man. He ordered Luke's furniture to be brought from the workshop and Grace's twiddly junk stored there instead. The house felt like its old self, happy too. Beda and Mwangi sang and gossiped at their work. Fairview was all right; Fairview had declared a separate peace.

Beda and Mwangi were as shocked as Ian when Grace returned suddenly after three months' absence, calling, 'Ian, come here, look what I've got.'

That voice again, spoiling the pleasure of his midday beer. He walked sadly to the kitchen door.

'I knew you wouldn't mind,' Grace said. 'Morrie was on his last legs.'

A new blue Volkswagen shone through recent dust.

'I left Nairobi practically at dawn and drove like the wind,' Grace said. 'It's safe if you go fast on the roads in daylight. I can only stay two hours, I must get back before dark. But you never answer my questions and I know how careless you are about business. I decided I had to come and make sure everything is in order.'

Ian brightened at the news of her departure but nerved himself for a scene when Grace saw the house. To his astonishment she said, 'Quite right, Ian. No sense using my good things when I'm not here.'

Ian hurried to the farm office to collect the papers and ledgers Grace wanted. She ate a snack lunch at her desk, having no time for talk.

'You've done splendidly, Ian, to keep things going in these dreadful times. But you are careless about money. Have everything ready for me, I'll pop in once a month and go over the books and take the chits back to Nairobi and send out the bills from there. Really, you needn't bother with the accounts. I can manage easily.'

Ian scarcely had a chance to speak before Grace whisked off in her blue car. He could bear a few hours once a month, especially since Grace would be too busy to trouble with him or the house.

On these blessedly brief visits, Ian began to notice that Nairobi agreed with Grace. He had the vague impression that she looked better and was more amiable. Grace saw herself, with ravishment, as a new woman. Mrs Milbank was responsible. Mrs Milbank's hairdresser cut Grace's shapeless crinkly hair short and dyed it so that it resembled a cap of some unknown auburn fur. Mabel, the beautician, prescribed a peach-toned foundation, a touch of rouge, blending powder, and showed Grace how to draw an outline around her narrow lips with a red crayon and fill in a wider softer mouth. Mabel said specs were no reason for a girl not to make the best of her eyes. Grace became adept with mascara and eye shadow. Mrs Milbank and Mabel together had the real brain wave: specs with pale blue tinted lenses so Grace would seem to be wearing stylish sunglasses. Finally, Mrs Milbank led Grace to a lingerie shop where Grace was introduced to the wonders of modern technology, a padded brassière.

New clothes completed the transformation. Feminine, floating, fragile, all shades of peach as advised by Mrs Milbank. 'Peach is your color, dear,' Mrs Milbank said. 'You haven't done yourself justice. I can see you've been too busy taking care of your husband but an attractive woman should never neglect herself.'

Grace did nothing to correct the assumptions of her darling friends at the Dorset. Somehow the idea had grown that Grace's was a wartime marriage to a man rather older who'd been turned into a neurotic recluse by his dreadful experiences in a German prison camp. Grace was the ideal of a devoted wife and of course her husband adored her, but still life must have been hard for her all those years alone on an upcountry farm. It was a joy to see the dear girl bloom before their eyes, so sweet in her manner, the youngest resident and everyone's pet. The older gentlemen were in the habit of saying, 'How's our pretty Mrs Paynter tonight?' The slightly less old gentlemen were more reserved in their gallantry but Grace sensed their admiration. Her middle-aged lady-friends were charmed by Grace's thoughtful little gifts and her deference and her pleasure in their company. At the Dorset, the whine almost vanished from Grace's voice.

Grace had waited in vain for Ian to speak of her appearance. Her pilot would have told her he had to fall in love all over again with a bewitching new woman. Her pilot would have noticed each small detail, from the pearls in her ears to the high-heeled sandals, and kissed her saying she looked her true irresistible self. Ian was blind, deaf and dumb. She burned with anger against the cold unnatural man who cared for nothing and noticed nothing except his farm. Her lifelong belief that a wedding ring guaranteed happiness had been crushed by Ian in less than two years of marriage. He could never make any woman happy. His wedding ring only guaranteed release from genteel poverty and rasping work but Fairview was as dull as any boarding school. Now, for the first time, she knew what happiness meant. She had everything she'd always wanted: this chic pretty person in the mirror, this delicious city life surrounded by doting friends, and the status of a married woman. Yet how much better to be a widow, all the advantages without the fearful drawback of Ian and Fairview looming ahead.

Partly because he knew all the *totos* and partly because he had to account for any new face or new absence, Ian spotted the little grayish, big-eyed creature at once.

'Ndola,' Ian said, 'where did you get this baby suddenly?'

Ndola was an old man in his fifties who cleaned the dairy; his wife Sita was an old woman with breasts like leather saddle bags.

'It is the child of my daughter. The one who works in the house of Asians in Kericho.'

'She looks sick,' Ian said.

'Yes.' And if she died, Ndola thought, it would be as well. His daughter would never bring in bride money; she was sixteen and any man could have her. This would not be the last child dumped on him. If a child came, you fed it. A sick child died.

Ian studied this wizened infant who did not cry, whose face looked strangely and pitifully wise, and said, 'Tomorrow morning I will take your wife and the baby to Karula to the doctor.'

Dr Parkinson was the Europeans' doctor, a kind bumbling man who grew show dahlias and loved bridge and felt that people either survived Africa or didn't. He held out little hope for this speck of black humanity. The child seemed to have been semi-starved from birth. Ndola's wife had no information about the first three months of the baby Zena's life but imagined that her whorish lazy daughter had not bothered to feed the child and brought it to Fairview when she saw it was going to die. It was not good to be near a death; someone might talk lies and the police would say you killed the baby yourself. Dr Parkinson doubted whether Ndola's wife would take the trouble to mix a formula but gave Ian the ingredients and the instructions.

Driving back to Fairview with the baby so bravely silent on Sita's lap, Ian came to a decision.

'Sita, you know the house for the man with the hat?' The imported houseboy, gussied up in tarboosh and white jacket, was a joke to the *watu*. The last of these passing servants had long since left Fairview but the rondavel, built for him, remained empty alongside the two small rondavels used by Beda and Mwangi. These round huts with their pointed thatch roofs stood forty yards behind the main house, screened out by a high cypress hedge.

'Yes, Bwana.'

'I want you and Ndola and the baby to move into that house. Ndola can weed the lawn, he will be a gardener. You will take care of the baby and I will see you every day when I finish my work.'

Ian was determined that this child should live. Perhaps because he was revolted by all the needless dying in the country. Perhaps from some sort of pride; the children on his farm did not die, they flourished like everything else growing here. In his kitchen Ian showed Mwangi and Beda and Sita how to prepare the first bottle. Now they had seen what they must do; no one was to forget; their most important job was to feed the baby Zena as the Daktari ordered. He would punish negligence.

Grace never knew that the unused servant's rondavel now housed a couple of old African farm laborers and a baby slowly fattening. Ian had been perfectly understood when he told Beda it was better not to worry the Memsaab with the problem of the sick child. Dr Parkinson watched the baby's recovery with interest. He wondered why Ian was so involved with little Zena but it wasn't his business and he did not gossip about his patients. The baby was nine months old when he tickled it professionally and it waved its now plump legs and arms and laughed. Dr Parkinson and Ian laughed too.

'We're a pair of sentimental fools,' Dr Parkinson said. 'She's all right now, old boy. No need to bring her in unless something goes wrong.

Cod liver oil. Takes care of everything. We'd die flat out if we had half the things Africans have. Very tough people. The old woman can look after the child. You've done your bit.'

The *watu* were mystified by the Bwana's concern for the baby Zena. The women had seen Sita's daughter arrive one morning on the farm lorry when it returned from Karula station. The driver had a busy arm around her; he stopped to let her off at the African lines before parking the lorry at the workshop. The next morning he took her back to Karula. They remembered that girl, she'd been a whore from the age of thirteen. They also remembered that Bwana Soft Voice had never spent a night away from Fairview nor traveled further than Nakuru or nearby cattle sales. He could not have flown on wings to Kericho to find the slut girl and make the baby. They talked and talked and finally concluded that Zena was like Bwana Looki's big brown dog with the squashed face, in the old days; Zena was Bwana Soft Voice's pet. Nobody wanted the child so she was lucky that Bwana Soft Voice had his peculiar notions.

Every morning after breakfast and every evening when the dairy was cleared and his office locked, Ian visited the rondavel behind his house. Zena knew his voice. The large solemn eyes watched until he came close; the delicate little hand curled around his forefinger; the baby smiled. You're better than roses, you are, Ian thought and then thought he really must be round the bend, what in hell did he mean by such an idea? Zena was fifteen months old when the Emergency officially ended.

Grace put off her return, writing that she was obliged to stay on a few weeks in Nairobi to see the dentist. Ian quickly wrote back, urging her not to hurry home. For two years and four months, they had enjoyed an ideal married life, apart. Neither of them considered the obvious solution. Had anyone suggested separation to Grace, she would have rejected the thought with fury. People would say Ian threw her out, she was a failure as a wife. Separation was as shameful as divorce. And she would have died rather than admit to her Dorset friends that Ian was not at all the worshipping husband they imagined.

Ian's view was simple. He married Grace of his own free will. She gave him no just cause to break a contract. It would be unfair and dishonorable to deprive her of a home. If Grace had a family the situation might be different, but she had nowhere to go. He told himself to buck up, grin and bear it, and it wasn't so bad. He felt at home with himself so it didn't matter how he felt with Grace.

Grace could no longer spoil his delight in his farm and his life. From the moment he watched the sun lift over the rim of the mountains to the moment he stood on the verandah in the cold night air for a last look at the stars, he was conscious of happiness. Too much time had been lost during the bloody Emergency; again George Stevens' workmen were imported to construct a second dairy, overhead piping, all the dreams Grace had listened to with concealed boredom long ago. More rondavels were built for more farm laborers, Kipsigis recruited by Simuni so that peace would reign among the *watu* and hopefully he would not be hiring drones. The men cleared arable land while he hurried to cattle sales, in search of grade stock for an increased herd. This intense growth of Fairview was joyful in itself but he had an extra private miraculous joy in Zena.

Zena had arrived wrapped in a scrap of dirty blanket. She was then wrapped in bathtowels from the house until Ian caught on to the idea of clothing. He drove to Nakuru and found a shop where he asked for all the clothing a baby would need, at various stages, until it was two years old. He came back with a small mountain of infant wear, a chest of drawers, a crib and a plastic tub. On a later trip he bought floor matting and an iron stove for Ndola's hut. These luxuries, unknown in any rondavel, were due to his fear of Zena catching cold in the wet season. Every Friday, he brought gifts from Karula for Zena. Every evening, he played with the tiny girl like a kitten to make her laugh. Since he tickled her with kisses, she had learned to kiss him too. Ndola and Sita, silent and dry and old, observed these goings-on without comment. They lived more comfortably and had more money because Bwana Soft Voice was foolish in the head.

But there was one foolishness which so shocked Ndola that he always left the hut, even in rain, to smoke outside; no man should behave like Bwana Soft Voice. Ian thought Sita rough and slapdash over Zena's bath. He rebuked Sita, but Sita was stubborn; she had washed her own children like this and resented the unnecessary work of washing Zena every night. The baby looked miserable under Sita's hands. Ian pushed Sita away and bathed the baby himself. This was probably the happiest single act of his life. It became a nightly game, soapy splashing and baby laughter, and the perfect end of the day.

After Ian tucked Zena in and kissed her goodnight, he walked back down the drive where he had left the Land Rover out of sight of the house and drove noisily home, amused by this deception. He had not planned to keep Zena secret from Grace; there was no reason to hide her. But he realized he loved Zena too much to let Grace intrude. He could hear Grace's voice questioning, bossing, arguing, jeering. No. Zena was entirely his; their life behind the cypress hedge belonged to them alone.

. . .

Immediately upon her return, Grace had said, 'Well, it's nice to be home. I'll have this dreadful stuff moved out tomorrow and my good things brought back.'

'Leave my big chair here.'

Grace opened her mouth to say this was absurd and would ruin the looks of the room. Something in Ian's face warned her not to.

Next morning, she said, 'I do hate eating breakfast on the verandah, it's too cold. And eight thirty in the morning. It was so lovely at the Dorset, ringing for breakfast in bed whenever I woke up.'

'Why don't you fix that with Beda? I intend to eat here, I like seeing the view.'

He could hardly conceal his satisfaction over this new arrangement. Fifteen quiet minutes to bolt eggs and bacon and fifteen minutes with Zena.

That evening when Ian came home from the visit behind the cypress hedge, Grace said, 'Ian, for God's sake, where did you store my things? They're an absolute mess, dirty, spotted, you might as well have kept them in the pigsty.'

Ian, unhearing, went to take his bath and change. Alone he'd worn pyjamas and dressing gown; he sighed as he put on fresh khakis. He settled by the fire with his book and his whisky. He had become fond of Jane Austen. The evening routine was a half hour with Jane Austen and two whiskies before dinner. Grace stood in front of him, furious.

'Ian!'

He was absorbed in *Emma*. Grace snatched the book from his hands.

'Ian, how dare you treat me like this?'

'What?'

'Oh, nothing. You pay more attention to your sheep. Or the *watu*. Much more attention to the damned *watu* when you know they hate us.'

'Sorry, did you say something?'

'Yes, I did. I said my good things are completely ruined. I'll have to start again from scratch.'

'All right. You can do what you like except I won't have any new servants. Beda and Mwangi were fine through the Emergency and I don't want uproar in the house. And you are not to touch the garden. I've made it the way I like and I will look after it. And my chair stays here. Otherwise, go ahead. May I have my book, please?'

Grace, dazed by receiving instead of giving orders, changed her tactics.

'I'll need to go to Nairobi a lot, to find the right things. I hope you won't mind.'

'Not a bit. Why don't you go every week? You might keep your room at the Dorset.'

'Oh no, that won't be necessary.' She had prepared for an argument; his swift agreement alarmed her.

Ian thought this an unexpected piece of luck. Perhaps she would be away several days a week, perhaps more. And when here, he calculated that out of sixteen waking hours he only had to see Grace for two hours and see was not the same as hear. When you got down to it, he didn't actually have to see her; she would be around, that was all, not much more of a nuisance than the tasteless rubbish she'd buy.

Though Ian had been inattentive and boring enough before she went away, Grace found Ian changed and worse. He wasn't surly as he had been after the ridiculous fuss about the roses, nor nasty as he was when they quarreled over the Mau Mau. He wasn't anything; that was the point. He behaved as if she weren't there. She would be making conversation at dinner like a civilized human being and Ian would finish his meal, leave the table, go to his chair and start reading. She bought a new radio in Nairobi and played it loudly in the evenings, read the novels she brought back from the lending library, stitched at needlepoint and lived for her frequent trips to the Dorset and the lovely chats and shopping and the pictures and bridge with her darling friends.

She knew she was a good wife, a real helpmate, Ian had absolutely no cause for complaint, he ought to be wildly grateful for all her work on his accounts and letters and bills and statements, she took an enormous burden from him. And she always asked if there was anything he wanted from Nairobi and searched for hardware and spare parts in the ugly remote industrial section, tiring herself to death for him. She tended his clothes, she kept his house pretty, she couldn't think of a woman who did more for a man. But she was anxious.

Something strange had happened to Ian; he was too happy, happier than she'd ever seen him. And he was always so encouraging about her departures. Yes indeed, what a good idea to go off to Malindi when her friend Miss Ball had a holiday. If Miss Greene wouldn't go alone but was dying to drive to Tanganyika and stay in that famous hotel on the side of Kilimanjaro, of course Grace must keep her company. It's called Travelers' Rest, she'd said, and I'm afraid it's frightfully expensive. Not to worry, and since it was such a long journey why didn't she stay ten days or a fortnight. All Grace's trips to Nairobi were welcomed. Ian never asked how long she would be away. Grace took with her uneasily the memory of Ian's smile when he said goodbye.

Though Mrs Milbank was her dearest friend and an older woman, Grace could not ask advice. She longed to fling herself on Mrs Milbank's motherly bosom and weep out her grievances and her confusion. He has never given me a present, never remembered my birthday or our wedding day, never taken me for an outing not even to the cinema in Nakuru, never paid me a compliment not even now when everyone says I look so pretty and attractive, never thanked me for all I do to manage our finances, he isn't human that's all. He doesn't see me or hear me or talk to me and he goes around as if he hadn't a care in the world and he was perfectly happy and I could drop dead right in front of him and he wouldn't notice enough to get me buried. No, no, she could not breathe a word of her trouble to anyone. She had a special standing at the Dorset as a woman loved, and loved by quite a wealthy man. She wasn't going to endanger her one happiness, her position at the Dorset.

Grace's uncertainty grew, month by month, though she could find no reason for this sensation of doubt. She began to study Ian for a clue which would explain his calm separate happiness. She had wondered if he met another woman at cattle sales but gave up that suspicion because of timing; he went and he came back. He was gone on Friday mornings in Karula just as long as it took to drive to and fro and stop at the bank and post office. Though she really dreaded it, she made a few sorties around the farm, to see whether he might have left Fairview without her knowing; but Ian was always to be found in some revolting place among cows or pigs or Africans. Thinking it over she decided she'd become a ninny from nerves; the very idea of Ian and a woman was ludicrous as who should know better.

One Friday she happened to be standing by the kitchen window when Ian came home for lunch. The rear seat of the Land Rover was loaded with parcels and bundles but Ian never bought anything for himself, his clothes were embarrassing, as if he hadn't a penny to his name.

She called, 'Ian, I do hope you've got yourself some new clothes.'

Ian was surprised to see her there; normally Grace summoned Mwangi to her presence. The period of baking goodies was long past.

'No. Presents for *totos*.'

'Oh, Ian really, don't you spoil them enough, what a way to waste money.'

'The *totos* are my greatest pleasure,' Ian said flatly. 'And what I spend on them is none of your business.'

Thank God he'd had the instinct not to speak of Zena. All day, when he was at work, Zena would have been at the mercy of that voice and those prying eyes and the meanness of Grace's nature. He had no talent for lying and was proud that he had instantly said 'totos'. Grace knew he had always been fond of the totos, plural, though he felt a bit guilty now because he was merely a walking toffee shop for the totos and the presents went to Zena at dusk. He couldn't be fair and equitable, he'd never counted the totos, they seemed to be born in litters. The truth was simply that his own child came first.

Grace puzzled over those presents for the totos. No gifts for her of course but anything to please the totos. She could picture Ian playing Santa Claus with the screeching, runny-nosed, smelly African brats clambering over him. But it seemed an implausible clue. For two weeks, she spied on Ian's Friday return from Karula, peering out of his back bedroom window. The Land Rover was regularly loaded. After lunch, Ian drove towards the African lines.

'Beda,' Grace said. 'How long has the Bwana been taking presents to the totos?'

Blank-faced, Beda said, 'I do not know, Memsaab.'

That was a mistake, one should never question servants. Grace checked a month of Fridays and concluded this must be it. Though grotesque for anyone else, it would be typical of Ian, the man disgusted by women, to have a passion for children. She gnawed at this thought. She remembered her first and only visit to the African lines when she had seen Ian covered with totos, while she did her best to keep clear of those grubby grabbing hands. She hadn't considered it, she had forgotten. 'The totos are my greatest pleasure.' My God. The man couldn't start a child but craved children. What difference did it make? Let him be a joke Daddy to a hundred black totos. He couldn't divorce her because she was childless, she hadn't refused his conjugal rights, he was unable to consummate their union. This was ridiculous, there was nothing Ian could do against her. She would ignore his abominable manners, she didn't intend to lose the advantages of marriage. He wouldn't dare go into a divorce court and say ... oh no, she was getting sick from imaginings. Anxiety festered and finally led to a cautious talk with Mrs Milbank.

'If only we had children,' Grace sighed. 'We never mention it but I sense that Ian would love a son to leave the farm to.'

Mrs Milbank offered a plate of small sandwiches provided by the hotel at tea-time and filled Grace's cup. They were having a private tea and chat in Mrs Milbank's room at the Dorset, sitting on the two stiff pink brocaded chairs on either side of the little tea table. Mrs Milbank thought of Grace's flat lean body, but her own was everywhere plump, with a large bosom, large hips, and just as barren.

'My dear, I know exactly how you feel,' Mrs Milbank said. 'It was our one sorrow. Of course when I was young like you, times were different.'

'How do you mean?'

'Well, in those days, no one adopted children, it wasn't done. But now everyone seems to be doing it. My niece Marjorie, the one in Wiltshire, has three sweet adopted kiddies. It's quite usual, I understand many people adopt children even when they have their own.'

Grace looked thoughtful.

'If I weren't so old,' Mrs Milbank said, 'I'd really consider adopting a little girl now. Our Vicar has been trying to place the most adorable baby. I told him he'd have no trouble at home but out here people seem so selfish. It's quite a problem because dear Mr Braithewaite is getting on and his wife's not strong. A darling blue-eyed baby girl with blonde curls. The child was simply chucked on the Braithewaites, I don't know how, the Vicar would never betray a confidence. I imagine it's the baby of a British soldier and one of the European typist girls. We saw enough of them billing and cooing together.'

Mrs Milbank glanced at Grace who looked more thoughtful.

'It would be wonderful if you took the baby, dear. I mean you have everything, a devoted husband, a beautiful home, plenty of money. And I feel it would make all the difference to you because you must be a bit lonely out there on the farm. If you don't mind my saying so, I think it might help your husband, bring him out of himself more, give him a new interest in life. And of course a child does bind people even closer together. Besides, I know how kind-hearted you are and it would be an act of real Christian charity.'

Grace was shaken by the suddenness of this idea. Her brain clicked like an adding machine. If she had guessed right, and she knew she was right, Ian was queer about children and using the *totos* as an outlet for his paternal feelings. Everyone said men always preferred their daughters; she could see Ian wouldn't want a boy from nowhere to carry his name but a girl was another matter. Instead of rushing off to spoil a horde of dirty African kids, he could pet and cuddle a clean pretty little white girl at home. He'd have to stop acting like a deaf-mute; the house wouldn't be ominously silent with a child in it. And as angelic Mrs Milbank said, a child binds people together; Ian couldn't work up some furtive scheme to get rid of her if they were parents. This might be a heaven-sent answer, startling though it first seemed. At any rate, she had nothing to lose by taking a look.

So Mrs Milbank, who had introduced Grace to a beauty salon, now introduced Grace to motherhood. She arranged a visit to the Vicar's house and Grace was enraptured by the pretty baby. Grace had never liked the children she once taught but this was different. A cuddly sweet baby of her own, a lovely child to dress up and show off; she imagined the picture and the words: young Mrs Paynter and her beautiful little girl. The least Ian could do was agree; it was entirely his fault that she hadn't become pregnant.

Ndola's daughter, the wayward sixteen-year-old, had coupled with her Asian employer or the employer's son or any stray Asian, for Zena was half-breed. Her hair was soft brown fluff, her skin copper-colored, her large eyes almond-shaped, not African round, her nose and lips finely formed. As a cattle breeder, Ian thought it a pity that Africans and Asians were not more warmly disposed to each other. Mixing the races produced a fabulous child.

Zena was now at the golden age of two. She called her grandparents Ndola and Sita having heard no other names. She called Ian Baba. Ndola and Sita, old and tired, not unkind but not interested, did not trouble to explain that Ian was Bwana the master, not Baba the father. Zena obeyed her grandparents without question, as caretakers. They had little to say to each other, less to her; she grew up in quietness, knowing she must not get under foot and must play by herself except for the few romping morning minutes and the evening hour with Ian. She ran on fat little legs to Ian's outstretched arms, while Ndola grunted distaste for this daily foolishness of pats and kisses.

'You're a beauty, that's what you are,' Ian said.

'Bootee?'

'Baba's bootee.'

He had carried her away from the rondavels to watch the fading sunset colors. They had a pattern for their hour.

'Now tell me what you see in the sky.'

'Red, awringe, grin, blue, *peenk!*'

'Very good. Shall we read our book?'

A devotee of farm catalogs, Ian had guessed there must be catalogs for everything and became a collector of toy catalogs. Aside from the teddy bear and rag doll, the big rubber ball and train to pull on a string, bucket and spade for her small sandbox, the plastic fish and frog to join her bath, Ian gave Zena alphabet blocks, chunky wood puzzles requiring her to fit pieces to form straight lines of color, round pegs for round holes, square pegs for square holes, a big abacus with colored beads and piles of picture books. They read these together, she poring over the pictures and watching words. She knew the stories by heart as he did with less enthusiasm. He was sure Zena would have learned to read to herself by the time she was four.

His child was beautiful and brilliant and healthy. Dr Parkinson kept saying, 'Ian, you really needn't bring her in for check-ups; she's about the healthiest child I know.' But Ian seized his chance every few months when Grace was away, to make sure. Any neighbors, seeing Ian and an old African woman and a *toto* on the road or at Dr Parkinson's, would think nothing of it. They all chauffeured the *watu* on errands of charity, it was a permanent part of the job.

Zena's delightful fingers had just pushed the last abacus bead for tonight's lesson. 'Twelf!'

'You're my clever girl too, you know that?'

'Clevah gul?'

'Yes, but I reckon we better not say that too much.'

'Not too much,' Zena said solemnly.

She could say anything she liked and as often as she liked, she couldn't possibly talk too much for him. Her voice sounded like music: low, soft, loving.

The drought was the worst in years. Most of last night and most of today he had been at Dick Gale's farm with a lorry-load of his *watu*, digging wide deep firebreaks against the fire that could be seen in the dark like a frightening long red snake sliding sideways down the. mountains. He smelled smoke everywhere and dreaded just one African careless with a cigarette; the dry grass would practically explode. There was also a plague of cattle thieving on the farms in the neighborhood and one of his herders had been rushed to Gilgil hospital with a spear wound in the stomach, delivered by a fellow Masai, those rotten *morani*, adolescent alleged warriors with ochre pigtails, bloody cattle thieves. His driver brought back from Karula rumors of an outbreak of foot and mouth disease around Thomson's Falls. Trouble always came like this, in bunches, and would be survived, but he was tired and took a third drink when Grace offered it, without noticing.

Grace remembered how a third drink had served her long ago. She broached the subject timidly but warmed up as she went along. At first Ian did not listen. Then words percolated past his trained deafness: baby girl, adoption. He began to listen with care and astonishment. He thought he knew Grace through and through and knew her to be lazy, selfish, interested only in money and what it bought her, a small-minded egotist playing the role of lady of the manor. She certainly didn't yearn for sex, she'd had plenty of time to hook on to a man if that was what she wanted. He had even hoped, when he saw how she dolled herself up and painted her face, that a man lurked in the offing and would carry her away with his blessing. Could this woman have one sincere and natural need? God, what a day. This on top of all else.

'Well,' Ian said.

'She's absolutely adorable, Ian, I know you'd love her.'

Grace waited in silence, remembering with anger bordering on hatred how she had waited before for this slow stupid man to take in an idea. Again her hands trembled and her head ached. She had lost the power to command Ian, she wanted to beat him but could do nothing except wait. Without his permission, young Mrs Paynter would not have her beautiful little daughter.

Ian thought about Zena. He had a child, he didn't want another. Grace had nothing, no work, no love of the land, no company. He wondered whether being a mother would make her happier and nicer. Or would it make her more shrill and complaining? He had no right to refuse, because of Zena. Comical, he thought, Mr and Mrs Paynter with their brown and white daughters.

'We haven't much room,' Ian said. Justice be damned if an adopted child meant sharing Grace's room.

'She'd sleep with me,' Grace said eagerly. 'But I don't know where to put the ayah.'

'What's the use of an ayah? If you don't mean to look after the child yourself, why adopt her?'

'Yes, of course, Ian, you're quite right.'

'How old is she?'

'Fourteen months.'

'Well, Grace, if you take this on, it will be your show entirely. I have more on my plate than I can manage. There'll be legal things to attend to, there'll be all kinds of things. If you're sure you can cope by yourself, it's okay with me.'

'Oh Ian! I knew you'd agree. A baby will be such a lovely common interest for us.'

He also didn't want a common interest. An interest for Grace would be quite enough. He foresaw pitfalls by the dozen but was too tired to think about it.

'You know the funniest sweetest thing, Ian. Those dear old Braithewaites haven't given the baby a name. They felt it was wrong; her new parents ought to choose. They just call her Baby. She's too young to notice, naturally. I've thought of a divine name for her; Mr Braithewaite can christen her.'

'Oh?'

'Joy,' Grace said. 'Isn't it lovely?'

'Fine,' Ian said and stopped listening.

Grace was gone for a month and a half. She wrote to Ian, reporting progress. She spent most of every day at the Braithewaites, learning from the ayah how to take care of little Joy. She had seen a lawyer. She was getting adoption papers and arranging to have Joy put on her passport. She had shipped baby furniture to Karula station. She was so sorry Ian couldn't leave the farm to come to the christening party. All too soon, the blue Volkswagen appeared on the long driveway with a baby in a carry-cot lashed to the front seat. Grace unpacked, while bossing Beda on furniture placement. 'The baby's bed *there*, can't you see?' She had prettied Joy in a ruffly little dress and was ready with the child in her arms, making an adorable picture, when Ian came back for lunch.

'Give Daddy a kiss, darling,' Grace said.

The baby recoiled from the strange man and began to cry.

'There, there, my angel,' Grace said. 'It's your farm smell, Ian. I should have waited until you've had a shower.'

Ian had long since realized that Grace was lazy. She worked in short bursts of frenzy on anything that concerned her, house furnishing, farm accounts, but otherwise passed her days with novels, cosmetics, the radio, solitaire, embroidery, if possible reclining. Now her working day began at six in the morning and ended twelve hours later, though Ian often heard the baby wail and Grace moving around her room in the night. She and Joy had breakfasted before Ian returned from his early morning chores. While he ate alone on the verandah, Grace washed and dressed the baby and herself, a slow process which sounded cheerful enough judging by Grace's crooning and baby gabble and laughter. At lunch, Joy was fed in a high chair alongside Grace. Grace talked only to the baby.

'Just another spoonful for Mummy, darling. There's my good little girl.'

The baby moved her head aside, spat out food, and cried. Grace seemed intent on stuffing the child until she choked.

'Maybe she doesn't want to eat so much, Grace, maybe she doesn't need all that.'

'Since when have you become an authority on the care and feeding of infants?' Grace said, with fury.

Soon Grace announced that one-thirty was too late for Joy's lunch; she ought to eat at noon.

'Fine,' Ian said.

'I haven't time to arrange two luncheons.'

'You and Joy eat when you want to. Mwangi will warm something up for me. I can't change the hours of the farm work.'

Ian was very quiet when he came home for his lunchtime shower and his warmed-over meal; Grace and Joy were asleep. In the evenings for an hour Grace described every detail of Joy's day and went to bed at eight thirty. Ian didn't believe Grace could keep it up; he waited for torrents of regret and blame. Grace was haggard, thin as a stick, but never complained or never of Joy. Though Ian steadfastly unheard her conversation, words sifted past his defences. Joy had picked a flower and given it to her, wasn't that adorable ... Joy tipped her plate on the floor at lunch and really and truly said 'bad', wasn't it divine ... The basic words were divine and adorable.

The divine adorable baby, however, did not look well; she was pale and puffed, simply too fat, and given to colds. If Joy sneeezed, Grace foresaw bronchial pneumonia. If Joy threw up, Grace imagined cholera or appendicitis. If Joy slept restlessly sweatily, Grace knew it was the onset of polio. Grace sent Beda on his bicycle to tell Ian that Dr Parkinson must come at once.

After the third of these visits, Dr Parkinson drove to the farm office, closed the door behind him and said, 'Ian, I want to talk to you.'

'Right.'

'I have many patients and some of them are actually quite ill. It's a forty-six-mile round trip for me, to visit a child who is not ill. She is kept out of the sun because your wife has some mad idea that her skin will be ruined for life. She is overfed, and bundled up like an Eskimo. There is nothing the matter with Joy except her mother. I find it difficult to talk to your wife. I don't think I've ever seen a woman like her. You'd imagine that Joy was the first baby on earth. But I will not come here again unless you send the driver with a note of your own; then I'll know it's serious. Meantime, here's a book to give to your wife. Tell her to read it, believe it and obey it.'

He handed Ian a paperback with a colored picture of a bonny babe on the cover.

'By a fella named Spock,' Dr Parkinson said. 'American but sound. I hope he can persuade your wife to be sensible, I certainly can't.'

'It won't do any good but I'll try.'

'How's Zena?'

'Fine, better every day.'

'Quite a contrast, isn't it?'

'You bet,' Ian said fervently. They smiled at each other.

Ian hesitated for three nights. Yes, he was sorry for poor sniveling Joy but scenes with Grace were such a terrible bore. As he knew, Grace took any suggestion as an insult to her mothercraft and snarled into the attack like a she-wolf. He didn't think Grace could actually kill the child with over-care, but he ought to make an effort to get Grace off old Parkinson's back. Braced for rage, he said, 'Grace, I couldn't have learned farming without books; raising children must be something on that order. Dr Parkinson left this for you. He said it was a sort of guide book.'

Grace did not hurl the book in the fire, abuse him for interfering and flounce from the room. Perhaps she was too exhausted. What would be the end of it? Grace in the Nairobi hospital with a nervous breakdown and the baby back at the Braithewaites with an ayah? Ian resigned himself to some kind of howling crisis but instead Grace grew almost rational. Either Dr Spock or experience had convinced her that the baby was not in imminent peril of death. The playpen was moved from the sitting room to the lawn. At least Joy would be exposed to a few hours of the morning sun.

Grace lived in terror that she would mishandle the helpless beautiful baby whose existence depended on her alone. If only dearest Joy could say what she wanted and how she felt. Grace hovered over the child as always but began to trust her ability to protect the little angel. Whenever the baby said Mama, and waved her fat arms as Grace drowned her in kisses, Grace's heart turned over. That breathless melting exalted sensation was her first experience of love.

Once, mistakenly, she believed that a wedding ring would secure happiness. Again, mistakenly, she believed that the delightful Dorset was everything she craved. She might have lived and died without knowng herself defrauded of love. Through loving this tiny person she had at last found true happiness. She lost the hunger of needing for herself; she wanted whatever her child needed. She no longer suffered from the monotony and isolation of Fairview and the presence of a dull withdrawn abnormal man. Fairview was a good healthy place for her baby.

This new emotion was of a power Grace could hardly understand. At night in her room, she stood over the baby's crib with tears of gratitude running down her cheeks. She kneeled by her child and prayed God to keep Joy always safe and well.

Since her return from glamorous Nairobi after the Emergency, Grace had abandoned housekeeping. She saw no point in a futile effort to order and plan interesting meals. Mwangi was a mule and Ian did not care what he ate. The house ran itself. Presumably Mwangi told the lorry driver what to collect for the kitchen. If she had to live at the back of beyond, at least she would spare herself annoying tasks. The drive to Karula was uncomfortable and she had no desire to meet the other farm wives.

But Joy loved outings and Grace loved to show off her bewitching two-year-old daughter. The farm mechanic rigged up a sort of seat belt and several mornings each week Grace drove the child to the Karula general store to buy sweets and toys and be seen. The other farm wives, shopping list in hand, were besieged by Grace and her conversation. Yes, Joy's very advanced for her age. Yes, isn't it a pretty frock, friends in Nairobi get them for me. Yes, everyone says her eyes are exceptionally beautiful.

The wives thought Grace was batty. What did Mrs Paynter mean, appearing in Karula dressed as for a garden party with her infant done up like a chocolate box, bows all over? And how frightfully bad for the child to be stuffed with toffees and put through tricks like a poodle. 'Kiss the nice lady, darling.'

Rose Farrell and Helen Gordon fled together from one of these visitations.

'Walk with me, Helen. I have to buy plimsolls for Jenny. God knows what she does with them, she can't eat them. I think there must be a huge plimsoll racket going on at Tanamuru Girls School.'

'How's Jenny liking it?'

'Fine. Not that she'll ever be a shining light of intellect but her manners are improved. Speaking of manners, I thought our Grace had hit rock bottom at those grisly Sunday lunches but she's surpassing herself with that unforunate child.'

'She's hard to take all right. Still, she can't help being so stupid. And I really believe she adores the baby. It's something in her favor. I'm positive she never gave a hoot in hell for poor Ian.'

'The child's pretty anyway.'

'You know who's lucky?'

'Who?'

'The ugly baby of her own that Grace didn't have. She'd have been a fiend to it.'

At the age of three, Joy had already learned how to control her mother. She could always get what she wanted. She had only to cry or feign sickness or snuggle and kiss and say, 'Mummy, Mummy I love you best,' words she had picked up from Grace. Joy did not try to conquer Daddy.

She scarcely saw Ian except on Sunday afternoons when he might be reading on the verandah. Daddy was no use to her.

Daddy observed Joy's slyness with pity and irritation. Poor beast, he thought, spoiled rotten, trained from the cradle to be a pain in the arse that everyone's going to hate. Joy inherited from her unknown parents her large blue eyes, her golden curls and her neat short nose, but had acquired Grace's whining voice. Having been assured that she was delicate, Joy also acquired the habit of complaint and a petulant expression. She could not amuse herself for a minute and demanded constant attention. She was quickly bored. 'I'm tired of that game, Mummy, play a new game.' On Sunday afternoons when he might have been with his lovely unspoilt clever little girl, he had to sit around and listen to Joy, who drove him up the wall, until the late milking made an excuse to sneak behind the cypress hedge.

Karula soon palled. 'I'm tired of that old place, Mummy. I want to go to Nairobi. Please Mummy, please Mummy.' Joy knew all about Nairobi; it was full of shops with pretty dresses for pretty little girls and toys for good little girls. Grace longed to show Joy to her Dorset friends; they were the ones who would truly appreciate her treasure.

At dinner, Grace said, 'I wonder if the drive to Nairobi would be too much for Joy, too tiring?'

'I don't see why.' By some mysterious inner antenna, Ian heard Grace when she said something to benefit him.

'My dentist ought to look at her teeth.'

'Grace, you deserve a holiday, you really do. You haven't left Fairview for what? Nearly two years?' It seemed forever.

'Twenty-three months,' Grace said. 'I measure time by Joy's growing.'

'Why don't you take Joy to Nairobi for a few weeks? There must be a garden at the hotel where she could play. Other children too. And you'd have your friends in the evening.'

In Nairobi, Grace felt that her life had reached a state of ultimate perfection, happiness piled on happiness. Mrs Milbank and Miss Greene and Miss Ball and the Braithewaites were dazzled by Joy's charm and beauty. They hadn't words enough to praise Grace's gift for motherhood. And Joy adored Nairobi. Grace had taught her to fear everything on the farm, from the Africans who were dirty and smelly and nasty to the land which was full of bad things like insects and snakes and wild animals and not a nice place for a little girl to wander. Joy was not the least frightened of traffic in Nairobi, nor of strange people in the hotel. She ran about the Dorset being pretty and petted. She loved window shopping with Mummy and the session at the beauty salon, where her curls were cut and fancily arranged. But Joy did not take to the few other children who happened to be staying at the Dorset. They were rude; they said 'shut up' when she told them how to play.

'Go out in the garden with those nice children, dear.'

'No, Mummy, no, I want to play with you.'

Grace thought this divine; in any case, Joy always did what she wanted. On the way home, Grace promised that they would have a holiday in Nairobi every month. Ian dimly heard how strangers had stopped in the street to admire Joy, how the whole Dorset was enslaved by Joy, and more of the same, but came alert when Grace said, 'I very foolishly promised I'd take Joy back every month because she was so happy at the Dorset, but now I've said it I'll have to do it, won't I, Ian? One must never break a promise to a child. I've made arrangements with the hotel for a special rate; it really won't be expensive.'

'As long as you don't eat into what I need for the farm.' Anything that got Grace and Joy away from Fairview was cheap at the price, but he thought it a wise tactic to seem somewhat grudging about money. If Grace knew how he blessed her absence she might not leave so readily.

Grace had given him one valuable idea which wasn't an excess in six years of marriage: a seat belt for Zena. The farm mechanic fixed a device of canvas straps to cross Zena's thighs and chest. For a week each month, Ian could safely take Zena with him in the Land Rover on his long bumpy morning drives over the farm. He had daydreamed this endlessly but the daydream was set in future time, Zena older, and for some reason unexplained by the daydream, Grace removed from Fairview. He hadn't hoped to have such joy so soon. Zena was speechless with excitement, her eyes enormous and her eyesight, Ian discovered, an African heritage. This was another of the many mysteries about Africans, they saw farther and faster than anyone when interested, saw nothing when bored.

'Baba, *look! Horses!*' Zena's picture-book culture.

'No, zebras. See the stripes?' He had not seen them, a small herd grazing in the sun far away.

'Where are they coming from?'

'I don't know. I don't know how long they'll stay either or where they're going. They're wild animals, they're free, they go where they want.' Well, with limits, but ecological lore would have to wait.

'Beauty?'

'Yes indeed.'

The Land Rover lurched and bounced on the farm roads; Zena gurgled with laughter. Worth it, to Ian, if she did nothing more than laugh. She had so little chance for laughter, growing up with the silent old people; that always worried him.

'Baba *look!* What is it?'

'Baboons. You see the baby baboons on the backs of their mothers?'

'Wild animals?'

'Yes.'

'Nice. Funny. Not beauty?'

'No, not beautiful but I love to see them. If we're lucky we'll see some wild animals every day. If there were no fences they'd be roaming all over the farm. I must have fences for the cattle though I wish I didn't. But the whole farm isn't fenced and anyway they get past the fences. This is what I love most, every day, if I can see wild animals here.'

'I love most too.'

Zena saw them all, when they were there to see, and saw them first. Ostriches running like mad dowagers along the fences, eagles sitting on fence posts, tommy leaping away from the noise of the Land Rover; distant giraffe. One morning she spotted elephants, the great travelers, moving slowly among the trees near Luke's burial ground. He stopped the Land Rover to gaze at those wonderful beasts.

'They're not afraid of anything,' Ian said. 'Except men. They are good and kind to each other and very clever.'

'Why are they afraid of men?'

'Because men shoot them. Can you see their heads?' Maybe she could; he saw only their enormous grey shapes.

'Yes, they have big teeth on the side.'

'Tusks, baby. They're made of ivory and ivory is worth a lot of money, so men shoot them.'

'You, Baba?' She was clearly distressed.

'No, never.' Not that the *watu*, who feared the *tembo*, didn't beg him to call the game warden and have them shot. He'd let them knock down anything on the farm rather than harm them.

'It's a *very* fine day if we see elephants, Zena. It doesn't happen often.'

The *watu* grew used to the small brown girl in the Land Rover with the Bwana. Bwana Looki, in the old days, took his big brown dog everywhere with him. Zena was accompanying him in his work and Ian explained the work as they went. Baba, does the milking machine hurt the cows when it pulls? No, not at all. What is that man doing, Baba? That man is Alhamisi and he is a mechanic, he fixes machines when they break. He is fixing the pump and by God's grace he will succeed or else I will have to get a fundi, a man who knows everything about pumps, to come from Nakuru. What does the pump do? It pushes water to many places on the farm so that we can all have water to drink, the people and the animals and the *shambas*. Nothing can live without water. Baba, does the big pig make all those *toto* pigs at the same time? Yes. How? A brief factual description of animal sex sufficed, neither of them being much interested.

The *watu* were not surprised to see Soft Voice stand by his Land Rover, holding the child's hand, while together they stared at Africa. Soft Voice was teaching Zena his religion but a new act of prayer had been added; Soft Voice lifted the child in his arms and pointed to the sky. *Mungo*, God, they told each other. Ian was showing Zena the clouds, cirrus and cumulus, sharing his wonder in the African sky. He was giving her all he had, his world, and knew it was a great deal for a four-year-old to understand, but month after month Zena learned with intelligence and love, as taught.

Zena had always been a smiling child and Ian could not doubt her happiness and still he worried. His little girl was growing up in isolation; children needed other children. Without much hope, he told Sita to walk the mile to the African lines where she could chatter with the other women and Zena play with the *totos*. Zena returned in tears, she didn't understand the *totos'* games, they pointed and stared and shouted at her. She was of course a foreigner, she wasn't their color, she lived a separate different life. Sita complained that her legs ached and it was *bure* anyway.

'I play with Bobby and Betty,' Zena said.

Ian loathed Bobby and Betty, golden-haired twins, hero figures of the first book Zena had read to herself. In his opinion, a more miserable pair of anaemic prigs had never existed but they were engraved on Zena's heart, her imaginary friends. She spent her days with them, she talked to them and about them; Ian was kept abreast of their activities and had to admit that they became less dismal as they developed in Zena's imagination. With love and the best intentions, he had put his child into a sort of prison. He seemed to have a special talent for prisons. Zena's extended back from the cypress hedge through a long stretch of *leleshwa* and lion grass to the fence at the public road. He made it as amusing as he could, with a swing and a pet lamb, which Zena named Mary, and toys and books, but he raged that he could only take Zena out on parole, by Grace's tacit permission.

When Grace began one of her devious conversations, Ian realized she was about to do him a tremendous favor. Living at this altitude all year round was bad for a child, Grace said, Joy ought to go to the coast for her health. Ian gave his usual falsely grudging consent. That was the first of the journeys to Malindi and lasted two weeks but, as Grace pointed out, she couldn't break her permanent promise of a week in

Nairobi. Malindi, Nyali, Bamburi; all for Joy's health. Soon Grace said that Joy ought to see the sights of East Africa as part of her education; it was absurd for the child to miss Kilimanjaro which was world famous, a splendidly long holiday at Travelers' Rest, and Mount Kenya, another long holiday in Nyeri with Miss Ball who was interested in the tree ferns, and Treetops, once visited by the Queen. Cannily, Ian said that Joy looked much healthier after the trips to the coast, having judged that this was what Grace and Joy liked best. By skilful manoeuvring, he could get them off the farm for two sure months in the winter and for joint vacations with the Dorset clique and the guaranteed week in Nairobi at the least.

Ian left supervision of the late milking to Simuni, giving himself afternoon hours with Zena as well as the morning Land Rover rides. Always proficient in the use of catalogs, Ian had found a correspondence school course for home teaching by parents stranded in outposts of civilization. They studied together. Unless he was making a muck of the grading system Zena was far ahead of her years. Since Grace did after all come home as a shackle on his freedom, Zena learned to prepare her lessons alone because Baba could not always spend so much time helping her. She didn't mind solitary homework, having Bobby and Betty for fellow pupils. Ian wished he had never given Zena that book, she should have started by reading the adventures of young devils instead of the mealy-mouthed inanities of the bloodless twins. He was stuck with Bobby and Betty and it would be cruel to criticize the child's only friends. But his little girl was too gentle, too docile, too quiet; she needed real lively children. In the back of his mind lay the dread that he was turning Zena into a misfit like himself, unable through lack of experience to join in the normal life of ordinary people.

When Grace and Joy were taking their long holiday at the coast, he could have brought Zena to live with him in the house. Ian thought of this with a yearning like hunger pains but decided that shuffling Zena back and forth from a European house to an African rondavel would badly dislocate the child. And besides, no: except for his old chair, the house was Grace's, tasteless and tainted by Grace. Considering the impression made on Zena by gruesome Bobby and Betty, it would be a major mistake if she got the notion that this house was the way a house should look. Everything on his farm was right and good for nourishing Zena's mind, but not Grace's house.

He was forced to deny himself a real life with Zena while Grace and Joy lived as they chose, returning to Fairview only because Daddy meant money and keeping up the pretence of a happy home. He was paying with pain for the inconceivable error of his marriage but Zena was paying too, unfairly, wickedly, though the child didn't yet know it. He would never be free of Grace and Joy for the simple reason that no one else would ever want them. Zena was the loser which he could not bear. He got drunk one night, mixing bitterness with whisky, and flailed around Grace's sitting room, kicking twee tables and hurling fringed sofa cushions at china ornaments, shouting 'Till death us do part', and ended the night in tears to wake with a grueling hangover and Zena still alone behind the cypress hedge.

Joy was equally isolated though neither she nor Grace noticed this. They lived in flawless harmony based on Joy getting what she wanted and Grace's adoring subservience. While Zena learned how to manage a farm, Joy learned how to manage hotels and the adults in them. Ian thought Joy was a hellish child, Grace's perfect product, but there was hope in the future because Grace would send Joy to boarding school, driven by snobbery to copy the local ladies. The girls at boarding school would either whip Joy into shape or murder her. For Zena there was no future like that, nothing to save her from an unnatural childhood.

Obviously, Joy and Zena should have been playing with each other since infancy, the reasonable solution for both children. He didn't see how he could have engineered it, knowing Grace's sentiments about all skin that wasn't one hundred per cent white. Grace might have softened after eleven years in Kenya, might even be secretly concerned over Joy's loneliness and surely Joy, born here, couldn't be a confirmed racist by the age of seven. More and more troubled by Zena's solitude, Ian invented and discarded and invented fresh schemes for bringing the little girls together. Away from Grace, Joy must have some human childish instincts, he couldn't utterly condemn a seven-year-old, and Zena would improve her.

This wavering idea was killed dead by Joy, lately returned from a grand hotel near Mombasa and accustomed to grand hotel service. Joy's presence at the dinner table was a recent hardship, a wretched half hour when Joy showed off her clothes and her grown-up manners. Beda was by no means the sort of servant Grace and Joy approved, but it was not his fault that Joy suddenly flung out her arm, to exhibit new silver bangles, and knocked a bowl of fruit salad from his hands. The bowl crashed to the table, spilling half its juicy contents on Joy's lap. She sprang up, shaking her dress, shouting. 'Look what you've done, *you stupid black baboon!*'

Beda stood as though frozen. Grace made angry clucking sounds and hurried to wipe Joy's dress.

Ian said, 'Apologize to Beda, Joy.'

Grace and Joy stopped their annoyed cleaning operation and stared at Ian.

'You heard me, Joy. Apologize to Beda.'

'Mummy!' Joy wailed; tears spurted from her eyes. Grace put a protective arm around her angel.

'How dare you, Ian? How dare you speak to the child like that? Of course she won't apologize. It's one of her best dresses.'

'Joy,' Ian said, his voice even and icy. 'Apologize to Beda.'

Joy was now wailing loudly, her face hidden against Grace's skirt.

'*Ian!* I will not tolerate such behavior. *You* apologize to Joy!'

'She will either apologize to Beda or go to her room and stay there until she does so,' Ian said, his voice unchanged.

'Darling, go to your room now, you wouldn't want to stay with your dress all wet and sticky. Mummy will be along in a minute.'

'Beda,' Ian said. 'I apologize for Joy and Joy will apologize later. We won't need anything more.'

Beda, still frozen, closed the kitchen door carefully behind him.

'Now, Ian,' Grace began, her eyes fiery, her voice a drilling whine. Ian got up from the table.

'You are never to speak to the child like that, do you hear me, Ian? And she's certainly not going to apologize to a clumsy stupid servant.'

'Joy will not leave her room until she can lower herself to an apology. Otherwise you can both leave the house. You're perfectly free to go at any time.'

He sat in his chair by the fire, seemingly undisturbed, seemingly deep in *The French Revolution*, and mocked himself for a fool, a real fool, a dangerous fool. In his idiot folly, he might have suggested that Zena play with that sickening child. There was no hope for Joy, deformed for good, and he didn't care. No doubt she and Grace would find plenty of company to their taste. But there was also no hope for Zena; she'd have to go on playing happily with Bobby and Betty, the little ghosts who proved that his child belonged nowhere.

'It's the Socialists!' Grace cried. 'Naturally they don't mind what happens to people like us! The Africans will take their pangas and murder us all!'

Grace had returned from Nairobi, hysterical with Dorset prophecies. The British Government had promised Kenya Independence next year. Whites would be ruled by blacks, as if blacks could manage the water works, the post, the trains, the electricity; name anything you could think of and imagine the hopeless botch they'd make. Quite aside from killing whites whenever they liked, and whites having to call them Bwana.

'You must sell the farm!' Grace shrilled. 'Ian, you *must*. We have to get out while we can. The Ethridges are moving to South Africa, you know that, don't you? I hear the Farrells are going back to England. People in Nairobi and Mombasa and everywhere upcountry are selling out while there's still time. None of us will be safe. It's too dangerous, it's terrible, life won't be possible here, I can't risk Joy.'

'Rubbish,' Ian said, turning a page of the *Kenya Weekly News*. The tone of Grace's voice, her wild eyes reminded him of the maddening early days of the Mau Mau rebellion. He didn't think he could bear this nagging idiocy a second time.

'I insist,' Grace said. 'I absolutely insist.'

'I don't give a damn who rules this country, I don't give a damn what happens to the water works or the mail or the trains or anything. Worst comes to the worst, Fairview can be self-sufficient. I'm staying here, this is my place. Besides which, I don't believe for a minute that Africans will butcher whites. No reason for it, once they've got what they want. I don't mind calling them Bwana. Why not?'

'You don't care what happens to Joy and me! And you haven't any pride, you'd lick the Africans' feet if that helped Fairview. You'll get on all right, it won't make any difference to you when we're all insulted and pushed around and probably in jail if not dead. You're a nigger lover!'

Ian rose from his chair and stood tall above her, his face rigid with distaste.

'That kind of gutter language may be acceptable among your friends, but don't ever use those words in front of me again. Never, do you understand?'

Ian stalked out to the verandah. Clean fresh air. How was he going to live with this odious woman under the new regime? She would whine about African outrages day and night, her usual contempt again turning into hate and fear. He found Grace huddled by the fire in tears.

'I'm thinking of Joy,' Grace said. 'I'm afraid for Joy.'

He always ended by being sorry for Grace. He didn't forgive her, he pitied her. She was so unattractive and so wrong-headed; he always ended by thinking how awful it would be to be Grace.

'Joy will be fine. Listen, Grace, talk to Helen Gordon, not those scared Nairobi people. You'll get a different angle. And the Farrells aren't leaving because they're spooked; they're leaving because Simon inherited a house and stable from an uncle in Oxfordshire; they're horse crazy, that's all.'

'Oh, Helen Gordon,' Grace said, sniffling. 'Why does everybody act as if Helen Gordon was so special? She's ridiculous. They could shoot her husband and burn down her house and she'd stay, just as long as she could keep her garden.'

There was nothing to do about Grace except not listen. Grace now drove to Karula every afternoon, feeding her fears on rumors in the general store and at the Sports Club. At dinner, she repeated these rumors accusingly to Ian's serene deafness.

Joy was bored with her doll's house under the jacaranda tree. Before that she had been bored with the beads she strung for necklaces and with her paint-box and coloring books. Mummy had stopped taking her to Karula, she said the daily drive was too tiring. Mummy said, 'You're my darling big girl now. Play by yourself for a little while. Mummy wants to rest.' She considered waking Mummy from her nap but she was cross with Mummy.

At morning lessons Mummy said sharply, 'Pay attention, Joy, you're not trying.' Her feelings were hurt and she cried and Mummy comforted her but also said they would work again after tea. Joy hated morning lessons; they were a bore too; everything at Fairview was a bore. She had learned the word from Grace.

Joy always obeyed Mummy about staying on the lawn to play; she had no desire to explore the hidden dangerous world of the Africans. But today, from spite and idleness, she decided to creep to the cypress hedge. She could run home to safety if there were snakes and nasty people. It was Mummy's fault for leaving her alone with nothing to do. Joy tiptoed behind the house and across to the hedge. She peeked around the corner and saw a brown girl on a swing. As there were no visible snakes or horrid Africans, she came closer.

'Who are you?' Joy said.

Zena had her back turned but jumped from the swing to face a girl who looked exactly like Betty, a beautiful pink and white girl with a blue bow in her golden hair and a blue and white polka-dotted dress and white sandals. A real Betty had come to play with her. She was so excited she could only stare in admiration. Beda and Mwangi spoke of this *toto*, the Memsaab's child, but Zena had never seen her. The cypress hedge was an impassable frontier. Sita said that the Memsaab lived on the other side and would beat Zena if she caught her.

'Who are you? Can't you talk English?'

'Zena,' with a warm smile.

'How old are you?'

'Nine.'

'What are you doing here?'

'I live here.'

Joy was not smiling. Zena wore a faded, patched pink dress, too small for her, which Joy recognized.

'Where did you get my dress?'

'Beda gave it to me.'

Grace had thrown it out. Beda brought everything Grace threw away to Zena. Fortunately Zena was the smaller child.

'You can't wear my dress.'

Zena said nothing.

'Where did you get that swing?'

'Baba gave it to me.'

'Who's Baba?'

Zena did not know how to answer. Why was the beautiful white girl looking at her with angry eyes and speaking in an angry voice?

'You heard me,' Joy said. 'Answer when I talk to you. Who's Baba?'

'The Bwana,' Zena said helplessly.

Joy thought about this but couldn't decide what it meant.

'Show me your house,' Joy said. Zena led her to a rondavel and Joy started to go in but drew back. Africans were smelly and dirty, as Mummy said. From the doorway, Joy saw rough wooden shelves with toys neatly arranged on them.

'Show me your toys.'

Obediently, Zena brought her toys from the rondavel and laid them on the table outside her grandparents' hut. Inside, Sita woke and stayed silent, listening. Mwangi and Beda and Ndola had walked together to the Asian duka on the road, this was the afternoon free time.

Joy studied the surprising collection of toys which were as good as her own. She knew it was not right for an African child to have anything like hers.

'You stole them,' Joy said.

'No! Baba gave them to me.' Tears began to leak from Zena's large brown eyes.

'Baba,' Joy said mockingly. 'You stole them. I'm going to show them to my Mummy.'

Joy collected as many of the toys as she could carry, a large flaxen-haired doll, a bag of glass marbles, a big rubber ball, the prettiest things she saw, and marched off beyond the cypress hedge. She had no intention of showing them to Mummy. She hid the toys in the doll's house, and was playing there peacefully when Mummy called her for tea.

Zena sat on the ground and wept. She knew what stealing was; Sita had not neglected her basic education. The police came for *totos* who stole. Joy had taken her best beloved doll, Betty, who closed her eyes to sleep, and her jewels, and the ball she and Baba played with.

Sita came out of the hut and said, 'Stop crying.'

'Why did she say I stole my toys and take them away?'

'I don't know. She can do anything she wants.'

Joy had discovered a fascinating occupation for the empty afternoons. She waited impatiently for Mummy to finish lunch and lie down in their room. Zena wasn't like the children she met in hotels who were rude and told her to go away and wouldn't play as she wanted. Zena was better to play with than Mummy or Mummy's friends, all kinds of new games she had never tried before. If Zena did not do what she ordered, quickly, she pinched Zena who cried and obeyed. Joy was specially fond of games in which she was the Queen, meting out punishment to Zena, the villain or slave. Zena did a lot of kneeling and begging for mercy as the Queen commanded, though her head was often cut off anyway.

Zena cried at night and woke to fear the coming afternoon. Sita had no sympathy for these tears and warned Zena not to tell Baba because that would bring more trouble for everyone. Abandoned by the only people who could protect her, Zena took to hiding like a hunted animal. She crouched behind a *leleshwa* bush and fled into the tall grass as soon as Joy appeared. She expected Joy to run after her and waited shivering to be trapped. But Joy did not follow. Zena stayed silent and motionless in the thick scrub. It was hard to keep so still and she never knew when Joy might creep up and pounce on her. She didn't feel safe until Sita called, 'She's gone. Come back now.' But it would start again tomorrow, it would never end. She wept at night in despair; Baba didn't love her. If he loved her, he would save her.

For once Joy couldn't run to Mummy to get what she wanted. She dared not brave snakes and wild animals and dared not shout to Zena in case Mummy heard and found her in this forbidden territory. Zena was a pig and a black baboon and she would really punish her, not play punish, when she caught her. She couldn't think of any way to reach Zena until Sita came yawning from her hut.

From Beda and Mwangi, Sita knew how the Memsaab ruled the house and spoiled her *toto* and how the Bwana allowed this as if afraid of the Memsaab. She didn't want a dispute with the Memsaab and the chance of losing the best rondavel on the farm. Though the white *toto* broke or stole all Zena's toys, she didn't actually injure Zena and Zena would have to get used to this sooner or later; Europeans were the masters. Sita never emerged from her hut until sure that the Memsaab's *toto* had left them in peace. Today she was fooled by the quiet; instead of stamping around and muttering threats, Joy stood glaring at the wilderness that hid Zena.

Joy was well aware of her power. Sita, being African, had to obey her. She ordered Sita to fetch Zena and Sita walked slowly into the bush, looking for the unhappy child. Joy slapped Zena hard for her attempts at escape.

'You do what I tell you or my Mummy will send you away from here,' Joy said.

That would be worse than all Joy's torments; she would never see Baba again.

Grace lay on her bed in the afternoons, trying to distract herself with novels and calm herself with aspirin, while her nerves felt like taut wires and she was eaten by fears of the future. Ian's selfishness was monstrous, criminal. On her worst days, she imagined Joy stripped and flung about like a rag doll by brutal laughing Africans. After Independence, no British soldiers would protect them against the murderous Africans. Her only comfort was Joy who was so gay and bright and such a darling considerate child, unlike Ian who had no consideration for anyone. To shame Ian by showing him this difference, she said, 'I'm always astonished by Joy's thoughtfulness. A little girl of eight but *she* worries about me. Today she said, "You need your afternoon nap, Mummy, you work so hard." I wish you had a tenth of her concern. But oh no, you don't care, you'll let us stay here to be attacked. . . .' Before Ian stopped listening, he wondered vaguely what tricks Joy was up to now.

Sita, wanting no trouble, tacked an old piece of cloth over the bare toy shelves. After Joy's first looting visit, Zena hid her books under her bed so that as usual Baba and she spent their evening hour studying and reading together. Ian saw nothing strange but something was very wrong. Instead of running to meet him with laughter and kisses, Zena cowered in a corner of the hut and waited for him to hold out his arms. Zena stopped working by herself in the afternoons, she had no samples of writing and finished arithmetic lessons to show him. When he asked for her notebooks, she shook her head and would not look at him. She read in a whisper, stumbling over words she had read easily before, close to tears. He was alarmed by this change and bewildered. What had happened? The child seemed afraid. He held her on his lap, reading to her, and her slender little body was stiff as if he had become a stranger.

Ian called Sita out of the rondavel and said, 'What have you been doing to Zena? She was never like this before. Have you been beating her? Tell me the truth.'

Sita said stonily, 'Not me.'

'Ndola?'

'Not Ndola.'

Ian found a moment to question Beda and Mwangi. 'Not me,' Beda said. 'Not me,' Mwangi said. 'Then who?' Ian asked. 'Don't lie to me. I know someone is frightening Zena.' He was up against the wooden faces of Africans who are unwilling to speak. They shrugged, all of them. When he asked Zena gently, rocking her in his arms, she buried her face against his chest and wept. The child only became almost her normal happy self during their week's holiday, when Grace and Joy were in Nairobi.

Ian took Zena to Dr Parkinson, having decided Zena must be ill, parasites maybe, one of the invisible African wasting diseases. Dr Parkinson reported bruises and scratches, nothing special. Zena could have got those playing in the bush. Yes, he agreed the child seemed different, nervous, perhaps the Africans were filling her with stories of evil spirits and black magic, upsetting her that way. Ian tried a new line of questioning and again Sita, Ndola, Beda and Mwangi said 'not me' and looked at him with the same wooden faces.

The rains put an end to Joy's interesting afternoons. Mummy said she would catch cold and must stay indoors, not that she wanted to get soaked and dirtied by the mud in the servants' quarters. She missed Zena, Zena was a good playmate who did as she was told. There was nothing to do in the long dull afternoons and Mummy went to their room with a book and left her alone to be bored. Grace was reading when Joy stood by the bedroom door and said, 'I *hate* it here!'

'Now, angel, we'll be going to the coast soon.'

'I hate it here. I don't want to live here. I want children to play with.'

Grace felt this as a knife wound. She knew it had to come, but so soon, so soon? Already she was not everything to Joy as Joy was to her. Before the prospect of Independence drove out all other fears, Grace had blocked from her mind the torturing thought of boarding school and her loneliness, separated from Joy.

Joy pouted and scuffed her feet.

'There's a girl here to play with.'

'Here? You mean an African? Oh darling, what a foolish idea, you wouldn't want to play with an African.'

Joy pouted more, hung her head, twisted her body.

'Where did you see her?' Grace asked.

Joy had not expected questions. She had never been scolded but she sensed trouble.

'In back,' Joy said sullenly.

'Beda's child or Mwangi's probably. Oh no, angel, they come from horrid dirty huts on a reservation somewhere.'

The wives of Beda and Mwangi, with assorted children, drifted in for visits when they saw fit and drifted off. Grace objected to this long ago. Ian said it was the custom, and he couldn't change it, and Grace didn't have to see the visitors. She would speak to Ian about this tonight, and sharply. Up to now during the day, on her specific orders, Beda and Mwangi kept their children in the African lines where they belonged.

'Not Beda's,' Joy said.

'Then Mwangi's, darling; it's the same thing.'

'No!' Joy shouted, furious with Mummy.

'Well darling, nobody else lives out there. Now be Mummy's good little girl and forget that silly idea. We'll play a lovely game together.'

'She's Baba's child,' Joy said.

'Who's Baba?'

'The Bwana.'

Joy had an active imagination and often made up stories, using words she did not understand. The child had no notion of what she'd said, of course.

'Let's play Snap,' Grace suggested. 'You find the cards and we'll play right here, nice and snuggly on the bed.'

Joy liked Snap, which she always won, and forgot Zena.

If Joy's story was true, Ian was giving in to the Africans even before Independence. Soon they would be all over the place, squatting and spitting in her garden. The blacks weren't rulers yet and her authority must be enforced: African children were forbidden to wander near the house where they might spread their disgusting diseases to Joy. But Joy should not be brought into it. After the unforgettable and unforgivable incident with Beda, she could see Ian taking the Africans' side, saying Joy had no business behind the house, blaming and upsetting Joy not the servants. She would find out for herself before Ian came home as if Joy had not alerted her. Grace quietly set her watch an hour ahead.

'Heavens, look at the time, darling. It's such a nasty wet night, wouldn't you love a picnic in bed? With the radio and whipped cream on your cocoa and delicious lemon pie?'

Joy was devouring lemon pie, the radio at full blast, when Grace took a torch and walked through the drizzle to the cypress hedge. She saw a lighted rondavel and approached the open door. Ian was sitting on a low stool, his back leaned comfortably against the wall. From beyond the doorway Grace smelled the African stench. Ian looked at home in this squalid place, smiling and easy. He held a small brown girl on his lap, stroking her hair while she read to him. When the child stopped, Ian lifted her up, hugged her close and kissed her cheek. 'You're Baba's clever little one. That was *very* good. Better every day. Tomorrow I'm going to bring you special presents from Karula as a prize for working so well.'

Grace turned and walked silently back to the house. She stood inside the verandah door, with the torch in her hand, too shocked to think or move. Then the meaning of what she had seen poured over her; she felt as if she were on fire, burning with hate, choked, gasping for air, burning. She stumbled towards Ian's room, the gunsafe, the shotgun, you don't have to know, just raise it and pull the trigger, deadly at close range, dead, dead, before he could bring his filth into her house. The noise of the radio stopped her at Ian's door. Joy terrified, Joy alone when they took her away. Oh God, no, I'm mad, I must think. Her legs were shaking, she leaned on chairs and tables, making her way back to the sofa by the fireplace.

Zena's sickness, whatever it was, had disappeared as inexplicably as it came. Perhaps she was quieter and less ready to laugh but she wasn't a baby any more that he could tickle and bounce on his knees. He had been desperately worried, knowing his child was unhappy and unable to help because he didn't understand. But it was all right now, the best sign being that Zena studied again in the afternoons and prepared her homework to show him and was eager to learn. And soon they would be alone, with Grace and Joy at the coast; he'd have the time he needed to play with her and cheer her up. Ian walked through the kitchen, whistling, and headed for his door not noticing Grace at the far end of the sitting room.

Whistling. He came here from that, whistling. The weakness left her, she sprang to her feet, powered by hate. She wanted to tear at his face with her nails, she wanted to scream at this monster, but was obliged to whisper. The radio still blared but Joy might not be asleep and voices carried, she could not risk Joy hearing.

'You are unspeakable,' Grace hissed. Ian turned to look at her with astonishment. 'There aren't any words for you, such filth, such vileness. That's what you were doing during the Emergency. No wonder you wouldn't leave here, you were sleeping with your African whore. And you keep your half-breed bastard right behind my house, where Joy could see her, where Joy *did* see her. How dare you live under the same roof with us? I wish I could kill you. You hear me? I wish I could kill you! *You nigger-lover!*'

Ian was transfixed. He stared at this familiar plain face, distorted by hate, he listened to the voice that he also knew too well, now whispering with a fury he had never heard anywhere, and he made no sense of it. It was too sudden. He opened his bedroom door and undressed and took his bath as usual. Lying in the hot water, he untangled what Grace had said, and understood what she meant, though he couldn't imagine how she reached this crazy conclusion. He felt nothing at all; whatever Grace thought was a matter of indifference. He had actually heard Grace say that she wished she could kill him, and he believed her, and he felt nothing. She might have been complaining of the weather.

Ian returned to the sitting room in clean shirt and khakis and mixed a whisky and soda at the drinks tray. He saw no reason to discuss Grace's lunatic accusation. Grace took this cool silence as the final outrage. The revolting beast expected her to accept what he had done?

'You listen to me, Ian Paynter,' Grace whispered. 'I will get a divorce and I will take every penny you have. You can live with your whore then, like an African, just like them, in a dirty rondavel, that's all you're fit for.'

'Divorce?' Ian began, dimly, to see a miracle solution to his life. He had to speak with caution and prevent himself from smiling.

'You heard me. Everyone in the country will know about you. You won't have a shred of reputation, every decent person will despise you, you won't be the big Bwana of Fairview, you'll be an outcast, you and your black whore and your bastard.'

'For a divorce,' Ian said mildly, 'you need proof. You'll have to find the woman first and then you'll have to find witnesses who have seen me with her. Just seeing isn't enough. They have to prove I was in bed with her. Do you think you can swing that?'

'Beda and Mwangi,' Grace said with loathing. 'They'll have seen you.'

'There's no woman out there, and Beda and Mwangi have seen nothing.'

'You mean you went away from the farm? Oh it's too horrible and disgusting to talk about. I can't bear to look at you. You make me sick. Being in the same room with you makes me feel dirty, covered with slime. Anyway there's your bastard, she's out there, I saw her.'

'You have to prove she's my child, don't you? Your word against mine. You'll never find any witnesses.'

Grace felt the sweat on her forehead, she was dizzy and shivering, she swallowed back a sudden rise of bile in her throat. She was torn apart, half mad with fury and a blood lust for revenge while Ian sat in his chair sipping his drink, calm, teasing her, mocking her, and winning. Witnesses would have to be Africans, Europeans wouldn't know this abominable story; and the Africans would be on Ian's side. She'd never get a word out of any of them. And if he said his whore was not there in the servants' rondavels, then she wasn't. How could she track down that woman; she might be anywhere in Kenya.

'Besides,' Ian went on. 'A huge scandal wouldn't be frightfully jolly for you and Joy. Would it? Scandal has a way of sticking to everyone. People might even laugh at you, you know, people do strange things.'

Grace collapsed on the settee and covered her face. She couldn't believe what was happening. Right and justice and honor and decency were on her side, and everything Ian said was true. Ian wouldn't care about scandal, he didn't care what anyone thought of him, but Grace could imagine the Memsaabs gossiping at the Karula Sports Club, poor Grace, she's been living all those years with Ian's black tart at her back door. Her friends at the Dorset would be horrified and sympathetic but all the same embarrassed, a sex scandal with an African wasn't the sort of thing nice people got mixed up in. And if she couldn't get a divorce, she couldn't punish Ian, the only way to punish him was to drive him from Fairview.

'If you think I'm going to live here, if you think I'm going to let you do this to me,' Grace said, incoherent with despair and hatred.

'No, I wouldn't expect you to stay. I suggest a legal separation. Something quiet and discreet so you and Joy won't have any unpleasantness and then you and Joy might move to England. You won't like it here anyway when the Africans are in charge.'

'That's lovely for you, isn't it?' Grace sneered. 'Get me and Joy out of the way and bring your whore here. Fill the house with kinky-haired bastards. I daresay you'd give us a measly allowance so we could live in a cheap boarding house.'

'Why would I do that? You can have half the profits, a settlement properly drawn up. I imagine you two could live quite well on that, and I'll be doing the work that keeps the profits coming in.'

Beda entered from the kitchen with a soup tureen. Ian waved him away, saying, '*Bado, bado.*'

Grace got up. 'I shall never eat with you again nor spend another night under the same roof with you. I never want to see you or hear from you. You'll get a letter from my solicitor. I mean to pack now and Joy and I will leave for Nairobi in the morning. I forbid you to see Joy. You're not fit to breathe the same air. I will take only our clothes and whatever toys Joy chooses. I don't want anything to remind me of this place and you ever. And I hope you suffer all your life as you've made me suffer.'

'Well, Grace, the main thing is that Fairview shouldn't suffer. Always remember the profits.'

Her beautiful angel was fast asleep. Grace began to pack, moving quietly. Her hands trembled so that it was difficult to fold Joy's dresses. That slow stupid man, Ian Paynter, had defeated her; she couldn't ruin him; she couldn't make him pay.

Words blazed in her mind. No wonder he wouldn't touch me, white women disgust him, the pervert, the liar, he only likes black flesh, no wonder he lived back of beyond and made no friends and kept white people away, no wonder, what did he do, go to the African lines and spend the afternoon in any hut with any fat stinking black woman he fancied, years of it, years; presents for the *totos*, lies, presents for his whores, married me as a smoke-screen, used me, made a fool of me, the best years, my youth, the horrible perverted sex monster, of course he let me adopt Joy, more smoke-screen while he kept his favorite bastard at hand for him, used Joy, used *Joy*, for years, all the time from the beginning, the sneaky cunning devil, no one knew, no one guessed, I'd have lived my whole life with this filth except for Joy, Joy saved me, Joy, Joy.

She had to sit down; she was exhausted by rage and bitterness. Never again sleep in that bed, I'd vomit if I thought of what had happened there, no, no, I must be calm and careful, Joy cannot know this not ever, it's my sacred duty to protect her, she must never know anything, I'll tell her we are leaving because an old friend is very ill in England, I'll think of something, she's so young, she won't question me.

Grace pulled the chair alongside Joy's bed where she could see that angelic face. Everything she loved, pure, unspoiled, and rescued thank God from this sewer of evil. Yes, rescued. Her hands had stopped trembling. She would be able to pack the last suitcases now. That was the main thing: Joy was rescued.

The ways of Providence were indeed mysterious and not painless at first sight. On second sight, the ways of Providence looked much more favorable. Joy would forget Daddy quickly; later she would tell Joy that Daddy was dead, as for any practical purpose he was. They would live in civilized England, instead of this backward country which anyway was on the verge of chaos, ruled by blacks. Bournemouth, Cheltenham? She needn't decide in a hurry, Joy loved living in hotels. And Joy could go to day school, sparing her the dreaded separation of boarding school. They would be together, she and her beloved daughter, and comfortably off, and no depraved man and no filthy Africans to trouble them. Grace longed for daylight, longed to get away, knowing how thrilled Joy would be: Joy hated Fairview, as she did. And fifty per cent was not enough.

The house had to be disinfected before he brought Zena to live with him. 'For the last time,' Ian said as Beda and Mwangi unloaded Luke's old furnishings. The two farm lorries were filled with all Grace's stuff and sent to the Nairobi saleroom. He might have kept the red nursery for Zena but it was Grace's doing and he wanted Grace expunged. Ian drove to Nairobi and ambled about like a helpless country bumpkin until he found a furniture shop. The Asian proprietor assured him that these pale blue things were 'a very fine suite for a young little lady'.

'I don't like the bunnies.'

The bunnies could be painted out, immediately, and where was the Bwana buying curtains and bedspread? The Asian's son led Ian to the Asian's cousin's shop where Ian was astounded by the quantity and variety of repellent material on sale and presumably bought. He was ready to give up when he saw a bolt of cloth, more or less the same color as the new furniture. It was patterned with small pink rosebuds. He showed the Asian the size of the windows as he remembered them; curtains and bedspread would be made at once by a glum African at a pedal sewing machine, and shipped with the very fine suite to Karula the next day.

Ian was too preoccupied to listen. He had suddenly thought of clothes. Since his first Nakuru effort, he had bought no clothing for Zena. But the child wasn't naked, how did she live? Clean little dresses, which he had taken for granted. From where? Joy's cast-offs, it had to be. He wanted to weep, thinking of Zena patiently accepting whatever Joy discarded all these years. He had much to learn and he must teach Zena to remind him, to ask; he couldn't bear the idea of her humility. But he also couldn't quite, as yet, bear the idea of a female clothing store. When Zena came with him, it would be different. Staring into shop windows, brooding on his carelessness, he saw a display of small shorts and striped T-shirts. Much better for the farm anyway. Zena would look enchanting, dressed like a little boy. He figured she was about the size of a seven-year-old male, and returned cheerfully to Karula with a stack of shorts and T-shirts.

He and Beda were behaving like a pair of old hens and enjoying it. Zena's room was ready, with bunches of flowers on the desk and bedside table, and the new boys' outfits in the bureau drawers. He felt a joyful elation he had markedly failed to feel long ago upon bringing Grace here. He went behind the cypress hedge, to bear the glad tidings.

'Zena, love, you're coming to live with me in the big house.'

Zena gave him a look of terror, wrenched away her hand and fled into the bush. He thrashed after her but she was well hidden. He found her sobbing in a sort of burrow behind a *leleshwa* bush. She must have made this hole herself and she certainly knew her way to it.

Ian carried the child in his arms to the swing under the Cape Chestnut tree and held her on his lap, soothing her while she cried as he had never seen her cry. He kept saying, 'Tell Baba, darling, tell Baba.' When she could speak, Zena said, 'No, Baba, please. The Memsaab's *toto* is bad to me, I don't want to live with her, please, Baba.'

So Ian learned at last the cause of Zena's unexplained sickness. If he had known, he wouldn't have let them go so easily; he would have driven them out with whips and thongs, the words springing into his mind; beaten them down the driveway, sent them bleeding and penniless from this place where the poisoned child of the poisonous woman had tormented his gentle timid little girl. How could anyone be so wicked, it was like trapping and baiting a young gazelle.

'Baba?'

'What?'

'Your face. Baba, your face is ugly.'

Hate was an ugly emotion. And now a useless one. Grace and Joy were beyond his reach, no doubt airborne. Grace had settled her business in Nairobi at speed. A letter from her solicitor demanded 60 per cent of the net profits of Fairview and he had agreed light-heartedly, with relief, by return of post. The only way he could punish Grace was by making Fairview fail. Hate was entirely useless, and a sort of victory for Grace.

He took a deep breath and let it out noisily. 'Better now? I blew the ugliness away.'

Zena nodded but she was still tense, like a little animal curled against danger.

'Listen to me, Zena. They are gone. The Memsaab and her *toto*. They are gone forever, they will never come back. Never, you understand that, don't you? We don't have to think about them, we will forget they were ever here. There's only us, together on our farm, for the rest of our lives. Now come home with me.'

Mrs Farrell called to the barman, '*Jambo* Samuel, coca cola *moja, baridi sana*.' She hurried across the tatty empty club room to Mrs Gordon who was reading her mail.

'Helen, have you seen Ian Paynter?'

'No, why?'

'I saw him at the post office, our throbbing social center. He had a

ravishing little brown girl with him, but ravishing. If you can imagine
Nefertiti as a child, wearing khaki shorts and a red and white striped
T-shirt.'

'Rose, dear, pull yourself together.'

'Why not? The Nilo-Hamitic tribes are all beautiful. How do we
know that isn't what Nefertiti was? The ancient Egyptians...'

'I'm not up to it.'

'Neither am I, really. Anyway you sidetracked me. The point is, this
beauty is obviously a half-breed. It's too extraordinary. I'm all of a
twitter. Instead of staring at his feet and mumbling, Ian looked me
straight in the eye, smiling all over his face, and said, "Mrs Farrell, may
I present my adopted daughter, Zena." I didn't know what to do. I tried
to shake hands with the child but she hid behind his legs and Ian just
laughed and patted her head and said benignly, "She's a bit shy, she'll
get over it." Coming from him, I ask you. And he looked radiant, I
don't think I've ever seen a man look like that.'

'That's good news. Grace was not one to inspire radiance.'

'But you know, it is rather weird. Grace and her film star kiddy
vanishing without a word and a few months later, Ian appearing with
this new child and she's not, repeat not, full-blooded African. What can
it mean?'

'Not what you think.'

'Oh, why?'

'Not Ian, anyone but Ian. I'd bet my last shilling.'

'Your opinions are universally respected, dear heart, but I'll bet my
last shilling they won't be shared this time.'

'Oh really, damn it to hell, I can see it starting all over again. Poor
Ian, they'll never let him alone. Why shouldn't he adopt a little girl, any
color, even green, if he wants to? You don't suppose he's had a jolly
good time with Grace and Shirley Temple, do you? I've always thought
he was the loneliest man I ever knew. And if he's happy now I wish to
God people would just be nice for a change and let him be happy. I'm
going to squash that rumor before it gets a good hold.'

'May I ask how?'

'I'll simply say I know all about the child, I've discussed it at length
with Ian, and any suggestion of hanky panky is rot. If you have a spark
of human decency you'll do the same. Your last good deed before you
leave.'

'Okay, but what do we do when they ask where Zena came from
etcetera?'

'We have the haughties, we say no one asks us about our children and it's rudimentary manners not to pry. After all, how do we know that Jenny is actually Simon's child, we take it for granted out of politeness.'

'Oh Helen!'

'Well, you get the general idea, don't you? And I'm going to have him to lunch with his new daughter as soon as Charles goes off to kill some more harmless wild animals.'

'That's a joke. He'll never come.'

'Yes, he will. He likes my garden.'

'How do you know, or has he been at your house secretly some time in the last ten years?'

'No, but he liked the garden then. And he'll need a woman friend for the girl. I'll make him come. And I long to help him with his borders, they haunt me.'

Zena had been chatting about school and gardening, for she was Helen Gordon's disciple, but grew silent as they neared Fairview. Helen Gordon could feel the child straining ahead towards home. She must have been wildly homesick this first term though Ian said her letters were cheerful. Helen Gordon felt a heavy responsibility; she had convinced Ian that Zena must go to school with other girls. She took it on herself to make the arrangements. Zena passed the scholastic tests with ease and after Independence no school could refuse a child because she had African blood. In fact, as Helen Gordon told Ian to calm him, Tanamuru Girls School accepted African students before Independence despite its reputation as the most stylish school for young ladies in East Africa.

'You don't want her to grow up knowing nobody except you and me, do you, Ian? No other children. She'll be a misfit, she won't know how to get along in the world.'

Mrs Gordon was not sure where or how the beautiful child would fit in the Republic of Kenya but then she was not sure about herself either. And it never hurt anybody to go to the right school. She had made careful inquiries and learned that the African students at Tanamuru Girls School were the daughters of Top People so she assumed the Africans were not all that different from the English in some respects.

Ian had forgotten his anxieties about Zena's solitude since they were so happy together and so sufficient to each other. Zena was blithely gay; his constant companion. The years behind the cypress hedge were unreal, part of an unreal past. He could not imagine life without her and resisted the idea of separation. But the word 'misfit' frightened him. Helen Gordon was right and he knew it though he agonized lest Zena be snubbed by white girls or mistreated; there might be other monsters like

Joy. He had written to Zena every day, in every letter he told her she could come home any time she was unhappy. He didn't say that he missed her so much he felt sick, the house was a tomb, no matter how hard he worked he couldn't work off his loneliness. He pulled the pages from the calendar in his office, waiting in desolation for the Christmas holidays. Helen Gordon was to call for Zena, as she would be in Nairobi that day. She took that on herself too, guessing Ian's profound reluctance to appear at a girls' school.

Now Helen Gordon turned away and walked out of sight around the house. She couldn't watch this silent rapturous reunion; Ian and Zena clinging together as if both had just escaped drowning. Perhaps she was wrong; she'd suffered untold misery when Charles shipped the boys to England but they were boys and there was no real choice and they had never been as close as a girl would be. Perhaps she had meddled, laid another paving stone on the road to hell. Perhaps they should be left alone to live their perfectly happy absorbed lives here; but what would Zena do when Ian died? If she had never known any place other than Fairview, made no friends, grown up a recluse like Ian? Ian was forty-four, Zena was twelve; Zena had a long piece of time to live without him.

There were noises of African welcome and laughter inside the house and then they came across the lawn, the sweet funny pair, the small girl with her arm around the waist of the tall man, his arm around her shoulders.

'Your roses are doing beautifully, Ian. I've never seen a new rose garden look like this. Let me know when you feel like coming to lunch.' She kissed them both and hurried off. Much as they liked her, she knew they didn't want her there a minute longer.

'Oh Baba,' Zena sighed.

'Yes.'

He understood everything Zena meant: to be together, here where they belonged, looking at the same view.

'I'll get out of my uniform and then can we drive to Luke's hill?'

'I thought you'd want to,' and had a picnic tea with thermos bottle ready in the Land Rover.

Zena came back in her farm uniform, khaki shorts and shirt, saying, 'I'm only comfy like this.'

They didn't talk on the way. The afternoon was hot, cloudless and windless. Dust hung in a curtain behind them and dropped in the still air. Ian felt Zena's joy when she saw a herd of grazing zebra. She was taking in the land through her eyes, regaining her home. Ian spread a plastic cloth on the grass at the edge of the ridge and Zena got the tea organized; this was one of their regular treats. After they had paid reverence to the view and their cups were filled, Ian said. 'Tell me.'

'You know our school uniform?'

'Yes.' Lucy had worn the same in a different color. Apparently natural law decreed that English schoolgirls or girls at English schools must wear that felt pot hat, blazer, pleated skirt.

'It was called nigger brown before Independence but now it's called dark brown.'

Ian took in his breath, all his worst fears were true; but Zena was having a simple schoolgirl's fit of giggles.

'Who told you?'

'Betty.'

Dear God, was Zena so lonely that she still depended on an imaginary friend?

'She's an African girl,' Zena said. 'She told me because it's so funny.'

'Is she a friend of yours?'

'Oh yes, everyone's my friend.'

'That's good,' Ian said uncertainly. Zena munched cookies.

'One day,' Zena went on, 'after sports, some of the older girls were talking and they asked me to come over. One of them, she's very pretty, her name is Isabel, she asked me about my mother.'

Ian had stopped breathing; he felt tears in his eyes. She would never go back to that rotten school, better grow up a misfit than grow up tormented.

'I said I didn't know, I'd never seen her,' Zena went on, still munching cookies. 'Then she asked about my father and I said you. Another girl, I forget her name, said I must be illegitimate. I asked how to spell it, it's got two l's with e after. So I could look it up, you see. Anyway Isabel said it was very romantic, and then they all said it was romantic, and Isabel said either my father or my mother or both must be very beautiful and I said you were. I looked up illegitimate. It means a lot of things but mainly not born in lawful wedlock.'

Ian didn't know what to do; this matter-of-fact instructive conversation affected him like being kicked in the stomach.

'Weren't you in lawful wedlock with my mother?' Zena asked.

'No.' That was God's truth, but what went on in her head? Of course Zena must believe he was her real father, having known no other, and he had never said he was or wasn't. He had never explained the circumstances of her birth for the idiot reason that he didn't think it mattered.

'Oh well, that's why you adopted me,' Zena said. 'So I could be your lawful daughter, I wasn't sure why. I wouldn't like to have a mother. I remember about the Memsaab not really but sort of.'

'Yes.' Bewildered, lost; was she telling him something he didn't hear?

'I'm the smallest girl in school. I don't mean the youngest, I mean the smallest. And I don't look like anybody else, the African girls are black and the European girls are white and then there's me. So everybody's my friend and the older girls say I'm their pet.'

'Zena, do you hate it there?'

'Oh no, Baba, I don't hate it. It's a very nice school. Lots of big trees and grass and flowers but you can't see anywhere, not like here, you can't look out and see the land and of course there aren't any wild animals. But if I can skip a form then it would only be five more years.'

Ian reached over and lifted her and sat her on his lap, enfolding her in his arms. 'You don't have to go back, you don't have to stay there five years, you can be here all the time right now.'

'Baba?' Zena said in a small voice.

'Yes, my little one?'

'Did you send me there because you were tired of me? Because you wanted to be alone on the farm?'

'Zena, how could you think that? I want you here every minute. I counted the days until the end of term. I love you better than anything in the world, the farm is terribly lonely for me without you.'

Zena snuggled closer and put her arms around his chest.

'I don't mind then.'

'Were you having sad thoughts all this time?'

'Well, I thought we lived here together and did lessons together and then all of a sudden I had to go to school, so I thought maybe.'

'No, dearest. No. Aunt Helen talked to me and said there were many things a girl needed to learn besides what she learns on a farm. I've lived here nearly twenty years now, and I don't understand much outside of Fairview. I wanted you to have more chances, but I won't keep you at that school if people hurt your feelings.'

'Nobody hurts my feelings, Baba. I told you. I was scared at first and cried in bed but so did other girls and I guessed they were scared too so I didn't feel so lonely. Then a girl called Joanna, she used to cry too, she said we'd be best friends and help each other. She lives on a farm near Thomson's Falls, they raise beef cattle, she's seen lions but she doesn't like them, she's afraid of them. Then we had parties in our dorm after lights out, you're not allowed to, eating sweets and cake and fruit and things, Aunt Helen sends me boxes so I have plenty. And they tell me funny stories and we laugh a lot. If you laugh you forget about being homesick. Anyway now I know millions of girls and they're all my friends.'

Zena unpeeled a somewhat melted bar of Cadbury's chocolate and began to lick it from the tinfoil. With chocolate on her nose, she giggled suddenly. 'I'm like Mary.'

'Mary?'

'Baba! You haven't forgotten Mary? My pet lamb?'

'Zena, love, I'm a bit confused but I think you are saying politely that Tanamuru Girls School is hell.'

'No, I'm not. Honestly. I think I'm saying that school's kind of silly, not like Fairview.' Zena licked her fingers and got up, tea and conversation finished, the sun magnificently sending afterbursts of light above the western mountains. Sounding very assured and brisk, she said, 'It's all right, Baba. Everybody has to go to school, all the girls know that. We better do what other people do. I don't suppose five years is really very long.'

They collected the remains of the picnic. Ian folded their table cloth and stowed the hamper in the Land Rover.

'You write to me or send me a telegram any time and I'll come and get you. You know that, don't you?'

'Yes, Baba, I do now.'

Mwangi had prepared a feast which left them waterlogged and stupefied. Zena had been reading aloud, in her dove voice, 'My Last Duchess'. They were both devoted to Browning as to Baroness d'Orczy, Conan Doyle, Robert Louis Stevenson, all the battered books in Luke's collection. Zena slept, in the curve of his arm, while Ian watched the fire burn down and tried to think of the future. After five years in that young ladies' establishment, would Zena find Fairview alien and uninteresting? A citified girl, not the responsible person Luke asked for, long ago, who'd inherit Fairview and guard it with love? Had he again got to work on building a prison for himself, a lonely old age? If so, what of it? He was trying to make sure there were no prisons for Zena. In any case, one day some sod would come along—black, white, copper-colored—to steal Zena from him. He only hoped the sod would be a good farmer.

What's the matter with you, Ian Paynter? Use your graying head. Think of the accidents. Who could ever have foreseen, when you were Zena's age, that you'd be here, the man you are, with this particular child as the center of your life? What about the accident that brought Zena, an infant more than half dead, to this farm? And the series of accidents that made her indeed your lawful daughter, and a bright steady little girl, able to cope with people much better than you can. Bad accidents too like going to the Karula Sports Club for the second and last time in nearly twenty years and meeting Grace. How does it cancel out? The worst, losing your family, against the best, Fairview and Zena? You won't know until you're dead, will you? And what's the point in worrying about the future? Let the future take care of itself, since you certainly can't. Be grateful now, man, be grateful.

He picked Zena up, still sleeping, and carried her to her room.